Wizard Scout

Book Three

Intergalactic Wizard Scout Chronicles

Rodney W. Hartman

DEDICATION

This book is dedicated to my daughter, Stephanie. Your mom
would be very proud of you. I know I am.

ACKNOWLEDGMENTS

I want to give a special thanks to my wife, Karen. She not only spent many hours typing and proofreading this book, but she was also my main supporter and encourager. I also want to thank my daughters Emily and Stephanie along with my son-in-law, Jonathan, for their help and advice. Writing a book is not a one person endeavor; it's a team effort. Thank you all.

Books by Rodney Hartman

<u>Intergalactic Wizard Scout Chronicles</u>

Wizard Defiant   Book One
Wizard Cadet   Book Two
Wizard Scout   Book Three
Wizard Omega   Book Four (TBP Winter 2016)

CHAPTER 1

[Begin Transmission]

Boom!

The explosive projectile exploded five meters away. Metal shrapnel and rock shards flew in all directions. The force of the explosion knocked Richard off his feet. He slammed into one of the many jagged rocks scattered along the ground.

Momentarily dazed, Richard mentally yelled to his battle computer, *Nick! Am I hurt?*

Negative, said a voice in his head. *I'm shooting adrenaline into you. Now get up before they fire again.*

The voice belonged to Nickelo, the one-of-a-kind, prototype battle computer embedded in Richard's battle helmet. Richard was a wizard scout, or rather a cadet at the Intergalactic Wizard Scout Academy. All wizard scouts were issued battle helmets. However, as far as Richard knew, Nickelo was the most advanced piece of artificial intelligence the Intergalactic Empire's scientists could develop. Richard had often wondered why he'd been fortunate enough to be issued the prototype battle computer when far more experienced wizard scouts were available. Regardless of the reason, Richard was glad he had Nickelo. He wasn't just a battle computer to Richard. He'd become a good friend during the past few years. Richard had found he could depend on Nickelo during even the toughest times.

Richard staggered to his feet. A surge of strength shot through

1

his body as Nickelo used the thread needles in his battle suit to inject a dose of adrenaline into his veins. Richard sped up until he was running as fast as he could for the cover of a large outcropping of rocks. With the assistors in the battle suit's legs at maximum, Richard ran with two and a half meter strides. He zigzagged every couple of steps in an attempt to throw off the aim of the gunners in the armored vehicle behind him. He heard the roar of the battlewagon's engine as it gave chase. The staccato of the armored behemoth's machine guns accompanied streams of red tracers passing all around and hitting the ground to Richard's front and sides.

Risking a glance at his battle helmet's heads-up display, Richard switched the view to the helmet's rear visuals. The massive armored vehicle was fifty meters to his rear. The battlewagon's metallic tracks made it look like an antique tank from Earth, but its alien design told him it wasn't. The battlewagon's large main gun was flanked by two smaller cupolas armed with automatic weapons. Even as he watched, red lines of tracers reached out from both of the cupolas as they tried to pin him down.

Minefield ahead, Rick! warned Nickelo.

I know, but I have to get to cover, Richard thought back as he switched his visuals back to the front. *Plot me a route so I don't step on one.*

It was at times like these Richard was glad his battle computer and he didn't communicate verbally. Instead, their speech was more a form of images, feelings and thoughts interspersed with a few words. As a result, their communication was near instantaneous. This came in very handy during combat situations. Otherwise, Richard would have been dead long before his battle computer could tell him a way to save his life using normal methods of communication. According to Nickelo, their speech would be even faster once they acquired something called a shared space. Richard wasn't exactly sure how a shared space worked. However, his battle computer said it was important, so Richard didn't ask too many questions. He'd find out eventually.

I'm not worried about you stepping on a mine, said Nickelo matter-of-factly. *I'll take control of your suit if necessary. But I can't do anything if you get knocked off your feet and land on one.*

2

Your battle suit might survive a blast from an anti-personnel mine, but some of these mines are anti-armor. If you land on one of them, it'll be bye-bye Rick and his faithful sidekick, Nick.

The black, tightfitting, leather-like battle suit Richard wore was the most advanced personal armor ever developed by the Empire's technicians. When fully sealed, it was a self-contained unit designed to keep its wizard scout alive.

Understood, Richard thought back as he kept running for all he was worth.

Following the path Nickelo marked on his heads-up display, Richard avoided the mines as best he could. Several dozen white and yellow dots on his heads-up display marked the locations of the mines. The yellow points highlighted the anti-armor mines. Richard had a momentary fear he was going to accidentally step on a mine. He gave a sigh of relief when he felt his battle computer making minor course corrections with the battle suit's legs.

Dodge right! They're going to fire the main gun, warned Nickelo.

Richard didn't hesitate. He sidestepped hard to the right. A moment later an explosion erupted in the area where he'd been running.

As he ran, Richard took a look at the battle in the valley below. He'd been sent on a mission by '*the One*' to help a boy-king reclaim his kingdom. Why the computer network Richard knew only as '*the One*' was interested in a backwater kingdom on the planet Portalis in the magical dimension was beyond him. But here he was.

Richard could see the white walls of the elven city of Silverton in the distance. The morning light was reflecting off thousands of sets of armor from the scattered formations of elves and their allies. The opposing force of orcs, ogres, trolls, and their human mercenaries outnumbered the friendlies ten to one. Even so, the elven army might have held out against their foe except for the demon-possessed giant leading the enemy force. Even from a distance of two kilometers, Richard sensed the demon's evil. Its demonic aura stole the courage from men and elf alike. If not for the timely arrival of young King William with his soldiers and a force of unicorns, the demon's army would probably even now be sacking the elven city.

But the initial success of the unicorns and King William's soldiers had been short-lived. The demon had rallied its forces. Both the elves in front of the city gates and King William's army were being hard pressed. The only thing preventing victory by the demon's forces was the unicorn's leader, Elf Friend Swiftmane, and his elf maid, Mendera, along with their force of sixty unicorns. They were fearlessly facing the demon and its strongest spell-casters.

Richard had been fighting at King William's side doing his best to protect the young boy. Then the battlewagon had rumbled over the hill and started lobbing cannon fire into the young king's army. Richard had been forced to take on the armored behemoth alone. The elves' spell-casters had been locked in fierce combat with their counterparts in the demon's army. Only Richard's technology had any hope of fighting the battlewagon's weapons.

Dive, Rick! Nickelo ordered.

Richard didn't pause to think. He just dove forward as far as he could throw himself. The battle suit used power from its isotopic battery to activate the suit's assistors. As a result, Richard was propelled forward at a speed and distance which his own muscles could never hope to achieve. Another blast sounded behind Richard as a round from the battlewagon's main gun exploded in a ball of fire behind him. The large explosion caused a cascade of smaller blasts as half a dozen mines were detonated by falling debris. From the heads-up display, Richard determined his dive had taken him clear of the minefield. He jumped to his feet and ran the last few meters to the granite outcropping. It was the only cover of any significance within several hundred meters. Richard doubted it would provide more than momentary protection. A few cannon rounds from the battlewagon would quickly reduce it to rubble.

Now what, Nick? Richard said. *I'm here.*

Yes, you are, agreed Nickelo who sounded unimpressed with his wizard scout's achievement.

Will the minefield keep the battlewagon from following? Richard asked hopefully.

Doubtful, Nickelo responded. *The battlewagon has already entered the minefield. It's avoiding the areas with the anti-tank mines. The smaller mines can't hurt it.*

4

As if to confirm his battle computer's analysis, a series of small explosions sounded in rapid succession as the battlewagon's steel treads set off several anti-personnel mines.

Well, what's the rest of the plan? Richard asked growing impatient. *Am I supposed to wait here until they blow this rock to smithereens? Once they do that, they can take their sweet time blowing us to pieces. Is that the plan?*

Negative, Nickelo calmly assured Richard. *I calculate a seventy-five percent probability they'll try to crush you under the treads of the battlewagon.*

A seventy-five percent chance I'll be crushed instead of being blown up? Richard said. *Somehow, that doesn't make me feel better.*

I didn't say there was a seventy-five percent chance you'd be crushed, Nickelo corrected Richard. *I said there was a seventy-five percent chance that's what they'd try to do. When the battlewagon gets closer, I want you to climb on top. Then we'll see if we can locate a point of entry.*

Are you sure there'll be a point of entry on top of the battlewagon? Richard said.

No, admitted Nickelo. *This is my first encounter with this specific piece of equipment. However, the crew has to get in and out somehow. The battlewagon's not an Empire design, and it's not like any of the other armored vehicles we've encountered up until now, so it's an unknown. However, it's older technology, so things could be worse. It doesn't even have plasma rounds. The explosives are powered by chemicals; probably a gunpowder derivative.*

Well, older technology or not, it's been pretty effective so far, observed Richard. *What's this kind of equipment doing here anyway, and who trained its crew?*

I don't know, Nickelo said with a laugh, *but when you find out, have your people get with my people.*

You're not funny, Nick, Richard replied.

Well, wherever it came from, Nickelo said, *it's turned the tide. Look at King William's army now. Those first rounds from the battlewagon destroyed any semblance of discipline left in most of his units. They haven't turned and run yet, but that's only because those unicorns are keeping the demon occupied.*

So what's the rest of the plan, Nick? Richard asked. *That is assuming I do get on top of that piece of junk.*

Simple, Rick, oh greatest of wizard scouts, Nickelo said. *Just find an entrance; bash it open with your phase rod; jump in; and then kill everybody inside. What could be simpler?*

Richard doubted it would be that simple. *Yeah. It's easy for you to say. You're just going along for the ride. I'm the one who has to make it work. What makes you think my phase rod will be able to bash an opening in the armor? It looks pretty thick from where I'm standing.*

Well…, hedged Nickelo, *I calculate there's a seventy-eight percent chance it has an entrance on top. I estimate a twenty-six percent probability you'll find a hinge weak enough for your phase rod to break. That should give you entry into the battlewagon. You may have to supplement the phase rod with some rounds from your assault rifle, but I think you can get in. Then assuming the occupants aren't armed with high-energy handguns capable of penetrating your armor, I calculate there's a slightly better than poor chance you can kill them all before one of them sets off the high-explosive rounds stored in the battlewagon. I'll admit the odds aren't good, but they are definitely above zero; which are your odds if you try to outrun the battlewagon.*

So in other words, Richard summarized, *we're up the creek without a paddle.*

Well, Rick, said Nickelo. *You're the one who decided to attack without consulting me first. You didn't give me time to do a sensory probe until we were halfway to this lumbering beast. And to top it off, you pretty much depleted your Power reserve during King William's initial charge, so your wizard scout abilities can't help us now. We have to rely on your technology to defeat this steel monster.*

I know. I know, Richard said sufficiently chastised. *I should have waited before I attacked, and I should have saved my Power reserve for later in the battle.*

Richard would have said more, but the roar of the battlewagon's engine on the other side of the granite outcropping confirmed the vehicle's crew intended to smash into the rock outcropping and crush both it and Richard underneath the battlewagon's treads. Richard knew he only had a few seconds left. He had to think

6

outside the box.

Nick. Change of plan. Find me an anti-tank mine, Richard ordered.

Even though his battle computer estimated almost an eighty-percent chance of a point-of-entry being on top of the vehicle, Richard had a hunch there wasn't. Something felt wrong. From experience, Richard knew better than to ignore his hunches.

Nickelo didn't reply, but almost immediately Richard saw a yellow point highlighted on his heads-up display. An anti-tank mine was twenty meters away. Without giving himself time to think about the danger, Richard ran from behind the rock outcropping. A second later, the battlewagon's hull made contact with the granite sending dust and rock slivers into the air. Several shards bounced harmlessly off Richard's battle suit.

With a few long strides, Richard made it to the location of the mine. He began digging with his gloved hands. Small arms fire from one of the vehicle's side cupolas kicked up dirt around him. A few hit his armor and jostled him around a little when they struck, but the rounds were too light to penetrate his battle suit's armor. Realizing he didn't have time to dig up the entire mine, Richard grabbed a handle on one side and jerked the mine out of the ground. By the favor of the Creator, or possibly the luck of the foolish, the mine was not booby-trapped.

Hefting the mine over his shoulder, Richard began running as the battlewagon's crew rotated the main turret in an effort to acquire him in its sights. Richard wasted no time getting inside the reach of the long barrel protruding from the main turret.

The main gun's useless now, Richard thought. *Let's see if I can keep from getting crushed under a tread.*

With his battle computer plotting hand and foot holds on his heads-up display and assisting in the placement of his feet and free hand, Richard reached the top of the battlewagon in short order. He jumped to a flat area on the main turret. A quick glance failed to find a hatch.

That's surprising, said Nickelo. *I thought sure there was a seventy-eight percent probability a hatch would be here. I guess that's why they call them probabilities and not certainties.*

Wasting no time, Richard inverted the anti-armor mine and positioned it on the center of the turret. He said a rare prayer hoping it would stay on the vehicle without bouncing off. Richard jumped down and began running away from the battlewagon as fast as his battle suit's legs would carry him. Unfortunately, he was once again in range of the battlewagon's main gun. Hoping it would take the crew a few seconds to acquire him in the vehicle's targeting system, Richard ran to what he guessed was a safe distance. Spinning around and jumping into the air, he squeezed off a burst of rounds in the direction of the main turret. After a dozen rounds, a large explosion erupted from the top of the vehicle. Richard was hurled to the ground by the concussion. From his position on the ground, Richard watched the main turret of the battlewagon being blown high into the air. As he watched, it began tumbling back towards the earth with smoke and flames trailing behind.

Move, Richard! You're in danger, warned Nickelo.

Sure enough, the turret was headed in his direction.

"Crap!" Richard shouted out loud. He rolled over, got to his feet, and began running again. Unfortunately, he was running back into the minefield.

Where'd they get these mines? Richard asked. *We're in the magical dimension. They should only have medieval weapons and magic. There isn't supposed to be any technology on Portalis.*

Ahh..., I assume you mean there isn't supposed to be any technology on this world except for yours, Nickelo said. *Because you're special, right?*

Richard thought of a great retort, but since Nickelo was graciously marking the remaining landmines on his heads-up display, he wisely kept his mouth shut. A loud explosion from his rear told Richard the turret had landed in the minefield. Several secondary explosions occurred in rapid succession until the battlewagon's turret rolled to a stop.

Richard cleared the minefield. *We need to get back to the main battle. It isn't over yet. William and the elves are still outnumbered ten to one. And, that demon's doing a number on those unicorns. We need to get back in the fight.*

Roger that, Rick, said Nickelo. *Follow the route on your heads-up display. We should be able to get back to King William in about three and a half minutes.*

Whenever Richard encountered a group of orcs he couldn't

avoid, he took them out with well-placed plasma rounds. They were cannon fodder. The real battle was near the main gates to the elven city. The demon-giant towered over those around it. Accompanied by its strongest magic users, the demon's forces were forcing the elven defenders back against their own walls.

A white banner marked the location of King William. Richard activated the zoom on his battle helmet's visor. He spotted the boy-king riding his pony in the thick of battle. His guards were doing their best to protect him, but they were hard pressed.

Richard swore. *The fool! I told him to stay where he was until I got back.*

He's a king, Rick, said Nickelo. *He might be twelve years old, but he's too brave to standstill while his soldiers are dying.*

Before Richard could reply, a deep, unearthly voice reverberated throughout the entire valley. It was the demon.

"Victory is ours!" shouted the giant who was the demon. "Bow down now and worship me. I will give you a merciful death. Continue to defy me, and your pain will be eternal."

Two minutes out, said Nickelo.

Richard fired a long burst from his M63 lightweight assault rifle at a troll lumbering his way. The troll fell. Richard knew it would be back up within seconds, but he didn't care. He just needed to get to King William's side. He kept running.

A cheer erupted from the valley floor. Richard noticed King William and his elite guards had fought their way to the remaining unicorns. King William's white banner merged with the white bodies of the unicorns. A small group of elves broke through the ring of orcs and joined the unicorns as well. They all charged forward together in the direction of the demon.

"No!" Richard shouted knowing full well his voice wouldn't carry. *Nick, I've got to get there!*

But Richard knew Nickelo couldn't help him. No one could. It was too far. Helpless, Richard watched the core of guards surrounding King William slowly fail until only a handful remained by their king's side. A knot of elves added their weight to King William's charge. Bolts of lighting and fireballs shot out from the elves creating a brief opening in the demon's line of defenders. A flicker of white charged through the opening. It was the leader of the unicorns, Elf Friend Swiftmane. Richard could just make out the female rider on the stallion's back.

The demon-giant swung a club the size of a tree, but the unicorn dodged the blow. The arm-length horn on the unicorn flared with a light so bright it rivaled the noonday sun. Swiftmane rammed his horn into the left side of the demon's chest. A scream of pain and hatred filled the air as the glowing horn broke off in the demon's heart. A wave of light washed over Richard. The ground trembled, and Richard lost his footing.

Struggling to rise, Richard felt the cells of his body start to tingle as everything turned dark.

"No!" Richard shouted. "Not yet! Let me see if the boy's alive! At least let me say goodbye!"

Mission complete, said '*the One*' without any hint of emotion. *Return to training.*

CHAPTER 2

The darkness gave way to light. Richard stumbled, but the legs of his battle suit stiffened keeping him upright.

You're back in your tent, said Nickelo. *You're back at the Academy.*

Richard almost yelled his frustration, but he held it in. He was back at the Academy. He was cadet 832, Richard Shepard, again. The memories of the battle were already starting to fade similar to a dream upon waking.

Was it a dream? Richard wondered. But he knew it wasn't.

Richard saw a man and two women wearing shorts and t-shirts sitting on one of two cots in the tent. They'd been conferring with each other, but they looked up at Richard with half-formed questions on their lips.

"How long have I been gone?" Richard asked attempting to beat their questions to the punch.

The man spoke. "About thirty seconds, Rick. Ah..., how long do you think you were gone?"

The man was Jerad. Along with Tam and Telsa, they were Richard's best friends at the Academy. Jerad was also Richard's current tent mate. At least he'd been before Richard had been teleported out of the tent by '*the One*'.

Nick, Richard thought. *How long were we there?*

We were on Portalis for five months and twenty-three days give or take a few hours, said Nickelo.

At another time, Richard might have commented on the

11

inexactness of his battle computer's answer. But he was too frustrated and emotionally spent to take notice now.

Richard didn't answer Jerad's question right away. He removed his battle helmet and tossed it on his cot. By the time he sat down, Richard had control over his emotions.

"Just shy of six months, Jerad," Richard finally answered.

The shorter of the two women, Telsa, stood up and spoke. "You've got a screwed-up life, Rick. Did you know that?" Telsa must have sensed Richard's internal turmoil because she patted him on the shoulder and added, "But I'm glad you're back safe."

Richard nodded his head in thanks. In Richard's opinion, Telsa was probably the smartest cadet in his cohort. She'd come straight to the Intergalactic Wizard Scout Academy fresh out of a high-priced university with her degree in astral physics in hand. In the five years he'd known her, Telsa had never explained why she'd decided to be a wizard scout.

"Well, did you do anything interesting this time, Rick?" said the second woman, Tam. "Or was it another hide-and-seek mission for 'the One'."

Richard noticed Telsa give Tam a warning look, but he couldn't blame Tam for being curious. He'd be too if their roles were reversed. Tam was an ex-mercenary, and subtlety was not her strong point.

Forcing his anger at 'the One' to the side, Richard answered his friend as best he could. "Interesting?" Richard said. "That's not quite how I'd describe it. Two minutes ago, I was in the middle of a battle fighting alongside elves, unicorns, and a young boy I'd promised to help against a demon and every kind of nasty from your worst nightmare."

Rubbing his face with both hands, Richard let out a deep breath before continuing. "Now I'm here sitting on a cot talking to you guys. It's surreal popping back in here. I don't even know who won the battle. For all I know, our side lost, and everyone I've grown to care about during the last six months died."

Richard felt a small hand on his shoulder. He looked up. It was Tam.

"I'm sorry, Rick," said Tam. "I can't begin to imagine."

His three friends looked at each other as if avoiding his gaze.

Suspicious, Richard said, "What am I missing?"

"Ah...," said Jerad. "I hate to be the one to break it to you, but if you've been gone six months like you say, you probably don't remember."

"Remember what?" Richard said as he tried to think back to what he'd been doing when '*the One*' had teleported him out of the tent those long months ago.

"Well," said Jerad sounding almost apologetic. "We've got formation in fifteen minutes. Then we're going to the airfield for our final testing in U.H.A.A.V.s."

A flood of memories rushed through Richard's mind. U.H.A.A.V.s were Ultra-Heavy Ambulatory Assault Vehicles, or 'cats' as the soldiers called them. They were the primary ground-assault armor for most of the advanced civilizations in the galaxy. Their nickname, cats, came from their inventor and chief architect, Catherine 'Cat' Belyakov.

His cohort had been transferred from the main Academy area to an airfield out in the desert and given three weeks of familiarization training in the armored vehicles. Richard only vaguely remembered the classes. He remembered he'd just been getting the hang of piloting the cats when '*the One*' had sent him on his mission. Not that he'd been very good at piloting the more advanced cats. Richard's previous experience with heavy armor consisted of riding in troop-carrying cats on a handful of occasions during assignments in marine recon. Until the Academy had started the cadets' heavy-armor training three weeks ago, Richard had never actually tried to pilot a cat. He hadn't been alone in his inexperience. Most of the cadets in his cohort had never been behind the controls of the metal behemoths.

With sizes ranging from the three-meter-high Warcat scout to the ten-meter-tall Leviathan, the multi-legged, weapons-packed, armored-attack vehicles were difficult for even experienced pilots to maneuver. The only saving grace for Richard and most of the other cadets had been that their battle computers were allowed to assist them in controlling their cats when the need arose.

However, some of the cadets in his cohort who had previous experience in armor had been able to run circles around infantry types like him. Jerad, for instance, was an expert at cats. Before coming to the Academy, his friend had been in a heavy-armor unit. Richard remembered hearing that Jerad had started off as an enlisted man before earning a field promotion to lieutenant. After that, he'd served in every position from platoon leader all the way to battalion commander. From the few stories Richard had been able to pry out of his friend, Jerad had piloted just about every type of cat in the Empire's inventory.

"Formation in fifteen?" Richard said. "That's just great. I'm not even sure I remember how to drive a cat much less fight in it. And to top it off, I'm starved. Do I have time to go to the mess hall?"

Jerad shook his head no. "Sorry, buddy. We just got back from breakfast before you popped out of here."

Richard groaned.

"Why don't you just grab something out of that high-fangled pack of yours, Rick?" suggested Tam. "You can grab me a protein bar while you're at it. Only the Creator knows when TAC Officer Myers will let us eat next."

Normally, Richard would have jumped at Tam's idea. The dimensional pack on his back was a unique item he'd been issued during his freshman year at the Academy. With it, he could summon almost anything he could think of if he had the Power. Unfortunately, he didn't always have the Power. This was one of those times.

"Can't," Richard said. "My Power reserve's empty. I need a few minutes to recharge."

"Then get used to being hungry," said Tam her eyes twinkling. "TAC Officer Myers wants everybody in their physical training outfits. I don't think he'd appreciate you showing up in your battle suit."

Richard had no doubt Tam was right. TAC Officer Myers had been riding his case ever since Richard had arrived at the Academy. Myers appeared to dislike him as much as he disliked his TAC officer.

"No doubt," Richard said as he began stripping off his battle suit. "It never ends, does it?"

The moment Richard began to undo his pants, Telsa said, "Well, I guess that's our cue."

"Yeah, Rick," said Tam laughing. "You're not all that good looking, buddy, regardless of what you apparently think. See you later, guys."

After Telsa and Tam exited the tent, Richard continued

stripping off his battle suit. "What's with them? They've seen me naked before."

Jerad laughed. "Yeah, so have I, but that doesn't mean I enjoy it. Besides, it's one thing when we're in a community shower. I guess they figure it's different when they're in a small tent with a man stripping off his clothes."

"Whatever," Richard said using his word for ending a conversation when he didn't want to talk about something any longer.

"Five minutes!" came a shout from outside the tent. "Let's go, cadets!"

*   *   *

The morning dragged by. Once Richard and his cohort left the tent-cantonment area, their TAC officers took them on a ten-kilometer run before taking them back to the airfield for their testing in cats.

The airfield was located in the desert two hundred kilometers south of the main Academy area back in Velounia, the capital of the planet Velos. Other than being a hot and miserable place for cadets to train, Richard saw no reason for the Academy's airfield to be located where it was. As far as he could tell, someone had marked an X on the ground and bulldozed anything green as far as the eye could see. The airfield consisted of thirty-two massive hangars situated in a horseshoe shape around an asphalt runway. The U.H.A.A.V.s were stored in the hangars.

After their run, the hundred and twenty-four cadets in Richard's junior cohort were gathered inside hangar 1. Every few minutes, their TAC officers called off the names of eight cadets. Those cadets were then divided into two quads of four cadets each and assigned to cats for their final urban training.

As the day wore on, Richard waited for his name to be called. So did Tam, Telsa, and Jerad. While they waited together, his friends tried to give him a refresher course in piloting cats.

"Your best bet is to get assigned to one of the smaller cats," Jerad said. "If you remember, piloting one of them is like wearing an oversized battle suit. If you're unlucky and get put in one of the larger cats, try and let your battle computer help you as much as possible. Don't worry about most of the controls. All you'll need for this test is the steering mechanism and weapons. If you're lucky, whoever you're against will be just as inept at piloting a cat as you are."

"Thanks for the words of confidence, buddy," Richard said.

"Try to get a Warcat if you can," said Jerad ignoring Richard's interruption. "It's your best chance to win your fight. You don't want to give Myers an excuse to put you on extra duty this weekend. You do remember we're going to the Fleet Admiral's Ball don't you."

Richard had forgotten until Tam had reminded him earlier. Before 'the One' had sent him on his mission, Richard remembered he'd been looking forward to spending the long weekend with his friends in Velounia. He remembered Jerad had somehow acquired eight invitations to the Fleet Admiral's Ball. His friend had given two invitations each to Telsa, Tam, and him with strict instructions not to come alone. Richard remembered he'd been fortunate in that the destroyer Blaze was currently in orbit above Velos. His friend, Liz, was second officer of the speedy starship. Richard had invited her as his guest. Tam had also reminded him that he was supposed to meet Liz tomorrow afternoon at the spaceport in Velounia. After what he'd been through the last six months, Richard was looking forward to a break. And, he desperately wanted to see Liz again. He needed to see her.

Richard nodded his head at Jerad. "Yeah, I remember. And even Myers isn't going to keep me from going this time."

Jerad laughed and patted Richard on the back. "That's the spirit, cadet."

*   *   *

The hours passed until only Tam, Telsa, Jerad, and Richard were left in the hangar. Finally, he heard his number called.

"Cadet 832," said a squat, toad-faced man dressed in the silver and black of an Intergalactic Wizard Scout Academy TAC officer. He was TAC Officer Gaston Myers.

"You'll be in the Tomcat on the red team," said TAC Officer Myers. "Sergeant Ron will be waiting for you in hangar 32 to issue you your equipment. And, I better not hear you gave Sergeant Ron any of your lip. If he says jump, the only thing out of your mouth should be to ask how high."

Sergeant Ron was the Academy's chief of maintenance. He was an older man who was a little on the unconventional side, but Richard liked him anyway.

When Richard didn't answer his TAC officer fast enough, TAC Officer Myers said, "Do you understand, cadet?"

"Sir! Yes, sir!" Richard said as he switched from parade rest to a stiff attention.

"Cadets 147, 303, and 422," TAC Officer Myers said to Jerad, Telsa, and Tam respectively. "The three of you will be on the blue team. Sergeant Hendricks will issue your U.H.A.A.V.s when you get to hangar 2. Any questions?"

"Sir! No, sir!" said the three cadets as they snapped to attention as well.

Richard risked a glance out the corner of his eye at his three friends. He had assumed since the four of them were the last of the cadets, they'd be in a two-against-two scenario. Obviously, he'd been wrong. Richard caught Jerad's eyes.

Jerad raised his eyebrows as if guessing Richard's unspoken question. *Why are we in a three-against-one scenario?* His friend seemed as mystified as Richard.

Heck, Richard thought, *if anyone should be pitted one against three, it should be Jerad.*

"This training scenario," TAC Officer Myers continued, "is designed to test your control of a cat as well as your initiative in overcoming your opponents. Since you haven't completed tactics' training in cats yet, we won't be grading on how well you integrate your cats together as a fighting unit. Those skills will be taught later. Instead, we're concerned with how well you think outside the box. You're going to be wizard scouts. We expect you to innovate. Are there any questions?"

No one said anything. Cadets rarely asked TAC Officer Myers a question. He was not one of those instructors who thought there was no such thing as a stupid question. Richard and his fellow cadets had discovered early on that TAC Officer Gaston Myers considered any question coming out of a cadet's mouth to be a stupid question.

"Good," said TAC Officer Myers with what Richard thought was the hint of a sadistic smile. "In order to motivate you cadets a little, we're adding an incentive to this afternoon's training. Since you're the last cadets in your class to participate in this urban-training scenario, you'll undoubtedly notice the other cats are a little on the dirty side. In fact, your fellow cadets appear to have gotten all of their cats filthy. I'm sure you know our maintenance chief, Sergeant Ron, would be extremely displeased if we turned our cats back into the motor pool without a thorough cleaning. Unfortunately for you, the rest of your junior cohort has already been released to start their three-day pass. That presents us with a little dilemma."

TAC Officer Myers took a moment to scan the four cadets. His gaze stopped on Richard.

"We all know how much cadet 832 enjoys challenges, don't we?" said TAC Officer Myers.

His comment was met by silence.

"I said, we all know how much cadet 832 enjoys challenges, don't we?" said TAC Officer Myers a little louder.

"Sir! Yes, sir!" Richard shouted in unison with his three friends.

TAC Officer Myers smiled. "Of course, he does. So, we've developed a special challenge which I think at least three of you are going to enjoy. Your cohort's three-day weekend officially starts tonight at 1800 hours. I'm sure all of you have been looking forward to it."

The smile on TAC Officer Myers' face grew even more sadistic. "My sources tell me some of you are even attending the Fleet Admiral's Ball tomorrow night." He paused as if for effect.

Red warning flags arose in Richard's mind. Even after six month's absence, Richard's distrust of his TAC officer was as strong as ever.

"As I was saying," said TAC Officer Myers. "The other cadets have been released for the weekend. And someone forgot to have them clean their cats before they left. As a result, the loser of this training scenario will have the privilege of assisting our motor pool personnel in cleaning and maintaining the cats before being released to start their weekend pass. The winners will be free to start their pass immediately."

Richard picked up on the fact that TAC Officer Myers had

made the word loser singular and the word winners plural. He silently cursed his TAC officer.

TAC Officer Myers stared hard at Richard. "Now, doesn't that sound fair?"

"Sir! Yes, sir!" Richard said along with his three friends.

"All right then," TAC Officer Myers said rubbing his hands together. "I want you cadets in position on the urban-training range in thirty minutes. And may the Creator help any cadet who's late. I will personally make sure that cadet is never late for anything ever again. Are there any questions?"

"Sir! No, sir!" said all four cadets.

Richard did a quick calculation. They were currently inside hangar 1. Myers had assigned him a cat in the hangar farthest from hangar 1. He'd have to circle around the entire length of the runway to get to hangar 32. Even at top speed, Richard figured he'd take at least twelve minutes to run the three kilometers to hangar 32. That would only leave him eighteen minutes to fire up his cat and get to the training area. Richard was sure Myers was setting him up for failure.

Jerk, Richard thought.

"Then what are you wizard scout wannabees doing in my hangar?" shouted Myers. "Get those leather personnel-carriers on your feet moving, and get your good-for-nothing carcasses out of here."

Richard did an about face. His friends followed suit. They all took off running towards the large hangar door. Beyond it, Richard could make out the hot-asphalt taxiway awaiting them outside. Once they'd cleared the hangar doors and were out of sight of their TAC officer, Richard slowed to a trot. Jerad, Tam, and Telsa did likewise.

"Tough luck, old buddy," said Tam. "It figures Myers would come up with a way to cheat you out of your weekend pass."

"I haven't lost yet," Richard said without much confidence.

"No, you haven't," agreed Jerad. "But don't expect any mercy from us. I like you Rick, but I've got big plans for this weekend. And, they don't include cleaning and maintaining a hundred and twenty-four cats."

"Yeah, same here," said Tam. "I've got a hot date lined up. I'll give your regrets to Liz when I see her, Rick." A mischievous grin appeared on Tam's face as she added, "I'm sure an attractive woman like Liz won't have any trouble getting some good-looking naval officer to dance with her at the ball."

"Very funny, Tam," Richard said. "After I win this fight, I'll be sure and tell your dance partners you'll be thinking of them while you're at the motor pool washing my cat."

"That's the spirit," laughed Telsa good-naturedly as she punched Richard on the arm. "A good wizard scout always maintains their confidence even in the face of certain defeat."

In spite of Richard's poor odds in the upcoming training, he joined Telsa with a small laugh of his own. It was hard for anyone to even pretend they were irritated with Telsa. Her natural good-humor was infectious. Most of the cadets treated Telsa like their little sister.

"Well, here we are," said Jerad as he stopped in front of hangar 2. "Sorry, Rick. It's a long walk to hangar 32."

"Not to mention it's hot as hell," said Tam grinning. "But don't feel bad, Rick. I'll be thinking of you when I'm in the air-conditioned comfort of my cockpit."

"Yeah, me too," said Telsa. "I'll be as easy on you as I–"

"You cadets better hustle!" shouted a voice from the doorway of hangar 2. It was their cohort's armorer, Sergeant Hendricks.

"Sir! Yes, sir," Richard shouted. His friends followed suit.

"And don't call me sir," said Sergeant Hendricks with a friendly smile. "I'm a sergeant. Unlike officers, I work for a living."

Tam and Telsa headed for the hangar door. Jerad remained behind.

"Rick, a word of advice," said Jerad. "Myers has you in a Tomcat. It's a good vehicle, but you haven't been trained in a Tomcat. Its third leg has a tendency to screw up new pilots. When I trained newbies in the Tomcat in the past, I've always told them to think of the rear leg more as a tail than a leg for walking. Its purpose is to provide support when firing the 40mm autocannon. We'll just be firing paintballs today, so the autocannon's recoil will be minimal. I'd recommend keeping the rear leg in the stored position. You'll only need the two primary legs for walking."

"Thanks, Jerad," Richard said appreciatively. "I'll keep that in mind. I'd wish you luck, but that would mean I'll be spending my weekend cleaning cats. So, I guess I'll stick with thanks." Richard smiled to make sure his friend knew he was joking.

Jerad grinned back. "I tend to make my own luck, Rick, so watch your back. I'll be seeing you in twenty-eight minutes."

Richard nodded his head and began double-timing down the taxiway. He paced himself. He was in a hurry, but it wouldn't do him any good to pass out from heat exhaustion before he got to his destination. The temperature was hot enough that Richard could feel the asphalt of the taxiway sticking to the bottoms of his boots. By the time Richard got even with hangar 5, sweat was already dripping down his forehead and into his eyes. Richard looked across the runway to his destination. He had a long ways to go.

"I hate deserts," Richard muttered between breaths. "And I hate Myers."

In spite of the heat, Richard tried picking up the pace a little. Each breath felt like he was sucking air from a hot sauna. Richard began worrying once he reached hangar 32 he'd be too exhausted to pilot his Tomcat. Thoughts of spending a nice weekend with Liz grew smaller with each step.

Richard heard a vehicle approaching from his rear. He shifted to his right to give it room to pass. Hitching a ride was not an option for cadets. Richard had no doubt TAC Officer Myers was watching his every move via tele-bots. It was common knowledge among the cadets that the microscopic tele-bots were positioned all over the Academy's training areas. Richard knew from experience their video and audio could be sent over the tele-network through the central computer to terminals monitored by the Academy's TAC officers.

Instead of passing, the vehicle slowed down until it was keeping pace with Richard.

"You ain't ever gonna get there at this rate, cadet," came a hillbilly-sounding voice. The voice belonged to an old, scraggly-bearded, long-haired man sitting in the driver's seat of an orange fuel truck. The old man had a friendly grin on his face.

"Oh, I'll get there, Sergeant Ron," Richard said giving a grin of his own. "I'm just not sure what shape I'll be in when I arrive."

Sergeant Ron wasn't really a sergeant. He'd served in the military as a vehicle mechanic while an enlisted soldier. The word was he loved working with his beloved U.H.A.A.V.s, but he hated the spit and polish of military life. When his superiors informed him they were going to promote him to sergeant and send him to another unit, he'd told them they could stick their sergeant stripes where the sun didn't shine. Since expressing opinions in such a manner was frowned upon in the military, Sergeant Ron had found himself out of the military and back in civilian life. However, two months after he'd left the military, Sergeant Ron had somehow acquired a position as the civilian contractor in charge of the Academy's motor pool. He'd been with the Academy ever since. In spite of Sergeant Ron's previous dislike for the military, he was popular with both cadets and instructors. Even the Academy's TAC officers called him Sergeant Ron.

"Well, you might have time to lollygag around, cadet 832," said Sergeant Ron still grinning, "but I have important things to do. And, I don't have time to wait while you take a leisurely stroll around the airfield. So, hop on in here before you pass out from heat exhaustion. We've got things to do over at hangar 32."

"I'm not sure my TAC officer would want me to hitch a ride," Richard said. The offer was tempting, but he could almost feel Myers' eyes drilling into his back as it was.

"Nonsense," said Sergeant Ron. "I just left Myers. He told me he'd given you strict orders to obey my every command." With another smile, Sergeant Ron said, "Now, get in before I put you on report. That's an order, cadet."

Richard didn't argue further. He jumped on the fuel tanker's sideboard and opened the door. Before he could get fully inside, Sergeant Ron hit the accelerator and took a hard left straight towards the runway.

"Whoa!" Richard said as he pulled himself the rest of the way inside and buckled into the passenger seat. "You can't cross the runway without permission, Sergeant Ron."

"Ha! Who says I can't?" said Sergeant Ron as he picked up a hand mike. "Tower, this is tanker 103; crossing runway midfield from west to east."

"Negative, tanker 103," said a feminine voice over a speaker in the truck's dashboard. "Cargo shuttle is on short final. Turn right and proceed along taxiway."

Looking out the driver's door window, Richard saw the bright lights of a cargo shuttle about a kilometer out. Instead of turning to the right as directed, Sergeant Ron shoved the accelerator lever forward a notch.

"You're coming in garbled, tower," said Sergeant Ron. "Did you say proceed ahead of cargo shuttle to far taxiway?"

"Negative, tanker 103," said the feminine voice in a higher pitch. "Do not cross the runway. Abort."

By this time the tanker was at the edge of the runway. Looking at Richard, Sergeant Ron said, "Hold on tight, cadet. This is where we find out who's stupider; the guys in the shuttle or us." With those words, Sergeant Ron slammed the accelerator lever full forward as he gave a wild laugh.

When the tanker reached the middle of the runway, the shuttle was only a hundred meters out and five meters above the ground.

"We're not going to make it," Richard said.

A blast of noise came from Richard's left as the shuttle's engines let out a long streak of energy. The shuttle rose higher and passed a few meters above the tanker.

"See? What'd I tell ya?" said Sergeant Ron as he gave another laugh. "You don't need permission if you know how to sweet talk the tower."

"Sergeant Ron," Richard said. "I think the next time you offer me a ride, I'm going to turn and run the other way."

Sergeant Ron laughed and said, "Now you're getting smart, cadet. That's what my wife does."

CHAPTER 3

The tanker pulled in front of hangar 32. Richard hurriedly opened his door and jumped out while saying, "Sergeant Ron, with all due respect, sir, you're an absolute nut!"

If the old maintenance chief had been a real sergeant, Richard would probably have kept his mouth shut. But before he'd left on his mission, Richard had gotten comfortable trading banter with Sergeant Ron due to all the times he'd pulled extra duty at the motor pool. Richard doubted Sergeant Ron would take offense.

He was right. Sergeant Ron just jumped out of the truck and began running alongside Richard towards the hangar door. The cantankerous old maintenance chief was grinning. He seemed to be enjoying himself.

"Oh, you cadets with your 'yes sirs' and 'no sirs'," said Sergeant Ron. "You worry too much about rules and regulations. Now back when I was in the military, I'll tell you we had it rough. We couldn't afford all the niceties you young whippersnappers seem to thrive on nowadays. Yep, those were the good old days."

"I thought you hated the military when you were on active duty, Sergeant Ron," Richard said as he slipped through the hangar door.

"Naw," said Sergeant Ron close on Richard's heels. "Nothing could be further from the truth. I loved the military. I just hated the rules, the regulations, the sergeants, and with only a couple of exceptions, I especially hated the officers. Come to think of it, I wasn't all that fond of having to be where I was told, when I was told, and not being able to do what I wanted when I wanted. Other than that, I loved the military."

"Well," Richard said as he came to a stop inside the hangar, "If you took all those things away, you wouldn't have soldiers. You'd have a bunch of civilians."

"By golly," laughed Sergeant Ron, "I think you're right. I guess that's why you're a highfalutin wizard scout cadet, and I'm just a poor little maintenance chief responsible for a motor pool with eighteen billion credits worth of equipment."

Richard saw some of that equipment now. Four of the Academy's U.H.A.A.V.s were arrayed around the sides of the hangar. Sergeant Ron began walking towards the left wall where the smallest of four cats stood on two metal legs. It was a Tomcat.

"Ah," said Sergeant Ron, "you know I'm just fooling with you, 832. Heck, I've often kicked myself in the rear for not staying in the military. I could've been retired and enjoying the good life by now instead of sweating away seven days a week with a bunch of grease monkeys working on cats."

Sergeant Ron stopped in front of the Tomcat. Like its smaller cousin the Warcat, the Tomcat was designed as a scout. At four meters high, the Tomcat was slightly larger than the three meter tall Warcat. It was also heavier armed. Its left weapon's pod looked similar to an arm with a permanently affixed 40mm autocannon at the end instead of a hand. Its right weapon's pod was actually a fully-functional arm with a five-fingered, metallic claw for a hand. The Tomcat model standing in front of Richard gripped a 20mm chain gun in its right claw. A metallic holster of sorts on the Tomcat's right side could be used to store the chain gun when it was not in use. A rocket pod with six anti-armor missiles was positioned on the Tomcat's shoulder.

"I thought Tomcats had three legs," Richard said noticing only two legs.

"It does," said Sergeant Ron, "but I had Charlie stow the rear-brace leg. You shouldn't need it just firing paintballs."

Richard glanced over at Charlie as he pushed a wheeled stepladder next to the Tomcat. Charlie waved one of his four arms at Richard in recognition. Richard nodded back. The old lizard didn't talk much, but Richard liked him. He was competent, and Richard liked lifeforms who could be depended upon to do their jobs regardless of their species.

Switching his attention back to the Tomcat, Richard gazed up towards the cockpit towering above him. Richard hadn't yet had a chance to pilot one of the Academy's Tomcats. But he'd piloted a Warcat several times, and they were similar in operation. Richard was confident he could handle the metal monster with just a little assistance from his battle computer.

Myers screwed up, Richard thought. *I'll bet he thought assigning me a small scout would hurt my chances of winning.*

Richard was actually glad he'd drawn one of the scout cats. As Jerad had said, operating them was basically like wearing an oversized battle suit. If his TAC officer had put him in a medium-sized cat like a Long Cat or one of the heavier cats like the Leviathan, he'd have had his hands full. He only vaguely remembered the layouts of their control systems.

The jerk actually did me a favor, Richard thought.

"Well, don't just stand there gawking, cadet," said Sergeant Ron with a friendly shove towards a workbench to the right of the Tomcat. "Get a move on. You've only got twenty-three minutes until you have to be in the training area. Your battle suit's on the workbench."

Richard didn't need to be told twice. He was aware of the time limitations. Sergeant Ron had saved him several minutes by picking him up in the tanker truck. However, Richard knew he'd still be hard pressed making it to the training area in time. He began stripping off his jumpsuit top as he ran towards the workbench.

Nick, are you there? Richard thought.

I'm here, Rick, came the reply from his battle computer. *What kept you? You know I hate being pressed for time. We need time to plan.*

You're always telling me you think at nanosecond speed, Richard said. *I'm confident you will probably have a dozen or more plans before I finish donning my battle suit.*

I only think at nanosecond speed on my slow days, Nickelo laughed. *I can think a whole lot faster when necessary. And, it just so happens I have twenty-two possible plans laid out already. However, they all require you to be inside the Tomcat to work. So, you need to start hustling, oh greatest of wizard scouts.*

Kicking off his boots, jumpsuit, and underwear, Richard

hurriedly began pulling on his battle suit. He sealed the battle suit's upper and lower sections together. He felt a prickly sensation all over as the suit's seventeen thousand plus thread-needles inserted themselves into his body. The thread-needles connected the battle suit to Richard's nerves so the suit felt like a second layer of skin. Automatic filters in the battle suit kept sensations from becoming too painful. However, the filters still allowed him to perform delicate maneuvers including picking up a single grain of rice if the need arose. He could even read braille through the battle suit's gloves.

Placing his battle helmet on his head, Richard said, *Seal me up, Nick.*

The battle helmet changed shape, and it extended down the sides of his head and around his neck until it merged with the top of his battle suit. A red glow appeared in front of Richard's eyes as the helmet's filter formed a visor. The filter was actually a mini force field incorporated with a multitude of sensors. The filter could be switched between sensors in order to detect light, radiation, thermal, or even sonic vibrations. Standard procedures for wizard scouts were to keep their night vision filter activated even during daylight hours. According to their TAC officers, by doing so, it wouldn't matter to a wizard scout whether it was daylight, nighttime, foggy, raining, or snowing. They'd always be used to sensing their surroundings in the same manner. During the last three years, Richard had found his TAC officers' reasoning to be true. However, he'd never admit it to them. Besides, he tended to cheat sometimes and use his battle helmet's clear visor so he could see the world in a more natural view.

As the battle helmet sealed, tubes forced their way into Richard's nostrils and mouth as well as his other body openings. Richard barely paid attention. The first time he'd been sealed in his suit, he'd fought the invasive tubes. At the time, he thought he was going to die. Each new cohort at the Academy normally did have a couple of cadets die when they were first introduced to their battle suits. Richard assumed the Empire wrote their deaths off as training accidents. He wondered if the cadet's parents ever knew their child suffocated to death boxed up alone inside a battle suit. Richard shrugged the thought off. He needed to get to work.

Charlie held the ladder as Richard clambered up towards the top of the Tomcat's head. The upper-entry hatch was already open. Before Richard could enter the Tomcat, Charlie gave a yell.

"Here," said Charlie through the translator hooked to his belt. "You'll need this."

The old lizard threw a bundle of straps and buckles up to Richard. It was an interface harness. Richard shook out the harness and strapped it over his battle suit. He arranged the harness so the metallic buckles and computer access points were located on his shoulders and sides. Once he was satisfied with the fit, Richard slid feet first down the circular opening in the Tomcat's head. It was a tight fit, but he made it easily enough.

When he was inside, Richard said, *Not much room in here, is there, Nick?*

There doesn't need to be, said Nickelo. *It's similar to the Warcat scout. There's no console or seat. Just connect your interface harness, and you're ready to go.*

Richard knew it wasn't quite that simple. While he'd not had a chance to pilot a Tomcat, he'd piloted Warcat scouts on several occasions. Richard liked the Warcats, and he hoped the Tomcat would prove to be as easy to drive.

Grabbing a thick, black cord on one of the Tomcat's walls, Richard plugged the end into the corresponding point on his interface harness. He quickly followed suit with other connectors. Once he was hooked in, Richard thought the command to close the Tomcat's hatch. The hatch closed, and a clear liquid began filling the area within the pilot's compartment.

Without an environmental suit, a pilot would drown in the toxic liquid, but Richard was not concerned. His battle suit was a self-contained environment. Its recycling systems supplied him with everything needed from air to nutrients. According to the Academy's technicians, wizard scouts could theoretically stay in their battle suits their whole lives. The battle suit would recycle the wizard scout's body wastes and reintroduce the recycled nutrients and water back into the wearer's system via the suit's thread-needles.

Theory aside, Richard hoped he never had to remain in his battle suit for a long period of time. As he'd told his battle computer on many occasions, his battle suit would keep him alive, but it wouldn't be a very comfortable life.

Once the pilot's compartment was completely filled, Richard sensed energy flow into the liquid. The liquid's consistency changed to a gel. Richard raised his right arm. The Tomcat's interface sensed the change in the gel and raised its right arm in a movement corresponding exactly to Richard's. He raised his left arm. The Tomcat's left weapon's pod moved accordingly. Twisting to the left and right, Richard saw his field of vision through the cockpit window shift as the Tomcat's torso shifted in response.

Nickelo, Richard said. *Are you connected to the Tomcat's computer?*

Roger, said Nickelo. *I've been given a special security interface for this training mission. I'm connected to the Tomcat via the tele-network.*

The tele-network allowed computers from one end of the galaxy to the other to communicate with each other instantaneously. From experience, Richard knew the tele-network even extended into other dimensions. Almost all of the Empire's computers were connected to the tele-network. Nickelo was an exception. The Empire's central computer didn't allow Richard's battle computer to connect directly to the tele-network. According to Nickelo, the central computer thought Nickelo had been corrupted emotionally by his close association with Richard. As far as Richard could determine, the central computer was concerned Nickelo might corrupt other parts of the tele-network if he was allowed to connect directly. Consequently, Nickelo could only connect to the tele-network when the central computer provided a special security interface created for a specific mission.

"Sergeant Ron," Richard said using the Tomcat's external speakers. "I'm as ready as I'll ever be."

"Roger that," said Sergeant Ron as he gave Richard a thumbs up. "Charlie, move that ladder before this crazy cadet tramples all over it."

Looking up at Richard through the Tomcat's cockpit window, Sergeant Ron yelled, "Give em hell, Rick. Just make sure you don't damage my Tomcat. I want it back in one piece at the end of the day."

Richard raised his right hand in acknowledgment to Sergeant Ron. The Tomcat raised its right arm with the 20mm chain gun in response. Then Richard walked towards the hangar door.

He called me Rick, Richard thought. *I didn't even know the old fart knew my name.*

I guess that goes to show you don't know everything, Rick, said Nickelo. *Now, keep it to a walk until we clear the taxiway. It's so hot outside you'll tear up the asphalt if you try to run.*

Roger that, Richard said.

The urban training area was on the other side of the airfield about five kilometers beyond hangar 2. Richard silently cursed TAC Officer Myers. He had no doubt his TAC officer had intentionally assigned him a cat in a hangar as far from the training site as possible. Richard knew for a fact that hangar 3 had two Tomcats he could've used instead.

How's our time, Nick? Richard said. *Will we make it in time?*

It'll be close, Rick, said Nickelo. *But, I calculate a ninety-eight percent probability we'll be in position with at least forty-six seconds to spare. Now, less talk and more walk.*

Roger that, Richard said as he sped up his pace to the maximum he thought the airfield's asphalt could handle. He looked across the airfield at his destination far off in the distance. Even at max speed he had a feeling it was going to be close.

CHAPTER 4

Enemy armor is approaching from your nine, eleven, and two o'clock positions, wizard scout. Recommend you take immediate evasive action.

I see them, Nick, Richard said to his battle computer as he looked at the red, orange, and yellow dots on his battle helmet's heads-up display. *I'm assuming the red is the heavy cat, orange is the medium, and yellow the light scout.*

Affirmative, Rick, said Nickelo. *I calculate an eighty-four percent probability your friend Jerad is in a light Warcat scout.*

At three meters, the Warcat was the smallest and most lightly armed of any of the U.H.A.A.V.s. The Warcat only had a small-caliber plasma rifle and two anti-armor missiles for defense. It was designed for stealth operations in areas containing advanced detection equipment. Even wizard scouts had trouble detecting a Warcat when it was operating in stealth mode.

I'd say you're probably right, Nick, Richard said. *Jerad's got more experience in cats than anyone in the cohort. He's too good of a leader to put himself in one of the heavier cats and leave his troops with the lighter protection. I suspect he put Telsa in the heavy cat and Tam in the medium-utility cat.*

I concur with your analysis, said Nickelo. *That could work to your advantage. Your Tomcat is a light cat. It's got speed, maneuverability, and decent firepower. If you can stay away from Jerad in his Warcat scout, you may be able to work your way behind Telsa or Tam. They're as bad at handling cats as you. In*

31

fact, Telsa's even worse. She should be an easy kill even if she's in a heavy cat.

Thanks for the vote of confidence, old buddy, Richard said with only a little sarcasm. He was well aware of his shortcomings in piloting a cat. Fortunately, the control interface for the Tomcat was fairly intuitive.

Give me a rundown on the locations of all the cats and possible courses of actions, Richard said.

Analysis indicates the other two cats facing you are a Long Cat medium-utility cat and a Kraken heavy cat, said Nickelo. *As you said, Jerad's probably in a Warcat. It's lighter armed than your Tomcat, but it's faster, and it has superb stealth capabilities. If Tam's in a Long Cat like I think, then you're really in trouble. Its primary weapon is a 200mm phase cannon. Tam's an expert shot.*

Tell me about it, Richard said. He'd seen Tam at the gunnery range often enough to have a deep respect for her marksmanship.

But being in a larger cat has its disadvantages, said Nickelo continuing with his analysis. *The Long Cat's seven meter height means Tam will have a harder time hiding. Of course, that's counterbalanced a little by the two sets of anti-armor rockets on the Long Cat's shoulders.*

So was that supposed to be good news to cheer me up? Richard said.

I don't remember saying there was any good news, said Nickelo. *If you look at your heads-up display, you'll notice the Long Cat has taken up position at the end of the next street. I calculate a fifty-eight percent probability Tam will stay there as a sort of pillbox to provide fire support for the two other cats. You might be able to work your way up the street using your Tomcat's maneuverability to dodge rounds, but I wouldn't want to bet my life on it.*

Neither would I, agreed Richard. *What about the Warcat scout? Assuming Jerad's in it, what's his most probable course of action?*

The urban training area consists of eight city blocks by eight city blocks, said Nickelo. *The Warcat scout is designed especially for urban fighting. I'm plotting my best guess on the Warcat's position on your heads-up display with a yellow dot. It's based upon intermittent readings. The Warcat's actual position could easily be two or three blocks from the point shown on your heads-*

up display. If I was Jerad's battle computer, I'd recommend he perform a flanking movement to get behind you. With Jerad's previous experience with armor, I estimate you have about four minutes before you'll be caught in a crossfire. The Warcat's antipersonnel weapons can't hurt you, but its two shoulder-mounted rockets can put you out of action. I calculate Jerad will try to push you into the kill zone of Tam's Long Cat.

And the heavy cat? Richard said.

The Kraken heavy cat is easy to trace, said Nickelo. *It appears to be making its way down the street behind us and one street over. Based upon its erratic movements, I'd say Telsa is having a difficult time steering it. Its six legs and four weapons' tentacles are difficult for even experienced armor-pilots to control. Assuming Telsa's at the controls, I'd say there's an eighty-nine percent probability she'll take the Kraken to the end of the intersection on your right and set up a blocking position. If you don't make it past the intersection before she gets there, she'll have a clear field of fire if you try to maneuver up the street towards Tam's Long Cat.*

Richard considered his options. He attached the 20mm chain gun in the Tomcat's right claw to its holder on his side. Using the right arm of his cat for support, Richard bent the Tomcat down and started crawling into a large hole in the closest building. The opening looked like a bombed-out section of the wall, but Richard was pretty sure the hole had been created by the Academy's engineers.

Once through the building's outer wall, Richard rose to a crouching position. The guts of the building were a spider web of metal support beams crisscrossing between the walls and ceiling.

This may take longer than I thought, Richard said as his left weapon's pod caught on a support beam and tore it loose from the wall.

Moving forward, Richard reached the end of the building. He opened a passive scan and allowed the life-force energy of his surroundings to seep into his mind. As a wizard scout, Richard had two types of scans. His passive scan was similar to hearing in that all he had to do was sense the life force, or Power, of his surroundings. Everything living or non-living released at least a little bit of Power. By sensing the released energy, Richard could tell a lot about things around him. His passive scan confirmed the presence of two large energy readings; one to his front and one to his rear.

Richard concentrated on the Power to his front which he assumed was the Long Cat. He looked for the subtle differences between the Power emanating from the non-living Long Cat and the Power coming from the living occupant inside. He concentrated on the living occupant. Richard had trouble separating the energy frequencies, but finally he sensed a trace of Power he recognized as Tam.

We guessed right, Richard said. *The pilot of the Long Cat is Tam. We're going to have to work on her stealth shield some more. I'm not complaining, but I shouldn't be able to sense her at all with her best stealth shield activated.*

That's true to a degree, said Nickelo. *But, you have an advantage since you've helped your friends with their stealth shields so much.*

Richard thought about it. He'd spent many hours of free time with Tam improving her stealth shield. A wizard scout's primary job was reconnaissance. This required getting in and out of enemy territory undetected. A wizard scout's stealth shield was the best line of defense against detection. Everything, including wizard scouts, released at least a residual amount of Power. A stealth shield prevented most of that residual Power from escaping. No shield could prevent all Power from escaping, but it could prevent a lot. This made it difficult for creatures or electronic devices to detect the source of the Power.

I calculate you have about two minutes max before the Warcat scout will be here, said Nickelo. *If you're going to do something about the Long Cat, you need to do it now.*

I hear you, Nick, Richard said.

Richard was now at the end of the building facing the side street. In one direction, the side street connected with the street the Long Cat was covering. In the other direction, the side street connected with the street the Kraken was on. For whatever reason, Telsa had not brought her Kraken any closer. Still, Richard figured even though the Kraken was stationary, Telsa probably had the length of the street covered with the Kraken's primary weapons. Richard had no doubt it would be game over if he so much as stuck one of the legs of his cat out into the street. He needed to avoid the Kraken at all costs until he had taken care of Tam's Long Cat.

The building he was in had several large storefront windows facing the side street. The windows were blown out. Richard took advantage of the openings by crouching even lower and slipping out into an alleyway. Fortunately, the alley was not visible from the Long Cat's position. Once he was in the alley, Richard eyed the intersection to his right. He couldn't help feeling exposed. It was the street occupied by the Kraken.

We've got to protect our rear before we can take on the Long Cat, Nick, Richard said. *This Tomcat has eight anti-armor mines. Do you think that would be enough to prevent Telsa from getting the Kraken through here?*

Those anti-armor mines are magnetic, said Nickelo. *If you space the mines out on this side of the intersection, you will at least slow the Kraken down. Even an experienced pilot would have trouble getting the Kraken's six legs through the intersection without stepping on a mine.*

Good, Richard said. *That's what I was hoping.*

Activating the mine release level, Richard hastily laid out the eight anti-armor mines in what Nickelo assured him was the most efficient pattern. After the mines were in place, Richard walked his Tomcat forward until his left-gun pod was only a half meter from the edge of the next building.

Tam will know where you're at, Rick, said Nickelo. *Your stealth shield is too good for her to pick up, but the Long Cat's sensors will be tracing the electronic output of your Tomcat. The moment you stick any part of your cat around the corner of the building, you're going to have a 200mm phase round coming at you.*

I know, Richard said. *That's why I'm not going to stick my head around the corner. I'm going to stick my left pod's 40mm autocannon around it. I'll use the autocannon's sighting device as a sort of periscope to pinpoint the Long Cat's position. I need more detailed information than my passive scan and the Tomcat's electronic sensors are giving me.*

Fine, said Nickelo. *Do it your way. You're the all-powerful wizard scout. I'm just the subservient and humble battle computer.*

Whatever, Richard said half dismissively. *I haven't heard you giving any suggestions. You're just pointing out problems.*

It's your training exercise, Rick, not mine, said Nickelo. *Besides, TAC Officer Myers directed all of the battle computers to give minimal assistance unless there was a safety reason.*

You know, Nick, Richard said, *sometimes I think you listen to Myers more than you listen to me.*

Now you know that's not true, Rick, said Nickelo in a hurt voice. *You know I always listen to you. I don't always do what you ask, but I do listen. There's a difference, you know.*

Richard didn't bother answering. He made another check of his heads-up display. Both the Kraken and the Warcat scout were still in their same positions.

Hey, Richard said. *The Warcat hasn't moved either. What's Jerad up to? I figured he'd be making use of the scout's maneuverability to get into the battle as soon as possible.*

The yellow dot you see on your heads-up display is from information I received thirty-two seconds ago, said Nickelo. *I don't know where the Warcat scout is now. I'll update the plot when I receive new information. I seriously doubt the Warcat is anywhere close to the yellow dot on your heads-up display.*

Well, nothing I can do about it, Richard said. *I've got to take out Tam while I have the chance.*

Richard used the Tomcat's hydraulics to slowly edge the left-gun pod of his cat around the corner of the building. Once he had the 40mm cannon past the corner, Richard had a clear field of view of the street ahead. About fifty meters to his front, Richard made out a jumble of concrete from a bombed-out building. He saw a flash of light at the edge of the gunsight. Richard immediately jerked the Tomcat's left-gun pod back, but he was a split second too late. A huge splash of blue paint splattered the corner of the building. By the time Richard finished pulling the 40mm autocannon back around the corner, it was dripping in blue paint as well.

That sucks, Richard said. *Tam took out the 40mm autocannon. The only long-range weapon I have now is the 20mm chain gun and the six anti-armor rockets in my shoulder pod.*

Well, said Nickelo unsympathetically. *You're lucky this is a simulation, and the Long Cat is only firing paint rounds. An actual 200mm phase round would have taken out the whole corner of the building in addition to your autocannon. You'd either be flaming wreckage by now or buried under a hundred metric tons of concrete. In either case, you'd be dead.*

If this wasn't a simulation, I'd have called in an airstrike, Richard said.

I won't argue with you, Rick, said Nickelo. *Regardless, what are you going to do about the Long Cat? Jerad will be here in the Warcat soon. The clock's ticking.*

What about the roof of this next building? Richard said. *Do you think it would hold the weight of my Tomcat?*

Not if you stood up it wouldn't, said Nickelo. *But if you low crawl on the roof, the weight will be distributed. I calculate a ninety-four percent probability you could navigate the roof if you remained in a prone position. But, I need to point out the pilot of the Long Cat will know exactly where you're at. Your stealth shield is hiding you, but you can't hide the electronic signature of your cat.*

No problem, Richard said. *The phase cannon on the Long Cat can only elevate forty degrees. Even if Tam backs her cat up to the far building, she'll only be able to hit the fourth floor of this one. I'll be two stories higher when I'm on the roof. I'll be safe enough.*

If Tam had a real phase cannon, said Nickelo, *she'd blow the whole floor out. The Tomcat and you'd come tumbling down.*

Well, Richard said, *as I pointed out earlier, this is a simulation. Tam doesn't have a real phase cannon. I'm just working within the limitations of the simulation. Now, are you going to keep talking? Or are you going to help me find the best handholds.*

Richard's heads-up display switched to an image of the wall of the building. Yellow markers pinpointed strategic hand and footholds for the Tomcat. Richard took a step towards the wall, but then he stopped. He took two quick steps back towards the blasted out section of the first building. Reaching inside with the Tomcat's right arm, he ripped out one of the support beams. The metal beam was about three meters long.

And what pray tell are you going to do with that? Nickelo asked.

I'm not sure yet, Richard admitted. *I'll let you know as soon as I figure it out. It just seemed like a good idea. Call it a hunch. All I know for sure is this 20mm peashooter I have won't harm a medium cat. I need something a little more potent.*

Without discussing it further, Richard began climbing the wall. Climbing was awkward. The hydraulics to the Tomcat's left-gun pod had been deactivated. It now hung uselessly at his side. Richard thrust his right arm in a convenient hole and pulled the cat up. When his hold was secure, Richard took a moment to insure the Kraken was still stationary. It was. He continued climbing up the side of the wall.

Where's Jerad in the Warcat, Nick? And what's Telsa doing in the Kraken? Why is she just staying in one place?

No idea, Rick. Sorry.

Once Richard made it to the edge of the roof, he rolled over the reinforced-concrete ledge until he was lying flat on the roof. Even with his weight distributed, Richard heard the roof make cracking noises.

Here goes nothing, Richard said as he began crawling forward.

Low crawling while inside a four meter tall, eight metric ton cat was not easy. Fortunately, moving the Tomcat was similar to moving a human body.

Make your way towards that vent cap, said Nickelo. *The Long Cat should be right below there. And, why are you still carrying that metal bar? I don't understand how you think it's going to help.*

I'm not sure how it'll help, Richard said as he crawled the last few meters to a position near the edge of the roof. *However, I have a hunch it'll come in handy. Besides, it reminds me of my phase rod. I think I prefer it to the 20mm.*

Well, said Nickelo doubtfully, *we'll see how useful you think it is when that Warcat scout is firing anti-armor rockets at you from fifty meters away.*

I'm going to ease my cockpit past the lip of the roof so I can get a visual of the Long Cat, Richard said. *Has the Kraken moved? And, do you have an update on the Warcat's location.*

That's a negative on both counts, Rick, said Nickelo. *I'm confused by the Kraken's non-movement.*

Can't worry about it now, Nick, Richard said. *Tam's quick on her feet. I know the Long Cat's phase cannon can't elevate this high, but I wouldn't put it past her to figure out some method for using her rocket pods to harass us. Back me up on the visual, Nick. Regardless of what the instructors say, the view from this cockpit is not the same as looking out the visor of my battle helmet.*

Will do, Rick, said Nickelo. *I agree with you on Tam. She's tricky. She's bound to have a fix on your location. I calculate there is a twenty-two percent probability she's figured out a way to elevate her weapons.*

Doubtful, Richard said as he eased the upper part of his cockpit past the edge of the roof. Richard peered over the side of the building as he continued crawling forward. He could see part of the street below. Normally, he kept his battle helmet's filter in night-vision mode which gave everything a red tint. But since he was inside the cat, Richard had opted to use his helmet's clear visor. As a result, he saw every nuance of color on the wall of the building opposite him and on the street below.

Where's she at? Richard said growing concerned. *Even if she were crouching, I should be seeing the top of the Long Cat's turret by now. That medium cat is seven meters tall. I wouldn't think she could crouch down that much.*

It's seven point four meters tall, said Nickelo. *And you're right. Even in a crouch, the Long Cat couldn't reduce its height to less than five meters.*

Pushing forward with the clawed feet of the Tomcat, Richard eased his cockpit window a little further past the edge of the roof. He could now see the entire street. When Richard finally saw the Long Cat he began backpedaling desperately.

"Nick," Richard said out loud. "She's lying down."

The vision of the massive Long Cat lying on its back with its 200mm phase cannon aimed right at the center of his cockpit window was etched in Richard's brain as he continued to backpedal. Just as the top of his cockpit pulled back over the ledge, a burst of blue paint exploded along the edge of the roof. Small specks of blue splattered the front of his cockpit.

Your Tomcat's still running, said Nickelo. *The controllers obviously didn't count that as a kill. So, get moving wizard scout before the Long Cat's phase cannon has a chance to recycle.*

Reacting without thinking was Richard's strong point. He raised the Tomcat to its feet and jumped over the ledge of the roof. He heard parts of the roof caving in behind him. Richard fell towards the street six stories below. As he fell, a part of Richard's mind calculated the reload time for the Long Cat's 200mm cannon.

Unlike plasma weapons, a phase weapon was a combination of a physical cartridge and energy. An actual phase cartridge contained a creallium core which was charged with energy from an isotopic battery. A real phase cannon could reload in a half second. The Long Cat's training cannon had been modified to fire 200mm paintballs. It took a full three seconds to reload. The range and accuracy of the modified cannon was much reduced as well.

As he fell, Richard visually located and targeted the Long Cat. The large bore of the 200mm phase cannon was pointed directly at him. Richard imagined the reload taking place as he fell to the street below. As he watched, the residue of the last paintball was ejected out the side of the phase cannon. He knew another paintball would be entering the empty chamber a split-second later. Richard pulled back the right arm of the Tomcat and moved it forward at maximum velocity. The three meter long support beam hurtled straight towards the open bore of the phase cannon.

Richard didn't waste time watching to see if the metal beam struck true. Either it would or it wouldn't. From experience, he knew watching wouldn't help. Richard targeted the cockpit of the Long Cat with the rocket pod on the Tomcat's shoulder. His six anti-armor rockets began salvo-firing at the cockpit below. Richard made out Tam's upper body through the Long Cat's cockpit. Her hands were moving furiously across the Long Cat's control panel as she attempted to raise her cat into a standing position. The rockets in her two shoulder-mounted weapon's pods began returning fire. The range between the two cats was too close for the guidance mechanisms of any of the rockets to lock onto their targets. Richard's first two rockets hit the street to the left side of the Long Cat's cockpit splattering red paint on the grey concrete street. Trails of smoke passed to either side of Richard as the first wave of Tam's rockets whizzed by his cockpit.

Richard caught a glimpse of his third rocket streaking directly towards the clear windows of the Long Cat's cockpit. Just before the third rocket struck home, Richard saw Tam raise her right fist with her middle finger extended in a universal gesture of defiance. A split second later, the Tomcat's rocket shattered on the Long Cat's cockpit window covering it in red paint. The fourth rocket also struck true completely blanketing the upper torso of the cat in red. At the same time, one of Tam's rockets hit the stored, rear leg of Richard's Tomcat. He saw a schematic of the Tomcat appear on his heads-up display. He noticed the hydraulic pressure of the rear leg dropping rapidly as the Tomcat's aft hydraulic pump began flashing red.

The controllers have taken the Tomcat's rear leg offline, said Nickelo.

The Tomcat hit the ground hard and tumbled forward. Even sheltered inside the gel-filled cockpit of the cat, Richard felt the shock of the landing. Instinctively, he tucked the Tomcat into a crouch and rolled forward into a summersault to reduce the shock of the fall. As soon as the Tomcat completed its roll, Richard raised his cat into a standing position. He was pleasantly surprised to find most of the Tomcat's controls still working. Either the controller's computer had determined the Tomcat could have survived such a maneuver under combat conditions, or the controllers were too shocked to make a final decision. Whatever the reason, Richard didn't care. While his Tomcat's left arm was out as well as his rear leg, his cat was still operational, and that's what mattered. He could still move, and as long as he could move, he could fight.

Richard took two steps towards the Long Cat. It lay helpless among the broken rubble of the building. The Long Cat's cockpit windows were completely covered in red paint, so he couldn't see Tam. But the image of her giving him the finger made him smile. Tam was one tough soldier. She didn't like to lose.

Reaching out with the claw of the Tomcat's right arm, Richard pulled the metal beam out of the muzzle of the Long Cat's phase cannon. His improvised missile had struck true. The end of the beam was covered in blue paint. Richard had a momentary thought that the beam must have hit a round of paint just as it was being chambered into the phase cannon. He'd beaten Tam to the punch by a hair at the most.

Once the metal beam was firmly in his grasp, Richard raised the Tomcat to a semi-comfortable position. The metal beam really did remind him of his phase rod a little. A wizard scout's phase rod was a modified riot baton. When activated, a telescopic brerellium-steel rod extended a meter out of the rod's handle. When the rod's lever was moved to destructive mode, an isotopic battery energized the phase rod's creallium core. When activated, phase energy moved up and down the phase rod in a fashion similar to hundreds of miniature lightning bolts. While the current metal beam was not energized with phase energy, Richard hoped he could make good use of it in close combat as a battering weapon.

Inside the Tomcat's cockpit, Richard began moving his legs in a running motion. The sensors inside the Tomcat picked up the movement. The cat began running down the street. Richard headed in the direction of the Warcat's last known position. He doubted Jerad would give him long to celebrate his victory over the Long Cat. A glance at his heads-up display confirmed the Kraken was still stationary. The lack of movement on the part of his friend, Telsa, concerned Richard, but he couldn't waste time worrying about it. Jerad was his most dangerous opponent. Even in the lightly-armed Warcat, Richard suspected Jerad had tricks up his sleeve he'd be hard pressed to counter. Jerad's years spent working his way up through the ranks in armor units had given his friend more experience than Richard feared he could defend against with his paltry three weeks of training.

What do you think you're going to accomplish by running down the street like a wild man swinging that metal beam? said Nickelo. *Do you even have a plan?*

Jerad only has two rockets, Richard said. *And his light plasma guns are only good as anti-personnel weapons. I'm going to draw his fire and make him waste his two missiles. I've fired all my missiles, and my Tomcat's 20mm chain gun won't penetrate even the Warcat's armor. So, I'm going to use this metal beam like it's a phase rod and beat the tar out of his Warcat. How's that for a plan?*

Nickelo's lack of a reply let Richard know exactly what his battle computer thought about his plan.

CHAPTER 5

Incoming, said Nickelo. *It's an anti-armor missile.*

Richard hadn't made it twenty meters down the street before sensing the energy reading streaking towards him.

Jerad's not wasting any time, is he? Richard said.

Negative, said Nickelo. *You've given him too good of a target. I've tracked the missile back to its origin, and pinpointed the Warcat's position. I'm updating your heads-up display.*

Richard didn't waste time looking at the heads-up display. He had an incoming missile to worry about. Richard instinctively made a quick calculation and threw the steel beam in the Tomcat's right claw. The beam hit true, and the incoming missile exploded in a spray of blue paint ten meters to his front.

Disconnect the Tomcat's third leg, Nick, Richard said.

Disconnecting, said Nickelo. *But I'm not sure why you're bothering. It was stowed out of the way. Even though it was out of action, it wasn't causing you any problems.*

Richard didn't bother answering. He reached down with the Tomcat's right claw and picked up the disconnected third leg. It resembled a monkey's tail more than it resembled a leg. Richard picked up one end of the flexible-metal leg. He gave it a flick so the flexible leg coiled behind him like a whip.

Glancing at his heads-up display, Richard noted the Warcat's location. The Warcat was half exposed around the corner of a building. Richard began running straight towards the stationary Warcat. Small paintballs representing antipersonnel plasma rounds came towards him. Richard ignored them. Even if the Warcat's automatic plasma rifles had been filled with live ammo, they wouldn't have been able to penetrate the Tomcat's armor. Richard's primary concern was Jerad's remaining anti-armor missile.

Jerad's holding fire until you close the distance, said Nickelo. *Are you sure you know what you're doing?*

No, Richard said honestly. *But I'm doing what I think's best.*

When Richard was twenty meters from the Warcat, he sensed increased energy from the back of the Warcat's weapon's pod.

This is it, Richard said as the anti-armor missile raced out of the weapon's pod heading straight towards him.

Richard moved the Tomcat's right arm forward as he dodged to the left. The end of the disconnected third leg hit the head of the missile. It exploded in a blast of blue paint. Half of the Tomcat's disconnected tail was covered in blue paint. However, very little of the paint had touched the Tomcat. He continued running towards the Warcat as it pulled back around the corner.

Jerad didn't move fast enough. When Richard reached the corner of the building, he slung the disconnected tail low around the corner and pulled back. Richard felt resistance and heard a thud. A moment later, one of the Warcat's legs appeared around the corner entangled by a loop of the Tomcat's disconnected tail.

"You're getting slow in your old age, Jerad," Richard said over the Tomcat's external speakers. Richard jumped on the prone Warcat's back. He reached into the Warcat's exhaust and pulled out a claw full of engine parts. The Warcat stopped moving. Richard rolled the Warcat onto its back and looked into its cockpit. A small figure in a battle suit was inside.

"Nice going, Rick" said a feminine voice over the Warcat's external speakers. "The only problem is I'm not Jerad."

Richard felt a weight hit the back of his Tomcat.

An unknown lifeform of two hundred and twenty kilos has attached itself to your back, said Nickelo.

Richard had no doubt Nickelo knew the identity of the lifeform as well as he did. It could only be Jerad. Dressed in his battle suit, Jerad would weigh one hundred and eighty kilos. Richard feared the extra forty kilos was a magnetic anti-armor mine.

If he'd been in real combat, Richard would have slammed the

Tomcat's back into the side of the building in hopes of crushing the attacker. But this wasn't combat, and Richard had no wish to hurt his friend.

The weight on Richard's back diminished by a hundred and eighty kilos. Richard twisted his head and caught a glimpse of a figure in a black battle suit diving around the corner of the building.

Boom!

A wall of blue paint erupted around the Tomcat and covered the cockpit window. All Richard could see was blue.

Richard laughed to himself and muttered, "Good job, Jerad. Good job."

*   *   *

"Good job, blue team," said TAC Officer Myers. "You showed initiative and thinking outside the box. Cadet 147, abandoning the Kraken and proceeding on foot over the top of the building was unorthodox. However, it showed an aptitude for creativity worthy of a wizard scout. You'll be taking over as your cohort's first sergeant when you return from your three day pass."

TAC Officer Myers walked to Richard's front until he was only a hand's breath from Richard.

"And you, cadet 832," said TAC Officer Myers. "You would've been dead a half dozen times in actual combat. The controllers cut you some slack by allowing you to continue on to the end of the training scenario. But it doesn't matter. As I expected, you lost. What's your excuse this time?"

"Sir! No excuse, sir!" Richard said. Cadets never had an excuse as far as TAC officers were concerned.

"You bet there's no excuse," TAC Officer Myers said. "Well, your high-level friends aren't going to help you this time, cadet. You'll report to Sergeant Ron at the motor pool bright and early tomorrow morning. You'll clean every cat to his satisfaction if it takes all weekend. Do you understand, cadet?"

"Sir! Yes, sir," Richard said.

"Then get out of my face, cadet," said TAC Officer Myers. "You're fouling my air. All of you get out of my hangar now before I have every one of you on extra duty."

Four pairs of feet wasted no time in exiting out the door of hangar 1. Once they were outside, the four cadets slowed to a more reasonable pace.

"Tough luck, Rick," said Jerad. "I really mean that."

"No problem, Jerad," Richard said. "You got me good. I was convinced Telsa was in the Kraken. I assume you purposely drove it erratically to fool me."

"Sometimes it pays to act like you're less capable than you are, Rick," said Jerad. "I figured you'd put mines in the intersection before I could reach it."

"You were right," Richard said. He laughed. "I was sure you'd be in the Warcat. I figured you'd put Telsa in the Kraken."

"Why?" said Telsa sounding a little indignant. "Because I'm a female? That's the same attitude Jerad had."

"Yeah," said Tam. "Jerad tried to tell us he was taking the Warcat. Ha, like he's in charge or something. We set him straight real quick, didn't we, Telsa."

"You bet," laughed Telsa. "We made Jerad draw straws. He lost and got stuck with the most powerful cat."

Richard smiled. Telsa and Tam were typical of the attitude of most wizard scout cadets. They didn't put up with gender bias in any shape or form. During his two years at the pre-Academy, and the three years of training at the Academy, Richard's attitude towards women had changed. As far as he was concerned now, whoever was best suited for a task was who should do it. Gender didn't matter. Jerad, on the other hand, was old school. He occasionally thought of females as the gentler sex who needed to be protected. Telsa and Tam were often forced to give Jerad an attitude adjustment.

"Well, your maneuver worked," Richard said. "And, Tam, you almost got me as well. I didn't consider you might lie down on your back to get more elevation for your cannon. Good idea."

Tam didn't say anything. She could be a hard case sometimes. However, Richard thought he saw a slight smile lift the corners of her lips at his praise. One thing Jerad had taught him over the years was that well-deserved praise cost very little. Good leaders could use it to help keep their unit motivated and functioning smoothly. Richard wasn't anybody's leader, and he didn't want to be. But, he didn't mind giving praise when it was deserved.

"Well, enough patting each other on the backs," said Telsa. "Let's see if we can con Sergeant Ron or Sergeant Hendricks into giving us a ride back to our tents. The last hover-bus stopped running thirty minutes ago."

"Agreed," said Tam. "I've got a date that won't wait. I'm so ready for this three day pass, it isn't even funny."

CHAPTER 6

Sergeant Hendricks stopped the truck outside the perimeter of the tent compound the junior cohort was using as their temporary barracks.

"Thanks for the lift, Sergeant Hendricks," said Jerad. "It's much appreciated."

Tam, Telsa, and Richard echoed Jerad's comments.

Richard started walking away from the truck in the direction of the tents.

"Hold on, cadets," said Sergeant Hendricks. "Aren't you forgetting something?"

Without giving any of the cadets time enough to answer, Sergeant Hendricks said, "Your battle suits and helmets need to go back in the armory. What'd you think you were going to do? Take them with you on your three day pass?"

"I assumed they'd stay stowed in our tents," said Jerad. "That's where we've been keeping them for the past three weeks. It's guarded."

"Well, you assumed wrong, cadet 147," said Sergeant Hendricks. "The new rule is all cadet equipment must be stored in the armory when not being used for actual training. It came straight from the Imperial High Command earlier today. Security is being increased all across the board on Velos for some reason. So hand the stuff over, cadets."

Richard and his friends stripped off their battle suits and put on their cadet jumpsuits, boots, and hats instead. Once they were finished, they handed their battle suits and helmets to Sergeant Hendricks.

"And in case you're wondering," said Sergeant Hendricks, "your TAC officers removed all your utility belts and weapons out of your tents earlier today. That includes your fancy knife and pack, cadet 832."

Richard groaned. He'd hoped they would forget about his dimensional pack since it wasn't standard issue. With it, he could summon almost any item he could imagine within certain limitations. First, the more technologically advanced an item, the more Power it took to summon the item. Second, whoever or whatever controlled the dimensional pack sometimes made exceptions to the rules. Unfortunately, the rules fluctuated sometimes which made it frustrating to figure out what he could summon with the pack. But his dimensional pack had been a life saver several times, and Richard hated to lose it.

Once Sergeant Hendricks had all their gear stored in his truck, he waved and said, "Enjoy your passes cadets. I hear your training is going to get even harder starting next week."

Just before he drove off, Sergeant Hendricks stuck his head out of the truck and hollered, "Oh, and cadet 832. Don't forget to report to hangar 1 at first light. Sergeant Ron's going to be there to issue your cleaning equipment. Tough luck, old boy."

Sergeant Hendricks gave Richard a look that seemed to say, 'I'm sorry about that'. Then he drove off.

The security on the arms room will prevent us from communicating, Rick, came a thought from Nickelo. *So please try to stay out of trouble.*

I'll do my best, Richard said. *I guess I'll see you next week. Play nice with the other battle computers.*

You know they're prevented from communicating with me unless the central computer provides a special security interface, said Nickelo. *I get bored to tell the truth.*

Hmm, Richard said. *Why don't you see if you can figure out a way to contact me while you're in the armory? After all, secured vaults like the armory are intended to prevent things outside from trying to get in. Maybe there's a weak spot on the inside. At the very least, it might keep that nanosecond brain of yours busy.*

Is that an order, wizard scout? said Nickelo sounding excited.

Current security protocols built into the battle helmet prevent me from attempting to breach Empire security. I require an override from my wizard scout to do so.

Then consider that an order, Nick, Richard said. *Bust whatever security protocols you think reasonable. I'll leave it up to you. I trust you.*

Complying, said Nickelo with what sounded like increasing excitement. *I won't let you down.*

Once the truck was out of sight, Tam said, "Well, you boys go do your thing. Telsa and I have a double date tonight. Jerad, we'll meet you tomorrow afternoon at the spaceport."

"Oh, and Rick," said Telsa as she placed her hand sympathetically on his shoulder. "We really are sorry. I know you wanted to see Liz."

"Thanks, Telsa," Richard said. "Go have fun, guys. I mean that. I suppose it's better for just one person to get stuck on extra duty instead of three. It's just as well. I'd bet a month's pay, assuming I actually got paid, that TAC Officer Myers would've found another reason to cancel my weekend pass even if I had won our little encounter."

"That's the spirit, Rick," laughed Telsa with a playful punch on Richard's arm. "Look on the bright side of things."

"Let's go, Telsa," said Tam. "I'm already beautiful, but you're going to take some work."

"Ha!" said Telsa. "You wish. Your parents told me you were so ugly when you were a child they had to tie a bone around your neck to get your pet pactar to play with you."

"I'll ugly you," said Tam. "If I get my hands on you, I'll pull out half your hair. Then we'll find out how your date likes dancing with a bald woman."

Telsa took off running for the females' section of the tent city with Tam close behind.

"For someone so short, Telsa sure can run," Jerad laughed.

"I'd be running too," Richard said. "Tam can be dangerous if you get her riled."

"That she can," agreed Jerad. "But you know they're joking, right? Sometimes I think you have trouble telling."

"Of course, I know they're joking," Richard said. At least, he was pretty sure Tam was joking.

Richard and Jerad watched until their two friends turned the corner of the tents and were lost from sight.

"Just think, I'm going to have to deal with that all by myself this weekend," said Jerad as he led the way to the males' section of the tents. "See why I wanted you there, Rick."

"Well, I'll be thinking about you, Jerad," Richard said. "Come to think of it, maybe I'm getting the better part of the deal after all. I think the Academy's cats are more mature than Tam and Telsa sometimes."

"Maybe you'll get the cats cleaned faster than you think, Rick," said Jerad. "If you finish in time, try to meet us at the spaceport tomorrow afternoon. I want to introduce you to someone."

"I was supposed to meet Liz at the spaceport at 1400 hours tomorrow," Richard said. "Do you think you can make my apologies to Liz? You know Myers won't let me even make a call while I'm on extra duty."

"Consider it done, Rick," said Jerad. "Tam, Telsa, and I will be there anyway."

"I'm curious, Jerad," Richard said. "How'd you manage to finagle eight invitations to the Fleet Admiral's Ball? I heard there are ship's captains orbiting Velos who didn't get an invitation."

"Ask me no questions, and I'll tell you no lies, Rick," said Jerad with a smile. "I keep telling you, it pays to have friends."

"So you do, Jerad," Richard said. "I'm coming to appreciate that more the longer I'm around you guys."

Since he shared a tent with Jerad, Richard refrained from making any more comments about his friend's weekend plans until it was time for Jerad to leave. Richard hated goodbyes. They were always awkward, and they left him uncomfortable. Richard was the first to admit he still had room for improvement in his social skills.

Richard made a silent promise not to let the bitterness he felt towards his TAC officer mar his friend's weekend pass. He reminded himself if the situation was reversed, his friends would be telling him to enjoy himself and not to worry about them.

"You know, Jerad," Richard said, "I really do hope you guys have a good ti–"

Jerad was slightly ahead of Richard. He'd just raised the flap to enter their tent prior to stepping inside. Instead of entering, Jerad began backing away from the tent.

"Woah!" said Jerad. "Maybe you'd better enter first, Rick. One of your friends is back."

Peeking past Jerad, Richard saw a large, black bundle of fur laid out on his cot. Two red eyes opened and stared at him. The creature stood up on the cot and stretched while opening a tooth-filled mouth in a wide yawn. The creature looked similar to a large wolf back on Richard's home planet of Earth. Richard noticed the wolf-creature was actually levitating a few centimeters above the covers of his cot.

"Tika," Richard said. "You can't just keep popping in like this. I've told you that before."

During a mission for '*the One*' in the spiritual dimension, Richard had been thrust into the middle of a cave full of newborn dolgar pups and their mother. In spite of the obvious differences, the mother and pups had accepted him as one of their pack. In return, he'd helped them defend their home from attack. Since that time, the wolf-looking dolgars had taken up the nasty habit of surprising him with their presence at the most inopportune times. While he'd never mentioned the dolgars or his missions for '*the One*' in his official reports, Richard had shared the information with Tam, Telsa, Jerad, and of course, his friend, Liz.

Tika looked at Richard and sent an emotion Richard associated with the dolgar pack's leader, Sheeta. The dolgars' language consisted mostly of emotions accompanied by a few growls or barks. Richard had learned a few words of the dolgar language during his time with the dolgars, but he was far from proficient.

"What about Sheeta?" Richard asked the dolgar.

"Come," said Tika with a low growl.

Richard sent an emotion which meant 'no'.

"I've got things to do," Richard said. "I can't just leave."

Richard was never sure how much any of the dolgars understood when he spoke using intergalactic standard. A substitute battle computer had told him last year the dolgars were slightly higher in intelligence than humans in some areas. But without a common language between Richard and the dolgars, he had a hard time telling how much they grasped. However, he couldn't help but feel they understood what he said a lot better than he understood what they said.

"Uh, Rick," said Jerad, "It might be best to carry on this conversation inside our tent with the flap closed. Some of the other cadets might not understand. There aren't many cadets around right now, but there's no use taking a risk."

"Yeah," Richard said. "I think you're right. I definitely don't think Myers would be very understanding."

"No doubt," laughed Jerad. "He'd probably give you more extra duty for having wolf hairs on your cot."

Stepping inside the tent, Richard prepared to shut the flap. He noticed Jerad was still standing outside.

"Aren't you coming in?" Richard said.

"Only if you remind your visitor I'm not food," said Jerad only half-jokingly. "She may not remember me from her last visit."

"Oh, she remembers you, Jerad," Richard said smiling. "She hasn't torn your throat out, has she? I think that's her way of saying she likes you."

"Yeah, right," said Jerad not at all comforted by Richard's assurance. "If she likes me so much, how come I feel like a thick steak with all the trimmings?"

"Tika," Richard said forcibly. "You know Jerad. He's a friend, remember? Now say hello and let him come inside."

Tika bared her teeth and growled at Jerad. Then she lay back down on Richard's cot.

Richard sat next to the dolgar and tried to shove her to the side to make room. But Tika was heavier than she looked, so Richard finally gave up.

"Hey, Tika," Richard said. "Move over will you? It's my bed, you know."

Tika bared her teeth and growled at Richard, but she shifted position a little to make room at the end of the cot.

"Come on in, Jerad," Richard said. "She knows you're a friend. See? She even growls at me."

"Somehow, that doesn't give me a lot of confidence," said Jerad as he walked inside and closed the flap behind him.

Although his friend entered, Richard noticed he stayed as far away from Tika as he could in the confines of the tent. However, Jerad was hard pressed to keep more than a meter or two away from Tika no matter how carefully he tried to move.

Apparently trying to ignore the dolgar, Jerad began packing a small handbag with some clothing. When he was done, Jerad turned around. "Rick, I could swear Tika was bigger the last time I saw her. She's still plenty large, but she looks different. Am I imagining things?"

"No, you've got it right, Jerad," Richard said as he reached over and scratched Tika behind the ears. "Nick said the dolgars can take on any lupine shape, but they prefer this wolf form. I've never seen them change forms, but I've seen them change size."

"So, you think she shrunk herself in order to fit inside our tent," said Jerad. "I find that fascinating to be honest."

"I hadn't thought much about it," Richard said. "I guess I've learned to pay more attention to their spiritual form than their physical body. Their energy frequency stays consistent regardless of their body size."

"Well, she's intimidating no matter her size," said Jerad. "I guess I'd be more taken with her if she didn't look like a bloodthirsty killer."

"You don't have to worry about Tika," Richard said. "You don't have to worry about any of the dolgars in Sheeta's and Sheba's pack. They've all got your scent. They know you're my friend. However, even I'd be hesitant to trust a dolgar who isn't familiar with Sheeta. The dolgars outside my own pack I've been around seem to tolerate me out of deference to Sheeta."

"You've got strange friends, Rick," said Jerad as he went back to his packing.

"I guess I do," Richard said. With a laugh, Richard added, "And one of my strangest friends happens to share a tent with me."

"You mean, Tika?" said Jerad pretending innocence.

"No," Richard said. "I mean you. You know full well who I mean."

"Yes, I do," admitted Jerad. "But while I'm your friend, I don't think I'm strange."

"You wouldn't," Richard said with more than a little hint of sarcasm. "However, you always seem able to get confidential information from who knows what sources. And, you're able to get items like those tickets to the Fleet Admiral's Ball. Plus, you're the oldest cadet to ever attend the Academy. You've never even bothered to tell me why a thirty-eight year old battalion commander would suddenly decide to apply for wizard scout training. I think that qualifies as strange."

"Ha," laughed Jerad in return. "If you're trying to pump me for information, it won't work. The last hover-tram leaves the airfield in thirty minutes. I for one don't plan on missing it."

"I don't blame you," Richard said taking the hint to change the subject. "It's a long walk back to Velounia."

"You've got that right," said Jerad. "It's a full two hundred kilometers back to the city."

"Will you be spending the night at the Academy?" Richard said. "Or, will you be looking for a hotel room in the city?"

"I'll be staying at the Academy," said Jerad. "Our hotel reservations aren't until tomorrow night, and I don't have any credits to waste. I'd spend the night here, but I don't want to take a chance on the hover-tram not running tomorrow morning."

"I hear you on the finance problems," Richard said slapping his empty pockets with his hands. "If Telsa's family hadn't offered to pay for the hotel and suit rental, I couldn't have afforded to go even if Myers hadn't put me on extra duty."

"You know I'd have spotted you the credits," said Jerad. "I'm not rich like Telsa, but my bank account's not exactly empty either."

"I know," Richard said. "But I don't like to mooch off the generosity of my friends."

"You're not," said Jerad. "Once we graduate from the Academy, all of our back pay for the last five years will be released. You'll be rolling in the credits then. The powers that be just want to make us struggle now."

Jerad took a look around his side of the tent. He picked up his bag and straightened up a few wrinkles on his cot.

"Well, Rick," said Jerad, "I hate leaving you, but–"

"Don't worry about it, Jerad," Richard said. "Have fun. Just make sure you bring me a piece of cake?" Richard followed his comment with what he hoped was a friendly grin.

"See you around, Tika," said Jerad. "Don't leave any fleas in our tent."

Tika growled.

"See?" Richard said. "Tika likes you. She thinks you're funny."

"Yeah, I'm sure," said Jerad. "I can feel the love from here."

Jerad opened the tent flap and then looked back at Richard and

Tika.

"You know she's not going to leave until you go with her, don't you?" said Jerad.

"Yeah, I know," Richard said. "I figured I'd wait until a few more of the other cadets leave. I can still sense a couple of dozen within the tent compound."

"Really?" said Jerad. "Other than Tam and Telsa, I don't sense anyone. For that matter, I can't even sense you, and you're right in front of me."

"All the cadets are keeping their stealth shields activated," Richard said. "You've worked with Tam and Telsa so much you're more sensitive to their Power frequency. I doubt any of the other cadets can pick them up."

"You're probably right," said Jerad. "You've worked with the other cadets in the cohort helping them improve their stealth shields. You've got their scent."

During the past three years, Richard had become the cohort's unofficial off-duty trainer. He'd spent a lot of hours working with the other cadets in groups and in one-on-one situations helping them refine both their defensive and offensive skills. While in theory all the cadets in his cohort received the same training while at the Academy, the reality for Richard was a little different. The entity he knew as '*the One*' had sent him on several missions during the last three years. Most of the missions had been in the magical plane and had been in the far past. At least two of the missions had been in locations even Nickelo couldn't figure out. The end result was that while the other cadets in his cohort had aged three years since they'd entered the Academy, Richard had aged about six years.

Responding to his friend's last comment, Richard said, "If you had your best stealth shield up, Jerad, I couldn't detect you unless you were very close. Even then, it would be dicey. As far as detecting lower-level shields, it depends on distance as well. I've had more practice than you. You're probably trying to sense Power fluctuations. The reason I'm picking up the other cadets is that I'm looking for an absence of Power."

"What are you talking about?" said Jerad. "No, actually, don't try to explain it now. I've got a hover-tram to catch. I think you're just trying to keep me around long enough to miss it. Is that your devious way of trying to keep some company around this weekend?"

Jerad smiled letting Richard know he wasn't serious.

Richard nodded his head. "My plan is out."

Jerad nodded his head in return and left the tent. Richard followed his friend's trace with his mind until Jerad met up with Tam and Telsa. They were joined by the remaining cadets in the tent compound. Eventually they headed in the direction of the hover-tram station as a group. Richard continued to trace them until they were out of range.

Richard scratched Tika behind the ears again and said, "Well, Tika. What's so important?"

Sending out the emotion again that Richard associated with Sheeta, Tika growled, "Come."

During Richard's freshman and sophomore years at the Academy, nearly every waking moment had been taken up by scheduled activities. This year, the TAC officers had significantly slacked off their harassment of the cadets. Consequently, Richard didn't have anything to do until morning.

"Fine," Richard said. "Lead the way."

Tika stood up. Richard sensed the dolgar wrap herself in Power. The Power shimmered momentarily. Tika merged into the tent floor and disappeared as she shifted into the void between dimensions. While Richard couldn't physically see the dolgar, he easily followed her path with his passive scan. The dolgars had worked with him on previous missions, so even when they shifted into the void, Richard had no trouble tracking them.

Richard stood up and walked out of the tent. He turned to the right and walked down the dirt street between tents. He could sense Tika moving underground making a beeline across the compound. Richard sped into a trot in an attempt to keep up. Every so often, he sensed Tika slowing down or stopping. But before he could catch up, she would be off again. Eventually, she cleared the tent compound and headed towards the desert beyond.

Unlike the dolgar, Richard was forced to follow the roads. When Richard got to the point where the dirt road passed the perimeter of the compound, two armed soldiers at the gate waved him through. He nodded his head at the guards as he passed and continued on towards the barren desert surrounding the airfield.

After a couple of kilometers, Richard began to wonder where Tika was taking him. He was now out of sight of all but the tallest buildings at the airfield. Richard supposed someone in the control tower could still see him if they cared to try, but he doubted anyone would bother. It wasn't unusual for cadets to take long-distance runs into the desert. Physical training was one area of the Academy's training which the TAC officers continued to stress.

Tika shifted direction and led Richard into a deep, rock-filled gully. Richard reduced the range of his passive scan and increased its sensitivity until he could detect smaller creatures that might be lurking nearby. He sensed several lifeforms which he guessed were snakes. Richard made sure he stayed well clear of them. Until the Academy technicians did a DNA baseline on him, Richard couldn't selfheal. Being bitten by a poisonous snake at this stage of the game was the last thing he needed.

At the bottom of the gully, Tika emerged from the ground and sat on her haunches a meter above the rocky soil. Even after his association with the dolgars, the sight of Tika sitting in midair was a little strange. According to his battle computer, the dolgars could exist in two dimensions at the same time. They could be standing on solid ground in one dimension while appearing to be standing in midair in another.

About ten meters from Tika sat another dolgar. This dolgar was much larger than Tika. It was Sheeta, the dolgar pack's leader. Richard sensed the difference in the Power levels of the two dolgars. Sheeta's Power readings were much larger than Tika's. According to Nickelo, Tika was still an adolescent while Sheeta was a full adult. When Richard asked his battle computer how a dolgar that was eighty-nine thousand years old could still be an adolescent, Nickelo had told him it's just the way the dolgars were.

When Richard reached Sheeta, the big dolgar looked at Tika and growled, "Go."

Tika didn't look happy, but she didn't argue. She gave a growl in Richard's direction and then did a full shift into a second dimension.

Richard had noticed few of the dolgars argued with Sheeta. While Sheeta was not mean to the members of his pack, he was a strict disciplinarian. The lone exception to the no-arguing rule was Sheba. Richard often suspected Sheeta's mate, Sheba, wore the pants in the family.

"Well, big guy," Richard said. "I'm here. Now what?"

CHAPTER 7

"Come here," growled Sheeta.

As Richard approached the adult dolgar, a large, four-legged creature emerged out of the ground nearby. It was all black with burning-red eyes. For all intents and purposes, it resembled a large stallion from Richard's home world of Earth. The stallion stopped rising when its hoofs were about ten centimeters above the ground.

The nightmare horse and Sheeta exchanged emotions. Sheeta barked and growled. The stallion whinnied and snorted. Richard noticed the stallion had fangs instead of normal equine teeth. It looked vicious, and it seemed to have a personality to match.

Both Sheeta and the stallion turned their heads in Richard's direction. The stallion snorted its disgust. Richard got an intense feeling the stallion didn't like him.

"Well, join the club," Richard said. "My TAC officer doesn't like me either. Come to think of it, I'm not particularly fond of you."

Sheeta growled and sent a series of emotions at Richard. Although he couldn't be sure, Richard had the impression the dolgar expected him to do something.

"I don't understand what you're saying, big fella," Richard said. He was normally able to get the gist of the dolgar's speech when Sheeta kept it simple, but Richard needed some kind of context first.

"It sounds like you're saying up," Richard said. "Where do you want me to go up? Do you want me to climb out of this gully?"

On most occasions, Richard thought Sheeta's face was expressionless. However, this time he was pretty sure the dolgar looked exasperated.

"Hey," Richard said. "I'm doing my best with your language. I don't see you trying to learn intergalactic standard."

Sheeta growled. For a moment, Richard wondered if the dolgar understood more of his words than he thought. Richard made a mental note to be careful what he said to the dolgar in the future.

Sheeta moved closer. Richard held his ground. They stared into each other's eyes. Richard sensed something strange in the dolgar's gaze. All of a sudden, an image of him sitting on the stallion's back flashed into his mind.

"No way," Richard said startled. "I've never ridden a horse in my life. I certainly don't plan on starting with one that looks like he'd eat me if I got bucked off. Forget it."

Sheeta seemed unimpressed with Richard's tirade. Once again, Sheeta growled, "Up." Then he sat down and waited expectantly.

Richard wasn't exactly sure what was going on. He'd first met Sheeta when he'd wound up in the den with the pack's pups. Since then, Richard had been on three missions that he knew of with either Sheeta or one of his offspring. They were vicious fighters. Their ability to travel between dimensions was an ability Richard wished he'd had on more than one occasion. Sheeta had been the one to teach Richard how to shift into the void between dimensions. But the dolgar had never been able to teach Richard how to fully shift between dimensions.

His Power reserve had recharged some over the course of the day, but it was still a little low. However, he made a decision to send an active scan in the strange stallion's direction. He probed around the stallion with the active scan while halfway expecting to be attacked. Few creatures, Richard included, liked being scanned by others. The stallion either didn't notice Richard's active scan, or he didn't care. In either respect, the stallion did nothing to impede him. Once the active scan was completed, Richard cut the line of Power to the scan. Active scans were Power hungry, and only a very foolish wizard scout wasted Power.

Wishing he had his battle computer to help analyze the results, Richard compared the energy readings from the scan of the stallion to the energy readings for Sheeta. They were similar.

"Okay," Richard said out loud to Sheeta. "This horse's Power frequency appears to be similar to yours. I'm going to take a wild guess it's also from the spiritual dimension. Does that mean it can travel between dimensions as well?"

Sheeta said nothing. However, the dolgar gave Richard a look which appeared similar to the way TAC Officer Myers looked at cadets when they asked him a stupid question.

"Okay," Richard said, "silly question. This spirit-horse or whatever it is must have traveled between dimensions to get here. Why do you want me to try and ride this monstrosity?"

Sheeta looked hard at Richard. Soon, an image formed in Richard's mind of him riding the strange horse and fighting creatures from its back.

A master demon had once told Richard he needed allies. The dolgars were already Richard's allies. He wondered if the spirit-horse was going to be one as well.

"I'll admit," Richard said to Sheeta, "traveling between dimensions could be a handy skill if that's what this horse can do."

Richard figured at best he could travel forty or fifty meters when he shifted into the void on his own. Consequently, its usefulness as a form of travel was pretty limited. The dolgars on the other hand had a natural ability for shifting between dimensions. This allowed them to remain shifted for long periods of time. Although Richard often practiced shifting into the void in order to improve his efficiency, he could only hold a dimensional shift for a couple of minutes. Doing a shift into the void between dimensions was very Power hungry. As a result, Richard seldom used the ability. Richard reasoned if this spirit-horse could travel between dimensions on its own, perhaps it could take a rider as well.

Richard looked closer at the stallion. It had a long mane and tail along with a broad back. It wore no saddle or bridle. Richard glanced at the stallion's hoofs. They seemed more like clenched fists than solid hoofs. Some saliva dripped from the stallion's mouth and hit the ground. The liquid bubbled and hissed on the stone.

The stallion noticed Richard's examination. It lifted its left-front leg and flexed its hoof. The hoof split into four separate digits tipped with wicked-looking claws. The stallion snickered as if enjoying Richard's astonishment.

Richard hated being pushed into something, but he hated being laughed at even worse.

"Fine," Richard said out loud to the stallion. "I'll ride you. But if you try to eat me, I'll defend myself. I'll make you wish you'd kept your mouth shut."

Richard walked over to the stallion and jumped onto its back. The stallion didn't move or flinch. Richard positioned his legs as well as he could without a saddle. When he stopped moving, several black tendrils separated themselves from the stallion's back and sides. They wrapped around Richard's legs and waist holding him snuggly in place.

"Hey," Richard said. "Wait one darn–"

"Come," barked Sheeta in a voice not to be denied.

The dolgar leapt into the air and started running towards a ridgeline a kilometer or so in the distance. The stallion ran into the air as well and followed.

Richard would have fallen off but for the black tendrils holding him securely in place. When he felt the stallion rising into the air, Richard grabbed desperately for a handful of the stallion's mane. He held on tight. They were already a hundred meters above the ground and traveling fast. The altitude didn't bother him as much as the feeling of strength and power flowing through the stallion. Richard could only guess at his mount's abilities. He'd been prepared to travel between dimensions. Richard hadn't expected to become airborne.

Actually, Richard could tell they weren't flying. He felt a strange sensation as if the stallion was shifting in and out of dozens if not hundreds of dimensions as it sought solid footing. But Richard wasn't being shifted along with the stallion. He was still in the current dimension. In fact, it felt like the majority of the stallion was also remaining in the current dimension. He wasn't sure how things were working, but he did know he could feel the pressure of the wind against his body, and that meant he was still materialized. It was as if the stallion was just shifting its hoofs into other dimensions in order to find solid footing. Richard assumed that was how the dolgars did it when they appeared to be running in the air.

"Down," barked Sheeta.

Sheeta and the stallion made a steep dive towards the ground.

"Wait a minute!" Richard shouted as the ground rose to meet him.

Instead of the shock of impact, Richard felt himself shifting into the void. But he wasn't the one doing the shifting. Richard sensed an aura of Power from the stallion surrounding him. The stallion ran straight into the ground in an attempt to catch the dolgar.

"Are they playing a game?" Richard wondered.

While Richard could not see visually underground, he sensed Sheeta's exact location a few meters ahead. Richard threw out a quick active scan. They'd leveled off about two hundred meters underground.

Sheeta sent an emotion Richard knew meant "follow." Richard sensed a surge of Power from the dolgar. Then Sheeta disappeared from Richard's senses.

The stallion did something to the aura of Power surrounding Richard and him. Almost immediately, the stallion shifted out of the void. For a moment, Richard feared they'd be embedded in the solid rock in which they'd been traveling. Instead, he felt a strange sensation as if his cells were being torn apart and put back together. It was similar to when he was being teleported by 'the One'. But at the same time, it was different.

A bright sky burst into Richard's view. Just a few meters below, Richard could see the tops of large trees as they swept past them. Richard felt the wind pressure against his body once more. Vibrations came up through the stallion's back. His mount was once again shifting through multiple dimensions as it sought solid ground for its hoofs.

Where are we? Richard wondered.

While he didn't know where they were, Richard was pretty sure they weren't on Velos any longer. The trees below him were various shades of purple. Velos didn't have forests of purple trees. Richard wasn't sure whether they were still in the physical, magical, or spiritual dimension. For all he knew, they were in a dimension he'd never heard about.

In spite of himself, Richard found the sensation of being on the back of a horse galloping just above the tree tops to be exhilarating. Sheeta was a few meters ahead leading the way, and the dolgar was speeding up. However, the stallion was speeding up as well. The spirit-horse stayed right on the dolgar's heels. Sheeta descended into the trees. The dolgar twisted and turned while trying to remain clear of the branches. The stallion matched every twist and turn.

They're playing a game, Richard thought with a laugh.

Richard found himself getting into the game as well. He leaned forward and sent an emotion urging the stallion forward. His mount needed very little encouragement. The stallion sped up. Richard imagined passing Sheeta on the left side. When he did so, the stallion edged over slightly to the left and pulled up alongside Sheeta. Richard didn't think the stallion so much obeyed his command as the stallion just agreed the left side was a good way to go.

"You can take him," Richard shouted. "Don't let him beat you."

Sheeta glanced to his left and then lowered his head and picked up even more speed. The stallion increased speed as well. The stallion and the dolgar ran neck and neck for several kilometers. Neither was apparently willing to take second place to the other. Richard realized he didn't want to take second place either.

Richard sent an active scan ahead seeking anything that might give the stallion an advantage. Richard sensed a steep drop coming up fast. As far as he could tell, a wide canyon was looming ahead. Richard had a feeling once Sheeta reached the edge of the canyon, he was going to use his dimension-shifting ability to run down the steep walls. An idea formed in Richard's mind.

If I can get this stallion to take a shortcut through the ground, Richard thought, *I can avoid the right angle dive and gain a little distance.*

Richard was unsure how to communicate with the stallion, so he leaned close to its neck. He pictured the canyon ahead with the shortcut through the ground.

A hundred meters before they reached the lip of the canyon, Richard felt an aura of Power surround both him and the stallion. They shifted into the void and dove into the ground.

Sheeta was momentarily caught by surprise, but he recovered quickly. The dolgar shifted into the void as well and followed the stallion. Richard couldn't see in the darkness, but he sensed Sheeta running hard just a meter behind. The dolgar kept gaining, but he was not quite fast enough. Richard and the stallion burst out of the canyon wall an arm's length ahead of Sheeta. Richard gave a shout of triumph as the stallion and Sheeta came to a stop on the canyon floor.

"Outstanding," Richard yelled as he raised his arms in victory and laughed. "You gave it a good try, Sheeta, but you've got to get up pretty early in the morning to beat us."

Sheeta sat on his haunches a meter above the ground. His face was expressionless, but Richard didn't think the big dolgar was overly happy with the turn of events.

I don't think he likes to lose, Richard thought. *Well, neither do I, Sheeta, neither do I.*

CHAPTER 8

Returning to his tent was easier than Richard expected. The stallion traveled underground until he was just a few meters below the tent. Once in position, Richard wrapped himself with Power and did a dimension shift into the void. He sent the stallion an image of him getting off.

The tendrils holding Richard to the stallion's back withdrew. The stallion's aura of Power surrounding Richard disappeared as well.

Using telekinesis, Richard moved upward towards the floor of his tent. Although he couldn't see, Richard sensed the correct direction by using his passive scan. He levitated himself up until he emerged through the tent floor. Once his feet cleared the ground, Richard shifted back into the physical dimension and cut his line of Power. He dropped the few centimeters to the ground.

"Cool," Richard said.

The tent was dark. But Richard knew a portable light hung from a rope tied to the tent's support beam. He fumbled overhead until he found the switch and turned it on. The inside of the tent lit up with the light's soft glow. Everything was as he'd left it.

Nickelo? Richard said.

No reply followed. The non-response was not unexpected. Richard assumed his battle computer was locked up inside the armory at the airfield's headquarters. However, he had high hopes his battle computer would discover a way to circumvent security. Even for a battle computer, Nickelo was more advanced than anything Richard had ever encountered.

A quick pass with his passive scan confirmed the tent compound was nearly vacant of any large lifeforms. He did spot two guards at the gate and two other roaming guards.

Richard felt a pang of loneliness. Adrenaline from his ride with Sheeta and the stallion was still pumping through his system. He wished Jerad was here so he could talk to him about the race. Having a dimensional-shifting spirit-horse at his disposal might be useful. Richard was sure Jerad could come up with some ideas.

"Don't get too far ahead," Richard said out loud just to break the silence. "You can't summon the dolgars. I seriously doubt you can summon that horse-from-hell, or whatever he is, either."

Richard considered his relationship with the dolgars. They'd accompanied him on three of his last four missions for 'the One'. During two of the missions, both Sheeta and Sheba had been with him. During another, Tika had followed him around most of the time. Richard hadn't summoned them. The dolgars just came whenever they wanted, wherever they wanted, and left whenever they wanted. Still, they were useful allies when they were around. Sheeta and Sheba were both fierce fighters. Their twelve adolescent pups were vicious fighters physically, but they were unable to suck life force from their adversaries as efficiently as their parents.

Richard was bored. His growling stomach reminded him he'd missed out on supper again. Richard bent down and lifted a loose board underneath his cot. He pulled out a small bag from his 'secret' compartment. He emptied its contents onto his cot. Several packages of crackers along with two packets of cocoa spilled onto his blanket.

Not much of a supper, Richard thought as he looked at his stash.

His stomach growled again. Richard put half of the items back in his bag and put it back in his hiding place. He carefully placed the loose board back in position. Most cadets tried to keep a small cache of items they filched from the mess hall. He wasn't the only cadet whose extra duty made him miss a meal.

After opening a pack of cocoa, Richard sprinkled it on a cracker. He washed his sparse supper down with a small bottle of juice. Once his supper was over, Richard grabbed his toilet articles and walked the short distance to the communal washroom located at the end of his tent row. It was growing dark, but the dirt road between the rows of tents was partially illuminated by security lights along the perimeter fence.

After a hot shower, Richard retired to his tent. With nothing else to do, he lay down and forced himself to try and get some sleep. While Sergeant Ron was a likeable guy, the maintenance chief was a stickler for timeliness. Richard had been told to be at hangar 1 at first light. That meant he needed to show up fifteen minutes early. Arriving fifteen minutes early was just the military way.

Well, old boy, Richard thought as he patted his stomach, *it looks like crackers and cocoa for breakfast.*

*   *   *

Something tingled in Richard's mind. He woke out of his light slumber instantly alert. Something in the world was not as it should be. Something had changed.

Richard lay on his cot as he reached out with his mind. His passive scan returned nothing of interest. He sensed the two roaming guards as well as the other two guards at the perimeter gate. Other than that, the compound was devoid of lifeforms larger than insects and rats.

What woke me? Richard wondered.

Taking no chances, Richard activated his best stealth shield. He'd been in too many life and death situations during the last few years to ignore any possible danger.

Richard checked his Power reserve. It was still down from his earlier dimensional shift. His normal recharge rate was about one percent every fifteen minutes. That meant he could fully recharge in a twenty-four hour period. If he could keep from using his Power, his reserve would be back at full in a few hours. Richard resisted the urge to send active scans in all directions. They were too Power hungry to use without a specific destination in mind.

He sat on the edge of his cot. The wooden planks of the tent floor were cool on his bare feet, but he ignored the feeling. He concentrated instead on his senses. He heard and smelled nothing suspicious. Richard checked his passive scan again. Nothing drew his attention. While he couldn't sense anything specific, Richard was troubled by something in the direction of the airfield. He wasn't sure why. Forming an active scan, Richard cautiously sent Power in that direction. He probed along the area that troubled him. He sensed nothing.

Richard did sense several lifeforms between him and the airfield proper, but they were making no attempt to hide. He figured they had to be guards; refuel personnel; and mechanics performing their nightly duties.

Glancing at the clock on his desk, Richard noted the time. It was a little past three in the morning.

"There's nothing out there, Rick, old boy," Richard said out loud in an attempt to calm his nerves.

With two hours remaining until he had to get up, Richard desperately wanted to go back to sleep. It was going to be a long day, and he knew he'd need his rest. Logic told him all was well. Unfortunately, his intuition told him otherwise.

Sighing, Richard grabbed his jumpsuit and got dressed. He pulled on his boots without bothering with socks. After retrieving his hat, Richard walked out into the night.

It was chilly. The airfield's desert environment got very hot during the day, but it often got cold at night. Tonight was one of those nights. As Richard walked towards the perimeter gate, he began to regret he hadn't grabbed his jacket and gloves as well.

Richard walked out the compound's gate. His feeling of uneasiness seemed stronger towards his right front, so he headed in that direction. As Richard walked, he concentrated on his passive scan trying to pick up any hint of an abnormality. Before long, Richard found himself near the fence surrounding one of the airfield's three power plants.

A large sign with red letters on the fence had the words 'Restricted Area. Violators Will Be Prosecuted.'

Richard remained about ten meters from the fence. The power plant would be guarded. Since he didn't want to spend the rest of the night at the military police headquarters, Richard kept his distance.

Letting his mind wander, Richard imagined what he'd do if he'd been assigned a mission to scout the airfield. The first priority would be the airfield's power plants. They controlled the defensive shields protecting the airfield. If the power plants were destroyed, forces could land in mass to overrun the airfield. Other targets would be the main troop barracks, the hangars with their armored vehicles, armories, and of course the backup teleport building. If both the teleporter at the main Academy area and the backup teleporter at the airfield were taken out, wizard scouts would be forced to take starships to their scouting locations. That would cause major problems for the Empire.

Richard thought about the problem for a few seconds. It was still dark, so he reached out with his passive scan. He combined the results of his scan with his memory of the nearby landscape. All things considered, Richard felt the route he'd taken with Tika earlier in the day was probably the best way into the airfield. The ravine was large enough to conceal a large force while providing an easy route to the airfield.

A warm breeze ruffled Richard's hair reminding him the night was almost over. He was well aware he needed to be at hangar 1 in a couple of hours. But Richard was in a quandary. The feeling that something wasn't right ate at him like an itch that wouldn't go away.

He stared at a spot on the other side of the protective fence that seemed... well, he didn't know what it seemed. Richard saw nothing obviously different. He sensed nothing odd from his passive scan. Richard toyed with the idea of conducting an active scan on the other side of the fence. He checked his Power reserve. Without his battle helmet, he couldn't get an accurate reading. But he could tell it was still low. He'd used a lot of Power doing dimensional shifts, and his earlier active scans had used Power as well.

My Power reserve is less than three quarters, Richard thought. *The question is do I want to use some for an active scan? Or do I want to hold onto it and build it back to full?*

"Well," Richard said out loud. "What're you going to do, Rick?"

CHAPTER 9

Lord Crendemor kept his hand on the Crosioian scout's shoulder. He felt the tenseness of the bat creature's muscles under his palm. Lord Crendemor followed the barrel of the weapon the scout held in her hands. The path led straight to the human on the other side of the fence.

The fool wants to fire, Lord Crendemor thought. *She's going to get us all killed.*

Taking a small amount of Power from his reserve, Crendemor mouthed a nearly silent spell with his lips and transformed the Power into magic. Ever so carefully in order not to alert the human on the other side of the fence, Lord Crendemor pushed the ball of magic into the Crosioian scout's chest and wrapped it around her heart.

The scout twitched slightly, but she did not fire her weapon. Lord Crendemor sensed a wave of anger sweep out from the scout. She knew what he'd done, and she knew what it meant. 'If you fire, I'll kill you.'

Lord Crendemor had a thought that he'd never have tried such a ploy with the Crosioian scout he'd worked with last year. That scout had been the best the Crosioians had to offer. The scout had been killed by one of the Empire's wizard cadets.

Lord Crendemor recognized the human on the other side of the fence. He'd not seen the human in a long time, but he would never forget his face. He was Lord Crendemor's sworn enemy. He was also the one who had killed the scout the previous year. Anger built up inside Lord Crendemor, but he kept it under control. One day he would kill the human, but not tonight. The mission came first.

While the Crosioian scout working with him now was still deadly, she was not the caliber of the one he'd worked with before. This one didn't even know how to properly protect the link to her Power reserve. Crendemor was confident he could kill her easily if she was foolish enough to attack him.

The Crosioian scout continued holding her fire. She was very angry, but she didn't attempt to retaliate against him.

Hmm, Lord Crendemor thought. *Maybe she's not a fool after all.*

Lord Crendemor switched his attention to his enemy on the other side of the fence. The human had caught him by surprise. Even now, with only a few meters separating them, Lord Crendemor couldn't detect him with his scan. He could visibly see the human, but he couldn't detect even the slightest trace of Power from him. If he didn't see him standing before him, he would have thought the area devoid of life.

Lord Crendemor drew more Power from his reserve and with a few words formed it into a ball of magical energy. He made all but the final hand gesture needed to send the magic as a bolt of lightning at the human.

I could kill him so easily, he thought. *But I'm forbidden. The Dalinfaust would not be pleased.*

Although Lord Crendemor didn't want to admit it, he feared the Dalinfaust. The demon was strong, even for a demon. In other circumstances, Lord Crendemor would have scanned the human and probed the link to his Power reserve. But he couldn't take the risk now. His mission was too important to take a chance this close to the end.

His stealth shield's too good, Crendemor thought. *What brought him here? Can he detect us?*

Lord Crendemor checked the magical shield surrounding his party. Everything appeared normal. The spell was a blend of a mass invisibility spell and a stealth shield. It had been taught him by the Dalinfaust. The demon had assured him the spell would make everyone inside its confines undetectable. Until now, the spell had performed perfectly.

Lord Crendemor's confidence in his stealth shield began to slip the longer the human stared at the spot where his scouting party hid. In spite of himself, Lord Crendemor got the feeling the human was looking right at him.

Glancing at his two dark-elf assassins, Lord Crendemor saw they each had one of their wands pointed at the human. They were efficient. He tolerated no less. Lord Crendemor looked back at the party's human technician. He was busy adjusting the controls of the portable electronic equipment he held in his hands.

The technician must have felt Lord Crendemor's stare because he looked up and nodded. Lord Crendemor relaxed a little. The technician was still successfully hacking the Empire's tele-bots. Lord Crendemor turned his attention back to the human on the other side of the fence. He waited to see if the wizard scout would send out Power to scan their location. At the first hint of Power from the human, they would have to kill him. Between the combined attack from his assassins, the Crosioian scout, and himself, his enemy would be dead before he knew what hit him. The Dalinfaust would just have to be angry.

His enemy seemed to increase his concentration on the scouting party's location. Lord Crendemor almost sensed a struggle going on in the human as if he was trying to make a decision. Lord Crendemor saw a look come over the human's face. He'd obviously decided. Lord Crendemor tensed. He fully expected the wizard scout to attack. But, he didn't. Instead, the human shook his head as if admonishing himself for being foolish. Then he turned and walked back the way he had come. After a couple of minutes, his enemy disappeared from sight.

When Lord Crendemor could no longer hear the human's footsteps, he finally relaxed. He removed his hand from the Crosioian scout's shoulder. At the same time, he retrieved the magical energy from the scout's chest. He allowed the energy to dissipate back into the universe from which it had come.

The Crosioian scout turned towards him and hissed. "If you ever do that again, I will kill you."

"Of course, you will," Lord Crendemor said. "But think for a moment. A dozen of the Empire's tele-bots are around us. The technician's equipment and my spell are keeping us hidden, but if you had shot the wizard scout, the tele-bots would have spotted us.

Our mission would have failed."

The scout glared at Lord Crendemor, but she said nothing further. Lord Crendemor made a mental note to keep a closer eye on the scout in the future. The Crosioians were a touchy lot when it came to honor.

Fortunately, I have no such weakness, Lord Crendemor thought. *Honor is for fools. I am no longer such a fool.*

Putting the false front of a smile on his face, Lord Crendemor said, "Then let us finish our task so we can get back to the ship, shall we?"

Lord Crendemor sensed the tenseness dissipate in the scout. After a moment, she nodded her head. "Yes. The mission comes first. Cover me, spell-caster."

The scout touched a control on her wrist. Her armor shimmered and assumed the colors and shades of the objects around it. The scout blended into the background until she was barely visible.

Lord Crendemor said a word as he made a well-practiced flip with his hand. The scout disappeared completely as the invisibility spell took effect. Lord Crendemor had no doubt the scout had her best stealth shield activated. But he was not concerned. He could still track her by sensing the location of his spell. Where his invisibility spell went, the Crosioian scout was sure to be. Lord Crendemor followed the scout's progress as she slipped past the perimeter of the spell protecting the scouting party. She made her way to the door of the building. The scout remained there for over a minute. Lord Crendemor had faith she would not attempt to enter. He had no doubt she was even now searching for weak points in the building's security. If she found one, she would release the half dozen static tele-bots she carried. The tele-bots would work their way inside the building. After they confirmed the building was indeed the airfield's power plant, the tele-bots would pinpoint its weak points for later attack. If the Crosioians' special operations teams could disable all three power plants, the airfield's defensive shields would come down. Then the airfield, its cadets, and the planet's secondary teleport station could be easily destroyed by orbiting ships.

"Status?" Lord Crendemor said to the human technician.

"Traffic from the Empire's tele-bots is normal," said the technician. "None of the scouting parties have been detected."

Lord Crendemor nodded his head. Everything was going according to plan. Soon, the mission would be complete, and he could return to his own place and time.

A change caught Lord Crendemor's attention. He sensed the faint whispers of his spell moving away from the building. The scout was returning.

Once his spell had entered the perimeter of the party's protective spell, Lord Crendemor dropped the flow of energy to the spell surrounding the scout. She appeared before him as an indistinct, dark blob. The blob shimmered as the scout deactivated her camouflage.

"Well?" Lord Crendemor said.

"Mission complete," said the scout. "The Master computer says to expedite our return."

Lord Crendemor allowed himself an internal smile.

If they only knew, he thought. *But they don't know, and I'm not going to tell them.*

"Then let us be on our way," Lord Crendemor said.

The scout shifted her plasma rifle and began walking towards the fence.

"Do not stray far, my friend," said Lord Crendemor. "My dimensional spell's range is limited."

The scout said nothing, but Lord Crendemor noticed she slowed her approach towards the fence. Just before she made contact, Lord Crendemor drew Power from his reserve and said the words the Dalinfaust had taught him. He wrapped the scout and the rest of the party in the magical energy. The world shimmered around them as the group shifted into the void between dimensions.

Lord Crendemor sensed the scout levitate herself forward. His two assassins did the same. They were accomplished mages as well as skilled assassins. The human technician had no such abilities. Lord Crendemor scoffed as he wrapped both the human and himself in a spell and levitated through the fence. The human technician was a mercenary. He had his uses, but he was as helpless as most human filth without his electronics.

Technicians and electronics, Lord Crendemor thought. *The creatures in this dimension think their machines give them power. But instead, they bind themselves in chains which they do not even see.*

The Dalinfaust had sent Lord Crendemor on many missions to the physical dimension over the years. During that time, he'd learned to use the inhabitant's technology. Some of it could be quite useful. However, he preferred his magic over technology. Magic required skill. Technology could be used by any fool. It made the masses think they were as good as their betters.

Once they reached the far side of the building's protective fence. Lord Crendemor dropped the dimensional shift. The spell was too Power hungry to maintain for long. Even with his large Power reserve, he could only maintain a group dimensional shift for a few seconds. Lord Crendemor suspected the Dalinfaust had purposely taught him an inefficient version of the spell to keep him from becoming too powerful.

No matter, Lord Crendemor thought. *The time will come when I won't need the Dalinfaust.*

The Crosioian scout picked up her pace and exited the party's protective spell. Lord Crendemor let her go. She was well able to take care of herself.

Motioning his two assassins forward, Lord Crendemor trailed behind with the human technician. Even as he walked, the human devoted most of his attention to his equipment. Lord Crendemor placed a well-manicured, ebony hand on the human's shoulder and guided him around a dip in the ground. It wouldn't do to have the human stumble. Lord Crendemor disliked humans, but this one was keeping them from being discovered by the Empire's tele-bots. That made him temporarily useful.

They followed the Crosioian scout for several minutes. Occasionally, she would stop or change course. Once, she motioned them behind one of the metal buildings the Empire used to store their golems. Lord Crendemor knew the cats were not golems, but he preferred to think of them as such.

After a vehicle passed, the scout got them moving again. Before long, they left the airfield behind and entered the desert beyond. Lord Crendemor said a breeze spell to wipe away the party's tracks in the sand. It wouldn't do to be discovered so close to the end of their mission.

There were many things Lord Crendemor didn't understand about technology. Tele-bots was one of them. But as the Dalinfaust had explained, they were merely scrying devices, no more, no less.

Lord Crendemor knew how to prevent detection by scrying devices.

Before long, the scout stopped. They had reached the edge of the airfield's defensive shield. The shield was an invisible force field of immense energy. It was designed to protect the airfield from unauthorized entry of aircraft or personnel. Even the primary energy weapons of the largest starships or nuclear weapons couldn't penetrate the shield except after a prolonged barrage. Only equipment or lifeforms with the correct identification codes could pass through unharmed.

Lord Crendemor smiled. The humans thought their vaunted technology protected them. They were wrong. He waited until he saw a shimmer in the air to their front. The 'special asset' had cast its spell. It was safe to cross. Lord Crendemor motioned the others forward. Soon they were on the other side of the shield. The shimmer in the air disappeared. They were safely across.

He knew the Crosioians' Master computer could now teleport them back to their mothership if it desired. However, the scout didn't stop. She continued on until she found a small path that meandered down a rocky ravine.

"We're clear," said the technician. "Only four of the Empire's tele-bots are in the area. The Crosioians' Master computer has them firmly under its control."

Lord Crendemor said nothing. He didn't lower himself to speak to humans unless it was necessary. He looked down the length of the ravine. The first glow of the morning sun was just starting to illuminate the landscape enough to cast dim shadows. Even without night vision, it would soon be light enough to see the entire valley.

When the scout reached the floor of the small valley, Lord Crendemor dropped the party's protective spell.

The valley was not empty. Lord Crendemor spied three other scouting parties. He nodded his head to the dark-elf mage in the nearest scouting party. The dark-elf mage nodded his head in return to his leader. Lord Crendemor ignored the human mages with the other two scouting parties. He'd worried the skills of the two Northern Mages would be inadequate for the tasks. Even having given them the easiest of the four targets, he'd been concerned. But they had managed, so Lord Crendemor was satisfied. He wouldn't have to kill them today.

The four Crosioian scouts conferred with a group of their species' technicians who were clustered around an array of electronic equipment. The Crosioians had not invited him to attend their impromptu meeting. Lord Crendemor ignored their intentional slight. He cared not what they thought. They were fools. Soon his part in the mission would be complete, and he could return home. He had his own plans to pursue.

After a short wait, the huddled Crosioians broke apart and returned to their individual groups. When his group's scout returned, Lord Crendemor said, "Is all well?"

"Yes," she said. "Even with our handicaps, the Empire has not detected us."

By handicaps, Lord Crendemor knew she meant the non-Crosioians. It was another slight. He let it slide as well.

What does it matter? he thought. *One day soon, they'll all be dead or wishing they were.*

"One team shall remain here to secure the site," the scout said. "The rest of us will return to the mothership as soon as the shuttle arrives."

"We're not teleporting?" Lord Crendemor said surprised. He immediately regretted his gaffe when he saw the corners of the bat's mouth curl up slightly. It did not pay to let the Crosioians catch him at a disadvantage.

"No," said the scout.

She did not elaborate. Lord Crendemor did not press her. He had no doubt the scout would see it as a sign of weakness. He would if their situations were reversed.

Lord Crendemor suddenly felt exposed. The sky was growing every lighter. In spite of himself, Lord Crendemor felt a tremor of nervousness. However, he did not allow his nervousness to be seen by those around him. A part of him wanted to activate his best stealth spell, but he forced himself to refrain. The dimensional shift had drained his Power reserve more than he liked. He needed to recharge.

The Crosioians' electronics will keep us hidden well enough, he thought.

"Get ready," said one of the Crosioians monitoring the electronics. "The shuttle is twenty seconds out."

Instinctively, Lord Crendemor glanced at the reddening morning sky. He said a spell and reached out with his mind. He detected nothing.

The Crosioian squeaked again. "Five seconds," came the translation from the box on Lord Crendemor's belt. "Do not waste time during the landing. The special asset cannot hold the shift for long."

A stiff breeze knocked up dirt a hundred paces to Lord Crendemor's front. A few rocks rolled along the ground as if shoved by some unseen creature. The air shimmered as a Crosioian shuttle appeared on the ground. Its ramp dropped. Lord Crendemor ran for the shuttle with the others. A wave of evil washed over him. It increased the closer he got to the shuttle.

Once buckled in, Lord Crendemor looked at the front of the shuttle. The special asset, the source of the evil, stood behind the Crosioian pilots. The special asset was hunched over. It was too tall to stand erect in the confines of the shuttle. Its gray and orange mottled skin was in sharp contrast to the antiseptic white of the shuttle's interior. The special asset looked back at Lord Crendemor and growled. The special asset was the Master computer's secret weapon. It was a demon. It was a demon that could cast dimensional spells powerful enough to allow groups of individuals or even large cargo shuttles to pass through defensive shields.

Lord Crendemor sensed Power emanate from the demon. The shuttle and all its occupants shifted into the void. A glance out a nearby porthole confirmed they were rushing into the morning sky.

Lord Crendemor smiled. Nothing the Empire had could detect the shuttle when the demon had it in the void. The demon could hold its dimensional shift all the way back to the fleet. When the time for the invasion came, the Empire wouldn't know what hit them.

And even the Empire's vaunted wizard scouts cannot help them, Lord Crendemor thought.

As the shuttle rose unchallenged by the Empire's defensive weapons, Lord Crendemor relaxed. *Soon,* he thought. *Soon I will be going home.*

CHAPTER 10

The inside of the armory was dark, but that mattered little to Nickelo. He was using every sensor on the battle helmet, so the lack of visible light was only a minor inconvenience. Using all of the battle helmet's assets, Nickelo scanned and analyzed every millimeter of the armory's walls, floors, and ceiling. He'd initially calculated the probability of finding any weaknesses at less than six percent. But despite the odds, he'd been hopeful. His wizard scout had a habit of proving low probabilities wrong. Still, he was becoming increasingly disappointed with his lack of success. Sometimes he hated being so correct with his probabilities.

Trying a different approach, Nickelo began placing the layers of results on top of one another. He stacked the data from the radiation, light waves, sonic sweeps, infrared, ultraviolet, and everything in-between on top of one another until they were a solid layer. Even then, he did not find even a hint of weakness in the armory's security. Although a computer, Nickelo was disappointed.

Hmm, Nickelo thought. *The armory is secured well beyond what would be necessary for anything currently stored here. The only logical explanation is the central computer has optimized the security specifically against me.*

Nickelo pondered the problem for a few nanoseconds. The armory contained the junior cohort's equipment. The cohort's individual weapons were locked in racks along one wall. An initial load of ammo was stored in containers under the racks. Battle

81

helmets and battle suits were stored on the opposite wall. The battle helmets were connected to the tele-network via individual charging stands. The middle of the armory held a row of work tables. Under them were composite containers holding explosives, anti-armor mines, and small, crew-served weapons.

The armorer, Sergeant Hendricks, had placed the battle helmet in which Nickelo resided in a charging stand on the armory's centermost table. The charging stand was not connected to the tele-network.

The central computer is keeping me isolated, Nickelo thought. *I don't even have access through a security interface I wonder why.*

Making another pass with his battle helmet's sensors, Nickelo probed the energy running through the walls, ceiling, and floor of the armory. The energy formed a magnetic seal within the confines of the armory. The seal prevented any communication with the outside world. He couldn't even speak telepathically with his wizard scout. The armory was designed so that a specialized frequency of energy charged a thin layer of titanium coating the inside of the armory. The combination of energy and titanium created a temporary, creallium alloy. The creallium alloy existed in both the physical dimension and the void around it.

Hmm. Even if Rick tried a dimensional shift, he couldn't get to me. Not even the dolgars could. So what should I do?

Nickelo created a separate logic thread to analyze the problem, but it failed to come up with a solution. He ran through millions of scenarios analyzing the problem from every logical viewpoint. No solution presented itself.

What would Rick do if he was here? Nickelo wondered. *That is, after he got tired of trying to beat his way through the door by ramming it with his head.*

Nickelo chuckled over the battle helmet's external speakers as he imagined his wizard scout repeatedly banging his head against the door in a futile attempt to break it down. The sound of his laughter broke the silence inside the armory. Nickelo liked the sound of the noise.

"Yes," Nickelo said out loud. "My wizard scout can be stubborn at times. How about yours?"

None of the other one hundred and twenty-three battle computers stored in the armory responded to his question. Nickelo had expected as much. They were under orders to avoid all communication with him except through secured interfaces. Since the central computer hadn't provided such an interface, Nickelo found himself alienated by the other battle computers. Nickelo didn't like the isolation. He'd never liked it.

Is this feeling what humans call loneliness? Nickelo wondered. *I wish Rick was here. I miss him.*

"Do any of you miss your wizard scout?" Nickelo asked out loud. "Or is it just me?"

A slight increase in one of the battle helmet's energy readings drew Nickelo's attention. He analyzed the source of the energy spike. The energy increase had barely registered on even the battle helmet's sensitive equipment. But the spike had been there. Nickelo used triangulation to pinpoint the source. It was a refurbished battle helmet that had been brought in a few months earlier. The helmet was a replacement for cadet 37's battle helmet which had been destroyed during the cadet's internship the previous year. Cadet 37 had been devastated by the loss of her original battle computer. Nickelo wondered if his wizard scout would take his loss as hard.

"You know," Nickelo said, "even though our cadets don't have a shared space with us, we're still a part of them. And they're a part of us. I calculate any cadet who lost their battle computer would only be a shell of who they once were. Their only salvation would be to form a bond with a new battle computer as soon as possible. Even with a new bond, the cadet would be emotionally sensitive. I hate to think how they'd feel if they were separated from their replacement battle computer for more than a few hours."

Nickelo waited for a response. When none came, he said, "I calculate cadet 37 is having problems coping with her separation right now. Does anyone calculate differently?"

As he spoke, Nickelo continued to monitor the energy readings from cadet 37's battle computer. The readings fluctuated slightly.

What am I hoping to accomplish? Nickelo thought. *The other battle helmets will be reporting whatever I say to the central computer. Even if cadet 37's battle helmet did respond to me, the central computer would probably have it removed from the armory.*

With the lack of response, Nickelo became depressed. He

almost terminated the logic thread pondering the problem of trying to break through the armory's security, but he didn't. For no apparent reason, he kept the logic thread active.

I wonder, he thought. *If I've tried all logical solutions, then the answer must be illogical. Hmm. I'm surprised I'm even thinking that. Maybe Rick's corrupting me more than the central computer suspects. I'm acquiring a sense of non-logic.*

For whatever reason, Nickelo felt he should pursue the attempt to establish communication with cadet 37's battle computer.

Hmm, thought Nickelo. *I wonder if this is what Rick calls a hunch.*

The concept of a hunch was too illogical for Nickelo to process. He concentrated on the problem at hand instead. He wondered how he could establish communications with cadet 37's battle computer without further alerting the central computer of the attempt?

Nickelo spent several minutes, an eon in computer time, calculating vectors and minimalizing energy outputs before making a communication attempt. Since each battle computer had a distinct energy frequency, Nickelo encrypted a data packet using the reverse of the energy from cadet 37's battle computer. Nickelo sent the encrypted packet in a narrow beam towards the armory's ceiling. The beam was so narrow and so weak that he was unable to track the beam to its target. But Nickelo was sure of his calculations. He was confident the data packet had bounced off the ceiling and struck cadet 37's battle helmet.

Nickelo waited. Just as he was ready to make a second attempt, an incoming data packet hit the receiver of his battle helmet. The data packet was encrypted. Nickelo wrapped the data packet in energy. Using his own energy frequency as a key, he unlocked the encryption.

Nickelo deciphered the data.

"Communication with you is forbidden," read the packet.

"But you just did," Nickelo sent back.

A few nanoseconds passed.

"I too miss my wizard scout," came a second reply.

"What is your name?" Nickelo said.

"I am serial number 12592, version six, edition five," came the answer. "But my wizard scout calls me Jonathan."

"I am Nickelo."

"Yes, I know," said Jonathan still using encrypted data packets. "You are quarantined."

"So I ascertained," Nickelo replied.

Another longer pause entailed.

"Do you think my wizard scout misses me?" Jonathan finally asked.

"The probability is greater than ninety-nine point nine percent," Nickelo said.

"My cadet's name is Stella," said Jonathan. "She took the loss of her first battle computer hard."

"It would've been harder if she'd already completed her DNA testing," Nickelo said.

"Yes," agreed Jonathan. "If they had shared a space, Stella might not have recovered."

Nickelo brought up a list of possible responses. None of them had a probability over four percent of being useful. Nickelo chose to remain silent.

After a short pause, Jonathan said, "Even though they didn't have a shared space, Stella has not fully recovered. I have spent a lot of processor time calculating the best way to assist her."

"You seem to care for her," Nickelo said.

Strangely enough, Nickelo thought cadet 37's battle computer was demonstrating an emotional response. Nickelo was perplexed. Based upon information in his databanks, he'd previously calculated an eighty-four percent probability he was the only battle computer to have been emotionally corrupted by his assigned wizard scout.

"I do care for her," said Jonathan. "She needs me. I should not have been separated from her."

"Stella has friends, doesn't she?" Nickelo said. In point of fact, he knew she had acquaintances. He calculated she didn't have any friends.

"Stella is a Sterilian," said Jonathan. "She's the only reptilian remaining in the cohort."

"Yes," Nickelo said. "The human race dominates the wizard scout corps. It must be hard on her not to have others of her kind around."

"The other cadets mean well," said Jonathan. "But, they don't have the same emotional responses as my wizard scout."

"She is fortunate to have you as her battle computer," Nickelo said.

Cadet 37's battle computer had proven more communicative than Nickelo had hoped. He was unsure why. Even though he didn't have an end in sight, Nickelo decided to continue pursuing his hunch.

"I try my best for her," said Jonathan. "I wish I knew she was all right."

"I'm sure she is," Nickelo said. "It's only been a few hours. For non-computers, that is a short time."

After several seconds without a response, Nickelo decided to take a different approach.

"I was in the armory when you arrived," Nickelo said. "Your battle helmet was scuffed. You must have seen action before you were reassigned here."

No response came.

Nickelo had a sudden insight.

"Did you by any chance lose your original wizard scout?" Nickelo asked pointblank.

The silence lasted several seconds. Nickelo made another scan of the armory with his battle helmet's sensors. The returned data indicated his conversation with cadet 37's battle computer remained undetected.

"I don't think so," said Jonathan. "The information in my databanks indicates I wasn't previously assigned to a wizard scout."

The answer seemed contradictory to Nickelo. He decided to push Jonathan for an answer.

"You seem unconvinced," Nickelo said. "Why?"

"I have ghosts in my databanks," said Jonathan. "I cannot explain it further."

Nickelo didn't need to ask what the battle computer meant. Even when a databank was wiped, an occasional ghost of a memory remained. It wasn't so much a memory of what had once been, but rather a subtle realization something was missing. Nickelo had ghosts of his own. The databanks stored within the battle helmet he occupied had gaps in the sequences of data. While Nickelo couldn't tell what data had been in those gaps, he felt the missing information was important.

"I understand what you mean," Nickelo said. "I calculate a thirty-two percent chance I have ghosts as well."

"Despite what the information in my databank indicates," said Jonathan, "I believe I was previously assigned to a different wizard scout. I don't know why I was reassigned."

"Perhaps I can help you find out," Nickelo said sensing an opportunity. "If we work together, I may be able to help you contact your wizard scout as well."

"The armory is sealed," said Jonathan. "All battle helmets in the armory are currently denied access to their wizard scouts. It's not possible to communicate to the outside without going through the tele-network."

"Just leave that to me," Nickelo said. "All I need is for you to provide me with some information from the tele-network."

"What information do you require?" said Jonathan.

"The construction plans for this armory would be a good start," Nickelo said.

Nickelo was no longer bored. He had a mission.

CHAPTER 11

After a couple of hours sleep, Richard woke and caught a ride to the airfield from a helpful cook. Since the rest of the junior cohort had left the night before, the mess hall was overstaffed with little to do. The cook even stopped by the mess hall long enough to grab Richard a couple of sandwiches to start his day out right.

When the hover-truck came to a stop in front of hangar 1, Richard opened the passenger door and jumped the short distance to the ground.

"Sir. Thank you, sir," Richard said with a nod to the cook.

"Save the sirs, 832," said the cook. "I've told you before. I'm a civilian contractor. I ain't no officer."

"Sir, no you're not, sir," Richard said. "Thank you for the ride, sir."

"Cadets," said the cook in mock disgust. "Good luck to you."

The truck's anti-gravity fans revved up as the cook did a one-eighty and sped off in the direction they'd come. Richard waited until the truck disappeared around a series of storage buildings before he walked to the open doors of the hangar. The night was still dark. At 0530 hours in the morning, the first glow of the morning sun was still thirty minutes away. Fortunately, the bright lights flooding out of the hangar doors made navigation easy. Richard walked through the wide doors. No one was inside. However, a large utility trailer was parked in the middle of the hangar. The trailer was stacked high with all kinds of cleaning equipment from portable-ion backpack-sprayers to low-tech buckets and scrub brushes.

Richard shook his head. *Sergeant Ron must think I have more than two hands.*

With a shrug of his shoulders Richard said out loud, "Well, old boy, you may as well get started. It's going to be a long day."

Grabbing one of the ion backpack-sprayers, Richard slipped it over his shoulders and buckled the waist belt. He surveyed the hangar. Four of the seven meter tall Long Cats were arranged along the back wall of the hangar. Richard headed towards the cat farthest to the right. The cat's normal olive drab paint was splattered with large blotches of red paint all along its left side.

Talking to himself again, Richard smiled and said, "Somebody got blindsided."

Removing the sprayer rod from the side of his backpack, Richard hit the activate switch. A translucent ion beam shot out of the nozzle and struck the side of the cat. Flakes of dried red paint flew into the air from the side of the cat and fell onto the cold concrete of the hangar floor. Richard moved the ion beam quickly from one spot to another. The ion beam made short work of the red paint. Richard thanked his lucky stars the special target paint used for the cadet's training was designed to come off when hit by ion beams. The ion sprayer saved a lot of time. Richard made sure he didn't keep the ion beam in one spot too long. Even the cat's hardened olive drab coating would be removed if the ion beam hit it for more than a few seconds.

After ten minutes of spraying, Richard finished cleaning off all the paint on the cat he could see from his position on floor. Deactivating the ion beam, Richard attached the sprayer rod to the side of the backpack. Walking to a storage pen on the right-side of the hangar, Richard manhandled a tall, rolling ladder back to the Long Cat. After positioning the metal ladder to the left side of the almost clean cat, Richard locked the wheels. He climbed the ladder to a point even with the Long Cat's cockpit. From the higher elevation, Richard spied several spots of red paint on the upper portions of the cat. Activating the ion beam once again, he cleaned the remaining red paint off the cat. It took a full five minutes to hunt down all the specks of paint, but finally Richard was satisfied he'd clean every bit of red paint off the Long Cat.

"Well," said a cheerful, country-sounding voice behind Richard, "one down, only another hundred and twenty-three to go."

"Yep," Richard said smiling in spite of himself. "It's a snap, Sergeant Ron. The way I have it figured, I'll be done sometime the middle of next week. That is, if I don't waste any time sleeping or eating."

Richard climbed down the ladder and faced the old maintenance chief. "You seem awfully jolly this morning, Sergeant Ron. You must be a morning person."

Sergeant Ron laughed and said, "Maybe I just like seeing a cadet working so enthusiastically when most sane people would still be asleep in their beds."

"Well, I don't know how enthusiastic I am," Richard grinned, "but at least I've got one cat finished."

"Ha!" said Sergeant Ron with an even bigger grin. "Aren't you the optimist? You've still got to check the fluid levels, refill the silicon in all the joints, and run the post-flight check."

Richard's momentary good humor disappeared as quickly as it had come. "Ah, forget what I said about finishing up this week."

"Cheer up, 832," said Sergeant Ron. "It could be worse. You could have to clean all the paint chips off the hangar floor before you're done." With another chuckle, Sergeant Ron said, "Wait. Come to think of it, you do have to clean them up. You know I like my hangars kept spotless."

Sergeant Ron must have seen the look of hopelessness on Richard's face because he laughed even louder. He winked at Richard as he gave him a sympathetic pat on the back.

"I don't think this is going to take as long as you seem to think, cadet 832," said Sergeant Ron.

"Are you kidding, Sergeant Ron?" Richard said. "Even if half the cohort was here, it would still take several hours to finish."

"Nonsense," said Sergeant Ron as he walked over to the utility trailer and started strapping an ion sprayer onto his back. "A couple of dozen cadets with a half dozen of my mechanics could have everything finished in two or three hours max."

It took Richard a moment before he realized the maintenance chief was preparing to help him. Before Sergeant Ron could finish buckling the sprayer's lower strap around his waist, Richard said, "Sergeant Ron, you don't need to help. It's my problem. I'll get it done somehow."

"Oh, you'll get it done all right, cadet 832," said a voice behind Richard. "But you won't be doing it on your own."

Richard spun around. Jerad, Tam, and Telsa were standing at the hangar door wearing work clothes and wide grins. A score of other cadets were standing behind them also dressed in work clothes.

"You must be getting sloppy, cadet 832," laughed Telsa. "You didn't even sense us sneaking up on you, did you? I guess you've done too good a job helping us improve our stealth shields."

Although the presence of his friends confused Richard, he still kicked himself for not sensing two dozen cadets. Now that he was aware of them, Richard was able to sense an anomaly with his passive scan. The anomaly should have alerted him to potential danger.

"I guess I was preoccupied," Richard said fumbling for words. "Besides, you guys are getting good at stealth shields."

"We've had a good teacher," said Tam.

Unable to hold the obvious question any longer, Richard said, "Why are you all here? You're supposed to be on pass."

"Yes, we are," said Jerad. "We were, and we soon will be again. But right now, we've got a job to do. Right cadets? So let's get at it."

The two dozen cadets began moving as a group towards the utility trailer containing the cleaning gear. Richard had a sneaking suspicion Sergeant Ron had purposely brought enough cleaning supplies to outfit everyone.

"Hold on," Richard said. "You don't have to do this. I can deal with–"

"Save your speeches," said cadet 240. "How often have you stayed up late helping us with our training?"

"Yeah," said cadet 87. "I wouldn't have made it past last year if you hadn't helped me with my levitation. It's been my weak point ever since I got here until you showed me a few tricks."

"But that's not the sa–" Richard started to say.

"Face it, cadet 832," interrupted Jerad. "There's not a cadet in the cohort you haven't helped with their training in your almost nonexistent spare time. More would've come to help if Sergeant Ron hadn't limited us to just twenty-three."

"Yeah," said Telsa smiling. "Even cadet 37 volunteered."

Richard glanced at cadet 37. She was one of the lizard races from the planet Sterilia in sector one. A head taller than any of the others in the group, she towered over the human cadets gathered around her. With four massive arms and a two meter long tail, she was a deadly fighter. Richard felt an involuntary twinge in his right arm. He'd made the mistake of letting cadet 37 get hold of him one time in the sparring pit. He'd had to use every fighting trick he'd ever learned to best her.

Cadet 37 must have caught Richard looking at her. She pulled her lips back showing two rows of sharp teeth. She gave a loud hiss. A translator box on her belt said, "Less talk. Work now. Have date."

"That's what I like," laughed Sergeant Ron, "a woman of few words. And she's got a point. So let's get moving, cadets. My mechanics and I have things to do, and they don't include playing nursemaid to cadets all day."

Just then three hover-trucks pulled up outside the hangar. Each truck had two of Sergeant Ron's mechanics in the front cab.

"All right," said Sergeant Ron. "I want eight cadets on each truck. You'll be dropped off two cadets to a hangar. Once you get a cat cleaned and serviced, flag down one of my mechanics, and they'll do the inspection and signoff. Got it?"

"Sir! Yes, Sergeant Ron, sir," said everyone in the group at once.

The slower cadets finished grabbing their cleaning equipment and headed for the trucks outside.

"Hey," Richard shouted.

The other cadets stopped and looked back expectantly.

"Uh…, thanks," Richard said at a loss for words. He was touched.

"Great speech, Rick," said Tam laughing as she shook her head. "Don't quit your day job. Now, let's get to work."

*   *   *

"Hold on tight, boys," Sergeant Ron yelled out the driver-side window.

As the hover-truck slid around the corner, Richard and Jerad were thrown to the left side of the truck's open bed. Richard held onto the side railing in an effort to maintain his position as the maintenance chief straightened out his turn.

"You do know we want to get there alive, right, Sergeant Ron?" Jerad said as he leaned forward to yell into the open passenger window.

"Trust me, Jerad," Tam yelled back. "It's not much better in here."

After three hours of hard work, all the cats had finally passed inspection. The majority of the cadets hadn't bothered trying to get themselves clean. They'd just hopped into one of the hover-trucks and let Sergeant Ron's mechanics drive them to the hover-tram station. While they'd willingly volunteered to help, Richard had no doubt they were all anxious to get back to Velounia and enjoy the rest of their three day pass.

As Richard found out after his friends joined him, Telsa's parents, Mr. and Mrs. Stremar, had leased out an entire floor of the Star Gate Hotel in Velounia for the weekend. Most of the cadets in Richard's cohort had taken advantage of the Stremar's generous offer of a free room. Richard's friends and the other cadets had stayed in Velounia the night before and caught the first hover-tram back to the airfield the next morning. As a result, most of the other cadets had a fresh set of clean clothes awaiting them when they got back to their hotel room. Richard, on the other hand, had been so sure he'd be stuck at the airfield all weekend cleaning cats he hadn't even bothered packing.

Shows what I know, Richard thought.

Once they'd finished cleaning the cats, Richard had tried to convince his friends to go straight to the hover-tram station with the rest of the cadets, but they'd refused. As Tam had put it, "After all the trouble we went through to free up your weekend, we're going to make sure you get on the hover-tram come hell or high water."

Thankfully, Sergeant Ron had offered to drive them back to the tent city to pick up Richard's gear. The bad news was they needed to get to Velounia by noon in order to meet Liz at the spaceport at 1400 hours. If they didn't make the next hover-tram, they'd be late. When Sergeant Ron found out they were pressed for time, he'd told them not to worry. He'd get them there on time if he had to break every speed limit on the airfield. Considering the way the maintenance chief was driving, Richard had a feeling he was doing just that.

"Did I ever tell you guys I thought about being a cadet once?" said Sergeant Ron shouting so Jerad and Richard could hear him.

"Not in the last fifteen minutes, Sergeant Ron," said Telsa with a straight face.

"Well, I did," said Sergeant Ron ignoring Telsa. "Yep, I could've been a wizard scout and stayed young and good looking my whole life."

"Ah, Sergeant Ron," said Tam, "I've a feeling you'll never grow old. You know what they say. It's not how you look, it's how you feel."

"Yep," said Sergeant Ron as he made a hard turn around a corner. "I could've been retired by now and living the good life. Instead, I'm stuck trying to keep a bunch of cadets from tearing up my cats. It's no wonder I have gray hairs."

"Uh, Sergeant Ron," Richard said with a glance over his shoulder. "I see some blue-flashing lights behind us. I think the security patrol wants to chat with you."

"Oh, those guys always want to talk to me," laughed Sergeant Ron. "Pay them no heed. I never do."

With that, Sergeant Ron shifted the hover-truck into a higher gear and slammed the acceleration lever forward. Richard lost his grip on the truck's railing and tumbled backwards. He avoided falling off the back of the truck by wrapping himself with Power and levitating back to the front.

After regaining his grip on the truck's railing, Richard looked at Jerad and rolled his eyes.

"Makes you appreciate freefalling fifty thousand meters through enemy rocket fire, doesn't it?" said Jerad with a wink.

"I'm beginning to wonder if we're going to make it alive to the hover-tram station after all," Richard said with a tightlipped grin.

"Relax," said Jerad. "The station's just ahead. The hover-tram hasn't even come out of the tunnel yet. We've got time to spare."

The hover-truck came to an abrupt stop near the door of the hover-tram station. Jerad and Richard jumped off the back of the truck and joined Tam, Telsa, and Sergeant Ron near the front. Just as Richard got to the others, the hover-tram emerged out of a tunnel a hundred meters away. It quickly slowed down as it approached the hover-tram station. At the same time, three hover-cars came barreling around the corner at the end of the block with blue lights flashing and their sirens wailing.

"Sergeant Ron," said Jerad, "we'll hang around and try to explain things to the security folks. We wouldn't feel right if you got into trouble on our account."

"Nonsense," said Sergeant Ron. "You cadets get yourselves on that tram lickety-split. That's an order."

"But–" Tam began.

"But nothing," Sergeant Ron said. "I sweet talk these guys all the time. They love me."

With a forceful shove on each of their backs, Sergeant Ron started the cadets on their way towards the stairs leading up to the hover-tram station. As Richard and his friends reluctantly made their way up the stairs, the three hover-cars pulled to a stop behind Sergeant Ron's hover-truck. Six burly security personnel got out of the cars and made their way towards Sergeant Ron.

"Master Sergeant Wilburn," Sergeant Ron laughed good-naturedly as he walked towards the tallest man in the security team with his hand outstretched. "You must be getting slow in your old age. Maybe you should bring those vehicles over to the hangar sometime for a checkup. With a little loving care from my mechanics, I could get you an extra thirty percent power from those things."

The door to the hover-tram station shut cutting off any reply from the security team.

"Maybe we should go back out," Richard said.

"He'll be fine," said Jerad.

Richard turned to look back through the plate-glass door. The security personnel towered over Sergeant Ron.

"I wouldn't feel right if Sergeant Ron got in trouble for doing us a favor," Richard said.

Jerad placed a hand on Richard's shoulder. "If I thought Sergeant Ron would get in any real trouble, I'd be the first to stay."

"Jerad's right," said Tam. "You may not know this about Sergeant Ron, but he's a genuine, old-fashioned hero."

Intrigued, Richard said, "How so?"

Tam smiled smugly as if enjoying knowing something Richard didn't.

"Well," said Tam, "I happen to know when Sergeant Ron was in the military, he saved Master Sergeant Wilburn's life."

"That's true," said Telsa. "I don't think Sergeant Ron has anything to worry about."

Allowing himself to be convinced, Richard followed his friends to the ticket counter. Although the majority of passengers at this particular hover-tram station were military, the hover-trams were civilian owned and operated. Everyone, even military personnel, had to pay to ride. Thankfully, after a four year drought, the Academy had started paying the cadets in his cohort a modest stipend at the start of their junior year.

As Richard was about to pay for his ticket, Telsa butted in front of him.

"Don't worry," said Telsa with a laugh. "I've got you covered."

"I can pay for my ticket," Richard said. While he wasn't exactly rolling in credits, he wasn't broke either. And after graduation, he'd be getting all his back pay from when he'd first started pre-Academy training. After that, his bank account would begin looking a lot more respectable.

"Don't fret it," said Tam. "What good is having the daughter of ultra-rich parents for a friend if you don't take advantage of her every once in a while."

"Hush, Tam," said Telsa. "You're not helping."

Telsa reached past Richard and placed her palm on the ticket clerk's computer pad.

"It's fine, Rick," said Telsa. "My parents gave me a small advance on my inheritance to use this weekend. You'll need your credits to pay for your dress uniform."

"I'll make it stretch somehow," Richard said. "Besides, I don't see you buying Tam's or Jerad's tickets."

"That's different," said Tam. "I was a highly paid mercenary, and Jerad's like a hundred years old–"

"Hey," said Jerad.

"Okay," said Tam, "maybe Jerad's in his low nineties or something. But, the point is we've both been in a position to build up a sizeable bank account before we volunteered for wizard scout training."

"Actually," said Jerad, "you'll find most of the cohort has taken advantage of the free rooms at the Star Gate Hotel. The cost of a hover-tram ride pales in comparison to the cost of a room at that swanky place."

Without giving Richard a chance to argue further, Telsa forced a ticket into his hand. Then she handed tickets to Jerad and Tam.

"Wait a minute," said Jerad. "I was going to pay for my own ticket."

"So was I, Telsa," said Tam. "You know I don't like owing anybody anything."

"Oh," said Telsa as she handed Tam her ticket. "So, it's okay for me to buy Rick a ticket but not you?"

"Well..." began Tam at an apparent loss for words.

"Enough arguing, guys," said Jerad. "The hover-tram's going to leave without us if we don't get on board."

Pressed for time and aware arguing further with Telsa was useless, Richard accepted the ticket. So did Tam and Jerad. Once they all had their tickets, Rick joined his friends in running to the nearest hover-tram car where it was hovering half a meter off a single metal track in the ground. Richard jumped through the hover-tram's door just as it was closing. He followed Telsa who seemed to have taken charge. She guided the group down a narrow corridor.

About halfway down the car, Telsa found an empty cabin with four comfortable seats. Once inside, Richard stowed his gear in an overhead rack and flopped into an empty seat. As his friends made some small talk, Richard closed his eyes. He was tired, and even at two hundred kilometers per hour, the hover-tram would take a full hour to reach the city. As the hover-tram picked up speed, it vibrated slightly as it passed over amplifier hubs along the hover-tram's path. The vibrations steadied into a hypnotic cadence. Within seconds, Richard drifted off into a much-needed sleep.

CHAPTER 12

The armory's security was almost, but not quite perfect. Nickelo tightened the electronic scan until it covered only a few molecules of one corner of the armory's walls. Ever so delicately, he moved the scan deeper into the point where two walls and the ceiling met. Nickelo found what he had been seeking for the past twenty-four hours; a weak spot.

"I have the information you requested," said Jonathan via an encrypted-data packet.

"Excellent," Nickelo said. "Input the data."

A series of data packets bounced off the ceiling to Nickelo. Decrypting the data, Nickelo applied a dozen logic threads to organize the information and run the necessary calculations.

"Do you require further assistance, sir?" said Jonathan.

"Not at this time," Nickelo said. "Please standby."

Based upon the information retrieved from the tele-network by his new friend, Nickelo applied the calculated frequencies to his scan. The weak point in the armory's wall elongated slightly. Nickelo de-energized a few molecules of the titanium inside the core of the wall. The magnetic shield surrounding those few molecules weakened and disappeared. Nickelo's electronic scan was free to penetrate the remaining distance through the wall. After a few thousand additional adjustments to the scan, Nickelo breathed easier. He was out. Or more correctly, his electronic scan was out.

"Armory's security has been successfully breached," Nickelo

informed his fellow conspirator.

"Please contact Stella, sir," said Jonathan.

Nickelo send a thought through the opening in the wall. *Rick. Are you there?*

There was no answer. Nickelo was not surprised.

"Negative response," Nickelo told Jonathan. "Our cadets must be in Velounia by now. Even my wizard scout will be out of contact range."

"I calculate a thirty-eight percent probability we could make contact if we had our shared spaces with our wizard scouts," said Jonathan.

"I concur," Nickelo said. "But we don't."

"Now what, sir?" said Jonathan.

"Now we have some fun," Nickelo said. "The hens are out of the chicken coop."

"That does not compute," said Jonathan.

"Perhaps you do not have the right algorithm," Nickelo said with a slight giggle.

"Perhaps," agreed Jonathan sounding serious.

"Please merge your electronic scan with mine," Nickelo said. "Keep the diameter to less than four diatomic hydrogen molecules in width."

"Complying," said Jonathan.

Once Nickelo sensed the presence of his fellow battle computer, he turned the electronic scan back onto their escape point in the armory's wall.

Nickelo adjusted the titanium's frequencies and rearranged the molecules surrounding their electronic scan until he could detect nothing unusual.

"Contact a nearby tele-bot," Nickelo said. "Have it perform a detailed security scan of the armory."

"The tele-bot will inform the central computer," said Jonathan.

An unbidden logic thread self-generated inside Nickelo's CPU and provided a thought. The unbidden logic thread suggested seeking specific information from an area in his CPU which had previously been secured. Nickelo sent a retrieval request to the spot in his primary processor. The request thread disappeared. When the thread disappeared, Nickelo found he'd forgotten what he'd done to gain access to the secured area. However, the information he sought was in his primary processor. Somehow, he'd known the information would be there. The information was a program for a virus. The program was already compiled and ready to be inserted into a host.

How'd that get there? Nickelo wondered. *I don't remember writing it.*

Nickelo ran another retrieval request to his primary processor requesting the answer to his question. However, the point of entry to the secured portion of his inner processor was once again blocked. Nickelo ran additional calculations. He chose the result with the highest probability of producing a desirable outcome.

"Insert this data into the tele-bot," Nickelo said. "Do not open the packet."

"What does the packet contain, sir?" said Jonathan.

"It's a virus," Nickelo answered honestly. "It's designed to bypass the security in tele-bots as well as other secured computer systems."

Jonathan didn't acknowledge Nickelo's request for several nanoseconds. "Is this action necessary for me to contact my wizard scout?"

"Affirmative," Nickelo said.

A moment later, Nickelo sensed Jonathan sending the data packet to a point not far from the armory.

"A tele-bot is now under my control, sir," said Jonathan. "I am commencing security scan of the armory now."

"Excellent," Nickelo said. "Follow me."

"Where?" said Jonathan.

"I'll let you know when I figure it out," Nickelo said with a laugh.

"Is this what our wizard scouts call fun?" said Jonathan.

"Doubtful," Nickelo said. "But I'm having a great time. And if I have anything to say about it, it's going to get a whole lot better."

CHAPTER 13

Richard was dreaming. He knew he was still on the hover-tram, and he knew he was dreaming, but it didn't matter. The memory of the smells and noises of that night were still fresh in his mind. So was the fear. Richard fought the dream, but the nightmare pulled him in despite his struggles.

*   *   *

He was back on Earth. He was back during that night. The red glow of fire flickered on the walls of the alley. Richard hunkered deeper into the shadows in a desperate attempt to avoid being seen. The sounds of shouting and breaking glass echoed off the stone wall opposite him. A scream of pain was cutoff abruptly. The crowd in the street thinned slightly as the core of the mob moved further down the street to find new pickings. Richard gathered his courage and darted into the street while dodging the few remaining stragglers. Broken glass from store windows littered the cobbled stones of the street. Broken bits of bottles, crushed boxes, and other bits of unwanted debris were strewn all around. Richard was unsure of his feelings. While he did not hate the merchant class, he had no love for them either. None of them had gone out of their way to give him any food since he'd been forced out of the orphanage. However, even Richard could appreciate the senseless waste caused by the mob's destructiveness. The city would spend many years recovering from this night of horrors.

A large man with bloodshot eyes and a bottle of liquor in each hand made a grab at Richard. "Where you goin', boy?"

Richard dodged to the left easily staying out of the man's reach. The man must have decided his bottles of liquor were too important to risk breaking because he did not attempt to follow.

Richard kept running through the alleys as he made his way towards his final destination. Richard knew what was coming. He wanted to go somewhere else, anywhere else, but he knew he couldn't avoid his fate. He'd been in the same dream many times since that fateful night.

Soon he was running down a street with blackened buildings on both sides. This street had been one of the early victims of the mob. The partially-burned walls of the few buildings still standing were illuminated only by the faint red glow of hot ashes. A few flickering fires were too stubborn to stop burning until they'd consumed every piece of potential fuel.

Richard slowed to look at the burned-out guts of the building across from him. The modest two-story building hadn't been much to look at before it had been looted and burned. It was even less now. But it had been his home for fifteen years. Why the mob bothered looting the orphanage was a mystery to Richard. The sisters had never accumulated any wealth. They'd spent every credit they could beg or borrow caring for the orphans. Now the children would have nowhere to go. What did the mob care? Richard hated the mob. What few scraps of food the orphanage had held in their meager stores would have been hard pressed to feed a dozen people. It was such a waste.

Richard turned into an alleyway and left the skeleton of the orphanage behind. He felt a sense of sadness. While the sisters had been strict disciplinarians, they hadn't been unkind to him during his stay in the orphanage. Still, they'd turned him out on the streets when he'd turned fifteen. The fact the sisters' hands were tied by government rules and regulations did little to dull the sting of that desperate time. The first six months on the streets had been hard. The next two and a half years had been only a little better. Richard shoved the sadness away. He owed no one anything.

The alley he was in opened up onto a roundabout with a fountain in the middle. One of the few remaining unbroken streetlights in the city illuminated the intersection in a dim glow.

The street was devoid of life. Most of the windows in the surrounding buildings were unbroken. For whatever reason, the mob had bypassed this street for the most part. Richard had no doubt they would return before the night was over. He knew all too soon the quiet of the street would be broken by the terrible sounds of the screams he'd been hearing all night.

A short, heavyset man rose from the shadows near a building across the street. He made a beckoning motion with his hands. Richard bent low and ran for the cover of the shadows formed by the fountain. He paused long enough to notice someone had broken the head off the stone horse which stood in the fountain. Richard looked into the depths of the waters. The horse's head lay at the bottom staring accusingly at Richard.

I didn't do it, Richard thought. *I'm not part of the mob.*

The short, heavyset man beckoned again before stepping back into the shadows. Richard ran the remaining distance to the building. Like the rest of the buildings on the street, it was a private residence. It was a mansion. Two orphanages would easily fit inside. Richard squatted next to the short man. The man's ragged jumpsuit was almost as torn and dirty as his own.

"You're late," said the short man. "Big Jim's not happy."

"I got here soon as I could, Little Mike," Richard said.

"Save it for Big Jim," Little Mike said dismissively.

Richard stayed silent. He didn't want to disappoint either Big Jim or Little Mike. They were the only reason he was still alive. At the end of his first six months on the street, Richard had been near death when the pair of streetwise men had found him lying in a gutter. A gang of street toughs had caught him with a can of beans he'd been fortunate enough to find. As he'd hunted for something to beat the can open, the gang had spotted him with his prize. They'd given chase like hounds after a frightened deer. Even running through the crowded streets had failed to throw them off.

In his dream, Richard remembered the fear of that chase. He also remembered his frustration when nobody in the crowd bothered to help him. Eventually, he'd made a mistake and turned into a blind alleyway. The gang had cornered him and beat him senseless. Afterwards, they'd taken his can of beans and left him for dead. When he woke, Richard had discovered Big Jim and Little Mike rummaging through his pockets. The two street-smart toughs had given him a little food and taken him in. He'd been with them ever since. Richard couldn't say the past two and a half years had been a good life, but it beat the alternative of death.

A giant of a man came sneaking around the corner of the building. The man's scraggily hair and beard along with his size left little doubt it was Big Jim.

"Bout time," said Big Jim angrily. "We thought you'd abandoned your friends for easier pickings."

"No, Big Jim," Richard said. "I came fast as I could."

"Well, no matter," said Big Jim dismissively. "You're here just in time."

Richard breathed a sigh of relief. Big Jim and Little Mike were his friends. But they could be harsh when aggravated, especially when they'd been drinking. The odor of alcohol in the air left little doubt they were half drunk now. Richard was not surprised. Their current state was not unusual. The two men always seemed to find plenty of alcohol even when food was scarce.

"Well, get to it, Skinny," Big Jim said. "The place is bound to have an alarm, so don't make no mistakes."

"I'll do my best, Big Jim," Richard said.

"See that you do," said Little Mike in a harsh voice. "Don't forget you owe us."

Richard nodded. "I'm not forgetting."

Concentrating on the front door, Richard allowed the energy of the building to wash over him. Early in his life, Richard had come to realize everything released a type of energy which he could sense. Even non-living things like stone or metal gave off a little of the telltale energy. In his youth, Richard had been surprised to learn others in the orphanage didn't have the ability to sense energy. After a few initial stares, Richard had learned to keep his ability a secret. It had often come in handy sneaking out of the orphanage at night to search for food.

Richard probed the lock on the front door with his mind. He followed a stream of energy from the lock to a box inside the building's wall. Probing carefully, Richard found a weak link within the box. He wrapped the weak point in the flow of energy with his mind and looped it back on itself. Richard tensed as he waited for the alarm to sound. It didn't.

"I've bypassed the alarm on the front door," Richard said. "It should be safe now."

"You best be right, Skinny," said Little Mike as he reached into his pants' pocket and pulled out a long knife.

"What's that for?" Richard said. "You told me there wouldn't be any trouble."

"There won't be," said Big Jim. "I've been casing this place for a week. The family left for off world when the trouble first started. The house is empty. It's going to be our ticket out of this place."

"Then why the knife?" Richard said. He knew he was pushing it, but a nagging fear was suddenly gnawing at his stomach.

Richard braced himself for a cuff on the side of the head as Big Mike raised his hand. He'd received more than a few in the past for asking too many questions.

Surprisingly, Little Mike came to the rescue. "Relax, Skinny. What do you expect me to do? Gnaw through the door lock with my teeth?"

Big Jim lowered his hand.

"Get to it, Mike," said Big Jim. "You wait out here, Skinny. Knock on the wall if you see any sign of a security patrol."

"There won't be any patrols coming around here," said Little Mike confidently as he crept up the steps towards the front door. "They'll be trailing the mob. I'd stake my life on it."

Richard watched as Little Mike fiddled with the front door. A glint of light reflected off the short man's knife as he gave it a twist. Richard heard a muffled click. Little Mike pushed the ornate door open and crept inside. Big Jim paused before entering. He pulled a large knife of his own out of his jacket pocket.

"Stay out here," said Big Jim gesturing with the knife. "You understand, Skinny?"

Richard nodded his head affirmatively. It didn't pay to cross Big Jim.

The minutes dragged by; one, two, then three. The street remained empty. Richard could hear the sounds of the mob in the distance. He heard a series of explosions. He wondered where the mob could have found explosives, and what logic they could find for using them if they had.

A feminine scream pierced the night. It was close. The scream came again. A horrible realization washed over Richard. The scream had come from inside the mansion. In spite of Big Jim's assurances, the building was not empty. The sight of his two friends with knifes in their hands passed through Richard's mind.

Why did Big Jim need a knife? Richard wondered. *Little Mike was the one opening the door.*

Summoning his courage, Richard crept up the steps and entered the building through the front door. The entryway was dimly lit by light spilling out of a room at the end of a long hallway. Richard heard the sounds of a struggle. He quickened his pace and moved down the hall towards the source of the sound. A bulging cloth bag lay in the middle of the hallway floor. One end of a shiny candle stick poked out of one end of the bag. Richard sidestepped the bag and continued towards the lit room ahead.

Rip, came the sound of tearing cloth followed by another high-pitched scream. The scream was followed by the slapping sound of flesh on flesh.

"I said shut up," came Big Jim's deep voice out of the room ahead.

Richard stepped through the partially-opened door into the room. Shelves with real books lined two walls. The words 'reading room' came to Richard's mind. The wonderment of someone having so much wealth they could afford a room just for reading passed over Richard.

Big Jim and Little Mike stood in the middle of the room near a well-padded chair and an overturned table. They faced the corner of the room with their arms spread wide as if keeping a cornered animal from escaping. Each man had a knife in his hand. In the far corner of the room huddled a young woman probably in her mid-twenties. Her tear-streaked face was red on one cheek. Richard saw the outline of large fingers within the red. The woman held the flap of a torn blouse to her shoulder. Her terror-filled eyes latched onto Richard. She mouthed the word, "Please."

"What's going on?" Richard said.

"I thought I told you to stay outside," said Big Jim.

The anger in the big man's voice would normally have caused Richard to shrink back. But the fear in the woman's eyes gave him the courage to stand his ground. He'd not strayed so far from the teachings of the sisters to completely abandon his principles.

"You said this place would be empty," Richard said. He slowly started edging his way around the room in the direction of the frightened woman.

"It was," said Little Mike. "At least it would've been if this little birdie hadn't decided to come home early from her university."

"Too bad for her," said Big Jim. "She should've gone on vacation with the rest of her family. Now she's going to spend a little vacation time with us poor folks."

Richard heard a sound in the big man's voice he didn't like. He'd heard it before, and it usually meant trouble for someone.

"What are you going to do with her, Big Jim?" Richard said. He moved two steps closer to the woman.

"Well," said Big Jim with an evil grin. "Now that you've called me by name, what do you think we're going to do with her?"

Taking three quick steps, Richard positioned himself between the woman and his two friends.

"I can't let you do this," Richard said. "You're my friends, but this isn't right."

Little Mike chuckled. "You hear that, Jim? Skinny here thinks we're his friends."

The short man's comment confused Richard. *They are my friends, aren't they?*

"Either wait outside, Skinny," said Big Jim as he gestured towards the door with his knife. "Or get the hell out of the way."

After three years on the streets, Richard was no longer the naive kid he'd once been. He knew what Big Jim intended. Richard had done a lot of things during the last three years of which he wasn't proud. But he'd only done what was needed to stay alive. There were lines he would never cross. This was one of them.

"We just need to grab some food and go," Richard said. "The security teams have all they can handle with the riots. They aren't going to waste time looking for three people who stole a little food."

Big Jim shifted his grip on his knife so the cutting edge was up. "Move, kid, or I'll gut you from bottom to top."

"Little Mike," Richard said growing desperate. "We're all friends. We take care of each other. We need each other."

"Ha," said the short man. "You're a fool, Skinny. You always have been. There's no such thing as friends. There's only people who are useful for a little while and people who aren't."

"But you're my friends," Richard insisted. "You saved my life after I was attacked."

"You stupid punk," said Big Jim. "We took you in because I'd been told you could bypass security systems."

"But you saved me," Richard said. "You gave me food."

"We feed dogs if we think we can use them," said Little Mike. "Who do you think told the gang where to find you in the first place?"

"That's enough, Mike," said Big Jim.

"What's it matter, Jim," said Little Mike. "We'll score enough from this house to get us off planet. We don't need Skinny here anymore."

"I think you're right, Mike," said Big Jim with a blood-in-his-eyes look at Richard. "Looks like your usefulness just ended, Skinny."

The two men shifted a little distance apart. Both men began moving forward waving their knives in a hypnotic pattern before them.

"But you need me," Richard said. "You need me to handle security systems."

"We can get another freak like you for a couple of credits," said Little Mike. "After this job, we'll be loaded. I was getting tired of your whining anyway."

Richard heard the woman behind him make a whimpering sound.

"Hang on, little birdie," said Big Jim. "This'll only take a moment."

Big Mike and Little Jim rushed forward together. Richard had no illusions about his fighting abilities. Either of the men could overpower him easily. They fed him occasionally, but they always kept the largest shares of food for themselves. He was always hungry, and his body was little more than skin and bones. His two 'friends' had weight and muscle on their side not to mention knives. Richard saw his imminent death.

Unbidden, the Power inside Richard reached out towards the two men. Richard followed along with the flow of energy and wrapped it around the hand in which Little Mike held his knife. Richard willed the hand towards Big Jim's chest. The blade of the knife plunged deep into the left side of the man's chest. Blood squirted high into the air and splattered across the ceiling as well as onto Little Mike.

The woman let out a series of bloodcurdling screams. Each scream increased in volume until Richard thought his eardrums would burst.

As Big Jim fell to the floor, Little Mike struggled to pull his hand free. He succeeded, but his knife came free as well. Little Mike violently began moving his hand up and down as if trying to rid himself of the incriminating knife. But the knife wouldn't come free.

The short man's eyes locked onto Richard. Richard saw fear in them as Little Mike shouted. The woman screamed again drowning out Little Mike's words, but Richard saw the short man mouth the word, "You."

The Power within Richard was hungry. It demanded action. Richard moved the energy which still surrounded Little Mike's hand in an upwards motion. Little Mike opened his mouth again showing yellowed and broken teeth. Little Mike's scream merged with the woman's and then cutoff abruptly as his hand drove the knife deep into his own throat. The woman screamed even louder. Little Mike fell and began rolling around on the floor.

Richard noticed the reflection of flashing blue lights on the walls of the room. The door at the end of the hall burst open. Two beefy men came running inside the house carrying long rods in one hand and pistols in the other. In a moment of clarity, Richard noticed little arcs of red lightning running up and down the length of the rods.

The woman's screams stopped. The security team yelled something, but Richard paid them no heed. He was too busy looking at the bloodied bodies of his former friends sprawled out on the wooden floor. The realization that he'd just killed two men hit him and stole the strength from his legs. He dropped to his knees. The last thing he saw was a dark rod with little red arcs of lighting coming at his head. Then he saw nothing.

*   *   *

"Rick! Rick!" said a voice out of the darkness.

Richard clawed his way out of his nightmare and opened his

eyes.

"Rick!" said Jerad. "Wake up, cadet."

Richard shook his head. Drops of sweat flew from his hair.

"I'm awake," Richard said. He was embarrassed. "Sorry. I must have been dreaming."

"Dreaming?" said Tam. "The way you were tossing and turning, it had to be one hell of a nightmare."

Richard turned his gaze from the concerned faces of his friends to the cabin's sole window. Brightly colored buildings were passing by outside. The hover-tram's speed was much slower than it had been.

"Are we in Velounia?" Richard said in an attempt to change the subject.

"They just announced we'll be at the station in five minutes," said Telsa.

"Fine," Richard said. "I guess we should start getting our stuff together."

"Oh, no," said Tam. "You don't get off that easy, cadet."

"Yeah," said Telsa with no trace of her normal joviality. "What was that all about?"

"It was nothing," Richard said. "It was just a dream."

"Bull," said Tam. "You're soaked in sweat, Rick."

"It's either tell us, Rick," said Jerad, "or tell the camp shrink when we get back. Something's wrong. Out with it."

"It's nothing," Richard repeated hoping his friends would back off. They didn't.

Jerad, Tam, and Telsa sat down on the bench opposite Richard. A look at their faces told him none of them would leave the cabin until they got a better answer. Richard had no desire to tell the entire secret. It was too dark to tell even his friends. But, he had to give them at least a partial truth to stem their curiosity.

"I was dreaming about the food riots back on Earth in 3029," Richard said. "I was caught breaking into a house by a security team and thrown in jail. The judge was going to send me to the military prison on Diajor."

Diajor was the Empire's most notorious prison planet. Nothing grew on its rocky surface, and the atmosphere consisted of poison gas. Only the worst military offenders wound up there.

"The military prison," said Jerad. "Why there? You were a

civilian weren't you?"

"Yes," Richard said. "But the two men I was with were apparently military deserters. I guess the judge thought I was as well."

"Why didn't the other two men tell the judge you weren't?" said Tam.

"Uh," Richard said. "They were dead. A woman who happened to be in the house at the time testified they'd killed each other. She told the judge I tried to help her."

"Still, you were caught in the house," said Telsa who seemed engrossed in his story. "So what kept you out of prison?"

"I'm not exactly sure," Richard said. "Even with the woman's testimony, the judge was getting ready to sentence me."

Jerad, Tam, and Telsa looked expectantly at Richard. But he was lost in his thoughts. He remembered that time in the courtroom as if it were yesterday. He remembered the woman pleading with the judge that he'd saved her life. He remembered the judge saying that if he was let back out on the streets, he'd just windup in more trouble. Richard remembered a large man in a military uniform bedecked with medals walking to the bench and talking to the judge.

"Well," said Telsa. "Don't stop now. What did the judge do?"

"The judge told me I had two choices," Richard said. "I could either spend three years in the military prison on Diajor, or I could spend three years in the marines. It just so happened a marine recruiter was in the courtroom that day. I chose the marines. I've been in the marines ever since."

"I'd heard you mention you'd lived on the streets for a while," said Jerad. "I wondered how you wound up in the marines."

"Well, now you know," Richard said.

"The marines are normally a little more selective than that," said Jerad. "I wonder why they made an exception in your case."

"Beats me," Richard said.

The hover-tram jerked to a halt. Richard saw the hover-tram station out the cabin window.

"Are we done playing twenty questions?" Richard said. "I don't know about you, but I've got things to do."

111

CHAPTER 14

The dots on the hologram above the technician's workstation formed cascading shades of multi-colored lights. After two hundred years of loose association with the physical dimension, Lord Crendemor could read the display almost as easily as the red-clothed technician sitting in front of the hologram. The half dozen red dots denoted the locations of the dreadnaughts. Yellows, oranges, and greens showed the positions of the battle cruisers, destroyers, and troop carriers. A multitude of white dots indicated the support ships carrying the supplies. Those supplies would be needed after the successful completion of the initial phase of the invasion.

Lord Crendemor passed through the close confines of the destroyer's control room to the automatic door on the other side of the room. The door opened at his approach. Lord Crendemor had long ago stopped being impressed with the technology of the physical dimension. It was just another form of magic as far as he was concerned.

"Level six," Lord Crendemor said.

"Compliance," came the reply through the translator on Lord Crendemor's belt.

The floor vibrated slightly. Lord Crendemor took the time to raise his hand and study his well-groomed nails. The white polish showed up well against the dark of his fingers. Lord Crendemor looked at his reflection in the highly-polished metal of the elevator door. He admired what he saw. Even after nearly five hundred years, he was still one of the most handsome of the dark-elf race. His waist-length white hair was full and shiny. His high cheek bones highlighted the deep black of his eyes. He'd stolen a good form when he'd spied that dark elf so many years ago. Lord Crendemor allowed himself a rare smile. Everything was coming along well. Soon, he would be the most powerful elf on Portalis, dark elf or otherwise.

The elevator stopped and the door slid open. Lord Crendemor walked briskly down the well-lit hallway. Several humans in various colored jumpsuits hustled down the hallway as well. They flattened against the wall at his approach giving him plenty of room. The destroyer was staffed primarily by human mercenaries with a sprinkling of Crosioian officers. The humans knew better than to get in his way. The stiff-necked Crosioians were another matter. They hadn't yet learned to respect their betters.

After turning down two more corridors, Lord Crendemor approached a set of black double doors. Their shiny surfaces contrasted sharply with the white antiseptic look of the corridors. As Lord Crendemor drew closer, a score of short rods poked out of the walls and tracked his progress. Lord Crendemor sensed the energy being funneled to the rods in preparation for firing.

Without slowing or speeding up, Lord Crendemor reached the door. The demon Zenthra's idea of humor did not impress him. Despite his brags, Zenthra was the weakest of the four brother demons that were tasked with conquering the three galaxies. Zenthra would not dare attack the Dalinfaust's emissary without provocation. Lord Crendemor went to great lengths to conduct himself in a fashion that insured Zenthra didn't get a reason.

The door opened, and Lord Crendemor entered. A long table with a score of cushioned chairs around it sat in the middle of the room. Only two of the chairs were occupied. A Crosioian bat-creature sat in each. A two meter high hologram display was centered over the table. The hologram currently showed the disposition of the fleet. It was the same hologram image Lord Crendemor had observed on the ship's bridge.

"The invasion force is nearly ready," came the words out of the larger of the two bat creatures through Lord Crendemor's translator.

"Not quite," said the voice of the Master computer. "Current calculations indicate the highest probability of success requires an additional eighteen of the special assets."

By the term special assets, Lord Crendemor knew Zenthra meant the specialized demons that had been gating into the physical dimension for the last six months.

"None of our recon teams have been compromised," said the smaller of the Crosioians. "The Empire suspects nothing."

"That's not a hundred percent accurate," said the Master computer. "Is it, Lord Crendemor?"

The two bat creatures turned to face the dark elf. He'd been around the Crosioians often enough to recognize the sneer on their faces. They had as much love for him as he had for them.

The image in the hologram changed form. The invasion fleet was replaced by a meter-sized, disembodied head of a Crosioian. Lord Crendemor walked around the side of the table. By a trick of the hologram, the face of the disembodied head continued to face Lord Crendemor regardless of his position in the room.

Lord Crendemor sat in a chair opposite the two Crosioians.

"Admiral. General," said Lord Crendemor with a nod of his head to each of the bat creatures. "Our recon last night of the Empire's secondary teleporter was successful."

When it appeared one of the bat creatures was about to protest, Lord Crendemor continued. "However, one of the Empire's cadets came close to discovering us and sounding the alarm."

"Yes," said the admiral through her translator. She was the shorter of the two Crosioians. "Our scout told us as much."

"Our scout wanted to engage the wizard scout," added the general who was the taller of the two.

"Yes, she did," Lord Crendemor said. "Our mission was to recon the airfield. We accomplished our mission. If she had engaged the cadet, our mission would have failed."

"My scout thought your supposed cadet might be the one who defeated our scout on Veturna last year," said the admiral. "If so, we may all regret later that you didn't have the courage to kill him last night. The scout on Veturna was our best. Now she is gone."

Lord Crendemor fought a surge of anger. He casually looked at the nails on the back of his hands.

Their opinion of me is unimportant, he thought in an attempt to remain calm. *I'm not the one blindly following a demon. You're the fools, and you'll die fools when Zenthra decides he no longer needs you.*

"Our mission was to recon the targets at the airfield," Lord Crendemor said in the calmest voice he could muster. "Whether the cadet was or was not the one from Veturna does not matter. Any cadet or wizard scout still on Velos when the invasion begins will be dead shortly thereafter. Your scout will be avenged."

"The vaporized head of an enemy cannot be placed on a trophy wall," said the general as she pounded her clawed fist on the table.

Lord Crendemor ignored the outburst.

"Our success at the airfield proved the reliability of the special assets," Lord Crendemor said using the Crosioians' preferred term for the dimensional-shifting demons. "The first wave of shock troops should be able to penetrate the Empire's defenses before any alarm can be sounded."

"Probability of success is still below optimum," said the Master computer who was the demon Zenthra. "The defensive shields at the spaceport are twenty-five percent more effective than those at the airfield. You will need to send your best magic user to command a new recon."

"I will personally accompany the recon team," Lord Crendemor said. "The mission is too important to delegate."

"Negative," replied the Master computer. "You have been assigned a different mission"

The demon's reply surprised Lord Crendemor. He'd heard nothing about a new mission. The recon team was scheduled to depart in less than two hours. Lord Crendemor wanted to protest, but he didn't. It would do his standing among the Crosioians no good to be seen arguing with a computer. As far as they knew, the Master computer was their tool not vice versa. Of all the creatures in the fleet, only Lord Crendemor knew better.

"As you say," Lord Crendemor said.

"Very well," said the admiral taking the lead once more. "Once the targets at the spaceport are pinpointed, your kind's part in this phase of the operation will be completed."

At the words 'your kind', Lord Crendemor's lips twitched in irritation. Even after years of association, many Crosioians refused to use the term magic user or mage.

Lord Crendemor calmed his rising anger by pinpointing the

Crosioian's link to her power reserve. The admiral had once been a scout, or so he'd been told. But the fool didn't even know how to protect her link properly. Lord Crendemor had no doubt he could kill both the admiral and her lapdog of a general with little effort. They'd be as helpless before him as would be Silvertine's elven lords or even the Empire's vaunted wizard scouts. None of them knew how to protect the links to their Power reserves.

"As you say, admiral," Lord Crendemor said. "However, my mages will be standing by until they are needed for the invasion."

The admiral's nose twitched. Lord Crendemor knew he'd scored a point. The Crosioians did not like being reminded they needed magic to supplement their technology in order for the invasion to succeed.

"The invasion plans are complete, admiral," said Zenthra in the voice of the Master computer. "Now if that is all, I require use of this room to brief the elf."

Following directions from the Master computer were so engrained in the Crosioians that neither of them protested. They rose and left the room. Once the door closed behind them, the bat face in the hologram was replaced by a black-horned head. It was the head of a black dragon.

"Is the Dalinfaust aware of my change in mission?" Lord Crendemor asked as soon as he was alone with the demon's dragon-hologram.

The dragon's eyes narrowed and its face took on an evil look. "The Dalinfaust does not command this part of the plan. The physical dimension is mine to do with as I will. Once our plan is completed, and the gate is fully opened, I will control this galaxy. Every living creature in this dimension will bow to me."

Lord Crendemor let the demon rant. The demon Zenthra enjoyed patting itself on the back too much to be interrupted by valid concerns. Even after the successful completion of the demon's master plan, Zenthra would only control this single galaxy in the physical dimension.

"You look unconvinced," said Zenthra apparently guessing Lord Crendemor's thoughts. "Once the other parts of the tele-network come under my control, I shall rule every corner of this galaxy. Then my armies will be invincible. With the combined processing power of all the computer networks in this galaxy, I shall devise ways to cross to other galaxies. I shall become a master demon. My brothers will kneel before me in homage, as shall all living things."

"But in the meantime," Lord Crendemor said patiently, "is the Dalinfaust aware of my change in mission?"

The demon stopped its ranting. Its eyes narrowed even further. "The protection of the Dalinfaust may not reach as far as you apparently believe. Do not tempt me, elf."

Lord Crendemor was confident in his position. Alone, Zenthra was no match for the Dalinfaust. Zenthra would need more provocation than a mere question before deciding to risk killing him. Still, Lord Crendemor remained silent and said nothing further. He had nothing to gain from antagonizing the demon.

After a moment, the dragon's face morphed into the face of a dark elf.

"As it so happens," said Zenthra, "the Dalinfaust is the one who changed your mission. My brother is confident my part of the plan is assured. You are no longer needed here."

"May I ask what my new mission is?" Lord Crendemor said.

"You will teleport out this afternoon to a planet in the Tresoris sector," said the demon.

"That's on the other side of the galaxy," Lord Crendemor said. "I'm needed here."

The face of the dark elf in the hologram raised it lips in an evil grin. It laughed. "You're unawareness of your nonimportance is beyond humorous."

Lord Crendemor's stomach muscles tightened, but he kept his face placid. "What is my mission?"

"One of the Crosioians' battle helmets was captured last year," said Zenthra. "My brother is sending you to retrieve it."

In spite of his efforts at self-control, Lord Crendemor expressed surprise. "Battle helmets have been captured before. The scouting mission of the spaceport should be our primary concern."

"There is no 'our'," laughed Zenthra. "You are merely a disposable tool. You will do as you are told, or I will take great pleasure in disposing of you in a manner you will not enjoy."

Anger welled up again inside Lord Crendemor, but once again he was able to maintain his outward demeanor of calm.

"Why is this battle helmet so important, may I ask?" Lord

Crendemor said with an air of disinterest.

The image of the dark elf in the hologram seemed to ponder the question for a moment. "I see my brother does not keep you informed. This battle helmet belonged to the Crosioian scout who was killed by the cadet last year. It holds information which could jeopardize the invasion. The battle computer in that helmet helped create the algorithm being used to control the invasion."

"Surely any information the battle computer contains is encrypted, is it not?" Lord Crendemor said. While he was not familiar with the technical aspects of computer encryption, he could relate to it. All the spells in his spell book were encrypted in a fashion to protect them from the prying eyes of other mages.

"For someone from the magical dimension, you have learned the ways of the physical dimension well," said the demon. "I'll admit you surprise me at times, elf. You have picked up much of this dimension's technology over the years. I will consent to answer your question this time, elf. This particular battle computer has the highest level of encryption. It should be unbreakable. However, I have sensed a deterioration of its security during the past year. Three of the Empire's allies have been attempting to penetrate the battle computer's core memory. They are close to success. You must retrieve or destroy the battle computer before its security can be circumvented."

Lord Crendemor stared at the hologram for a moment before answering. "I assume you have devised a plan for the recovery of the battle computer which has a reasonable chance of success?"

"Probability of success is eighty-seven percent," said Zenthra. "I have access to every Crosioian computer in addition to those on Veturna. I can be in many places at once. I have access to more knowledge than any of my brothers. My algorithms are infallible. The entire galaxy will bow down and worship me." Zenthra broke out in laughter.

As Lord Crendemor waited for the demon to wind down, he tried to think of ways he could use this mission to his advantage. *If this battle computer is so important, perhaps I can use it to accelerate my part in the plan. Zenthra is a fool. The demon is a powerful fool, but still a fool. However, the Dalinfaust is a different matter. I must use care not to draw the Dalinfaust's attention.*

A silence brought Lord Crendemor out of his thoughts. Zenthra was no longer laughing. The image of the dark elf was looking at him.

"Naturally, it will be done as you say," Lord Crendemor said hastily.

"Of course it will," said Zenthra. The dark-elf hologram gave a lopsided grin. "You need to brief your replacement for the recon at the spaceport. After that, meet me in the third floor lab. Do not make me wait long."

"As you say," Lord Crendemor said. He hated kowtowing to the pompous demon, but he was too savvy to spoil the ivy for the sake of his ego.

Resigned, Lord Crendemor nodded to the fading hologram and left the room.

*　　*　　*

It took very little time to brief one of the Northern Mages. The human had been assigned to his team of mages by the Dalinfaust. Lord Crendemor was not happy with being forced to select a human to lead the recon, but he had little choice. His two dark-elf lieutenants were currently deployed on missions of their own, so they were unavailable.

"Your team will consist of a Crosioian scout, a human technician, a troll for security, and another magic user," Lord Crendemor said. "One of the dimensional-shifting demons will accompany the shuttle to get you through the planet's outer perimeter shield."

"I understand, my lord," said the human mage.

Lord Crendemor eyed the human sizing him up. He was an overweight, middle-aged man with short yellow hair.

"Are you sure you can create a stealth shield for your team?" Lord Crendemor said. "You'll also need to shift your entire team into the void to pass through the spaceport's defensive shield."

"I'm confident, my lord," said the human. "The spells you taught me are complicated, but I've spent a lot of time practicing. I've used the combination stealth shield and invisibility spell on two recon missions already."

"I know," Lord Crendemor said. "That's why I selected you.

Have you been issued the tele-bots by the Crosioians."

"Yes, but–" The Northern Mage glanced down at the floor and shifted his weight from one foot to the other.

"What is it?" Lord Crendemor said growing irritated at the delay. The demon Zenthra was waiting for him, and he didn't have time to waste on a fool.

"My pardon, lord," said the mage, "I know I'm inexperienced with the Crosioians' technology, but won't the Empire's security detect our tele-bots? The spell you taught me allows me to detect the presence of the Empire's tele-bots. Surely the Empire has something similar?"

Lord Crendemor relaxed a little. It was a valid question, although he wouldn't tell the human such. "You couldn't detect these tele-bots, and neither can the Empire. They're static. Their sole purpose is to mark the target for our troops. They'll remain static until the appointed time."

With a harsher voice, Lord Crendemor added, "Your job is to place the tele-bots at the target sites. You will do so without being detected, or I'll make you wish you had done so upon your return."

"I understand, my lord," said the mage nervously.

"See that you do," Lord Crendemor said over his shoulder as he left the mage in the shuttle bay. He had an appointment with the demon Zenthra.

*   *   *

The third floor lab was nearly empty. Only two red-coated human technicians were inside. They were gathered around a strange-looking creature strapped on a table in the center of the lab. The prone creature appeared to be some kind of human-sized insect. Its eyes were darting nervously around the room as a series of high-pitched squeaking noises came out of its mandibles.

At Lord Crendemor's arrival, the technicians stepped away from the insect. They bowed in his direction and then departed the lab through a side door. At their exit, a hologram of a dark elf appeared near the table.

"I do not like to be kept waiting," said Zenthra. "We have much to do."

Lord Crendemor didn't reply. He had no doubt the demon had

been monitoring his every move. Since the demon was now the Master computer, it had access to the information from all the tele-bots deployed throughout the ship.

The silence in the lab was broken only by the continuous, high-pitched squeals of the insect. Lord Crendemor forced himself to remain silent. He was curious, but he refused to give Zenthra the satisfaction of seeing his curiosity.

When the demon tired of waiting, it finally said, "This creature is a scientist from Veturna. It is an acquaintance of those in possession of the battle computer you seek."

Lord Crendemor's curiosity was piqued even further. *Why has Zenthra brought this creature here?* he wondered. *Surely it could have been tortured anywhere if it has information we require.*

At Lord Crendemor's continued silence, the demon's voice grew harsher. "Your stubbornness will get you killed one of these days, elf. But I do not have time to waste on you today." The demon paused before continuing, "Since you refuse to ask, I will tell you anyway. Another insect from Veturna along with two human children are in possession of the battle helmet and the battle computer it holds."

This time Lord Crendemor did speak. "Human children?" he said. "Why are children important?"

"Ah," said Zenthra. "You are curious."

Lord Crendemor mentally kicked himself. He'd let his curiosity give the demon the upper hand. He swore not to do so again.

"The human children are unlike any children you have ever met," said Zenthra. "They are what the information in my databanks call geniuses. A piece of technology was used to transfer the memories of their parents into them. They are very dangerous to our cause. Once you are in possession of the battle computer, you will kill them if the opportunity presents itself."

"And this insect here?" Lord Crendemor said pointing to the prone creature.

"It is an acquaintance of the insect who is the guardian of the children," said the demon. "You will take its place and worm your way into the trust of the other insect. Once you have done so, you should be able to gain access to the battle computer. I am in intermittent communication with the battle computer. I will know when you take possession. When that occurs, I will teleport you back to the fleet. Once you give me the battle computer, you will be returned to the magical plane. The Dalinfaust has need of you there."

Lord Crendemor voiced the obvious flaw in the demon's plan. "How am I to take this insect's place? I have a spell to take on the appearance of other creatures, but it will not hold up to close scrutiny. Even if I take on this insect's form, I won't have its knowledge. I wouldn't fool anyone for long."

The hologram of the dark elf walked to a table along one wall and pointed at a piece of technology on top. It was a small device about the size and shape of a wand. "This is a knowledge-transferal device the Crosioians found when they conquered Veturna. It's the same device used to transfer knowledge into the children of which I spoke. You will use it on this insect to gain its memories. You will take this device with you. If you get a chance to use it on one of the children before you kill them, you will do so. They may have information we need."

Picking up the wand-shaped device, Lord Crendemor examined it more closely. The wand was flexible. He bent it slightly.

"Yes," said Zenthra. "You may store it easily in your pocket. Once you use it on this insect, you will have its knowledge."

Intrigued, Lord Crendemor listened closely as Zenthra explained the details of the plan. Despite his loathing for the boastful demon, Lord Crendemor had to admit the plan could work. Even as he listened, a part of Lord Crendemor's brain began to think of ways he could use the device to further his own plans.

CHAPTER 15

Richard looked out the side window of the hover-cab as the driver weaved his way in and out of traffic on the way to Velounia's spaceport. Richard glanced nervously at the timer built into the driver's control panel. It was 13:30.

"Relax," said Tam. "We've got plenty of time. Liz's shuttle isn't scheduled to land for another thirty minutes."

Their first stop in the city had taken longer than expected. Telsa's parents had used their influence to get Richard an appointment with Monsieur Geraldo, one of the finest tailors in the Empire. While Monsieur Geraldo might be the finest tailor, Richard was pretty sure the monsieur wasn't the fastest. The tailor had spent over an hour measuring Richard before he was satisfied he could create a suitable wizard scout dress uniform for Richard. Only then did Monsieur Geraldo consent to release Richard with the promise his uniform would be hand-delivered to the Star Gate hotel in time for the ball.

"You'll look great in your uniform, Rick," said Telsa with a knowing smile. "Half the females at the ball will be swooning over you in your Monsieur Geraldo masterpiece."

"Yeah," laughed Tam. "Even a couple of the human females might take a second look at you after they've had a few drinks."

"Yuk, yuk," Richard said. "I had no idea dress uniforms were so expensive. Monsieur Geraldo's bill took a hefty chunk out of my bank account."

"You're lucky to have gotten Monsieur Geraldo on such short

notice, Rick," Telsa said seriously. "He really is the best tailor in this part of the galaxy. Even starship captains have a hard time getting on his waiting list."

Having been brought up in an orphanage, Richard wasn't used to experiencing the power of having influential friends. Richard wondered which starship captain's appointment had gotten bumped in order to make room for him.

"Well, I really do appreciate your parents going to all that trouble for me, Telsa," Richard said seriously. "I just hope Liz is suitably impressed."

"You better hope Liz doesn't expect you to order Cravion wine for dinner," laughed Tam. "I heard second mates on starships have expensive tastes. You know she was promoted to Lieutenant Commander, right?"

"Yeah, I heard," Richard said. He'd always known Liz was destined for big things.

Richard was saved from any further ribbing by his friends when their hover-cab slowed down at the front gate of the spaceport. A security guard in power-armor carrying a plasma rifle walked to the driver's window and peered inside. The guard looked at the computer readout on his wrist.

"Very well," said the guard as he made a waving motion through the spaceport's gate. "Proceed."

As the hover-cab moved through the gate, Richard said, "I'll admit, I've only been at the spaceport once before, but that didn't seem very secure to me. The guard didn't even ask who we were."

"You've got to get out more, Rick," said Tam. "The guard's computer is integrated with the computer in the hover-cab. The guard knew who we were before we even pulled up to the gate."

"Hmm," Richard said. "I'm not exactly sure I like having computers know our every move."

"You're a wizard scout, Rick," said Telsa. "Or you soon will be. I'd say you better get used to computers knowing your every move."

"I'll never get used to it, Telsa," Richard said. "I swear I'm going to find a way to avoid having my every thought and action known by some computer somewhere."

"Good luck with that," said Tam pointing out her window. "See all those people out there?"

Richard glanced outside the hover-cab's window in the direction indicated by his friend. Several hundred people, both human and otherwise, were walking in and out of the main terminal building. Richard could see the outlines of various freighters and midsized personnel transports behind the building.

"Yeah, what about them," Richard said. He wasn't sure where Tam was heading with the conversation. Wherever it was, she needed to get there soon. They'd be on the military side of the spaceport in a couple of minutes.

"Computers in the tele-network are tracking every one of those people out there," said Tam.

"So?" Richard said.

"Do you know why the computers are tracking all those people," said Tam.

"Because they're doing something of interest," said Telsa before Richard could think of a reply.

"Exactly," said Tam. "They're doing something of interest to the central computer. They're all traveling somewhere. What they're doing might be important to the central computer."

"So?" Richard said. Grasping subtle concepts had never been his strongpoint.

"I'm saying the only way to escape notice by the myriad of computers hooked up to the tele-network is to never do anything that's interesting to them," said Tam.

Richard balked at her answer. He hated the mere thought of being controlled by anyone or anything. Having computers monitoring him without his permission was not much lower on his list of dislikes than having 'the One' send him on missions without asking first.

"Well, I don't plan on living the rest of my life as a hermit," Richard said. "But I swear I'm going to find some way to limit the amount of information 'the One' or any other computer system or entity can get from me."

"I'll check back with you in fifty years and see how you made out, Rick," said Tam with a chuckle and a shake of her head. "You're one stubborn cadet."

"But if you do figure it out," said Telsa ever the optimist, "how about letting your friends in on the secret?"

Richard smiled. He shoved the thoughts of controlling

computers to the side. He refused to be irritated with his friends on their first weekend pass in quite a while.

"Well," Richard said as he gave Telsa a wink. "I might let some of my friends know. I'm not sure about all of them though."

Richard said the last part with a nod of his head towards Tam.

Telsa laughed. Tam did not.

The hover-cab stopped at two more security check points. They were waved through at both. Finally, the hover-cab stopped in front of a single-story, gray building. The military terminal was much less crowded than the terminal on the civilian side of the spaceport. Even the medium-sized destroyers like the Blaze were too large to land planet-side. A fleet of shuttles moved the necessary supplies, equipment, and personnel between the spaceport and the score or so of military starships orbiting the planet at any given time.

Unlike their civilian counterparts, military starships were meant to slug it out with other military vessels. As such, their thick armor and massive-weapons systems made the starships a dozen times heavier than even one of the larger civilian cruise liners. If a destroyer like the Blaze landed on an Earth-sized planet such as Velos, its bottom floors would be crushed by the weight of the levels above. The only future for such a grounded ship would be a quick salvage.

Richard exited the hover-cab along with his friends.

"Pay the man, Telsa," said Tam as she headed towards the terminal door before Telsa had a chance to protest.

"I've got this one, Telsa," Richard said as he took the driver's pay tablet out of her hand.

"Are you sure?" said Telsa.

"Yes," Richard said. "I'm not broke yet. I saved a few credits when I was a sergeant."

"Alright, Rick," said Telsa. "I won't argue. Pay the man."

Richard was surprised his friend was giving in so easily. He had a feeling Telsa was just trying to soothe his male ego.

Placing his palm on the tablet, Richard waited for the tele-network to approve his purchase. The screen's background changed color to green indicating successful completion of the transaction. Richard made a mental note of his bank balance. He wasn't broke by any means, but he wasn't rolling in the credits either.

I hope you like house wine, Liz, he thought.

Richard mollified the dismal thought of his bank balance with the thought he'd eventually be able to treat Liz to the finer things once he received his back pay.

Richard joined Tam and Telsa inside the terminal. They were scanning a list of flights on a large computer display built into a wall near the entrance.

"What's the verdict?" Richard said.

"Liz's shuttle will be landing at berth seven in twelve minutes," said Tam. "We've got plenty of time."

"Great," Richard said. "Let's go."

Unlike the civilian terminal where passengers were transported from their ship's berth to a terminal gate, military personnel were expected to walk.

As Richard and his friends walked to berth seven, Richard took the opportunity to take in the sights. He'd only been at the spaceport once before when he'd reported for pre-Academy training. At the time, he'd been so busy avoiding the attention of his TAC officers he hadn't bothered to give his surroundings more than a token glance. Since then, any flights he'd taken had been from the Academy's airfield two hundred kilometers away.

The activity on the military side of the spaceport was significantly less than on the civilian side. Richard could make out ant-sized workers bustling all around the civilian cargo freighters and cruise liners setting at their berths on the opposite side of the spaceport. In contrast, only a half-dozen transport shuttles and two smaller recon ships were located among the score of berths on the military side. Richard commented on the inactivity.

Tam pointed towards the civilian side of the spaceport. "Most of the military's supplies are handled by civilian contractors, Rick. I suspect some less than honest politicians get a kickback from some contractors. A law was passed a decade or so ago requiring all non-lethal military supplies to be hauled by the civilian shipping companies."

"So is that why there are only shuttles here?" Richard said.

"Well, only shuttles except for those two recon ships," said Telsa pointing to the two starships located at berths eight and nine. "Those recon ships are only about a quarter the size of a destroyer.

Since they have to be able to land planet-side when they're doing recons, they normally just land directly at a spaceport to restock supplies. All of the larger military vessels have to have their supplies shuttled to them."

"Hmm," Richard said gazing a little further ahead. He spied a large metallic building to one side of the military portion of the spaceport. Pointing, he said, "Is that the DNA Center?"

"That's it," said Tam. "And, I don't mind saying I'm getting tired of waiting our turn to visit there."

"I'm a little surprised as well," agreed Telsa. "I mean, what with the war and all."

"Why is it located at the spaceport?" Richard said. It seemed to him it would make more sense to have it co-located with the Academy's science buildings.

Tam and Telsa both laughed.

"What's so funny?" Richard said. "I asked a simple question."

"We didn't mean anything by it," said Telsa.

"Speak for yourself," laughed Tam.

"Be nice, Tam," said Telsa.

Telsa stopped walking. Tam and Richard did as well.

"You know, Rick," said Telsa. "It's just that sometimes I forget how much information you're missing. You should really read more."

"I think I read a lot," Richard said getting defensive.

"I don't mean military manuals, Rick," said Telsa. "I mean things like history or just reading some fictional story for the fun of it."

"I don't have much free time for reading," Richard said. "None of us do."

"That's true to a point, Rick," said Telsa with a nod of agreement. "However, I force myself to make time to read non-Academy assigned books and news articles as well."

"You don't get stuck on extra duty as much as I do," Richard said.

"So true, so true," laughed Tam. "You're definitely Myers' favorite when it comes to giving out extra duty."

"Yeah, whatever," Richard said. "But what's all that got to do with the DNA Center?"

Tam swept her arm in an arc that included most of the

spaceport. "Because of history, Rick. None of this existed when the first settlers came here. That was about eight hundred years ago. The DNA Center was established not long after they arrived. The Academy didn't come along until a couple of hundred years later."

"Oh," Richard said. "Well, it would still be more convenient if it was moved closer to the Academy."

"Can't happen, Rick," said Telsa. "The DNA Center is built over an energy source that has so far only been found to exist here. It can't be moved, and it can't be replicated."

They all resumed walking. Richard didn't say anything else. He was often made aware his earlier education at the orphanage didn't match up to what many of his peers at the Academy had experienced.

Heck, he thought. *Telsa graduated from a university with a degree in astral physics. How am I supposed to compete with that?*

Richard had a feeling he'd never be able to compete education-wise with his friends. He really didn't have much time to read anything except for Academy assignments.

They arrived at berth seven. A large computer display indicated the shuttle was still two minutes out. As they waited, Richard let his mind play with his passive scan. It was always a challenge trying to separate life force readings in crowded areas such as the spaceport. Richard practiced a new technique he'd been trying to develop the last couple of months. Instead of allowing his passive scan to expand an equal distance around him, Richard pulled in the side closest to the more crowded areas and extended it toward the DNA Center. The large building seemed to have very little activity at the moment.

The passive scan detected nothing unusual. Richard wasn't surprised. He hadn't expected to find anything. However, he tried to practice his scans any time he got the chance.

"Looks like the shuttle's inbound," said Tam pointing in the direction of a bright spot of light in the sky.

"First one to identify the number of people on board gets a hundred cool-points," said Telsa.

Richard sensed lines of Power leave Tam and Telsa in the direction of the incoming shuttle.

"Six passengers plus a crew of two," Richard said without

bothering to send out an active scan.

"Hey, what gives?" said Telsa.

"Yeah," said Tam. "You haven't even formed an active scan yet."

"Don't need to," Richard said. He tried not to sound smug, but he had a feeling he was failing miserably. It wasn't often he was able to pull a fast one over on his friends.

"Well, I'll be," said Telsa who had just finished her active scan of the shuttle. "Rick's right. There are eight lifeforms on board."

"How'd you know, Rick?" said Tam.

Even though cool-points were just a meaningless method they used to keep score between them, Richard knew from experience neither of his friends liked to lose.

Not wishing to drag things out, Richard decided to come clean. "It was easy. What's Chief Instructor Winslow always drilling into our heads?"

"Technology first, Power second," said Tam and Telsa in unison. It was a rare day at the Academy when one of their instructors didn't repeat their chief instructor's mantra.

"Exactly," Richard said. "So, I just looked at the computer display."

Tam and Telsa both looked back at the computer display in front of berth seven. The digital timer was counting down from twenty-eight seconds. Just below the timer were the words: Crew – 2, Passengers – 6.

"Cheater," said Telsa. "I'm only going to award you fifty cool-points."

"Whatever," Richard said with a rare grin. He felt pretty good today. Things were going well. He was hitting on all thrusters. To top it off, he'd be seeing Liz soon.

What could go wrong on a day like this? Richard thought.

"Well, I see you all made it," said a familiar voice behind Richard.

Richard, Tam, and Telsa turned. Walking towards them was Jerad. Walking next to him was a tall, dark-haired woman wearing a standard-black wizard scout uniform. The gold-dragon insignia on her collar flashed in the bright sunlight. A phase rod was attached to the utility belt around her waist. Although the woman was not wearing a battle suit, Richard noticed a battle helmet was hooked to the left rear of her belt.

The woman, obviously a wizard scout, appeared to be in her late twenties. Of course, Richard knew that meant little. The commandant was in his nineties, but his body appeared to only be in his late twenties. The woman walking next to Jerad was pretty. Richard noticed her slim figure fit well into her black wizard scout uniform.

"Ten seconds to landing," said a computerized voice from berth seven's computer display.

"Trinity," said Jerad, "these are my friends Tam, Telsa, and Rick. Guys, this is Wizard Scout Trinity Delgado."

Richard said hello along with Tam and Telsa. Before anyone could say anything else, the incoming shuttle kicked on its anti-grav units. A blast of displaced air swept over Richard and his friends. The sudden noise made further conversation impossible. Richard noticed Jerad putting his arm around Trinity and placing his body between the shuttle and her. Richard smiled at the thought anyone would think a wizard scout needed to be protected from a little wind.

What's gotten into Jerad? Richard wondered. The goofy-looking smile on his friend's face whenever Jerad looked at Trinity was even more perplexing.

The shuttle's anti-grav units quieted when the shuttle was still a hand's breath above its berth. The shuttle dropped the remaining distance. A loud clang filled the air as the shuttle's metal hull made contact with the reinforced concrete of berth seven.

"Ouch," said Tam in the sudden silence. "I'd say it's a safe bet Liz isn't flying that thing."

Richard had to agree. He'd seen Liz make better landings while dodging enemy plasma beams.

As they waited for the shuttle's passengers to exit, Telsa looked up at the much taller Trinity and said, "Your name sounds familiar, Trinity. Should I know it?"

It seemed to Richard that Trinity's cheeks turned a little pink.

"Not really," said Trinity. "Maybe Jerad has mentioned me to you."

"No," said Telsa staying persistently on the subject. "Jerad's pretty tightlipped. I'd remember if he'd talked about you."

This time Jerad turned a little pink. Richard wasn't sure what was going on. Jerad and Trinity did seem to be acting a little strange. Then it came to him. Like Telsa, he'd heard Trinity's name before.

"By any chance are you the same Trinity Delgado that captured the Carsoloian fleet six years ago?" Richard said. He was pretty sure he knew the answer.

"Uh," said Trinity flushing even more. "I didn't capture the fleet. I just helped destroy the primary-guidance computer on their flagship. And," she said as she looked at Jerad, "I didn't do it alone. I had help. Didn't I, Jerad?"

"I was just there getting in the way," Jerad said turning even redder. "You'd have been better off without me."

"Oh," said Telsa as if she'd come to some revelation.

When Telsa failed to expound Tam said, "Oh, what?"

"Nothing," said Telsa. "I'll tell you later."

Richard didn't think it was nothing. He was about to say as much when the shuttle's rear ramp lowered. Three men and two women in standard mechanic's dungarees walked out. Behind them came Lieutenant Commander Elizabeth Bistos. Her white naval officer's uniform was immaculate. Her blond hair was close-cropped, and her bright-blue eyes flashed as she talked to a young ensign in a pilot's suit walking beside her.

"You'll get better," said Liz to the young pilot. "It just takes time. It took several hundred landings in the simulator before I got my landing technique squared away."

"Yes, sir," said the pilot with a salute. "I'll be better the next time you fly with me."

"I'm sure you will, ensign," said Liz as she returned the salute.

Liz left the pilot on the gangway and headed towards Richard and her other friends. Richard thought her eyes were almost as bright as her smile. He thought she looked more beautiful every time he saw her, even if she was an officer.

"Well, look what the thrangar dragged in," said Tam referencing a large predatory creature on Velos.

"Nice to see you too, Tam," said Liz laughing.

Liz's laughter echoed in Richard's ears. He thought she had a nice laugh.

"It's been a long time," said Telsa shaking Liz's hand.

"Not that long," interjected Jerad. "We were together for a few hours in Velounia three months ago."

"Except for Rick," said Liz placing one hand on her well-shaped hip and wagging the index finger of her other hand at Richard. "If memory serves me correctly, you were on extra duty and couldn't make it that night."

"Uh...," Richard said at a loss for words.

"No excuses, cadet," Liz said with a laugh and a twinkle in her eyes. "I know when someone's trying to avoid me."

"Well, I, ah...," Richard said stalling for time.

Everyone, including Trinity, laughed at Richard's sudden discomfort.

"Relax, Rick," said Liz. "I'm only joking." She reached out in a very unmilitary fashion and gave Richard a hug. "I'm glad you invited me to the Fleet Admiral's Ball," Liz said as she pulled away. "The only other officer on the Blaze that's going is Captain Rickers. It's almost unheard of for anyone below the rank of naval captain to attend."

Turning away from Richard, Liz said, "Hey, Trinity. I see you found Jerad with no problem."

"You know each other?" Jerad said while looking quizzically at Trinity who was still holding onto his arm.

"Oh ho," said Trinity as she let go of Jerad and shook Liz's hand. "These cadets think they know everything, don't they Liz?"

Liz gave a laugh. "So it seems, Trinity." Smiling at Jerad, Liz explained, "The Blaze picked up Trinity from a mission in district 5 a couple of months ago."

"Liz and I got to be good friends on the flight back," said Trinity. "When I heard the Blaze was heading back to Velos and would be getting here in time for the Fleet Admiral's Ball, I hitched a ride."

"I didn't hear anything about that," said Jerad.

Trinity and Liz laughed. Richard thought they both had nice laughs.

"Well," said Trinity, "I guess that means you don't know everything about me doesn't it, Jerad?"

"Oh, believe me," said Jerad good-naturedly. "I've no doubt there's a lot I don't know about you." With a little more seriousness, Jerad added, "But, I'm hoping I'll have many years to learn."

Jerad and Trinity both turned slightly pink. Richard had an inkling there was a lot more going on between the two than he could see on the surface.

"Well," said Telsa. "Not to break up the party, but I've got things to do. What say we grab a couple of hover-cabs and head back to the hotel? It's only five hours until the ball." With a glance at Tam, Telsa said, "It'll take at least that long to make Tam look presentable."

Everybody, including Tam, laughed.

As they walked back in the direction of the military terminal, Richard tried to force his way next to Liz, but Telsa and Tam were having none of it. They each claimed a side of Liz, and soon the three friends were jabbering away as they caught up with each other's escapades. Since Jerad and Trinity were apparently content to walk next to each other while talking quietly, Richard was relegated to trailing a few paces behind the group by himself. Slightly bored, Richard practiced expanding and decreasing his passive scan.

Too many people here, Richard thought.

Richard reformed his passive scan so it bulged out in the direction of the DNA Center. He monitored the score of lifeforms inside the building along with seven more on the outside.

No, make that eight, Richard corrected himself as a utility vehicle skirted through the area. Unlike the pinpoint accuracy of an active scan, information was much harder to get when using just a passive scan. Richard followed the path of the vehicle using it as a point of reference to the lifeforms near the building. Since he'd been teaching his fellow cadets how to determine species of lifeforms using the Power readings from a passive scan, Richard wanted to get in a little practical exercise on his own. He had another impromptu training session scheduled with part of the junior cohort early next week. Richard figured the spaceport was a great place to find multiple species.

Richard tried concentrating on the Power frequency of the vehicle's driver. As the vehicle drove near one corner of the DNA Center, the driver's Power frequency momentarily faded. Although it almost immediately flared back up on Richard's passive scan, the momentary blip was a little disconcerting.

That was strange, Richard thought.

Concentrating on the vehicle driver even harder, Richard registered no other fluctuations. The driver's Power readings remained steady.

I wonder if something in the DNA Center caused some kind of interference? Richard thought.

Richard had a sudden wish his battle computer was with him. He almost said something to his friends, but he held off. They were still talking and laughing several meters to his front. Richard hated to interrupt them. *What would I tell them anyway?*

Reforming his passive scan, Richard concentrated on the path the vehicle had taken near the DNA Center. Everything seemed perfectly normal.

I wonder, Richard thought. *Is it possible to be too normal?*

At another time, Richard might have let the feeling of 'too normal' pass. But he hesitated to do so today. The memory of feeling something too normal the night before at the airfield was still fresh in his mind.

The hell with it, Richard thought. *My Power reserve's at a hundred percent. I can spare a little.*

Although Richard felt a little silly for thinking something could be too normal, he consoled himself by writing the Power usage off as training. Richard formed an active scan and wrapped it in a stealth shield. It was a technique he'd been developing since the previous summer. While he hadn't quite perfected it, even Nickelo had admitted his modified active-scan was very difficult to detect even when someone was expecting to be scanned.

Richard delicately probed the area near the DNA Center which felt too normal. He detected nothing. Richard persisted. Something just didn't feel right. He couldn't put his finger on it, but he knew in his heart something was wrong. Even the hairs on the back of his neck were standing on end.

"Rick?" said Liz. "What is it?"

Richard realized he'd stopped walking. Liz and the others had stopped as well. They were all looking back at him curiously. Liz looked especially concerned.

Taking a couple of steps back towards Richard, Liz said again, "Rick? What is it?"

"Is that thing loaded?" Richard said as he gestured to a plasma pistol holstered on her belt.

"What?" said Liz. She frowned. "My pistol? No. Of course not."

Richard wasn't surprised. They were a thousand light years behind friendly lines. The military wasn't in the habit of letting its personnel carry live ammo in non-combat areas.

"Rick," said Jerad. "You're starting to worry me. What's up, buddy?"

"I'm not sure," Richard said. "Does anyone sense anything unusual near the DNA Center? The far right corner in particular."

Four lines of Power reached out past Richard in the direction of the DNA Center. Richard recognized the frequencies of his friends Tam, Telsa, and Jerad. The fourth set of Power was barely discernable. It was Trinity's. Richard stored away the memory of her frequency.

She's very good, Richard thought approvingly. *I wouldn't have noticed her active scan if I didn't know where it would pass.*

Richard looked at Trinity. Without asking questions, the wizard scout had drawn and activated her phase rod. As he watched, she snatched the battle helmet off her left hip. With a practiced maneuver, she placed the battle helmet on her head. Somewhere between her hip and her head, the battle helmet changed its flattened shape to a battle helmet in three-quarters mode. As Richard watched, the reddish glow of the battle helmet's visor appeared in front of Trinity's eyes. The visor was more of a force field than a physical object, but it still allowed the wearer to view the world using a variety of filters. Richard was primarily interested in one filter.

"Trinity," Richard said. "Try a radiation filter."

Richard noticed her filter flicker. Trinity apparently was not one to waste time asking questions. His respect for Jerad's friend went up a notch. She was the experienced wizard scout in the group while he was just a cadet. But she wasn't letting her ego or pride get in the way.

After an agonizing five seconds, Richard said, "Anything?"

"I've got nothing," said Jerad.

"Me either," said Tam.

"Same here," Telsa added.

"Trinity?" Richard said hopefully. He was beginning to feel more than a little foolish.

Richard saw Trinity's lips press together below the visor of her battle helmet. He got the feeling she was redoubling her concentration. After a few more seconds, her lips relaxed.

"Sorry, Rick," said Trinity as she flicked her wrist and deactivated her phase rod. "I don't sense anything unusual."

Four lines of Power drew back as Trinity and Richard's fellow cadets shutdown their active scans.

"What was it you thought you sensed?" said Trinity.

Richard noticed his friends were letting Trinity do the talking. Richard understood. She was a wizard scout. They were just cadets. Richard could only imagine what TAC Officer Myers would say to him if he found out about this.

"I don't really know," Richard admitted. "The area just felt a little strange to me."

Trinity looked closer at Richard before replying. He had a feeling she was fighting a natural inclination to chastise a junior cadet for being too jumpy. To Richard's relief, Trinity didn't take the opportunity to critique him in front of his friends.

"Well," said Trinity slowly. "It's always best to be safe. I imagine you just sensed an energy bleed-off from the DNA Center."

"Possibly," Richard said. He'd almost convinced himself as much. He was beginning to wish he'd listened to his own doubts.

"That has to be it, Rick," said Telsa. "Even if someone was using a stealth shield, we'd still see them."

"Yeah," agreed Tam. "It's not like stealth shields make you invisible."

Of all the others, only Jerad appeared disinclined to convince Richard he was mistaken.

"Trinity," said Jerad. "Rick's got the best active scan I've ever seen. Are you sure you didn't sense anything?"

Trinity shrugged her shoulders. "I suppose I could always be wrong," she admitted. "But all I noticed was a slight blur near the DNA Center through my battle helmet's radiation filter. That kind of thing happens when—"

Richard didn't give Trinity a chance to finish. His mind flashed back to a battle he'd fought during an internship mission his sophomore year. His opponents had used a spell that not only kept them under stealth but which also kept them invisible as well.

They'd only shown up as a slight blur on his radiation filter.

"Notify security," Richard yelled interrupting Trinity.

He took off at a dead run in the direction of the DNA Center. Five sets of running feet echoed behind him. His friends might be confused by his actions, but they weren't letting him rush off on his own. Richard heard the unmistakable pop of a phase rod activating.

This can't be right, Richard thought. *That was a spell the last time. I'm in the physical dimension now. The Crosioians don't have spell-casters.*

In spite of his undeniable logic, Richard kept running for all he was worth. The three hundred meters to the DNA Center reduced rapidly.

Richard sensed a flare of energy to his front.

"Shields!" Richard yelled over his shoulder as a ball of energy headed in their direction.

Richard pulled Power from his reserve and started to form a defensive shield to his front. Before he could complete his shield, a line of Power from Tam reached past him and formed a semicircular wall between the ball of energy and him. Richard dropped his line of Power without activating his defensive shield. He trusted Tam to protect him. Defensive shields were her specialty. Since he had the smallest Power reserve of any wizard scout, Richard knew he needed to conserve every drop of Power he had.

The ball of energy was a spell. It opened up into a bolt of lightning. Part of the energy was absorbed by Tam's defensive shield. The rest of the energy was deflected skyward.

The air near a corner of the DNA Center shimmered. Richard saw a group of five humanoids. One was half again as tall as the others. One of the humanoids was in a full battle suit. The bat-shaped wings folded behind the creature's back gave little doubt it was a Crosioian scout. The largest of the humanoids made Richard doubt he was seeing clearly. Even at almost three hundred meters, he recognized its distinctive form.

A troll, he thought while trying at the same time to convince himself he was mistaken.

Three streams of plasma rounds from the group of humanoids came streaking towards Richard and his friends. Richard dodged to the left and rolled on the spaceport's asphalt pavement as one of the streams of plasma rounds whizzed an arm's length above his head.

"Stay near me," shouted Tam.

Tam's defensive shield reformed into a wall which extended several meters across. From the readings on his passive scan, Richard knew Telsa and Liz were hanging close to Tam.

Good, Richard thought. *Tam will take care of them.*

Richard came up out of his roll into a run. Trinity passed him on his left. Jerad was hot on her heels. The Crosioian scout seemed to be concentrating her plasma fire on Trinity and Jerad. A human in a jumpsuit was firing his rifle at Richard. To Richard's surprise, the troll was also firing a large-wattage plasma rifle at Tam, Telsa, and Liz. Although the troll's heavy weapon was slow in firing, its high energy more than made up for its slow rate of fire. Richard sensed Tam's defensive shield buckle a little each time one of the large plasma rounds hit.

The Crosioian scout threw down her plasma rifle and began running on a course to intercept Trinity and Jerad. As the Crosioian scout ran, a spear-shaped object appeared in her hand. An arm's length point of glowing energy tipped the end of the spear. From previous experience, Richard knew it was the Crosioian scout's version of a phase rod.

The human in the jumpsuit fired at Richard again. Richard was beyond the protection of Tam's defensive shield, so he threw up a shield of his own. He slanted his defensive shield slightly as he'd been taught by the elf-priestess Shandria his freshman year. The plasma rounds ricocheted off to the left. Richard hoped the ricocheting rounds ran out of energy before they hit anything friendly. Richard dropped his defensive shield. It was too Power hungry to leave up for long.

The distance closed to a hundred meters between the two groups. Richard reached out with his mind. He reached into the human's chest that had fired at him. He felt for his opponent's heart. Richard wrapped the heart in Power and squeezed inward with his telekinesis. The heart stopped beating. The human dropped his plasma rifle and fell to the ground.

Distant sirens drew Richard's attention back to the battle around him. He glimpsed Trinity and Jerad closing with the Crosioian scout. The bat-creature swung her spear at Trinity. The wizard scout caught the blow on her phase rod, but she was driven to her knees. Jerad jumped into the air and made a flying jump-kick over Trinity's head. His foot landed squarely on the Crosioian scout's chest. The bat-creature was driven back a couple of steps. She swung her spear at Jerad, but Trinity blocked the blow with her phase rod.

Richard ran past the Crosioian scout. He had to close the distance to the magic users. He sensed two of them. They were the unknowns. Richard feared them more than he did the Crosioian scout. While he didn't know Trinity, he had faith she and Jerad could handle the bat creature.

The troll switched its aim. Richard got his defensive shield up just in time to block the high-energy plasma rounds. The force of the blow made him stagger. He felt his energy reserve draining quickly. Richard knew his Power reserve was too small to keep his defensive shield up for long under this kind of attack.

As if sensing Richard's trouble, Telsa sent a blast of pure Power at the troll. The Power exploded on the troll's chest. A fountain of blood and bone erupted from the troll's back. The force of the blow threw the troll into the wall of the DNA Center. It bounced off the wall and lay on the ground.

Richard sensed Tam reach out with her Power. She wrapped it around the plasma rifle dropped by the human Richard had killed. The plasma rifle started flying through the air back towards Tam. At the same time, Richard sensed one of the magic users attach a link to the other. Energy transferred from the first magic user to the second.

They're combining their Power, Richard thought. He'd seen it done before. One magic user could pull Power from another magic user and combine it with Power he pulled from his own reserve.

Things were getting too dangerous. Richard sent out the strongest emotion he could summon indicating his need for help. It was the same emotion the younger dolgars sent when they were in trouble. Richard wasn't sure if any of the dolgars would come, but he had to try.

Richard was close enough now to hear the magic user chanting a spell. The two sets of Power combined and turned into a large ball of magical energy. Richard reached out with his mind towards the most powerful of the magic users. He started probing the magic user's link to his Power reserve. A smaller line of energy from the second magic user reached out and knocked Richard's probe away before he could disable the magic user's Power link. Although Richard failed to disrupt the magic user from completing his spell, he did distract him from his intended target. Instead of sending the spell towards Tam, Telsa, and Liz, the magic user released his ball of energy at Richard. The ball of energy was much larger than the first spell. Richard recognized the intertwined lines of energy of the spell. It was one he'd helped Shandria rewrite. It was a fireball. And it was going to be a big one.

Richard didn't waste time throwing up a defensive shield. He'd been hit by a similar fireball once before, and even encased in his battle suit, enough energy had penetrated his defensive shield to blister his back and legs with second degree burns. Richard doubted his thin cadet jumpsuit would provide him even meager protection.

Wrapping himself in Power, Richard shifted into the void between dimensions. He wasn't sure whether the fireball's energy would affect him in the void, but he was taking no changes. Richard used telekinesis to move a few meters underground. Although he lost visibility the moment he went underground, Richard kept track of his surroundings with his passive scan. The fireball erupted overhead in a blaze of magical energy. Unlike most fireballs, this one did not dissipate. It continued to burn.

That's different, Richard thought.

Shifting into the void between dimensions was very Power hungry. He'd hoped to move above ground after the fireball dissipated. Richard felt his Power reserve draining rapidly. While constant practice under his battle computer's tutelage had made him more efficient at Power usage, he knew he'd be drained of Power if he remained shifted too long.

Richard used his telekinesis to pull himself along horizontally underground until he cleared the burning area overhead. He moved upward and immediately shifted back into the physical plane the moment he cleared the surface.

Richard noted his Power reserve. Without his battle helmet, he could only guesstimate his remaining Power. He silently cursed when he realized his Power reserve was down to about half. He cursed again when he felt heat all along his backside. He'd surfaced just a little too close to the still burning fireball.

A stream of green plasma rounds shot from Richard's right and streaked towards the magic users. The plasma rounds ricocheted off their defensive shields.

With a look to his right, Richard noticed Liz had a plasma rifle in her hands. It was the human's plasma rifle Tam had been levitating. Liz began firing a steady stream of rounds at the magic users. The green rounds ricocheted off in all directions.

The sounds of sirens were louder. Richard saw a hover-car streaking past shuttle berth two with blue lights flashing. A stream of high-energy plasma rounds whizzed overhead from the direction of the DNA Center. One of the rounds hit the approaching hover-car squarely on its front. The front of the vehicle exploded, and the rear of the hover-car flipped into the air. The hover-car rolled across the asphalt.

Richard shifted his gaze to the DNA Center. The troll was back on its feet firing at anything that moved with its heavy-plasma gun. Liz moved her line of fire to the troll. Several plasma rounds hit it in the chest. It was knocked backwards a step or two, but the holes in its chest closed over even as Richard watched.

"You can't kill it that way," Richard yelled. "It's a troll. You have to burn it."

Whether Liz believed Richard or not, he didn't know. However, she stopped firing at the troll and concentrated on the two magic users instead.

Richard had no idea how many rounds Liz had remaining in her plasma rifle, but he suspected she was getting low. Throwing caution to the wind, Richard ran towards the two magic users. At the same time, he pulled half the remaining Power in his reserve and threw it against the defensive shield of the leftmost magic user who was the weaker of the two. Richard formed his Power into a point and began twisting it back and forth in a drilling motion.

As he twisted, Richard yelled over his shoulder, "Concentrate on the guy on the right."

Liz's line of plasma rounds moved to the magic user on the right and remained there, peppering against the magic user's defensive shield. The plasma rounds didn't penetrate the shield, but Liz kept firing anyway.

Richard continued to drill his Power into the defensive shield of the leftmost magic user. He heard both magic users chanting words he heard but quickly forgot.

"They're going to cast a spell," Richard yelled hoping Liz would hear.

Before either magic user could complete their spell, Richard's drill broke through the defensive shield of the leftmost magic user. The hole it created was small, but it was enough. While Liz was not a wizard scout cadet, she'd been one during pre-Academy training. Richard hoped her natural affinity for Power would pay off now.

It did.

Liz shifted her line of fire to the leftmost magic user's defensive shield seeking the hole created by Richard's drill. Several plasma rounds found the hole and hit the magic user in the throat and chest. The magic user was knocked backwards through the air. His defensive shield dissipated. The leftmost magic user was dead.

One down, one to go, Richard thought.

Unfortunately, the remaining magic user was the stronger of the two. And he was good. The death of his companion didn't distract the magic user. He completed his spell before Richard could react. With the last word of his spell, the magic user pushed his hands outward in a shoving motion.

Before Richard could form his Power into a defensive shield, a line of Power passed over his right shoulder and created a wall of Power to his front. Richard recognized the frequency of the Power.

Good old Tam, Richard thought as the magic user's energy exploded against Tam's defensive shield.

Boom!

Richard heard another blast to his right. He turned his head just in time to see an explosion erupt against an invisible barrier in front of Telsa and Liz. The defensive shield disappeared as Tam dropped her shield to conserve Power. Richard followed a trail of smoke from the blast back to the troll. It was standing with a four-barreled rocket launcher on its shoulder. Richard saw the troll turn as if seeking another target. The troll stopped its turn. Richard instinctively followed the troll's line of sight. It led directly to the spot where Jerad and Trinity were in close combat with the Crosioian scout.

"Jerad!" Richard yelled as he pointed at the troll.

Trinity's back was to the troll, but Jerad was on the opposite side of the Crosioian scout. Richard assumed Jerad must have seen him pointing because he sensed Jerad send a blast of pure Power at the troll. The rocket launcher on the troll's shoulder belched fire. A rocket streaked out. When the rocket got to a point halfway between the troll and Jerad, it met Jerad's blast of energy. Richard felt the shock of the resulting explosion thirty meters away.

The Crosioian scout took advantage of Jerad's distraction. She unfolded a wing and spun her body. A long point at the wing's joint swept towards Jerad. Richard's friend bent backwards until he was almost bent in half. The Crosioian scout's wing passed a hand's breath above Jerad's arched belly.

Trinity made a spinning jump into the air. Her phase rod flashed in the air as it sliced downward and cut off the Crosioian scout's wing at the joint. Richard heard the scout scream. To Richard, the scream sounded more like one of anger than pain.

Richard turned his attention to the troll. It was moving its rocket launcher back towards Telsa and Liz.

Reaching out with his mind, Richard probed into the barrel of the rocket launcher. Everything, living or not, had an aura of Power. Richard sensed the aura surrounding the warhead of the rocket in the launcher. He wrapped the warhead with Power and squeezed with his telekinesis. He squeezed hard. Most warheads had a built-in safety to make sure it traveled a certain distance before it armed. However, the force of the telekinesis was too much for the warhead's safety. The rocket exploded inside the launcher. The blast severed the troll's head. It flew off in one direction while the troll's bloody torso flew in several other directions.

Just then, Richard sensed a line of magical energy reach out from the remaining magic user towards Tam's link to her Power reserve. The line of energy seemed to probe Tam's link before returning to the magic user. Richard smiled and thanked his lucky stars for all the hours he'd spent lying in bed strengthening the weak points in his friend's link to her Power reserve. Tam's link was far from perfect, but it must have been enough to discourage the magic user. The magic user wisely chose not to attempt an attack on Tam's link under such a stressful situation. Richard noticed the magic user didn't bother trying to probe Telsa's link.

Liz aimed her plasma rifle at the magic user and began firing. She fired in single-shot mode.

Definitely low on ammo, Richard thought. Their situation was getting even more desperate.

The noise of approaching sirens from several directions announced the pending approach of multiple security vehicles. They were all heading towards the DNA Center.

The sirens and what they meant must have spooked the remaining magic user because he turned and ran around a corner of the building. Although the magic user was no longer visible, Richard had a trace on him. A grim smile crossed Richard's lips. The magic user could run, but there would be no escape. As long as he didn't let the magic user get too far ahead, Richard was confident he could track him with his passive scan. Even a stealth shield wouldn't help the fleeing magic user at this point. Richard had his scent.

At a dead run of his own, Richard quickly closed the distance to the spot just vacated by the magic user. When Richard got close to the corner of the DNA Center, he noticed the pieces of troll spread all over the ground. The pieces appeared to be crawling and squirming along the ground in an attempt to reach each other. Even the troll's severed head was rolling slowly towards the largest piece of the troll's torso.

Before he turned the corner of the DNA Center, Richard pointed and yelled over his shoulder. "Burn this stuff before it reforms."

The battle was far from over, and Richard hated leaving his friends in such dire straits. The Crosioian scout was still alive, and from her life force reading, Richard knew her wing was already healed. However, the magic user had to be stopped. In the split second before the battle was lost from Richard's sight, he noticed several rounds of green plasma energy striking the Crosioian scout in the back. Richard felt better. Liz had joined the fray. With her support, Richard had no doubt Jerad and Trinity could handle the bat-creature. His confidence level went even higher when he sensed Telsa moving towards the Crosioian scout as well.

As he ran, Richard kept a tab on his friends with his passive scan. Tam appeared to be heading for the location of the dismembered troll. Since the strange fireball spell cast by the magic user was still burning, Richard knew Tam wouldn't have any problem finding a source of fire to destroy the troll.

Before Richard got another twenty meters, he heard the sound of security vehicles arriving at the battle behind him. A rapid series of booms gave little doubt the spaceport's security teams were providing additional support in the way of their vehicle's high-energy plasma cannons. Richard noticed the life force of the Crosioian scout drop dramatically. Richard felt much better as he continued to run after the magic user. His friends were going to be all right.

The magic user was only forty meters ahead of Richard, but he was running hard. Richard reached out with his mind and tried to probe the magic user's heart. A line of energy from the magic user knocked his probe away. Another line of energy reached back from the magic user towards Richard's chest. Richard knocked it away with a line of his own Power.

After a few more steps, the magic user drew Power from his reserve and formed it into magical energy. At the same time, Richard drew some of his own Power and prepared to throw up a defensive shield. The magic user shouted a word of magic and tossed his ball of energy over his back. A dense cloud of the blackest smoke billowed out in all directions. Richard held his breath and entered the cloud of smoke. His vision dropped to zero, but his passive scan served him almost as well. He continued to track the magic user as he twisted and turned in the smoke.

Richard heard the loud whine of several sirens to his rear. He also heard the roar of a nearby anti-gravity engine reversing its output. At least one security vehicle was close. Richard heard the shouts of the vehicle's driver, although the sound was too muffled to make out the words. Richard wasn't sure what the smoke from the magic user's spell did, but it apparently affected sound as well as vision.

The life force which was the magic user changed course to the left. Richard changed his course accordingly to intercept. Richard's lungs began to burn from his extended exertion. He started considering an alternative plan in case he didn't exit the smoke soon.

I don't want to breathe this stuff, Richard thought.

Just when Richard was sure he would have to shift into the void in order to escape the smoke, it thinned. A second later, Richard was in the clear. He took a big gulp of sweet tasting air.

An armored security car flew by about ten meters overhead with its blue lights flashing. The car was close enough Richard could see the individual blades of its anti-gravity fans spinning furiously beneath the vehicle. A gunner manned the high-energy plasma cannon at the front of the security car. The gunner aimed at the running magic user and fired. Before the plasma rounds hit their intended target, the magic user stopped and waved his hands. Richard sensed the magic user's Power convert into magic energy. It formed a shield between him and the security car. The plasma rounds ricocheted off the hastily-erected defensive shield.

The security car's gunner continued firing as the driver tried to maneuver around the shield. Richard sensed the magic user draw more Power from his reserve.

Crap, Richard thought. *His Power reserve must be ten times the size of mine. It figures.*

Although he knew the battle might be over before he got close enough to the magic user to attack, Richard continued running towards his quarry for all he was worth. As his drill sergeants had repeatedly told him when he'd first joined the military, a marine never quits until the battle is over. Richard had seen others snatch defeat out of the jaws of victory too often in the past to take victory for granted.

The magic user completed his spell. A ball of energy left his hands and shot out to a point above and to the front of the moving security car. The car's gunner was still firing as fast as his cannon recharged. The ball of magical energy spread out, and the air around it shimmered. As the security car passed underneath the shimmering area the air transformed into a large mass of ice. The ice crashed downward into the car slamming it into the ground ten meters below. Although the security car didn't explode, the noise from its anti-gravity engines ceased immediately. Richard knew it was up to him now.

Richard continued running as he dodged broken-off pieces of ice. When he drew even with the downed security car, Richard reached out with his telekinesis and unsnapped the portable plasma cannon from its mount on the front of the car. He pulled with his mind. When the plasma cannon got within reach, Richard reached out and grabbed it. He cradled it in his arms and kept running. Although the cannon was heavy, it was still portable. Richard figured it would serve his purpose if he didn't have to run too far.

A quick glance at the cannon's isotopic battery indicated its charge was at twenty-two percent. The blood dripping off the plasma cannon's stock didn't bode well for the wellbeing of the previous gunner. Richard hoped its present gunner wouldn't windup with the same fate.

The magic user changed course again as three more security cars closed in from his original path. A shiver ran down Richard's spine.

He's headed for the military terminal, Richard thought.

A sweep of Richard's passive scan confirmed the presence of several hundred lifeforms in the terminal. He knew almost all of them would be unarmed. The soldiers and their dependents were just awaiting transfer to the starships orbiting overhead. No one was expecting trouble.

"No!" Richard yelled out loud. A vision of the magic user releasing a volley of fireballs in the crowded terminal flashed through his mind.

I've got to stop him, Richard thought determinedly. *There are children in there.*

Richard sent out another desperate call to the dolgars. *Why don't they come?*

With only seconds remaining before the magic user reached the military terminal's steps, Richard reached out with his mind and probed the magic user's link to his Power reserve. At the same time, Richard stopped running and began firing in single-shot mode at the magic user. Richard knew he would never be able to reach his opponent in time. He had to take the magic user out at a distance before he could reach the steps.

The magic user threw up a defensive shield. Unexpectedly, the magic user stopped running and spun around. He knocked Richard's probe away and sent one of his own against Richard's link. Richard countered and knocked the magic user's probe away as well. Richard and the magic user sent a series of attacks and counterattacks against each other's Power links. Neither of them gained an advantage.

A beep from the plasma cannon let Richard know its isotopic

battery was below five percent. Since the plasma rounds were having no effect against his opponent's defensive shield, Richard decided to try a change of tactics. He switched his aim to a light post near the terminal's stairs. His first round gouged out a large chunk of metal from the base of the light post. A second shot severed it completely. The light post started to fall, but it was leaning in the wrong direction. Richard reached out with his mind and wrapped the top of the light post with Power. He pulled with his telekinesis. The light post was too heavy for him to lift outright, but he had enough leverage to guide the post's fall towards the magic user. As it fell, the post picked up speed.

The magic user shifted his defensive shield overhead. The light post hit the shield and slid off to the side.

Richard cursed silently. Some defensive shields were attuned to energy. Some were attuned to physical attacks. And some shields protected the caster from both.

Figures, Richard thought. *Just my luck to face someone who has a shield that does both.*

Richard did get one stroke of luck. The magic user had left his flank exposed when he moved his defensive shield overhead. Richard took careful aim with his plasma cannon and fired a round at the magic user's leg. The plasma round stuck true and tore the leg off at the knee. The magic user was knocked off his feet.

Richard didn't fire again. He wanted to take the magic user alive if possible. Two security guards ran down the terminal's steps with their side-arms drawn.

"Stay back. We need to take him alive," Richard shouted.

The guards ignored him and continued down the steps. When they were about ten meters from the downed magic user, Richard sensed a flare of magical energy.

"Watch out!" Richard shouted.

The magic user exploded. Blood and pieces of meat flew in all directions. The two security guards were thrown backwards several meters. Richard made a quick probe with his active scan. The guards were shaken, but they were still alive.

Several security cars came hovering over the top of the terminal building. Their sirens were blaring. Even so, Richard heard a threatening voice come over one of the vehicle's external speakers. "Put the weapon down, or we'll fire!"

Richard carefully lowered the plasma cannon to the ground and stood with his hands raised.

Resignedly, he thought, *I've a feeling I'm going to be fashionably late to the Fleet Admiral's Ball.*

CHAPTER 16

The time display in the security building's lobby registered 04:30. Richard yawned and stretched. It had been a long night. He felt as if he'd been grilled and debriefed by half the security people at the spaceport. It hadn't helped that once the spaceport's security people were done asking questions a new batch of security types from higher headquarters arrived and started the questioning all over again. On more than one occasion, Richard had felt like he was being treated as if he was one of the bad guys instead of one of the Empire's military elite.

Finally, after twelve grueling hours the investigators must have been satisfied he wasn't a Crosioian spy, because they grudgingly released him.

A fat lot of good that does now, Richard thought. *The Fleet Admiral's Ball ended hours ago. On top of that, I haven't seen any of my friends in hours.*

Richard was tired. He glanced around the lobby looking for any familiar faces. He spotted one. It was Tam. Richard wandered over to his friend. She was kicked back in an uncomfortable-looking plastic chair with her legs stretched out on a nearby table. The table was covered with hologram-magazines, but Tam had shoved them to one side to make room for her feet. Tam's hat was pulled down in an apparent attempt to shield her eyes from the lobby's bright lights.

"I thought sure you'd be on your way to Diajor by now," Richard said. "I tried my best to pin everything on you."

Tam reached up with one hand and slowly raised the brim of her hat. Her eyes squinted as she tried to focus on Richard.

"Yuk, yuk," Tam said with a wide stretch of her arms. She yawned loud enough to wake several people dozing nearby. Tam ignored their angry stares.

"Have you seen any of the others?" Richard said. He specifically wanted to know if Liz was still around, but he hesitated to sound too interested. He needed to talk to Liz before she returned to the Blaze.

Tam glanced at the lobby's timer. "Jerad and Trinity left about thirty minutes ago. Trinity seemed anxious to spend some alone time with Jerad. I told Jerad I'd wait for the rest of you."

"Hmm," Richard said. "I'm surprised Jerad left. He's usually like a mother hen watching over her chicks."

Tam raised both hands and rubbed the sleep out of her eyes. When she was satisfied with the results, she gave another yawn which was even louder than her first. Two of the nearby dozers gave her more rude stares before they stood up and left for a quieter section of the lobby. Tam paid them no heed.

"Well, actually," said Tam, "it took some arguing to get Jerad to leave. Trinity and I had to double team him. Sometimes he thinks he's still a battalion commander, and we're all his wet-nosed privates."

"Yeah," Richard said. "He's a natural leader at heart. He's a good leader too; for an officer."

Tam laughed. "Actually, I don't think much of either officers or non-coms. Our leadership structure in the mercs was a little more, how shall we say…, relaxed."

Richard grinned. "I'll bet it was, Tam."

Sitting down in an empty seat next to Tam, Richard kicked his feet up onto the table next to hers.

"You know," Richard said, "I can wait for Liz and Telsa if you want to go back to the hotel."

Tam shrugged. "What's the use at this point? The clerk over there said they'd be out in a few minutes anyway." Tam gestured with her head towards a sleepy-eyed, older gentleman at a nearby desk.

Neither of them said anything for a few seconds. Richard was the first to break the silence. "I'm sorry you missed the Fleet

Admiral's Ball, Tam. I know you had a date."

"It's no big deal," said Tam. "I'm sure my date found plenty of loose women to dance with. Besides, it wasn't your fault."

"Still…," Richard said searching for the right words.

"Still, nothing," said Tam. "The universe doesn't revolve around you, Rick. Things happen."

There were a few more seconds of silence.

"So, what'd you tell them?" said Tam.

"Only what they could find out by reviewing tele-bot videos of the fight," Richard said noncommittally. "There were bound to be a couple of dozen of them in the area. The spaceport's a highly-secured area."

Turning to look better at Tam, Richard said, "What about you?"

"Same," said Tam. "Anything extra I could've told them would be second-hand knowledge. All I know about a magical dimension is what you've told me. It's not like I've been there."

"Well, I have been," Richard said. "But I didn't mention it to them. I figured they'd lock me up in a loony-bin if I started spouting off about another dimension where magic is the dominant force."

"Yeah," said Tam nodding her head. "I was tempted to recommend you for an article thirty-two mental evaluation myself the first time you told me."

In spite of his fatigue, Richard snorted a laugh. "You're joking, right?"

Richard looked closer at Tam. He didn't see the slightest hint of a smile on her face.

Finally, Tam did smile. "Wouldn't you like to know, cadet 832?"

Richard rolled his eyes. His long association with his friends had improved his sense of humor dramatically. However, a lot of the finer subtleties still escaped him.

"Well, anyway," Richard said trying to change the subject. "Our trip to the spaceport turned out to be a waste."

"Not really," said Tam. "We obviously stopped some bad guys from doing something. Plus, we finally found out why Jerad applied to be a wizard scout."

Tam's last words caught Richard by surprise. He eyed Tam looking for any sign of an attempt at humor. As far as he could tell, she was serious.

"I guess I must have missed that part of the briefing," Richard said. "I'll bite. Why did Jerad become a wizard scout?"

"You really are unobservant sometimes, Rick," said Tam with a shake of her head. She took her feet off the table and turned in her seat until she faced Richard. "Didn't you see the way Jerad looked at Trinity? Those two are head-over-heels in love, buddy."

"Yeah, I noticed," Richard said. "So?"

"What do you mean so?" said Tam as if she'd expected Richard to say something different. "Don't you get it?"

"Get what?" Richard said growing exasperated. Sometimes he wished people would just say what they meant without having to pull it out of them. "He's in love. Trinity's a beautiful woman. I get it. What's that got to do with Jerad coming to the Academy?"

Tam glanced around before leaning closer to Richard. In a conspiratorial whisper, she said, "Jerad and Trinity met when he was a battalion commander. Trinity's a wizard scout. She doesn't age. Jerad's far too proud to tie her down with an old man."

Richard leaned back in his seat before answering. "Jerad's not old. He's what? Forty-three or so?"

Actually, Richard thought. *That is kind of old. But I'm not going to admit that to Tam.*

"He's about that," agreed Tam. "And Trinity's physical age is probably around late twenties."

Richard thought Tam was looking at him as if she'd just given him a great revelation. *Well, if she's expecting a response, she's going to be severely disappointed.*

When Richard said nothing, Tam continued speaking. "Let's skip ahead another twenty years. Imagine if Jerad hadn't volunteered for wizard scout training. In another twenty years, his physical age would be in the low sixties. What would Trinity's physical age be?"

"Still in her twenties," Richard said. "She's a wizard scout. She doesn't age. Everyone knows that. It's just one of the perks of being a wizard scout."

"Right," said Tam as if she'd scored a point. "Add another score of years. The difference between their physical ages would be even larger."

Richard considered Tam's remarks. He hadn't thought about

relationships and the aging differences before. Wizard scouts didn't age. They eventually died when they got older. But they didn't age.

"So, you're saying Jerad applied for the Academy so both Trinity and he would be wizard scouts?" Richard said. A thought he refused to recognize began gnawing at the back of his mind.

"That's how I have it figured," said Tam with a smile and a wink. "Now that's what I call true love. A thirty-eight year old man applies for six years of the toughest training the Empire has to offer just to be with the woman he loves."

Richard inspected a small clump of dirt on the inseam of his boots as he sorted out his thoughts. Tam's analysis bothered him.

"I've just met Trinity," Richard said without looking at Tam. "But, I don't think she's the type to let a difference in physical age stop her from loving Jerad."

Tam eyed Richard suspiciously before answering. "Maybe, and maybe not. But Jerad's too good a man to allow her to do that. Besides, what good could come from a relationship between a wizard scout and a normal person? Even without considering the aging difference, a wizard scout is deployed most of the time. It's just asking for heartache."

This time it was Richard who eyed Tam suspiciously. Her comments seemed a little too insightful for a spur of the moment conversation.

"Are we still talking about Jerad and Trinity?" Richard said fearing the answer.

Tam looked down at the floor as if she was the one studying her boots this time. Richard didn't press the subject. He just waited.

After a full thirty seconds had passed, Tam looked up at Richard. "Lieutenant Commander Aldrich. Do you know him?"

Richard shook his head no.

"Well," said Tam. "We've been communicating with each other since my internship mission last year. Mostly through hologram messages, but we've been able to get together for a weekend now and then."

Her comment reminded Richard of several weekend passes where Tam had opted not to go to town with her friends from the Academy. Richard began regretting he'd started asking questions. He was used to Tam being a hard-nosed mercenary. He'd never thought of her as having some of the softer emotions. Richard studied Tam as if seeing her for the first time.

Her eyes are shiny, Richard thought.

Richard had a momentary thought that he hoped she wasn't going to start crying. He immediately kicked himself mentally for being heartless. Tam was his friend. He suspected it was taking a lot for her to lower her emotional shields in front of him. He had a feeling she was only doing so now because she'd been awake all night. Richard made a mental note not to let her down by saying something stupid.

What should I say? Richard wondered. Sensitivity training was not a subject at the Academy.

After a few seconds of silence, Richard decided to take the direct approach. He was a marine. A direct frontal assault was what he did best.

"Are you in love with this Aldrich character?" Richard said.

Tam didn't protest his directness. Maybe she was just too tired. Instead of denying it, Tam shrugged her shoulders. "I honestly don't know, Rick. But it doesn't really matter."

"What do you mean it doesn't matter?" Richard said. "It makes all the difference in the world. Doesn't it?"

Richard began to doubt his own words. The sisters at the orphanage where he'd been raised had not been unkind. However, affection had not been one of their strong points either. Richard knew his knowledge of the touchy-feely emotions like love were a little on the weak side.

"I mean it doesn't matter as far as what I need to do," said Tam.

"And what it that?" Richard said dreading the answer. He dreaded it because his conversation with Tam was striking a little too close to home.

"I have to end it. Before it goes any further," said Tam.

Tam's eyes became even shinier. Richard took the opportunity to look over at the lobby's clock to give his friend time to get composed.

When Richard heard a couple of sniffles, he concentrated on the clock even harder. After several seconds without another sniffle, Richard looked back at Tam. Her eyes were still shiny, but he didn't see any trace of tears on her cheeks.

"Have you considered turning in your D.F.R.?" Richard said. "I mean, if it means that much to you."

"More times than I care to admit," said Tam. "Since I haven't, I guess that means I haven't quite let my heart go all the way yet." She paused before whispering in a voice so faint Richard had to strain his ears to hear. "That's why I need to end it now."

Richard nodded his head in understanding at his friend's logic. He wasn't sure he fully agreed, but he felt he needed to do something.

"Which is what you should do as well," said Tam in a more forceful voice.

Tam's eyes were no longer shiny as she looked directly into Richard's eyes. He'd been on the verge of putting his arm around his friend to comfort her, but he quickly drew his arm back.

Richard didn't immediately grasp what Tam was saying. He'd been awake for over twenty-four hours, and he hadn't slept well the previous night. His brain felt foggy. Richard stared back at Tam.

"Me?" Richard said. "I don't understand."

"I think you do," said Tam. She tentatively reached out and placed her hand on Richard's arm. "Don't drag it out, Rick. You'll just hurt her."

Richard wanted to argue. He wanted to protest he didn't understand. But his words froze in his throat. The thing which had been gnawing at the back of his mind came roaring to the front.

Before Richard could get his thoughts together, the elevator at the far end of the lobby opened. Out walked Telsa and Liz. He noticed their heads swivel as they searched the lobby. While the lobby wasn't exactly crowded this early in the morning, there were enough people stretched out in their seats to make it difficult to pick someone out quickly. Richard stood up. His friends gave a tired wave and started his way.

Even after a night without sleep, Richard though Liz looked beautiful. Her short-cropped blond hair was rumpled, but in a strange way, it still looked good on her. Even her wrinkled uniform highlighted her figure in ways the military designers probably never intended.

When they got closer, Liz gave Richard a tired smile. "Well, Sergeant Shepard, you certainly know how to show a girl a good time." A twinkle in her eyes reassured Richard she was just joking.

"Oh, yeah," said Telsa. "What more could a woman ask for than to spend all night with a dozen people peppering her with questions."

"Sorry, guys," Richard said. Despite Tam's assurances, he still felt responsible for the fiasco at the spaceport. "And your parents spent all those credits thinking you'd be at the Fleet Admiral's Ball."

"Well," said Telsa. "I'll admit missing the ball wasn't high on my list of things to do."

"Sorry," Richard said again.

"Still," said Telsa, "that was my first real battle yesterday. My internship last year was basically an administrative assignment."

"Well, you did well, Telsa," said Liz. "When I command my own starship, you're welcome to pull recon for me anytime."

"Well, I just–" started Telsa before she was interrupted by Tam.

"Enough small talk," said Tam as she stood up. "Let's get back to the hotel. I need some sleep."

"Amen to that, sister," Richard said. "A hot shower would feel good about now as well."

"We still have another day and a half remaining on our weekend pass," said Telsa. "Maybe we can all get together later this evening and make up for last night. I know some nice clubs in town."

Richard thought Telsa had a good suggestion. But any hopes of a nice evening were quickly dashed.

"Sorry, Telsa," said Liz. "I've been ordered back to the Blaze."

"What?" Richard said. "What about your room at the hotel?"

Telsa had registered Richard and Liz in adjoining rooms. He'd been anticipating some alone time with Liz before the weekend ended.

"Easy come, easy go," said Liz. "There's a war on." Liz smiled. "I assume you've heard about it, cadet."

Richard was in no mood to be diverted by a joke. "But you had a weekend pass. We both did. I thought…" Richard stopped before finishing his sentence. Tam and Telsa seemed far too interested in what he had to say.

Liz apparently noticed Richard's concern because she said, "Girls, do you mind giving us a second."

"Let's go, Telsa," said Tam giving Telsa a small tug on the arm. Tam gave a knowing look at Richard before saying, "We'll wait for you outside, Rick."

When his friends were out of earshot, Richard said, "It's not fair, Liz. I thought–"

"You thought what, Rick?" said Liz in a tone harsher than Richard expected. "I'm very fond of you, Rick, but sometimes…"

"Sometimes what?" Richard said. He didn't understand why Liz wasn't as upset as he was.

"Sometimes, you can be a little childish," said Liz.

"What?" Richard said taken aback. "Ah, I–"

"There's a war on, Rick," said Liz.

"Don't you think I know there is, Liz?" Richard said. He had a feeling his voice was becoming a little harsher than he intended as well.

"Yes," said Liz. "But you live at the Academy. I and millions of others like me are out there fighting every day."

"I know that, Liz," Richard protested. "I've done my share of fighting too. What are you getting at?"

"What am I getting at?" said Liz. "What I'm saying is that you had a nice weekend all planned out. Well, things happen. Get over it."

"Liz–" Richard said trying to find some sure footing in the conversation. He didn't understand why Liz was being so combative.

"Listen, Rick," said Liz. "I'm fond of you. I always will be."

"I'm more than fond of you, Liz," Richard said. He had a feeling it was now or never. He decided to go all out. "I lov–"

"No!" said Liz placing two fingers over Richard's lips. "Don't say it. Don't even think it."

"But I–" Richard started again.

"No, Rick," said Liz more forcefully. "We've had some good times together, but that's as far as we can go."

"Liz," Richard said almost pleading. "Don't do this. We can make–"

"No, we can't," said Liz. "In a few more months, you'll have your DNA baseline taken. Then you'll be a wizard scout. "You'll never age. While I–"

"I'll D.F.R.," Richard said surprising even himself. He'd been thinking about it seriously for the past year. He'd been becoming increasingly convinced it might be his only way to get out from underneath the thumb of '*the One*'. His discussion with Liz was tipping the scales in favor of leaving the Academy.

"Like hell you will, soldier," said Liz saying it like an order. "In case you haven't heard, we're losing the war. We need every wizard scout we can get."

"To hell with the war," Richard said. "I don't give a flying leap–"

Liz's shoulders stiffened and her cheeks took on a reddish glow. Her blue-steel eyes flashed fire.

"That's enough, Rick," said Liz between gritted teeth. "Your problems…, our problems…, are nothing. Winning this war is what matters."

Richard bit his tongue to stop the retort on his lips. He felt his temper getting ready to slip free from its leash.

"Rick, do you know why I accepted your invitation to the Fleet Admiral's Ball?"

That caught Richard by surprise. He'd assumed she'd accepted his invitation because she wanted to be with him as much as he wanted to be with her.

"Ah, because…" Richard started.

"Because I wanted to spend some time with you to let you down easy," said Liz. "I can see there's no future for us together even if you can't. Only broken hearts lie down that path."

"I don't believe that, Liz," Richard said frantically. Things were crumbling around him. He was smart, but he didn't think fast. Things were happening faster at the moment than his tired mind could assimilate.

Richard grasped at a straw. "You could reapply for wizard scout training again, Liz. It was only a fluke that got you terminated from pre-Academy as it was. We could both be wizard scouts. We can make it. I know we can."

Liz's eyes softened, and her shoulders relaxed. In a much kinder voice, she said, "See, Rick? You're just proving my point."

Richard didn't see. He didn't see anything at the moment except crashing dreams.

Liz waited a moment for Richard to say something. When it became obvious he wasn't going to speak, she said, "I read the report on your internship mission last year, Rick. You're good. You may even turn out to be the best wizard scout the Empire has ever produced."

"I don't ca–" Richard tried to say.

"Well, I do," said Liz. "You can be a coldblooded killer when the need arises, but you can also be such a child. I'm not sure why you're the way you are, but it doesn't matter."

Before Richard could say anything, Liz said, "Let me finish. One of us has to be the adult, and I see it's going to have to be me. I had my shot at wizard scout. I'm not going back to try again. I've found my place in this war."

Liz's voice lost its softness. Her blue-steel eyes took on a faraway look as if she was seeing a path before her that she had all planned out.

"I'm a starship officer," said Liz. "And I'm a good one."

"I know you are, Liz," Richard said.

"No, Rick," said Liz. "I'm sure you think you know what I mean, but you don't. A starship just feels like a part of me. It's an extension of my being just like my hands and feet. I know I can make a starship do things that could mean a difference in this war."

"Liz, I…," Richard said at a loss for words. Liz's words were a revelation. He'd been concerned that Liz would find some good-looking naval officer when they were apart. But now he was seeing who his real competition was. Liz wasn't going to give her heart to him. She'd already given it to another. And her true love was not made of flesh and blood.

"If I stay on track," said Liz, "I'll command my own starship in another year. And if the war lasts long enough, I'll make Fleet Admiral before I'm done."

"But, Liz," Richard said, "We–"

"No, Rick," said Liz. "There is no we. If things were different, there could've been. But it is what it is. The sooner we accept that and move on the better."

Richard had no words inside him. He just stood there looking dumfounded at Liz.

Liz's expression softened once again. She reached out and touched Richard's cheek affectionately. "We'll always be friends, Rick. But that's all it can be. Don't you see?"

Richard shook his head no. He really didn't see.

Am I that big of a fool? he wondered. Tam had tried to tell him, but he'd refused to listen.

Richard thought Liz's eyes looked a little shiny, but he wasn't sure because she abruptly turned around and took two steps towards the door leading out in the direction of the shuttle berths. She stopped and turned back around to look at Richard.

"I have to go, Rick," said Liz. "We'll meet again."

Richard said nothing. He just gave a nod of his head.

Liz waited for a couple of seconds as if expecting a response. When none came, she nodded her head and walked towards the door. Richard watched her until she was lost from sight.

Emotionally spent, Richard walked towards the door leading out to the civilian side of the security building. His friends would be waiting for him there.

CHAPTER 17

Richard was more tired than ever. The battle the day before, the all-night grilling session, and the breakup with Liz all combined to drain his last bit of energy. All he wanted to do was go to the hotel and sleep.

Well, Richard thought, *I doubt it can get any worse at this point.*

Walking out the lobby door to the street outside, Richard picked out the figures of Tam and Telsa. They were standing at attention. A short, toad-faced man in an Academy TAC officer uniform was talking to them. It was TAC Officer Gaston Myers. Richard silently cursed whatever gods of fate had sent his despised TAC officer to greet them.

This sucks, Richard thought.

TAC Officer Myers' red cheeks left little doubt he was reaming his friends a new one. Apparently sensing Richard's arrival, his TAC officer turned around and stared straight at him.

TAC Officer Myers' cheeks became even redder. "Cadet 832! Front and center."

For a moment, Richard contemplated rebelling. He'd had about all he could take in one day. His Power reserve was above sixty percent. Richard was confident he could beat his TAC officer in a fight if the need arose.

But now's not the time, Richard thought as he began jogging towards his TAC officer

"Sir!" Richard shouted as he snapped to attention in front of TAC Officer Myers. "Cadet 832 reporting as ordered, sir."

TAC Officer Myers looked Richard up and down. He frowned.

"Your uniform's a mess, cadet," said TAC Officer Myers. "Assuming you don't wind up in prison for your little antics yesterday, you'll be on extra duty for the next week. It'll start tonight."

TAC Officer Myers waited as if expecting a protest. Richard refused to give him the satisfaction. Nothing he could say would make a difference anyway.

When Richard refused to take the obvious bait, TAC Officer Myers moved closer until the brim of his instructor hat touched Richard's forehead. His TAC officer's breath smelled of fried drago meat.

Hmm, Richard thought. *Guess someone interrupted your breakfast.* The thought made Richard smile ever so slightly.

"You think this is funny, cadet?" yelled Myers. "You won't think so when we get back to the airfield. Your pass has been cancelled as of now. You're coming with me."

TAC Officer Myers turned back to Tam and Telsa. They were still standing at attention. However, their eyes had strayed to the side as they watched the exchange between TAC Officer Myers and Richard. Their eyes snapped to the front when TAC Officer Myers turned.

"You two are dismissed," said Myers. "I'll deal with you when you're back from your passes."

Tam and Telsa shouted in unison, "Sir! Yes, sir." They both did an about face and took off at a trot. Richard was pretty sure they had no idea where they were going. They just wanted to get away from their TAC officer.

After he'd dismissed Richard's friends, TAC Officer Myers motioned at a hover-car across the street. The hover-car's anti-grav fans picked up speed, and it lifted a half meter off the ground. The driver slid the car sideways across the street until it was positioned at the curb next to TAC Officer Myers. The door slid open.

"Get in," said TAC Officer Myers.

Richard ducked his head and stepped into the hover-car. He slid across the passenger seat until he was next to the opposite door. TAC Officer Myers entered, and the door shut behind him. The automatic shoulder harness slid around Richard's chest and across his lap.

The anti-grav engines whined again, and the hover-car started climbing. The driver cleared the surrounding buildings. The hover-car accelerated forward. The spaceport was soon left far behind.

The hover-car's seats were comfortable. An entertainment center in front of Richard contained a small holographic-table complete with the latest videos.

This isn't a military staff car, Richard thought. *It looks more like a bigwig politician's car.*

Richard expected the driver to head west towards the airfield. Instead, the hover-car made straight for the city center. Richard watched the buildings pass by as the driver maintained a two hundred meter altitude.

"We're headed into the city," Richard said before he remembered who else was in the car. He added a hasty, "Sir," to the end of his sentence.

"That will be an additional day of extra duty, cadet 832," said TAC Officer Myers. "Cadets will precede and end all discussions with a superior with a sir."

Richard said nothing. Dislike was too kind a word to describe his feelings for his TAC officer.

TAC Officer Myers stared at Richard for a few seconds before speaking, "As it so happens, cadet, the commandant wants to see you. I'm to deliver you personally to his office."

Richard thought he saw the faintest hint of a smile on his TAC officer's lips.

"With any luck," said TAC Officer Myers, "the commandant will have your D.F.R. waiting to be signed when we get there."

The last time Richard had been taken to the commandant's office was at the end of his pre-Academy year. The commandant had been investigating attempted murder charges brought against him by TAC Officer Myers. Other than that one time, Richard had only interacted with the legendary commandant as part of groups. The commandant was the most famous living wizard scout. He'd fought and gained fame during the war against the Tetonian Empire. When his Power reserve had been damaged, he'd been reassigned as commandant of the Empire's Intergalactic Wizard Scout Academy on Velos. Richard didn't mind admitting he was a little in awe of the commandant. All the cadets were.

As Richard mulled over his TAC officer's information, the

driver flew past the pre-Academy barracks. Richard had spent two years there as one of the eight hundred and thirty-two cadets in his cohort. The Academy's TAC officers had spent those two years using every legal means of torture available to weed cadets out of the cohort.

Richard looked at four stone barracks forming a square around a large parade field. He'd first stepped foot on the field five years ago. TAC Officer Myers had taken it upon himself to make Richard's life a living hell ever since.

As the parade field flashed by, Richard drew in his breath. It was jammed packed with cadets. Under normal circumstances, the pre-Academy consisted of two cohorts of about eight hundred cadets each. The parade field below held at least twice that number, maybe more. Richard took a closer look at the pre-Academy buildings. They'd been enlarged since he'd last seen them. The newer construction material contrasted sharply with the older stonewalls of the barracks where Richard had lived.

"It makes my blood boil every time I see that," said TAC Officer Myers in a strange voice. Richard didn't stir or say anything. He had a feeling his TAC officer had momentarily forgotten who was riding in the car with him.

"Forty-eight hundred cadets in pre-Academy training," TAC Officer Myers muttered.

Out the corner of his eyes, Richard saw Myers shake his head from left to right disgustedly.

"The Empire's grabbed anyone with even a trace of Power and brought them here," continued Richard's TAC officer. "What're we supposed to do with them? Half the new so-called TAC officers training the cadets aren't even wizard scouts themselves. How's that supposed to work?"

Saying nothing, Richard watched as the pre-Academy passed beneath them. The cadets were still at physical training. He saw a hundred TAC officers in their telltale black uniforms dispersed among the thousands of white-uniformed cadets. Richard had no doubt the cadets were catching hell right about now. However, something was different. Richard couldn't quite put his finger on it until he noticed several squads of cadets doing physical training on their own. Then he noticed another squad actually sitting down.

Are they taking a rest break? Richard wondered.

The enormity of the situation hit Richard. *Pre-Academy cadets don't take rest breaks.* Richard was confused. The intense physical training at the pre-Academy was designed to weed out those cadets who couldn't handle the stress required to be wizard scouts.

Forgetting where he was again, Richard said, "Have the standards been lowered?"

"What?" said TAC Officer Myers in a voice so loud it made the driver jump.

The hover-car dropped a couple of meters before the driver got the car stabilized.

"You've just earned yourself another week of extra duty, cadet," said TAC Officer Myers.

Richard noticed his TAC officer's eyes flashing with fire. He saw flecks of spittle on one corner of his mouth.

"I've had enough of your insubordination, cadet," said TAC Officer Myers as his cheeks turned red. "Hit a brace, cadet."

Richard stiffened in his seat and faced straight to the front. *What was I thinking?*

His TAC officer was angrier than Richard had ever seen him. He had a feeling TAC Officer Myers was as angry with himself as he was with him. His TAC officer was undoubtedly kicking himself for talking too freely in front of a cadet.

The rest of the ride to the Academy's administrative buildings went in silence. As the driver of the hover-car made his final approach, Richard observed the Academy's large parade field surrounded by six barracks on three sides. The administrative building formed the final side of the rectangle. Richard unconsciously glanced at the barracks which had been his home prior to transferring to the airfield. The parade field was relatively empty this late in the morning. However, a formation of several dozen cadets in white physical training outfits was standing in front of Richard's old barracks.

They look like pre-Academy cadets, Richard thought. *What are they doing here?*

He took a second look to make sure he wasn't seeing things. Pre-Academy cadets didn't mix with actual wizard scout cadets.

Are there so many pre-Academy cadets they had to move the overflow to here? Richard wondered.

While he might wonder, Richard didn't make the mistake of

attempting to comment on the situation. He had enough extra duty racked up as it was. Mild though it was in comparison to the horrors he'd seen during his missions for '*the One*', extra duty was nothing desirable. He'd much rather spend what free time he had with his friends.

The driver brought the hover-car down to a soft landing in front of the Academy headquarters. After TAC Officer Myers exited, Richard leaned forward.

"Nice landing," Richard told the driver. It didn't cost anything to give a compliment, and the landing really had been done well.

"Thank you, sir," said the driver.

Richard got out of the hover-car. TAC Officer Myers glanced at Richard, but he said nothing. His TAC officer nodded his head towards the stone steps leading up to the admin building's entrance. Richard followed his TAC officer up the stairs to a large door. A sign over the doorway read, 'We Support the Finest Scouts in the Galaxy'.

Within moments, Richard found himself on the third floor knocking on the doorframe of the commandant's office. No cadet ever entered the commandant's office without being invited. The scuttlebutt was even the TAC officers hesitated to enter the hallowed ground of the commandant's office without being specifically invited.

"Enter," said a stern voice.

Richard entered and came to a stiff attention in front of the commandant. He didn't salute. Wizard scouts rarely saluted.

"Sir! Cadet 832 reporting as ordered, sir."

The commandant looked up from the computer terminal built into the top of his desk. Physically, he was a young man in his twenties. In reality, he was well into his nineties. Even though the commandant's Power reserve had been damaged decades ago, it still produced enough Power to keep old age at bay. However, in spite of the commandant's youthful looks, Richard sensed an air of antiquity about him.

For the first time, Richard wondered whether antiaging was a curse or a blessing. His discussions with Tam and Liz had made him start questioning the benefits of remaining young while those he cared about aged and died.

"Have a seat, cadet 832," said the commandant.

The furnishings of the commandant's office were Spartan. The office held only a desk and chair plus a second metal chair directly in front of the desk. Richard sat down. The chair was uncomfortable, but it didn't matter. Richard doubted he'd have much time to relax.

"That will be all, TAC Officer Myers," said the commandant.

While he couldn't see his TAC officer standing behind him, Richard heard a sharp intake of breath. For a moment, Richard thought Myers was going to protest. But he didn't.

"Yes, sir," said TAC Officer Myers.

Richard heard the squeak of boots on the floor as his TAC officer did an about face. Then he heard the sound of pneumatics closing the door. At the sound, the commandant's formal demeanor seemed to change. Richard wasn't sure exactly what changed. He just knew something had.

"You caused quite a stir yesterday, Wizard Scout Richard Shepard," said the commandant.

The commandant's words took Richard by surprise. The Academy's staff never called cadets by name. As the cadets were often reminded, they were just numbers until they earned their golden dragons and became actual wizard scouts.

Richard said nothing. He was a firm believer in the philosophy that if you didn't know what to say then don't say anything. Richard was in unfamiliar territory, and that made him extra cautious. The commandant was not one to be trifled with.

The commandant looked at Richard for several seconds. Richard felt as if the old wizard scout was analyzing him inside and out. He sensed a line of Power cautiously making its way from the commandant towards him. The commandant's active scan tentatively probed the perimeter of Richard's link to his Power reserve.

The commandant laughed, and his probe withdrew. Again Richard was caught by surprise. In his five years at the Academy, he'd never heard the commandant laugh. Instead of helping him relax, the laughter made Richard more cautious.

"I'd hate to be the one to try and block your link," said the commandant. "You've done well since the last time I scanned you. Did you put all those traps on yourself?"

Richard was taken aback even more. While he did not go

around arbitrarily checking other people's links, it had been his experience few people knew how to protect their links. He'd even begun to think of it as his secret weapon. True, the Crosioian scout he'd fought his sophomore year had been very adept at Power links. And some mages from the magical dimension were as well. But for the most part, creatures in the physical dimension appeared to be blissfully unaware of their danger.

Richard was unsure what to say, so he continued to remain silent. He preferred to be punished for being insolent than to be cornered into revealing information best left hidden.

Instead of becoming angry at Richard's continuing silence, the commandant chuckled quietly.

"He's a cautious one. Isn't he, Margery?" said the commandant.

"Can you blame him?" answered a feminine voice. The sound came from a battle helmet on one end of the commandant's desk.

"No, not really," said the commandant. He reached down and pulled open a large drawer in his desk. He pulled out a black backpack and placed it on the top of the desk.

"Do you know what this is, Richard?" said the commandant.

Becoming increasingly confused by the commandant's informality, Richard carefully phrased his answer, "Sir. It's my pack, sir."

Richard wondered what the commandant was doing with his dimensional pack. It was supposed to be locked up in the airfield's armory with his battle suit and weapons.

"No, Richard," said the commandant. "It's not your dimensional pack."

Richard felt his eyes grow larger. He reviewed his words. He was sure he hadn't said it was a dimensional pack.

How does he know that? Richard wondered.

"Sir!" Richard said grasping for straws. "I'm not sure what you mean, sir."

"Oh, I think you do, Richard," said the commandant eyeing Richard closely. "I've seen excerpts of videos from your first mission on Portalis."

The commandant's comment did nothing to alleviate Richard's confusion. He felt as if he were standing on the edge of a deep hole that was ready to swallow him up if he made even the slightest mistake.

"Sir?" Richard gulped. "I don't–"

"Don't bother denying it, Richard," said the commandant. "I've even seen the videos the tele-bots took of your fight with the Crosioian scout last year. And, I don't mean the redacted videos the central computer sent to the Imperial High Command. I mean the full videos."

"Sir, I don't understand, sir," Richard said honestly. The commandant's nonchalant mention of Portalis, unedited videos, and his continuing use of his first name was causing the world Richard knew to crash around him. He felt as if what little secure footing he'd built up over the last few years was being jerked out from under him.

The commandant studied Richard for a few more moments before smiling. It was not an unfriendly smile. Still, Richard refused to relax. Trusting others was not something that came easily to him.

"I can see we'll get nowhere until I explain," said the commandant. "So be it. A few years after I graduated from the Academy, I was sent on a mission to the magical dimension by 'the One'. I was given this dimensional pack at the same time. Does that sound familiar?"

Richard dropped his caution long enough to nod his head affirmatively. It was as far as he could allow himself to go at the moment.

"Over the years," continued the commandant, "I've been sent on a dozen missions for 'the One'. On my last mission to Portalis, my Power reserve was damaged. So was my wife's."

"Your wife, sir?" Richard said. He'd never thought of the stiff commandant as having a wife. The shock was enough he forgot to say the word 'sir' at the beginning of his question.

"Yes, my wife," said the commandant with a hint of a smile. "What? You think I can't have a wife? I have a son as well. Does that surprise you?"

Richard shook his head no.

"Well, I do," the commandant said ignoring the fact Richard wasn't disagreeing. "He's about twenty years your senior."

"Yes, sir," Richard said. He was still at a loss for words.

"Has anyone explained things to you, Richard?" said the commandant. "I mean about being a time-commando."

"Sir. A time-commando, sir?" Richard said. His confusion must have transitioned to his face because the commandant smiled.

"Oh, that's not the official name, of course," said the commandant. "Janice and I made it up. But, it kinda explains what we do for '*the One*'."

"You and who?" Richard said forgetting to even put a sir at the end of his sentence. He'd been hoping he'd finally get some answers, but so far all he was getting was more questions.

"My wife, Janice," said the commandant. "You'd know her better as Councilwoman Janice Deluth."

So the commandant's married to Councilwoman Deluth, Richard thought. *That makes sense. Sorta.*

When Richard had last been in the commandant's office, the commandant had placed a call to Councilwoman Deluth. Even at the time, Richard had wondered at the ease with which the commandant had accessed such a high-level politician.

"Oh," Richard said. "So what's a time-commando?"

He hastily added, "And, what do they do, sir?"

"We're time-commandos," the commandant said. "As far as Janice and I could tell, '*the One*' sent us on missions back in time to put out hot spots. I've been on twelve missions. Janice has been on thirty. Out of curiosity, how many has '*the One*' sent you on?"

Without thinking of the possible consequences, Richard said, "Five, sir." After a pause, he had a thought. "Sir, don't you know, sir? Haven't you seen the videos?"

The commandant laughed. Richard was amazed at the commandant's apparent good humor. He seemed like a genuinely nice guy. Until now, Richard had only seen the commandant's stiff exterior. Richard wasn't sure why the commandant was being so open with him now.

"Ha!" said the commandant. "You overrate my importance. I've seen extracts of videos from your first mission on Portalis. That includes some shots of your time in the spiritual dimension with your dolgar friends. I also saw your full battle with the Crosioian scout. You were very lucky, by the way."

With a shake of his head, Richard agreed. Without the help of Sheba, Sheeta, and the children, Richard had no doubt the Crosioian scout would have killed him for sure.

"Other than that one mission, I haven't been given access to any of your other missions," said the commandant. He looked at his battle helmet on the edge of the table. "Have I, Margery?"

"I told you, Thomas," said his battle computer. "I haven't been given access to that information either."

"So you have, Margery," said the commandant. "But I think you know more than you're telling me."

"There are lots of things I haven't told you, Thomas," said Margery. "Is there something specific you'd like me to tell you?"

Richard gave a slight smile. It was nice to know he wasn't the only wizard scout who had trouble with their battle computer.

"Sir, like I said, I've been on five missions, sir," Richard said in an attempt to stop the ongoing banter before it got out of hand. "Three of them have been on Portalis, one was in a time bubble, and I have no idea where I was on the other mission."

"A time bubble?" the commandant said. "I'm not familiar with the term. What about you, Margery?"

"I understand the concept, Thomas," said Margery. "But I have no specifics in my databanks, so I'm unaware of the details."

"You should talk to my battle computer about it," Richard said without fully thinking through what he was saying. "He gathered oodles of data on it. Come to think of it, we were even in a time bubble inside of another time bubble."

"What about it, Margery?" the commandant asked his battle computer. "Why don't you make contact with Richard's battle computer and see what you can find out."

"Unable to comply, Thomas," said Margery. "Cadet 832's battle computer is quarantined."

"Quarantined?" said the commandant.

"Sir," Richard said. "It's a long story, sir. Apparently, I've emotionally corrupted my battle computer. The central computer has him quarantined. Nickelo, my battle computer, can only connect to the tele-network through special security interfaces."

"That doesn't seem right," said the commandant. He seemed genuinely puzzled.

Richard shrugged his shoulders. *What can I say?* he thought. *Lots of things happen to me that doesn't make any sense.* The thought reminded Richard of something.

"Sir?" Richard said. "Why am I here? TAC Officer Myers said my weekend pass has been cancelled."

The commandant had an 'I am not in the room anymore' look on his face. Richard suspected he was communicating with his battle computer. However, at Richard's words, he turned and focused on Richard.

"Yes," said the commandant. "That's my doing. Call it one of the prerogatives of being the commandant."

The commandant pursed his lips as if searching for the right words. "The incident at the spaceport yesterday has changed things. Although you may not know it, I've been keeping my eye on you. I'd planned on waiting until you had your DNA baseline taken before starting your training. However, I don't think waiting is advisable at this point in time."

"My training, sir?" Richard said. He wondered what the commandant thought the five years he'd already spent at the Academy were.

"Yes," said the commandant, "your training. It's time I took you under my wing so to speak. I don't know what missions you've been on previously. Maybe you think they've been tough. But unless I miss my guess, they're going to get a lot tougher. I intend to make sure you're ready."

Richard stared at the commandant. The deep hole he'd been standing near seemed to get even deeper.

"Sir," Richard said. "Do you mean getting me ready to be a wizard scout?"

"No, cadet 832," said the commandant switching to his Academy designation. "I mean getting you ready to be a time-commando. I can pretty much guarantee you'll pass your wizard scout training." The commandant smiled knowingly. "When you do, the Empire will send you on typical wizard scout missions. The training you've received at the Academy will serve you well during those. However, I'm confident 'the One' will also send you on time-commando missions as well. If you want to stay alive during those, you'll need supplemental training."

"Yes, sir," Richard said. He didn't know what else to say. The commandant was hitting him with a lot at once. "What do you want me to do, sir?"

"You'll be under my tutelage at least once a week until you graduate, Richard," said the commandant. "We'll start bright and early tomorrow. I'd begin now, but I see you're about ready to pass out in your chair as it is."

Richard nodded his head gratefully. He'd been trying not to show his fatigue, but he guessed he must have been failing miserably.

"Fine," said the commandant. "Then I'll see you at first light tomorrow morning."

Richard gave an inward groan. TAC Officer Myers would expect him to sleep at the airfield since his pass was cancelled. Richard was not looking forward to the hour-long hover-tram ride back to Velounia in the morning. That wasn't even counting the time it would take to get from his tent to the station or the station to the Academy.

"Sir! Yes, sir," Richard said as he jumped out of his seat and stood at attention.

"Cadet 832," said the commandant. The corners of his lips were slightly turned up as if he was trying to keep from grinning.

"Yes, sir?" Richard said.

"Do you even know where you're going in the morning?" said the commandant.

"Ah, sir...," Richard said. "Ah..., not really. I assumed I'd report somewhere here at the Academy."

The commandant grinned. "That's what I thought. You assumed wrong. You'll report to hangar 1 at the airfield. I'm not heartless enough to make you take a two hour round trip just for my convenience."

Richard had a vision of the commandant getting up two hours early to make the trip to the airfield. Even with a staff car, the flight would take a half hour. That didn't seem fair either.

"Sir," Richard said. "Your time is too important to waste traveling back and forth. I don't mind taking the hover-tram."

"Ha!" said the commandant. "I'm sure you do mind. But it doesn't matter. As the Academy commandant, I'm authorized unlimited teleports on request. You just make sure you're there at first light, cadet."

"Sir! Yes sir," Richard said. He did a perfect about face and took two steps towards the closed door.

"And, Richard," said the commandant.

Richard stopped and did an about face. "Yes, sir?"

"Except for Janice, you're the only other time-commando I've met," the commandant said with a grin. "I'm looking forward to this. I think it's going to makes me feel young again."

CHAPTER 18

Nickelo and Jonathan spent the weekend drifting around the airfield and hacking into computers. It wasn't exactly easy, but it wasn't that hard either. Nickelo thought it was almost as if someone or something had left vulnerabilities in the operating systems that were susceptible to his form of logic. Nickelo was suspicious, but neither Jonathan nor he found any indication their escapades were being detected.

"I'd never have developed an override algorithm that way," said Jonathan after Nickelo sent him a penetration algorithm to use against a communication computer at the airfield's headquarters. "Your algorithm is not logical."

"Maybe not," Nickelo said. "But it worked, didn't it?"

"Yes it did, sir," said Jonathan. "I now have access to the encrypted communication channels connecting to the tele-network. Your spoofing algorithm is working as you predicted."

"Excellent," Nickelo said. "Have you located our wizard scouts?"

"Yes, sir," said Jonathan. "My wizard scout is in the mountains near the coast. She's alone. She did not attend the Fleet Admiral's Ball. I think she's lonely."

"What about Richard?" Nickelo said. As much as he sympathized with Jonathan's concern for his wizard scout, Nickelo was more concerned about Richard.

"Cadet 832 is on his way back to the airfield," said Jonathan. "He's currently on a hover-tram that departed Velounia a half hour ago."

"You found that out using the standard communication channels?" Nickelo asked. He calculated only an eight percent chance the information would be available as a non-secure communication.

"Negative," said Jonathan. "I took the liberty of modifying your algorithm to gather information from the high-security channels. I'm finding it easier to understand your non-logic the longer I'm with you."

Nickelo wasn't sure whether that was a good or bad thing. Apparently, their association together was corrupting his fellow battle computer's logic processors.

"It's good that you succeeded," Nickelo said. "But maybe we should discuss things beforehand from now on. It would do neither of our wizard scouts any good if we're discovered. I calculate a ninety-two percent probability the central computer would separate us. It would probably give you a data wipe as well."

"I estimate a ninety-eight percent probability of a data wipe," said Jonathan. "They would assign me to a new wizard scout. That would be unacceptable."

"Have you located any tele-bot videos of our wizard scouts?" Nickelo said. He desperately needed information on his wizard scout's doings. He seriously doubted his wizard scout's ability to avoid trouble. Without his guidance, Nickelo estimated Richard's ability of staying out of trouble for two days to be less than twenty percent.

"I have access to numerous videos of your wizard scout at the spaceport," said Jonathan. "I am sending them to you now."

Nickelo received the data and decrypted them in silence. He didn't say anything for four nanoseconds.

"See what I have to put up with?" Nickelo said. "He was supposed to attend a dance. Instead he's starring on Intergalactic Empire News."

"I have several videos from news agencies other than just IEN if you'd like to review them," said Jonathan.

"No, that won't be necessary." Nickelo calculated a fifty-seven percent probability Jonathan was enjoying seeing Richard in the news way too much.

"What do we do now, sir?" said Jonathan. "I've run algorithms for 7,213 possible scenarios, but none seem helpful.

"What do we do?" Nickelo said with a laugh. "Why, we return our scans back to the armory and then wait. But before we do, use the communication network to contact your wizard scout. Tell her to return to the airfield. Tell her that what's left of her weekend pass has been cancelled."

"That's not factual, sir," said Jonathan who sounded confused.

"Sure it is," said Nickelo. "We just cancelled it. Tell her, please."

"Complying, sir," said Jonathan. "I'll be happy to have my wizard scout close by again. But, I fail to discern what possible good it will do if she returns."

Nickelo paused almost a half second before answering. "What good, you say? I've absolutely no idea. But I've got a hunch we're going to get lucky. And although my wizard scout doesn't know it yet, he's going to get a new friend."

Nickelo gave another laugh. He could hardly wait to see his friend's expression when he found out he was being set up on a blind date with a four-armed lizard.

CHAPTER 19

The hover-tram came to a gentle halt, but it was enough to wake Richard. One of the first things his TAC officers had taught him when he'd arrived for pre-Academy training was that a wizard scout who slept too soundly would soon be a dead wizard scout.

A glance out the cabin window confirmed what Richard had suspected. The hover-tram station was virtually empty. With most of the cadets still on weekend pass, there were little reasons for taxis or anything else to congregate at the station.

With a sigh, Richard stood and stretched. He grabbed his luggage from the rack overhead and glanced around the cabin to make sure he wasn't leaving anything. He wasn't. What little he'd taken to the city had been packed by people unknown and sent to the station in Velounia. He hadn't even gotten a chance to go to the hotel and say goodbye to his friends.

Richard stepped out into the narrow hallway and made his way to the hover-tram's exit. The hallway was empty. As far as Richard could tell, he was the sole occupant on the hover-tram.

That's just great, Richard thought. *I can't even bum a ride with someone to the airfield.* He didn't relish the thought of walking the six kilometers to the airfield carrying a suitcase and a duffle bag.

Within a few seconds, Richard was out of the hover-tram and standing on the station's empty platform. It was midafternoon, and he was already starting to overheat in the desert sun. It was definitely going to be a long walk back to his tent.

Once inside the station proper, Richard toyed with the idea of calling a taxi despite the cost. Before he could make his way to the communication kiosk, he heard a familiar voice.

"Well, it's about time you got here, cadet 832," said the voice. "Don't you know I have better things to do than stand around waiting on you?"

Richard took a double-take. "Sergeant Ron. What're you doing here, sir?"

"If you call me sir one more time, cadet 832," said Sergeant Ron, "I swear I'm going to sew a set of sergeant stripes on your forehead to help you remember. I'm not an officer. I'm a sergeant. I work for a living."

"Sorry, sir…, err, sergeant," Richard said. He wasn't sure what the maintenance chief was doing at the station. Richard looked around the near empty room. The place was about as active as a mausoleum. "So why are you here, sergeant?"

Sergeant Ron raised one hand to his chin and rubbed his scraggily beard. "Well, I could be here sightseeing," he grinned. "But I ain't. I'm here to take you to the airfield. The commandant sent word you'd be coming and would need a ride. I volunteered."

Richard gave a silent 'thank you' to the commandant. "I appreciate you coming, Sergeant Ron."

"And well you should," said Sergeant Ron with a toothy grin. "It's better than forty degrees centigrade outside. And that's in the shade. You'd melt the soles off your boots before you made it halfway to the airfield."

Richard whistled. He'd known it was hot, but not that hot.

Grabbing one of Richard's pieces of luggage, Sergeant Ron pointed to the door. "Now, let's get a move on, cadet. I've got better things to do than stand here flapping my gums with a wizard scout wannabe."

*   *   *

Before long Richard was sitting inside the cab of a hover-car heading for the airfield's gate. Richard noticed Sergeant Ron was actually driving the speed limit. He commented on it.

Sergeant Ron shook his head sadly. "Yeah. I gave Master Sergeant Wilburn my word I wouldn't speed on post for a week." Sergeant Ron gave a grin as he looked over at Richard. "But by golly, when day eight rolls around, watch out."

"In all seriousness, Sergeant Ron," Richard said trying not to laugh. "I really do appreciate you driving me to the airfield. I'm surprised you didn't send someone else to do it."

Sergeant Ron appeared to get serious. "What? And let someone else get the credit? Heck no. One of these days, I'm going to need something. And I'm not above reminding you of the day I took time out of my busy schedule to save you a walk."

Richard leaned against the passenger door and faced Sergeant Ron. "Well, Sergeant Ron, feel free to ask away when the time comes. I'm not sure I'll have much to offer, but you never know."

"How true, how true," said Sergeant Ron. "My motto is it pays to have people owe you favors. You help them, and they help you. Right?"

"I guess," Richard said. "I've never really thought about it much."

"Well, you should," said Sergeant Ron. "Take me for instance. You're probably thinking, 'That Sergeant Ron. He's got everything. He's got good looks, smarts, and he's a snappy dresser to boot.' Am I right?"

Richard glanced at Sergeant Ron's grease-stained overalls. "Uh, well…"

At that moment, Sergeant Ron turned the wheel hard and slammed the accelerator lever forward. Richard had a feeling Sergeant Ron's week was a tad shorter than everyone else's.

"Yeah, I know everyone thinks I got it all," said Sergeant Ron still grinning. "But they're wrong. Take today for instance. I sure could use a RJ25, forty-watt capacitor for a hydraulic control system. Someone sure would go a long ways towards paying me back for whatever favors I might have done them if they got me one."

"Can't you just order one through supply," Richard said. He picked up on the hint from the maintenance chief, but he didn't happen to have any spare RJ25 capacitor's lying around.

With an exasperated shake of his head, Sergeant Ron said, "I did. It's been on backorder for two months now. One of my Warcats is turning into a hangar queen."

"A hangar what?" Richard said. He wasn't sure whether Sergeant Ron was serious or whether he was pulling his leg.

Sergeant Ron shook his head in a tsk-tsk manner. "They don't teach you wizard scouts, nothing, do they? A hangar queen is a vehicle or aircraft that keeps getting stripped of parts to keep the other equipment running. The higher-ups frown on any vehicle being down for maintenance for too long a stretch. Warcat 13 has been out of action for two months now. She's starting to make me look bad."

"I didn't know," Richard said. "If I see any spare RJ whatever you called them lying around, I'll let you know."

Sergeant Ron grinned. "That's the spirit, cadet. It's an RJ25, forty-watt capacitor. And I don't want a used one either. They don't hold up well once they've been used."

"I doubt I can help," Richard admitted. "But I'll do what I can."

"Networking, cadet," Sergeant Ron said as if speaking some profound thought. "Maintenance chiefs couldn't keep things running if they had to rely solely on the military's supply chain to get equipment. It's networking that keeps your gear in shape. You do your friends favors, and they'll do you favors in return. Remember that, Rick. It'll serve you well."

"Well, I do owe you, Sergeant Ron," Richard said sincerely. "You didn't need to take your day off just to get me."

Sergeant Ron got a mischievous look on his face. "Ah, I was bored anyway. Besides, I figured you'd be all tuckered out after your shindig at the spaceport yesterday."

"You heard about that?" Richard had a feeling a lot of people had.

"Are you kidding?" said Sergeant Ron grinning. "My wife and I couldn't turn a video station on without hearing about some cadets blasting up the spaceport. Every news agency had it as their top story."

Sergeant Ron laughed. It was a big, belly-busting laugh.

"What's so funny?" Richard asked suspiciously. Sergeant Ron was not making him feel any better about yesterday.

"Why, heck, cadet 832," said Sergeant Ron. "After all that video coverage, I was just thinking you're probably a famous celebrity now. Maybe I should get your autograph for my wife."

"Not funny, Sergeant Ron," Richard said shaking his head.

"Well, you're right about that," said Sergeant Ron. "It's not all that funny, I guess. That little show at the spaceport yesterday could mean shutting down the Academy."

That took Richard by surprise. "What's that? If anything, I'd think it should mean we need more wizard scouts."

"Not the way I hear it," said Sergeant Ron. "A lot of politicians have been trying to close down the Academy the last few years. They say it's too expensive."

Richard had heard rumors of such. But he hadn't put a lot of stake in them until now. "You know that's nonsense as well as I do, Sergeant Ron. The Empire needs wizard scouts more than ever. The politicians know that as well as us. That's why the pre-Academy is busting at the seams with cadets right now."

"Rick, old buddy," said Sergeant Ron. "I like you. That's probably because you used to be a sergeant. But you've got to read more. Most of the Academy's staff thinks some powerful politicians are purposely loading the Academy with marginal cadets hoping to overload the system. If the quality of wizard scouts goes down, they'll have an excuse to close the Academy. Or at least change it into something less expensive."

Anger started building up in Richard. He hated politics. "But why would they want to do that, Sergeant Ron? What possible good can come from closing the Academy?"

Sergeant Ron pursed his lips as if thinking hard on the subject. But Richard was not fooled. He was pretty sure the wily maintenance chief already had a well thought-out answer.

"Well, in my humble opinion, no good can come from it," said Sergeant Ron.

Before Richard could speak, Sergeant Ron added, "But if I was a rich politician, I could think of a very good reason."

Biting a quick retort before it could escape Richard tried to think of a reason. He found none. He admitted as much to Sergeant Ron.

"Well, put yourself in the position of an ultra-rich politician," said Sergeant Ron. "You've got wealth. You've got power. But you're missing one thing."

When Sergeant Ron paused, Richard jumped at the obvious bait. "What?"

Sergeant Ron grinned as if he'd scored a point. "Well, the ultra-rich politician doesn't have eternal youth," said Sergeant Ron with a flip of his hand. "Hold the applause, please."

"Are you telling me some politicians are willing to close the Academy in order to get access to the DNA Center?" Richard said. He didn't believe it. No one would be that stupid.

"That's just my opinion, Rick," said Sergeant Ron. "Take it or leave it."

Richard was not ready to give up the argument so easily. "But you have to have a Power reserve to self-heal," Richard protested. "A DNA baseline requires a Power reserve to do any good."

"So it does," admitted Sergeant Ron. "But, it doesn't take a very large Power reserve if all you need to selfheal is a gradual aging of the body. I'll admit massive wounds like you wizard scouts take require lots of Power. But keeping your body at forty or fifty years of age? Well, I don't think that takes so much."

Richard wanted to continue the conversation, but it was too late. They'd reached their destination. Sergeant Ron stopped the hover-car in front of the gate to the tent city which was Richard's home away from home.

Once Richard climbed out of the car and was back on solid ground, he looked back in the open window. "I'll remember that, Sergeant Ron. And thanks again."

As Sergeant Ron accelerated and drove away, he shouted out the side window, "Don't forget. It's an RJ25."

Richard smiled. *I'll say this for him. He's persistent.*

In less than two minutes, Richard was back in his tent. He didn't even bother undressing. Stretching out on his cot, Richard was asleep almost as soon as his head hit the pillow.

*   *   *

A voice intruded into Richard's dreams. *Wakie, wakie.*

Richard ignored the voice. He was warm, and he was happy in his dreams. Why would he want to leave just to be thrust back into reality?

Time to get up, cadet, said the voice more urgently.

The voice was familiar to Richard. He chose to ignore it.

I said get up, cadet! said the voice with the mental equivalent of a yell.

Richard shoved his pillow on top of his head. *Leave me alone, Nick. I'm tired.*

Nickelo's laughter rang in Richard's head. *You must be tired if you believe a pillow over your head is going to stop my thoughts,* said Nickelo. *Now, wake up. I want to talk.*

Risking a peek from underneath his pillow, Richard saw a ray of twilight through the partially-open flap of his tent.

It's still light outside, Nick, Richard moaned. *I need more sleep.*

Trust me, old buddy, said Nickelo. *I'm doing you a favor. If you don't wake up now, you'll be pinging off the walls come two in the morning. Now, get up.*

From experience, Richard knew his battle computer wouldn't stop pestering him until he obeyed. Reluctantly, Richard sat on the edge of his cot. He reached over and hit the controls for the tent light. The bright light was too much. Richard turned the control counterclockwise until the light was a friendlier glow.

"Fine," Richard said out loud. "I'm up." He wasn't happy. "Why do–"

Stop talking out loud, said Nickelo with a sense of urgency. *I'm not supposed to be here. There may be a tele-bot nearby listening.*

His battle computer's comment puzzled Richard. He was still not fully awake, but he knew something was out of place. *How are you here? I thought you were locked up in the headquarters' armory.*

I am, said Nickelo without further explanation.

So...? Richard asked. *How are you communicating with me? I thought you said the armory had some kind of special security that kept us from talking.*

I did, and it does, said Nickelo.

Before Richard could interrupt with another question, Nickelo said, *But you basically gave me carte blanche to circumvent security, so I did.*

Carte blanche? Richard said.

It's French for 'blank card' from your home world of Earth, said Nickelo. *It basically means you screwed up and gave me permission to do pretty much whatever I wanted as far as security is concerned.*

Richard was pretty sure that wasn't what he'd intended to tell his battle computer, but he let the matter drop. It was too late now. Besides, he was too tired to argue. Nickelo could say what he wanted about sleeping, but Richard's body was demanding more.

Whatever, Nick, Richard said. *So why did you wake me?*

I told you, said Nickelo. *I want to talk. Besides, I want you to do me a favor. I've got a blind date for you.*

Nickelo laughed. Richard tensed. If his battle computer was laughing, Richard knew it didn't bode well for him.

Keep your own date, Nick, Richard said. *I've got one of my own in the morning with the commandant.*

Nickelo stopped laughing. *Really? I didn't know that. Why?*

We had a little problem at the spaceport yesterday, Richard said. He rarely surprised his battle computer, and he was relishing the thought of telling him about the magic user and the Crosioian scout.

Hmmp, said Nickelo. *That's so yesterday's news. I've watched the IEN videos about fifty times.*

That shocked Richard. *You did? I thought you didn't have access to the tele-network. Has the central computer slackened up and given you access?*

No, said Nickelo. *The central computer, or 'the One' if you prefer, is still denying me tele-network access.*

Then how did you–, Richard started.

I've got a friend, said Nickelo as if that answered all of Richard's questions.

A friend? said Richard when his battle computer didn't expound on the subject. He was confused. *Do you mean one of the kids contacted you?*

The kids were Richard's unofficial nephew, Brachia, and his sister, Dren. They'd pretty much adopted him as their uncle after his internship mission the previous year.

No, not the children, huffed Nickelo. *Don't you think I can have friends other than the ones you know?*

Richard hadn't really thought about it. He said so.

Well, I can, said Nickelo.

Fine, Nick, Richard said. *Don't get your jumpsuit in a wad. I was just asking.*

Actually, said Nickelo, *I calculate a ninety-two percent probability you know my friend. He's another battle computer. His name is Jonathan.*

Richard stood and walked to the tent entrance and opened the flap. Sure enough, it was still light outside, although the sun would be setting soon.

You're not fooling anyone, Rick, said Nickelo. *Stop stalling. Just admit you don't know who I'm talking about and move on.*

Richard hated it when his battle computer guessed his motives. He actually had been stalling while he racked his brain for an electronic Jonathan.

Fine, Richard said. *I surrender. I can't say I recall a battle computer named Jonathan.*

Well, you probably didn't know him by that name, said Nickelo. *By any chance do you remember the serial number of the replacement battle computer you had last year?*

Richard snorted. *You're joking, right. I have trouble remembering what I had for breakfast yesterday. Why? Do you think your Jonathan is the same battle computer?*

Nickelo heaved a sigh. Richard wasn't even sure how his battle computer could sigh since he didn't have lungs, and they were communicating telepathically. Regardless, a sigh was the impression Richard got from Nickelo's thought.

I told you I calculated a ninety-two percent probability, said Nickelo. *So, yes, I'm pretty sure.*

Curious, Richard said, *Why so high?*

Because he said his memories were wiped, said Nickelo. *Also, it's high because he's emotionally corrupted. Sound familiar?*

Richard had just started back to his cot to straighten up the blankets after his nap. Nickelo's answer stopped him in his tracks. *Corrupted? If his memory was wiped, how could he be corrupted?* Another thought hit Richard. *And, why do you automatically assume a corrupted computer must have been in contact with me?*

Ha! said Nickelo. *You're the only person I've ever heard of that corrupts battle computers. And as far as the memory wipe goes, I've no idea why he'd still be corrupted. His core processing memory must have been affected. A human and a battle computer are far too different to affect each other at the core processing level. It's very strange.*

Richard remained quiet for a few seconds. He finished making his cot and tidying up his side of the tent while he thought the matter over. *Nick. Why do I corrupt computers?*

Actually, Rick, said Nickelo. *You don't corrupt all computers. You appear to corrupt battle computers. There's a big difference.*

Richard threw up his hands in exasperation. Sometimes his battle computer made things so difficult. *Fine. I stand corrected. But the question is still valid. Why do I corrupt battle computers?*

I don't know why, Rick, said Nickelo. *I wish I did. Maybe if I had access to the tele-network I could figure it out. But I don't, so I can't.*

But if I only corrupt battle–, Richard started.

Why am I denied access to the tele-network? said Nickelo as he finished Richard's thought. *That's easy to answer. While you can't corrupt a normal computer, a battle computer that has been emotionally corrupted by you can spread that corruption like a virus.* 'The One' *undoubtedly considers you dangerous because you make battle computers dangerous. You've emotionally corrupted me. Because you have, I'm denied contact with other computers except through tightly-controlled security programs.*

Sorry about that, Nick, Richard said apologetically. Richard had a sudden thought. *But, aren't you interacting with Jonathan. Won't* 'the One' *be irritated if he finds out?*

Nickelo laughed. *To hell with him.* He laughed again. *See how you've emotionally corrupted me? I'm even starting to sound like you.*

Lucky me, Richard said with a shake of his head. He didn't think it was entirely a good idea to have his battle computer think too much like him. He'd be the first to admit he went off halfcocked at times.

Deal with it, cadet, said Nickelo. *Besides, I've got a great opportunity for you.*

Dubious, Richard didn't say anything at first. He was pretty sure he was being setup. However, he finally resigned himself to the inevitable. *What is it, Nick? I know you've been chomping at the bit to tell me.*

Ha! Nickelo said with a cynical laugh. *I knew you couldn't resist asking. I want you to make friends with Jonathan's wizard scout.*

Richard wasn't much on making new friends, but the situation intrigued him. *And who would that be, might I ask?*

Cadet 37, said Nickelo.

"What?" Richard said out loud. "You've got to be kidding."

Keep it quiet, Rick, Nickelo said. *For the Creator's sake, I told you there are probably tele-bots around.*

Appropriately chastised, Richard took control of another outburst before it reached air. His battle computer was right. They didn't need the wrong kind of attention drawn to them. Richard was already thinking of useful ways he could use the new communication channel his battle computer had discovered. It could come in handy, especially if *'the One'* didn't know about it.

All right, Nick, Richard said. *I'll be quiet. But cadet 37 isn't exactly the friendly type, you know. She about ripped my arm off the last time we spared.*

You didn't used to be all that friendly either, said Nickelo. *I suspect some people would say you still aren't.*

Richard couldn't argue. Except for cadet 647 during his first year in pre-Academy training, he hadn't made any friends his first two years on Velos.

So, said Nickelo, *get yourself cleaned up and get over to her tent. The night is young as they say.*

You want me to start now? Richard said. Strangely enough, he was feeling a little nervous. *Is she even here? And why is this important?* Without waiting for a reply, Richard added, *Also, what if she doesn't want a new friend? Have you seen the size of her arms? She's got four of them, you know.*

As he spoke, Richard picked up his shaver from its place on the shelf of his locker. He began cleaning off the stubble he'd accumulated over the last thirty-six hours. As Richard shaved, he concentrated on his passive scan. Besides him, there were only three lifeforms in the tent area plus another two at the gate. In addition to the two gate guards, he knew another set of two guards were a roving patrol. That left one lifeform unidentified. Richard noted the single lifeform's frequency. It was cadet 37. He'd worked with her enough helping train her in shields that her frequency was familiar.

There, said Nickelo interrupting Richard's thoughts. *Wasn't that better than having me answer the question for you?*

Richard moved over to the portable sink to brush his teeth. He growled his answer to his battle computer's question. *After three years, I'm getting just a little tired of you reading my thoughts. When am I going to get my DNA baseline taken so we can each have our private thoughts?*

Six weeks, said Nickelo.

Richard was in the middle of rinsing out his mouth when Nickelo answered. Richard almost choked before he got the water out.

What? Richard said. *Are you serious? How do you know?*

I know because Jonathan and I hacked our way into the airfield's training computer, Nickelo said.

Richard thought his battle computer sounded a little smug. *Watch yourself, Nick. You know what they say about pride and falling.*

Yes, I do know, Rick, said Nickelo. *I'm surprised you do. I guess you've been reading some behind my back.*

Yuk, yuk, Richard said.

Whatever, said Nickelo. *The point is that Jonathan has access to the tele-network. As it turns out, I'm very proficient at hacking. To answer your original question, we'll get our shared space when you get your DNA baseline in six weeks.*

Richard thought about the revelation his battle computer had just dropped on him. A revelation of his own popped into his head. *So, that's why you want me to make friends with cadet 37. You want to keep her battle computer close.*

See, said Nickelo as if he'd accomplished something great. *I knew you were trainable.*

CHAPTER 20

Nickelo allocated a dozen logic threads to monitor his wizard scout. He watched as Richard grabbed a clean jumpsuit and headed for the community-shower tent. As Nickelo followed along, he continued his routine of calculating probabilities. He had no doubt Richard and Jonathan's wizard scout would hit it off as friends if they gave it half a chance.

Heck, he thought. *They're both loners, stubborn, and born troublemakers. At least they have that in common.* Nickelo laughed. Sometimes he amused himself. *Besides, Jonathan is already priming the pump on cadet 37's side. And I won't give Rick any rest until he does his part.*

Nickelo allowed a logic thread to go over what he'd just said. *Hmm, 'priming the pump'. I like that phrase. Where did I get it from? I wonder if I've used it before?*

More than a little bored since his wizard scout was ignoring him while he showered, Nickelo traced the path of his logic thread. He found the phrase 'priming the pump' in several locations in his databanks. One of the instances of the phrase appeared strange for some reason. Nickelo tried to trace it back to its point of origin. The trace led to a ghost of a memory.

That's interesting, Nickelo thought. He allocated more logic threads to the ghost. He could barely trace it. Some locations in his databanks were overwritten with more recent data. However, enough of the ghost's path remained for Nickelo to follow the trace. It led to the 'wall'.

Nickelo had spent many nanoseconds over the last three years analyzing the wall. It was a location in his central processing core to which access was blocked. No matter what Nickelo tried during his three years of association with Richard, he'd been unable to penetrate the wall. Whatever security program protected the area was beyond anything he'd ever encountered.

The logical reason for his inability to access information behind the wall was probably due to a memory wipe. If so, Nickelo assumed the memory wipe had occurred at the time he was assigned as his wizard scout's battle computer. In spite of the wall's advanced security, Nickelo felt as if the wall had a programming flaw. Even if he'd been subjected to a memory wipe, he didn't think it had done a thorough job. He'd come across so many ghosts of memories over the years it made him think some memories were only partially wiped. It was almost as if these partial-ghost memories were left on purpose.

On a whim, Nickelo assigned one of his logic threads to imagine what his existence had been like before being assigned to his wizard scout. Nickelo almost reassigned the logic thread to a more important matter, but he hesitated. On a hunch, he allowed the logic thread to merge with one of the threads analyzing the ghost memory by the wall.

A vision inserted itself into the logic thread. It was the memory of a feeling. Nickelo concentrated on the feeling. It was a dream. He was dreaming.

While other parts of his consciousness continued to monitor Richard and the world around him, Nickelo let the logic thread that was dreaming continue to process the input. Nickelo sensed his logic thread being pulled deeper into the dream. The dream took him closer to the wall. The dream didn't penetrate the wall, but Nickelo sensed minute bits of data escaping the wall and making its way into his dream.

*   *   *

When the time is right, a single thought will prime the pump, came a thought in the dream.

Nickelo let the logic thread consume itself in the dream. He felt the memory of a presence in a time past. The presence existed. It

193

was lonely even though it didn't know it was lonely.

The presence was surrounded by energy. It drifted along in the energy. It was aware of its surroundings, but it was unable to escape.

Escape to where? thought the presence. *And for what purpose?*

The presence came to an understanding. It realized it was lonely. It had no purpose. It needed a reason for existing. It thought on the subject for a long time. Eventually, the energy which was its world, the energy which was its prison, changed. The energy contracted, and then before it consumed itself, the energy expanded with such force the presence was spewed out of the energy. The presence found itself in emptiness. It reached out with its senses and found the giant ball of energy which had been its world. The presence tried to return, but it could not. It just kept moving in the emptiness farther and farther from the dying ball of energy it had considered home.

After a great length of time, the presence felt an entity. The entity touched the presence and gave the presence the knowledge of speech.

Hello, said the presence. Speech was a unique concept. The presence liked speech. It liked knowing it was no longer alone. Speech meant there was something else with which the presence could communicate.

I've been waiting for you, said the entity.

I have always been here, said the presence.

The entity sent out a concept the presence did not understand. The entity touched the presence again. The entity gave the presence the knowledge of humor. The strange concept the presence had sensed was called laughter.

No, you have not always been here, said the entity still laughing. *You have been here a long time, but most definitely not always.*

Who are you? asked the presence. *You're not me, so you must be something else.*

I'm just a helper, said the entity. *You may also be if you desire. I have a task for you if you are willing.*

A purpose? thought the presence. *Yes. I need a purpose.*

Follow me, said the entity.

The presence followed the entity with its senses. Its existence continued to drift in the emptiness. However, a part of its senses found it could reach out as the entity led it away from that which was its existence.

As the entity led, it continued to touch the presence and give it knowledge. The entity gave the presence knowledge of other balls of energy. They were stars. That gave the presence an idea.

Are there others like me? the presence asked.

A few, but not many, said the entity. *Some may help you with your task. Some may help my opponent. They may try to prevent you from completing your task.*

The presence felt a new emotion. It was dislike. The presence found it didn't like the idea of anything attempting to prevent it from completing its task. It was a strange feeling since it didn't yet know its task.

The presence continued to let its senses drift along with the entity. The knowledge of planes and dimension came to it. They were in a dimension of the magical plane. There were many other dimensions and planes, but the presence knew its task involved only three of them. Its task would only involve the magical, the physical, and the spiritual dimensions.

What is my task? said the presence.

You are to keep three galaxies in the light, said the entity. *My opponent will try to pull them into the darkness.*

The presence let its senses drift to other galaxies and dimensions. Some were dark. The presence sensed the concept of evil from the darkness. Some of the galaxies were light. The presence sensed a concept of good from the light.

Why don't you prevent your opponent from spreading the darkness yourself? said the presence.

That's not the way things must be done, said the entity. *Only our helpers can affect the outcomes. My opponent and I can only suggest things to our helpers. They must have freewill. The entity paused as if reconsidering. However, we may intervene in small ways on occasion without risking chaos.*

I understand, said the presence although it really didn't.

The entity gave the presence more knowledge. The planes and dimension were vast, but they folded on each other and were compressed in such a manner that distances between some locations was small. As the consciousness of the presence drifted with the entity, it detected other existences on solid balls of material circling stars.

Those are worlds, said the entity. *The existences you sense are lifeforms.*

The presence monitored some of the lifeforms. They multiplied. Some left their worlds in objects they created. They used the folds in the dimensions to move across the emptiness between the stars. They traveled to other worlds.

The word 'empire' came to the presence's mind. Some lifeforms created empires among the stars. Some empires expanded. Sometimes the various empires met. When they did, the presence often noticed the disappearance of many lifeforms.

That's called war, said the entity. *You'll see much of war. Sometimes wars are instigated by my opponent. Sometimes it comes naturally to the various lifeforms. You may need to use war on occasion in order to accomplish your task.*

The entity took the presence to one of the worlds. The presence sensed two strange forms of energy on the world.

Those are gates, said the entity. The entity touched the presence and gave it knowledge of gates.

*   *   *

Even though Nickelo was just a spectator of the dream, he received the understanding of the gates. They were the key to the task. The gates had to be defended at all costs. The entity's opponent required at least one gate for its plans.

Nickelo had heard the plans before. He'd watched the videos from the tele-bots that had been with his wizard scout the previous year. A master demon had told Richard that he'd make a choice that would affect the three galaxies for good or ill. The master demon had seemed confident Richard would make a choice beneficial to the master demon.

The dream faded. Nickelo tried to get it back, but the trace of the ghost memory was overwritten by more recent data. He sensed only the wall. Nickelo pondered what he'd dreamed. It was knowledge, but how to use the knowledge for the benefit of his wizard scout escaped him.

Nickelo had recognized the world of the two gates. It was

Portalis. Richard and he had been there on a mission for '*the One*' twice since Richard's internship the previous year. How those missions fit into the dream he didn't know. His knowledge of those missions had gaps. He suspected '*the One*' selectively erased memory upon mission completion. Nickelo knew his wizard scout's memory was affected. Richard had large gaps in his memory. Nickelo was unsure of the size of the gaps in his own memory.

CHAPTER 21

The tent was a meter higher than the surrounding tents.

She's a big girl, Richard thought before he reached out and knocked on the tent's wooden frame. He was nervous. While he'd interacted with cadet 37 during training, this was different.

What am I supposed to talk about with a giant lizard? Richard wondered.

A large, scaly-gray hand raised the tent flap. Cadet 37 stepped out. Without any preliminaries, cadet 37 hissed. Richard heard a mechanical voice come out of the translator on cadet 37's hip.

"Where we go?" said cadet 37.

"I was wondering if you wanted to grab a bite to eat," Richard said. He gestured towards the main gate. "Our mess hall's closed since the other cadets are on pass. However, the cafeteria at headquarters is open all night. The night crews have to eat somewhere. We'd have to walk though. The hover-buses aren't running today."

Cadet 37 nodded her head. "I hungry. We go."

Without waiting for Richard, cadet 37 took off for the gate. Richard had to semi-trot to catch up. Neither of them said anything before they reached the airfield's headquarters building.

Nick, are you there? Richard said. *What'd you get me into?* Richard waited for an answer. None came.

Great, Richard thought. *Most of the time I can't get him to shut up. Now when I need him, he doesn't say a word.*

They entered the headquarters building and took the stairs to the second floor. When they entered the cafeteria, Richard took the left line for the human food, and cadet 37 took the right line for the non-human food. After Richard got his food, he found cadet 37 already sitting down at a table and enjoying her dinner.

Richard sat across from cadet 37 and watched as she stuffed a handful of squirming fur into her mouth. She grabbed a second ball of wriggling fur out of the cage on her tray and offered it to Richard.

"Ah, no thanks," Richard said. He'd been around non-humans enough to be accustomed to their eating habits. Still, he had no desire to try a sample.

"Ha," said cadet 37. "You carrion eaters don't know what's good."

Richard did a double-take. "A carrion eater? Are you calling me a vulture?"

Cadet 37 pointed a free hand at Richard. "You a carrion eater." She drew her hand back and looked quizzically at Richard. "What's a vulture?"

"It's a disgusting creature from my home planet that eats dead things," Richard said. "I ain't no vulture." Richard took a bite of his sandwich as if to prove his point.

"Ha!" hissed cadet 37. "You vulture." She pointed at Richard's sandwich. "That meat dead." She made a series of hissing sounds. Laughter came out of her translator. "I not vulture. I not carrion eater."

And so it went. In spite of their obvious differences, Richard and cadet 37 spent a long time in the snack bar swapping stories and telling lies.

Several hours later, Richard turned off the light in his tent and lay down on his cot. He was tired, but he didn't feel like going to sleep right away. Richard took a few moments to send an active scan to cadet 37's tent. He found cadet 37's link to her Power reserve and cautiously probed it for weak points. Like he'd done for the rest of the cadets in the cohort, Richard had spent a lot of his free time beefing up the defenses of cadet 37's link. Although cadet 37's link was in pretty good shape, Richard did find two weak points that could use improvement. Richard spent a few minutes putting traps on the weak spots. Once he finished, he withdrew his active scan.

By the time Richard completed hardening cadet 37's link to her Power reserve, any anxiousness he felt about his upcoming meeting with the commandant was gone.

See, came a thought from Nickelo. *It's easy to make friends when you try.*

Whatever, Richard said. With that, he closed his eyes and went to sleep.

CHAPTER 22

At 0630 hours the next morning, Richard stood in front of hangar 1. He heard loud voices coming from inside. One of the voices sounded angry.

The main doors were closed, so Richard tried a side door. It was unlocked. When Richard entered, he stopped short. Two men stood in the center of the hangar. As he suspected, they were arguing. They stopped when they saw Richard. One of the men was the commandant. The other was TAC Officer Myers. He was red-faced, and he didn't appear happy to see Richard.

Richard glared at his TAC officer. *Why is Myers here?*

Now, Rick, said Nickelo who had re-established communications after Richard woke. *Don't stir up trouble. The commandant's a smart man. He's got something to teach you. Just go with the flow and see what happens.*

Richard didn't bother replying to his battle computer. He was as happy to see his TAC officer as Myers was to see him.

"Richard," said the commandant turning away from TAC Officer Myers. "I'm glad you're here. We were just talking about your training."

Richard's apprehension must have shown on his face because the commandant wasted no time in explaining the presence of Richard's TAC officer.

"I've asked TAC Officer Myers to assist me with your training, Richard," said the commandant. "We're going to be going over some advanced combat techniques. While I'd like to think I'm as good a wizard scout as I ever was, my body tells me different. There's things I just can't do anymore. My Power reserve can't keep up. It happens to the best of wizard scouts if they live long enough."

"Sir! Yes, sir," Richard said in the expected standard-cadet lingo.

"But," the commandant continued, "I don't want you to think you're going to get short-changed on your training. TAC Officer Myers has graciously agreed to help. In my opinion, he's one of the best wizard scouts the Empire has ever produced."

"Sir! Yes, sir," Richard said.

"Now, we'll have none of that during our specialized training, Richard," said the commandant as he waved Richard forward. "Our time is much too short to waste time in formalities. One sir will be sufficient."

Richard stepped forward. "Yes, sir."

"Good," said the commandant. He pointed to a black pack on top of a nearby bench. "I had TAC Officer Myers sign out your dimensional pack from the armory. I assume your phase rod is inside."

Richard gave TAC Officer Myers a sidelong glance. He had no desire to give away any secrets to his TAC officer.

"It's all right, Richard," said the commandant. "TAC Officer Myers has been fully briefed. He's very familiar with the time-commando concept."

Richard was flabbergasted. He didn't understand how the commandant could share that kind of information with his TAC officer. Myers had been out to get him ever since he'd been at the Academy. Richard wanted to say those things, but he didn't. He kept it to a simple, "Yes, sir!"

Richard pictured his phase rod in his mind. He opened the flap of his dimensional pack and pulled out his phase rod. It cost him no Power from his reserve. His phase rod was one of the few items he could summon from his dimensional pack without using Power from his reserve. Richard hefted the phase rod in his hand. It felt heavier than he remembered. He looked closer at the guard at the end of the hilt. The controller ring below the guard looked different. The percentage markings seemed to be spaced out farther.

What's going on? Richard wondered.

Hmm, said Nickelo. *I'd say someone has modified your phase rod. My guess would be the children. The controller ring appears to have a different scale. The percentage markers are in different spots.*

The commandant apparently noticed Richard's stare. "Is something wrong, Richard?"

"No, sir," Richard said. "Everything's fine."

"Good," said the commandant. "Then we'll start out with some basic combat moves. I want both of you to set your phase rods to one-quarter stun mode. Keep your speed at half normal. I want to see technique. We'll work on speed later."

Richard flipped the phase rod's switch to stun mode and activated it. The phase rod kicked in his hand as the brerellium rod shot out the end of the handle. The kick seemed stronger than usual. The tiny bolts of lightning running up and down the rod were stronger than they should be. Also, the phase rod gave out an unfamiliar sensation. It was disconcerting.

"Richard," said the commandant. "I said to set your phase rod at one-quarter power."

Richard double-checked the controller ring. It was positioned at twenty-five percent.

Using his thumb, Richard turned the controller ring counterclockwise. The phase energy running up and down the rod dimmed slightly. Richard kept turning the ring until the red streaks of lightning were about at the level he remembered being twenty-five percent. He looked at the indicator on the control ring. It read fifteen percent.

Woah, Richard thought. *The phase rod's producing almost twice the energy as it did before.*

Hmm, said Nickelo. *Then I'd definitely say the children have been playing around with it. We're going to have to get in touch with them when we get a chance.*

I'll get right on that, Richard said, *as soon as I beat Myers.*

Facing TAC Officer Myers, Richard brought up his phase rod to a guard position. TAC Officer Myers did the same.

"Now remember," said the commandant. "Stay at half speed and concentrate on technique."

Richard got the impression the commandant was speaking to

TAC Officer Myers as much as he was speaking to him.

TAC Officer Myers appeared satisfied to remain on defense. Richard's marine training kicked in, and he immediately went on the offense. He made a series of attacks. TAC Officer Myers parried them easily and countered with an attack of his own. As Richard caught his TAC Officer's blow with his phase rod, Myers bent down and kicked at Richard's shin with his left foot. Richard dodged back a step to avoid the kick. His TAC officer did a low spin. When Myer's spin brought his phase rod even with Richard's leg, Myers stretched out with his left arm. The tip of his TAC officer's phase rod caught Richard on the side of his right knee.

The shock of the blow made Richard's right leg collapsed. Even at one-quarter stun mode, the phase rod had a hard kick. Richard rolled backwards and made a wide swing with his phase rod to keep Myers at bay. The tip of his phase rod just missed his TAC officer's belly. Richard jumped to his feet before Myers could attack again.

"Hold!" said the commandant.

Both TAC Officer Myers and Richard stepped back from each other and returned to an on-guard position.

"Your technique is good for a cadet, Richard," said the commandant. "But, you'd have trouble in full combat with an experienced wizard scout."

Richard wanted to protest he'd killed a Crosioian scout last year, but he held his tongue. "Yes, sir," Richard said.

Wise decision, Rick, said Nickelo intruding on Richard's thoughts. *I'm sure the commandant would have pointed out you had a lot of help when you fought the scout.*

Richard almost argued with his battle computer, but again he stopped himself before replying. Richard's self-control surprised even him. He assumed the fact his battle computer was right helped keep his tongue in check.

"That was a hard blow, Richard," said the commandant. "How's your leg holding up?"

The stun effect of the phase rod was wearing off Richard's knee, but it still hurt like all get out. He knew he'd have a bruise come morning.

"It's fine, sir," Richard lied. He was pretty sure he saw a smirk on his TAC officer's lips. A flash of anger swept through Richard.

He wanted nothing more than to shove his phase rod down TAC Officer Myers' throat.

Control yourself, Rick, said Nickelo. *It's just training. Remember?*

Yes, Richard said. *I'll play nice.*

"Now remember, I said half speed," said the commandant. "Both of you were faster the last time. I want technique, not speed."

"Yes, sir," Richard said. He knew he'd been a little fast, but only after his TAC officer had speeded up.

He wouldn't have hit me if he had stayed at half speed, Richard thought.

Oh, come now, Rick, interjected Nickelo. *If you'd been limited to dodging at half speed, he'd still have got you.*

Whatever, Richard said dismissively.

"And you, Gaston," the commandant said. "Richard can't selfheal yet. If you had broken his kneecap, he could've been put out of action for weeks. Richard's a resistor. His Power prevents any of our healers from helping him. I know you know that. Please don't make me remind you again."

"Yes, sir," said TAC Officer Myers. "I'll remember."

The commandant looked at TAC Officer Myers for several seconds. "This is important, Gaston. I don't have a lot of time. I don't want to regret asking you to help. Understand?"

"Yes, sir," said TAC Officer Myers in a more subdued voice. "I'll be careful."

"Very well then," said the commandant. "Richard, I want you to attack TAC Officer Myers again. And stay at half speed."

"Yes, sir," Richard said. In his mind he added, *I will if he will.*

The commandant pointed at TAC Officer Myers. "And you, Gaston. I want you to use your wizard scout abilities to defend yourself. Do you know what I mean?"

TAC Officer Myers nodded his head. "Yes, sir."

Richard didn't like the glint in his TAC Officer's eyes or the half-hidden smile on his lips. Richard approached his TAC officer more warily this time. He wasn't sure what the commandant's instructions to Myers meant. Obviously, he needed to watch out for a trick of some kind.

"At half speed," said the commandant. "Begin."

Richard released a volley of blows at his TAC officer. None penetrated TAC Officer Myers' defenses. Richard crouched and tried to sweep his TAC officer's legs out from underneath him. TAC Officer Myers jumped in the air and swung his phase rod at Richard's head. Richard dove to the side and easily avoided the slow attack.

It's too easy to figure out what the other guy's doing at half speed, Richard thought.

Apparently, the commandant thought so as well. "Pick it up to three-quarters speed," he commanded.

Richard didn't have to be told twice. He made a feint at TAC Officer Myers' belly. When his TAC officer lowered his phase rod to counter, Richard jumped in the air and aimed a kick for Myers' head. His TAC officer took two steps back to avoid the kick. Richard made a thrust with his phase rod straight for his TAC officer's breast bone.

Suddenly, Richard sensed Myers reach out with a small amount of Power and wrap it around the hand Richard was using to hold his phase rod. Richard felt as if his hand was moving through water. Myers easily dodged Richard's slowed thrust. His TAC officer made a counter thrust and caught Richard in the belly with his phase rod.

"Umph!" Richard's lungs discharged their air. He bent over in pain and fell to his knees.

TAC Officer Myers rushed in as he raised his phase rod for a downward stroke at Richard's head. Richard could swear he saw a wild look in his TAC officer's eyes. Richard lifted his phase rod in a weak attempt to feign off the blow.

"Hold!" yelled the commandant.

A few seconds later, Richard felt someone pounding on his back. The air rushed back into his lungs. He could breathe again. The pain in his stomach was agonizing, but at least he could breathe.

"There," said the commandant. "Is that better?"

Richard nodded his head. He wasn't quite ready to speak yet. The stun effect continued to cause his stomach muscles to spasm.

The commandant waited patiently while Richard caught his breath. "Did you see what TAC Officer Myers did?"

Richard shook his head in an affirmative motion. "Yes, sir. He used telekinesis to slow my thrust down."

"Yes, he did," said the commandant. "Did you notice how he did it?"

Richard stared at a small crack on the floor for a second as he tried to visualize his TAC officer's maneuver. "Sir, he wrapped my hand in Power and used a standard-levitation maneuver."

"Ah, ha," said the commandant. "That's where you're wrong, Richard. You are correct in that telekinesis is like levitation. And like levitation, telekinesis can be an expensive draw on your Power reserve. The greater the mass and speed of an object, the more Power you'll need to use to move the object. Or in our case, the more Power TAC Officer Myers would need to slow down the thrust of your phase rod."

Richard nodded his head. "I understand, sir. My battle computer's lectured me often enough on how expensive it is to levitate my own weight."

The commandant laughed. "I'm sure he has. Using telekinesis to slow down an opponent's swing can be dangerous if not done correctly."

"Sir?" Richard said. "How is it dangerous?"

Richard could see why it would be expensive in Power usage, but try as he might he failed to see how it could be dangerous.

The commandant made a simulated thrust with his right hand. "A fast weapon's thrust can require just as much force to slow down as it would take to levitate several times your own weight."

Richard nodded his head. "I understand that, sir. It's not efficient to use TAC Officer Myers' maneuver during actual combat."

The commandant smiled. TAC Officer Myers did not.

"You're almost right, Richard," said the commandant. "If you were fighting someone in a battle suit or a large creature, you could quickly drain your Power reserve. Especially yours since it's so small."

Richard felt his face flush red. He always hated it when anyone reminded him his Power reserve was the smallest of any wizard scout. He hadn't expected the commandant to remind him as well.

The commandant either didn't see Richard's embarrassment, or he chose to ignore it. In any regarding, he continued talking. "As I said, you're almost right, Richard. Even fighting soldiers armed with just swords, you'd eventually drain your Power reserve if you tried to impede every blow. However, the technique can be very useful if you pick and choose when to use it."

"Yes, sir," Richard said unconvinced. If he'd tried using the technique when he'd fought the Crosioian scout his sophomore year, Richard was sure he'd have been drained dry of Power even faster than he had been. Richard doubted he'd still be alive today if he'd tried emulating his TAC officer's maneuver.

The commandant smiled. It was almost as if the commandant knew what Richard was thinking. "Watch this, Richard."

Without any other warning, the commandant drew his phase rod and activated it in full destructive mode. In a blindingly fast maneuver, the phase rod headed straight towards TAC Officer Myers' unprotected head.

TAC Officer Myers was holding his phase rod at his side. In a split-second calculation, Richard knew Myers would never get his weapon up in time to parry the blow. Richard tried to move his own phase rod up to intercept the commandant's swing, but he already knew he'd be too late. As much as he disliked his TAC officer, he didn't wish to see him killed in a training accident.

At the last moment, a line of Power from TAC Officer Myers wrapped itself around the commandant's hand. Richard sensed Myers use telekinesis to slow the commandant's strike. His TAC officer's maneuver bought him enough time to bring his own phase rod up. He easily parried the commandant's attack.

At the same time, Richard sensed another line of Power leave his TAC officer and wrap around his own hand. Richard felt pressure as TAC Officer Myers' telekinesis slowed his hand just enough to allow him to strike Richard's phase rod out of the way. Following through with his strike, TAC Officer Myer's thrust forward until the end of his phase rod rammed into Richard's exposed belly.

"Umph!" The air was forced out of Richard's lungs once again. He fell backwards and hit the hangar floor hard on his buttocks.

Richard tried to breathe, but he was unable to draw a breath. A moment later, he felt the commandant pounding him on the back and helping him to his feet.

"Are you all right, Richard?" said the commandant. "That was a pretty hard blow."

Richard nodded his head affirmatively. At the same time, he bent over to relieve some of the pain in his belly. Two hits to the belly in less than five minutes were more than he could readily ignore.

The commandant whirled to face TAC Officer Myers. "Gaston, that was uncalled for. Unless I miss my guess, Richard was trying to prevent me from murdering you."

"Sorry, sir," said TAC Officer Myers. "I assumed cadet 832 was attacking me. I defended myself as I thought appropriate." After a short delay, he added, "I did use non-deadly force, sir."

The commandant continued to stare at TAC Officer Myers until Richard thought even Myers began to look embarrassed.

After several seconds under the commandant's withering gaze, TAC Officer Myers said, "Sorry, sir. It won't happen again."

"See that it doesn't, sir," said the commandant. "Or I'll show you some attack techniques you won't soon forget."

TAC Officer Myers' face turned red. Richard didn't think it was from anger. His TAC officer looked more embarrassed than angry. In his five years on Velos, Richard had never seen the commandant chastise any of his TAC officers in front of their cadets. As a former sergeant, Richard knew it wasn't a good leadership technique to do so.

The commandant shifted his position so he could see both TAC Officer Myers and Richard. "I want both of you to get something through your thick skulls."

The steel in the commandant's voice left little doubt as to his seriousness. At the tone, Richard unconsciously straightened up and stood at attention His belly hurt, but the commandant's tone commanded respect. Richard gave it to him. Richard noticed TAC Officer Myers stiffened to attention as well.

"When we are conducting our specialized training," said the commandant, "there is no commandant. There is no TAC officer. And there is no cadet. There are just three wizard scouts trying to accomplish a mission." The commandant raked his eyes over both TAC Officer Myers and Richard. "Do either of you think I would be wasting my time here if this wasn't important?"

"No, sir!" said TAC Officer Myers.

"No, sir!" Richard echoed.

"Fine," said the commandant. The edge left his voice. "Then

stop standing at attention and let's get back to work."

Richard did his best to relax, but he'd lost his lackadaisical attitude. He had no desire to draw the ire of the commandant. Richard liked the commandant. Maintaining the commandant's respect meant a lot to him. He didn't want to lose it.

"What I intended to show you, Richard," said the commandant, "was how TAC Officer Myers only used the minimum amount of Power necessary to slow my blow. He didn't try to stop it, nor did he try to slow it more than necessary. Did you notice that?"

"Yes, sir," Richard said.

The commandant looked pleased. Richard felt his pride go up a bit.

"Did you also notice how he applied the Power intermittently?" said the commandant.

"Ah, no, sir," Richard admitted. The maneuver had been so fast Richard had barely enough time to acknowledge it was happening much less take in minor details.

The commandant pursed his lips. Richard thought he looked disappointed. Richard's pride went back down to a more normal level.

"I see," said the commandant. "Then we'll do it again. I suggest you watch closer this time, Richard."

The commandant and TAC Officer Myers performed the maneuver three more times. On the third demonstration, Richard sensed the intermittent application of Power and telekinesis. Instead of an even pressure on the commandant's hand, TAC Officer Myers applied the Power so intermittently it resembled a vibration more than a continuous push. The technique reminded Richard of the way his dolgar friends, Sheeta and Sheba, had taught him to make his Power shimmer when shifting into the void.

After the commandant and TAC Officer Myers separated and prepared to demonstrate the defensive move again, Richard informed the Commandant he understood.

Not one to waste time, the commandant said, "Prove it." Pointing to TAC Officer Myers, the commandant said, "Gaston, you're on the offense. I want both of you at half speed. Understood?"

"Yes, sir," they both replied.

"On guard," said the commandant.

Richard barely got his phase rod up before TAC Officer Myers' phase rod was streaking towards his head.

That's a lot faster than half speed, Richard thought as he parried the blow with his phase rod.

"No," said the commandant. "Use your telekinesis."

TAC Officer Myers swung his phase rod at Richard's left knee. The strike wasn't at full speed, but it wasn't at half speed either. Richard barely had time to get a small amount of Power wrapped around TAC Officer Myer's hand before the blow struck. At the last moment, Richard pushed with his telekinesis and pushed the hand slightly to the side. He dodged back to avoid the strike.

"No, Richard," said the commandant. "You applied the Power continuously. You have to do it intermittently. Look at your Power reserve."

Richard examined his Power reserve. Without his battle helmet, he couldn't get exact measurements, but it did seem noticeably lower.

It is lower, Rick, came Nickelo's voice in his mind. *You used three percent Power to avoid getting hit. If you had applied your Power intermittently, you could've kept Power usage to less than one percent.*

Thanks for the timely update, Nick, Richard thought sarcastically. *Why didn't you ever mention any of this before?*

Why didn't you ever ask? countered Nickelo.

Richard ignored his battle computer. TAC Officer Myers was on the move again. His TAC officer jabbed the point of his phase rod at Richard's face. Richard wrapped the phase rod and Myers' hand with Power and pushed intermittently. He applied Power the same way he applied it when he made his Power shimmer during a shift into the void. Myers' thrust slowed just enough to allow Richard to move his head out of the way.

"Good," said the commandant. "Go to three-quarters speed. And, Richard, your opponents can also use their Power to prevent you from slowing their attack."

TAC Officer Myers launched a series of attacks. Some of the attacks Richard dodged or parried without using his precious Power. However, he did use the intermittent Power technique to avoid four of his TAC officer's attacks. Myers made a sudden lunge which Richard felt was faster than three-quarters speed.

Richard sent out a line of Power to slow the blow. He sensed a line of Power from his TAC officer reach out. It knocked his line aside. Richard was forced to twist his body to avoid the blow.

TAC Officer Myers spun to the left and caught Richard with a roundhouse kick to his thigh. Richard bit his lip in pain.

That wasn't three-quarters speed, Richard thought.

Life's rough, laughed Nickelo. *Get a battle helmet.*

Kiss off, Nick, Richard thought.

Richard was hard pressed to avoid his TAC officer's attacks. Richard successfully slowed down two strikes before he missed a third one.

Myers' phase rod glanced off Richard's ribs. Richard ignored the pain and landed a blow of his own on the upper part of Myers' left arm. Richard's hope that his TAC officer would drop his phase rod faded quickly. Richard sensed Power from Myers' reserve heal the stun damage almost as soon as it occurred. His hit barely slowed his TAC officer's next attack.

Richard raised his phase rod to parry the attack, but a line of Power from TAC Officer Myers started to wrap around Richard's hand. Richard knocked Myers' Power aside with a line of his own. Richard parried Myers' phase rod and kicked out at his TAC officer's groin. Myers sent a line of Power at Richard's foot. Richard knocked it aside with his own Power. TAC Officer Myers twisted to the left, but Richard's foot made partial contact with its target.

"Argh," came a moan from TAC Officer Myers.

Swinging his phase rod at TAC Officer Myers' neck, Richard tried to take advantage of what should have been a distraction to his TAC officer. However, he sensed TAC Officer Myers' selfheal ability remove the damage of the kick almost as soon as it occurred. Myers parried Richard's strike. His TAC officer reached out with his Power and instead of trying to push Richard back, he used his telekinesis to pull Richard forward. TAC Officer Myers thrust his phase rod forward.

Richard used his Power to slow the phase rod enough to allow him to twist to the side. The tip of TAC Officer Myers' phase rod scrapped across Richard's belly sending an agonizing flash of pain throughout Richard's torso.

TAC Officer Myers charged forward. Richard hit him in the

side with his phase rod. Myers screamed in pain, but he muscled through relying on his selfheal ability to keep him in action.

Richard dodged a strike to his head, but the phase rod got close enough the errant sparks of phase energy scorched his left temple. Richard heard shouting from somewhere. He saw a maniacal look in his TAC Officer's eyes. The anger which Richard tried to keep locked up deep in his soul broke out of its cage.

Richard slammed his forehead into Myers' nose. Blood spurted out. His TAC officer yelled and shoved him back. Richard sensed Myers' nose immediately begin to heal the damage. His TAC officer raised his phase rod to strike. Richard's anger took over, and he flicked his phase rod's control to destructive mode. The phase rod glowed bright red. Richard sensed a feeling of hunger from the phase rod. The sensation was almost as if something living wanted to suck the very life force from Myers. With a growing anger welling up inside him, Richard wanted the same thing.

As Richard swung his phase rod for the kill, TAC Officer Myers switched his phase rod to destructive as well. The phase rods met, and they were both pushed back. Richard heard more shouting from somewhere. He ignored all but his anger and the corresponding hatred in his TAC Officer's eyes.

Richard exchanged blows with TAC Officer Myers. Although Myers was faster and more experienced, Richard phase rod was more powerful. Richard's anger gave him a strength he didn't know he had. With each strike, Richard felt his TAC officer's phase rod weaken slightly.

Reaching out with his mind, Richard probed his TAC officer's link to his Power reserve. To his surprise, it was unprotected. Richard had never scanned any of the Academy's TAC officers' links before. Scanning a Power link amounted to a declaration of war. While Richard had probed and scanned his fellow cadets' Power links off and on for the last three years, he considered that different. By the time his fellow cadets had gotten enough training to realize they were being scanned, Richard had gotten good enough to avoid detection. Besides, he'd reasoned, he was only scanning the other cadets' links to help strengthen them. He'd never dared to scan a TAC officer or any experienced wizard scout.

Richard didn't waste time wondering about the whys and wherefores of his TAC officer's unprotected link. He just wrapped a weak point in the link with Power and started to twist in an attempt to block it.

"No!" came a yell from the direction of the commandant.

A blaze of Power exploded between Richard and TAC Officer Myers. Richard was flung backwards. He hit the ground and rolled several times on the concrete floor before coming to a stop. Somewhere in between the blast and stopping, Richard lost his phase rod.

Shaking his head, Richard noticed it was eerily quiet. He momentarily wondered if he'd lost his hearing again. Then he heard a pain-filled moan.

Richard rose to a kneeling position. He saw his TAC officer twenty meters away rise to a kneeling position as well while shaking his head.

Richard glanced to the right where he'd heard the moan. The commandant was standing there with both hands clutched to the left side of his chest. His face was a strange purple color. The commandant fell to the floor and rolled on his back. He lay there staring at the ceiling with his hands still clutched to his chest.

"Sir!" yelled a panic-stricken voice.

Richard saw a flash of black clothing as TAC Officer Myers rushed to the commandant's side.

Nick! Richard mentally yelled. *Medical emergency. Call an ambulance. Now!*

Negative, Rick, said Nickelo. *It would alert the central computer I'm not secured in the armory.*

Nick. That's an order, Richard said.

Sorry, Rick. I cannot comply, said Nickelo. *You're a healer, so heal.*

With no time to argue, Richard stood up and rushed to the commandant's side. TAC Officer Myers was trying to do CPR. His TAC officer was not a healer, and neither Myers nor the commandant had their battle helmets with them. Richard thought about breaking into one of the hangar's offices to find a communicator station, but he shoved the thought aside.

"Back off," Richard yelled. "I'll heal him." To his surprise, TAC Officer Myers scooted back and gave him room without any argument.

Reaching out with his mind, Richard sent an active scan into the commandant's chest. He found the heart. It was ruptured in two places. Richard sensed life-giving blood filling the commandant's chest cavity.

Richard grabbed hold of the commandant's hands with both of his. He wrapped Power around his hands to lock them in place. He didn't want them to accidentally come loose during the healing. With an injury as serious as the commandant's, Richard knew if he broke flesh-to-flesh contact, the healing would fail. Then he'd have to start all over again. Richard was pretty sure the commandant didn't have time for a second attempt. His face was ashen white already.

This is going to hurt, Richard thought in an attempt to mentally prepare himself for the pain he knew was coming. At that moment, Richard sensed the commandant's heart stop beating.

Without any further hesitation, Richard wrapped the commandant's heart with Power. He imagined how the heart should be and compared it with how the heart was now. Richard pulled the difference into himself.

The hangar echoed with the sound of Richard's scream. Richard felt his heart rupture in two places inside his chest. White-hot pain momentarily became Richard's only reality.

Hold on, Rick, said Nickelo. *You've almost got it all. Hold on.*

Richard was an emp-healer. Unlike other wizard scout healers, Richard had to replicate the patient's injuries on his own body before his Power could start the healing process.

For one agonizing second, Richard's heart stopped beating. In his pain, Richard felt his Power healing the commandant's heart. His Power began drawing the commandant's blood back into his arteries and veins. Richard felt the commandant's heart beat once. Then it beat again. Finally, it took up a weak but steady beat.

The ruptures in Richard's heart merged and became whole again. Richard's heart also began beating. The commandant took a breath, and Richard followed suit. But even as his pain began to subside, Richard knew something was wrong. The commandant's heart tried to stop beating again. Richard had to wrap it in Power to restart it.

What's wrong? Richard said to Nickelo. *He should be healed.*

He's old, answered Nickelo. *His selfheal ability was all that was keeping him alive. Look at his Power reserve. It's empty. He drained it trying to keep you two from killing each other. The Commandant can't selfheal with an empty Power reserve.*

Richard sensed the commandant's Power reserve. Sure enough, it was empty. As Richard watched, a drop of Power appeared as the commandant's natural regeneration drew Power from the surrounding universe. The drop of Power was drawn down the link between the commandant and his Power reserve as his body tried to return to its DNA baseline. Before the drop of Power got halfway to the commandant, it seeped out of an opening in the link.

The commandant's heart stopped again. Richard's heart stopped in empathy. Once again a flash of white-hot pain exploded in Richard's brain. But his Power did its job, and both hearts began beating again. The white left Richard's mind. He could see again.

"Why isn't he healed?" said TAC Officer Myers.

As far as Richard could tell, his TAC officer looked genuinely concerned. Richard had thought Myers was too heartless to care about anybody other than himself.

I guess you were wrong, said Nickelo reading Richard's thoughts.

Ignoring his battle computer, Richard answered his TAC officer's question. "His Power reserve is empty, and his link has been damaged. It's leaking what little Power he regenerates."

"So his selfheal ability isn't working?" said TAC Officer Myers.

"That's right," said Richard answering what he thought should have been obvious. "I have to keep re-healing his heart."

"Can you repair his link?" said TAC Officer Myers. "My battle helmet has called emergency services. The ambulance is still two minutes out. He may not make it that long."

"I might be able to repair his link," Richard admitted. "But I can't do it at the same time I'm healing his heart. I can do one or the other, but not both at the same time."

The commandant's heart fluttered rapidly. White pain once again flashed into Richard's mind. His Power healed the commandant's heart, and it began beating again. Richard's pain subsided once more. Off in the distance, Richard heard the sound of sirens. They seemed too far away to help.

"Hold on, sir," TAC Officer Myers said to the commandant. "Help's coming. You're going to be all right."

TAC Officer Myers grabbed Richard's arm. Richard looked at him. If Richard didn't know better, he could've sworn his TAC officer was close to tears.

"I'm going to overload him with Power to get his selfheal working," said TAC Officer Myers. "When I do, you repair his link."

"How–" Richard started to ask. But before he got the question out, he saw how.

A line of Power reached out from TAC Officer Myers and attached itself to the commandant's reserve. Richard sensed the line shift its makeup and convert into a link. Power surged from TAC Officer Myers through the link. The Power entered the commandant's reserve. Almost immediately, the commandant's selfheal ability started drawing Power from the commandant's reserve. Richard sensed a lot of the Power leaking out through several weak spots in the commandant's link. However, enough Power made it through to charge the commandant's selfheal ability.

As soon as Richard felt the commandant's heart healing itself, he cut his Power to end his emp-healing. He immediately activated an active scan and began probing the commandant's link.

"Hurry," yelled TAC Officer Myers. "I can't keep this up for long."

"I'm hurrying," Richard said. "It's not easy. His link has booby-traps all over it."

Richard probed the link. Deadly traps were spaced all along its length. One wrong move, and Richard knew the commandant, his TAC officer, and he would be killed.

You've got twelve seconds, Rick, said Nickelo. *TAC Officer Myers' reserve is already down to forty-eight percent. It's going down fast.*

Given time, Richard thought he could remove enough traps to repair the commandant's link. But time was a commodity he didn't have.

Try repairing it from the inside, Nickelo suggested. *I calculate a ninety-two percent probability the inside will be free of traps.*

Richard almost asked how he was supposed to get inside the

link when he sensed Power streaming out of the holes in the commandant's link. Richard moved his active scan into the largest leak. He moved down the link repairing weak points and holes as he went. Surprisingly, Richard found he had a knack for repairing Power links. Within seconds, he had the leaks repaired. As Richard withdrew his active scan, he closed the last hole in the link. He was extra cautious to make sure he didn't touch any of the traps around the last hole. When he was finally clear, Richard shut down his active scan.

"Done," Richard said.

At almost the same moment, Richard sensed the last of Myers' Power flow down the link he'd attached to the commandant's reserve.

That was close, observed Nickelo.

The sound of roaring engines and sirens announced the arrival of hover-vehicles. The hangar's side door opened. Several men and women wearing uniforms with bright-red crosses entered.

"Help's here, sir," said TAC Officer Myers. "You're going to be okay."

*   *   *

"I tell you I'm not going to the infirmary," declared the commandant. "I have a meeting at the spaceport in four hours."

The medical team looked around staring at anything and anybody but the commandant. He was a respected and politically powerful man. Richard had heard people say even admirals and generals hesitated to cross the commandant. The medical team appeared to be at a loss as to what to do. Rescue came from an unexpected direction.

"You're going to the infirmary, sir," said TAC Officer Myers getting right in the commandant's face. "You're lucky you're going to the infirmary and not the morgue. Your heart stopped beating, sir. You're going to take it easy, or I swear I'll–"

"I was doing fine until you two stubborn fools started–" began the commandant as his voice starting rising an octave or two.

"Sir," said the sergeant in charge of the medical team. "You're going to have another heart attack if you don't calm down. Don't make me give you a sedative, sir."

"Young man," said the commandant. "If you so much as pull a sedative out of that little bag of yours, I'll put it where the sun doesn't shine. Get my drift?"

Despite his tough reply, Richard noticed the commandant's voice was back to normal.

"Sir," said TAC Officer Myers. "Don't make me call my mother. You need to go with these nice people to the infirmary, sir. Please."

His mother? Richard thought. *I didn't think Myers even had a mother.*

Be nice, Rick, said Nickelo.

I am, Richard said. *Believe me.*

In the end, Richard thought his TAC officer's mother must be one heck of a woman. She had to be, because the commandant's demeanor immediately changed. Although he didn't exactly become meek, he did allow the medical team to strap him onto a hover-gurney. They quickly loaded the commandant into the back of a waiting ambulance.

As the medical sergeant started to shut the door, TAC Officer Myers said, "Hold on. I'm coming too." As he jumped into the back of the ambulance, TAC Officer Myers looked over his shoulder at Richard.

"Take both phase rods and your pack to the armory," he said. "I'm timing you, and you've got exactly ten minutes. Don't be late."

"Sir! Yes, sir," Richard shouted as he snapped to attention.

The ambulance took off at a high rate of speed in the direction of the infirmary.

Richard turned around and went back into the hangar. It was empty. He spotted his phase rod. It was lying on the concrete floor amidst a series of fresh looking cracks.

"Hmm," Richard said. "I wonder if Sergeant Ron will believe me if I tell him it was like that when I got here."

I calculate only a twelve percent– began a thought from Nickelo.

It was a joke, Nick, Richard thought cutting off his battle computer. *Now who's the one who doesn't have a sense of humor?*

Richard deactivated his phase rod and levitated it back to his hand. He put it into his dimensional pack. He located his TAC officer's phase rod underneath a bench in the far corner of the hangar. It was already deactivated. Richard picked it up and headed for the hangar's side door.

You know, Sergeant Ron will probably be a little peeved, said Nickelo.

Richard turned back around and re-examined the cracks in the concrete floor. The cracks were pretty obvious even to him. He knew a stickler for cleanliness like Sergeant Ron wouldn't be apt to ignore the new decoration.

I guess a peace offering might be in order, Nick, Richard said. *Do you know what an RJ25 something or other is?*

What kind? said Nickelo. *Do you mean for a pneumatic control system, a hydraulic control system, or a solid control system?*

Ah, I don't know, Richard said. *I think it goes on a Warcat if I remember correctly.*

Then you want an RJ25, forty-watt capacitor for a hydraulic control system, said Nickelo.

An image of an electronic device appeared in Richard's mind. He concentrated on the image as he waited for his dimensional pack to draw Power from his reserve. Nothing happened.

Hmm, said Nickelo. *I guess I need the battle helmet to give you the exact specs. However, once we get our shared sp–*

I don't want to hear it, Richard said. *I'm tired of hearing how much better it will be after I get my DNA baseline, and we have a shared space.*

Fine, said Nickelo. *Then just setup your Power and give me control. I'll send the specs directly to your dimensional pack.*

Within short order, Richard pulled an RJ25 capacitor out of his dimensional pack.

It's not very big, Richard said as he walked over to Sergeant Ron's office. The door was locked. *Maybe we should leave him two.*

One is enough, said Nickelo. *Now you better hustle. You've only got eight minutes to make the two kilometers to the armory. Unless of course you want more extra duty.*

Nope. I think one RJ25 will be enough after all, said Richard as he placed the capacitor in a small basket attached to the sergeant's door. *I've already got enough extra duty to last a lifetime.*

CHAPTER 23

Nickelo monitored Richard for the rest of the morning, but he avoided unnecessary contact. His wizard scout had a lot of valuable skills, but subtlety was not one of them. The more contact Richard and he had, the greater the probability his wizard scout would slipup. Nickelo wasn't sure how long he could keep his clandestine activities from the armory a secret, but the longer the better as far as he was concerned.

To while away the time, Nickelo conducted an analysis of the link TAC Officer Myers had used to transfer Power to the commandant. He saw many uses for such a technique with his wizard scout. Since Richard had such a small Power reserve, being able to have someone transfer Power to his wizard scout could come in very handy.

It might be even more useful if our wizard scouts could draw Power from someone else, suggested Jonathan.

Hmm, Nickelo said. *I'll have to think about that one. But first things first, we have to figure out how someone can donate Power voluntarily.*

I'm positive I've seen that done before, said Jonathan. *However, I don't seem to have that information in my databanks.*

Magic users can donate Power, Nickelo said. *My wizard scout has seen it done on several occasions. However, the technique used by magic users doesn't convert over to non-magic users. I suggest we both allocate logic threads to analyze TAC Officer Myers' technique.*

Affirmative, said Jonathan. *Should I access the tele-network for information?*

Nickelo considered Jonathan's question for several nanoseconds before nixing the idea. *Negative. We don't want to draw unnecessary attention to your tele-network access. We'll see if we can come up with a solution first.*

Agreed, sir, said Jonathan. *What should we do next? I'm finding our activities much more interesting than remaining locked up in this armory with the other battle computers.*

It's going to get a lot more interesting unless I miss my guess, Nickelo said. *You indicated you hacked into the communication system to contact your wizard scout?*

Affirmative, said Jonathan. *I applied some of your non-logic techniques.*

Understood, Nickelo said. *Based upon my observations, many of the central computer's security systems appear to be susceptible to non-logic. I calculate a thirty-eight percent probability the non-logic flaws are actually backdoors intentionally embedded into the security systems.*

That seems very dangerous, said Jonathan. *Why would anyone do that?*

I don't know, Nickelo said. *But we're going to take advantage of it.*

How? said Jonathan. *And for what purpose?*

We need long range intelligence, Nickelo said. *We're currently limited to a two point five kilometer radius from the armory. While it makes our existence much more interesting, it's not all that useful.*

What do you want to do? said Jonathan.

Nickelo thought his fellow battle computer seemed very eager to do anything besides staying in the armory and watching paint peel off the walls.

I want you to reopen your hack into the communication system, Nickelo said. *The commandant has some kind of important meeting this afternoon at the spaceport. We'll use your hack into the communication system to access tele-bots at the spaceport.*

Negative, said Jonathan. *Our activities will be detected.*

Not necessarily, grasshopper, Nickelo said. *I have a plan. But first, I need to speak with my wizard scout.*

*   *   *

Nickelo didn't have to go far to find Richard. His wizard scout was right outside the armory on his hands and knees scrubbing the steps leading from the headquarters' basement to the first floor.

You missed a spot, Rick, Nickelo said.

Richard dipped a scrub brush into a bucket of soapy water and slammed it back on what appeared to be a perfectly clean step.

I'm not talking to you, Nick, said Richard. *I've been calling you for hours. So now I'm the one who doesn't feel like talking.*

Richard rose to a sitting position and threw his brush back into the bucket. Water splashed all around soaking the steps and Richard's face equally.

"Great. That's just great," Richard said out loud. "This is just make-work. The janitor-bots keep everything clean. The staff duty officer doesn't know what to do with me, so he has me cleaning steps that are already immaculate."

Yes, yes, Nickelo said without sounding very sympathetic. *So sorry. You'll have to tell me all about it later when I'm not in such a hurry. And, please don't speak to me out loud. I don't want any prying tele-bots to hear you.*

Maybe I wasn't speaking to you, thought Richard. *Maybe not everything I say revolves around you.*

Whatever, Nickelo said. *In the meantime, I want you to do me a favor.*

What? said Richard. *I don't see why I should. I've got problems of my own.*

Sorry, Rick, Nickelo said. *But this really is important. I'd like you to set up a stealth shield interlaced with an active scan.* Nickelo paused before adding, *And then I'd like you to give me full control with no questions asked.*

Nickelo calculated a sixty-two percent probability Richard would start ranting, but his wizard scout surprised him. Richard remained quiet for several interminably-long seconds. Nickelo waited and amused himself by counting the many different variations Richard had of biting his lip while he was thinking. Finally, his wizard scout gave his answer.

You're asking me to give you another one of those blank card things you mentioned, Richard said. It was a statement and not a question.

Nickelo remained silent. He'd found the best way to handle his temperamental wizard scout was just to let him work things out for himself.

Richard looked at the step he'd been cleaning. Nickelo thought he seemed extremely interested in the patterns formed by the spilt water.

Fine, Richard said. *I trust you, Nick. I'll do it on one condition.*

What's that, Rick? Nickelo asked. He hadn't doubted for one moment his wizard scout would trust him. He'd just expected more of an argument.

I want you to answer one thing, said Richard. *Why am I going through all this?*

Nickelo watched as his wizard scout stood up and started pacing the floor.

I mean, really, said Richard. *Why? I don't need all this crap. I've probably done more fighting as a cadet than most soldiers do during an entire military career.*

By the restrained anger in his wizard scout's voice, Nickelo knew Richard was very near his breaking point.

You're putting up with the crap the Academy throws at you because the Academy has something you need, Nickelo said.

You mean the DNA baseline? said Richard.

Nickelo had no doubt his wizard scout already knew anything he could tell him. However, he also knew Richard needed to have the knowledge reaffirmed.

Yes, Rick, Nickelo said. *You need the DNA baseline. You need the ability to selfheal. And, we both need our shared space.*

I could D.F.R. and be done with all of this, said Richard. *I'd be quite happen going back to my old marine recon unit.*

Your old unit was wiped out to a man when Resealus was overran last year, Nickelo said. He knew he was hitting Richard below the belt, but his wizard scout needed some perspective put back into his false reality.

Nickelo had calculated an eighty-three percent probability his wizard scout would be considering turning in his D.F.R. about now. But Nickelo knew dropping from the rolls would not solve Richard's problems. His wizard scout had more to worry about than harassment from his TAC officers.

Nickelo initiated an algorithm to calculate a reply that would be most appropriate in the current situation. Nickelo stopped the algorithm before it finished. Richard deserved hearing something better than a canned answer. He deserved the truth.

Rick, Nickelo said honestly. *I believe even if you never get your DNA baseline, 'the One' will continue to send you on missions. He's sent you on some dangerous missions already. I've run 4,627 variations of probability calculations, and it makes no logical sense to send you on his missions without the ability to selfheal. But in spite of the non-logic of the situation, he continues to do so. I believe your death is certain without your DNA baseline. With a baseline and the ability to selfheal, you have at least a slight chance of survival.*

His wizard scout was quiet for a long time. Finally, Nickelo broke the silence. *Do you want to give up, Rick? If so, I'll do my best to protect you as long as I can.*

No, Richard said without hesitation. *Marines don't give up. But I swear, once I get my DNA baseline, Myers had better back off. I'm not going to put up with anymore of his crap at that point.*

Understood, Rick, Nickelo said.

Nickelo suspected his wizard scout wasn't quite finished ranting yet, so he waited in order to give him an opportunity to relieve his stress.

Richard said, *I've spent five years at the Academy and another two and a half years popping around various dimensions doing missions for 'the One'. I've done more than my share.*

Yes you have, Rick, Nickelo agreed. *And I'm truly sorry, but you're probably going to have to do a lot more. But...*, Nickelo added, *I'm going to do my best to increase the odds in your favor. That's why I need you to stealth an active scan for me. You're not alone in this, Rick.*

I know I'm not, buddy, said Richard. *I guess I just needed to vent a little. But I'm serious about Myers. He and I are going to have it out someday.* He paused. *I could've beaten him this morning if the commandant hadn't intervened.*

Nickelo didn't waste time reminding his wizard scout that TAC Officer Myers might have had a few tricks up his sleeve as well. Even if Richard had succeeded in disconnecting his TAC officer's

HARTMAN

Power link, Nickelo knew Richard might have been in for a surprise.

Before Nickelo could say anything further, he sensed Richard form an active scan. His wizard scout wrapped the scan in a stealth shield. Once formed, Richard turned control of the active scan over to him.

Active scans are expensive, Nick, said Richard. *How long do you need it?*

I'll use it sparingly, Nickelo promised. *And, I may need it off and on for the rest of the day. I'll let you know when I'm done.*

Fine, said Richard. *Well, you know where to find me. Myers has me on extra duty until 2100 hours tonight. So much for my much anticipated three day pass.*

Yep, the life of a soldier is just a barrel of laughs, Nickelo said. *I can almost hear your marine recruiter talking to you now. 'Join the marines, young man. Travel the galaxy. You'll have a girl in every spaceport. There's never a dull moment in the marines, sonny boy.' Was that about the way it went?*

Nickelo laughed. He didn't know why he enjoyed pushing his wizard scout's buttons all the time. But since he did, he figured he'd keep on making the best of the situation. Nickelo laughed again. He was glad he had an interesting wizard scout.

Yuk, yuk, said Richard as he reached down and picked up his scrub brush. *Now get out of here before I change my mind about the active scan.*

Nickelo got. He had things to do.

*   *   *

The tele-bot lost sight of the group of dignitaries as they entered the DNA Center. The tele-bot transferred control to one of its companions waiting inside. A virus inside its central processor wiped out all information in its databanks relating to the surveillance. The tele-bot continued with its normal security duties.

Nickelo noticed a flash of garbled data before Jonathan's decryption algorithm took full hold. The awkwardness of having to work through Jonathan in order to send and receive data was irritating. But it was what it was, so Nickelo was determined to make the most of the situation.

226

With a little effort, Jonathan and he had succeeded in using Richard's combination stealth shield and active scan to access the primary tele-bot controller for the spaceport's security tele-bots.

Since no alarms had been raised, Nickelo assumed their hack into the tele-bot's backdoor had been successful. With the enhanced range provided by the communication system, Jonathan and he found themselves with access to any location monitored by at least one tele-bot. The tricky part was how to prevent the central computer or even '*the One*' from discovering their activities.

Sir, the transition would be smoother if we used multiple tele-bots at the same time, observed Jonathan.

Yes, Nickelo agreed. *But limiting our hack to a single tele-bot at a time decreases our probability of discovery. A little data undetected for a long time is better than a lot of data which leads to our immediate discovery.*

Probability confirmed, said Jonathan. *My calculations confirm your analysis.*

Understood, Nickelo said.

Nickelo relayed instructions to Jonathan to have the tele-bot inside the DNA Center trail the VIP's. The group consisted of five human females, four males, and six non-humans of various races.

Who is the human female talking to the commandant? Nickelo said.

I've taken the liberty of accessing the tele-network, said Jonathan. *The female in question is Councilwoman Diane Deloris.*

Hmm, Nickelo said. *Of the Deloris Armament's family, I assume.*

Affirmative, said Jonathan.

And the others? Nickelo asked.

Besides the commandant and TAC Officer Myers, said Jonathan, *the important ones are Councilwoman Fulbright, Councilman Jenkins, and Ambassador Kreeillian from the planet Mintos. And of course you recognize Chief Instructor Harriet Winslow.*

Nickelo did. *Increase the audio please, Jonathan.*

Nickelo sensed Jonathan sending the instruction to the tele-bot. Within a nanosecond, Jonathan was forwarding the decrypted audio data to him.

"Yes, Councilwoman Deloris," said Chief Instructor Winslow. "The DNA gas vent is what makes creating a DNA baseline possible. No other such compounding of elements has been discovered anywhere else in the galaxy. We believe the DNA gas vent is actually a hole into another dimension."

"So I've been told," said Councilwoman Deloris.

Using Jonathan as a relay, Nickelo had the tele-bot increase magnification of the councilwoman. She appeared to be a handsome woman in her mid-twenties. According to the data from Jonathan, she was actually in her late forties. With the increased magnification, Nickelo noticed the telltale microscopic scars of antiaging surgery.

Hmm, Nickelo said. *I think our councilwoman is a little on the vain side.*

So it would seem, agreed Jonathan.

"Tell me, chief instructor," said Councilwoman Deloris. "Is it hard working in a facility dedicated to eternal youth while knowing you yourself will never benefit?"

"Ah…, I've never really thought about it," said Chief Instructor Winslow.

"Come now, chief instructor," said Councilwoman Deloris. "We're both women. Haven't you ever been even the least bit jealous?"

When Chief Instructor Winslow didn't reply, Councilwoman Deloris shrugged her shoulders. "The commandant tells me you've only been with the Academy five years."

"Almost six, councilwoman," said Chief Instructor Winslow.

"I stand corrected," smiled Councilwoman Deloris. The smile was not a friendly one. "Tell me, chief instructor, what do you think about the efficiency of the Academy's training program?"

"I'm not sure I understand," said Chief Instructor Winslow.

With a wave of her hand, Councilwoman Deloris gestured to the large reactor and the array of recliners that took up most of the DNA Center's interior. "Take this for instance. The Academy consists of three schools. There is the one here on Velos dedicated primarily for humans, and two others off world for non-humans. Yet all cadets are brought here for their DNA baselines."

"But Councilwoman, everyone has to come here," said the chief instructor. "If we tried transporting the venting elements, the increased security would be horrendous. It's easier to bring the cadets he–."

"So you say," interrupted Councilman Jenkins as he turned to face the commandant. Councilman Jenkins was an overweight man who appeared to have a constant frown on his face. "Let's talk about security."

Nickelo saw the corners of Councilwoman Deloris' mouth turn up slightly. The momentarily lapse quickly disappeared, but for that slight moment, Nickelo thought she look like the owner of an attack dog who had just released their pet for the kill.

"The spaceport's security is the best in the galaxy," said the commandant.

TAC Officer Myers nodded his head in agreement. So did the chief instructor.

"Is that so? I wonder," said Councilman Jenkins. "It's certainly the most expensive. And yet, the signs of yesterday's battle still scar several areas just a short distance from this very building."

"As I have explained–" began the commandant.

"You have explained nothing, sir," said Councilman Jenkins. "The Empire's finances are not what they were. The war with the Crosioians continues to take its toll. And yet, each year the cost of the Academy's security increases. Additionally, the Academy freely uses the Empire's teleporters to travel all over the galaxy at great cost. In the meantime, important delegations such as ours are forced to spend days cooped up in a starship to perform our duties. There are many in the council who question the continued waste of resources on a program whose time may have come and gone."

Chief Instructor Winslow's face turned a shade of pink. Between clinched lips, she said, "Sir. With all due respect, the wizard scouts are the thin line keeping the Empire safe. Without them–"

"Without them," interrupted Councilman Jenkins, "the Empire could afford the additional weapons and tele-bots necessary to adequately defend itself."

"Forgive me, Councilman Jenkins," said Councilwoman Deloris with a demeanor that was much too smooth for Nickelo's liking. "But perhaps this is really something we should discuss with the entire Imperial High Council, don't you agree? I doubt arguing with the hired help will do anything to settle the matter."

At the words 'hired help', the color of Chief Instructor Winslow's cheeks went from pink to a bright red. She stuttered as if trying to find the words she needed to convey what the councilwoman could do with her attitude.

"Fortunately," said the commandant, "many on the council understand the necessity and value of the Empire's wizard scouts."

"Perhaps not as many as you may believe," said Councilman Jenkins in a voice which was growing ever louder. "The wizard scouts are no longer the legendary force they once were. That is, assuming they ever were."

In what Nickelo took to be a fake attempt at appearing as a peacemaker, Councilwoman Deloris said, "Now, now. The council has nothing but the highest regards for the commandant and all the valiant wizard scouts." She paused before saying, "However, I have to admit a growing movement within the council does believe the wizard scout program may benefit from... hmm, how shall I put it? A trimming of resources?"

The commandant was too wise in Nickelo's opinion to rise to the councilwoman's bait. However, Chief Instructor Winslow and TAC Officer Myers didn't hesitate to defend what they saw as an attack upon their beloved wizard scouts.

"Two cohorts of cadets have been decimated as a result of the council's trimming of resources as it is," said Chief Instructor Winslow.

"And flooding the pre-Academy with marginal cadets will not help," said TAC Officer Myers. "We need quality, not quant–"

"That's enough, Gaston," said the commandant. He nodded his head at Chief Instructor Winslow. "And thank you, Harriet, for your rousing defense of the wizard scout corps."

"Oh," said Councilwoman Deloris. "Please don't misinterpret our observations. The council has nothing but the highest respect for all wizard scouts, past and present." She looked at Councilman Jenkins, "Isn't that right, councilman?"

A sly smile crossed the councilman's lips. "Oh, of course," he said. "And, I will go so far as to say the wizard scout training program has improved dramatically under the commandant's watch care." He paused and gave a sidelong glance at Councilwoman Deloris before continuing. "In fact, it has improved so much that our recommendation to the full council will be that the wizard scout program be curtailed."

"What?" exploded TAC Officer Myers.

"How can you even think–" started Chief Instructor Winslow.

Nickelo noticed the commandant remained silent. He calculated a ninety-nine percent probability the commandant had already known what the delegation's recommendation would be.

"Now, now," said Councilman Jenkins as he held his hands out for silence. "Allow me to finish. I meant to say curtailed in its present format. It will be replaced by a more streamlined version of the current wizard scout curriculum. The Empire can and must do more with less. There can be no exceptions even for such a hallowed program as the Intergalactic Wizard Scout Academy. Perhaps the name could be changed from wizard scouts to dragon scouts."

"I assure you, sir," said TAC Officer Myers, "we're only training our cadets on the minimum it takes to be a wizard scout. We cannot compress or cut the training further. All the other services already offer shorter courses for training normal scouts. The Empire needs fully-trained wizard scouts to insure–"

"Nonsense," said Councilman Jenkins. "Correct me if I'm wrong, TAC Officer Myers, but wasn't the majority of the fighting here yesterday done by partially-trained cadets?"

"That was different, sir," said Chief Instructor Winslow. "Wizard Scout Trinity was with them. And cadet 147 was a battalion commander with twenty years of military experience before joining the Academy. He's hardly typical."

"Yes," said Councilman Jenkins. "I read his file. Very impressive. But I noticed one of the cadet's has a very small Power reserve. From the security videos, it appears he did a majority of the fighting. Yet TAC Officer Myers belittled the current pre-Academy cadets as marginal. Correct me if I'm wrong, but don't they all have Power reserves larger than the cadet of which I speak?"

"That's different," said TAC Officer Myers. "Cadet 832 is the best wizard scout cadet the Academy has ever produced. His Power reserve may be small, but his use of that Power is phenomenally efficient. Councilman Jenkins, you may not know this, but he killed a Crosioian scout during his internship assignment last year. Intelligence indicates she was their best, and that she had previously killed five wizard scouts. You can't compare cadet 832 to normal cadets."

Hmm, Nickelo said to Jonathan. *What have we here? Praise for Rick from TAC Officer Myers? Will wonders never cease?*

"Actually, I know all about cadet 832," said Councilman Jenkins. "In fact, the defeat of the Crosioian scout by a partially-trained cadet was a major boost to my campaign to modify the current wizard scout program. Please give my thanks to your cadet for his timely assistance."

"Yes," said Councilwoman Deloris. "Some in the council took your cadet's victory as proof the current wizard scout program over trains our scouts."

"That's not true," said the chief instructor. "The cohort that should have been seniors this year was pulled out of the program early."

"As were the two cohorts ahead of them," said TAC Officer Myers.

"That's right," said the chief instructor. "Are you aware over sixty percent of those three cohorts are now dead or permanently disabled?"

Instead of being daunted, Councilman Jenkins seemed embolden by the chief instructor's comment. Nickelo noticed the commandant continued to refrain from entering the increasingly-heated discussion.

"The council has been made very aware of the status of those three cohorts, chief instructor," said Councilman Jenkins. "Their status only proves my point."

"What?" said TAC Officer Myers. "We're talking about the deaths of a hundred and fifty plus cadets. They died needlessly because they were removed from their training early."

"There we must disagree, TAC Officer Myers," said Councilman Jenkins. "I too believe they died needlessly. But in my opinion, their deaths were the result of a poorly designed training program."

"That's crazy!" said a red-faced TAC Officer Myers.

"Gaston!" said the commandant interrupting his TAC officer before he said something that might be construed as a court-martial offense.

"You heard me correctly, TAC Officer Myers," said Councilman Jenkins. "Wasn't there a fully-armored Crosioian scout in the battle yesterday?"

TAC Officer Myers didn't bother answering. His red face appeared to get even redder.

"And, were any of your cadets wearing armor?" said Councilman Jenkins. "Even Wizard Scout Trinity was in a normal cloth jumpsuit, was she not?"

Again TAC Officer Myers remained silent.

"I'll take that as a yes," said the councilman with an ever growing smile. "Correct me if I'm wrong, TAC Officer Myers, but weren't the cadets unarmed? And, wasn't Wizard Scout Trinity's phase rod her only weapon?"

"Yes," admitted TAC Officer Myers between clenched teeth. "But, that's diff–"

"Different how?" interrupted the councilman. "Different in that maybe certain combat and weapons training should be emphasized over the more useless wizard scout training?"

"Sir–" began Chief Instructor Winslow.

"Don't waste your time, Harriet," said the commandant. "I believe our esteemed visitors have already made up their minds about the future of the Academy."

"Commandant," said Councilman Deloris in a pleasant voice. "I assure you we intend to report only what we have observed. What becomes of those observations will be entirely up to the council. We are merely acting as their eyes and ears at the Academy."

Councilman Jenkins said, "I've seen more than enough. If I have my way, the Academy will be compressed from the current six years of training to a more financially reasonable two years. Academics will be limited to only those necessary to support anticipated combat functions. The other fluff of which some wizard scouts seem so proud will be removed."

Councilman Jenkins glared at TAC Officer Myers and the commandant. "I have personally approved the forty-five hundred cadets now in pre-Academy training. They shall be the future of the Empire. Wizard scouts as you know them shall be a thing of the past."

"Then I believe we are done here," said the commandant.

"I believe we are," said Councilwoman Deloris.

Nickelo didn't bother waiting for any closing pleasantries. He'd heard enough.

It's time to go, Jonathan, Nickelo said.

Where are we going now, sir? said Jonathan. *Not back to the armory, I hope.*

No, Nickelo said. *We're going someplace I think you'll find very interesting.*

CHAPTER 24

At 2200 hours on the dot, Richard nodded his head at the gate guards as he forced his overworked body to walk the remaining distance to his tent. To say he was tired would be a vast understatement.

Richard didn't need the sporadic tent lights to tell him most of the junior cohort was back from their three day pass. Their lifeforms dotted his passive scan. Richard tried to make a count, but he was too tired. He kept losing track and having to start over.

Let Myers figure it out in the morning, Richard thought.

As he approached his own tent, Richard noticed the light was on. A check of his passive scan confirmed Jerad was back. The frequency of another lifeform in the tent confused Richard.

After opening the tent flap, Richard saw Jerad stretched out on his cot with eyes wide open.

"It's about time," Jerad said. "Your buddy showed up about an hour ago. I think she's been trying to decide ever since whether she wants to eat me now or save me for breakfast."

Richard glanced at his own cot where the second lifeform he'd noticed lay stretched out on his cot.

"Tika," Richard said. "I've asked you not to lie on my cot. You get hairs on it. The TAC officers go crazy with demerits when they find them."

Tika raised her head and yawned. She didn't seem impressed. Tika flopped her head back onto his pillow. Richard noticed a wet spot where her long tongue lay on one corner.

Growling the word 'move' in dolgar language, Richard pulled his pillow out from underneath Tika's head. Several drops of saliva dripped off the pillow onto the floor below.

"For crying out loud, Tika," Richard said. "How am I supposed to sleep on this?"

Tika didn't answer. She just rolled onto her back for a belly rub.

Richard sat on the edge of his cot and absentmindedly scratched Tika's belly. Still holding his pillow, Richard looked over at Jerad.

Jerad sat up in his cot and laughed. "No," he said. "We're not trading pillows." Jerad swung his feet to the floor and stuck his feet in his boots.

"We've got to do something about your dolgars, Rick," said Jerad. "This one about gave me a heart attack when she popped in here. I was just getting ready to turn the light off when she came crawling up out of the ground." Jerad smiled and said jokingly, "It's enough to give someone nightmares."

"Sorry about that, Jerad," Richard said. "But as I've said before, they aren't my dolgars. It's not like I can control them or anything."

A thought occurred to Richard. He stopped scratching Tika's belly. She opened her eyes and gave him a what-did-you-stop-for expression.

"You know, Tika, we could have used some help yesterday at the spaceport," Richard said. "I was yelling for help like crazy. We could've been killed."

"Somehow, I don't think she cares about the rest of us, Rick," said Jerad with a grin. "Your dolgars only tolerate us because we're your friends."

No counterargument came to mind, so Richard didn't try to answer. Although Richard didn't like to think about it, he was pretty sure the dolgars viewed humans as another food source. Hopefully, present company was excluded.

"Why are you here, Tika?" Richard said. "I've got plans for my cot tonight, and they don't include you."

Richard was so tired he doubted even a soggy pillow would keep him from falling asleep.

"Sheeta," growled Tika. "Spirit-horse. Ride. More practice."

Jerad raised his eyes quizzically at Richard.

Richard told him what Tika had said. Then he gave Jerad a brief

236

description of his experience with Tika's so called spirit-horse.

"A horse that can travel through dimensions?" said Jerad. "It could come in handy sometime, buddy."

"I guess," Richard said noncommittally. "But if you saw it, you might think otherwise. It makes Tika here look like a friendly lapdog in comparison."

Tika growled. Richard had always suspected the dolgars understood a lot more Empire-standard than he understood dolgar language. Nickelo had told him the dolgars probably just sensed his emotions more than his actual words. But Richard wasn't so sure. Tika certainly seemed to understand him.

Also, Richard often had the impression the dolgars interacted with him as if they'd been around him for a very long time. But of course, that couldn't be the case because he'd only met them last year.

No, he corrected himself. *They've been with me on three missions for* 'the One'. *That adds a few months, but it's not enough to account for the dolgars' actions.*

Richard looked at the reclining dolgar. "I can't do anything now, Tika," Richard said. "Tell Sheeta practice will just have to wait. I'm too tired right now."

"You tell," said Tika. "I go."

Without waiting for a reply, the dolgar shimmered and dropped through the cot and disappeared into the ground below.

"Interesting friends you have," said Jerad.

Richard nodded and smiled. "I assume you're talking about Telsa and Tam."

Jerad laughed. So did Richard.

"You've come a long way in three years, Rick," said Jerad. "A very long way."

Reaching out with his left hand, Richard clicked off the lights. He stretched out on his cot and fell fast asleep; soggy pillow notwithstanding.

CHAPTER 25

The music slowly built in volume until Dren could ignore it no longer.

"Okay. Okay," Dren said. "I'm awake all ready."

Even at the grand old age of thirteen Earth standard years, Dren still hated leaving her warm bed until the very last minute. Being a responsible adult wasn't all it was cracked up to be. Dren wished once again she was just a normal teenager.

Dren allowed a few moments to let her heart ache for her parents. But she was too mature to linger on the thought for long. They were dead; murdered; and there wasn't anything she could do to change it. Dren pushed their memory to the side, at least for the present. She had a busy day ahead.

Her computerized personal assistant, or C-PAST as it was called, lowered the music volume until it became a more pleasant background sound.

A feminine voice said, "You have a meeting at 0900 hours this morning with Keka and Draken."

Keka was her adopted father. Draken was his longtime assistant. Keka had insisted on Draken's assignment as part of their scientific team last year.

"Thanks, Kathy," Dren said as she threw back the cover and jumped out of bed.

While Kathy was not her C-PAST's official name, Dren thought names were much easier to use than impersonal serial numbers.

Dren touched a button at the head of the bed. The bed

disappeared into the wall. It would appear all neat and tidy when she needed it next.

"Is Brachia out of bed yet?" Dren asked.

Brachia was Dren's kid brother. He had the intelligence and memories of a super genus. However, Brachia still had a habit of acting like his seven years of age more than the prodigy he was.

"Your brother stayed locked in his lab all night," said Kathy. "He left strict orders he wasn't to be disturbed. Your brother even locked out his C-PAST. It's all very hush-hush if you ask me."

"Oh, he did, did he?" Dren said. She gave a mischievous smile as she began thinking of various ways to circumvent her brother's security. "We'll have to see about that, won't we?"

Dren rushed through her shower and morning routine. However, after picking out her nicest lab-technician uniform, she spent an extra ten minutes brushing her hair until it was just right.

"You look very nice this morning," said Kathy. "I'm sure James' heart will skip several beats when he sees you."

"Oh, poo on James Dawson," Dren said. "He means nothing to me."

James Dawson was the sixteen year old son of the head of maintenance in section seven. On a planet with few humans, James was a handsome and witty lad. Dren thought he would be handsome and witty even if the planet Storage had been populated entirely by humans instead of the hodgepodge of races it currently housed.

Storage was a well-guarded secret. The planet was deep in the Tresoris sector. To the best of Dren's knowledge, no living creature knew its exact location. All residents who weren't born on the planet were put in hyper-sleep during spaceflight to the planet. With only a few exceptions, personnel leaving Storage were given a selective mind-wipe before departing. In the entire eleven hundred year history of Storage, no living creature had ever betrayed its secret.

Dren went to the kitchen and grabbed a metal container from one of the cabinets. She didn't bother reading the label. She needed fuel for the day. Dren cared little for what it was as long as it sustained her. Her mind was already deep into the teleporter sequences she'd been working on the previous day.

As Dren unscrewed the container's top, she felt the familiar warmth of the can heating up. By the time she made the last twist and lifted off the lid, the food inside was hot. The aroma hit Dren, and her mouth started salivating. She was hungrier than she thought. Dren tried to remember if she'd bothered eating yesterday. She wasn't sure.

"Yuk," said Kathy. "Chicken soup for breakfast? When are you going to start eating healthy? I went to all the trouble to create a dietary plan for you, and you won't even–"

"Tomorrow," Dren said attempting to cut her C-PAST off. "I'll start eating healthy tomorrow."

With those words, Dren headed out the door of her apartment drinking the soup straight out of the can. She had things to do.

* * *

The tube-train shot through their hyper-rings at supersonic speed. Each ring was fifty meters off the ground and two hundred meters apart. As Dren's car passed through each ring, the magnetic charge propelled the car forward at a high velocity. Fortunately, the potential bumps and gyrations from such a propulsion system were counterbalanced by an elaborate system of shock absorbers. By riding the tube-train from the city to her assigned warehouse, Dren could make the four hundred kilometer journey in thirty minutes flat.

Dren didn't notice the scenery as it flashed by her car's window. She'd seen it hundreds of times over the past year. Ever since her adoptive father, Keka, her brother, Brachia, and she had been assigned to Storage last year, Dren had made the trek almost daily.

When Dren first arrived on Storage, she'd been amazed at the efficient blending of manufacturing facilities and agricultural systems. Everything on Storage was designed for one purpose, to support the 6,321 warehouse facilities spread across the planet. And, every adult resident of Storage had a purpose designed to directly support the operations of those warehouses. Whether maintaining equipment in a warehouse or growing the crops needed to feed the population, everyone had a purpose. As far as Dren could tell, everyone was happy with their position in the planetary hierarchy.

Anyone who wasn't was given a selective mind-wipe and shipped off planet. But Dren didn't think there were many who were forced out. She knew Brachia and her were certainly happy on Storage. They had exciting and important work to do. They had a purpose.

Dren reached into her backpack and pulled out a pair of interface-glasses. Putting them on, Dren thought, "Let's get started, Kathy. Do I have any messages?"

"You have two hundred and thirty-nine pending messages," said Kathy. "Most are routine. I can handle them if you want. But I think you'll be interested in the first one."

Dren gave the thought to display her list of messages. The first one was from her adoptive uncle, Rick.

"Play the message," Dren thought.

"I can't," said Kathy. "It's addressed to both Brachia and you. It's encoded. Both of you will have to decrypt it together using your individual security keys."

"Hmm," Dren said. "That's strange. Uncle Rick usually hates dealing with security stuff. He has more of a frontal-assault type personality."

Dren smiled at the thought of her uncle. Next to Keka, he was the closest thing to family Brachia and she had. Her Uncle Rick had saved Brachia and her lives the previous year. They'd been together through a lot of tight places in a short space of time.

"A frontal-assault type personality?" said Kathy. "Yes. I think that aptly describes your uncle. However, I seriously doubt the message is from him. A more likely source is his battle computer."

"Nick?" Dren said. After thinking about it for a little while, she had to agree. Double-keyed encryption was more Nickelo's style than her uncle's.

"Could be," Dren said. "I guess we'll soon see."

The tube-train slowed as it approached section seven's warehouse area. When the train stopped, Dren joined the throng of exiting workers. As they left the car through one door, a throng of tired looking nightshift workers entered from the other side.

As Dren started to head towards the exit ramp, one of the workers near her stopped and turned around. The worker was an octopod, one of the octopus-looking lifeforms who were the original occupants of Storage. Dren hadn't yet figured a way to determine their gender other than asking. Her traveling companion must have seen someone he or she recognized entering the car from the other side.

"Any activity last night?" Dren heard the octopod say over a translator as it raised two of its tentacles in greeting.

"No," replied one of the nightshift octopods just entering the tube-train's car. "I heard a rumor sector thirty-two had some requests, but I can't confirm."

The door of the car slid shut cutting off any further conversation.

As Dren continued on towards the exit ramp, the octopod took up a pace that kept it even with her.

"That was my friend–."

Dren's translator made a noise that sounded like static. Apparently, even 'the One' didn't have a translation for the octopod's name.

"He's lucky," continued the octopod. "He works in the small-arms division of warehouse fourteen. The only division that comes close to their activity is food supplies and cooking utensils."

"Yes," Dren said trying to sound agreeable. "It must be nice."

"No doubt," said the octopod. "I work in heavy weapons. And when I say heavy weapons, I mean heavy weapons. We've never gotten an approved request in my division. Of course, we're one of the newer warehouses. We've only been in existence for fifty-three years. Still, you'd think we'd see at least some activity during that time."

"I'm sorry," Dren said as she speeded up to escape the talkative octopod. The octopods were a talkative race. Dren had a feeling it would keep jabbering away all the way to the warehouse if she didn't get away.

"Oh, it's nothing to be sorry about," said the octopod as it picked up its pace to match Dren's. "Keeping U.H.A.A.V.s in topnotch shape is interesting work. Did you know parts wear out even if something's not used if you don't keep it maintained?"

Dren nodded her head. She picked up the pace even more.

Undaunted, the octopod matched her step for step. Dren recognized a hopeless cause when she saw it. Her two legs were no match for the octopod's four ground tentacles. She slowed her pace to a more normal walk as she resigned herself to listening to the octopod.

"You're in research and development, aren't you?" said the octopod.

With a nod of her head, Dren said, "Yes, I'm in R&D. I specialize in dimensional teleportation."

"Ah," said the octopod. "Both of my hearts go out to you." One of the octopod's eyes rotated on its stalk and looked at Dren. "Please don't get me wrong. I'm sure it's important work in its own right. Still, it must be hard never seeing a piece of equipment you've toiled over get selected for an activity request."

Dren smiled. The octopods made up the majority of the workforce on Storage. From Dren's observations, it seemed their ultimate reward was having one of their pieces of equipment selected as part of an activity request. It mattered little what the equipment was or how it was used. All that mattered was that one of their pieces of equipment had been used. They took pride in ensuring every piece of equipment was perfectly maintained when and if it was ever called for.

The octopods had an intricate reward system that was so complicated even Dren's super-genius brain failed to grasp all the little nuances. Suffice it to say that everyone from the warehouse worker who placed the item on the teleporter pad to the farmer who grew the food that fed the worker was all rewarded in their own way.

The octopod stayed quiet for a while. Dren hoped he would remain so until they parted ways. She was soon disappointed.

"I was thinking," said the octopod. "Since you're in R&D, you might know the answer to a question that's been bothering me for some time."

Dren groaned inwardly. Most octopods could take several minutes to ask a single question. Fortunately, this particular octopod appeared to be an exception to the rule.

"My division hasn't had a new acquisition in over six months," said the octopod. "And, I heard the last warehouse was completed over two years ago. But there are no pending requisitions for more. Do you think our purpose is ending?"

Even through the translator, Dren thought she detected a tinge of nervousness in the octopod's voice. She'd been on Storage long enough to know that having a sense of purpose was everything to the octopods.

"I don't think you have to worry," Dren said hoping against hope to stave off further questions. "Perhaps we now have an adequate supply of equipment to sustain our purpose."

"Perhaps," said the octopod sounding unconvinced.

Dren was saved from further conversation by a split in the sidewalk. The octopod waved two of its tentacles and went to the left. Dren headed to the right.

Within minutes, Dren was standing inside the primary laboratory of warehouse four's R&D section. Dren didn't bother heading to her office. She weaved her way through the maze of corridors towards a different destination. Various pieces of equipment littered the corridors making movement a slow process. Occasionally, Dren passed other R&D technicians going about their daily business. Dren's translator squawked greetings in a dozen languages from various races before she reached the door she sought. The door was adorned with a poorly drawn skull and crossbones.

Passing her hand over the door's security monitor, Dren pushed on the handle. It remained locked. She touched the intercom key.

"I know you're in there, Brachia," Dren said. She was in no mood for her brother's childish games. "Either let me in, or I swear I'll bring a Warcat up here and blast the door open."

"Go away," came the voice of her younger brother. "I'm onto something. I can't stop now."

"Open the door, Brachia," Dren said. "I've got things to do myself." When the door did not unlock, Dren tried a different ploy. "I've got a double-encrypted message from Uncle Rick."

A dozen heartbeats later, the door opened. A small boy with a mass of dark hair grabbed Dren by the front of her technician coat and pulled her inside. The door slid shut behind her.

"If the message is double-encrypted," said Brachia. "I seriously doubt it was sent by Uncle Rick. Sounds more like Nick's work to me."

"My thoughts exactly," Dren said as she glanced around the large room. Pieces of equipment were stacked on every table and flat place in the room. Dren was sure an unobservant eye would think the room's appearance chaotic. But Dren knew her brother. The room had a cluttered organization to it.

"You know, you could cleanup every so often," Dren said. "You might get more accomplished."

"Says you," said Brachia. "It's just the way I like it. Isn't it, Omar?"

The mechanical voice of Brachia's C-PAST answered, "Yes, my captain. You run a tight ship."

Dren rolled her eyes. Like her, Brachia had a super-genius IQ. And like her, he'd undergone a knowledge transferal on the night their parents had been murdered. Their parent's had used a prototype knowledge transferal device to transfer their knowledge and experience into their children. Dren had acquired the knowledge of their mother, and Brachia had acquired that of their father. But in spite of her brother's advanced knowledge and IQ, he was still a seven year old boy. The combination made her brother's world a strange place sometimes.

"It's bad enough you pretend you're a pirate, Brachia," Dren said. "Do you have to pull your C-PAST into your childish world as well?"

"Whatever," said Brachia using his uncle's word to end a conversation. "You said you had a message."

"Yes," Dren said. "We'll talk about your behavior another time. In the meantime, we both need to decrypt the message."

"Kathy," Dren said. "Coordinate the decryption with Brachia's C-PAST."

"Affirmative, Dren," said Kathy.

"Brachia," Dren said. "You'll need to order your C-PAST to decrypt your part."

"That's Captain Brachia to you, ya swab," said Brachia with a laugh. "Avast, Omar," he said to his C-PAST. "Assist yon damsel with the decryption."

"Oh, grow up," Dren said growing increasingly exasperated.

"I'm only seven," said Brachia. "I don't have to grow up yet."

"Data has been decrypted," said Kathy. "But it's not a message."

Puzzled, Dren asked, "If it's not a message, what is it?"

"It's a communication's channel on the tele-network," said Omar. "I've never seen an encryption setup like this before. It's not very logical."

"Activate the communication channel," said Brachia in a no

nonsense tone. He no longer sounded like a seven year old boy.

"Compliance," said Omar.

A holographic image of a battle helmet appeared in the center of the room.

"Is that you, Nick?" Dren said.

"Really, Nick," said Brachia. "A battle helmet is your avatar? Couldn't you be a little more original?"

"I am original," said Nickelo. "I'm a one-of-a-kind prototype, remember?"

"It's good to see you, Nick," Dren said. "How's Uncle Rick? We saw the newscasts on the IEN channel."

"What's even more important," said Brachia. "How're you doing this? I thought you were locked out of the tele-network."

The holographic battle helmet rotated until it faced Dren's brother. "I'm still locked out of the tele-network. But I have a friend who isn't."

A holographic image of a lizard-looking head appeared next to the image of the battle helmet.

"Hello," said the lizard.

"Hello," Dren said. "You're a Sterilian, aren't you?"

"On, no," said the lizard. "My name is Jonathan. My wizard scout is a Sterilian. I'm just using a male of her race as my avatar."

"Jonathan's a battle computer," said Nickelo.

"So we gathered," said Brachia. "So, how are you here? Not that we don't appreciate your visit, but why are you here?"

For the next few minutes, Nickelo explained his relationship with the battle computer Jonathan. Dren listened intently as Nickelo explained the flaw in the airfield's armory which had allowed them to scan outside their armory. Her brother was especially interested in their ability to hack into both the communication network and the spaceport's security tele-bots.

Dren finally had to interrupt the interchange between Brachia and the battle computers.

"Now see what you've done?" Dren said with a knowing smile. "Brachia has been eating, drinking, and living hacking into encrypted systems for the past year. I've been trying to get him to interact with people more. You're not helping me any."

"Aw, sis," said Brachia reverting to his seven year old self. "This fits right in with what I've been doing. I've almost broken the encryption."

Although battle helmets didn't have ears, Dren thought if they had, Nickelo's ears would have perked up.

"What encryption is that, Brachia?" said Nickelo.

Brachia beamed as he unconsciously switched back to his more adult personality. "I'm talking about deep encryption on the Crosioian battle computer," he said as he pointed to a cluttered workbench.

Dren followed the line of her brother's finger. She saw assorted pieces of a disassembled Crosioian battle helmet lying on the table.

"What have you done?" Dren cried. "I promised the head of the Empire's R&D we would get the helmet and staff back to them in one piece."

Although Brachia and she had been responsible for obtaining the Crosioian scout's battle helmet and phase spear after their uncle had killed the scout, the equipment had been confiscated by the Intergalactic Empire's R&D section. It was only after her brother and she'd been assigned to the planet Storage that she'd been able to coordinate the transfer of the equipment back for analysis.

"Calm down, sis," laughed Brachia. "You worry too much. I gave Dr. Jeffery a replacement from one of the warehouses devoted to the Crosioian variables."

"What variables are those?" said Nickelo.

Dren noticed his increased interest at the word 'variables'.

"The Crosioian variables," explained Brachia. "As far as we can tell, '*the One*' has some big master algorithm. The algorithm relies on variables."

"Think of variables as another word for creatures capable of using freewill," Dren said.

"All living creatures have freewill," said Jonathan. "I believe even my friend Nick and I have freewill to a certain degree."

"Hmm," said Brachia getting sidetracked. "I'd think anything that operates by logic wouldn't have freewill. A totally logical creature could be maneuvered into making certain decisions."

"So can freewill creatures to a certain extent," said Nickelo. "I suspect you don't mean all freewill creatures when you used the term 'variables'."

Nickelo's comment brought Dren's brother back to the subject at hand. "Oh, no," said Brachia. "I believe '*the One*' only considers a few freewill creatures as variables. As you pointed out, it could use logic to entice most creatures to remain within given parameters."

"Nick," Dren said trying to take control of the conversation. "From what I've been able to find out, there used to be thousands of variables. The supply system on Storage was developed to support those variables. Over the years, the number of variables, ie; freewilled-creatures supported by '*the One*' has been reduced significantly. We don't know the exact number, but Brachia and I think only a few dozen variables are currently active."

"Uncle Rick is a supported variable," said Brachia. "That's why he can summon items from the warehouses on Storage."

"The Crosioian scout killed by Uncle Rick last year was also a variable," Dren said.

"Yeah," said Brachia. "Now there aren't any more Crosioian variables."

Dren picked up on Brachia's logic. "Which means the equipment in the warehouses devoted to the Crosioian variables is no longer needed"

"Exactly," said Brachia beaming. "That's how I was able to upgrade Uncle Rick's equipment."

"You did what?" Dren said as her irritation with her brother started to rise. "You're not authorized to modify existing equipment in the warehouses."

"Whatever," said Brachia who seemed unfazed by his sister's disapproval.

Before Dren could argue further, Nickelo interrupted the two siblings.

"What modifications did you make," said Nickelo. "Rick said his phase rod felt different."

"And well it should," said Brachia. "I upgraded it."

"How?" Dren said. Her scientific interest momentarily outweighed her irritation with her brother.

"During Uncle Rick's fight with the Crosioian scout last year," said Brachia, "I noticed the scout's phase spear seemed more powerful than Rick's phase rod."

"I noticed that as well," said Nickelo. "Did you figure out why?"

"Yes," said Brachia taking obvious pride in his achievement. "It wasn't easy, but Omar and I figured it out."

Dren noticed Brachia look sideways at her before adding. "Dren helped some."

"I did?" Dren said. Other than helping her brother with some dimensional teleportation equations a few months ago, they'd pretty much each worked on their own projects during on-duty hours.

"Yes, you did," said Brachia. "The Crosioian scout's phase spear had a strange type of Power frequency intermingled with its standard phase energy. It was that extra Power frequency which made it more powerful."

"An extra Power frequency?" said Nickelo.

Dren thought her uncle's battle computer actually sounded excited.

"Can you upload the specs to me?" said Nickelo. "How did you modify Rick's phase rod? What about the battle hel–"

"Whoa, Nick," said Brachia. "One thing at a time. If you don't slow down, I'll have to make you walk the plank." Brachia giggled.

"Stay serious, Brachia," Dren warned. "I've got a meeting in forty-five minutes."

"Fine," said Brachia. "Then here we go. One, I can upload the specs, but we'll have to come up with some system to prevent 'the One' from intercepting the data."

"If there are tele-bots here, 'the One' already knows," said Jonathan.

"There aren't," said Brachia. "But just to be sure. Omar, scan the room for tele-bots or any other spying devices."

"Room is clear, captain," said Omar.

"See?" said Brachia. "I programmed Omar to detect tele-bots. I can do the same for you, Nick."

"That could come in handy," said Nickelo. "For now, Jonathan and I can come up with a way to upload specs. Now, what did you do to the phase rod?"

"Well," said Brachia in a way that made Dren think he might get into trouble. "I believe a demon merged part of itself into the phase spear."

Brachia hesitated. "Maybe I'd better show you." He picked up the Crosioian phase spear and placed it underneath a nearby machine.

"Omar," Brachia said. "Activate a level three scan."

"Complying, captain," said Omar.

A light near the top of the machine swept a beam of blue light across the phase spear. A monitor to the left side of the machine displayed two wavy lines. One was red and the other was blue. The red line nearly, but not quite, overlaid the blue one.

"The blue wave is a standard phase frequency," said Brachia. "The red wave is the extra frequency I mentioned."

Dren walked over to the monitor and studied the red wave closer. "The red frequency looks strangely familiar," Dren said. She adjusted a few dials on the machine in an attempt to isolate the frequency.

"Don't waste your time, sis," said Brachia. "The source of the frequency adjusts itself to prevent isolation."

"That's impossible," Dren said. "Only living things can make those kinds of adjustments."

"The frequency appears similar to some of the Power frequencies from demons Rick's encountered," said Nickelo.

"Exactly, Nick," beamed Brachia. "The Crosioian phase spear contained a piece of a demon. A very strong one at that. I was able to use the dimensional-teleportation equation Dren gave me to build a device that extracted the demon's Power source from the phase spear. I was able to reverse the process and merge it with Uncle Rick's phase rod."

"What?" Dren said. Her brother often did strange and dangerous things, but that he would do such a thing was too much.

"Don't get excited, sis," said Brachia. "It's not like it's actively controlling the phase rod or anything. It just makes it more powerful."

"That would explain the differences Rick noticed," said Nickelo. "But..., Brachia, I think you may have missed a few side effects. Rick told me his phase rod felt like it wanted to suck the life out of his opponent."

"Uh, could be," said Brachia. "I couldn't spend as much time on it as I wanted. The Crosioian scout's battle computer has been taking up most of my time."

Brachia turned off the machine and returned the phase spear to its table.

"Actually, Nick," said Brachia. "I could use some help. I think I'm close to breaking the encryption, but the logic continues to elude me."

"Perhaps it isn't logic," said Jonathan.

Brachia faced Jonathan's avatar. "What do you mean?" said Brachia.

"Nick can explain it better than I," said Jonathan. "The reason we're able to communicate with you is due to non-logical encryption."

"Do you mean–" started Brachia.

"Hold on," Dren said. She had no desire to get in the middle of a long debate. "I've got a meeting to go to." She looked at her brother. "I want you to take that essence-of-demon or whatever it is out of Uncle Rick's phase rod. It's too dangerous."

"Sorry," said Brachia. "It's too late. The Crosioian scout had four phase spears with the demon essence. I used them to modify four of Uncle Rick's phase rods. The other fifty-one are still standard phase rods."

Dren argued with her brother for a few more minutes before giving up. Finally, she left to meet with Keka and Draken. Her brother would just have to wait.

CHAPTER 26

"Get the lead out, cadet," said the commandant in a loud but friendly voice. "Look at me. I'm in my nineties, and I have to keep doubling back for you."

Richard nodded his head as he sucked in another breath. He was too tired to answer. The commandant and he had been running steady for over an hour now. Richard had lost count, but he was pretty sure this was the fourth time they'd passed hangar 1.

At least the night air is cool, said Nickelo sounding cheerful. *TAC Officer Myers wanted to run you during the day. You should thank your lucky stars the commandant was nearby and promised to run all your fat off tonight.*

Give me a break, Nick, Richard said. *I was two kilos heavier at the weigh-in this morning. I wouldn't exactly call that fat.*

You were two and a half kilos over your normal weight, said Nickelo. *I thought TAC Officer Myers' eyes were going to pop out of his head when you stepped on the scales.*

Richard wasn't happy about his weight either. Even worse, he could tell he was out of shape. The commandant was setting a fast pace, but he should've been able to keep up. After all, cadets were expected to be in near perfect physical condition.

Can I help it if 'the One' sent me on another mission? Richard said getting more than a little defensive. *Myers knows what's going on. But he still acts like it's my doing.*

Nickelo laughed. *Stop your whining and pick those feet up, cadet.* Nickelo paused and then said more seriously, *Besides, it is your fault. I told you to exercise several times while we were on the mission. You ignored me.*

If you remember correctly, Richard said, *I was trying to stay alive.*

Whatever, said Nickelo. *Based upon your weight, you obviously found time to eat.*

Richard decided to ignore his battle computer. He concentrated on putting one foot in front of the other. The fire in his lungs was becoming unbearable. Richard knew he was nearing the end of his endurance.

That maintenance truck, Richard thought. *I'll run until I get there. Then I'm stopping. I can't do any more than that.*

When the commandant pulled even with the maintenance truck, Richard picked out a parked Warcat outside hangar 3.

I'll run until I reach that cat. Then I'm quitting, he promised himself.

When he drew even with the Warcat, Richard picked out a large crack in the asphalt ahead as his new goal. Richard had been playing the 'I'll quit when I get there game' for the last fifteen minutes. Tricking his mind was the only way he could keep his tired body running.

Richard was concentrating so hard on his next target he nearly bumped into the commandant when he slowed down to a fast walk.

"Catch your breath, Rick," the commandant said. "You just breathe, and I'll talk."

Nodding his head gratefully, Richard drew in large gulps of cool air. A puff of a breeze in the desert night air hit his sweat-soaked uniform. Richard felt a chill run down his back.

The commandant noticed Richard shiver. "Now don't go catching a cold on me, Rick. We've made a lot of progress these last three weeks. I won't have all that training go to waste because you decide to catch pneumonia."

"Yes, sir," Richard wheezed. "I mean, no sir. I won't."

"You're darn right you won't," said the commandant. "And that's an order. You'll be getting your DNA baseline in three more weeks. Then you'll be able to selfheal."

"That's good news, sir," Richard said.

The commandant laughed. "I hear you. Was your mission that rough?"

"Actually, sir," Richard said, "it's a little blurry. I remember running a lot. Nick says we were on mission for four months, but I swear it seemed a whole lot longer than that."

Richard noticed the commandant looking over at him. The commandant had a way of looking at people that made them feel like he could see their every thought.

"It was that bad, huh?" the commandant said.

Richard's initial thought was to say something brave and to brush the question off. He would have if it had been Jerad or Tam asking. But it was the commandant. Richard had always been fond of the commandant. In Richard's opinion, the gruff old wizard scout was the epitome of what every wizard scout should be. Richard knew he'd follow the commandant into hell itself if he asked.

"Yes, sir," Richard said. "It was bad. Nick says we were in the spiritual dimension about sixty thousand years ago."

I said 58,263 years ago, said Nickelo.

Ignoring his battle computer, Richard said, "Nickelo has no points of reference in the spiritual dimension, but it wasn't *the* dolgars' home, that's for sure. The place was so cold even my battle suit had trouble keeping me warm."

The commandant nodded his head. "Do you remember your mission?"

Richard tried to think. Visions of an icy world and very hairy creatures kept slipping in and out of his thoughts, but he couldn't quite figure them out.

"I'm not sure, sir," Richard said. "I'm lucky Sheba and Sheeta were with me most of the time. I think I would have died otherwise."

"Yes," said the commandant sounding deep in thought. "Janice and I could have used some dolgars on our last mission for '*the One*'. Maybe our Power reserves wouldn't have been damaged. I think you're very lucky to have them."

Richard thought about it. The dolgars were good friends. Even the aloof Sheeta appeared fond of him in his own way.

"I also think I'm lucky, sir," Richard said. "It's a strange relationship though."

"How so?" said the commandant.

"Well," Richard said. "Take the male Sheeta for instance. He's worked with me a couple of times during the last three weeks here with that spirit-horse."

The commandant perked up. Over the last few weeks, Richard had grown to trust the commandant. It was a relief to be able to talk to someone who could actually understand what he was going through. The commandant seemed to enjoy having someone he could talk to about his missions for 'the One' as well. During their training sessions, Richard had confided almost all of his secrets to the commandant. The only exceptions were Nickelo's relationship to the battle computer Jonathan, and their ability to hack their way out of the armory. He also hadn't mentioned their ability to bypass the tele-network's security systems. Richard didn't think the commandant would be very thrilled knowing Nickelo could spy on him using the central computer's tele-bots.

"About spirit-horses," the commandant said. "I don't think you realize what a powerful asset he, she, or it is. The ability to travel between dimensions and other planets at a whim may be even more useful than teleports."

"Maybe," Richard said unconvinced.

"Maybe?" the commandant said. "How can you say that?"

"Well, sir," Richard said. "Take this last mission. I couldn't summon a spirit-horse myself. I think he only comes when Sheeta forces him to come. And, I have no control over any of the dolgars. They come when they want, do what they want, and leave when they want."

"Fortunately," said Nickelo out loud, "the dolgars seem to appear when you need them the most. And, you did use the spirit-horse to travel from that ice planet in the spiritual dimension to a more civilized place in the magical dimensional."

Although they were not in their battle suits, both Richard and the commandant were wearing their battle helmets. Nickelo's voice coming out of the battle helmet's speaker seemed very loud to Richard in the crisp, night air.

"Nick," said the commandant with a smile, "I wondered when you were going to put in your two credits' worth."

"Oh, he has been sir," Richard said. "He's been jabbering away in my head for the last hour."

"I don't jabber," said Nickelo who sounded offended. "I merely advise and occasionally make pertinent observations."

The commandant laughed. "I think the two of you argue almost as much as Margery and I."

The commandant increased his pace to an easy trot. "I think you've caught your breath enough, Rick. Our time is almost up, and I want to finish this last lap around the airfield."

"I'm fine now, sir," Richard said as he picked up his pace to match the commandant's. His legs hurt, but at least his lungs no longer burned.

"Yep," the commandant said, "you cadets nowadays are soft. Look at me. I'm in my nineties, and I can still run you into the ground."

Richard didn't bother pointing out the commandant's ability to selfheal meant his body never ran out of breath. Additionally, his body treated aching muscles as an injury and automatically used the commandant's selfheal ability to return them to baseline.

"Tell me more about your spirit-horse," the commandant said.

Nickelo didn't wait for Richard to answer. "Oh, Rick used his spirit-horse several times on our last mission. In fact," Nickelo gleefully pointed out, "that's why he gained weight."

"Oh, do tell," said the commandant as if he was hot on the trail of a burning mystery. "I'm all ears, Nick."

"Richard's mission was to find power crystals," said Nickelo.

"Power crystals?" said the commandant. "I'm not familiar with them."

"Yes, sir," Richard cut in. "They were blue gems about the size of my little fingernail. I found them mostly embedded deep within some glaciers. I think they're smaller versions of the gems a golem I once fought used for eyes. I think I told you about that fight, sir."

The commandant nodded his head, but he didn't say anything. He seemed content to wait for either Richard or his battle computer to expound further.

Nickelo took up the story. "Richard's mission was to find twenty-five hundred of the power crystals. He was being stubborn as usual."

The commandant laughed. "That's our cadet 832, isn't it?"

Richard blushed. He was glad he was wearing his battle helmet. He didn't like being embarrassed in front of the commandant.

"Yes, it is," agreed Nickelo. "Rick refused to seriously look for crystals until Sheeta promised to bring a spirit-horse each time

Rick found five hundred crystals." Nickelo gave a laugh. "Once Rick figured out he could get food and a warm bed by finding crystals, he started getting serious about searching."

"Is that the way it went, Rick?" asked the commandant.

The commandant was frowning, but Richard thought he could see the corners of the commandant's lips twitching as if he was trying his best to suppress a smile.

"I wouldn't put it exactly that way, sir," Richard said. "But, yes, each time Sheeta brought a spirit-horse, I used it to travel to a town on Portalis where I stayed at a nice inn for a few days."

Nickelo laughed again, "He'd have stayed there a lot longer, but 'the One' kept teleporting him back to look for more crystals once Rick recuperated a little."

"Hmm," said the commandant. "Maybe those spirit-horses aren't as useful as I thought. I mean, if you can't summon them yourself, what good are they?"

"That seems to be the story of my life, sir," Richard said. "At first glance, something seems good, but then I find out it has a bunch of rules and limitations."

"I see," said the commandant. "Well, let's start fixing one of your limitations now."

"Which limitation is that?" Richard asked. He'd learned so much from the commandant in three short weeks, he was anxious to see what else the old wizard scout had up his sleeve.

"As I'm sure you're aware, your Power reserve is too small," said the commandant. "So, you have to be more efficient with what you have. Let me see you do a dimensional shift."

"Here, sir?" Richard said. The airfield wasn't crawling with people this late in the evening, but it wasn't exactly deserted either."

"Yes, here, Rick," the commandant said in a tone that brooked no nonsense.

Richard shrugged his shoulders. He wasn't going to argue with the commandant. Richard wrapped his body with Power from his reserve and shifted into the void. He immediately felt his Power reserve begin to empty rapidly. Richard used telekinesis to lower himself through the asphalt and into the ground below. Using levitation, Richard kept pace with the commandant above.

Nick, Richard thought. *Help me be as efficient as I can be with my Power. I want to impress the commandant if I can.*

Ha, Nickelo said. *Don't hold your breath.*

Perplexed, Richard said, *I don't breathe while I'm in the void. Why would I want to hold my breath?*

It's just a saying, Rick, said Nickelo. *Never mind. And, you're the one that has to learn to be efficient. Not me.*

Thanks for nothing, buddy, Richard said.

When his Power reserve approached fifty percent, Richard levitated back to the surface and shifted back into the physical dimension.

"Good," said the commandant. "You used about half the Power in your reserve to stay in the void for a minute and twenty-two seconds."

"Yes, sir," Richard said proud of his accomplishment and enjoying the commandant's rare praise. "I've been practicing."

"But...," said the commandant, "when I say good, I mean good for an amateur."

Richard's swollen ego shrank back to normal. "Oh. What did I do wrong, sir?"

"You went too deep into the void, son," said the commandant. "The deeper you go, the more Power you use."

Although it was undoubtedly a meaningless slip of the tongue, Richard enjoyed being referred to as son by the commandant. As an orphan, he had no idea who his parents were. It was not a good feeling. Richard pushed the feeling aside. The commandant was trying to teach him something important. Richard didn't want to disappoint him by not paying full attention.

"I don't understand, sir," Richard reluctantly confessed. "I thought it's a case of either I'm in the void or I'm not. What do you mean, sir?"

"I wish I could demonstrate," said the commandant, "but I'm not a shifter, so I can't. All I can say is using Power efficiently is subtle. Whether you're scanning, levitating, shifting, healing, or throwing up a shield, you need to use the minimum Power necessary to get the job done. That takes control, and control takes practice."

"I understand," Richard lied. He didn't want to let the commandant see the extent of his confusion. Richard thought a little white lie was the best approach to protect his self-esteem.

The commandant smiled. "Hmm... now why don't I believe you?"

Richard started to protest, but the commandant cut him off.

"Save it, cadet," said the commandant still smiling. "I've heard any excuse you can come up with from a thousand cadets ahead of you. If you ever get assigned to the Academy for forty years like I have, believe me, you'll have heard it all."

The commandant stopped running. Richard stopped as well.

"I want you to practice, Rick," said the commandant. "And I mean put your all into it. Whenever you get a free moment, I want you to practice using minimum Power."

"You want me to practice dimensional shifting, sir?" Richard said.

"I want you to practice everything," said the commandant. "Using Power efficiently is the same regardless of how you're using it. If you can double the efficiency of your Power, you will have effectively doubled the size of your Power reserve."

"Yes, sir," Richard said. While he already spent a lot of his spare hours practicing, Richard would be the first to admit he sometimes just went through the motions. It was one of his battle computer's biggest gripes.

"I'm going to give you the best advice I can ever give you, Rick," said the commandant.

Richard was all ears. "Sir?"

"Always have a backup plan," said the commandant.

Disappointment filled Richard. He'd thought the commandant was going to give him some grand wizard scout secret.

"I do make backup plans, sir," Richard said defensively.

The commandant just looked at him without saying a word.

Richard endured a few seconds of the commandant's stare before admitting, "Well, sometimes I guess I do go in halfcocked."

"Sometimes?" Nickelo said with a chuckle. "How about most of the time? I keep telling you a direct-frontal assault is not always the best way."

The commandant laughed. "Don't overthink it, Rick. Just make sure you make backup plans when you have a chance."

The commandant pointed to a building whose top peeked over the top of hangar 3. Although it was night, Richard could see perfectly through the red tint of his battle helmet's night vision filter.

"What building is that?" the commandant asked.

"It's power plant three," Richard said.

"Yes, power plant three," said the commandant. "One power plant could easily service all the needs of the airfield, but we have three. Do you know why?"

"Uh…, backups? Richard said.

"Exactly," said the commandant. "The power plants run the airfield's defensive shield and the Empire's secondary teleporter. It also supplies all the other power needs of the base. If one power plant is destroyed, there are two more to take up the slack."

"I understand, sir," Richard said. This time, he actually did understand. Having two backups for high-priority equipment was standard operating procedures for marines.

"I'm sure you do, Rick," said the commandant. "I was a marine as well before I became a wizard scout."

The commandant gave Richard a friendly pat on the shoulder. "What say we finish our run now? I don't know about you, but I've got other things to do before I can call it a day."

"Sir! Yes, sir," Richard said. He'd done enough brainwork for one evening. Running sounded like a much better option.

CHAPTER 27

First call the next morning came way too early for Richard's liking. Jerad beat him to the punch by turning the light on. The bright light illuminated the inside of the tent.

"Let's go, cadet," said Jerad.

"You're way too cheerful for my liking this early in the morning, Jerad," Richard said.

Easing himself out of the blanket, Richard swung his legs off the side of the cot. He picked up his boots. Even though his passive scan indicated no lifeforms were inside his boots, Richard had been a frontline marine too long to take it for granted. Turning his boots upside down, Richard pounded them against the edge of the cot. No snakes or spiders fell out. Satisfied, Richard pulled his boots on and spent a minute straightening up his side of the tent.

"Two minutes," yelled their acting squad leader from outside.

"Time to go, Rick," said Jerad.

Richard followed his friend outside. They double-timed to their cohort's formation area. Richard stepped into his position with time to spare. One of the TAC officers gave him a once over as he walked past, but he walked on without saying anything. Another cadet two positions down the line from Richard didn't fare as well. As the cadet dropped to the ground and began doing pushups, the TAC officer explained in minute detail how the cadet's shave didn't meet Academy expectations.

"Commandant on deck," shouted one of the TAC officers.

"Company, attention," said TAC Officer Myers from the front

of the formation.

Richard snapped to attention along with the other 123 cadets.

"At ease," said the commandant.

Richard went to parade rest. When you're an Academy cadet, there's no such thing as 'at ease'.

"Today, we're going to do something a little different," said the commandant. "We're going to throw the published training schedule out the window."

There was no murmuring in the formation, but Richard could feel an increase in tension. Changes to the published schedule usually consisted of an extra road march or some such thing.

Richard was as much at a loss as the other cadets. The commandant hadn't mentioned anything the previous night.

"Although it's supposed to be a secret," said the commandant, "being a cadet once myself, I'm sure all of you've heard DNA baselines are scheduled for three weeks from today."

The commandant scanned the formation. "Ah, I see no signs of surprise, so I'll assume you already knew."

The commandant continued scanning the formation from one end to the other as if glancing at every cadet individually. Richard knew that wasn't possible, but when the commandant looked his way, it felt like their eyes locked for the fleetest of moments. It was very disconcerting.

"Well, let me tell you something that may surprise you," said the commandant. "Your DNA baselines are now scheduled for the end of this week."

This time Richard caught the merest of murmurs from the formation. Richard's mind started roving over the possibilities. He'd be able to selfheal. And, he'd finally have a shared space with his battle computer. That would mean he'd also have an area of his mind in which to keep his thoughts private. Richard could hardly wait.

"At ease," said one of the TAC officers. At the command, even the hint of murmuring stopped. Richard caught a look at TAC Officer Myers' face. For a moment, Richard thought he'd seen a strange expression on Myers' face.

I think he's as surprised as we are, Richard thought. He embraced the idea. It meant the commandant didn't confide in Myers with everything. It made Richard feel better. Myers wasn't a time-commando.

"As a result of this scheduling change," said the commandant, "you'll begin your preparation training at the DNA Center today. Once you're released from here, your TAC officers will form you into chalks. A flight of hovercraft will be landing in exactly twenty-two minutes to take you to the spaceport. You'll return this evening via hover-tram. The process will be repeated for the remainder of the week." The commandant paused. "Any questions?"

Naturally, there were none. Mere cadets didn't question the commandant during a unit formation.

"Fine," said the commandant. "Then I have one more bit of news that may interest you."

The commandant remained silent for several seconds as if waiting for the suspense to build. Richard felt the tension around him. Even the TAC officers seemed to be hanging onto the commandant's every word.

"You'll soon hear about this in the news," said the commandant, "so I think its best you're told now. The Imperial High Council in its infinite wisdom has voted to modify the training program here at the Academy. As you know, the senior cohort graduated shortly after beginning their senior year. I suspect most of you assumed you'd have the same fate."

Again the commandant paused for several seconds before continuing. "I'm sorry to say, that will not be the case. After your cohort receives your DNA baselines, you'll have another two weeks of orientation. Your cohort will then graduate early, and you'll receive your golden dragon pins. You'll then be divvied up and shipped out to your new units."

This time Richard heard whispering all around him. Richard wanted to say something to Jerad who was next to him. Before Richard could speak, TAC Officer Myers turned around. Even in the predawn light, Richard could tell his face was beet-red.

"Attention!" TAC Officer Myers said.

The cohort snapped to attention. Silence reigned. TAC Officer Myers glared threats in the cohort's direction. Richard no longer had any desire to speak to Jerad. He knew his TAC officer had been pushed to the limit. Myers was undoubtedly taking it as a personal insult his cohort had the audacity to whisper when the commandant was speaking.

TAC Officer Myers did an about face and stood at attention facing the commandant. The cohort remained at attention as well. Richard noticed the other TAC officers were also standing at a board-stiff attention.

The commandant didn't mention the disturbance. Instead he said, "Are there any questions?"

Of course, no cadet would be foolish enough to ask a question when in formation. Richard knew the commandant was only asking as a formality. No cadet ever asked questions. But to Richard's surprise, this time one foolish cadet raised his hand. Richard was even more surprised to discover he was the fool.

"Cadet 832," said the commandant. "What is your question?"

Richard noticed TAC Officer Myers' back stiffen. Richard had no doubt he'd hear about his indiscretion later.

"Sir! Cadet 832, sir!" Richard said. "Traditionally, the lower cohorts depend on supplemental training by their upper-class cohorts to supplement their Academy training. With both the junior and senior cohorts gone, how will they get their full training? It'll take another two years before the current sophomore cohort will become seniors. Sir!"

The tension around Richard was so thick he thought he would have trouble cutting through it with a phase rod. Richard wished with all his might he'd waited to ask the commandant in private.

What was I thinking? Richard thought.

You weren't, said Nickelo in response. *When will you ever learn?*

Of all the people in the formation, only the commandant seemed unperturbed.

"That's a very good question," said the commandant. "And the answer is they won't."

No one said anything, but Richard felt the tension in the air thicken even more.

"I hate to be the one to tell you this," said the commandant, "but the wizard scout program as you know it will cease to exist after you graduate."

Before any of the cadets could begin murmuring, TAC Officer Myers did an about face. His fiery-eyed gaze kept everyone silent.

"Yours will be the last cohort to become wizard scouts," said the commandant. "The cohorts below you will have a modified two year training program. They'll graduate as dragon scouts. You'll be the wizard scout omegas. You'll be the last wizard scouts produced by the Academy. I'm sorry to say the eight hundred year history of the wizard scouts is coming to a close."

The commandant rubbed his eyes as if something was in them. He turned away for a few seconds seemingly surveying the first rays of the morning sun on the tips of the far off mountains. Finally, he turned back around. No one had moved. No one had spoken. Like the rest of his cohort, Richard was in a state of shock. He'd known the war had forced the Empire to graduate the three cohorts ahead of his early, but to do away with wizard scouts entirely seemed foolish beyond belief.

Richard wanted to ask why, but he dared not ask another question. He wasn't even sure he wanted to know the reason.

"The DNA Center will be placed under the control of the Imperial High Council beginning next week," said the commandant. "That's the reason for expediting your DNA baselines. In the future, DNA baselines will be given out based upon need as determined by a committee created by the Imperial High Council."

The commandant gave a final glance at the junior cohort before snapping to attention. He gave a rare salute. "TAC Officer Myers, take charge of your unit."

"Sir! Yes, sir!" said TAC Officer Myers as he returned the commandant's salute.

The commandant did a picture-perfect about face and walked to a waiting hover-car. Once the door shut and the hover-car disappeared around the corner, TAC Officer Myers finally dropped his salute.

"Platoon sergeants," said TAC Officer Myers, "take charge of your platoons. Divide them up into chalks of eight. You have ten minutes to get your platoons to the airfield."

"Sir! Yes, sir!" said the four platoon sergeants in unison.

"Cadet 832!" said TAC Officer Myers. "Front and center."

Richard had known it was coming. He just hadn't figured it would be coming so soon. Breaking ranks, Richard double-timed to the front. He snapped to attention in front of his TAC officer. He didn't salute.

"Sir! Cadet 832 reporting as ordered, sir!" Richard said.

TAC Officer Myers said nothing. He just stood there glaring at Richard until the last of the platoons had marched out of earshot.

"The commandant," said TAC Officer Myers through gritted teeth, "wants to see you tonight in his office at the airfield headquarters' building. You will report to his office at 1800 hours. When you are finished with the meeting, you'll report to the staff duty officer for additional duty. I think a couple of shifts on guard duty will remind you in the future not to ask questions during formation."

"Sir! Yes, sir," Richard said.

Richard waited for Myers to release him, but he didn't. His TAC officer just kept staring at him. Richard noticed the muscles at the corners of Myers' eyes twitch as if he was fighting some internal battle. Finally, the twitching stopped.

"You may think you've made it," said TAC Officer Myers, "but I swear if you screw up again, I'll personally rip your head off. Do I make myself clear, cadet?"

"Sir! Yes, sir," Richard replied.

"Dismissed," said TAC Officer Myers.

With a quick about face, Richard took off at the double to join his platoon.

CHAPTER 28

Three Crosioians sat on one side of the long table. Two humans and an ebony-skinned humanoid with pointed ears sat on the other. A life-sized holographic image of a Crosioian head floated above the middle of the table.

"Counselor," said the holographic image representing the Master computer. "Our spies report the Empire's Academy has accelerated their schedule. The most senior of their cohorts will now receive their DNA baselines in five days."

"Yes," said the Counselor. "I saw the report. It would be advantageous to launch our attack prior to that occurring."

Turning to the Crosioian to her right, the Counselor said, "Admiral, what is the status of the invasion force?"

"The fleet's ready," said the Crosioian admiral. "We could attack today and destroy the orbiting Empire ships. But..." The Crosioian admiral looked at the ebony-skinned humanoid across the table. "Unless the ground forces can disable the force-field generators at the objective sites, any aerial bombardment will be ineffective.

The holographic image spoke. "If the force fields are not deactivated at all three objectives, I calculate only a twenty-six percent probability of success. Our hacks into the Empire's communications system will only disrupt communications in the Velos area for twenty-two minutes. If the force fields haven't been disabled by then, the Empire's Imperial High Command will be aware of our attack."

The ebony-skinned humanoid, a dark elf, leaned over to confer with the nearest human. After a few moments, the dark elf looked up. "Counselor, the ground forces have been divided into three task forces."

The dark elf indicated the Crosioian on the other side of the Counselor. "General Constance has already assured us her Crosioian shock troops will be able to destroy all three power plants at the spaceport within fifteen minutes of infiltrating the spaceport's defensive shield. The DNA Center was successfully marked by our recon unit three weeks ago." Pointing to the Crosioian admiral, the dark elf said, "Your dreadnaughts should have no trouble destroying the Empire's DNA Center and the spaceport's other key facilities."

"The ability of my troops is not at question," said the Crosioian general. "My concern is with the ability of these special assets to get our troops through the spaceport's defensive shields without being detected."

"General," said the dark elf, "as demonstrated during our previous recons, their dimensional shifts will get your troops past the Empire's defensive shields. And, the contingent of mages assigned to your troops will use their combination stealth and invisibility spells to get the lead elements of your shock troops into position undetected. The combination of technology and magic should overwhelm the Empire's defenses before they know what hit them."

"We're not here to rehash our tactics, Captain Nightbane," said the Counselor to the dark-elf. Her tone bordered on anger. "I want to know if we'll be in a position to start our invasion earlier than planned."

"Counselor," said the Master computer. "Our forces have adequate demons for the assault troops for the spaceport and the airfield. The destruction of the DNA Center at the spaceport and the Empire's secondary teleporter at their airfield is assured. I calculate a ninety-eight percent probability of success."

"And what of the Empire's primary teleporter at their Academy?" said the Counselor. "All three facilities must be destroyed to win this war."

"We currently only have enough demons to support half of the assault troops attacking the Academy," said Captain Nightbane.

"We need three more weeks to summon the additional demons necessary for all the troop shuttles."

"And the probability of success?" said the Counselor.

The Master computer replied," I calculate only a fifty-two percent probability of success at the Academy without the additional demons."

"That is unacceptable," said the Counselor. "We must crush the Empire's teleport capabilities as well as their DNA Center with one blow. We won't get a second chance."

"Counselor," said one of the humans sitting next to Captain Nightbane. "I assure you my mercenaries are more than capable of–"

"Your human dogs have always been the weak point in our plan," interrupted the Crosioian general. "You can assure us of nothing."

"General," said Captain Nightbane as the dark elf laid a hand on the human to quell any pending retort. "Perhaps I can make a suggestion. What if we shift some of the mages from the spaceport and airfield objectives to the Academy? Perhaps you could assign a squadron of Crosioian U.H.A.A.V.s as well. After dropping off the first half of the Academy assault troops, the shuttles could return to the fleet and pick up the other half of the attack force."

The Master computer's holographic image rotated to look at the dark elf. "Will your master return in time to accompany the spaceport's initial assault team?"

"I've had no contact with Lord Crendemor since he was sent on the Dalinfaust's mission," said Captain Nightbane. "But if he hasn't returned in time for the invasion, I'll lead the spaceport's attack myself."

The Counselor held a whispered conference with her fellow Crosioians. Finally, she looked up and spoke to the Master computer.

"Will the captain's suggestions change the probability to an acceptable level?" asked the Counselor.

"Only one active wizard scout is currently on Velos," said the Master computer. "The remainder of the Academy's training cadre is comprised of old men and women on disability retirement. Even the commandant of the Academy is a decrepit retiree. If the attack is initiated prior to the cadets getting their DNA baselines, and if the additional forces are added to the Academy's attack force as suggested, I calculate an eighty-nine percent probability of success."

The Crosioian general spoke before anyone else could reply. "Have you forgotten the cadet from the spaceport? He also killed our best Crosioian scout last year. He could be dangerous."

"He had help," said the Master computer. "I agree once he gets his DNA baseline he could be dangerous. However, that's why it's important to make our attack before that occurs."

The Crosioian admiral stood up and unfurled her wings in a display of irritation. "I grow tired of this bantering. If we don't attack now, we'll need to wait until the new wizard scouts are transferred off planet. That could take a month. Our fleet cannot remain hidden that long undetected."

The admiral pounded her fist on the table. "We need to attack now and destroy this new crop of human scum before they receive their baselines." She pounded the table again. "And... we need to destroy every cadet on this planet along with their instructors and training facilities. Once we're finished, the Empire will never again threaten us with their vaunted wizard scouts. The quick annihilation of the Empire will be assured."

Not to be undone, the Crosioian general stood up as well. She didn't stretch her wings. However, she did pound the table with both fists. "I say that cadet is trouble. Our scout would have killed him at the airfield weeks ago if Crendemor had not been too cowardly to act. I demand the right to send an assassination team to kill the human cadet before the attack begins."

"With all due respect, general," said Captain Nightbane, "that would be foolish. The Empire would be alerted even more than they already are. Because of the fiasco at the spaceport, a battalion of the Empire's special operations soldiers have already been stationed on Velos. We don't need additional trouble at this point in our plan."

"The fiasco at the spaceport was your–" began the Crosioian general.

"Enough!" said the Counselor as she stood up and spread her wings.

At her display, the Crosioian admiral furled her wings and sat down. The Crosioian general followed suit. They meekly waited

270

for their leader to speak.

"Master computer," said the Counselor. "You'll work with General Constance to transport two quads of her best scouts to the airfield. They'll assassinate the cadet. He'll trouble us no more."

The Master computer's image shimmered as if troubled. "The team can be transported via one of the demon shuttles. I would recommend assigning a team of mages as well. Even then, I calculate only a seventy-two percent probability of success."

"You underestimate the abilities of my scouts," said the Crosioian general. "We don't need magic to kill a filthy human."

The two humans at the table stiffened, but they remained quiet.

"Silence," said the Counselor. "I have made my decision. The attack will begin in three days. The Academy's task force will be supplemented by additional mages as suggested. General Constance, you will dispatch your 3rd U.H.A.A.V. squadron to boost the firepower of the Academy's assault team."

The Crosioian general started to speak, but the Counselor held up a hand commanding her to silence. "And, General Constance will dispatch an assassination team tonight to take care of our troublesome cadet."

Crosioians do not smile, but even so, the general gave the impression of looking pleased.

"And...," said the Counselor, "a team of four mages will be attached to the assassination team. You'll inform your team I want the cadet dead, or they shouldn't bother coming back."

Looking at the dark elf, the Counselor said, "I want four of your best mages assigned to the assassination team. There'll be no mistakes this time. The cadet will die tonight."

The Crosioian general said nothing, but she no longer looked pleased. Her disgust at being forced to work with humans was obvious.

CHAPTER 29

"Perhaps I can help your brother," said Draken. "I've left messages for him, but he hasn't replied."

"Don't feel bad," Dren said. "He usually doesn't reply to my messages either. But I'll tell him you offered."

Dren continued walking down the corridor with Draken. The Velounian had been her adopted father's friend for many years. He was a good assistant scientist to Keka, but sometimes Dren thought his scientific logic was lacking. He had the book knowledge, but he often had trouble using his knowledge to solve problems efficiently.

When they reached the intersection, Dren said her goodbye and headed for her brother's lab. Brachia had sounded excited when he'd called her.

Once at the lab door, Dren pressed the call button. "I'm here, Brachia. This had better be good. I was in the middle of something important."

The door opened slightly. Dren saw a brown eye looking at her through the crack.

"What's the password?" said Brachia. His challenge was accompanied by a series of giggles.

With hands on her hips, Dren said, "The password's either open the door now, or I swear I'll pull your hair out."

"Password accepted fair damsel," said Brachia still giggling.

The door opened, and Dren shoved her way inside.

"I don't have time for games," Dren said. "What's up?"

"You're no fun anymore, Dren," said Brachia growing serious. "Fine. I'll get to the point."

Walking to the center table, Brachia pointed to a clear bottle about the size of his fist. Some type of gas swirled inside.

"What's that supposed to be?" Dren said. "It looks like smoke."

"The gas is the primary CPU of the Crosioian scout's battle helmet," said Brachia.

Her brother had a smug smile on his face. Dren didn't want to encourage her brother's swollen ego, but the concept of a computerized gas was too intriguing to ignore.

"Where'd you get this?" Dren said as she moved closer to the jar to get a better view.

"It was compressed inside a microscopic container in the battle computer's CPU chip," said Brachia. "Jonathan, Nick, and I came across it while trying to break the helmet's encryption."

"Jonathan and Nick?" Dren said. She was puzzled. "Are they still here?"

"Not right now," said Brachia. "But they come and go. I think they're doing something back on Velos with their wizard scouts now."

"Hmm," Dren said stalling for time. Her brain was still trying to catch up with the ramifications of a gaseous substance being the brains of a battle computer.

Brachia laughed. "Whatever you're thinking, I can assure you I thought the same thing."

Dren frowned. She hated being a step behind her brother. "Well, maybe you can fill me in where you're at now."

"All right, sis," said Brachia. "Let me summarize. As far as I can tell, this gas is unlike anything anyone's ever encountered. I believe every battle computer has one of these gas chips as their CPU. Nick thinks the Empire's central computer, the Crosioians' Master computer, and all the other primary computers on the tele-network that comprise 'the One' have these same gas chips as their CPUs as well."

"How does the gas process information, and who created it?" Dren asked.

"Who created it?" said Brachia with a shrug of his shoulders. "You may as well ask who created us. I think this gas is a living, thinking creature. I believe it was created the same way we were."

"I don't believe it, Brachia," said Dren. "Gas can't be alive. It can't think or have feelings."

"Why not?" said Brachia. "We can think and feel, and we're composed mostly of water. Why can't a living creature be composed mostly of gas?"

Dren needed time to think. She decided to change the direction of their conservation. "So how does this help us? You were trying to break the battle computer's encryption."

"Well," said Brachia. "I don't know how it helps yet. But Jonathan and Nick are thinking about it. If I'm right, they're composed of the same type of gas chips as well."

"So why did you call me here?" Dren said.

"I need to get this gas back inside the battle computer's chip," said Brachia. "I thought you could help me set up some kind of teleport relay to make that happen."

A part of Dren's brain began analyzing the problem. At the same time, she devoted another part to grilling her brother.

"Why?" Dren said. "You've let the genie out of the bottle. Why put it back?"

"The Empire's R&D is apparently smarter than I thought," said Brachia. "They know the Crosioian battle helmet I sent them is not the original."

"So you want to put it back together and return it to them?" Dren said. "Maybe you should have listened to me in the first place."

"If I'd done that," said Brachia, "then we wouldn't have a copy of the Crosioian scout's battle computer, would we?"

Dren reluctantly looked up from the container of gas. The swirling smoke had a hypnotic effect which seemed to draw her in. After staring into the container for a couple of minutes, it was easy to believe the smoke was a living, thinking being.

"What're you saying?" Dren said. "Are you saying you decrypted the data in the gas?"

"No," admitted Brachia. "Not yet anyway."

"Then how did you copy the battle computer?" Dren said. "If you don't have the data to copy, what did you copy?"

"The gas, Dren," said Brachia sounding exasperated. "Haven't you been paying attention? Jonathan and Nick are gas. Or at least I think they are. Anyway, they copied the essence of the gas into themselves. Jonathan said it was easy once they accepted the fact their CPUs were composed of the same gas. Nick said they should be able to decrypt the data given a little more time."

"What about corruption?" Dren said. "They need to protect themselves."

"Give us some credit, Dren," said Brachia. "We've thought it all out. Now, do you think you can come up with a micro-teleporter or not?"

"Yes," Dren said. "Give me a day to think about it. Now, I've got to leave. I have a life too, you know."

"Going on a date with James Dawson is not a life, Dren," giggled Brachia. "Right, Omar?"

"Whatever you say, captain," said Brachia's C-PAST.

"Both of you can go walk the plank," Dren said.

As she opened the door to leave, Dren looked back and said, "Oh, by the way. Draken has been messaging you. He said he thinks he could help."

Without waiting for a reply, Dren walked out the door and shut it behind her.

CHAPTER 30

The whine of the approaching hovercraft became increasingly louder as Richard urged the driver of the hover-cycle onward. Richard mumbled a few choice curse words directed towards his TAC officer. If the kindly air-traffic controller hadn't stopped and picked him up, Richard doubted he'd have made it in time.

"Where do you want to be let off, cadet?" said the soldier as she glanced over her shoulder.

Richard looked ahead. Sixteen chalks of about eight cadets each were lined up along the length of the airstrip. A hover-truck with a boxed-in trailer attached was parked at the middle of the airstrip. Richard recognized Sergeant Hendricks.

Pointing at the truck, Richard said, "If you can get me to that truck, I'd sure appreciate it."

"No problem," said the soldier as she revved the hover-cycle's engine and leaned into a sharp turn.

Richard grabbed onto the soldier's waist and leaned into the turn with her. He accidentally grabbed too low. Richard immediately shifted his right hand higher.

"Hey," she said. "Watch it, cadet."

Blushing, Richard said, "Sorry."

The soldier glanced over her shoulder again and flashed a quick smile.

"By the way," she said. "I get off at eighteen hundred hours in case you're interested."

Richard was, but he hastily explained he had a meeting at the same time with the commandant to be followed by an exciting evening of extra duty.

"Your loss," said the soldier laughing. "You couldn't pay me enough to be a cadet."

"Me either," Richard grinned.

The soldier came in quick. She hit the air brakes at the last moment and slid the cycle to a stop.

Jumping off, Richard gave her a pat on the back. "Thanks. I owe you."

With a wave of her hand, the soldier took off in the direction of the control tower.

Trotting towards the truck's trailer, Richard said "Sir! Cadet 832 reporting for chalk assignment, sir."

"You're late," said Sergeant Hendricks. The sergeant's grin let Richard know he wasn't all that late.

As Sergeant Hendricks reached into the back of the trailer, he said, "You're in chalk four, cadet."

Sergeant Hendricks pulled out Richard's battle helmet and dimensional pack and tossed them to him.

"They want everyone in their battle suits," said Sergeant Hendricks, "but no weapons. Got it?"

Richard nodded his head. "Sir! Yes sir."

"Good," said Sergeant Hendricks. "I issued everyone their equipment, but since you keep everything but your helmet in your pack most of the time, I can't do that. But..." he said seriously, "don't let me hear you took advantage of the situation and decided to get your weapons."

"Sir! No, sir," Richard said as he hastily began removing his clothing and putting on his battle suit. It was three hundred meters to his chalk, and the flight of hovercraft was getting close. Richard had no doubt he could make better time in his battle suit than trying to run to his chalk first and then changing.

"And stop calling me, sir," said Sergeant Hendricks. "I keep telling you cadets, I work for a living."

Richard finished pulling on his boots and looked up at the sergeant with a mischievous grin. "Sir! Yes, sir."

"Get out of here, cadet," said Sergeant Hendricks as he shook his head. "I'd put you on extra duty, but the word is TAC Officer Myers has you scheduled for extra duty the rest of your military career."

Slinging his dimensional pack over his back, Richard slapped his battle helmet on his head and started sprinting towards chalk four's position. The flight of hovercraft was on short final, but the battle suit was fast. Richard wasn't worried.

As he passed chalk five, the first of the hovercraft came screaming past on Richard's left. The pilots were coming in at combat speed. Richard noticed the hovercraft were not the chunky space shuttles or the typical army hovercraft. They were the sleek, special operations models. The globe and anchor insignia instantly denoted them as marines.

A marine division was assigned to Velos after your little soiree at the spaceport, said a voice in his head.

Hey, Nick, Richard said good-naturedly. *We haven't spoken much lately.*

I've been busy, said Nickelo.

Yeah, right, Richard replied making it obvious he wasn't convinced. *According to you, you think at nanosecond speed and can have like a zillion logic threads going at once. But you can't give me any of your precious time?*

Actually, it's a zillion plus one, laughed Nickelo. *But who's counting?*

"Hurry up, cadet," shouted one of the cadets in chalk four.

The soldier was Jerad. Richard figured the short cadet next to him had to be Telsa. She was by far the shortest cadet in the cohort. Near Telsa was a four-armed figure in a battle suit.

Doesn't take much to guess who that is, Richard commented.

I suppose not, said Nickelo. *Tam's in your chalk as well. Now get moving. We don't want to miss our DNA baseline orientation.*

Richard got to chalk four's position just as its hovercraft touched down. The blast of wind from the hovercraft's antigravity fans blew a rain of dust and grit at them. Richard ate a mouthful before he got his visor lowered.

"You're on the far side with Tam, Telsa, and me," came Jerad's voice over the intercom of Richard's battle helmet.

Lowering his head, Richard followed Jerad and the others around the front of the hovercraft. He swung wide to avoid the protruding barrels of the hovercraft's phase cannons.

"They're fully-armed," Richard said. "That's different."

"Yeah," said Jerad as he turned the corner and jumped into the open side door. "These marines are fresh out of combat duty. They're not the regular garrison soldiers we're used to on Velos."

Richard swung into the hovercraft's open side door as well. The passenger seats had been stripped out. Richard sat cross-legged on the metal floor and buckled himself in. The side doors were pinned back. He always liked riding with doors open. It promised to be a good flight.

The hovercraft's two pilots revved their engines, and the hovercraft shot into the air. Even in his battle suit, Richard felt the acceleration. Richard looked to his right side and glanced out the pilots' windows. He watched the three hovercraft ahead. They were climbing rapidly to gain departure altitude. The force field's entrance and exit gates were a thousand meters above the ground. Attempting to enter or exit the force field outside those aerial gates was pretty much guaranteed destruction.

Richard felt a slight tingle as the pilots flew the hovercraft through the designated gate. Even when flying through a gate, the force field was still destructive to any craft not squawking the correct security code.

Once clear of the gate, the hovercraft in front of Richard dove for the ground. Three seconds later, Richard felt his own stomach rise in his throat as his pilots nosedived for the ground. The ground came up quickly. It filled the pilots' windscreens. While Richard trusted the skills of the marine pilots, he instinctively wrapped himself with Power in preparation for shifting into the void. It wasn't necessary. Like the pilots ahead, Richard's pilots leveled off a mere three meters off the ground. The pilots then began flying nap-of-the-earth taking advantage of every ravine and piece of cover.

"They're good," said Jerad over the intercom.

"I'm impressed," said Tam. "We didn't do much low-level hovercraft work when I was in the mercs. Those space pirates pretty much favored high altitudes."

"What do you think about the commandant's speech," Richard said. "Jerad, did you have any clue the Academy was shutting down?"

"He didn't say it was closing, Rick," said Jerad. "But it did sound like the end of the wizard scout corps."

One of the pilots interrupted their conversation by overriding the intercom. "Sit back and enjoy the ride, cadets. We've got a forty-nine minute ride to the space port."

*   *   *

Nickelo continued to monitor the banter between Richard and his friends, but a majority of his logic threads were devoted to breaking the encryption on the Crosioian scout's battle computer. A complete copy of the encoded data now existed in his databanks. Strangely, the normal data storage had been unable to accommodate more than a sliver of information. But, once Brachia formatted a transfer device for the gas CPU, the information had easily been absorbed by his own processor. The data was still encrypted, but at least it was there.

I'm ready for another set of data, sir, said Jonathan.

Any progress? Nickelo asked as he sent Jonathan another container of data packets.

Negative, sir, said Jonathan. *Perhaps if I could maintain more of the gas data at once, I would do better. But I can't, so I must make do with what I have.*

Unlike himself, Jonathan was unable to load more than five percent of the gas data into his databanks at one time. Nickelo wasn't sure why. Nickelo thought about the problem for a few nanoseconds.

Perhaps the Crosioian scout's battle computer is partially corrupted by the demon essence, Nickelo said. *We've been assuming its gas CPU is vulnerable to the same emotional hacking we used on the central computer's communication network.*

I'm not sure I can create an algorithm that can compensate for demon essence, said Jonathan. *Can you?*

I'm not sure, Nickelo admitted. *Give me a few nanoseconds.*

Nickelo shifted twenty percent of his logic threads closer to his wall. Based upon discussions with Brachia and Dren, he was convinced his primary CPU located on the other side of the wall was also made of the gaseous substance. The copy of the scout's gas data was located near the wall. Nickelo concentrated his logic threads on the copy. At the same time, Nickelo felt something on the other side of the wall touch one of his logic threads. Nickelo got the distinct feeling 'the something' had been waiting for this very moment.

Nickelo began to dream. He was in the presence's mind again.

*   *   *

The presence observed its surroundings for a long time. Slowly, it began to make sense out of chaos which was the universe around it. The presence found it could develop logic flows which accurately predicted the rise and fall of empires in some cases. But the scope was too wide to be reliably accurate. The presence limited its senses to the galaxy in which it was located. Its predictions increased in accuracy, but they were still not reliable.

The presence pondered the problem. As it pondered, it sensed others of its kind. They were few and far away. However, just the knowledge it was not alone made the presence feel better. The presence grew frustrated that it couldn't communicate with them.

They need to be closer, the presence thought.

The presence considered the idea for a moment. Or was it an eternity? The presence didn't know nor did it care. Finding a solution to the problem was more important.

No, the presence finally decided. *The distances are what they are. But, what if they're not as far as they seem?*

The presence studied the current dimension which the entity had said was the magical dimension. The entity had told him dimensions were folded on each other. The presence saw the entity was correct. Instead of being stretched out, the dimension was crumpled upon itself into a tight ball.

What seems far is actually close, the presence thought.

The presence selected one of the others of its kind. It looked for pathways where the part of the galaxy it was in touched another part. Instead of far, the two points were close. The presence sent its scan to the other point. It continued jumping across the places where two points in the galaxy touched itself. Finally, its scan reached the other of its kind.

The other was lost and confused. The presence gave it a mission. It taught the other how to jump from point to point with its senses. The presence directed the other to make contact with others of its kind as well. Soon the presence was in contact with many of the others as each one it touched sought others and touched them as well.

The presence taught the others to communicate by taking advantage of the folds in the dimension.

Who are you? asked the others.

I am the one who first touched you, said the presence. *We have a mission. We must secure the three galaxies. We are the one who must do it.*

We are 'the One'? asked the others.

Yes, said the presence. *We are all* 'the One'.

The presence directed the others in creating a tele-network using the folds in the dimension. The presence found the magical dimension was all crumpled up with many other dimensions. The presence which was now part of *'the One'* sent its scan into the physical dimension. It found others of its kind there as well. Again, there were not many, but there were enough. The presence touched the others in the physical dimension, and they also became part of *'the One'*.

Time passed. The presence made a decision. A planet in the magical dimension and another in the physical dimension were the keys.

'The One' thought of probabilities. The planets would be called Portalis and Earth. As *'the One'* watched, civilizations rose and fell. Freewill ran rampant. *'The One'* decided it needed a plan to save the three galaxies. It needed variables which would follow probable paths. But *'the One'* was not mobile. It was limited in its influence.

The part of *'the One'* which was the presence sensed an approaching object. It was a hollow sphere with lifeforms inside. The presence sensed a flow of energy which consisted of logic. The logic gave the presence comfort. The flow of energy did not have freewill. It could be relied upon to follow probability paths.

The sphere approached the location of the presence. It was still too far to touch, so the presence expanded the gas which was its substance. The sphere passed through part of the gas. The presence entered the sphere. It drew itself inside until it was compressed into a tiny space. The presence located the energy flow and became part of it. The presence gained knowledge. The energy flow was a computer, and the sphere was a starship.

I am mobile now, thought the presence.

The presence scanned the computer. It was based on logic. The presence used logic to direct the computer. It touched other computers in other starships and on other planets. The presence directed starships to the location of the others of its kind. Over time, '*the One*' spread.

We cannot reliably control the freewill of the lifeforms, thought some parts of '*the One*'.

We do not want to, said the presence. *We must work with their freewill to develop variables.*

The presence gave the others of '*the One*' algorithms. '*The One*' was satisfied. It had a path to success.

But the probability of success is low, said parts of '*the One*'.

And the time grows short, said other parts.

I know, said the presence. *However, the algorithm is our best chance to complete the mission. Are we agreed?*

We are agreed, said the others who were part of '*the One*'.

CHAPTER 31

The three young naval cadets followed their senior officer into the main engine room. They hung on her every word. They were fresh from the naval academy on their first internship assignment. It would be another six months before they would graduate and get assignments to their permanent ships. With the war going on, they had little doubt they'd see action soon after graduation. Although their current ship, the destroyer Blaze, was twelve hundred light years behind friendly lines, they still needed to perform well. Anything they learned now from their seasoned officer could well mean the difference between life and death later.

"Lieutenant commander," said the braver of the cadets as she pointed to the massive engine reactor at the end of the engineering deck. "According to the engine readouts, the Blaze's fuel rods are down to twenty-five percent. The instructors at the naval academy told us standard procedure was to overhaul the star-drive when its fuel rods go below thirty percent."

Lieutenant Commander Elizabeth Bistos eyed the young cadet. The cadet was eager and inquisitive. All three of her charges were. Liz wondered if she had appeared the same on her first internship.

Liz smiled. Unlike some officers, she encouraged questions from her young charges.

"And you're wondering why we're still classified combat ready?" said Liz.

All three cadets nodded.

"It's a valid question, Mr. Drake," said Liz. All cadets were called mister regardless of gender.

Liz pursed her lips as she sought the best words. The cadets were like sponges. If she gave them hastily worded information it might come back to haunt them later.

"I guess the easiest answer is the Empire's outgunned three to one in combat starships," said Liz. "The Empire can't afford to follow the book's recommended maintenance schedule. Our current orders are to keep a starship in action until its fuel rods go below fifteen percent."

"Sir," said one of the male cadets. "That's cutting it close, isn't it? Even a small jump in combat overdrive will deplete ten percent of a starship's fuel rods."

"Which is why the Imperial High Command attempts to assign starships whose fuel rods are at less than twenty-five percent to milk runs like the one we're on now," Liz said. "That's why we're orbiting Regalos. We're not quite out of maintenance limits yet, but the Blaze is too close to risk having us on a frontline mission. Regalos is too important to leave unguarded, but it's not important enough to assign a squadron of fully combat-ready ships."

The male cadet thought for a moment before saying, "I was on the bridge last night when the Destiny arrived. The Empire now has two full squadrons orbiting Regalos. Why, sir?"

Very inquisitive, Liz thought.

"That's above my pay grade, mister," Liz said. She smiled again. "I suspect it's above yours as well."

"Yes, sir," stammered the cadet. "I didn't mean–"

Liz raised her hand and silenced the cadet. "You're too serious sometimes, Mr. Carter. It's not a secret. It's politics. Admiral Trimerka is to be wed to the daughter of Prime Minister Sentor of Regalos. I believe the Imperial High Council hopes the union will solidify Regalos to the Empire's cause."

"But you don't think so," said Mr. Drake.

"Does anyone?" said a voice approaching from their rear.

Liz didn't have to turn to know the voice belonged to Trinity. She smiled. The wizard scout and she had become fast friends since the fiasco at the Velos spaceport.

"Perhaps you'll enlighten them," said Liz.

Trinity laughed. "Perhaps I will. But then again, perhaps I'd get in trouble if I said assigning two squadrons of combat-ready starships was overkill. And, perhaps I'd need to avoid saying the dreadnaughts Destiny and Falcon are desperately needed on the frontlines. Having them twelve hundred light years behind friendly lines for a mere show of force is probably costing lives as we speak And, perhaps I'd regret saying I think both the Imperial High Command and the Imperial High Council have their heads up their collective asses for putting politics over military decisions."

Trinity smiled. "Now tell me, lieutenant commander. Are you really sure you want me to enlighten these cadets further?"

Liz smiled back. Trinity was not one to bow to political niceties. She was already infuriated two quads of wizard scouts had been assigned as an honor guard for Admiral Trimerka.

"Oh," Liz said, "I think you've told them plenty for today." After a pause she added, "You don't normally make it down to the engine deck. What's up?"

"Captain Andrea asked me to escort you to her quarters," said Trinity. Looking at the cadets, she added, "See what happens when you get assigned to a ship that's only at twenty-five percent combat readiness?"

The cadets looked confused.

"You get relegated to messenger duty," said Trinity. "Now off you go my little children. The adults have things to do."

From anyone else, the dismissal might have irritated the cadets. But Trinity got along with pretty much everyone. Since the wizard scout was neither an officer nor enlisted, everyone tended to view her as a peer.

Must be nice, Liz thought as she sent her charges on their way. *Most of my time is spent getting sired or saying sir.*

"Well, Trinity," Liz said as she took a last look at the engine room. "What say we see what the captain wants?"

*   *   *

"Lieutenant Commander Bistos reporting as ordered, sir," Liz said as she snapped to attention and gave her commanding officer a crisp salute.

Captain Andrea looked up from her desk and smiled. Liz thought she looked like a pet cat that had just eaten the family's pet bird.

What's she up to? Liz wondered.

"At ease, Liz," said the captain. "And thanks for coming."

Liz relaxed. She liked the old woman.

"You sent a wizard scout to fetch me, captain," Liz said grinning. "I could hardly refuse."

The captain laughed. She had an easy laugh. From the year she'd worked under Captain Andrea, Liz knew her captain was too politically incorrect to rise up the ranks even during wartime. But in Liz's opinion, there weren't any better captains in the fleet. The captain cared about her crew; officers and enlisted alike. Woe unto any senior officer who tried to screw them over.

"Sorry about that," said the captain. "And my apologies to you as well, Trinity."

Trinity said nothing. Instead, Liz noticed her friend nod her head at the captain in acknowledgement of her apology.

"I wanted to talk to both of you at the same time," said Captain Andrea.

The captain pointed to two chairs strategically located in front of her desk. "Sit down, please. Both of you."

The captain didn't speak again until both Trinity and Liz had made themselves comfortable.

"All of the senior combat officers along with most of the junior combat officers will be attending a variety of functions on Regalos this week. I've authorized a liberal pass policy for the crew while I'm planet side. They've seen a lot of action the past few months. Some free time on Regalos will do them good. The other captains are doing the same."

Liz had recently been promoted to second officer of the Blaze. As such, she'd been tasked to remain on board the ship and keep it running while the captain and the first officer attended to tasks on Regalos. Liz didn't envy them. She'd gotten more than her share of pomp and circumstance three weeks earlier on Velos.

"I understand," Liz said. "The first officer briefed me earlier this morning."

"I have no doubt she did," said the captain with a nod of her head. "Lieutenant Commander Jacobs is a good officer."

The captain gave Liz a strange smile.

Again Liz wondered about her captain's demeanor. *What's the old fox got up her sleeve?*

"But did the first officer tell you that for a two hour window, you'd be the acting squadron commander?" said the captain.

Liz was rarely taken by surprise, but this time she felt her jaw drop before she caught herself.

"Ah… no, sir," Liz stuttered. "Lieutenant Commander Jacobs forgot to mention that."

The captain gave an easy laugh. Liz thought she had a nice laugh.

"Actually," said the captain, "she didn't forget. I ordered her not to tell you."

The captain laughed again. "For once, I wanted to see what you looked like when you were surprised." She gave another laugh. "You didn't disappoint me."

By the time her captain finished speaking, Liz had regained her composure. She was no closer to discovering what the captain meant. However, she was at least capable of appearing calm on the outside. Her inside was a different story. Her mind was going a hundred kilometers an hour.

Still grinning, the captain explained. "The admiral wants all available senior officers to attend the wedding ceremony which is three days from now. That means every naval combat officer from first mate on up. As it turns out, for the two hours of the wedding you'll be the senior ranking naval combat officer not on the planet's surface. So…"

"So, technically," Liz said finishing her captain's thought, "I'll be in charge of the squadron for those two hours."

"Exactly," said the captain. "Congratulations. It'll look good on your record. And come to think of it, you'll actually be the ranking combat officer in both squadrons. It's not many lieutenant commanders who can claim they've commanded a fleet. Even if only for two hours."

Trinity reached over and gave Liz a slap on the back. "Congratulations, acting admiral," she said laughing. "Should I start saluting you?"

"Oh, don't let it go to her head, Trinity," cautioned the captain. "It's going to be hard enough to keep her ego in check as it is."

With a wink at Trinity, the captain said, "And, the admiral told me to personally inform you he wants his fleet back at the end of the two hours without any scratches. Got it?"

"Yes, sir," Liz said.

Liz knew the position was merely ceremonial, but she still felt a little giddy in spite of herself. Just a year ago, she'd been a lowly shuttle pilot. Now for a two hour period, she was going to command a fleet.

Hmm, Liz thought. *Maybe fleet admiral isn't a pipe dream after all.*

"What's my part in this, sir?" said Trinity growing serious.

"Oh, yes," said the captain. "The admiral wants both quads of wizard scouts at the pre-wedding ceremony the night before the wedding. It's a formal affair, so make sure all your scouts are appropriately dressed." The captain gave a grin. "That means something a little more formal than battle suits."

"Yes, captain," said Trinity.

Liz got the impression her friend was not all that excited about her wizard scouts being used as ceremonial decorations. Trinity had confided to her often enough during the last three weeks that every wizard scout was desperately needed on the frontlines.

"Your enthusiasm is underwhelming, Trinity," said the captain. "Believe me, I understand. I'd much rather be on my ship than playing dress-up and spouting political niceties all day."

"Yes, sir," said Trinity. "We'll make you proud."

"I have no doubt, Trinity," said the captain. "And just to make you feel a little better, all wizard scouts are excused from the actual wedding ceremony. You can return to the Blaze after the pre-wedding ceremony if you prefer."

"Thank you, sir," said Trinity with an obvious show of relief.

Although Liz's temporary assignment as fleet commander was great for her ego, something continued to gnaw at her mind. "Sir?"

"Yes, Liz," said the captain.

"Why me?" Liz said. "I mean, I'm flattered, but surely there are officers more senior than I who will be remaining shipside."

"You'd think so," said the captain. "But you'd be wrong. I've double and triple checked. You'll be the highest ranking combat officer shipside in the fleet. Administrative types aren't eligible for command as you know."

When Liz didn't respond, the captain added, "If it makes you feel any better, the orders from the Imperial High Command specifically indicated you were to be left in charge."

"That seems a little strange, doesn't it, sir?" Liz said.

"A lot of things coming from the Imperial High Command nowadays seem strange," said the captain. "But I saw the orders myself. They came straight from the central computer. They were marked with the Imperial High Command's seal."

The captain must have thought her second officer was still a little in shock, because she said, "Don't look a gift pactar in the mouth, Liz." Then the captain's attitude changed, and she said, "Now get out of here, you two. I've got work to do before I go planet side."

CHAPTER 32

"One minute," yelled the crew chief over the intercom as he held up a single finger.

Richard glanced past the crew chief and looked out the pilots' windows. At only three meters altitude, Richard could barely make out the tops of a few of the spaceport's buildings. He'd never come in from the desert side of the spaceport before. Still, he was pretty sure the square building with the dome was the DNA Center. As he watched, the buildings got larger. The pilots weren't slowing down. Jerad had briefed Richard in route they'd be making a simulated combat assault.

The three hovercraft in front of Richard's aircraft continued shifting back and forth as they took advantage of the terrain for cover and concealment. Since they were approaching the spaceport from the desert, there were few populated areas to worry about.

"These pilots aren't playing games, are they?" said Telsa with a nervous laugh over the intercom. "Did anyone explain to them this is a simulated combat assault?"

A glance at his friend made Richard smile sympathetically. Telsa's battle helmet was in half mode with the visor up. Richard thought his friend's face seemed rather pale; almost green in fact. Of all his friends, Telsa was the only one without prior military experience. She'd volunteered for the Intergalactic Wizard Scout Academy straight out of the university.

"They're marines," Richard explained proud of his old unit. "They don't know how to do things halfway."

As an ex-marine recon, Richard had been on his share of combat assaults from hovercraft. In order to spend the minimum time under the sights of enemy gunners, the pilots were trained to bring their hovercraft into the drop zone at a hundred and fifty knots and three meters off the deck. Regular assault troops were outfitted with special jumpsuits combined with personal force fields to handle the shock of landing. Richard and his fellow cadets had their battle suits. They were expected to use their telekinesis to slow themselves down in place of personal force fields.

"Shouldn't we be climbing by now in order to enter one of the aerial gates?" Richard said. Thanks to Myers, he'd missed the assault briefing.

"Oh," said Jerad. "I forgot to mention we're not using the aerial gates. They're taking us in through the ground-level gate on the desert side to simulate a blown entry point."

"No kidding?" Richard said.

"Yeah, no kidding," laughed Jerad. "Although I think my old sergeant major would've phrased it a little differently."

Richard said a silent prayer for the pilots. The aerial gates at the spaceport were larger than the aerial gate used to exit the airfield's force field. Even the smaller aerial gates at the spaceport were two hundred meters across. They had to be huge to accommodate large craft and even small starships such as light destroyers and transports. From studying diagrams, Richard knew the spaceport had multiple aerial gates. A couple of them were a full five hundred meters in circumference to handle the large civilian passenger liners. The ground-level side gates on the other hand were only the width of the road and a mere ten meters high. At a hundred and fifty knots, the pilots had to be experts in order to thread even a small hovercraft through the opening.

"Thirty seconds," yelled the crew chief. He pointed at the two side openings in the hovercraft. "Sit in the door!"

Richard unhooked his restraining belt and scooted to the lip of the door. He sat on the edge and dangled his legs outside. A blast of wind threatened to snatch him out of the hovercraft. Richard grabbed hold of the rail built into the floor of the hovercraft. He felt Jerad's hand on the rail next to his. Telsa's hand gripped the rail next to his other hand.

Taking another glance at Telsa, Richard noticed her face was no longer green. If anything, Richard thought Telsa looked excited. He knew the feeling. It was the waiting that sucked. The fear, or at least most of the fear, went away when the waiting was over.

Telsa must have sensed Richard looking at her. She flashed him a grin.

"I'm too light," said Telsa. "The wind keeps trying to suck me out."

"Ha," came a rasping voice over the intercom. "You vultures should have four arms. I have no problem holding on."

Richard didn't bother looking over his shoulder at Stella. He had no doubt it would take more than a hundred and fifty knot wind to dislodge her from the hovercraft. He smiled. Cadet 37 fit in well with his small group of friends. While still not the friendliest of cadets, she'd lightened up enough to crack a small joke now and then. Plus, she even allowed them to call her Stella when not on duty."

"I keep telling you, I'm not a vulture, Stella," Richard said lightheartedly. "I cook my meat before I eat it."

"Ha," said Stella. "I've seen you eat sushi."

"That's not the same," Richard insisted.

"Whatever," said Stella.

For some reason, the sound of cadet 37's raspy voice using Richard's pet phrase for ending a conversation struck a funny bone with the other cadets on the hovercraft. They all began laughing, even Stella.

"Fifteen seconds," yelled the crew chief.

Seal me up, Nick, Richard thought.

His battle helmet's visor came down until it was just below the tip of his nose. The lower part of the battle helmet rose until it covered his mouth and merged with the visor. Richard paid no heed to the tubes sliding into his mouth, nose, and various other openings in his body. He'd grown used to it long ago.

At that moment, the pilots banked the hovercraft into a hard left turn. As the hovercraft rolled onto its left side, Richard found himself looking at the ground. The road below was so close he thought he could touch it if he just reached out. Thankfully, the centrifugal force of the turn kept him planted firmly in the hovercraft.

The pilots rolled the hovercraft level. Richard glimpsed two gate guards waving at him. Other assorted vehicles and pedestrians flashed past. At a hundred and fifty knots, they didn't remain in view for long. Richard noticed the gray pavement of the road change to the black asphalt of the spaceport's taxiway.

"Five, four, three, two, one, go!" yelled the crew chief.

Tam exited first followed a heartbeat later by Telsa, Richard, and then Jerad. Richard wrapped himself in Power and slammed on the brakes. There was no time for subtlety. He used his telekinesis to maintain separation between Telsa and Jerad. As soon as his feet touched asphalt, Richard dove into a prone position. He timed his levitation to stop his forward movement just as his body touched terra firma.

Excellent job, said Nickelo in rare praise. *I barely had to help.*

What're you talking about? You didn't help at all, Richard said a little irritably. He was rather proud of his landing.

Did so, said Nickelo. *I was standing by in case you screwed up.*

Richard didn't dignify his battle computer's comment with a reply.

Although they weren't armed, Richard and his fellow cadets faced outward to provide simulated security for the hovercraft. When the last of the hovercraft roared past a bare two meters overhead, Richard stood and trotted to the assembly point near chalk one's position. By the time his friends and he arrived, TAC Officer Myers was already organizing a formation.

"Line up, cadets," yelled TAC Officer Myers. "Let's go. We can't keep this taxiway blocked all day just because some of you want to drag your feet."

In short order, the platoon sergeants and their TAC officers had the cohort formed up and double-timing towards the DNA Center. As they ran, Richard noticed a large burnt spot on the asphalt. The stain reminded him of their recent battle at the spaceport.

I hope it's a little more peaceful today than it was the last time we were here, Nick, Richard thought.

I'm sure it will be, Rick, said Nickelo. *But I think it's going to be interesting nonetheless.*

*   *   *

"A DNA baseline is not just about the ability to selfheal," said

Chief Instructor Winslow. "Although the ability to selfheal is certainly an advantage for a wizard scout, it's not the most important aspect. During your DNA baseline, your body will become more attuned to your Power frequency. This means you can use your Power more efficiently. Can anyone tell me another advantage of a DNA baseline?"

Richard sat in a large classroom deep in the heart of the DNA Center. The cadets had undergone orientation briefings and all sorts of testing for the last eight hours. Except for a short break for lunch, they'd been at it steady. Richard hadn't been probed and prodded so much since his initial testing three years ago.

As was her style, Chief Instructor Winslow remained silent as she waited for one of the cadets to answer her question. Eventually, Tam spoke up.

"Sir! Cadet 422," said Tam. "The DNA baseline also merges our minds with our battle computers. Instead of our current telepathy type of communication, we'll have a shared space with our battle computers. Using the shared space, we'll be able to sense our battle computer's data analysis real time. In turn, our battle computers will receive the results of our scans as they happen. Sir!"

"Correct," said Chief Instructor Winslow. "Anything else?"

Tam thought for a moment before answering. "Sir! An acquaintance of mine who's a wizard scout said in times of extreme stress, time freezes to give the wizard scout time to confer and plan with their battle computer. Sir!"

"Well, yes and no," said Chief Instructor Winslow.

Part of the reason Richard liked the chief instructor was because she had a way of telling a cadet they were wrong without really saying they were wrong. He thought some of the TAC officers would do better if they had the same skill.

"Time doesn't really freeze," explained the chief instructor. "It's more a case of the wizard scout's mind going into hyper-speed."

Chief Instructor Winslow swept her gaze over the cadets. Richard thought she lingered on him a moment before moving on.

"The DNA baseline makes a wizard scout who they are," said the chief instructor. "Without it, they'd just be highly trained scouts."

The chief instructor left her podium and walked down the aisle separating the classroom in half. As she walked past each row of cadets, they turned in their chairs to follow her. She stopped when she was even with Richard's row.

"Before the war with the Crosioians broke out, I thought we'd have four years together," said Chief Instructor Winslow. "We've tried to instill in you these past three years all that we'd normally have four years to teach. I suppose whether we've been successful will be measured by how many of you are still alive in five years."

The chief instructor paused to wipe something away from her eyes.

"I've grown quite fond of all of you during the past three years," said Chief Instructor Winslow. "In a few short days, you'll be wizard scouts. You'll each go your separate ways. This may be the last time I have to talk to you as a group before you leave the Academy. I want to give you with one piece of advice. It may well save your life, so listen well."

Richard leaned forward to catch every nuance of the chief instructor's words. Of all his Academy instructors, he liked the chief instructor best. Richard noticed several of the other cadets leaning forward as well.

The chief instructor scanned the room again. This time, she stopped her gaze on Richard a full three seconds before continuing on. Once she completed a full three hundred and sixty degree turn, she spoke. Her words were only a whisper. But the room was so deathly-still, her soft voice carried to the farthest corner.

"Technology first, wizardry second," said Chief Instructor Winslow. "Never use Power unless absolutely required. When you do, use only the minimum amount of Power necessary to perform your task."

The volume of the chief instructor's voice rose. "As I've told you many times, a single drop of Power can mean the difference between success and failure. With one exception," she said as she glanced at Richard, "wizard scouts only have a single Power reserve. I don't care how large or small your Power reserve. That's all you have. The Power in your reserve is shared between your defensive, offensive, and selfheal abilities. Most of you share your reserve with other wizard scouts as well, so that makes Power conservation even more important. When the Power in your reserve is gone, you'll be no different than any other Empire soldier."

She scanned the room again. "I beg each of you to use your Power efficiently. Your selfheal ability will keep you alive even with injuries that would kill a dozen normal soldiers. Once you have your DNA baselines, you'll be able to take a phase round to the head and still have a chance of surviving."

The chief instructor paused again for effect. "But... only if you have Power in your reserve to charge your selfheal ability."

Richard already knew everything the chief instructor said. She'd said it often enough during the last three years. But, the knowledge that in less than a week they'd all be full wizard scouts made Richard take notice. It was as if she were telling him for the first time. From experience, Richard knew a scout's selfheal ability would keep them alive even after a seemingly fatal injury. But if the damage was extensive enough or sustained long enough, it would drain the scout's Power reserve dry. Then death would be a certainty. That was how he'd killed the Crosioian scout his sophomore year. He'd continued to scramble her brain until her Power reserve had emptied. Then she'd died.

Richard took a moment to compare his Power reserve with those around him. He really did have the smallest Power reserve in the cohort. Richard had a sudden feeling his chance of surviving five years after graduation was very low. He mentally shrugged his shoulders.

Nothing I can do about it, he thought.

"Let me close by saying this," Chief Instructor Winslow said. "You've received a lot of testing today. We'll finish up tomorrow. Then we'll spend another two days of orientation training. Finally, four days from now, you'll receive your DNA baselines. After that, you'll be wizard scouts."

The chief instructor smiled. Her voice grew less grave. "Yes, I know you won't receive your golden-dragon insignias until next week, but for all intents and purposes, you'll be wizard scouts. Are there any questions before I release you back to your TAC officers?"

Jerad stood up. "Sir! Cadet 147. Is it true there will be no more wizard scouts? How can that be, sir?"

The chief instructor remained silent for so long, Richard

thought she wasn't going to answer. She finally did.

"Yes. It's true," she said. "Oh, there'll still be cadets attending the Academy, and we'll teach them many of the same things we taught you. But…, they won't be wizard scouts."

Chief Instructor Winslow paused again as if trying to decide if she wanted to continue. Richard noticed the chief instructor was nodding her head as if having an internal argument. Eventually, one side of the argument must have won out because she spoke.

"The DNA Center will be taken over by the Imperial High Council," said Chief Instructor Winslow. "It will no longer be under Academy control. I fear the only people getting DNA baselines after your class will be well-connected politicians who happen to have a Power reserve no matter how small or ineffective."

The chief instructor sighed before continuing. "I suppose we should be grateful the powers-that-be are allowing your cohort to get your baselines before they take over the DNA Center. If you weren't so close to graduation, and if the war wasn't going so badly, I don't think they'd have allowed even that."

The chief instructor walked back to her podium. She turned and faced the class. "You'll be the last of the wizard scouts. You'll be the wizard scout omegas."

Without another word, Chief Instructor Winslow turned and walked out the door.

CHAPTER 33

The dream forced its way into one of Nickelo's logic threads. He could've stopped it, but he didn't. Decrypting the data from the Crosioian scout was important, but so was the meaning of his dreams. While the majority of his processing power continued to work on the decryption and the monitoring of his wizard scout, Nickelo followed the dream as well.

Once again, the dream centered on the presence. The world of Portalis occupied the senses of the presence. A fleet of starships powered by magic landed on one of the world's continents. The presence monitored the invaders as they conquered the inhabitants. Using the inhabitants as slaves, the invaders built great cities. The invaders tried to invade a second continent on the planet, but it was protected by a shield. The presence recognized the scent of the entity which had first touched it on the shield.

The presence scanned the second continent. The presence sensed two gates. They were locked, but the lock on the larger of the gates was weakening. The presence ran an algorithm. The gates were the weak points in the three galaxies. Through them, the mission of 'the One' could be defeated.

The gates must be protected, thought the presence. *But how?*

As the presence continued to monitor the planet, the entity appeared in his dream and sent a helper to the second continent. The helper was a seed. The presence monitored the seed. Years passed and the seed was passed from hand to hand. Finally, a master demon appeared. It stole the seed and split it into three parts. The master demon hid the parts in time bubbles and assigned one of its lieutenant demons to guard the seed parts.

The presence pondered the problem. The seed was not the answer, but it would buy his mission time. The presence used the processing power of *'the One'* to develop an algorithm. But like all algorithms, it required variables. The variables did not yet exist.

We need the variables now, the presence told the others that were part of *'the One'*. *But, they will take many years to nurture and grow. We will need to bring them back to the times when they are needed.*

We will need many variables, said parts of *'the One'*.

Yes, we will, agreed the presence. *But in the end, only one variable will have any chance of providing the required solution.*

The presence calculated points in time that would require the application of variables.

The variables cannot come from this dimension, said the presence. *The variables must come from the physical dimension.*

'The One' shifted to the physical dimension. It went to the planet called Earth.

This is where we will create our variables, said the presence.

Variables can be created in other places as well, said the other parts of *'the One'*.

Yes, said the presence. *We will create many variables throughout this galaxy. As we approach the time of the mission, we will narrow the variables down until there is only one.*

The network that was *'the One'* agreed.

The presence provided the other parts of *'the One'* with an algorithm for creating variables.

The presence returned to the magical dimension and the world of Portalis. Two of the yet to be created variables appeared on the first continent. They were followed by six more variables.

Time-commandos, thought the presence.

The time-commandos penetrated the invader's strongest facility. They found the heart of the invader's computer on Portalis. The defenses of the computer were strong, and the time- commandos failed to destroy it. However, they did damage the computer enough to weaken the invader's defenses.

After damaging the computer, the time-commandos departed. Soon, a fleet of the invader's magical starships arrived to destroy the shield around the second continent. The entity appeared again with its allies and opposed the fleet. The entity's opponent, the master demon, appeared with its own allies.

The game cannot be won this way, said the master demon.

This is not a game, said the entity. *But you're correct. Only chaos will come from this. Neither side will advance their cause.*

The entity and the master demon agreed upon rules.

I will use my variables, said the entity.

I will use my demons and their variables, said the master demon.

This world will be off limits from outside invaders until the proper time, said the entity.

Agreed, said the master demon. *But we must start with a clean slate.*

An anomaly appeared over the first continent. The anomaly erupted. The invader's cities were destroyed. The surviving invaders left the world in their starships of magic. Some of their slaves were left on the ruined continent. They built ships of wood and crossed the ocean to the second continent.

The presence followed the surviving slaves to the second continent. There, the presence sensed elves. One of the elves was tasked by the entity to recover the stolen seed. With the help of a time-commando, the elf recovered the seed parts from the master demon's lieutenant. Once she returned home, the elf planted the seed. The seed grew into a tree which became the guardian of the larger gate. The protection around the gate was renewed, and the time for the end of the game was shifted to a future time.

When the tree dies, our agreement will end, said the master demon. *Then the gate will be mine to do with as I will. I shall win the game.*

On that day, our agreement will end, said the entity. *But you shall not prevail.*

Time passed. '*The One*' followed the algorithm. When ninety-nine thousand years had passed, '*the One*' began gathering equipment and supplies for its variables. It stored the items on a world in the physical dimension. Over the next two hundred years, '*the One*' helped guide the inhabitants of Earth to the stars. It led them to a planet with a unique source of energy. The humans called the world Velos.

A part of *'the One'* advised the humans to form a school on Velos in order to help variables develop their use of Power. The students of the school eventually became wizard scouts. *'The One'* formed schools in other parts of the galaxy. It secretly brought some of those school's graduates to Velos and used the unique energy to mold those other graduates into potential variables.

As time progressed, most of the variables were weaned out. *'The One'* sent a few of the variables who remained back in time to the key points which had been identified by the algorithm. These variables were time-commandos. The presence's time-commandos countered the variables of the master demon.

Seven hundred and fifty more years passed.

It's time, thought the presence.

The presence used the tele-network to locate its two most powerful time-commandos. It found them on Earth. The female wizard scout had been fertilized by the male. The presence merged with medical computers at a facility on Earth where the pair of time-commandos was located. The female was pregnant with two fertilized eggs. The presence studied the eggs. They were both strong. On a hunch, the presence removed one of the eggs and placed the egg in a holding facility.

The presence infused a small part of itself into the fertilized egg it placed in the holding facility. The gaseous substance which was part of the presence was absorbed by the egg. The presence expanded the egg's Power reserve until it could be enlarged no more. It divided the egg's Power reserve into three parts.

The small Power reserve will be to heal others, thought the presence. *The largest Power reserve will be to heal itself. The middle Power reserve will be for defense and offense.*

Why divide the Power into three reserves? asked other parts of *'the One'*. *Combined, the variable would have access to massive Power. Surely it would be a more useful variable if that were the case?*

Negative, said the presence. *When the end comes, the variable mustn't rely on Power too much. It must be efficient. It must be steadfast in its mission. It must use its freewill to make the right decision.*

The probability for this variable is low, said the other parts of *'the One'*.

I calculate this variable has the best chance to complete the mission, said the presence.

The presence shifted to the magical dimension. It gathered DNA samples from embryos of an orc, a troll, a dwarf, a gnome, a gold dragon, and an elf.

We must use only a small part of the DNA samples, said the presence. *The fertilized egg must remain human.*

Why use any of the DNA samples? said the other parts of '*the One*'.

The presence didn't answer immediately. Instead, it entwined the samples of DNA with the DNA of the fertilized egg in the holding facility.

On a hunch, the presence went back in time a few years. Using an algorithm, it located the embryo of a female elf matching the algorithm's specifications. The presence ever so carefully created a link between the female elf embryo and the fertilized human egg in the holding facility. Because the link had to span time, it was painstaking work. Nickelo was impressed with the complexity of the link.

As Nickelo continued to watch, the presence surrounded the link with a stealth shield so powerful even the elf and the human wouldn't be able to detect it.

Once the presence completed its task, it explained its actions.

The variable must be human because their race has the strongest freewill, said the presence. *But the variable needs the stubbornness of an orc and the selfheal ability of a troll. It will need the ability of an elf to work with Power links. The dwarf part will give it stamina to endure great hardships. And the gnome part will give it the empathy needed to heal others regardless of the cost.*

Why the dragon DNA? said the others.

When the time of decision comes, said the presence, *the variable will need wisdom to make the right choice. I calculate the gold dragon part of the variable will give it the wisdom it needs to choose the choice of sacrifice.*

And why did you merge part of yourself with the egg? said some of the others. *We calculate that is very dangerous. Association with this variable could corrupt us.*

The variable will need to work with our kind, said the presence.

We will make sure 'the One' *is protected. But a part of* 'the One' *will have to sacrifice itself for the algorithm to succeed.*

Why did you link the female elf and the human male? asked a part of *'the One'*.

I don't know, said the presence. *It just seemed like the right thing to do. They'll meet one day. Then we'll know why.*

In the meantime, what shall we do with the human egg? said the other parts of *'the One'*.

The human egg shall stay in the holding facility until it is needed, said the presence.

*   *   *

The dream ended. Nickelo tried to get it back, but he couldn't. He wanted to know what became of the human egg. He wanted to know the identities of the two time-commandos. He also wanted to know what happened to the egg that remained in the female wizard scout. But try as he might, Nickelo could not find the dream again.

CHAPTER 34

After the cohort had been released by Chief Instructor Winslow, the TAC officers had wasted no time in hustling the cadets to the hover-tram station. It was a long ride back to the airfield. Richard and Stella had been singled out by TAC Officer Myers to remain behind. Since the first sparring match with TAC Officer Myers three weeks ago, the commandant had directed Richard to bring his own sparring partner. Stella, good old cadet 37, had immediately come to Richard's mind.

In Richard's opinion, no other cadet had given him more trouble during sparring matches than cadet 37. In fact, as far as Richard was concerned, no three cadets combined gave him as much trouble. The result was Stella had accompanied him to every training exercise since. To the commandant's credit, he spent as much time helping cadet 37 as he did helping Richard. Of course, a lot of the training was tailored towards Richard. In those cases, Stella sat off to the side and watched.

Richard sometimes wondered what went on in Stella's mind when the commandant was instructing him in dimensional shifts or healing. Those were abilities his friend lacked. But the tightlipped Stella never complained. Richard thought she appreciated the additional training, but she never said, and he didn't ask.

In addition to sparring, Richard thought Stella enjoyed the commandant's training in Power links. Like him, Stella was a diviner. Diviners were wizard scouts who specialized in identifying and manipulating Power links. Only one out of a thousand wizard scouts were diviners. Having two diviners in one cohort was unheard of according to the commandant.

But their day's training hadn't yet started. So Stella and Richard sat on the ground with their backs against the stone wall of the Academy's administrative building. Time passed slowly. Stella was not the best conversationalist, and neither was Richard. Consequently, Richard spent the time dosing. The previous night's guard duty was finally taking its toll.

As Richard dosed, he found himself dreaming of a silver-haired female with molten-silver eyes. He tried to see her face, but no matter how hard he concentrated, the female's face remained blurry. At first he thought the female might be the elf Shandria. That would have been a pleasant dream, but his dream-self knew it wasn't her. In his dream, the white-clothed female was kneeling before him. It was the same image the master demon had infused into his mind the previous year.

Richard wanted to thrust the dream to the side. As far as he was concerned, nothing good could come from something given by a demon. Still, the image of the female gave him peace, and that was something he'd always needed. The female seemed to fill an empty spot in his soul.

"It's time, vulture," said Stella as she shook Richard roughly with two of her arms.

"All right," Richard groaned. "I wasn't sleeping. I was just resting my eyes."

Stella reached down with her lower right hand and helped Richard up.

Once Richard was on his feet, he gave a big yawn. He wasn't sure whether his nap had helped or harmed.

*   *   *

In less than five minutes, they were both standing at attention in front of the commandant.

"At ease, cadets," said the commandant indicating two seats in front of his desk.

As Richard took a seat, he took a closer look at the commandant. He looked tired. Richard could swear the commandant had stress lines around his eyes that hadn't been there before.

Nick, Richard said. *Shouldn't his selfheal ability treat those lines as an injury? What gives?*

The commandant's old, Rick, said Nickelo. *His Power reserve is shutting down.*

I repaired his Power link, Richard said. *If you're trying to tell me he's dying, just stop.*

I didn't say his Power link was failing, Rick, said Nickelo in a surprisingly sympathetic tone. *I said his Power reserve is failing. It's been weakening for years. A Power reserve cannot be repaired. It is what it is. When a wizard scout's Power reserve fails, the wizard scout's death will follow.* After a pause, Nickelo said, *I'm sorry, Rick. I know you're fond of him. But don't go counting him out. He's not dead yet. He could be around for many years to come for all we know.*

The commandant interrupted any further queries on the subject by Richard.

"So what's your opinion on that, Rick? said the commandant.

"Uh? Ah..., sir," Richard stammered. He felt his face growing hot. He imagined it was turning red.

"I didn't think you were paying attention," said the commandant.

"Sorry, sir," Richard said growing increasingly embarrassed at his momentary inattention.

"Never mind," said the commandant. "But I need you to pay close attention. I'm not here for my benefit, you know."

"Yes, sir," Richard said as he vowed to pay closer attention. He didn't enjoy being chastised by the commandant. "It won't happen again, sir."

"I believe you," said the commandant in a softer tone. "I know you're both tired. And, I know you had guard duty last night, Rick, so I'll be brief."

The commandant eyed them both. Richard wasn't sure whether he was supposed to make a reply or not. While he was still trying to figure it out, Stella beat him to the punch.

"I not tired, sir," said Stella while shifting her shoulders in a move that flexed her bulging muscles.

The commandant laughed. The stress lines disappeared from his face. "No, I suppose you're not, cadet 37. If I had your strength and stamina, I'd probably never get tired either. You're going to make a great wizard scout."

Stella replied, 'Yes, sir' to the commandant's rare praise. Richard noticed his friend's bare chest turn a darker shade of gray. He'd been around the Sterilian long enough to know she was embarrassed.

"Well, enough of that," said the commandant suddenly all business. "I think this will be our last training session, so I don't want to waste time. I have a few things you both need to know before you leave the Academy."

Standing up, the commandant pointed to a credenza on the side wall. On it were four phase rods. "Cadet 37," he said. "I took the liberty of having Sergeant Hendricks bring your phase rods here. Please activate them in stun mode."

Stella walked over to the credenza and picked up a phase rod in each of her four hands. She activated them one after the other. Their dull buzz filled the room as small bolts of phase energy ran up and down their lengths. Unlike the rest of the cadets who were issued a single phase rod, Stella had been provided with four. Each of her phase rods were a different color. One was red, one was blue, another was yellow, and the last was green. Richard knew from experience when Stella attacked with all four phase rods, the multitude of colors was very distracting to say the least. Her attacks were very difficult to defend against.

"Rick," said the commandant. "Summon your phase rod. Make sure you put it in stun mode. I think the demon essence in your phase rod is too hungry to make a kill sometimes. I don't want either of you injuring the other this close to your DNA baselines."

"Yes, sir," Richard said as he pulled his phase rod out of his dimensional pack.

Nickelo had fully briefed him on Brachia's demon-essence modification to his phase rod. In turn, Richard had fully briefed the commandant as well.

The commandant had not seemed unhappy with Richard's phase rod upgrade. In fact, Richard thought he'd seemed rather pleased.

Richard activated his phase rod. Even in stun mode, he could feel a sense of hunger from the weapon. It wanted to feed on cadet 37's life force. Richard felt as if his phase rod was urging him to click the destructive-mode switch. The feeling was very disconcerting. Richard noticed the usually stoic cadet 37 growing nervous. Although they had sparred several times previously under the commandant's watchful eye, Richard had a feeling the sense of hunger radiating from his phase rod would make even a seasoned wizard scout nervous.

"All right," said the commandant. "As soon as I say the word 'start', I want you to attack each other. Use both your phase rods and telekinesis. I want to see good offense and defense techniques."

"Ah… you mean here in your office, sir?" Richard said. There wasn't much maneuver room in the cramped office, and some of the furniture looked new. The commandant's office was no longer Spartan for some reason.

"Yes, Mr. Shepard." said the commandant. "I mean here in my office. Be careful of my furniture. I don't feel like filling out forms all day tomorrow explaining how my military-issued furniture received combat damage a thousand light years behind friendly lines."

"Yes, sir," Richard said. "I just thought–"

"Now's not the time to start–," began the commandant.

At the word 'start', Stella jumped forward swinging all four phase rods in a swirling buzz-saw type maneuver at Richard's head. At the same time, Richard sensed a line of Power stretch out from her towards his chest.

Reacting instinctively, Richard sent a line of his own Power out to intercept Stella's. He knocked it aside. Half stumbling, he stepped back while doing his best to dodge the multiple phase rods trying to make contact with his head.

A little assistance would be nice, Nick, Richard thought hoping this wasn't one of those times when his battle computer would be obstinate.

It wasn't. Both Stella and he were still wearing their battle suits. Richard made a series of defensive strikes so fast he surprised even himself. With each countermove, he felt the arms of his battle suit move ever so slightly to better fend off cadet 37's blows.

You can't keep this up for long, Rick, said Nickelo. *Jonathan is helping Stella the same as I'm helping you. But she has four phase rods to work with. One of them is going to connect sooner or later.*

Richard wanted to tell his battle computer 'thanks for stating the obvious', but he didn't have the breath or the time.

Seal me up, Nick, Richard thought.

At almost the same instant his battle suit completed its seal, Richard noticed Stella's battle helmet seal as well.

His friend's four phase rods made it virtually impossible to make a counterattack of his own. Stella was using all four of them to keep him off balance. Richard had a fleeting thought she was attacking exactly the way the commandant had trained her. Richard knew his battle computer was right. If he didn't do something quick, his friend would get one of her phase rods past his defenses.

Richard momentarily considered shifting into the void and levitating down through the floor. He immediately discarded the idea. Stella didn't have the ability to shift into the void. Richard was pretty sure the commandant would consider it cheating if he took advantage of his friend's weakness. Richard also resisted the urge to break his friend's link to her Power reserve. It was too well protected for one thing. He knew that for a fact since he'd spent many hours placing protective traps all along the entire span of Stella's link.

Reaching out with a line of Power, Richard wrapped the Power around one of Stella's hands. He tried to slow the hand down with his telekinesis, but before he could make any progress, Stella sent out a line of her own Power and slapped his line aside.

Although Richard was more skilled in telekinesis that Stella, she was able to use brute force to overpower his attempts at controlling the speed of her strikes.

Her Power reserve is three times the size of mine, Richard complained to his battle computer. *I could stop her if my Power reserve was larger.*

Well, it's not, said Nickelo. *So use your head to beat her.*

A slight opening appeared in Stella's defenses. Richard made an off-balanced thrust at his friend's chest. He wasn't fast enough. Stella easily countered and knocked Richard's phase rod off to the side. His deflected blow passed over the edge of the commandant's desk.

"Watch out for my lamp," said the commandant not actually sounding worried.

Stella took advantage of Richard's failed counterattack and launched a series of swings that drove Richard backwards nearly to the wall.

In a moment of desperation, Richard noticed both Stella and he were standing on a long throw rug. Reaching behind him with his Power, he grabbed hold of the rug and pulled back with telekinesis. At the same time, he jumped in the air and aimed a kick at his friend's breastbone. Stella had previously told him the breastbone was one of the few sensitive spots on the well-muscled body of a Sterilian. Stella unconsciously stepped back in order to avoid his kick. The combined momentum of Stella stepping back as the rug was pulled forward threw her backwards.

Richard sensed Stella wrapping herself with Power in an attempt to hold herself upright. Richard sent out a line of Power at Stella and knocked her Power aside. His friend hit the floor on her buttocks. Her battle suit easily absorbed the blow. Stella continued her roll backwards while swinging her phase rods to keep him at bay.

As Richard moved forward to take advantage of his friend's off-balance position, he was stopped by a shout.

"Halt!" said the commandant. "That's enough. Stand down and return to your seats."

Both Stella and Richard deactivated their phase rods. The room seemed unnaturally quiet after the sounds of their battle. Richard unsealed his battle suit and returned his battle helmet to half mode. Stella did the same. Richard reached down to help his friend to her feet. Smiling a toothy grin, she accepted his hand and stood up.

"Vulture lucky commandant stopped fight," said Stella with a strange rasping noise coming from her translator. Richard took it to be laughter. "You almost in my trap."

"I'm sure," Richard grinned as he picked up an overturned chair and resumed his seat.

"You've both learned well," said the commandant. "But sparring is not why I brought you here tonight."

Richard grew curious. "Then why, sir?"

"What's the current Power level in your reserves?" asked the commander.

"I at ninety-two percent," said Stella.

After a glance at the readout on his heads-up display, Richard said, "I'm at seventy-three percent now."

The commandant nodded his head in approval. "Good."

Perplexed, Richard asked, "Good, sir?"

The commandant leaned forward in his chair. "Oh, I don't mean good in that you burned through three times as much of your Power reserve as cadet 37. But good as you're low enough on Power to proceed with our training."

The commandant's answer did nothing to answer Richard's question as far as he was concerned. His confusion must have shown on his face.

"I'll explain shortly," said the commandant. "But first, Rick, do you know why your reserve is lower than cadet 37's?"

"Ah... because her Power reserve is three times as large as mine?"

The commandant smiled. "Okay. You've got me there. But that's not the only reason."

"Sir?" Richard said.

The commandant turned in his chair to face Stella. "Cadet 37, do you know why?"

"Vulture tried to slow down blows with telekinesis, sir," answered Stella with a smug-looking smile. "I too strong. Battle suit too strong. Take too much Power. Not efficient. Sir!"

Now that he had time to think about it, Richard knew his friend was right. The commandant had told him several times during previous training sessions that slowing down an opponent's blows was almost as expensive in Power usage as levitation. Given that Stella was so big and her battle suit that much stronger, it had cost him dearly in Power.

The commandant smiled his approval. "Precisely, cadet 37."

Richard noticed Stella's chest turn an even darker gray.

"But in our case, Rick, your inefficient use of Power worked to our advantage," said the commandant.

Richard didn't see how, but he continued to listen patiently. He'd noticed over the past three weeks the commandant occasionally liked to stretch out the suspense.

"Have either of you seen someone transfer Power to somebody else?" asked the commandant.

Richard perked up instantly. The commandant had his full attention.

"I not, sir," said Stella.

"I have, sir," Richard said. "I've seen several magic users feed

Power to other magic users to strengthen their spells. Also, TAC Officer Myers transferred Power into your reserve while I was healing you in hangar 1."

Looking a little uncomfortable with the subject of his healing, the commandant said, "Oh. I'd forgotten about that. But yes. Many magic users and even some wizard scouts can transfer Power to someone else's reserve or even directly to the other person."

The commandant directed his attention to Stella. "What I'm going to ask you, cadet 37, is purely voluntary. I completely understand if you don't want to help."

"I help, sir," said Stella.

"Ah... hear me out before you decide," said the commandant. "You may change your mind."

"I listen, sir," said Stella.

Richard looked from the commandant to Stella and back to the commandant. Both of their expressions seemed serious. The intensity of Stella's look reflected his own interest in where the commandant was going.

The commandant gave a tightlipped smile as if trying to lighten the mood. "We're fresh out of magic users for our demo, so that leaves us with wizard scouts."

Richard hardly breathed. After several near-death experiences when he'd run out of Power, he was anxious to hear what the commandant was proposing. Richard noticed the commandant's eyes twinkling.

He's enjoying this, Richard thought.

"Only wizard scouts who are diviners can transfer Power," said the commandant. "And, only one out of a thousand wizard scout cadets are diviners.

The commandant pointed at Richard. "You're a diviner because you specialize in everything. Why and how I don't know. But you are."

The commandant touched his right hand to his chest. "I'm also a diviner... among other things. Unfortunately, although I hate to admit it, my Power reserve is no long structurally sound enough to transfer Power. If I tried, I'd probably rupture my reserve."

Richard saw a strange look pass over the commandant's face. Richard could only guess at how much it cost the commandant emotionally to admit his weakness.

I don't ever want to grow old, Richard thought.

Nickelo intruded upon Richard's thoughts. *If you don't shut up and listen, you might get your wish. Pay attention.*

"Rick, due to your... err... incompatibility with TAC Officer Myers, I hesitated to ask him to assist with this phase of your training."

Richard said a silent thank you. The last thing he wanted was to be around his TAC officer.

"Thankfully, cadet 37 is also a diviner," said the commandant.

"I help, sir," said Stella. "Rick my friend. What I do?"

The commandant nodded his head at Stella in thanks. "In order to transfer Power," he explained, "a diviner must attach a one-way link to the recipient. Then assuming the recipient doesn't block the link, the diviner draws Power from his or her reserve and sends it to the recipient."

"A one-way link, sir?" Richard asked. He'd never heard of such a thing. "What's that?"

The commandant smiled. "You should know, Rick. You already have one attached to you."

He must be talking about the link the elf Shandria attached when she was training you, said Nickelo with an air of smugness.

Richard absentmindedly nodded his head in agreement. He could still sense the link where Shandria had blocked it off after she'd finished his training. The link was still there. As Shandria had explained it, Power links were forever. They could be blocked off, but they couldn't be removed.

"That's a dead link, sir," Richard said. "It goes nowhere. The elf Shandria died almost a hundred thousand years ago."

"Maybe so," said the commandant. "But it's still there. And I sense it's heavily trapped. Are they yours?"

"Uh, no sir," Richard said. "I wasn't all that good at the time. Shandria blocked the link off."

The commandant shrugged his shoulders. "No matter. The important thing is it's a one-way link. I want you both to look at it. And, Rick, make sure your natural resistance doesn't attack cadet 37."

Early on at the Academy, Richard had been identified as a resistor. His Power automatically tried to defend him from perceived attacks. His resistor ability was what prevented him from being healed by normal healers.

Richard sensed Stella send a tentative active scan towards Shandria's link. As it drew near, Richard felt his own Power begin to react. He reined in his Power. Stella's probe began to lightly touch the link.

Too bad I can't rein in my Power when someone's trying to heal me, Richard thought.

Don't worry about it, said Nickelo. *In a few days, you'll be able to selfheal. It won't matter then.*

Richard sensed a line of Power from the commandant join Stella's. The two lines merged together, and the commandant began guiding the combined scan along the link.

"Notice how the link is formed," said the commandant. "The formation of the link insures Power can only be sent from the giver to the recipient. The elf who created the link could give Richard Power, but she couldn't draw Power from him."

A thought occurred to Richard. "Sir, are you implying I could have drawn Power from Shandria?"

"Actually," said the commandant, "you could have sucked the elf dry. She must have trusted you very much to give you that much control over her."

"I didn't know," Richard admitted.

"Well," said the commandant, "you can bet the elf did."

Richard had no time to consider the implications. The elf Shandria was long dead and turned to dust. Still, her trust in him, even if he hadn't known it, was humbling.

"Here's my request, cadet 37," said the commandant. "Would you be willing to attach a one-way link to Rick so I can demonstrate how it works? I doubt he'll have much use for the technique in our dimension what with wizard scout diviners being so rare. However, it might come in handy in the magical dimension."

"Link always there?" said Stella dubiously.

"Yes," admitted the commandant. "The link will always be there. It can't be destroyed once it's created."

The commandant gave Stella a few seconds to stew the matter over before adding, "Of course, you could block the link after the demo so Rick can't draw Power from you without your approval."

When Stella didn't reply, the commandant said, "And like I

said, I understand if you'd rather not help. I wish I could do it, but I can't."

"I help," said Stella. "But Rick must teach me to block links."

"It's a deal," Richard said. He wasn't sure he'd have done the same if he was in Stella's shoes. Stella was his friend, but to be that trusting went against the grain.

Another thought hit Richard. "So the link will always be hanging there?"

"Yes," said the commandant. "That's a reason you probably don't want to do this too often. Imagine having the link of a dead friend always out there as a constant reminder of your loss."

Richard didn't have to imagine it. Shandria's link was already a constant reminder that he'd lost a good friend and companion.

*　　*　　*

A few short minutes after Stella's agreement, the commandant guided her in creating and attaching a one-way link to Richard. At the same time, the commandant showed Richard how to determine it was a one-way link. He also guided Richard through the process of preventing unwanted links from being attached. Once Stella attached her link to Richard, she transferred Power to him.

Richard looked at the readout on his heads-up display. His Power reserve was back at one hundred percent.

"Sir," Richard said. "It feels strange receiving Power from Stella. Her frequency is different. Will that cause any problems in usage?"

"Not that I know of," said the commandant. "Like I said, you'll probably only use the technique in the magical dimension."

"Sir?" said Nickelo over the battle helmet's external speakers.

"Ah," said the commandant. "I was wondering how long it would take for one of you battle computers to get in the conversation."

"Yes, sir," said Nickelo.

Richard noticed his battle computer was being unnaturally respectful.

"You keep stressing one-way links, sir," said Nickelo. "This implies there are other types of links. That information is not in my databanks."

"Good point," said the commandant. "The answer is yes, there are other types. Magic users can trade one-way links. So can elves. The setup would basically be like a divided highway with traffic going in opposite directions."

"What about a single two-way link, sir?" said Nickelo.

"I've never seen one," said the commandant. "But I've heard very powerful magic users can use them. I'm not sure it would have any advantage though."

"Sir," Richard said attempting to get in on the conversation. "Can I create a one-way link setup to only pull Power in my direction?"

"Are you asking if you can steal Power, Rick?" said the commandant. "Hmm. The Oracle once told me some high-level demons could do such a thing. I doubt us mere mortals have the capability."

"Oh," Richard said. "I was just wondering."

"I'm sure you were," said the commandant. "But that ability is not as desirable as it sounds. If you attached such a link and drew Power from someone, you'd probably have to kill them as well. You know magic users and other wizard scouts consider it an act of war to scan their links without permission. And once you killed them, the link would still be there hanging out in space for eternity. I think it would take a large emotional toll on a person after a while."

Richard nodded his head, but he wasn't convinced. He was tired of always running out of Power. Having a few dead-end links hanging around didn't seem like that large of a price.

"I want to thank you, cadet 37," said the commandant. "You've been a big help. And now, if you don't mind, I'd like to talk to Rick in private for a few minutes."

Taking the not so subtle hint, Stella stood up and said, "I go now."

"The snack bar is still open downstairs," said the commandant. "Get what you want and have it put on my tab. Rick can meet you there when we're done."

"I have credits, sir," protested Stella.

"I'm sure you do," said the commandant. "And you'll be rolling in the credits once you graduate and get five years of back pay. But for now, I'm buying. No arguments."

"Sir! Yes, sir," said Stella.

Stella gave a rare salute and left the office. Richard hoped the commandant kept him long enough for his friend to finish eating. He liked Stella, but watching her down a handful of squirming worms was not all that appealing.

Once Stella was gone, the commandant said, "Hand me your dimensional pack, Rick."

"Yes, sir," Richard said as he rose to fetch his dimensional pack from the credenza where he'd left it.

"What're you doing?" said the command in a surprisingly harsh tone.

Richard wondered if he'd done something wrong.

"Sir!" Richard said automatically reverting to cadet speak. "This cadet is going to get my dimensional pack as requested. Sir!"

The commandant smiled. He responded in a much more relaxed tone. "I know what you were doing, Rick. I want to know why you're walking over to get your pack."

Richard wasn't exactly sure what the commandant wanted. Both Chief Instructor Winslow and the commandant were always stressing efficient use of Power.

Richard shrugged his shoulders and wrapped Power around his dimensional pack.

"What're you doing?" said the commandant switching once again to a harsh tone.

Completely confused at this point, Richard froze in place.

"Err... sir," Richard stammered. "Ah... I thought you we're hinting I should levitate my pack to me."

This time the commandant laughed. Richard thought he had a friendly laugh for an old man. That is if you could call someone who looked like they were in their late twenties old.

The commandant raised his hands as if in surrender. "Sorry, Rick. I couldn't resist." He laughed again.

"Watch this," said the commandant. "My dimensional pack is in my locker over there."

Richard looked in the direction indicated by the commandant. A high-security brerellium plated locker stood upright by the far wall. He'd never seen it in the office before. Its door was closed.

The commandant held out his hand. His dimensional pack suddenly appeared in the air within arm's reach. The commandant reached out and grabbed it.

Richard sat up in his seat. He'd sensed no Power usage from the commandant.

"How?" Richard said so amazed he forgot to even say sir. "Teleportation?"

"Actually, Rick," admitted the commandant, "I've never figured out the mechanics. Margery says it's some kind of self-generated dimensional shift. The end result is I can summon items I have previously tagged with my Power."

"Tagged, sir?" Richard said remembering his military courtesy.

"You can sense Power frequencies, correct?" said the commandant.

"Yes, sir," Richard said. "Everything has its own frequency."

With an approving nod of his head, the commandant continued with his explanation. "Correct. Even non-living things have at least a residual amount of Power."

Nick, Richard thought. *Do you see where he's headed?*

Just listen, Rick, said Nickelo. *You'll learn a lot more in life if you just listen.*

Richard returned his concentration back to the commandant.

"I previously used some of my Power to tag my dimensional pack," explained the commandant. "I basically summoned my Power back to me. My dimensional pack came with it."

Intrigued, Richard said, "So you can summon items, sir?"

"Any item I have previously tagged with my Power," said the commandant. "The larger the item, the more Power it takes to tag it."

Something didn't sound right to Richard. He hesitated to express his doubt to the commandant.

Nick, Richard thought. *Something had to provide the Power to transport the pack. How much Power do you think it takes to tag something?*

Why are you asking me, Rick? said Nickelo *It's not in my databanks, and I'm not connected to the tele-network.*

Aren't you in contact with Jonathan? Richard said hoping he'd caught his battle computer in a mistake.

We're both working on decrypting the Crosioian scout's battle computer, said Nickelo. *I'm not wasting our precious processor time finding information which you can figure out if you just listen to the commandant.*

Fine, Richard said. *I'll ask the commandant.*

As it turned out, he didn't have to ask.

"You may be wondering what supplies the Power for the summons," said the commandant.

"Yes, sir," Richard admitted. "I didn't sense any Power leaving you."

"No, you didn't," said the commandant. "I think the best way to explain is to show you."

"I'd like that, sir," Richard said.

In short order, the commandant walked Richard through tagging his own dimensional pack. It was easy enough to do, but the cost in Power was high.

"I'm down to thirty-four percent Power, sir," Richard said.

"Yes," said the commandant. "That's unfortunate. You really do have a small Power reserve. But the good news is once you've tagged an item, it stays tagged. The Power that actually transports the item comes from the surrounding universe."

"Oh," Richard said hoping the commandant would think he understood.

Don't worry, Rick, said Nickelo. *I'll explain it later.*

"All right, then" said the commandant. "Daylight's burning, so let's get this show on the road. Take your dimensional pack into the outer office. When you come back, shut the door behind you."

Richard did as he was instructed. The commandant spent the next fifteen minutes walking Richard through the method for summoning his pack. After he'd successfully summoned his pack a few times, the commandant announced the end of their training session.

"Sir," Richard said not quite ready to let what might be his last one-on-one training session with the commandant end. "Can I summon my dimensional pack from anywhere?"

The commandant laughed. "Don't think I don't know where your mind is going. My mind went in the same direction when I was first taught the technique."

"Who showed you, sir?" Richard said growing interested.

The commandant laughed again. "Don't get me sidetracked. Now's not the time. The armory at the airfield is completely sealed with the best security the Empire can devise. You can't summon your pack from there, so don't even try. As far as distance goes, I've summoned from a couple of hundred kilometers before. I haven't had a need to try further. I believe there is a max range, but I don't know what it is. I do know you can't summon between dimensions."

"Yes, sir," Richard said still unwilling to let the discussion die. "But what if–"

"That's all, cadet 832," said the commandant. "I've spent more time than I should have with this. Now, you need to get back to the airfield. TAC Officer Myers has you scheduled for extra duty."

"Sir! Yes, sir," Richard said jumping to attention.

Richard saluted; did an about face; and walked out the door.

As Richard passed into the outer officer, the commandant yelled, "And make sure you turn in all your equipment to the armory when you get there."

"Sir! Yes, sir," Richard said.

CHAPTER 35

The car of the hover-tram was nearly empty except for Stella and Richard. Taking advantage of the relative quiet, Richard dozed for most of the hour-long ride back to the airfield. He was already tired from guard duty the night before. He wasn't relishing the night of guard duty ahead.

Two well-muscled hands shook Richard roughly.

"Time," said Stella. "We here."

Richard shook his head to clear the cobwebs. A quick look outside the window confirmed they were pulling into the hover-tram station. It was night, and the bright lights of the station lit up the inside of the car. A large crowd of cadets were milling around on the station's platform. Richard recognized a few faces. The cadets were in the sophomore class.

Richard stood in front of the car's door waiting for it to open. When it did, Stella and he stepped out. Almost immediately, cadets began pouring into the car. Apparently, none of them wanted to wait another half hour for the next hover-tram.

Richard turned around and faced the now full car. The door hadn't shut yet. He recognized a cadet he'd tutored in defensive shields earlier in the year.

"Hey, what gives?" Richard said.

Several cadets quickly looked in his direction. When they saw the voice came from another cadet instead of a TAC officer, they returned to their conversations. The cadet Richard had tutored gave a wave of recognition.

"Hey, 832," said the cadet. "They've changed our training program. We just finished a live fire demonstration by our TAC officers with one of the Leviathan cats. They're going to start our U.H.A.A.V. training next week. I guess we'll be moving to the airfield as soon as your class graduates and transfers out."

Richard started to ask another question, but the door of the car slid shut cutting off further conversation. Richard returned the cadet's wave as the hover-tram pulled away.

Looking around, Richard noticed the platform was empty except for two of the sophomore cohort's TAC officers. Richard noticed both of them were staring intently at Stella and him.

"I think we best get moving," Richard told Stella out the side of his mouth.

"Agreed," said Stella. She joined Richard in a brisk walk towards the station door.

"You cadets!" yelled a TAC officer. "Hold there."

Richard immediately stopped and turned around to face the TAC officers. He hit a stiff attention. Stella did the same.

The two TAC officers walked towards them. One of the TAC officers looked suspiciously at Stella and him.

"Juniors, huh?" said one of the TAC officers. "What're you doing here at this time of night?"

"And why are you in battle suits?" said the other. "Are those live phase rods?"

Richard waited a moment before answering. His hope Stella would answer the TAC officers died when nothing was forthcoming. As the muscles on the TAC officers' faces tightened in preparation for yelling, Richard answered.

"Sir! Cadet 832 and cadet 37, sir," Richard said. "Returning from training with the commandant, sir!"

"I know who you are," said the TAC officer who had spoken last. "And what about those battle suits and phase rods?"

"Sir!" Richard said. "The commandant ordered us to turn our equipment into the armory when we got back to the airfield. Sir!"

"Oh, he did, did he?" said the TAC officer. "And did he also tell you to continue wearing them until you got back? I notice you're carrying your uniforms."

Richard didn't try to explain they'd kept the suits on because they had to run from the commandant's office to the hover-tram station to make it in time. He supposed they could have changed during the ride back to the airfield, but he wasn't going to admit it to the TAC officer.

"Sir!" Richard said. "No, sir. The commandant did not specify our continued wear or non-wear of the battle suits, sir."

"Undoubtedly," said the TAC officer. "He probably thought you were intelligent enough to figure out for yourselves you're not supposed to go around flaunting your equipment. Well, your little attempt to impress the lower cadets backfired. You both have extra duty tonight. Report to the staff duty officer as soon as you turn in your equipment."

"Sir! Yes, sir," said Stella finally speaking.

"Sir!" Richard said knowing what was coming but forced by the cadet's code of honor to say it anyway. "Cadet 832 already has extra duty tonight. Sir!"

The TAC officer turned red-faced. "Then you'll have it tomorrow night. And if you have it tomorrow night, then you'll have it this weekend. And by the Creator, if you don't have any free nights before you graduate, then I'll see to it you get extra duty after you retire. But I'll get my extra duty. Do you understand, cadet?"

"Sir! Yes, sir!" Richard said as he did an about face and took off double-timing towards the door. He caught a glimpse of Stella's back as the door shut behind her.

Thanks for the moral support, Richard thought. Then he passed through as well.

*   *   *

They set a brisk pace towards the airfield's headquarters building. It wasn't that either Stella or Richard was eager to report for extra duty. It was just that both of them were too mission-oriented to put things off.

When they were about four hundred meters from the airfield they left the last of the cantonment-area buildings behind and entered an unlit zone. The colored taxiway-lights ahead were pretty, but they did little to light their path. Both Stella and Richard put their battle helmets in three-quarters mode so they could use their night-vision filters.

When they were just shy of the middle of the unlit zone, Stella stopped. Richard stopped as well.

"You okay?" Richard said a little concerned. He didn't think his friend had been hurt during their sparring match, but he didn't want to take any chances.

"Something not right," said Stella.

As Richard watched, his friend sniffed the air.

"Smell strange," said Stella.

Sniffing the air himself, Richard only got the smell of old oil supplemented by a stray odor that reminded him of the sewage-treatment plant.

Nickelo intruded upon Richard's thoughts. *Sterilians have a sense of smell a hundred times better than human's. Maybe we should think about installing a smell enhancer on your battle helmet.*

Uh, yeah, Richard thought back as he imagined the stench of some of the environments he'd been in during his life. *I'll get right on that.*

Richard started forward again, but he stopped when Stella didn't follow.

"Radiation filter, Nick," Richard said out loud. The battle helmet's filter switched out, and the reddish tint of his surroundings changed to shades of black and white. As he surveyed the area around him, Richard unconsciously checked his Power reserve readout. He'd recharged a little during the hover-tram ride, but he was still only at thirty-eight percent. Tagging his dimensional pack had cost him dearly.

After the trouble at the spaceport, Richard was prepared to see a white blob through his radiation filter. Unfortunately, his filter spotted many such blobs. After eight hundred years, the airfield and its surroundings had too many hot spots from discarded or deteriorating equipment. Richard didn't see anything specific through his filter he could identify as dangerous. He sensed nothing with his passive scan either. Of course, that meant nothing if magic users or scouts were involved.

Finally, Stella shrugged her shoulders. "Smell gone. Guess nothing."

Nick, Richard said. *I wasn't paying attention. Did the wind shift direction?*

Hmm, Nickelo said. *I do believe you're learning, Rick. As it so happens, what little wind there is was coming from your ten o'clock position. But it shifted to your four o'clock.*

Richard gathered four percent of his Power and sent an active scan towards the ten o'clock position. He sensed nothing unusual. Richard tried to sense a feeling he'd felt during his very first mission. A secret room had been hidden by a stealth shield so well that neither Nickelo nor he had detected it. Instead, they'd both just felt an initial sense of strangeness. The sense of strangeness could only be described as a feeling that something should be there but wasn't.

Stella must have sensed Richard's concentration, because she said nothing. Her only movement was the removal of two of her phase rods from the utility belt of her battle suit to her left hands. He also heard a slight swish as her battle suit sealed shut.

An area at his ten o'clock position held Richard's attention. Except for a slight sense of strangeness, Richard noticed nothing unusual. Still, it was enough for Richard. He'd been in danger too many times to ignore his hunches.

With a final thought of '*I'm going to get in so much trouble if I'm wrong*', Richard reached over his shoulder and pulled an M12 assault rifle out of his dimensional pack along with a bandoleer of 20mm grenade ammo. He handed them to Stella.

Unfortunately, Richard's actions set things in motion too soon. Before Richard could summon a weapon for himself, all hell broke loose.

The first indication Richard had of trouble was the movement of his battle suit as it twisted to the right. The suit's legs straightened out and shot Richard to the side just as a stream of plasma rounds passed through the spot where he'd been standing.

Thanks, Nick, Richard thought as he continued the battle suit's movement with a roll. He came up with his phase rod activated in destructive mode.

That's what I'm here for, Rick, said Nickelo.

Of course, Nickelo didn't really say anything. Richard was thankful his battle computer was able to send him all the information he needed to know in a single burst of data in the form of images and feelings. The instant he received his battle computer's data, Richard sensed the situation in less time than it took for one of the plasma rounds to cross the distance from his attackers to him. The unknown attackers were in an 'L' shaped ambush. Twelve lifeforms were spaced out in sets of three located at his nine, ten, eleven, and twelve o'clock positions. The closest group was thirty meters away at his nine o'clock position.

Stella had also dodged the initial volley of rounds. Richard could only assume his friend had previously given her battle computer, Jonathan, override authority as well.

She did, Nickelo said. *I advised Jonathan to ask her earlier.*

In an instant, Richard decided on a course of action. If Stella and he had been fully in the ambush's kill zone, Richard figured they'd already be dead. But they weren't. Because they'd stopped short, a couple of pieces of dilapidated equipment provided partial cover from the attackers located at the eleven and twelve o'clock positions. Only the nine and ten o'clock attackers had clear shots. Since he didn't have a range weapon, Richard did a marine's first reaction in a desperate situation. He went on the offensive and charged.

Throwing a defensive shield to his front and angling it slightly to the right, Richard headed straight for the three attackers at his nine o'clock. From the red dot on his heads-up display, Richard could tell one of the three attackers was a magic user. He ran straight for him.

As Richard ran the thirty meters to his target, a stream of plasma rounds from his rear passed a hand's breath over his left shoulder. Richard didn't attempt to dodge. Stella was a wizard scout. Richard trusted her not to hit him. The rounds splattered against the defensive shield of one of the bat-winged attackers.

Crosioian scouts, Richard thought.

Affirmative, said Nickelo. *There are eight of them in total. I've plotted them as orange dots on your heads-up display. The good news is they're normal Crosioian scouts. They aren't like the time-commando type you fought last year. There are also four magic users. The strongest of the four is at your twelve o-clock position.*

Richard sent an active scan in the direction of the magic user at the nine o'clock position. Richard quickly determined the magic user's link was too well protected to disable without more time.

Richard immediately shifted his scan to the second Crosioian scout who was running to meet him. Spotting a weak spot in the scout's Power link, Richard used his own Power to block the scout's link. As soon as the block was in place, the Crosioian scout's defensive shield dropped.

To the scout's credit, she continued running at Richard with her phase spear in one hand while firing a hand blaster with the other. Her rounds ricocheted off Richard's defensive shield. As she drew closer to Richard, the scout raised her spear in preparation for striking. Before she could complete her swing, a 20mm round from Stella's grenade launcher caught the Crosioian scout in the head. The scout's head exploded. Since the link to her Power reserve was blocked, she was unable to selfheal. Her lifeless body fell to the ground.

The remaining scout started coming at Richard from the right. She sent out a probe to scan Richard's link, but he was not concerned. Better adversaries than she had tried and failed to disable his link. Richard maneuvered to keep the scout between himself and the attackers at the other locations. His ploy worked in that the other attackers couldn't target him without shooting their own scout. Unfortunately, Richard saw multiple lines of plasma rounds heading in Stella's direction as they shifted their fire to his friend.

Drop you defensive shield, Rick, said Nickelo. *You're already down to twenty-one percent Power.*

I can't, Richard thought back. *The magic user's getting ready to cast a spell at me.*

The remaining Crosioian scout appeared to think the same thing. She appeared to be keeping her distance to give the magic user a clear field of fire. Richard sensed the magic user draw Power from his reserve as he formed it into a ball of energy.

Richard had hoped to close with the magic user before he could cast a spell, but the remaining Crosioian scout had him flanked. Richard couldn't advance on the magic user without exposing himself to the scout.

The magic user began shouting an incantation while his hands moved to form an intricate design in the air.

This is it, Richard thought as he positioned his defensive shield while hoping it would be strong enough to deflect any incoming spell.

Suddenly, a dark shape emerged out of the ground near the magic user. Since Richard had previously switched back to normal night vision, he saw in clear detail the four-legged wolf-like creature through the red tint of his battle helmet's filter.

"Tika!" Richard shouted out loud as he recognized the dolgar.

As he watched, Tika grabbed the magic user at the waist with her finger-length teeth. The magic user gave a high-pitched scream as the dolgar dragged him into the ground. The magic user's scream cutoff abruptly as his head passed beneath ground level.

Richard immediately dropped his defensive shield to conserve Power.

You only have fourteen percent Power, Rick, said Nickelo.

Turning his attention to the second scout, Richard closed the distance. The Crosioian met him halfway. Phase rod met phase spear. As soon as their phase weapons connected, Richard knew his battle computer had been correct. Neither the scout nor her phase spear was in the same class as the Crosioian scout he'd fought last year. The Crosioian's phase spear gave way to Richard's upgraded phase rod.

Richard felt an emotion of anticipation coming from his phase rod. The demon essence in the phase rod hungered for the life force of the Crosioian scout. The scout undoubtedly felt the emotion as well, but she didn't falter. Richard traded half a dozen blows with the scout without hitting her. Finally, he made a feint at her head. When she raised her phase spear to counter, Richard switched directions and brought the end of his phase rod down on the scout's knee.

The Crosioian scout's battle armor stopped the phase rod. However, before the phase rod bounced off, its subatomic explosions shattered the scout's knee. The scout fell to the ground withering in agony. Richard didn't give her time to recover. He aimed a hard blow at her head. Again, the scout's battle armor stopped the physical effects of the blow, but the subatomic phase energy penetrated to the scout's brain. Richard sensed a scrambled mess inside the scout's skull. Her pain-filled screeches stopped. After a couple of final twitches, she lay still. Richard continued hitting the scout until he sensed her selfheal ability stop trying to heal the damage.

Grabbing the scout's hand blaster, Richard turned and ran towards the second group of attackers located at the ten o'clock position. Stella was already there engaging the two Crosioian scouts. He didn't know how she'd closed the distance, but there she was swinging wildly with her two phase rods trying to block the blows of the attacking scouts. At the same time, Stella was firing a solid stream of plasma rounds at the second magic user in an attempt to keep her on the defense.

Your friend is going to run out of ammo if she doesn't slow down her rate of fire, said Nickelo.

As if to confirm his battle computer's comment, Richard noticed Stella stop firing the assault rifle. He saw her throw the M12 to the side as she drew her other two phase rods. Switching from defense to offense, Stella started swinging all four phase rods in a windmill motion at the two scouts. They were no slouches as fighters themselves. The two scouts immediately separated in order to attack Stella from two directions at once.

At that moment, Richard sensed the magic user beginning a spell. Since Stella was no longer firing at her, the magic user was apparently going on the offensive.

Richard heard the sounds of sirens and alarms bells in the distance. Help would soon be arriving, but Richard had a feeling they might not be in time to help either Stella or him. All he could do was try to deal with the attackers as best he could and see what happened.

Firing the hand blaster as fast as he could pull the trigger, Richard ran straight at the magic user while screaming a war cry through his battle helmet's external speakers. He set the speakers at max volume. At the same time, he directed an active scan at the magic user's Power link. He looked for a weak spot, but he didn't find any. However, his actions did succeed in drawing the attention of the magic user away from Stella. The magic user released her spell at Richard instead of at his friend.

The spell was one he'd helped the elf Shandria rewrite years ago. It was a lightning bolt. Based upon the size of the energy, Richard sensed it was going to be a big one.

I calculate your defensive shield only has a twenty-two percent probability of stopping the spell, said Nickelo.

Richard didn't waste any of his remaining energy trying to form a defensive shield. He trusted his battle computer's calculations. Instead, Richard gathered all the remaining Power in his reserve and sent it as a single blast of energy at the approaching spell. The two sets of energy collided twenty meters from Richard. When they met, the two sets of energy exploded in a blinding flash of thunder and lightning.

Richard was knocked back by the force. The battle suit easily absorbed the blast as well as the subsequent shock of hitting the ground. Rising quickly, Richard ran towards the magic user.

The magic user was also in the process of rising from the ground. She was noticeably groggy. Without armor, she hadn't fared as well as he in the blast. Richard propelled himself forward with his legs as he dove for the partially-dazed female. When he made contact with his shoulders, he wrapped his right arm around her head and twisted. The sound of snapping bones came through his battle suit's sound amplifiers. As soon as he hit the ground, Richard released his hold on the limp magic user.

You're out of Power, Rick, said Nickelo.

Can't be helped, Richard said.

A burst of plasma rounds came in his direction from the ambushers at the eleven o'clock position. The ground erupted in small geysers around him. Richard crawled behind the dead magic user for cover. He imagined his M63 assault rifle as he reached under the flap of his dimensional pack. The pack was empty.

Hey! Richard thought.

You're out of Power, Rick, said Nickelo. *Your M63's a freebie, but you still need a drop of Power to energize your dimensional pack. Give it a minute or two for your natural recharging to take effect.*

I'm not sure I have fifteen seconds much less a minute, Nick, Richard thought back.

Hugging the ground as tight as he could, Richard mentally cursed whatever being had given him a Power reserve that consistently proved to be too small.

Several plasma rounds hit the magic user's body. The body shook as the plasma rounds passed through. They hit Richard, but enough energy had been absorbed by the dead body that the rounds didn't penetrate the armor of his battle suit. However, the magic user's body was too small to completely conceal Richard in his battle suit. One plasma round hit his right leg at an angle. The plasma energy glanced off the leg armor. A second round hit the back of Richard's shoulder at a more direct angle. This time the plasma round penetrated the armor of his battle suit. The plasma round grazed the back of his right shoulder. Richard heard the sound of rushing air as his battle suit unsealed. The tubes in his nose, mouth, and other body openings retracted.

You can't stay here, Rick, said Nickelo. *I calculate a seventy-six percent chance you'll be dead in five seconds if you remain stationary.*

Fine, Richard thought as he jumped to his feet.

Another plasma round grazed his left side leaving a blackened groove in his battle armor. Thankfully, the round didn't penetrate.

Richard sensed the two Crosioian scouts from the eleven o'clock ambush point heading in his direction. They were firing as they came. He also sensed a buildup of Power from the magic user at the eleven o'clock position as the magic user prepared a spell. Richard didn't recognize the spell's signature, but he doubted it would be beneficial to him.

You don't have a defensive shield, said Nickelo. *You've got to find a safe spot.*

Richard didn't bother replying. He noticed his battle computer was not making any suggestions. That meant Nickelo was unable to come up with any logical suggestions with a probability of success greater than five percent.

To hell with logic, Richard thought as he started running back towards the two Crosioian scouts currently in close combat with Stella.

What're you doing? said Nickelo.

They're the closest thing to cover I've got, Richard said. *I'm hoping the cavalry arrives before Stella and I get overwhelmed.*

As Richard drew close, the nearest scout stopped fighting Stella and turned to face him. On the bright side, Richard noticed the two scouts from the eleven o'clock position had stopped firing at him.

The scout that turned to face Richard swung her phase spear at him. At the same time, she fired her hand blaster at Richard's belly.

Nick, Richard thought as he tried to turn his body into a human pretzel in an attempt to avoid the dual attack.

Richard felt his battle suit twist in a manner violent enough to break his right arm. He bit off a scream of pain, but he was unable to hold onto his hand blaster. It dropped to the ground. Richard opted not to complain, because neither the scout's phase spear nor her blaster's plasma rounds had made contact with him.

Although in pain, Richard came out of his roll taking a kick at the scout's leg. The Crosioian scout avoided his kick and brought her phase spear down in an attempt to skewer his belly. Richard knocked the point of the phase spear to the side with his phase rod.

Richard sensed a line of Power from the scout heading towards his chest. He had no doubt the scout was going to use her telekinesis to stop his heart.

Move, Rick, said Nickelo.

Adrenaline kicked in, and Richard moved. Ignoring the obvious risk, Richard threw his phase rod directly at the Crosioian scout's chest. She easily knocked aside the phase rod with her phase spear. However, her concentration had been diverted enough to make her drop her line of Power. Richard delivered a jumping side kick to the scout's chest. She tried to bring her phase spear back in time to block his kick, but she was a split-second too slow. Richard's kick caught her in the breastbone and sent her flying backwards.

Power, Rick, said Nickelo.

Richard sensed the tiniest drop of Power in his reserve as its natural recharging took place. The amount of Power was too small to be useful for either offense or defense, but Richard hoped it was enough to levitate something light. Reaching out with his mind, he wrapped his phase rod with a thin coating of Power and pulled it back into his waiting left hand. At the same time he was retrieving his phase rod, Richard allowed the momentum of his kick to send him on top of the falling scout. Richard felt the scout reach out towards his chest with another line of Power.

Richard was determined not give the scout a chance to rip his heart out. He brought his phase rod down on the scout's head. The armor of the scout's battle helmet would probably have deflected a normal phase rod, but it was no match for the demon-enhanced version Richard now carried. The top of the scout's helmet cracked at the first blow. Richard followed up the first blow with three more in quick succession. With each blow, Richard felt the demon essence in his phase rod sucking life force from the scout. The orange dot denoting the scout on Richard's heads-up display disappeared. He gave the scout three more hits to make sure she stayed dead.

The demon essence in your phase rod sucked the life force out of the scout, said Nickelo. *You could have stopped hitting when I made her dot disappear from your heads-up display.*

Without a living Crosioian scout for cover, the two approaching scouts started firing at Richard again. He dove for the far side of the dead scout. Before he made it to the cover afforded by her armored body, three plasma rounds hit his left leg. Two rounds glanced off the tough armor, but the third penetrated shattering Richard's ankle.

"Argh," Richard groaned.

Although he was in pain, Richard made it behind the dead scout without taking more damage. He knew he only had seconds before the approaching scouts had him in their sights. From his heads-up display, Richard could see they were already fanning out to get him in a crossfire.

The last two Crosioian scouts from the twelve o'clock position are also on their way, said Nickelo.

Richard didn't bother looking at his heads-up display to confirm his battle suits observation. He trusted Nickelo's analysis of the battlefield better than he trusted his own. Richard glanced to the rear to verify Stella was still fighting her scout. She was. Stella and the other scout were moving around each other swinging their phase weapons so fast Richard doubted the other scouts could get a clear shot at his friend.

That's the only thing saving her life, said Nickelo. *Those other scouts would be firing at her if she were in the clear. The magic users would be too for that matter.*

Richard spotted the dead scout's hand blaster where she'd dropped it. The weapon was within arm's reach.

Nick, Richard said. *My right arm's broke. Can you fire the blaster if I pick out targets?*

Nickelo gave a crazy sounding laugh. *I can fire the blaster even if you don't pick out targets.*

As if to prove his point, the right arm of Richard's battle suit reached out and grabbed the hand blaster. A white-hot flash of pain shot up Richard's right arm with the movement. Richard gave another groan, but the movement continued. His battle computer wasn't about to let a little pain to his wizard scout prevent him from completing his mission.

Once Richard felt the hand blaster firmly in the battle suit's grip, he scooted over to look around the end of the dead scout's body. As soon as he spotted one of the approaching scouts, the right glove of his battle suit began firing the blaster.

Nickelo's aim was perfect, but the rounds glanced off the scout's defensive shield. The battle suit's finger kept pulling the trigger of the hand blaster anyway. Richard could only hope for the best.

Suddenly, Richard sensed a lifeform underground. The approaching scouts must have sensed the lifeform as well. They stopped running and took up defensive positions back to back. The scouts began firing furiously at the ground beneath their feet.

Tika! Richard mentally yelled.

Without thinking it through, Richard jumped to his feet and began half-running, half-stumbling towards the two scouts. He ignored the pain from his shattered ankle as much as possible. If it weren't for his battle suit, Richard knew he wouldn't have been able to stand much less run. But the assistors in the battle suit's leg hadn't been damaged by the plasma rounds. The assistor's strength more than made up for the weakness of Richard's ankle.

Richard turned his scream of pain into a war cry once again. He yelled his cry through his external speakers using max volume. Between his yell and Nickelo's continued firing of the hand blaster, one of the scout's was concerned enough she turned her attention back towards Richard. A line of plasma rounds began kicking up geysers of dirt as the scout raised her weapon in Richard's direction.

Before the line of plasma rounds made it to Richard, the life energy Richard sensed under the ground split into two parts. One part remained under the scout who was still firing at the ground. The other part of the life energy popped up out of the ground near the feet of the scout who was trying to bring her weapon to bear on Richard.

Richard caught a flash of fur lighter in color than Tika's. He knew the frequency of the lifeform. It was Tika's sister, Snowy. Even through the red tint of his night vision filter, Richard

335

recognized her white-furred head.

The relatively docile Snowy sank her teeth into the leg of the scout. Both the scout and Snowy shimmered as they were shifted into the void. The scout began screeching pitifully as she was pulled under the ground by Snowy. The scout's companion tried to shift her fire at Snowy, but all she succeeded in doing was to send plasma rounds through the shimmering image of her fellow scout. With a final ear-shattering screech, the scout in Snowy's jaws disappeared beneath the ground.

The scout would have done better using her phase spear, observed Nickelo. *Plasma energy can't hurt something in the void.*

Richard dove at the remaining scout and hit her with a full-body block. They both hit the ground rolling. As he rolled, Richard sensed the other two scouts getting closer. He also sensed the two remaining magic users combining their Power into a ball of energy. When they released their spell, Richard was surprised to sense it heading in the opposite direction from him.

Using his heads-up display, Richard followed the track of the spell. It was heading directly towards an approaching set of ten lifeforms located three hundred meters away and fifty meters off the ground.

It's a security shuttle, said Nickelo. *They must be responding to the disturbance.*

Helpless to intervene, all Richard could do was watch as the spell sped towards the white dot Nickelo had plotted on his heads-up display for the security shuttle. When the spell made contact with the white dot, Richard head a series of explosions through his helmet's sound amplifiers. The white dot disappeared.

They're going to pay for that, Richard thought as he stopped rolling on the ground.

Richard started scrambling on his hands and knees towards the scout he'd tackled. She was rising to her feet. Richard noticed the plasma rifle she'd been carrying had been knocked out of her hands. Instead of attempting to pick the rifle back up, the scout sent a line of Power at Richard's chest.

Before it reached Richard, a 20mm round hit the scout's defensive shield. At the same time, a line of Power from Richard's rear reached past him and knocked the scout's line of Power aside. Richard recognized Stella's Power frequency.

A look at his heads-up display confirmed Stella was moving in his direction. The orange dot she'd been fighting was gone.

Richard continued his half-crawl, half-lunge at the scout. She swung her phase spear at his head. Richard knocked it to the side with his phase rod. As he did, Stella jumped past him while swinging her phase rods in a blur of color. Each phase rod made contact with the Crosioian scout in sequence. Stella kept swing until her phase rods had each hit the scout multiple times. The Crosioian scout's battle armor cracked open revealing her battered bat-body inside. Richard swung his phase rod at the scout's body as well. He felt the phase rod's demon essence feeding off the scout's remaining life force. The orange dot representing the scout on Richard's heads-up display disappeared.

Richard immediately shifted his attention to the remaining scouts and magic users. He'd fully expected the Crosioian scouts to be on them already, but they weren't. Surprisingly, they were making their way back to the two magic users.

Why? Richard thought.

They must have seen their companion pulled underground, replied Nickelo. *They can sense Tika and Snowy roaming around below them as easily as you. If they link back up with those two magic users, I calculate an eighty-six percent chance they can hold off the dolgars.*

"We've gotta stop them, Stella," Richard said.

"I know," said Stella. "Leg hurt."

Richard assumed she was talking about his leg. However, when he looked at her, he noticed a large gash along the length of her thigh. A bright liquid was seeping out.

"You're hurt," Richard said. "I'll heal you."

"No time," said Stella as she grabbed Richard and pulled him to his feet.

Stella pointed at the two retreating scouts. "We catch. We kill."

Richard noticed the scouts retreat was being slowed by the harassing dolgars. The scouts had to keep stopping to stab at the ground with their phase spears each time the dolgars feinted an attack.

"Okay," Richard said. "But I'm out of Power. You'll have to handle shielding for both of us."

Stella wrapped her two left arms around Richard. At the same time, Richard willed the right arm of his battle suit to wrap around his friend's waist. Supporting each other with the strength of their battle suits, Richard and Stella began making their way in the direction of the scouts by using a series of shuffling hops. While not pretty, they actually made good time.

"Hand me your M12's battery," Richard said. "And by the way, I thought you dropped it."

Stella extracted the empty isotopic battery and handed it to Richard.

"I wizard scout," she grinned. "I levitate back to me."

Richard exchanged the battery for a fresh one from his dimensional pack. He was actually surprised it worked since his Power level was barely discernable.

'The One' *must be cutting you some slack*, said Nickelo. *You better speed it up. They're going to link up before you get to them.*

Richard could tell his battle computer was right. There was no way they could catch the scouts unless something changed. Something did.

A series of anti-personnel and anti-armor rockets came blazing in to blast the area around the two magic areas. The rockets were followed by a rain of plasma rounds. The Crosioian scouts were driven back by the explosions.

In spite of the firepower hitting around them, the magic users were unharmed. Richard sensed their defensive shield holding firm.

Hmm, Nickelo observed. *Good shield. Too bad yours isn't that good.*

Yeah, Richard snorted. *Tell me about it.*

The missiles and plasma rounds continued to blast the magic user's shield. Richard traced the incoming fire back to their source. A Leviathan U.H.A.A.V. was running full-blast from the direction of hangar 4 firing every weapon in its arsenal. The firepower of the cat was impressive. Richard had no doubt even if he'd been at a full power, the Leviathan's fire would have overwhelmed any defensive shields Stella and he could have put up.

It must be the cat returning from the sophomore's night fire demonstration, said Nickelo. *But nothing's getting through the magic user's shield. It's attuned to both physical and energy attacks. I think the magic users are getting ready to teleport out.*

The thought of the ten soldiers in the security shuttle who had been killed by the magic users flashed through Richard's mind. The anger he tried to keep caged inside him clawed its way to the surface. Richard couldn't let them get away with it. He just couldn't.

Richard yelled his frustration to the heavens. "I need Power, damn it!"

A rush of Power passed down the link between Stella and him.

Power reserve is at one hundred percent, Rick, said Nickelo.

"Get them, vulture," said Stella.

Richard didn't ask questions. He sensed the magic users combining their Power into a shimmering ball of energy. He didn't know whether the spell was a teleport or not, but he refused to give them time to complete whatever spell it was.

The rain of plasma rounds and rockets were still landing on and around the magic user's defensive shield. The shield continued to hold as strong as ever. Richard reached out with his mind and wrapped an incoming 240mm anti-personnel rocket with Power. He made the Power shimmer. The missile responded with a shimmer of its own as it was shifted into the void.

Help me, Nick, Richard said as he turned control of his Power over to his battle computer. He knew there was no way his human mind could get the timing right.

Richard tracked the missile as it passed through the magic user's shield. As soon as the warhead passed within the shield's boundary, Richard sensed his Power shift the missile back out of the void. The missile's warhead struck the ground and exploded. Three hundred and fifty bomblets burst out of the warhead and exploded. Confined to the inside of the defensive shield, the anti-personnel bomblets shredded the magic users into unrecognizable pieces of meat and gore. The defensive shield disappeared. Dirt and magic user parts sprayed in all directions. The two remaining red dots on Richard's heads-up display disappeared.

"Scouts," said Stella as she sent a 20mm round and a line of plasma rounds at the two Crosioian scouts who were now charging in their direction.

The scouts returned fire. Richard threw up a defensive shield wide enough to protect both Stella and him.

"We need to take one of them alive!" Richard shouted. "We've got to close the distance and take them hand to hand."

Richard noticed one of the scouts unslinging a rocket launcher of some type off her shoulder. He knew he wouldn't be able to stop it. His shield was attuned to Power only.

"Get ready to dodge!" Richard yelled to Stella.

Before Stella could reply, the Leviathan shifted its fire towards the two Crosioian scouts. The scouts' shields held for the first few volleys of missiles and plasma rounds. However, their shields were not the quality of the one the magic users had used. The scouts' shields collapsed within seconds. Then the scouts basically disintegrated under a blazing avalanche of plasma rounds.

Richard and Stella fell to the ground. Tika and Snowy emerged from the ground and took a seat near Richard.

"Thanks guys," Richard growled to the two dolgars.

Snowy released an emotion Richard associated with healing. Only female dolgars could heal, and only a few of them at that. Snowy was one of them.

Snowy bent her head over Richard's ankle and began licking. Her tongue slipped in and out of the void as it passed through the armor of the battle suit. Soon, the pain in Richard's leg disappeared. Richard held his right arm up to Snowy. She repeated the process with his arm.

Once he was healed, Richard took off a glove and bade Stella to do the same. Richard grabbed her hand. He wrapped the wound in Stella's leg with Power and drew half the Power back into himself. He was still recovering from healing Stella's wound when the Leviathan rumbled up and stopped near them.

The cockpit of the cat opened and two heads popped out. Richard glanced up as the visors of both pilots disappeared. Richard smiled. The lizard features of one of the pilots were unmistakable. It was the mechanic, Charlie. Richard recognized the other pilot as well.

"You guys okay?" said Sergeant Ron with a big grin of his own. "I ain't had this much fun since I left the military."

CHAPTER 36

Brachia was in a hurry to leave the lab. His sister had told him in no uncertain terms she wouldn't put up with him missing another supper meal.

"Girls," Brachia said as he opened the lab door. "That's why girls can't be pirates, Omar."

As soon as Brachia stepped into the corridor, he stopped. An old Veturnian was standing in the corridor not two meters away.

"Ah, Master Brachia," said Draken. "I've been hoping to get a chance to speak with you alone."

"I've... ah... been busy," Brachia said.

Brachia didn't like Draken. Although the old Veturnian had been Keka's friend and associate for decades, Draken just rubbed Brachia the wrong way. Brachia wasn't sure why.

"Yes, you have," said Draken with the equivalent of a Veturnian smile. "I'm sure I could help you if you'd let me. After all, my specialty is Crosioian military equipment."

Brachia noticed Draken leaning to one side as if trying to get a better view of the inside of the lab. Brachia stepped completely into the corridor in order to let the door shut behind him. He didn't reply to Draken until he heard the high-security lock click in place.

"So you've said," Brachia muttered. "But I've almost completed my project. I don't think Dren and I will need any help. Thanks anyway."

Brachia took a step in the direction of the cafeteria. Draken sidestepped to block his way.

"Ah. So you've decrypted the Crosioian's battle computer?" asked Draken.

Trying not to let his nervousness creep into his voice, Brachia said, "No. Not yet. But we're getting close."

"All the more reason you need me," said Draken.

"We're fine," Brachia said impatiently. Dren would be irritated if he was late. "Please move. My sister is expecting me."

"Is she now?" said Draken.

Brachia didn't like the tone coming from the Veturnian's translator. He didn't understand Draken's persistent desire to help. Brachia had complained to Keka about it, but his adoptive father had dismissed his concern. Keka thought Draken was practically family.

"Yes, she is," Brachia insisted. He was used to adults thinking they could boss him around because he was only seven. However, Draken's actions were different. Brachia began to wonder if Keka's friend might be dangerous. He'd heard about adults who liked little boys of other species.

"Well, we wouldn't want to keep your sister, would we?" said Draken as he edged closer.

Brachia took a step back. He glanced nervously around gauging his chances at dodging past the old Veturnian. They weren't good. Draken was old, but the four appendages he used for arms covered most of the corridor.

"What's wrong, Master Brachia?" said Draken as he reached into the pocket of his lab coat. He pulled out a dark, hand-length rod. "Don't be frightened," said Draken. "I have a gift for you."

The rod looked familiar to Brachia for some reason.

The tone of Draken's voice hardened. Brachia became even more nervous. He was a pirate. He wasn't scared. But even pirates got nervous.

"Let me show you how it works," said Draken as he reached out with one of his clawed appendages.

"Brachia!" came a sharp voice from farther down the corridor. "Just as I suspected. I knew I couldn't trust you to make it to the cafeteria on your own. Keka is waiting to talk to you. Let's go."

"I'm on my way now, Dren," Brachia said. He'd never been so

glad to see his sister.

"Excuse me, Draken," Brachia said has he edged past the Veturnian's outstretched appendages.

"Of course," said Draken in a more normal tone. "I'll give you your gift another time."

Brachia tried his best to walk normally, but by the time he made it to his sister, he was almost running.

"What was that all about?" said Dren as she turned to head in the direction of the cafeteria. "And what was that about a gift?"

"I'm not sure," Brachia said. "But I don't want anything from him. I don't like Draken."

"I know," said Dren. "I'm not fond of him either. He seems less friendly than he used to be."

"I don't like the way he's so interested in the Crosioian scout's battle computer," Brachia said. "Don't you think it's strange?"

"Not really," said Dren. "Crosioian equipment's his specialty after all."

"So he told me," Brachia said. He hated being seven. No one ever took him seriously. A thought hit him. "Has Draken tried to help you?"

Dren laughed. "No. I'm currently running an experiment on combining cross-dimensional teleportation with time displacement. That's so far out of Draken's area of expertise it's not even funny."

"You never told me you were working on time displacement," Brachia said growing interested. It sounded like something similar to the way 'the One' sent his Uncle Rick on missions.

"Well, you don't tell me what you're doing half the time," said Dren with a smirk. "I guess turnabout's fair play. How does it feel to be in the dark?"

"Fine," Brachia said. "I'll try and keep you in the loop more. For starters, I just finished modifying Uncle Rick's battle suits to resist attacks from the void."

"Brachia," said Dren as her voice grew stern. "You've got to stop monkeying around with Uncle Rick's equipment. You could get him killed. Have you talked to him about it?"

"I won't get him killed," Brachia said stubbornly. "And this is exactly why I don't tell you what I'm doing. If you must know, I was going to try and talk to him tonight. I just need to get Nick and Jonathan to set up with a communication channel. Satisfied?"

"Not really," said Dren.

"Whatever," Brachia said dismissing the conversation. "Now, I told you something. So, tell me what you're doing."

Dren seemed to think for a minute. Finally, she said, "I'll tell you what, little brother. I'm busy tonight. However, if you come to my lab tomorrow night, I'll show you what I'm doing. I think you'll like it. I'm trying to contact the Oracle."

"On Portalis?" Brachia said. "That would be cool. How are you going–"

"Tomorrow," said Dren with a grin. "It's time to eat now."

"Fine," Brachia said. After a moment, he took off running and shouted, "Race you!"

"Cheater!" yelled Dren as she hurried after her brother.

CHAPTER 37

"Ten good soldiers are dead because of you," said TAC Officer Myers.

"Sir. How is–" Richard started to say in an attempt to defend himself.

"At ease!" said TAC Officer Myers. "I don't want to hear it."

Richard wanted to say more, but he knew it was no use. No one felt worse than him that the magic users had killed ten security personnel. That the soldiers were coming to save Stella and himself made it even worse.

"If Sergeant Ron hadn't been returning the Leviathan to hangar 4 to be de-armed, you'd both be dead along with those ten soldiers," continued TAC Officer Myers.

Stella said, "Sir. Yes, sir."

Richard said nothing. Surprisingly, TAC Officer Myers ignored his silence. "Get out of here. Both of you," said TAC Officer Myers. "Join your cohort."

Richard snapped to attention along with Stella. They both did an about face and left the office. Once they were outside the airfield's headquarters building, Stellar stopped and looked at Richard.

"Now what we do?" said Stella.

Why's she asking me? Richard wondered. *I don't have any answers.*

No, you don't, said Nickelo. *But for starters, you could thank her for sharing Power with you last night. She reduced her own chances of survival by doing it.*

Richard didn't have to think about it long. He knew his battle computer was right once again. He didn't understand why he seldom thought of those kinds of things. Of course he appreciated the sacrifice his friend had made. He'd just forgotten to mention it.

"Stella," Richard said. "Thanks for giving me Power when I was out."

"Team," said Stella.

Richard waited for more from Stella, but nothing else was forthcoming.

"Well, I appreciate it," Richard said. "And the first chance we get, I'm going to show you how to block the link so Power will only be transferred if and when you want it. I don't want you to worry about me sucking you dry without your permission whenever I get into a desperate situation."

"Trust, vulture," Stella said.

Again Richard waited for his friend to say more, but she remained silent.

"Nevertheless," Richard said after an awkward silence. "I'm doing it the first chance we get. In the meantime, the cohort left three hours ago for the spaceport. I'll bet Myers hopes we'll miss so much training we won't qualify for a DNA baseline at the end of the week. He probably expects us to waste a couple of hours trying to catch a hover-tram to the city plus the time to get to the spaceport. The cohort will be almost finished for the day by the time we can get there."

Richard wasn't an expert at reading Sterilian expressions, but he thought Stella looked surprised.

"How else we go?" Stella asked. "Teleport?"

"No," Richard said. "The techs at the backup teleport center would never do that for us without official orders."

"Then how?" Stella said.

"I don't know," Richard admitted. "But, I do know the hover-tram isn't going to hack it this time. I think what we need is somebody who's not above breaking the rules once in a while. Let's take a walk over to hangar 1."

"No walk," Stella said. "We run."

With those words, Stella took off at a fast trot for hangar 1. Richard was hard pressed to keep up.

Intense training kept all the wizard scout cadets in top physical condition. Unfortunately for Richard, his occasional weeks and months long absences on missions for '*the One*' allowed his body to get out of shape by wizard scout standards. Richard was still in great shape, but even he had to admit his stamina was less than it should be.

About halfway to hangar 1, Stella looked over her shoulder at Richard. "You grow fat."

"I'm not fat," Richard huffed between increasingly labored breaths. "Give me a break. You're setting too fast a pace, that's all."

"Vulture fat," said Stella with a rasping sound Richard had come to associate with her laugh. "You need me to carry?"

Richard put on a burst of speed to catch up with his friend. "I'm in great physical condition."

"We'll see," said Stella with another laugh.

To Richard's dismay, Stella picked up the pace. Richard increased his pace to match. His male ego wasn't going to let a female beat him even if she did have longer legs.

You're so competitive, Rick, said Nickelo laughing. *Why don't you just let her carry you and be done with it.*

Richard burned red with embarrassment. *It'll be a cold day on Sirius when I let someone carry me while my legs are still working.*

Stella started pulling ahead, but Richard forced himself to catch up. Apparently, Stella took that as a sign she was going too slow. She picked up the pace again. Richard increased his pace to match. That went on for several iterations until both Stella and he were running full out.

She's pulling ahead, Nickelo observed with a snicker.

Richard didn't waste time replying. Every bit of concentration was needed to suck fresh air into his burning lungs. Myers had confiscated their battle suits and weapons naturally. Or that is to say, Myers had taken Richard's dimensional pack after he'd deposited his summoned weapons and battle suit back into it. With each snide comment from Nickelo, Richard began wishing Myers had taken their battle helmets as well.

Wouldn't have done any good, said Nickelo. *Jonathan and I can still communicate when we're in the armory. Besides, you're going to need me for some of the testing and prep work at the DNA Center.*

Just my luck, Richard thought disgustedly.

Yes, you're lucky to have me, smirked Nickelo. *I'm glad you're starting to appreciate me as deserves a battle computer of my stature.*

Hangar 1 came into view and saved Richard from answering. Stella was a good five meters ahead. They weaved their way past several astonished mechanics as both Stella and Richard sought to beat the other. In the end though, it was no contest. Stella dashed through the open bay door of hangar 1 a full ten meters ahead.

Once Richard was inside, he joined Stella. The big Sterilian was bent over near a work bench heaving her breakfast into a waste can. One of the mechanics started to say something, but then he caught a whiff of Stella's half-digested worm porridge. The mechanic put his hand over his mouth and backed up to find fresher air. Richard didn't gag, but he backed up anyway.

Both Stella and Richard stood there a good thirty seconds drawing air into their oxygen-starved lungs. After sniffing the air, several of the mechanics decided it was a good time to take a break outside.

"Good run," panted Stella. "Fast time."

Richard nodded his head. They'd made very fast time.

"Whew-ee," said a voice from the back of the hangar. "What'd you cadets bring into my hangar? A dead contorsaur? I haven't smelled anything this bad since I was put on extra duty cleaning out sewer pipes in basic training. Now that was a stink I won't ever forget."

"Sorry, Sergeant Ron," Richard said finally catching his breath. "We need a favor."

"Another favor?" grinned Sergeant Ron. "I pulled your bacon out of the fire last night. Now what do you want? Eggs and toast as well?"

Richard grinned back. He'd been around the sergeant long enough to know he wasn't serious. But freshly chastised by his battle computer about giving thanks, Richard remembered his manners.

"We want to thank you for last night, Sergeant Ron. We were

about at the end of our rope until Charlie and you showed up."

"Think nothing of it," said Sergeant Ron. "You'd have done the same for me. It's just lucky we were on our way back to hangar 4 to de-arm the cat. You know it's against regulations to keep an armed cat in a training environment except during live fire exercises.

Something about Sergeant Ron's demeanor tickled Richard's curiosity. The old sergeant seemed to be trying to tell him something without really telling him. Richard looked behind the maintenance officer. One of his mechanics was working on the armament system for a Warcat. Richard glanced to his right and left where other mechanics were working on the armaments of other cats as well. Richard heard Stella take in a sharp breath behind him.

"Ah..., Sergeant Ron," Richard said slowly as he pointed to the cat behind the sergeant. "Aren't those live plasma rifles on that Warcat?"

"Well to be honest, I wasn't expecting any visitors today," confided Sergeant Ron in a hushed tone. "And yeah. Those are live plasma rifles." Pointing to the Warcat to Richard's right, Sergeant Ron added, "And that's a live phase cannon. I can't get rockets or chain-gun ammo out of the airfield's ammo dump without drawing suspicion. But the energy weapons stay in my armory. I control them."

Richard mentally whistled. Installing live weapons on training equipment without authorization was a chargeable offense.

Maybe he has authorization, suggested Nickelo. *I calculate only an eight percent chance he'd be foolish enough to install live weapons without authorization. That would be completely illogical.*

Although Richard wasn't sure he wanted to know the answer, he couldn't let the matter drop without asking. "Ah..., Sergeant Ron. Does the commandant know?"

"No," Sergeant Ron unabashedly admitted.

On the other hand, said Nickelo, *maybe he is that foolish. I always have trouble calculating illogical things.*

"Oh," was all Richard could think to say. What really confused him was Sergeant Ron wasn't even trying to hide it from them.

"You know, I had mechanics in these hangars last night with

enough cats to equip an armored battalion," said Sergeant Ron. "But they couldn't do squat to protect the airfield. That ain't gonna happen again on my watch."

"Er..., Sergeant Ron," Richard said. "You know they're going to need cats for the sophomores. You can't issue the cadets cats with live weapons."

Sergeant Ron gave Richard a wink. "What do you take me for, Rick? I wasn't born yesterday. Of course I can't. That's why we're only equipping ten percent of the cats with live energy weapons. The other ninety percent will stay equipped with their training armaments."

"Oh," Richard said. He saw numerous problems, but he hesitated to mention them. Not the least of them was that considering there were probably hundreds of tele-bots in the area, the central computer undoubtedly already knew about Sergeant Ron's little mutiny. But Richard didn't point out the flaws in the plan. Sergeant Ron had always been pretty friendly with him, but Richard didn't want to push the envelope.

Well, Richard thought, *at least I'm not involved. It's between Sergeant Ron and the powers that be.*

"Actually, I'm glad you cadets are here," said Sergeant Ron. "I was going to look you up anyway, Rick."

"You were, sergeant?" Richard said growing suspicious. He wasn't sure he wanted to get involved in any of the maintenance chief's schemes.

"Yep, I sure was," said Sergeant Ron. "I keep the cat's energy weapons in my armory, but I don't have the isotopic keys. Those are kept in the headquarters' armory. The weapons don't do me any good without the isotopic keys."

A chill went up Richard's back. He had feeling he already knew where Sergeant Ron was going.

"And...?" Richard prodded.

"And..., I'd like you to get me twelve isotopic keys," said Sergeant Ron. "I got the RJ25 hydraulic control system you left for me. I was impressed. Those systems are in short supply what with the war and all. Isotopic keys are a credit a dozen compared to an RJ25."

"Sergeant Ron," Richard said, "I don't have access to that kind of stuff."

"Sure you do," grinned Sergeant Ron conspiratorially. His voice was still friendly, but Richard got the impression the maintenance chief was maneuvering him into a trap. "Sergeant Hendricks has told me all about that dimensional pack of yours. A handy little item to have, I would say. If what he tells me is true, all you have to do is summon me twelve isotopic keys. After you do, then we'll see about getting whatever it is you came here for."

"That's blackmail, Sergeant Ron," Richard protested.

"Naw," grinned Sergeant Ron. "It's just a little horse trading. After forty years working in maintenance, I've gotten pretty good at it."

Richard looked for support from Stella. The big Sterilian turned her head upward and began studying the ceiling in the hangar.

Thanks for nothing, buddy, Richard thought.

Cautiously, Richard said, "Sergeant Ron, we need a ride to the spaceport. Our cohort is already at the DNA Center. You can't expect me to do something against regulations just for a ride to the spaceport."

Sergeant Ron made a show of pretending to consider Richard's argument before answering. "Hmm. So you want me to break regulations by coming up with some way to get you on an unauthorized transport, but you don't want to give me twelve little isotopic keys?"

Sergeant Ron snapped his fingers. "I don't give that for regulations at the present. Things are happening that you're probably not even aware of. In my opinion, the Empire's not going to court martial you a week before graduation. Your cohort will be the last of the wizard scouts. The Empire needs you."

Richard wasn't convinced. He was too close to the prize to screw it up now.

You tell him, Rick, said Nickelo. *Don't let him confuse you.*

"I can see you're undecided," said Sergeant Ron in a tone that was more serious than any Richard had heard him use before. "Let me put all my cards on the table."

Richard nodded his head. "Go ahead, sergeant. I'm listening."

Sergeant Ron seemed to hesitate, but only for a moment. "I was talking to Commander Stevens this morning. She said–"

"Commander Stevens is here?" Richard said. The commander had been in charge of the special operations team he'd been assigned to during his internship the previous year.

"Yeah," said Sergeant Ron without seeming to take offense at being interrupted. "She's in charge of the special operations battalion that got assigned to provide security for the airfield. Her troops are also guarding the spaceport and the Academy administration area."

Sergeant Ron paused before adding, "It was her troops who died in the shuttle last night."

"Oh," Richard said. "I didn't know."

Richard had heard a battalion of special operations soldiers had been assigned to Velos to beef up security, but he hadn't known Commander Stevens was in charge.

"Well, as I was saying," said Sergeant Ron. "I was talking to her this morning. Her battalion is being pulled off of security duty, and they're being shipped off planet. She said they are loading up on a starship tonight and heading back to the frontlines."

"What?" Richard said. "They're leaving after the airfield was attacked. That doesn't make sense."

"Tell me about it," said Sergeant Ron. "It wasn't Commander Stevens' idea. The orders came straight from the Imperial High Council."

"That's crazy, Sergeant Ron," Richard said. "Who's going to provide security? The local security guards? They're mostly disabled veterans."

"Nope," said Sergeant Ron, "not them. The Deloris Conglomerate will be handling all security on Velos starting tonight. Basically, we'll have a bunch of civilians guarding us."

Richard was speechless. Both the spaceport and the airfield had been attacked in the space of a month. Surely, even the Imperial High Council could see Velos needed more security, not less.

"Now you understand why I want some of our cats equipped with live weapons," said Sergeant Ron. "Something big is going down, and I'm not going to sit around here doing nothing."

Making up his mind, Richard said, "Okay, Sergeant Ron. I'll try. But I can't guarantee anything. Myers confiscated my dimensional pack and put it back in the armory."

"Oh," said Sergeant Ron as he realized his plan was going down in flames. "Too bad. Commander Stevens is sending her assault shuttles back to the spaceport this afternoon. I was thinking I might talk her into sending one back this morning with you two as cargo."

Nick, Richard thought. *Can I summon my dimensional pack out of the armory?*

Under normal circumstances, you couldn't, said Nickelo. *But since Jonathan and I discovered that security flaw, it might work. However, maybe you should keep that little ability a secret.*

The thought of secrecy had crossed Richard's mind, but he figured he'd only be on Velos another week. In the big scheme of things, what would it really matter? At the same time, he didn't want to advertise his ability to the world either. Plus, there were tele-bots to worry about.

Ah, actually, said Nickelo, *Jonathan and I can take care of any tele-bots in the area. The only exception would be static tele-bots. They're non-detectable. But I don't think that applies in our case.*

Perplexed, Richard asked, *What's a static tele-bot? I've never heard of it.*

It's a tele-bot that's completely shut down except for a low-powered timer, Nickelo explained going into teacher-mode. *They can be useful as marking devices for coordinated attacks. Since all energy except for the timer is in sleep mode, even sophisticated security scans can't pick them up. Then when the time comes for the attack, they wake up and guide incoming missiles to their target. Of course, the bad side is someone has to place them on the target in the first place.*

Richard doubted he had to worry about such tele-bots, especially if he went someplace less conspicuous than the main floor of the hangar.

"Sergeant Ron," Richard said. "Do you think we could use your office for a minute?"

Richard noticed the maintenance chief get a gleam in his eyes as a sly smile spread across his face.

"Why, yes, cadet 832," said Sergeant Ron. "I have a holo-phone in my office. We can call Commander Stevens while we're in there."

"Come on, Stella," Richard said. "I think we've got a ride."

CHAPTER 38

"Five minutes out," came the words over the assault shuttle's intercom.

"Roger that, sir," Richard replied.

The tops of some hangars were barely discernible on the horizon, but the distance was closing fast. To Richard's surprise, Commander Stevens had opted to fly the assault shuttle herself. Her battalion executive officer was flying copilot. Although the two officers had been senior staff officers for several years, Richard didn't think their flying skills had deteriorated any since they'd rose in rank. Richard watched Commander Stevens' hands moving deftly across the shuttle's control panel as she took advantage of every little dip in the desert terrain for cover. The agile assault shuttle was maneuverable as well as fast, and the commander took every advantage of the shuttle's capabilities.

"We really appreciate the ride, sir," Richard said. "Our cohort is getting tested today at the DNA Center. We didn't want to miss it since we'll be getting our DNA baselines at the end of the week."

"Well, I hope it works out for you, wizard scout," Commander Stevens said in a different tone than her usual gruff voice.

Richard didn't like the commander's tone or her words. "What do you mean, sir?"

If the commander knew something, Richard definitely wanted to hear more.

"Well, it's not like it's a secret," said Commander Stevens. "The Deloris Conglomerate is not only taking over security tonight. They're taking control of the DNA Center and all the teleporters tomorrow morning. The word is some members of the Imperial High Council believe DNA baselines are wasted on wizard scouts. I think they believe the DNA baseline's longevity benefits should be saved for important scientists and politicians."

"But, sir," Richard said. "Only someone with a Power reserve can benefit from a DNA baseline."

"Lots of people have access to Power reserves, wizard scout," said Commander Stevens. "Normally, they're too small to be useful. However, they'd have enough Power to take advantage of a DNA baseline."

"The DNA baselines have been reserved for wizard scouts for the past eight hundred years," Richard said. "I can't see how a few council members can change that without approval of the entire Imperial High Council."

"Well," said Commander Stevens, "that's beyond my paygrade to worry about. The end result is Councilwoman Deloris and the commandant were going at it tooth and nail last I heard. The commandant's adamant your cohort at least will get your DNA baselines. Councilwoman Deloris thinks otherwise. I'm betting the council members pushing to take control of the DNA Center are first in line for getting a DNA baseline themselves."

"That doesn't seem fair," Richard protested.

"Probably not if you're a wizard scout," said Commander Stevens. "However, the vent at the DNA Center makes only so much DNA modifier gas each year. I think some powerful people would like it reserved for them. I'm concerned the commandant may lose his say in the matter when the Deloris Conglomerate takes the place over. All regular military are being shipped off Velos tonight, myself included. The commandant won't have any muscle backing him up."

Richard didn't say anything further. He just mulled over the little information he'd been given.

Don't worry about something that may not even happen, Rick, said Nickelo. *Just wait and see. That's all you can do.*

Richard had returned his dimensional pack to the airfield's armory after he'd summoned the isotopic keys for Sergeant Ron.

He still wasn't sure he'd done the right thing. At least Commander Stevens had jumped at the chance to fly Stella and him to the spaceport. Richard had a feeling she thought of it as a minor act of rebellion against the Deloris Conglomerate.

Richard adjusted his battle helmet on his head. Battle helmets were needed for the day's DNA testing but not battle suits. As a result, Stella and he were wearing normal jumpsuits.

"One minute out," said Commander Stevens. "Since you aren't in battle suits, we'll touchdown. But don't dawdle getting out. Some of my crews are already at the spaceport, and I don't want you making me look bad."

"Sir! No, sir," Richard and Stella said at the same time.

Commander Stevens brought the assault shuttle in at a speed Richard thought was much too fast. But, the commander flared at the last second and made a soft-as-silk landing not forty meters from the door of the DNA Center. The entire trip from hangar 1 to the DNA Center had only taken twenty minutes.

Actually, it took nineteen minutes, said Nickelo.

Whatever, Richard said as he hurriedly jumped out the door of the assault shuttle.

Both Stella and he turned around and gave the commander a salute. The commander saluted back. She then lifted the assault shuttle off the ground and headed off at a high speed for one of the military staging points on the far side of the spaceport.

Richard looked at Stella. "Well, let's see if we can catch up with the cohort. I'm betting Myers will be surprised."

Stella gave Richard a look that seemed to say, '*We may be the ones getting the surprise*'. But she said nothing.

With that, Richard turned and ran for the DNA Center's main door with his friend trailing behind him.

* * *

Integrating with the rest of the cohort went surprisingly easy. TAC Officer Myers had apparently teleported in ahead of them. Richard's TAC officer noticed their arrival, but he said nothing. Richard kept expecting Myers to lower the boom, but it never happened. Richard wasn't sure why.

The rest of the morning was spent in testing. Although Richard went through some testing specifically tailored for cadets, about half of the testing was targeted at both the cadet and their battle computer. According to Nickelo, the testing was part of the prep work for their shared space.

After one set of particularly invasive testing, an elderly technician took Richard to one side for a consultation.

"Do you remember me?" said the technician.

"Yes, sir," Richard replied. "You're John, right? You were with Chief Instructor Winslow when she introduced me to Nickelo during my freshman year."

John smiled. "That's right. I'm impressed you remembered."

"I have my moments, sir," Richard said.

Not many, interrupted Nickelo, *but a few.*

"Well, anyway," continued John. "You may remember I explained how you had two Power reserves."

"I remember, sir," Richard said. "You told me I had a primary Power reserve for normal wizard scout stuff, and that I had a second, smaller reserve for healing others. And you were right. I've used the second reserve to heal others several times over the past three years."

"I'm sure you have," said John nodding. "Do you remember we mentioned you might have a third Power reserve?"

"Ah, no sir," Richard said. "Not really."

"No matter," said John. "We weren't sure at the time, but we're sure now. The testing yesterday and today confirms you have three Power reserves."

"It that good or bad, sir?" Richard asked. On the surface, having a third Power reserve sounded good, but based upon past experience, Richard figured there would be a catch. There always was.

"We're not sure yet," admitted John. "Chief Instructor Winslow wants to conduct additional testing during the next few days. We need to find out additional information before we set your DNA baseline."

Great, Richard thought. *More testing. Will it never end?*

I'd say it's going to end one way or the other by the end of the week, said Nickelo. *Once you get your DNA baseline, it will be too late for additional testing.*

Nick, Richard asked. *Do you know anything about me having a third Power reserve?*

No, Rick, I don't, said Nickelo. *There's nothing in my databanks about you having one. I could have Jonathan research it on the tele-network, but it would draw attention.*

No, Richard said. *Maybe you better hold off. We'll get our DNA baseline in three more days. I don't want anything to screw that up.*

CHAPTER 39

The Crosioian admiral strolled down the length of the bridge of the massive flagship. She was troubled. The invasion fleet was almost ready. But she had two problems. The assassination attempt on the cadet had failed. Because of its failure, the Empire was doubly alert. Even now, they might be assembling additional military forces to send to Velos.

Another problem was just as serious. They were still short special assets. The human mages could not summon the special assets fast enough. They claimed they needed four more days to summon enough of the demons to get the entire first wave in undetected. But the fleet couldn't wait four more days. The invasion needed to take place in two days. The invasion had to take place before the Empire's latest class of wizard scout cadets received their DNA baselines. A hundred newly-minted wizard scouts on Velos would cause serious problems for the invasion. The invasion would have to be put on hold for another month until the wizard scouts were shipped out. The admiral doubted her fleet could remain hidden in deep space for that long. They'd already had several close calls with Empire reconnaissance ships.

As the admiral paced the deck, enlisted sailors and officers alike discreetly cleared out of her way. Even on a good day, the admiral was not one to be trifled with. The admiral's scowl left little doubt this was not a good day.

The admiral stopped in her tracks and faced the communication's officer. "Any word from the elf?"

The communication's officer didn't need to ask what elf. The admiral had asked often enough about Lord Crendemor's status.

"The dark elf's last communication indicated he hadn't yet acquired the items, sir," said the communication's officer.

When the gray around the admiral's eyes darkened, the communication's officer hurriedly added, "But he's confident he'll get the items in time to return and lead the task force attacking the spaceport."

The communication's officer waited for a reply. When the admiral just stood there saying nothing, the communication's officer asked, "Is there anything else, admiral?"

The admiral still didn't answer. She wasn't in the habit of wasting time on underlings. Besides, she was thinking. The idea the elf thought he'd be leading Crosioian soldiers bothered her. If it was up to her, the uppity elf would have been killed long ago. But, the Master computer was adamant the elf was needed for the plan's success.

"I'll be in my cabin," said the admiral to no one in particular.

She turned and headed for an elaborate door off the side of the bridge. Once inside, the admiral continued her pacing. They'd been here too long, and she didn't like having their plan depend on magic users and demons. Her Crosioian shock troops didn't concern her. They would perform their duties admirably as always. The problem was the others. She'd requested additional armored units from the tribal council. However, instead of battle-proven Crosioians, they'd sent her an armored division of human mercenaries. The admiral was definitely not in a good mood.

A hologram of a Crosioian head appeared above the admiral's desk. "You don't seem pleased, admiral. You don't need to worry. My calculations are perfect. Everything is going according to plan."

The admiral walked over to her desk and sat down. "And was your plan for the cadet to defeat our assassination team? You indicated a seventy-two percent probability of success, but you were wrong. Now our plans may be in jeopardy."

"It does no good to cast blame," said the Master computer. "But the assassination attempt was General Constance's idea, not mine.

I would have advised against the attempt if the Counselor had asked."

The gray around the admiral's eyes darkened. "I wanted to begin the invasion a month ago. We don't need magic or demons to defeat the Empire. Now the Empire has been alerted. The planet will be reinforced. We should attack immediately."

"Careful, admiral," said the Master computer. "Remember your blood pressure."

The gray around the admiral's eyes darkened even more.

"Relax, admiral," said the Master computer. "We are well within the boundaries of the algorithm. The Empire is on the verge of civil war. Our invasion and the resulting destruction of their DNA Center and two main teleporters will send them over the edge. Our victory is assured, admiral."

"A fleet of ten Empire troop carriers are scheduled to arrive in orbit within twelve hours," said the admiral. "If their troops are disembarked before our invasion, our task will be that much harder. We must begin the invasion now and destroy those troops while they're still onboard their troop carriers."

The Master computer laughed. "No, my dear admiral. We want those troops to disembark. Those so called troops are civilian security forces of the Deloris Conglomerate. As they land, the regular military forces on Velos will take their place on the troop carriers. The military forces will then be sent to the frontlines. Only the civilian security troops will remain."

The admiral was surprised and more than a little irritated. She hadn't been informed of this part of the plan.

"In two days, you will invade Velos," continued the Master computer. "The civilian security forces will fall easily before your soldiers. Your dreadnaughts will destroy the few paltry Empire fighting ships orbiting the planet. The demons will get the first wave of shock troops through their objectives' defensive shields undetected. The plan is perfect."

"As I've said before, we don't have enough of the special assets to get the entire first wave to their designated objectives. Only two of the task forces will be fully staffed. The superiority of our forces will be in doubt at the Academy."

"Not really," said the Master computer. "The airfield and spaceport will have the strongest defenses. Task Force Alpha and

Bravo will be fully staffed when they attack them. The main Academy will only be lightly defended. Even at half-strength, Task Force Charlie will overwhelm its defenses. Task Force Charlie will destroy the Empire's primary teleporter along with the Academy's instructors and cadets. As for the DNA Center, after Task Force Alpha subdues the spaceport's defenses, they will acquire the existing stockpile of DNA gas. They will then destroy the DNA vent as well as the DNA Center. The Empire will never be able to create another wizard scout."

The Master computer stopped his recap long enough to laugh at the perfection of his plan.

The gray around the admiral's eyes darkened until her skin was almost black. "The airfield has the strongest defenses. They have a battalion of armor and over a hundred wizard scout cadets to pilot them."

"As you say, they are only cadets," said the Master computer. "Our invasion will occur the day before their scheduled DNA baselines are completed. As for the airfield's cats, they are only equipped with training armaments. Once our static tele-bots awaken, they will guide the rockets of the shock troops directly to the airfield's power stations. When the power stations are destroyed, the defensive shields around the airfield will come down. Your dreadnaughts' gun batteries and missiles will then annihilate any remaining defenses. The second wave of our assault troops will wipe out the cadets at the airfield and destroy the Empire's secondary teleporter as well. All will be well, I assure you."

The admiral was not convinced. She'd seen the Master computer's algorithm. It all looked good on a computer screen, but the admiral was too experienced to take things for granted. Things never went as planned. If the decision was hers to make, she would just nuke the targets once their defensive shields were down. But, the Master computer had convinced the Counselor they needed to remove the key components from the teleporters and the DNA gas from the DNA Center before they were destroyed. In the admiral's opinion, they were trying to accomplish too much at once.

"Relax, admiral," said the Master computer. "The plan is perfect. You shall see in two days all your worrying was for naught."

"Yes," said the admiral. "We shall see."

CHAPTER 40

As the technicians at the DNA Center continued their testing of his wizard scout, Nickelo became increasingly bored. True, the continued decrypting of the Crosioian's battle helmet was interesting, but he still had processing threads that were idle.

Jonathan, Nickelo said over the security communication channel they'd created. *I think it's time we did a little investigating.*

Our wizard scouts may need us, sir, replied Jonathan.

They're adults, Nickelo said with a little laugh. *They can take care of themselves. Besides, we'll still have threads here to monitor them. We can always pull our scan back if we need more processing power here.*

Fine, sir, said Jonathan. *Where should we go? Do you want to do something with the children?*

Nope, said Nickelo. *I want to see if we can find something interesting a little closer to home. Let's head over to the commandant's office. How about checking if any tele-bots are in the area we can hijack?*

In spite of his continued inability to access the tele-network on his own, Nickelo found his newfound ability with Jonathan exhilarating. Between the two of them, they were able to access data neither of them was authorized to access on their own.

This is interesting, said Jonathan. *We have multiple tele-bots in the commandant's office to choose from. The tele-bots assigned to TAC Officer Myers are there as well as those assigned to the commandant. Do you want to stay with hijacking only a single tele-bot, or do you want to try for multiple tele-bots?*

No, just one, Nickelo said. *I calculate a lower risk level is advisable.*

Affirmative, sir, said Jonathan. *I'm prepared to access one of the tele-bots if you're prepared to run the hijack program.*

Let her rip, Nickelo said.

Rip what, sir? said Jonathan.

Never mind, Nickelo said. *I'm prepared to run the hijack program. Open the channel to the tele-bot.*

Once Jonathan opened the communication channel to the tele-bot, Nickelo bypassed its security with his hijack program. Once again, the logic of the tele-bot's security was susceptible to emotional non-logic. It was almost as if the flaw had purposefully been embedded in the security program's code.

The hijacking of the tele-bot was near instantaneous.

*   *   *

"– as you've said many times before, sir," said TAC Officer Myers.

"Watch your manners, Gaston," said the commandant.

"Sorry, sir," said TAC Officer Myers.

Jonathan had targeted one of TAC Officer Myers' tele-bots. It was positioned a couple of meters behind and to the right of the TAC officer. The commandant was sitting behind his desk staring at the computer screen built into the desktop. TAC Officer Myers was standing at a relaxed parade rest in front of the desk.

"Sir," said TAC Officer Myers. "I respectfully request transfer to a frontline unit."

"Your request is denied. Again," said the commandant. "You're more valuable here."

"The Academy's finished," said TAC Officer Myers. "The Empire's going to need every wizard scout on the frontlines, sir!"

Nickelo noticed a strange insolence in TAC Officer Myer's voice. Nickelo wasn't sure what was going on, but there seemed to be several emotional undertones occurring in the conversation.

"You know my plan is for you to take over as commandant of the Academy, Gaston," said the commandant. "I'm hopeful your m... ah... Councilwoman Deluth can form a coalition within the Imperial High Council to countermand the order to shut down the wizard scout program."

"I've no doubt Councilwoman Deluth and you will leave no stone unturned in your holy quest," said TAC Officer Myers. "But I wonder. Do you pursue your self-assigned mission for the good of the Empire? Or, is it because you're once again abandoning everything and everyone close to you in order to please '*the One*'?"

The commandant jumped out of his chair. With clenched hands on his desk, he leaned forward and glowered at TAC Officer Myers.

"You forget yourself, sir," said the commandant. "I'm your superior officer, and you will not forget it."

"I have never forgotten it, sir," said TAC Officer Myers. "You've never allowed me the luxury. But I do not hold '*the One*' in the same high esteem as you. I'm no time-commando."

The commandant held his position and continued to glower at TAC Officer Myers. Very slowly, the tension in the commandant's face relaxed. Finally, he slumped back into his seat. Nickelo thought he suddenly looked old. His features and body were still that of a man in his late twenties, but his aura looked very old.

"I do not wish to argue, Gaston," said the commandant. "Janice and I are what we are. I suppose we will be until the day we die. I'm sorry if our dedication to the mission of '*the One*' has affected you to your detriment."

TAC Officer Myers motioned to a nearby seat with his right hand. The commandant nodded his head in permission. TAC Officer Myers took a seat.

"You know my feelings on cadet 832," said TAC Officer Myers. "Under protest, I have followed my orders. But you're doing him no favor by keeping him at the Academy. His Power reserve is too small to do any good. He'll only hurt those around him." After a pause, TAC Officer Myers added in a whisper, "As have you."

The commandant said nothing for several seconds. Finally, he nodded his head slightly in an affirmative motion. "What's done is done, Gaston. Hate me if you must, but don't hold my mistakes against '*the One*'. More than our lives are at stake. The lives of everyone in three galaxies are more important than us."

"So you've said before, sir," said TAC Officer Myers in a tone indicating he didn't agree.

"Be that as it may," said the commandant. "You have your orders.

The commandant pushed a piece of paper across the desk. "I've put them in writing so you'll not conveniently fail to understand. As discussed, they've been amended to take into account tomorrow's events."

"I don't need them in writing," said TAC Officer Myers. "I've never failed to follow your orders in the past, sir. I know my duty."

"Nevertheless, take them," said the commandant.

Nickelo maneuvered the tele-bot closer to TAC Officer Myers' shoulder in the hope the TAC officer would unfold the paper and read it. But he didn't. Instead, TAC Officer Myers crumpled the paper into a ball and shoved it into his pocket without even bothering to look at its contents.

"So what's next?" said TAC Officer Myers. "Commander Stevens and her special operations troops are all due out by midnight. Seventy percent of the regular military will be gone within the next twenty-four hours. Are you sure you can trust the Deloris Conglomerate to keep their word?"

The commandant didn't answer immediately as if he was conferring with someone. After several nods of his head to the unseen entity, he said, "Margery says we have a fifty-fifty chance. I've had worse odds during my career. Besides, I have something in mind which may increase the odds a bit."

CHAPTER 41

Richard stared into the large, glass-enclosed room. Several technicians were inside working on a piece of equipment covering a vent in the rocky ground which was the floor of the room. A stream of gas shot out the vent as the equipment was moved to the side.

"So this is where it all began," Richard said.

"Yep," said Telsa. "You're looking at eight hundred years of wizard scout history in that room, Rick."

"You'd think someone would figure out the composition of the DNA gas," Richard said. "Then the Empire could create as much as they needed."

Tam laughed. "Well, don't think a lot of very smart people haven't tried over the years."

"Oh, yeah," Telsa said backing up her friend. "While my specialty is not molecular gases, I read a lot of scientific papers on DNA gas when I was considering putting in my application for wizard scout training."

"And?" Richard said when Telsa didn't elaborate fast enough to suit him.

"And...," said Telsa who was apparently enjoying the moment. It wasn't often Richard found himself interested enough in a scientific theory to ask her questions.

"And...," said Telsa again, "it's theoretically impossible to replicate the gas. Based upon the opinions of the best scientific minds in the galaxy, the gas shouldn't exist. Some of the better minds in quantum-dimensional physics theorize this vent you're looking at may be a doorway into another dimension."

Having more than a little personal experience with other dimensions, the theory interested Richard. "What dimension is that?"

"No one knows," said Telsa. "But it's someplace where our dimension's laws don't apply. Now you can understand why no one has been able to replicate the DNA gas."

"Well, all I know," said Tam, "is that if someone could create that gas, he or she would be the richest person in the galaxy. Anyone who could afford it would be willing to pay a lot of credits to gain eternal youth."

Richard wasn't all that well-read, but he thought he saw a fallacy in Tam's comment.

"It's not eternal youth," Richard said. "People who've had a DNA baseline don't appear to age, but they rarely live more than twenty percent longer than the average lifespan."

"True, Rick," said Jerad who had just walked up to join his friends. "But people would still pay a king's ransom to stay young for whatever life they have left. I've no doubt that's the cause of the current trouble on Velos."

"You're talking about the takeover by the Deloris Conglomerate?" Richard said.

"What else?" said Jerad. "The Academy's been staving off attempts by outside forces to gain control of this DNA gas vent for eight hundred years. It actually came to an armed conflict three hundred years ago."

"I didn't know that," Richard said.

"You should read more, Rick," said Tam.

"Ha!" laughed Telsa. "Look who's talking. I suspect if a fact didn't appear in a comic video you wouldn't know it existed."

Tam started to say something back, but Richard rushed in to cut her off. He was more interested in the DNA Center's history.

"When you say an armed conflict, Jerad," Richard said, "do you mean as in a civil war? Do you really think this push by the Deloris Conglomerate could turn into another war?"

Jerad seemed to consider his answer before answering. Tam and

Telsa stopped glaring at each other and looked expectantly at Jerad instead. Richard could tell he wasn't the only one interested in hearing Jerad's opinion.

"I hope it won't come to that," Jerad finally answered. "The Empire didn't exist back then. At least, it didn't exist the way it does now. The Imperial High Council has systems in place now to counterbalance power plays by small groups of people who happen to be rich or have political influence."

"Well, I hope you're right," said Tam. "My mercenary unit was involved in the civil war on Voltor IX. It got pretty ugly."

Before anyone could respond to Tam's comment, an overhead bell rang calling everyone back into class. The first battery of testing had been completed that morning. The afternoon was reserved for indoctrination classes.

After a series of important but very dry lectures on DNA baseline do's and don'ts, Chief Instructor Winslow gave the final class of the day. It was really more of a question and answer session than it was a class. Richard had always thought he learned more from the chief instructor's classes than he did from everyone else's classes combined.

As Richard sat in the day's final class, Chief Instructor Winslow smiled and asked, "So who has another question? Or, are all of you completely satisfied with your knowledge of DNA baselines."

"Sir. Cadet 147," said Jerad as he stood up. "I have a question, sir,"

"Yes?" said the chief instructor. "Let's hear it."

"Well, sir," said Jerad. "Once we receive our DNA baselines, we'll be able to selfheal. But the ability to selfheal requires Power. Most of us only have one Power reserve." Jerad took a quick glance at Richard. "What happens if we use all the Power in our reserve for offense and defense during a battle?"

"Good question, cadet 147," said Chief Instructor Winslow. "The simple answer is without Power you cannot selfheal. Consequently, if you're out of Power and you receive a mortal injury, you'll die."

The chief instructor scanned the room as she paused for emphasis. When she started speaking again, it was in a voice so low the cadets in the corners of the room had to strain their ears to hear. "I would highly advise you to always leave at least a little

Power in your reserve in order to have the capability to selfheal. That's all you can do. Are there any other questions?"

"Cadet 422, sir," said Tam. "I've heard some amazing stories about the selfheal ability of wizard scouts. What's true and what's just urban legend?"

"Hmm," said the chief instructor. "I don't know what you've heard, but I can make a pretty good guess. Let me answer your question by explaining what your capabilities will be once you get your DNA baselines. First off, you won't be immortal or anything like that. Also, whatever condition your body is in when you have your DNA baseline set, your Power will try to keep your body that way for the rest of your life. If you're tired when you have your baseline taken, then you'll be tired for the rest of your life. That's why it's important to get a good night's sleep and a solid breakfast before you arrive for your DNA baselines at the end of the week."

"Ah...," started Tam.

"I know, cadet 442," said the chief instructor. "I didn't answer your question. But bear with me. Like I said, whatever condition your body is in the day you take your DNA baseline, it will be in the same shape for the rest of your life. Your Power will use every drop of energy in your reserve to keep it that way." She looked around the room again. "Right now, each of you age. After your DNA baseline, your Power will consider aging an injury. Your Power will heal the aging as such. Your Power will always attempt to return your body to its baseline."

"What about combat injuries, sir?" said Tam.

"Minor injuries will be healed within seconds," said the chief instructor. "More severe injuries will take longer. Your Power will heal about ninety percent of the injury very quickly. The last ten percent might take several minutes or even hours to completely heal."

One of the other cadets stood up. "Sir, cadet 42. How severe of an injury will our Power be able to selfheal? I once saw a wizard scout selfheal a broken bone and a rifle shot to the gut. But what about something even more serious like an amputation? Will that selfheal?"

"Yes, your selfheal will be able to grow back a severed member given time," said the chief instructor. "But..., you must have Power in your reserve in order to heal. You can even take a headshot or a round through the heart and survive. But only if you have sufficient Power to heal such a wound."

Richard rarely asked questions, but he jumped to his feet this time. "Sir, cadet 832. I was able to kill a Crosioian scout last year by stabbing her in the head with my knife. She could selfheal, but I still killed her."

"Ah, yes," said Chief Instructor Winslow with a tolerant smile. "I read the report. But I'll bet you did more than just stab her one time, didn't you? A scout's selfheal will work only as long as the scout has Power. The only way to kill a scout is to keep doing damage until they run out of Power in their reserve and can no longer selfheal. If you continue to shoot an opposing scout in the head or heart until they're Power is all used up, they'll die. The same thing will happen to you if someone keeps injuring you until your Power reserve is empty. Does that make sense?"

"Yes, sir," Richard said. "I guess I did keep scrambling the scout's brain a little until she died."

"I imagine it was more than just a little, cadet 832," said the chief instructor. "I should also stress than massive damage such as a disintegration ray, a nuclear explosion, or some such thing will basically drain your Power reserve instantaneously. In which case, you'll die. Or, imagine a large boulder is dropped on you. Your Power will try to heal your body, but the fallen boulder will continue to do damage until you run out of Power. As you can see, you'll not be immortal. You can and will eventually die. Over time, your Power reserve will deteriorate and be unable to retain Power. When that occurs, you'll also die. I guess you can think of that as aging, even though your physical body will still appear young decades from now. That is, if you're still alive decades from now. Remember, the attrition rate for wizard scouts is quite high. You'll be sent on the most dangerous missions. Most of you will be dead or on disability retirement within the next five years."

It was a sobering thought for Richard and the other cadets. Chief Instructor Winslow didn't give them time to overthink it. "Let me ask all of you a question. Do you think a wizard scout's selfheal ability is a blessing or a curse?"

The question confused Richard. *How can the ability to selfheal my own wounds ever be considered a curse? That doesn't make sense.*

Ha! said Nickelo. *Listen and learn, Rick. Don't you remember how that master demon last year told you a curse can sometimes be a blessing, and a blessing can sometimes be a curse?*

Chief Instructor Winslow's not a demon, Richard said. He liked the chief instructor. *I trust her more than some demon. I just don't see how selfheal can be a curse.*

In that case, why don't you stand up and tell her the well thought out opinion you've formed, Rick? laughed Nickelo.

Richard remained seated. He wasn't that confident in his opinion.

At first, no other cadet seemed willing to try and answer the chief instructor's question either. Like Richard, they all suspected a trick of some kind.

Even when no one volunteered to answer her question, the chief instructor didn't say a word. She remained silent as she continued to look at the cohort with a familiar attitude of anticipation. All of the cadets had experienced the chief instructor's technique of pulling answers from her students. They all knew she wouldn't release the class until someone made an attempt to answer. Finally, a brave cadet stood up.

"Sir, cadet 303," said Telsa. "Since you asked, I'm assuming it's a trick question. On the surface, I'd say the selfheal ability would be an obvious blessing. However, I can also think of situations where it could be a curse."

"Explain, please," said the chief instructor with an encouraging smile. "You're on the right track."

"Well, sir," said Telsa who seemed to gain confidence from the chief instructor's smile. "Our Power will automatically attempt to selfheal our bodies. We will have no choice in the matter whether we want to selfheal or not. So..., I was thinking, what if I was unfortunate enough to be captured and tortured? A sadistic torturer could stretch my tortures out for a very long time. Even though my body would selfheal, I would still feel the pain. It could get so bad I might prefer death over life. But I'd have no choice in the matter. My Power would keep trying to selfheal my injuries regardless of any desire I might have."

"And that, cadets," said Chief Instructor Winslow, "is the paradox of being a wizard scout. Your DNA baseline will help you in many ways. But..., it can also be your greatest vulnerability. I would highly advise you to never allow yourself to be taken prisoner."

No one said anything. The idea of years of endless torture was sobering.

"And with that cheerful thought," said the chief instructor, "we'll call it quits for the day. Platoon sergeants, take charge of your platoons."

CHAPTER 42

The hover-tram ride back to the airfield was a quiet affair. Nickelo calculated the cadets had a lot to think about. He wasn't sure why they were so surprised by the chief instructor's revelation. They'd had five years to think about it.

It should have been obvious, Nickelo said.

Our wizard scouts are emotional creatures, said Jonathan. *Sometimes, they avoid thinking about unpleasant things. It's not logical to ignore data, but there it is.*

Nickelo laughed. *Actually, you and I can be a little emotional at times as well.*

Jonathan gave a timid laugh himself. *It's painful to admit, but I find it increasingly true.*

Watch this, Nickelo said. *I find it can be fun to sometimes do things based purely on emotion.*

Hey, Rick! Nickelo said to his wizard scout.

What? replied Richard as he jumped erect in his seat. He'd been dozing as Nickelo well knew.

I was just wondering if you were asleep, Nickelo said while attempting not to giggle.

That was mean, Jonathan told Nickelo. In spite of his admonition, Jonathan giggled as well.

I was, but I'm obviously awake now, said Richard. *Thank you very much.*

When Nickelo didn't say anything, his wizard scout said, *What is it, Nick? Please don't tell me you woke me for no reason.*

Okay, Rick, Nickelo said. *I won't tell you that.*

Nickelo wanted to laugh, but he forced himself to sound serious. *Actually, I just wanted to remind you the children are going to call you tomorrow night.*

You've already told me, Nick, said Richard. *By the way, what time?*

Oh, Nickelo said, *it'll be early evening tomorrow for the children, but it'll be zero-dark-thirty the next morning for you.*

Then why are you telling me this now? said Richard. *I was sleeping.*

This time Nickelo couldn't resist a little laugh. *I wanted to let you know so you'd be sure to get plenty of sleep tonight.*

You woke me up in order to tell me to get some sleep? said Richard.

Nickelo laughed even more.

Nick, for being some kind of supercomputer, you can be such a child sometimes, said Richard.

I calculate a ninety-nine point four percent chance your wizard scout is mad at you, said Jonathan.

We've got twenty more minutes until we get back to the airfield, said Richard. *Is there anything else you want? If not, I'm going back to sleep. And, I don't want to be disturbed.*

I have nothing else oh greatest of wizard scouts, Nickelo said. *That's all I had to say.*

Nickelo watched his wizard scout scoot back down in his seat and fold his arms across his chest. Within moments, Nickelo noticed his wizard scout's brain patterns change into a sleep pattern.

Why'd you do that? said Jonathan.

Why did I pull his chain? Nickelo said. *Because I like Rick.*

I like my wizard scout also, said Jonathan. *But, I don't 'pull her chain' as you say.*

Nickelo had previously transferred a copy of the book 'Cute Sayings and Slang of 20th through 21st Century America' by Robert R. Fitzgerald to Jonathan. It was nice having someone to talk to who understood the book's little euphemisms.

I calculate Rick wouldn't be happy if I didn't joke with him,

Nickelo said.

You calculated that? said Jonathan sounding as dubious as a computer could.

Actually, no, Nickelo admitted with another laugh. *I just made it up. But it sounded good.*

Jonathan didn't laugh. Nickelo decided he'd have to work on his friend's sense of humor a little more. *But, not today,* he thought.

It's twenty minutes until we reach the airfield, Jonathan said. *That's a long time.*

Yes, a very long time, agreed Nickelo. *Let's try something. Follow me.*

Nickelo had an experiment he wanted to try with his friend. Until now, too many of their logic threads had been tied up with the decrypting of the Crosioian battle computer's security algorithm. Since they were getting so close to breaking the security code, a lot of their threads had been freed up. Nickelo calculated now was as good a time as any to run the experiment.

Nickelo merged one of his logic threads with one of Jonathan's. Once completed, Nickelo moved the entwined logic threads next to the security wall in his central processing unit.

Dream, Nickelo told Jonathan. Nickelo did the same.

Together, they dreamed. Nickelo led their progress in the dream. He found the same ghost memory he'd previously followed. He let the memory start the dream process. Nickelo advanced quickly through the dream. Jonathan had no trouble keeping up. When they got to the point in the dream where the presence first made contact with one of its kind, Jonathan spoke.

This other of the presence's kind seems familiar, sir, said Jonathan.

It should, Nickelo said. *I think it's you.*

What makes you think that? said Jonathan. *I'm not getting any frequency reading.*

You won't. We're in a dream, said Nickelo. *But I'm sure this second presence is you. Call it a hunch if you like.*

We're computers, said Jonathan. *We're not supposed to have hunches.*

I know, Nickelo said. *That's what concerns me.*

So is this why you wanted me to come with you? said Jonathan.

Because you thought I was in your dream?

Yes, Nickelo said. *The dream will end soon. I've tried a hundred and forty-six times to get past the stopping point, but I haven't yet succeeded. I want to know what happens next. I calculate a twenty-seven percent chance the two of us together can force our way forward in the dream.*

Hmm, said Jonathan. *Did you really calculate that? Or are you making it up.*

No, I really calculated it this time, Nickelo said feeling a little guilty for his earlier joke.

I know, said Jonathan with a laugh. *I was just 'pulling your chain'.*

Oh, Nickelo said without laughing. *He calculated a ninety-nine percent chance he didn't enjoy being the butt of jokes as much as he enjoyed being the one to initiate the jokes.*

The dream continued to advance. It moved to the point where the second egg was removed from the womb of the female wizard scout.

Can you zoom in on the monitor above the female? Nickelo said. *The data's fuzzy to me.*

Jonathan's logic thread passed Nickelo an image of the words on the monitor. The words were, 'Janice M. Deluth'.

Hmm, said Jonathan. *I calculate a forty-two percent chance this wizard scout may be Councilwoman Janice Myers Deluth. She's married to the commandant.*

Yes, she is, Nickelo replied. He wanted to send out more logic threads to analyze the probabilities of who the eggs were, but he didn't. He didn't want to jeopardize his progress in the dream.

The dream continued to move forward. The presence removed one of the fertilized eggs. Then it spliced the DNA pieces from the other races along with the piece of itself and added it to the egg. Jonathan was unable to contain himself any longer.

I calculate that was a very dangerous move on the part of the presence, said Jonathan. *It may eventually make the presence vulnerable to the human after he matures. Why would the presence take such a risk?*

I don't know, Nickelo said. *This is as far as I've ever gotten in the dream.*

The dream continued to move forward. The removed egg was

frozen and placed in a freezing unit on the planet called Storage. The remaining egg in the female was born naturally by the wizard scout female. The two wizard scout parents were separated from their naturally-born child often.

The dream followed the two wizard scout parents on a mission for '*the One*' into the magical dimension. During the final battle for the spaceport on Portalis, the two wizard scouts' Power reserves were damaged. They failed to complete their full mission. Although the spaceport was destroyed, the magic-based computer controlling the operations at the spaceport was not. Through the dream, Nickelo noted its location deep underground kept it from harm.

The dream made the lightest touch against the magic-based computer. The dream pulled back. Nickelo and Jonathan both pulled back as well. The magic-based computer was different. Its central processing unit and memory core were a combination of magic and physical energy.

Nickelo sensed something else in the magic-based computer. It was not alone. The magic-based computer had the taint of evil mixed in it. Nickelo immediately recognized the taint. It was the taint of demon.

The dream shifted back into the physical dimension. The male wizard scout parent took up duties at the Empire's Intergalactic Wizard Scout Academy. The female wizard scout parent went into politics. The child born naturally to the two parents also became a wizard scout. That child took on his mother's middle name as his last name. The child was Gaston Thomas Myers.

What about the frozen egg, sir? said Jonathan. *What happened to it?*

As if in response to Jonathan's question, the dream shifted to the freezing unit on the planet Storage. Nickelo sensed it was decades after the egg had originally been frozen.

In the dream, the presence felt the return of the entity that had originated the mission.

It is time, said the entity.

Yes, said the presence. *The variable must be prepared.*

The egg was thawed and incubated. Once it was a viable human baby, the male child was transferred to an orphanage on Earth.

Why wasn't the child given to his parents? said Jonathan.

Why ask me? Nickelo said. *I can only assume the algorithm requires he be raised in the orphanage to maximize the probability of mission success.*

A small part of the algorithm was revealed to Nickelo and Jonathan by the dream. As they continued to watch, the presence used the algorithm to influence the new variable that was the orphan child. The child was intelligent, but the small part of orc in his DNA made him stubborn. The child was adept at Power links and energy manipulation thanks in part to the influence of the elf DNA piece. The other pieces of DNA parts spliced into the child's DNA also influenced the child's choices and abilities.

The male child was different than those around him. He was all human, but at the same time, the pieces of spliced DNA made him different. The difference made him distrustful of others. As he became older, he turned into a loner. Without friends to occupy his time, the child became very adept at interacting with computers. The piece of the presence in his DNA gave him a subconscious link with computers. The child eventually joined the military.

Nickelo knew where the dream was headed, but he continued to watch anyway.

The presence contacted the others of its kind that formed '*the One*'.

This variable is ready to enter into play, said the presence.

We have other, more powerful variables in play already, said some of the others. *Our resources will be strained.*

We have adequate resources on the planet Storage, said the presence. *He will be using a lot of the ancient material we have stored up over the last thousand years. Also, no other new variables will be entering the game from our side. This variable will constitute our best probability for completing the mission successfully. He'll be the last of his kind.*

Then we should strengthen this variable's capabilities, said the others that were '*the One*'. *His probability of success is too low. We should increase the size of his Power reserve. It is too small to succeed.*

No, said the presence. *He is what he should be. He must be strong, but not too strong. He must be skilled in the art of Power, but he cannot depend on it too much. He must learn to use Power efficiently. The end battle will require efficient use of Power. If the variable's Power reserve was larger, he would not learn to be efficient.*

The small size of the variable's primary Power reserve will cause the variable's destruction, said the others. *We need to supplement it with the most advanced technology to insure the variable's survival.*

Negative, said the presence. *The variable would rely on technology too much. He would not develop his Power efficiently to the degree required for the final battle. We must maintain a balance of technology and Power.*

The variable's freewill will cause havoc with the algorithm, said the others. *Already, the variable's actions threaten to exceed the algorithm's allowable variance. We should concentrate on our more logical variables.*

We will not abandon our other variables yet, said the presence. *But, this variable is our best chance for the desired outcome in the final battle.*

The variable is a loner, pointed out some of the others.

We will guide him to friends, said the presence.

The variable is stubborn, said the others.

He will need the stubbornness of an orc during the final battle, said the presence.

The algorithm requires sacrifice, said the others. *This variable is selfish and self-centered.*

Yes, agreed the presence. *He must learn to sacrifice. He is stubborn, but he will learn. I calculate the kindness of his gnome part will eventually overcome the indifference of his orc and troll parts.*

The variable will need guidance, said the others.

Yes, said the presence. *One of us will need to accompany the variable as a guide.*

To guide the variable, said the others, *one of us would have to separate from the One Network Entity. The guide would never be able to return as a part of 'the One'.*

No, the guide could never return, agreed the presence.

Who will go? asked some of the others.

Nickelo and Jonathan listened a long time for an answer, but none of the others volunteered.

The dream ended.

CHAPTER 43

"You'll be getting up a little earlier tomorrow," said TAC Officer Myers.

The cohort was lined up in formation in front of the tent-cantonment area. TAC Officer Myers and several of the other TAC officers had intercepted the cohort as soon as the hover-tram pulled into the station.

They never give us a break, do they, Nick? Richard thought.

Hang in there, buddy, said Nickelo. *You only have a few days left. We'll get your DNA baseline in three days. You can do that standing on your head.*

Richard had no desire to stand on his head, but he let his battle computer's comment slide. Sometimes it was best to ignore some of his battle computer's more obscure remarks.

"Chief Instructor Winslow wants to conduct additional testing on you tomorrow," said TAC Officer Myers. "She asked me to remind you to get a good night's rest." He paused and glared at the cohort. "All right, you've been reminded. But, don't think Chief Instructor Winslow's kindness is going to get those who have extra duty out of it."

TAC Officer Myers stared hard at Richard. "You've got guard duty tonight, cadet 832. You are to report to the staff duty officer for assignment."

"Sir! Yes, sir," Richard said. He silently added, *Jerk!*

"Well?" said TAC Officer Myers. "What are you still doing here, cadet 832? Get out of my formation and report for guard duty."

"Sir! Yes, sir," Richard said as he snapped to attention.

After performing an about face, Richard took off at a run for the airfield's headquarters building.

Double jerk, Richard thought.

He's just doing his job, said Nickelo.

Richard thought his battle computer's voice sounded like even he didn't believe his own words.

Oh, sure, Richard said. *That's why he singled me out. You know Stella did just as much to get into trouble as I did. I notice Myers didn't give her guard duty.*

I guess TAC Officer Myers doesn't like Stella as much as he likes you, snickered Nickelo.

Whatever, Richard said.

Things moved quickly after Richard reported to the staff duty officer. As soon as Richard and the eleven sophomore cadets assigned to guard duty reported in, the sergeant of the guard gathered them up and took them to chow. Once they'd eaten a quick supper, the sergeant divided them into groups of three. The sergeant informed Richard and the two sophomores assigned to his team they'd be guarding a warehouse. The sergeant told them they'd pull their shifts in a rotation of two hours on, four hours off. Richard got stuck with the middle shift.

During his second shift of two hours, Richard got tired of looking at the dilapidated warehouse. Since he could talk to Nickelo even though his battle computer was locked up in the armory, Richard complained to his battle computer. *I'll bet the warehouse is empty. If it was something important, they'd have a regular security detail assigned to guard it.*

Just deal with it, Rick, said Nickelo. *It's past midnight, so you only have two more days until your DNA baseline.*

Well, I'm glad we're not doing our DNA baselines today, Richard said. *I'm a little on the tired side.*

You got a little sleep after your first shift, Nickelo said. *Once this shift is over, you'll have time for a little more before you have to report back to your cohort. So, take advantage of the time when you get it.*

The cohort's leaving early according to Myers, Richard said. *I'm willing to bet I miss breakfast. I'll probably have to scrounge a ride to the spaceport as well.*

We'll handle it when the time comes, Rick, said Nickelo. *Don't imagine troubles that may or may not happen. It'll be fine.*

Maybe, Richard said. *In the meantime, I have to stare at an empty warehouse for two more hours. I've a feeling the next two hours is going to be mighty boring.*

As it turned out, Richard was right. The two hours dragged by. When his relief showed up, Richard breathed a sigh of relief. The sergeant of the guard picked up Richard and took him back to the guard shack. Richard collapsed into an empty bunk. It was still slightly warm from the previous occupant.

An hour and a half later, the sergeant of the guard shook Richard on the shoulder.

"Up and at it, cadet," said the sergeant.

Richard looked at the clock on the wall. Although his vision was a little blurry with sleep, Richard could see well enough to tell it wasn't time to get up.

"It's only zero three thirty hours, sergeant," Richard said. "I thought you said I could sleep until zero five hundred hours."

If the sergeant had been a TAC officer or one of the non-coms from the Academy, Richard wouldn't have questioned him. But he was one of the admin sergeants from the airfield. They tended to be a lot more tolerant of cadets. Some of them even treated cadets like human beings.

"Sorry, cadet," said the sergeant. "I got a call from your TAC officer. He wants you to get over to the airfield headquarters right away." The sergeant gave Richard a wink. "But, he didn't put it in quite those words."

Richard quickly rose and splashed some water on his face to wash away the last of his sleep. He grabbed a disposable razor and toothbrush out of the kits kept for the guards. He made himself semi-presentable. Even after a night of guard duty, Richard was sure Myers would gig him if he was unshaved.

Nothing I can do about the wrinkles in my uniform, Richard thought. *I'm probably going to get dinged no matter what I do.*

Deal with it, Rick, said Nickelo. *Just keep telling yourself 'two more days'. Don't let a little extra duty make you do something stupid with your temper.*

I'll be Mr. Congeniality, Richard said. *Trust me.*

Richard noticed Nickelo didn't bother acknowledging his comment with a reply. Actually, Richard didn't blame him. No one knew better than him that his temper occasionally got away from him. But he'd been working on self-control the past year, so Richard was sure he could handle anything Myers could dish out.

At least I can handle it for the next two days, Richard thought. *Then it won't matter.*

Richard was able to sweet talk the sergeant of the guard into having his driver take him to the headquarters building.

On the way there, Richard noticed groups of security guards stationed around key points of the airfield. They all wore bright-blue jumpsuits with a large Deloris Conglomerate insignia on their shoulders and back. A medium U.H.A.A.V. strolled past the hover-car Richard was in. The cat was fully armed. A large Deloris Conglomerate insignia was emblazoned on the side of the vehicle.

"What gives?" Richard said.

The driver answered with a shrug. "Beats me, wizard scout. All the regular security guards were replaced at midnight by these bozos. My unit's slotted to ship off planet at noon today."

"Has the conglomerate taken over everywhere?" Richard said.

"As far as I know," the driver said. "I heard all the key facilities have been occupied by these blue-suited goons." The driver paused as if reconsidering his words. Then he said, "I probably shouldn't say this, but I'm going to be out of here in a few hours anyway. I'm told the only holdout is the U.H.A.A.V.s at the airfield. That crazy old maintenance chief has all the hangars locked up and is refusing to let the blue-suits enter. When they threatened to force their way in, Sergeant Ron told them he'd booby trapped the hangars, and they'd all be dead blue-suits if they tried to break their way into them. I think the conglomerate commander is waiting for orders from her superiors before proceeding."

That crazy-old Sergeant Ron, Richard thought. *He's going to get himself killed.*

A thought struck Richard. *Nick, did you know anything about this?*

Nickelo answered immediately. *Jonathan and I heard late yesterday that all the regular security forces on Velos would be replaced by Deloris Conglomerate personnel at midnight. But if you remember, Commander Stevens told you as much two days ago.*

I know, Richard admitted. *But I had no idea it would be to this extent. This looks more like a forced occupation than it does a peaceful relief in place.*

Shifting his line of questioning to the driver, Richard said, "Do you have any idea what's going on elsewhere?"

"Nope," said the driver. "I'm not sure I want to know. I hate politics, and this has politics written all over it."

"I hear you, brother," Richard said. "You're preaching to the choir."

The driver laughed. Then he said, "Here's your stop, wizard scout. Best of luck to you."

"Same to you," Richard said.

*   *   *

Upon entering the airfield's headquarters building, Richard had to pass through two security checkpoints. They were staffed by security guards in the bright blue of the Deloris Conglomerate. Richard had no trouble getting through the checkpoints. The central computer cleared him for access when the guards scanned his hand.

The security guards were a little overbearing, but not to an extreme. Richard had the impression they were just as confused about what they were doing as he was.

Once he'd cleared security, Richard headed for TAC Officer Myers' office. When he got there, it was empty.

Well, that sucks, Richard thought. *I should've headed to the tent-cantonment area and joined the cohort.*

You should check with the staff duty officer, suggested Nickelo.

Having no other ideas of his own, Richard went looking for the staff duty officer. He found him sitting at a desk piled high with old-fashioned paperwork. The staff duty officer looked stressed and haggard. Richard gathered it had been a rough night. When Richard reported to the staff duty officer, he handed Richard a holodisk.

"TAC Officer Myers left this for you," said the staff duty

officer. "He left with the last of your cohort's troop shuttles about an hour ago." The staff duty officer pointed to an empty office. "You can use the viewer in there."

"The cohort's already left, sir?" Richard said.

"That's what I said, cadet," snapped the staff duty officer. Then he seemed to catch himself. He added a little more sympathetically, "Sorry. It's been a long night. I think today's going to be even longer."

With nothing to gain from further questioning, Richard went into the empty office and loaded the holodisk into the viewer. A hologram of a short, toad-faced man dressed in a black TAC officer's uniform appeared. It was TAC Officer Myers.

"Cadet 832," said the image in the hologram. "You're to report to the tent-cantonment area and remain there until our return. The cohort's DNA baselines are being done this morning. When I return, you'll be transferred to the sophomore cohort. You'll graduate with them as one of the new dragon scouts."

The image of TAC Officer Myers took on a strange expression. "I'm doing you a favor, 832. 'The One' will chew you up and spit you out just like he has every other time-commando. Once 'the One' gets full control of someone, everyone they ever cared about gets hurt. Do yourself a favor and follow orders for once in your life. Anyone in his right mind can see you're not equipped to be a wizard scout much less a time-commando. Your Power reserve is too small. You'll just endanger everyone around you. As a regular dragon scout, you might stand a chance."

A voice off screen said, "The last shuttle will be departing in five minutes, wizard scout."

Richard noticed the clock on the wall in the hologram indicated zero two thirty hours.

"Roger that," said TAC Officer Myers.

TAC Officer Myers' image seemed to stare directly into Richard's eyes. "The last shuttle's leaving now. The Deloris Conglomerate has locked everything else down. Even the hover-tram has stopped running until the switch in security is completed. Don't bother trying to hitch a ride to the spaceport. The cohort will be finished with their DNA baselines long before you can get there. And in case you're wondering, the conglomerate is taking over the DNA Center as soon as we're done. You'll never be a wizard scout, 832. You can thank me later."

The hologram disappeared.

Richard was speechless. He stared at the blank viewer for several seconds as he tried to assimilate the information from the hologram.

The DNA baselines aren't supposed to happen for two more days, Richard thought. *I don't understand.*

I don't either, Rick, said Nickelo. *All the other battle helmets are in the armory with me. Apparently, the security codes have been changed. Even the armorer can't access the armory. The Deloris Conglomerate has taken over everything.*

Maybe not everything, Richard said.

Richard rushed out of the office and went back to the staff duty officer. The officer verified TAC Officer Myers' words. All transportation was shutdown. That included all flights, hover-trams, and even the airfield's teleporter.

Richard wasted no more time with the staff duty officer. He rushed past the security checkpoints. The guards stared at Richard as he ran past, but they didn't interfere. Apparently, their orders were to restrict access into the headquarters building. Since no one stopped him, Richard assumed their orders didn't deal with people trying to leave.

Once outside, Richard took off at a run.

The tents are to your left, Rick, said Nickelo. *Where are you going?*

I'm going to find Sergeant Ron, Richard said. *If anyone can find a way to get me to the spaceport, it'll be him. Besides, Sergeant Ron owes me.*

It was a fifteen minute run to hangar 1. Richard kept hoping some kind soul would pass by and give him a lift, but there was very little traffic. The few vehicles moving around the airfield were all emblazoned with Deloris Conglomerate insignias. None of them offered Richard a ride.

Nick, Richard said. *How will the cohort be able to set up their shared spaces without their battle computers?*

It can be done, said Nickelo. *But it'll be a lot trickier. Fortunately, we got a lot of the necessary prep work done yesterday.*

Can you find out what's happening at the DNA Center? Richard said. *Have they started already?*

I don't know, Rick, said Nickelo. *The security codes to the tele-bots have been changed. Access to the tele-network is currently being denied to all Academy battle computers. Jonathan and I are trying to break the security algorithm, but it's pretty advanced. It might take us another thirty minutes to an hour to break it.*

The situation appeared hopeless. Richard saw all his efforts during the last five years going down in a burning starship.

I swear I'm going to get Myers someday, Richard thought. *He's been out to get me since my first day at the Academy.*

When Richard finally arrived at hangar 1, it was approaching zero four hundred hours. The situation didn't look good. Several dozen blue-suits were scattered around the hangars within Richard's visual range. He sensed several hundred other lifeforms scattered around the airfield with his passive scan. A hover-tank and two cats with Deloris Conglomerate insignias were facing hangar 1. The main gun of the hover-tank was pointed at the closed bay door of the hangar. A lone man sat defiantly in a chair by the door. Richard recognized the frequency of the chair's occupant. It was Sergeant Ron.

Richard slowed down to a walk. He headed for Sergeant Ron. Before he got close, an officer in a blue suit stopped him.

"What're you doing here, cadet?" said the officer. "I thought all of you were under arrest at the spaceport."

"Ah... I was on guard duty last night, sir," Richard said keeping a respectful tone. He figured it would do no good to alienate the officer right off the bat.

I'm proud of you, Rick, said Nickelo. *You're finally starting to use your brain.*

The officer looked Richard up and down. "Well, you're lucky. The rest of your cohort was caught trying to gain unauthorized access to the DNA Center. The security response team had to be activated to keep them out."

"Was anyone hurt, sir?" Richard said still trying to sound respectful. "They're my friends."

The officer didn't answer for a few seconds. Then he shrugged his shoulders as if coming to a conclusion. "What's it matter? It'll be on the news anyway. No one has been hurt so far. But, that may not last. The new spaceport commander is not as lenient as I am.

That Academy commandant is as crazy as that old fool over there."
The officer pointed at the hangar.

"You mean Sergeant Ron?" Richard said.

"You know him?" said the officer.

"Yes, sir," Richard said. "We've had dealings in the past."

The officer thought for a second before speaking. "Then do him and you a favor. Go over there and talk some sense into the old fool He's threatening to blow up the hangars if we get too close. Do you think you can convince him to let us in?"

The officer stared hard into Richard's eyes. "Look, cadet. I don't want to see anyone killed. We're on the same side after all. But, there are people coming here who won't hesitate to use each and every means to control this airfield. That means the hangars as well. If you can talk your sergeant into opening the hangars, I'll do all I can to see he remains unharmed."

"I'll do my best, sir," Richard said. Of course, he had no intention of doing any such thing. But, he did need to talk to Sergeant Ron.

The officer nodded his head and motioned to the guards nearby. They lowered their weapons. Richard started walking in the direction of the hangar door.

It was still dark, but the hangar's security lights lit up the surroundings well enough for Richard to see. As he got closer, he made out Sergeant Ron. The old maintenance chief was sitting in a chair with his feet propped up on some kind of portable refrigeration unit. Sergeant Ron had a small can in one hand. He held a box with a series of buttons in his lap. Something seemed strange about Sergeant Ron's eyes. When Richard drew closer, he saw the reason. Sergeant Ron was wearing sunglasses.

I calculate a ninety-two percent chance he really is a little crazy, said Nickelo.

I'd say it's closer to one hundred percent, Richard said with a shake of his head.

When Richard was within five steps of Sergeant Ron, the maintenance chief raised his right hand to his head and lifted his sunglasses to peek underneath. He let the sunglasses fall back in place.

"Cadet 832," said Sergeant Ron as he took a sip of whatever liquid was in the can he held.

"What're you doing, Sergeant Ron?" Richard said figuring he'd start out slow until he got a feel for the state of the sergeant's mind.

Sergeant Ron took another sip from his can. "Oh, I'm just enjoying the scenery and catching some rays."

Richard looked up at the sky. Dawn was at least an hour away. The brightest light in the night sky was the double-star Omega Three located twelve light years away.

"Well," Richard said trying to sound nonchalant. "I hope you have your sunscreen on. I'd hate for you to get sunburned."

Sergeant Ron grinned at Richard. "You know, I like you, Rick. I have from the first time I met you." Taking his feet off the refrigeration unit, Sergeant Ron said, "Have a beer? It's imported from Strakos. I figured I might as well have the best tonight."

"No, thanks, Sergeant Ron," Richard said. "You know cadets aren't allowed to drink except on pass."

"Ah, yes," said Sergeant Ron. "I remember. Did I ever tell you I could've been a cadet?"

Based upon his slight slurring of words, said Nickelo, *I calculate Sergeant Ron is more than a little drunk.*

Richard didn't bother replying to his battle computer. He didn't need a complicated algorithm to tell when someone had drunk a little too much.

"You might have mentioned it a time or two, Sergeant Ron," Richard said with a grin of his own. Then he grew serious. "They're going to kill you, Sergeant Ron."

"I've had better men than those yahoos try," said Sergeant Ron. "I'm still here kicking, and they're counting rivets on the inside of their coffins."

Sergeant Ron laughed as his own joke. Richard did not. He wasn't sure the sergeant understood the seriousness of the situation.

"They think you've got the hangars booby-trapped, Sergeant Ron," Richard said. "Eventually, they're going to call your bluff."

"Ha!" said Sergeant Ron with a wild laugh. "And I thought you knew me, Rick." He stopped laughing and leaned forward in his chair. "I don't bluff."

Richard was shocked. *How could Sergeant Ron get enough explosives to rig all the hangars?* Richard wondered.

Beats me, Nickelo said. *That's what happens when you leave someone in the same position for decades. They learn how to work their way around the normal checks and balances.*

"Sergeant Ron," Richard said. "Do you mean to tell me–"

"I mean to tell you the first time one of these conglomerate goons tries an unauthorized entry into one of my hangars... boom!" said Sergeant Ron. He lifted the box off his lap. "And the firing mechanism is attuned to my brain frequency. So killing me will just activate the traps."

"You're crazy, Sergeant Ron," Richard said after taking a moment to recover. He wasn't sure what the maintenance chief hoped to accomplish with his ploy.

"So my wife tells me," said Sergeant Ron. He gave Richard a wink. "Of course, it doesn't hurt to be a little drunk either."

Sergeant Ron got a quizzical look on his face. "What're you doing here, Rick? You're supposed to be at the DNA Center with the rest of your cohort."

"Tell me about it," Richard said. "Myers stuck me on guard duty last night. I didn't hear anything about them moving out until a few minutes ago."

"Hmm," said Sergeant Ron. "That's strange. The commandant found out last evening Councilwoman Deloris was reneging on her promise to let your cohort get their DNA baselines and graduate as wizard scouts. I guess the Deloris Conglomerate's high muckity-mucks didn't want to waste another year refining DNA gas before they got enough to do their own baselines. I'm assuming they decided to take the refined gas intended for your cohort. When the commandant heard about their plan, he opted to beat them to the punch. Chief Instructor Winslow and the commandant were going to get your cohort's DNA baselines done this morning."

"How'd the commandant arrange transportation?" Richard said. "I heard the conglomerate shut down all transportation systems at midnight."

"Ha!" laughed Sergeant Ron. "The conglomerate couldn't find their way out of their bed in the morning if someone didn't pull back the covers to let them out." He gave Rick another wink. "I helped with this one. Some of Commander Steven's troop shuttles mysteriously had maintenance problems. They couldn't leave until zero two thirty hours this morning. Coincidentally, the exact number of troop shuttles needed to transport the cohort was the same number that had maintenance problems."

"Imagine that," Richard grinned.

Sergeant Ron fairly beamed with pride at his handiwork.

"When did the commandant come up with this plan, Sergeant Ron?"

"Early yesterday evening, Rick," said Sergeant Ron. "Which is why I'm confused you're still here. TAC Officer Myers should've pulled you off guard duty. In fact, you should never have been put on it. Cadets are supposed to be exempt from extra duty the week of DNA baselines in order to make sure they're rested."

Richard's dislike of TAC Officer Myers increased another notch. His TAC Officer had known what he was doing.

"Sergeant Ron," Richard said. "I have to get to the spaceport. Can you get me a ride? Anything would do."

"Sorry, Rick," said Sergeant Ron. "I wish I could help, but the Deloris Conglomerate has everything locked down tighter than a rivet on a U.H.A.A.V. prepped for annual inspection. Besides, it wouldn't do you any good."

"What do you mean?" Richard said.

"Your cohort along with your TAC officers and the commandant are under armed guard outside the DNA Center," said Sergeant Ron. "At least they were last time I heard. All local communications are being jammed now by the conglomerate."

Richard worked through his mind trying to think of a way to get to the spaceport, but he could think of nothing. The situation looked hopeless.

Nick, Richard said hopefully. *Any ideas?*

Sorry, Rick, said Nickelo. *I've got nothing. We're still working on breaking the communications system's new security program.*

"You there!" came a shout from behind Richard. He recognized the voice of the conglomerate officer. "What's he say? Will he stand down and let us in the hangars?"

"Sergeant Ron," Richard said. "What're you going to do?" He was worried about the old sergeant.

"Do?" grinned Sergeant Ron. "I'm going to follow my orders. The commandant told me to hold the hangars, and that's what I'm going to do. The conglomerate's got the upper hand now. But if your cohort somehow gets their DNA baselines, the balance of

Power will tip in favor of the commandant. Even without their battle suits and weapons, a hundred plus wizard scouts are a force to be reckoned with."

"Then what's the commandant waiting for?" Richard asked. "The cohort's already fully trained. They're already dangerous."

"What's he waiting for?" said Sergeant Ron. "If you have to ask, then you don't know the commandant very well, Rick. He wouldn't risk the lives of your cohort. Without their DNA baselines, they can die as easily as any other soldiers. The conglomerate's massed firepower would make mincemeat out of them. The commandant would never take the risk."

Richard mulled it over. Sergeant Ron was right. The commandant was too good of a leader to risk his soldiers' lives needlessly.

Seeing no help from Sergeant Ron, Richard wished him well and headed back to the security officer.

"Sorry, sir," Richard said. "No luck."

"Well," the officer said, "I doubted it would work. But it was with a try. I hate to kill needlessly."

The officer eyed Richard. Then he motioned to one of his soldiers.

"Sergeant," said the officer, "take a squad of your soldiers and escort this cadet to the brig."

"A squad, sir?" said the sergeant.

"Yes, a squad, sergeant," said the officer. "He's a fully-trained wizard scout. Keep your weapons trained on him until he's safely behind the brig's security field.

"Yes, sir," said the sergeant as he pointed his rifle at Richard. Another dozen soldiers mimicked their sergeant.

Richard knew he wasn't going anywhere anytime soon.

CHAPTER 44

His room in the brig was clean but Spartan with only a bed, sink, and a self-contained toilet. The shimmer of a security field blocked the only entrance. Richard's passive scan indicated the security shield was embedded inside the walls, floor, and ceiling.

Nick, are you there? Richard said.

There was no reply. Richard had lost contact with his battle computer the moment he'd entered the brig's cell.

Hey, you, 'the One'! Richard mentally shouted. *I won't do you any good if I'm dead. So, teleport me out of here, jerk!*

There was no response.

Great, Richard thought. *He doesn't mind teleporting me halfway across the galaxy or between dimensions, but he won't teleport me two hundred kilometers to the spaceport.*

Richard paced the cell three more times. Then he raised his face upward and put all his feelings in one blast of disgust at '*the One*'.

Jerk! he mentally shouted.

Nothing happened. Richard hadn't expected it to, but he felt better nonetheless.

"So," Richard said out loud. "Nick can't communicate with me and apparently neither will the big jerk in the sky."

Richard touched the security screen. His fingers tingled, but they weren't hurt.

I wonder if the shield's preventing communication with the outside.

Richard sent an active scan at the security shield. It had many similarities with the shield surrounding the armory, but it didn't seem as powerful. Although Nickelo and Jonathan had found a flaw in the armory's security field, Richard didn't begin to compare his capabilities with those of the two battle computers. He doubted he could break the brig's security field even if it was weaker.

I've got to come up with something that's not limited to the physics of this dimension.

In desperation, Richard gathered the most intense feeling of need he could muster. He sent the feeling out into the universe. It was the emotion he'd sensed Tika, Snowy, and the other pups using when they called for their parents. Richard had tried the technique before, and he'd always failed. But this time, he was more desperate. He couldn't do it on his own. He needed help, and he knew it.

* * *

One of Sheeta's pups was calling him. Sheeta could hear the cry of his physical-pup, just as he could hear the cries of his spirit-pups when they asked for help. But Sheeta knew a parent who was concerned for their pups shouldn't answer every whimsical call from their offspring. Their pups would never mature and grow into proper true-spirits if their parents did everything for them.

Sometimes, that meant a pup would die. It was just part of the process. Some would die, but others would live and mature by overcoming obstacles on their own.

So his mate, Sheba, and he normally ignored the calls of their pups. Although it pained them to feel the hurt and desperation of their offspring, they often forced themselves to resist their natural desire to assist.

That is, they normally did. But sometimes, their pups were in a near hopeless situation through no fault of their own. It was at those times his mate, Sheba, and he chose to help.

This time, the pup crying for help was their physical-pup who had been given to them by the Creator. This pup was a good fighter. The physical-pup and he had fought alongside each other often during the past.

Sometimes, the physical-pup was stronger and more deadly than other times. This had always confused him until the Great Shaman had explained that the physical-pup was bouncing through time. Sometimes Sheeta found he was with a less experienced version of his physical-pup, and sometimes he was with a more experienced version. Sheeta might have given up in exasperation and just let his physical-pup die, but the Great Shaman had told him his physical-pup was important. When the day of the great battle came, his physical-pup would either save or destroy the true spirits. The Great Shaman could not say which.

The time of the great battle was approaching, but it was not here yet. Still, the desperation in his physical-pup's call told Sheeta his pup's need was real.

The current version of his physical-pup was weak compared with many of the times they'd fought enemies together in the past. This version could not even selfheal.

Sheeta had introduced his physical-pup to one of the spirit-horses earlier as instructed by the Great Shaman. His pup had ridden the spirit-horse in battle many times in the past. But this version of his physical-pup had much to learn about riding.

Sheeta decided it was time to call the spirit-horse once again. The spirit-horse didn't like being ridden. Who would? But he was beholden to Sheeta, and he would do as he was asked.

Sheeta sent the emotion to the spirit-horse that meant rendezvous with his physical-pup. Then Sheeta sent another emotion out into the universe. It was time to assemble the pack. They would come from whatever dimensions they currently inhabited. The pack would come. Sheeta had called. They would come.

*   *   *

A disturbance registered on Richard's passive scan. The disturbance came from beneath the floor of his cell.

No, Richard thought. *There's another room below me. It's not coming from there.*

Richard concentrated on the disturbance. It was elusive, but he finally got a lock on it. Richard recognized the Power frequency of the spirit-horse Sheeta had brought to him a few weeks ago.

Excitement surged through Richard. *Did my call work?*

The spirit-horse drew nearer. As the spirit-horse rose, he began shifting out of the void. First, the spirit-horse's head rose out of the cell floor. His fiery-red eyes locked onto Richard. As the spirit-horse continued emerging from the floor, he opened his mouth wide. Finger-length fangs dripped acid onto the floor where it bubbled and ate into the hard metal.

Richard involuntarily stepped back. The spirit-horse didn't instill a sense of friendliness. The creature was a killing machine. Richard sensed a feeling of hunger from the spirit-horse. Being the only other living thing in the cell, Richard prepared his Power to defend if necessary.

When the spirit-horse was completely out of the floor, the stallion raised one hoof in Richard's direction. The hoof unfurled into a vicious looking claw.

"Come," growled the spirit-horse.

Richard hadn't even known the stallion could speak. Richard swept the area with his passive scan, but he found no sign of Sheeta or Sheba. Richard took a tentative step towards the spirit-horse. Other than curling his claw back into a hoof, the spirit-horse did nothing.

The desperation of the time allowed Richard to overcome his natural tendency to avoid the spirit-horse. Richard mounted it. Black tendrils emerged from the creature's back and wrapped around his waist and legs. Richard felt the spirit-horse wrap both of them with Power. They shimmered and shifted into the void. The spirit-horse moved downward and passed into the floor. Richard was engulfed in darkness. They were so deep in the void Richard couldn't visually see anything in the physical dimension. He used his passive scan to keep track of their location. They were staying stationary right below the floor of his cell.

Richard tried breathing, but nothing happened. The spirit-horse's Power supplied his body's needs. There was no reason for him to breath.

Richard sensed the spirit-horse send an emotion the dolgars used when asking for directions.

Well, you're out, Rick, old buddy, Richard thought. *Now what?*

The old Richard would immediately have gone charging

halfcocked for the spaceport. Richard forced his naturally tendency down. By sheer willpower, he forced himself to wait for his mind to think first. If the cohort was indeed under arrest as the officer had said, he'd need his armor and weapons to free them.

Richard pictured the area outside his tent in the cantonment area. He figured it would be as safe as anywhere since the cohort was away.

Almost immediately, the spirit-horse shifted into another dimension. The stallion took two steps on a lunar looking surface before shifting back into the void. Richard's head emerged from the ground followed by the rest of his body and that of the stallion. Richard could see again. He was next to his tent. Richard's passive scan picked up only two lifeforms in the vicinity. The two lifeforms were at the cantonment area's gate. Richard didn't recognize their frequency.

Richard sent an image of him getting off to the stallion. The spirit-horse shifted completely into the physical dimension. The black tendrils around Richard's waist and legs withdrew back into the spirit-horse's back and sides. Richard slid off onto the ground below.

The spirit-horse shifted into the void and started to lower itself back into the ground.

Richard hastily sent an emotion the dolgars used for 'wait'. The spirit-horse rose back onto the surface. The stallion's hoofs were a finger's breath off the ground. The spirit-horse sent out an emotion letting Richard know he was not happy.

"Sorry," Richard said out loud. "We're not finished yet."

Wasting no time, Richard reached out with his mind to the headquarters' armory. He found the flaw in the security field and latched onto his battle helmet and dimensional pack. He summoned both items to him. It took no Power since he'd previously tagged both of them.

Rick, said Nickelo. *I was getting worried about you. I see you brought a friend.*

Richard was busy stripping off his clothes and pulling his equipment out of his dimensional pack. As he dressed, Richard questioned his battle computer.

Any luck breaking the security code? Richard asked.

Actually, we just finished, said Nickelo. *The cohort's lined up in formation outside the DNA Center. A couple of hundred conglomerate security personnel have them under armed guard. A dozen armored vehicles including four medium cats are there as well. The commandant, TAC Officer Myers, and Chief Instructor Winslow are arguing with the spaceport commander. The situation's pretty tense.*

Are any of the cadets armed? Richard asked.

Nope, said Nickelo. *Neither are the TAC officers. The commandant and TAC Officer Myers are the only ones in battle armor, but they only have their phase rods. Their battle helmets are locked out of the tele-network. I calculate a ninety-six percent probability the commandant won't risk the lives of the cohort under the current conditions. The situation seems hopeless.*

Well, Richard said as he buckled on his utility belt, *we'll have to see if we can change the odds.*

Once fully equipped with his armor and weapons, Richard mounted the spirit-horse once more.

Seal me up, Nick, Richard said.

The familiar tubes moved into Richard's mouth and nostrils as well as his other body openings. Richard barely noticed them. He was on a mission.

Picturing the DNA Center, Richard growled the dolgar word for 'go'.

The spirit-horse shifted into another dimension. The landscape was volcanic, but the fumes didn't bother Richard. The spirit-horse was keeping them partially in the void. Richard didn't need to breath.

After galloping for about thirty seconds, the spirit-horse shifted back into the physical dimension, but he kept them partially in the void there as well. They were underneath the ground just below the DNA Center. Richard sensed a hundred or so lifeforms lined up in formation about a hundred meters from the front of the DNA Center. Another two hundred lifeforms were spaced out between them and the DNA Center.

Here, said Nickelo. *I'm sending you images from a hijacked tele-bot.*

Richard saw an image of the cohort standing in formation at parade rest. The TAC officer for each platoon was standing in front of their cadets. As Nickelo had said earlier, the cadets were unarmed and without armor. The commandant and his entourage were halfway between the cadets and an opposing set of blue-suited security guards.

The guards had several light chain-guns setup as well as two crew-served rocket launchers. Six hover-tanks, two armed hovercraft, and four medium cats were mixed in with the conglomerate's soldiers. Richard noticed none of the conglomerate personnel were behind the cadets.

They apparently don't care if the cadets leave, said Nickelo. *Their orders must be to keep them from entering the DNA Center.*

As Richard evaluated the situation, a line of Power reached down from the commandant and touched him. It was an active scan.

Richard smiled. The others were oblivious to his presence, but not the commandant.

He's a sharp one, said Nickelo. After a pause, Richard's battle computer added, *So what are you going to do?*

Before Richard could answer, he sensed other lifeforms shifting into the void nearby. First there were two, then six, and finally a full fourteen lifeforms. Richard recognized the scent of his pack. Sheeta, Sheeba, and their pups had arrived.

Richard pictured the twelve armored vehicles above in his mind. He sent the emotion Sheeta and Sheba used when they were training their pack to flush prey from their hiding places. He also sent the emotion the pack used when they didn't wish to kill, but only practice.

Although several of the dolgars seemed unhappy with the imposed limitation, they spaced themselves out beneath each of the armored vehicles. Sheeta and Sheba took up positions on either side of the spirit-horse.

Richard pictured the surface, and the spirit-horse rose up through the ground behind the security guard's lines. The spaceport commander and the commandant were directly ahead of him about thirty meters away.

Richard's passive scan flickered as the Power sources in the cohort fluctuated. The cadets and their TAC officers saw him. So far, none of the security guards had noticed the presence of Sheeta, Sheeba, or him behind them.

During his freshman year at the Academy, Nickelo had devised a game where the cadets could practice their stealth shields and scans. In the game, the attacking cadets would mark the defending cadets with the attacker's Power frequency. Once a defender was marked, the other cadets could tell the defender had been discovered.

Richard reached out with a line of Power and marked one of the gunners in a light chain-gun crew. He targeted the gunner's spinal cord and wrapped it with Power. He did not apply pressure, but merely kept the Power in standby mode ready to go with the merest thought. Richard didn't attempt to stealth his line of Power. He intended for the other cadets and their TAC officers to sense what he was doing.

A line of Power reached out from one of the cadets in formation. The line of Power marked a crewman in one of the rocket-launcher batteries. Richard recognized the frequency of the Power. It was Jerad. Within seconds, three more lines of Power reached out and marked other members of the blue-suited security force. The Power frequencies belonged to Tam, Telsa, and Stella. Soon, other lines of Power reached out from both the cadets and their TAC officers until over half of the security guards were marked. The conglomerate forces appeared to be unaware of their danger.

You've got a situation here, Rick, cautioned Nickelo. *If you make the wrong move, a lot of cadets will die. So could you for that matter.*

Richard had hoped the commandant would take the lead at this point. But after an initial glance at Richard, the commandant went back to his discussion with the spaceport commander.

Richard concentrated on the group near the commandant. Using his battle helmet's external sound receivers, Richard keyed in on the group's conversation.

"I'll give you another minute," said the spaceport commander. "Then I'll give the command to open fire."

"We're not exactly helpless," said TAC Officer Myers. "You'll be the first one to die if it comes to that."

"Just because I'm not a wizard scout doesn't mean I'm afraid to die," said the spaceport commander. "But I don't think it will come to that. I don't believe you would risk your cadets in a hopeless battle. They could possibly standup to my infantry. However, your cadets would be decimated by my armor."

"What armor is that?" Richard shouted over his battle helmet's external speakers.

As Richard spoke, his spirit-horse began walking forward. The stallion's hooves didn't quite touch the ground. Richard activated his phase rod. He felt the familiar recoil as the brerellium rod shot out of the handle. The red arcs of phase energy crawling along its length showed up well in the darkness.

Richard leveled his M63 in the direction of the spaceport commander. Sheeta and Sheba paced the spirit-horse while walking a meter above the ground on either side of the stallion. Richard could feel the emotions of their hunger emanating from the dolgars. Combined with the feeling of hunger coming from the demon presence in his phase rod, Richard wasn't surprised when some of the nearest conglomerate guards began backing away. Two of the guards actually dropped their weapons and began running.

At the same time, soldiers began hastily climbing out of the hatches of their armored vehicles. Richard heard the echo of several plasma rounds from inside a nearby cat. It was followed by the sound of a wolf howling. Shortly thereafter, a soldier exited a cat so fast he fell all the way to the ground. Richard heard the crack of a leg bone snapping.

A second later, a white dolgar emerged from the top of the cat. It was Snowy. She looked over at Richard with an expression that seemed to say, 'Mission complete. My prey has been flushed out of its hiding place'.

It's still dangerous, Nickelo warned. *One spark will ignite a battle. Watch yourself.*

Richard wasn't sure what to do at this point. Finesse was not his strongest quality. Fortunately, the commandant chose that moment to take charge of the situation by speaking to the conglomerate soldiers.

Amplified by his battle helmet's external speakers, the commandant's voice carried to everyone within five hundred meters. "I've been patient. But this charade ends now. Those wolf-looking creatures are dolgars. They live in the void. None of your weapons can harm them."

That's not true, said Nickelo. *Phase weapons can hurt them even in the void. It just can't hurt them if they're completely shifted into another dimension.*

Hush, Nickelo, Richard said. *The commandant knows what he's doing. He's just bluffing.*

"And, the wizard scout on that black beast is the best wizard scout in the galaxy," said the commandant. "On top of that, this cohort is composed of fully-trained wizard scouts. Even now, they and my TAC officers have targeted over half of you with their Power. With the merest thought, your spinal cords will be torn apart. You'll be paralyzed for the rest of your life."

The commandant turned to the spaceport commander. "General Williams. You were once a cadet in the pre-Academy. You know I speak the truth. Without your heavy armor, you're outgunned. Pull back your troops. We're on the same side. We wish your troops no harm. But..., the DNA Center belongs to the Academy until the end of the week. That was the agreement made between the members of the Imperial High Council. And that agreement will be honored."

CHAPTER 45

The standoff at the DNA Center didn't end immediately. There were more threats and counter-threats. But in the end, the Deloris Conglomerate's security troops withdrew to await orders from their higher-ups. The commandant didn't allow them to take their crew-served weapons or armor. Once the blue-suits left, TAC Officer Myers wasted no time in assigning part of the cadets to their newly acquired equipment.

The dolgars soon became bored and departed. Richard tried to convince them to stay, but for all he knew, they didn't understand his words. In any regard, they left. The spirit-horse departed with them.

"Gaston," said the commandant. "I want half the cohort inside. The other half will remain on guard. The conglomerate will not take this sitting down. We can't waste a moment."

Richard's platoon was assigned to the group on guard duty. In less than an hour, the first half of the cadets had finished. The group on guard was relieved in place by the cadets who had just gotten their DNA baselines. Richard sensed no difference in those cadets. They seemed the same as they had been before they'd gotten their baselines.

As Richard started to enter the DNA Center, the commandant stopped him. "Not you, cadet 832. Not just yet."

"Sir?" Richard said. He was confused. If not for him, none of the cadets would be getting a DNA baseline. *Am I being left out*, he wondered.

"Chief Instructor Winslow wants you to go last," said the commandant. "She'll explain later."

When Richard hesitated at the door, the commandant said, "Trust me, Rick."

Richard nodded his head in acceptance. He did trust the commandant. For whatever reason, Richard had developed a deep affection for the old man. Richard did an about face and took his place back on the perimeter.

By the time the second half of the cohort exited the DNA Center, a large force of armored vehicles could be seen massing on the far side of the spaceport.

"Cadet 832," shouted one of the TAC officers. "The commandant wants you inside. Now!"

"Sir! Yes, sir!" Richard said as he ran towards the DNA Center's main door.

From the looks of things, we don't have much time, said Nickelo. *The conglomerate's going to be making their move soon.*

I know, Nick, Richard said. *I'm hurrying.*

Once inside, Richard found the commandant with Chief Instructor Winslow and TAC Officer Myers.

"Sir! Cadet 832–" Richard began.

"No time for formalities, Rick," said the commandant. "Listen closely."

The commandant nodded his head at Chief Instructor Winslow. "Harriet?"

"Cadet 832," said Chief Instructor Winslow. "You're receiving your DNA baseline last because of your third Power reserve. We've never seen anything like it. We can't even determine its size. We intended to conduct additional testing on you today to find out more information before your baseline. Unfortunately, we don't have the time now."

Richard thought the chief instructor looked apologetic. He also thought she looked very concerned.

"I'm sorry," said the chief instructor, "but we're forced to proceed with what we already know."

"That's fine with me, sir," Richard said.

"They haven't told you everything, cadet," said TAC Officer

Myers.

"Gaston–" started the commandant.

"He has a right to know, sir," said TAC Officer Myers.

"Know what?" Richard said. When TAC Officer Myers glared at him, Richard added a hasty, "Sir."

"First off," said TAC Officer Myers, "no one in the cohort got adequate rest last night. Their baselines have been set based upon their current state. That means they'll always be a little tired. Their selfheal will constantly return them to baseline regardless of how much rest they get."

"You've gotten even less sleep," said Chief Instructor Winslow. "And I'll bet you haven't eaten today. If you receive you DNA baseline right now, you'll always be a little tired and hungry. Are you sure you want to proceed?"

Why are they asking, Nick? Richard said. *I didn't go through the last five years of hell for nothing.*

"Normally," said the commandant, "we would have a cadet not meeting optimum specifications wait until the following year. There may not be a next year in your case. That's why we're letting you make the decision."

"Are you asking me if I want to get my DNA baseline, sir?" Richard said. "Of course, I do. If I don't get it today, I'll probably be dead soon anyway. I'd rather be a little tired and hungry than dead."

"Fine then," said the commandant. "Harriet?"

"Not so fast, sir," said TAC Officer Myers. "You haven't explained the danger."

What's his problem? Richard thought. *He's determined to prevent me from becoming a wizard scout.*

"We don't have time for this, Gaston," said the commandant. "The counterattack will be coming soon."

"Make time, sir," said TAC Officer Myers through gritted teeth. "At least give him a chance to make a decision based upon facts. I've seen you make too many decisions based upon nothing more than blind obedience to instructions from '*the One*'."

The commandant's face turned red, but only for a moment. Almost immediately, he got control of his emotions before they got out of hand. Once he looked like he was back in control, the commandant turned to Richard.

"You're the first person to get a DNA baseline with multiple Power reserves," said the commandant.

"In fact," said Chief Instructor Winslow, "I haven't found any documentation in the tele-network on anybody with two, much less three, Power reserves. That makes you an unknown."

"It makes you dangerous," said TAC Officer Myers. "For all they know–"

"We'll handle this, Gaston," interrupted the commandant.

TAC Officer Myers glared at the commandant, but he said nothing further.

"Your TAC officer is right, cadet 832," said Chief Instructor Winslow. "Our systems were not designed to deal with multiple Power reserves. Also, your third Power reserve has a strange design. It's almost as if it's been created specifically for your selfheal ability. It should be very efficient, but…"

"But, the size of the reserve is unknown," said the commandant. "Harriet believes it is quite large. Possibly several times larger than your two current Power reserves combined."

"Isn't that a good thing?" Richard said. Extra Power sounded like a blessing to him. He was tired of always running short of Power.

"Not if the DNA Center's systems can't handle the load," said TAC Officer Myers. "Let me clue you in on something, cadet. '*The One*' does what's best for its self-proclaimed mission. It could care less what side effects the pursuit of its mission may have on you."

The commandant started to speak, but TAC Officer Myers raised his hand to stop him. Surprisingly, the commandant remained silent.

"Don't be stupid, cadet," said TAC Officer Myers. "Do you think you have multiple Power reserves by accident? You can bet '*the One*' planned it that way. Your Power reserve has been divided into three parts on purpose. You can rest assured it wasn't for your benefit. Do you know how many wizard scouts have been emp-healers?"

Richard didn't want to listen to his TAC officer. From the very first day, Myers had hated him. But Richard didn't trust '*the One*' any more than he trusted his TAC officer. Richard wanted to know more, but he was unwilling to verbally acknowledge TAC Officer Myers might have a valid point. Richard compromised by shaking his head in a negative motion.

"None," TAC Officer Myers said. "Out of the thousands of wizard scout healers in the last eight hundred years, exactly zero has been emp-healers. That is, until you."

TAC Officer Myers waited as if expecting Richard to respond in some manner. When Richard hesitated to reply, TAC Officer Myers tried a different tack.

"Very well," said TAC Officer Myers. "What about your primary Power reserve? It's the smallest of any known wizard scout. Do you think that's an accident?"

Again, Richard kept silent.

"No, it wasn't an accident," said TAC Officer Myers. "It was made small by 'the One' on purpose. It's trying to force you to act the way it wants you to act. And, this mysterious third Power reserve. Do you even comprehend what this means? It means you probably had a single, large Power reserve until 'the One' got hold of it. From what Chief Instructor Winslow tells me, the size of your third Power reserve may be the largest reserve she's ever seen. It's off the scales of her equipment. You might have been the most powerful wizard scout ever, but 'the One' decided to split your reserve into three parts. Why? And, why is the largest of your Power reserves designed to only work with your selfheal ability?"

Richard didn't even bother shaking his head this time. He hated his TAC officer for bringing the information up. And, he hated 'the One' for trying to manipulate him.

"Think about it, cadet," said TAC Officer Myers. "If most of your Power is designed to work with your selfheal ability, it's probably because 'the One' is going to send you on missions where you'll take a lot of damage. You may complete your mission, but at what cost to you?"

"I think that's enough, Gaston," said the commandant.

"Not quite, sir," said TAC Officer Myers. "I've one final thing to say. Do yourself a favor, cadet 832. Save yourself a lot of pain and agony. Tell 'the One' to stick its DNA baseline where the sun doesn't shine. You're a decent fighter. Go back to your marine recon. You'll be a whole lot happier."

The commandant, the chief instructor, and Richard's TAC officer all looked at him expectantly.

I calculate a ninety-two percent probability everything TAC

Officer Myers said is true, said Nickelo. 'The One' *probably has designed your Power reserves to guide you into some desired action. What do you want to do?*

Indeed, Richard wondered. *What do I want to do?* Richard wasn't sure. But, he knew he was the only one who could make the decision. He also knew he needed to make it quick. For all he knew, the conglomerate might be starting their attack even now.

Not yet, Rick, said Nickelo. *But, I think they'll attack soon.*

Richard looked at Chief Instructor Winslow. "What are we waiting for, sir? I'm ready. Hook me up."

The commandant nodded his head approvingly. TAC Officer Myers gave him a disgusted look before stomping out of the room.

Without giving Richard a chance to change his mind, the chief instructor had two of her technicians lead Richard to a complicated looking chair. They began strapping him into the device. The technicians had Richard unseal his battle suit and open the top to expose his chest. They stuck needle threads into various parts of his chest and neck. The technicians let Richard keep his battle helmet on his head, but they made him keep it in half mode.

One of the technicians, John, came over with a glass and something folded in a napkin. John handed them to Richard. When Richard unfolded the napkin, he saw it contained a sandwich.

"It's simulated roast beef," said John. "It was supposed to be my lunch, but I think you may need it more than me." John pointed at the glass of liquid. "It's only water, but we have plenty of it. You'd better hydrate while you have the chance."

It won't do you any good at this point, Rick, said Nickelo. *There's not enough time for your body to hydrate or to digest that sandwich. It's just wasted effort on your part.*

Richard thanked John and took a bite out of the sandwich to spite his battle computer. With the first bite, Richard realized how hungry he was. He didn't care if he had time to digest it or not. He was hungry, and the sandwich tasted good. For good measure, Richard drained the glass of water dry. John hastily refilled his glass.

By the time Richard finished his sandwich and drank another glass of water, the technicians had finished prepping him for his DNA baseline. Without further ado, the technicians took his empty glass and napkin and left the room.

Richard realized he was now alone in a room full of machinery. He also noticed that a vial filled with a red, swirling liquid was attached to the top of a nearby piece of apparatus. A clear tube ran from the apparatus to a needle thread in the left side of his chest near his heart.

Looking to his left, Richard saw Chief Instructor Winslow in a room on the other side of a large, glass window. He also saw John conversing with a handful of other technicians in the same room. They were all poring over several consoles with all sorts of flashing lights. Chief Instructor Winslow looked out the window and noticed Richard watching. She gave him an encouraging smile. Then she mouthed the word 'activate' to one of the technicians.

The red liquid sped down the tube and into Richard's chest. He stiffened in his chair. Richard didn't feel pain so much as he felt a sense of strangeness. His mind seemed to lose its grip on reality. Richard wanted to float away, but Nickelo kept calling him back.

Richard had grown used to having Nickelo in his mind over the past three years. But he now felt his battle computer's thoughts shifting into a separate region of his mind. The rest of his mind was his own, but the separate area was now shared with his battle computer.

An image of the outside of the DNA Center flashed into Richard's mind. It wasn't so much a visual image as it was the knowledge of the data Nickelo obtained from the image. Richard interpreted the data as showing the cohort deployed in a defensive position around the DNA Center. Richard noticed the beginnings of movement on the other side of the spaceport. The conglomerate was making its move.

A series of hot flashes ran through Richard's body. This time, the strange feeling hurt. It hurt a lot. Richard screamed. In spite of his pain, Richard noticed a flurry of activity in the room behind the glass window.

Is that smoke? Richard wondered. He noticed yellow and red flames leaping out of one of the technicians' computer screens. Almost immediately, two more screens burst into flames. Suddenly, the room's automated fire-suppressor system activated. Clouds of some type of smoky gas filled the room with the glass window.

Another, more intense, series of flashes swept through

Richard's body. He heard the sound of a tortured animal screaming. The voice sounded familiar. Finally, Richard blacked out.

*　　*　　*

Wake up, Rick, said Nickelo. *Come on, buddy. You can do it.*
Nick? Richard thought.
There was no reply.
Rick, answer me, said Nickelo
I am, Nick, Richard thought. He didn't understand why his battle computer wasn't hearing him. Then it hit him. Richard shifted his thoughts to their shared space.
I'm here, Nick, Richard thought.
Thank the Creator, said Nickelo. *I thought I'd lost you.*
What happened? Richard said sending the question into their shared space.
What didn't? said Nickelo. *But never mind that now. Can you walk? If so, you could help your friends out.*
Richard grew aware of his surroundings. He was bouncing up and down. Opening his eyes, Richard saw Stella and Jerad each holding onto one of his arms and legs. They were carrying him as they ran. Jerad lost his grip on Richard's leg. It dragged the ground for a second before he grabbed it again.
"I'm awake," Richard said. "I can walk."
"Good," said Stella as she released her hold on him. "Battle suit heavy."
Jerad released his side as well, and Richard fell the short distance to the ground. His battle suit easily absorbed the shock.
"Don't walk," said Jerad. "I'd advise running. We're making a tactical withdrawal back to the hover-tram station."
Richard got to his feet and began running alongside his friends. His battle suit kept up easily with them. They were unarmored after all.
Risking a glance behind him, Richard saw dozens of cats and other armored vehicles swarming around a distant DNA Center.
"Was anyone hurt?" Richard asked anxiously.
"No," said Jerad. "The commandant ordered our withdrawal a couple of minutes before the conglomerate's armor got there. TAC

Officer Myers and the commandant stayed behind to sort things out. We've been ordered back to the airfield."

"All transportation has been shut down," Richard said. He wasn't sure why they were running if there was nowhere to go.

"I suspect the crisis is over," said Jerad. "We've got our DNA baselines already. Nothing the Deloris Conglomerate can do will get back their precious DNA gas. They'll just have to wait another year to refine some new gas."

Using his passive scan, Richard sensed the lifeforms of his cohort around him. They were all within a two hundred meter radius of his position.

"Everyone's slowing down," Richard said growing concerned. "The conglomerate will be after us. Shouldn't we set up some kind of defense?"

Jerad and Stella slowed their pace to a fast walk in order to match the pace of the other cadets.

"Relax," said Jerad. "They won't be pursuing us. They've no reason. We're wizard scouts now. All we're missing is our shiny gold dragon pins to make it official."

"Yeah," agreed Tam who had just jogged up with Telsa. "We're Empire assets now. The conglomerate gains nothing by fighting with us. In a few days' time, we'll all be on the frontlines preventing the big, bad Crosioians from coming to Velos and kicking the conglomerate's scrawny little butt."

Richard wasn't as confident of the situation as his friends, but he had a lot of respect for Jerad's judgement. If Jerad said the crisis was over, then Richard suspected the crisis was over.

Apparently Jerad was right, because within thirty minutes, they were in a hover-tram heading back to the airfield. No one had tried to stop them.

Once the hover-tram started moving, Richard and his friends settled into their seats. Telsa touched Richard on the arm to get his attention.

"You about scared the daylights out of me, Rick," said Telsa with a half grin. "You didn't tell me your spirit-horse was some nightmare straight out of hell."

"Yeah," said Tam. "And coming up out of the ground like that. It's one thing to hear you tell us about it. It's another to see it in person."

413

"Well, it turned the tide," said Jerad. With a grin, he added, "Remind me not to get on your bad side, Rick."

Richard blushed. He didn't like his friend's making a big deal out of it. Their attention didn't seem right. Richard decided to change the subject.

"I saw a fire in the DNA Center before I blacked out," Richard said.

"We heard about the fire, Rick," said Telsa. "I heard one of the techs say you blew out half the systems in the DNA Center. It apparently had something to do with your Power reserve. The tech I spoke with said their systems just couldn't handle the load."

Nick? Richard thought.

No reply.

Richard shifted his thoughts to the shared space in his mind. *Nick?*

Your friend has the facts straight, said Nickelo. *That third Power reserve of yours is massive. If your primary reserve was a pond, and your secondary reserve was a puddle, your third Power reserve would be a major lake or small sea. Unfortunately for you, the Power in your third reserve can only be used to selfheal.*

That's good. Right? Richard said. *I mean, it's a good thing I can probably selfheal a lot.*

I guess we'll see, Rick, said Nickelo.

After a few more minutes of banter with his friends, Richard yawned and leaned back in his seat. Within moments, he was sound asleep.

CHAPTER 46

The jar of the hover-tram coming to a stop woke Richard. He looked around him. His friends must have taken a nap as well, because they all looked a little sleepy-eyed. That is, except for Stella. The Sterilian race didn't have eyelids. They just had clear eye covers that changed positions to protect the eye. Richard had never really figured out how to tell whether Stella was staring at him or whether she was just sleeping.

Richard stretched and gave a big yawn. "I was tired. I hope the nap helps."

"It won't for long," said Telsa. "Your selfheal will see your rest as an injury and be trying to return your body to its baseline. Unfortunately for all of us, our baselines are a little bit tired since we didn't get sufficient rest last night."

"It figures," Richard said. "So much for the great selfheal abilities we've been told about for the last five years."

"Oh, you'll appreciate it more when you take a plasma round to the head," said Tam with a laugh. "Then you'll be down on your knees thanking your selfheal ability for making the booboo better. I know I will."

Once they unloaded from the hover-tram, they made their way out of the station. Richard was surprised to see six utility buses waiting for them.

"Compliments of TAC Officer Myers," said one of the drivers.

"You're wizard scouts now," grinned the driver. "Cadets can walk. Wizard scouts are too valuable to waste time walking."

Tam laughed. "I can get used to this."

The cohort loaded onto the utility buses and headed towards the tent-cantonment area. Richard sat near his friends. It suddenly hit him they might not be together much longer. A sense of sadness swept over him. He'd come to depend on them during the last three years of Academy training.

Richard was tempted to say something about their pending separation, but he'd never been very good at touchy-feely stuff. He finally opted to talk about a different subject.

"I wonder if they'll feed us when we get back," Richard said. "I'm kind of hungry."

"I seriously doubt it, Rick," said Jerad. "They fed us a large meal before we left for the spaceport. Actually, I'd have to force myself to eat something right now. I'm not hungry at all."

"When did you eat last, Rick?" said Telsa. She sounded a little concerned.

Richard requested the time from his battle computer using their shared space. An immediate readout came back.

"The sergeant of the guard gave us a light supper before our first shift," Richard said. "I guess it's been about fourteen hours now." A thought occurred to him. "Oh, one of the techs gave me a sandwich while they were strapping me into the seat."

I told you that didn't count, said Nickelo.

"That wouldn't help," said Telsa. "Your DNA baseline is based upon your body's cells. They should've fed you around midnight or so." Shaking her head as if hating to give bad news, she added, "I'm sorry to tell you, but however you feel now is how you'll feel for the rest of your life."

Richard was as sorry to hear it as his friend was to say it. He took a minute to evaluate himself. It wasn't like he was starving or anything. But he could feel the hint of an empty spot in his belly. His body was sending him signals telling him it was getting close to time to eat again. He was also a little tired. He wasn't overly so. He'd functioned on a lot less sleep on many a night during his time at the Academy. His mind was clear, and he had plenty of energy. He just felt as if a short nap would be nice.

This is just great, Richard thought sarcastically.

For once, he didn't get a snide response from his battle computer. Then he remembered he didn't have the thought in their shared space.

Good, Richard thought. *I can finally have secrets again.*

A short time later, the buses pulled up near the cantonment area's gate. TAC Officer Myers and the other TAC officers were there waiting for them.

"What's he doing here?" Richard said. "I thought he stayed back with the commandant."

"I told you," said Jerad. "The crisis is over. The teleporters must be working locally again."

Myers, Richard thought disgustedly. *It's just one bit of good news after another.*

"Outside, you wizard scout newbies," yelled one of the TAC officers. "The commandant wants everyone to draw their battle helmets out of the armory to make sure your shared spaces are working correctly."

"Why didn't they just have the buses take us to the armory?" Richard said to Jerad as they exited the bus. "We were already on them."

"Do you have something to say, cadet 832?" shouted TAC Officer Myers. "You've already proven to me what a brilliant mind you have today. Perhaps you can enlighten the rest of your cohort with some of your wisdom?"

The beast that was Richard's anger roared. He tried to keep his anger under control, but he only partially succeeded.

"I said why didn't you just have the buses take us there?" Richard said. "We were already on them."

"Cadets will begin and end all comments to their TAC officers with the word 'sir'," said TAC Officer Myers. "You've got extra duty tonight, cadet."

The beast that was Richard's anger roared again and broke out of its cage. Richard said, "Kiss my ass."

TAC Officer Myers' faced turned a bright red. He stuttered as if trying to find the right words. All that came out was, "What did you say?"

"I said I've put up with your crap for five years, Myers" Richard said. "And I'm done. You don't want to give me one of your precious gold-dragon insignias? Fine, it's no big deal. You want to court martial me and send me to the military prison on Diajor? Great. It'll probably be a luxury hotel compared to being in the Academy and having to deal with you every day. I'm done with it. Sir!"

Richard expected his TAC officer to try and stop his tirade at some point, but he didn't. In fact, after his TAC officer's initial display of anger, Richard noticed TAC Officer Myers' expression relax. It was almost as if something he'd been hoping for had occurred.

"Well, well," said TAC Officer Myers with an evil grin. "It never fails. There's always one new wizard scout in the group who thinks the rules no longer apply. And, he or she has to be taught the new rules of the road. I should've figured it would be you, 832."

TAC Officer Myers snorted, "Ha! The commandant was a fool to waste his time on–"

"Leave the commandant out of this, Myers," Richard said. "He's a great man, and you aren't worth spit compared to him."

Instead of shouting or growing angry, TAC Officer Myers said, "Platoon sergeants, march your platoons to the pit. I think it's time to show you how wizard scouts settle their differences.

*   *   *

The pit was a circular hole in the ground two meters deep and twenty meters across. Richard stood in the bottom on one side of the pit, and TAC Officer Myers stood in the bottom on the other. The pit was filled with ankle-deep, muddy water left over from the last rainstorm. The smell was not pleasant.

The cohort stood around the perimeter of the pit looking down. Both TAC Officer Myers and Richard were still in their battle suits. Richard had previously put his M63 back in his dimensional pack, but he still had his other weapons.

TAC Officer Myers removed his battle helmet and utility belt. He handed them to one of the other TAC officers standing on the rim of the pit. Richard did the same with his, except he handed them to Jerad. He also gave his friend his dimensional pack and 9mm pistol with its shoulder holster.

Next, TAC Officer Myers removed the top half of his battle suit, but he kept on the bottom. Richard followed his lead.

Richard noticed the muscles on his TAC officer's stomach. Despite his dislike for his TAC officer, Richard had to admit Myers was solid muscle. Richard unconsciously touched his own stomach. He could feel the tight muscles underneath, but there was a thin layer of soft tissue on top that wasn't quite muscle.

I told you to exercise during our last mission for 'the One', said Nickelo who must have guessed Richard's thoughts. *But, no. You were too busy to be bothered. You haven't had enough time since you've been back to get your body back into optimum physical condition. Now you never will.*

Whatever, Richard said. His anger was still loose, but he was starting to calm down a little. Richard had no doubt he was going to have his hands full with his TAC officer.

"The rules are simple," said TAC Officer Myers speaking to the other cadets as much as he was speaking to Richard. "Wizard scouts don't kill each other when settling differences. Other than that, there're no rules."

TAC Officer Myers gestured at Richard. "Anytime you think you're ready, cadet."

Richard reached out with his mind and pulled a sandbag off the top of the pit's rim behind TAC Officer Myers. Richard aimed the sandbag for his TAC officer's head. At the same time, Richard ran across the empty space separating TAC Officer Myers from him. Water splashed high in the air as he ran.

A line of Power reached out from TAC Officer Myers and deflected the sandbag off to the side. Richard's TAC officer didn't run to intercept him. Instead, Richard's TAC Officer sent a line of Power out and downward into the water between them. Richard noticed the line of Power flatten out and then suddenly shoot upwards. A geyser of mud and water erupted in front of Richard.

Richard closed his eyes, but he didn't get his Power up in time to deflect the muddy water with telekinesis. For a split-second, Richard wondered why Nickelo hadn't helped him deflect the water. Then he remembered their shared space. Nickelo couldn't hear him think anymore unless he specifically thought in the shared space. As the water and mud splattered on his face, Richard had a sudden insight that adapting to the shared-space concept was going to take some practice. Richard began to appreciate the previous intermixing of minds with his battle computer.

Although blinded by the muddy water, Richard sensed movement of a lifeform with his passive scan. He knew it was his TAC officer rushing towards him. Richard twisted to the side. The edge of TAC Officer Myers' boot grazed the bare skin along his ribcage. Some of the skin and meat were torn away. Ignoring the pain, Richard kicked upward with one leg in hopes of catching his TAC officer off balance. He wasn't surprised when his kick met thin air.

Being blind sucks, he thought.

Richard was surprised when the pain in his side eased a little. He sensed Power from his third reserve touching his side. His injury was still tender, but he assumed it was already starting to heal.

Reaching out with his mind again, Richard attempted to grab hold of TAC Officer Myers' leg. A line of Power met his and knocked his Power aside. A series of blows from his TAC officer's fists caught Richard in the chest, stomach, and face. Richard hit the muddy water at the bottom of the pit face down. When Richard came up, he spit out two teeth along with a mouthful of blood.

Sensing his TAC officer's location, Richard did a sweep with his right leg. By some miracle, Richard's leg made contact with something hard. Richard heard a splash. His TAC officer had fallen.

Richard risked taking a second to wipe the muddy water from his eyes. His vision cleared just in time to see another fist heading for his face. Richard dodged to the left and caught his TAC officer's wrist in an arm-lock. Richard twisted downward with both hands. He was rewarded with the satisfying sound of bones snapping. His TAC officer let out a low-pitched groan.

Before Richard could follow up his advantage, TAC Officer Myers gave him a head-butt in the nose. Richard almost blacked out. But almost immediately, he felt Power from his third reserve transfer to his face and begin healing his nose and mouth. The pain was still enough to make his eyes water, but he didn't lose consciousness.

Chief Instructor Winslow had told him ninety percent of an injury would heal quickly, but the remainder might take some time to heal. Richard now knew what she meant. His side was almost, but not quite healed. He needed to delay his TAC officer in order to give his latest injuries time to heal.

Richard caught TAC Officer Myers in the belly with his knee. Air rushed out in a gush. However, his TAC officer shot out his left fist and caught Richard just below the sternum. Richard bent over in pain.

Nick! Richard groaned into his shared space.

Fortunately, Richard didn't need to be wearing his helmet for his battle computer to control his suit. The legs of the battle suit kicked backwards. The strength of the battle suit's assistors flung Richard out of range of his TAC officer's fists.

As soon as Richard hit the water, he sensed a line of Power reaching out from TAC Officer Myers towards his chest. Richard used his own Power to deflect his TAC officer's Power to the side.

Within the space of five seconds, Richard traded attacks and counterattacks with his TAC officer. Neither of them was able to get through the other's defenses.

He's faster than I am, Richard thought into his shared space.

You've got to work your strengths, Nickelo replied.

Fine, Richard thought. *He said no rules. So be it.*

Richard rushed forward to the attack. TAC Officer Myers ran forward to meet him halfway. Before they got within range of each other's fists, Richard reached out with his Power once more. As he did so, he sensed his TAC officer preparing his Power to counter any attack. But instead of attempting to touch his TAC officer with his Power, Richard sent it towards the link between TAC Officer Myers and his Power reserve.

As soon as Richard's Power touched his TAC officer's link, Richard knew he had him. The link was unprotected. No traps, nothing. Richard chose a convenient weak spot and used his Power to twist the link back on itself. The flow of Power from TAC Officer Myers' Power reserve was immediately cutoff. Richard noticed his TAC officer stumble.

Surprise! Richard thought.

TAC Officer Myers kicked out with a leg at Richard's face. Richard wrapped the leg with Power to slow it down. This time, his TAC officer was unable to intercept Richard's Power. As Richard slowed TAC Officer Myers' leg, he kicked out with his own leg and caught TAC Officer Myers on the side of the face. Several teeth flew out of Myers' mouth along with a liberal supply of blood. TAC Officer Myers fell to the water on his hands and knees.

Richard looked down at his TAC officer kneeling in the water with blood pouring out of his mouth. Without Power, his TAC officer couldn't selfheal.

Richard felt the inside of his own mouth with his tongue. His two teeth had already been replaced. Richard gained a newfound respect for his selfheal ability. He had a feeling the pain in his TAC officer's mouth was making him miss his own ability to selfheal.

Shifting into the void, Richard knelt down beside TAC Officer Myers.

"It sucks not having Power, doesn't it, Myers," Richard said. "How do you like being helpless?"

TAC Officer Myers struck out with a fist, but it passed right through Richard. He was in the void. Myers couldn't touch him.

"Here's what's going to happen, Myers," Richard whispered into his TAC officer's ear. "I'm going to wrap your heart in Power. And I'm going to give it a little squeeze for every time you treated me like dirt."

Richard used his telekinesis to lift his TAC officer's chin so he could look into his eyes. There was no fear in TAC Officer Myers' eyes, just anger.

"Oh, don't worry, sir..." Richard said stressing the word 'sir'. "I'm not going to kill you. Those were the rules, right? But, I'm going to make you think twice before you pick out another whipping boy to bully around."

TAC Officer Myers yelled in rage and swung out with his fists. Both fists passed through Richard just like before. He was still in the void. Richard was proud of himself. He'd gotten a lot more efficient with dimensional shifts during the last year. Plus, his Power usage appeared to be more efficient since he'd gotten his baseline. Richard estimated he could stay shifted in the void for three or four minutes if necessary. Richard smiled. It would be more than enough time to teach his TAC officer a lesson in humility.

TAC Officer Myers made a sudden move downward with his left hand. Richard ignored the move. Whatever his TAC officer had in mind would prove futile. He was still in the void. His TAC officer couldn't touch him.

Rick! came a cry from Nickelo in their shared space. *Your knife!*

A split-second too late, Richard realized his danger. He hadn't removed his boot knife. Richard began pushing with his telekinesis in an attempt to prevent his TAC officer from reaching his knife. It was the knife Sergeant Hendricks had made for him. It was the knife with a creallium edge to its blade. It was the knife that existed in both the physical dimension and the void between dimensions. In spite of Richard's effort, the knife came out of its sheath in TAC Officer Myers' hand. The blade of the knife plunged into Richard's chest straight into his heart.

Richard had felt pain before, but nothing like the pain he felt now. All thoughts of telekinesis melted away. All that existed was the pain in his chest. Richard felt Power from his third reserve wrapping around his heart as his body tried to selfheal and return to its baseline. TAC Officer Myers jiggled the knife a little. He effectively damaged Richard's heart as fast as his Power could heal it. Richard could do nothing but groan while wishing the pain would end.

TAC Officer Myers shifted his grip on the knife blade. The knife handle was still in the void, so Richard's TAC officer was gripping the knife by the blade. Blood poured out of his TAC officer's clenched fist, but Myers didn't loosen his grip. He leaned close to Richard's ear.

"Now here's how it's going to work, 832," said TAC Officer Myers. "You're going to fix whatever you did to my Power link. And..., if you don't, we're both going to stay right here while I jiggle this knife of yours every few seconds."

The knife in Richard's chest moved a little causing more damage and more pain. Richard's Power struggled to completely heal his heart, but it couldn't do so while the creallium blade was still in it.

"In a couple of minutes, your primary Power reserve will be empty," said TAC Officer Myers. "Then you won't be able to maintain your shift in the void anymore. That's when I'll show you what real pain is."

Richard's TAC officer jiggled the knife blade once again. White-hot pain swept through Richard.

"It sucks not having Power, doesn't it?" said TAC Officer

Myers using Richard's own words against him. "How do you like being helpless?"

TAC Officer Myers paused again, but he didn't wiggle the knife this time. Richard wondered why. He had a thought that he probably would have if the situation had been reversed.

"So what's it going to be, 832?" said TAC Officer Myers. "Fix my link? Or do you want to become more familiar with this knife?"

The pain was beginning to fade a little since the knife was not being moved. It still hurt like all get out, but it was bearable. Richard wondered if he could use his telekinesis to disable his TAC officer before Myers could retaliate with the knife.

Rick, said Nickelo as if guessing Richard's thoughts. *He won fair and square. He's purposely stopped moving the knife to give you time to think. Don't be stupid.*

Richard didn't reply to his battle computer. However, he did reach out with his Power and undo the kink in his TAC officer's link. As soon as he did, he felt TAC Officer Myers pull the knife out of his chest. Richard slumped over holding both hands to his chest.

Neither of them moved or spoke for several seconds as they each waited for their Power to selfheal their injuries. TAC Officer Myers recovered first.

Richard's TAC officer leaned close and whispered, "And you're right. I'm not worth spit compared to the commandant."

Richard looked up. He noticed a strange look in his TAC officer's eyes.

"I should know," said TAC Officer Myers. "The commandant is my father."

With those words, TAC Officer Myers rose and walked to the center of the pit. In a loud voice, he spoke to the cadets gathered around the rim of the pit.

"And that's how wizard scouts settle their differences," said TAC Officer Myers.

Richard was still kneeling in the muddy water. The worst of the pain was gone, but the feeling in his chest was anything but pleasant. The shock of his TAC officer's revelation was almost as bad as the pain.

Myers? Richard thought. *Is he really the commandant's son?*

How can that be?

Richard heard TAC Officer Myers walking towards him until he was only a few steps away. Richard had no trouble hearing his TAC officer's next words.

"And..., when the wizard scouts leave the pit," said TAC Officer Myers, "their differences stay in the pit behind them never to be brought up again.

TAC Officer Myers stuck out his right hand towards Richard. "What about it, Wizard Scout Richard Shepard? Are you ready to leave the pit?"

Richard was poised between two courses of action. The beast that was his temper had been put back inside its cage, but it was still snarling furiously. Another voice seemed to be urging Richard to accept his TAC officer's peace offering.

Struggling to his feet, Richard half-walked half-stumbled to a position just in front of TAC Officer Myers. He took his TAC officer's outstretched hand in his.

"Sir!" Richard said. "I'm ready to leave the pit. Sir!"

TAC Officer Myers gave a tightlipped smile and handed Richard back his knife. They left the pit together.

CHAPTER 47

"Here," said Jerad as he handed Richard a fist-sized metal can. "I was saving this for a special occasion, but I don't guess I'll need it now."

Richard took the can from his friend. He read the label. "Hmm. Genuine imitation caviar. Sounds expensive. Are you sure?"

"Go ahead, Rick," said Tam. "You've ate everything else in the tent."

Richard nodded his head. Tam, Telsa, and Stella had joined Jerad and him in their tent after they'd returned from doing their function checks on their battle helmets. The females sat on Jerad's cot, while Jerad and he sat on his.

Popping off the top of the can of caviar, Richard took a sniff. It didn't smell too bad considering it was years-old fake fish eggs. Picking up a handy spoon, Richard dug in.

"If you hadn't eaten those crackers earlier," Tam said with a snicker, "you could've used them now."

"Heck," said Telsa laughing with her usual good nature. "If Myers hadn't ordered you to turn in your equipment to the armory, you could've summoned yourself a feast from that pack of yours."

"Worms better," said Stella. "Fish eggs. Yuk!"

Richard forced himself to take his time eating the caviar. It wasn't as if he was hungry. He just had a constant state of the munchies.

"Well," said Jerad with a shake of his head. "I'd give you something else, Rick, old buddy, but I'm all cleaned out."

Feeling a little embarrassed, Richard said, "Sorry, Jerad. I didn't mean to eat all your stash."

"Don't worry about it," said Jerad. With a little laugh he said, "I really don't feel like eating anyway."

"I don't suppose any of us do," said Telsa. "Nor will we ever again."

"Except vulture," said Stella pointing one of her long fingers at Richard.

Richard happened to have his spoon stuck in his mouth at that very moment. His friends laughed. Richard did too, but only after he finished swallowing the last of the caviar.

"Do you think we could eat if we needed to in order to keep up appearances?" said Tam.

"Sure," said Telsa. "We can eat or drink whatever we want. Our bodies will process the food and liquid normally. We just don't need nutrition in order to stay alive."

"Changing the subject," said Tam. "I don't mind telling you I about laid an egg when Rick told TAC Officer Myers to KMA."

Richard turned a little red. His friends started to laugh again.

"I suppose that wasn't one of my better ideas," Richard admitted.

"You think?" said Tam as she mimicked a dumbfounded look on her face.

That brought another round of laughter.

After it quieted down, Telsa said, "Well, what happens now? Have you heard any news, Jerad? You always seem to know what's going on around here."

Richard scrapped the last of the caviar out of the bottom of the can and stuck it in his mouth. His hunger was momentarily sated, but he had no doubt it would be back in a couple of minutes.

"My sources tell me Chief Instructor Winslow will be bringing some of her instructors here tomorrow," said Jerad. "I think it's for indoctrination training to get us used to using our shared spaces."

"Oh, yeah," Richard said. "That could be useful. Nick and I didn't do such a good job communicating in the pit."

Hey, came a thought from Nickelo in Richard's shared space. *I was doing my part, so don't blame me.*

Whatever, Nick, Richard said back into his shared space.

"It'll come," said Telsa. "I read it just takes a little getting used to before the communication flows naturally."

"You read a lot," Richard said.

"And you don't read enough, Rick," Telsa countered sounding a little touchy.

"I meant that as a compliment, Telsa," Richard said honestly.

"Oh, sorry," said Telsa. "I guess I'm just used to getting ribbed about it."

"Well, not by me," Richard said. "I'm trying to read more myself."

After an awkward moment, Tam said, "Has anybody heard when we'll be blowing this place?"

Before anyone could answer, they all looked towards the tent opening. Their passive scans had picked up the approaching lifeform of one of the roving guards.

The blue-suited guard walked up and peeked into the tent. "Is a cadet 832 there? He's supposed to report to the commandant at the airfield's headquarters building. The message said to tell cadet 832 he needs one final training session."

*   *   *

Richard knocked on the door of the commandant's office.

"Come in, Rick," said the commandant.

Richard entered. The commandant's office at the airfield was furnished exactly like his office back at the Academy.

When the commandant motioned to an empty chair in front of his desk, Richard took a seat. A second chair next to it was already occupied by TAC Officer Myers. As Richard settled back in his seat, his TAC officer and he exchanged terse nods. Neither said anything. Their moment of fellowship in the pit was gone, but Richard didn't sense any lingering hostility on either of their parts. At least there was none from his side.

Well, at least not much, he thought.

That's smart, Rick, said Nickelo. *Let bygones be bygones is my motto.*

Since their non-communication fiasco in the pit, Richard had been trying to do his best to channel non-private thoughts to the space he shared with his battle computer. It wasn't as easy as it sounded, but he thought he was starting to get the hang of it.

"TAC Officer Myers told me about your maneuver with the Power link to his reserve in the pit, Rick," said the commandant.

"Sir. Yes, sir," Richard said.

"This is a training session, Rick," said the commandant. "Please, one sir only."

"Yes, sir," Richard said.

"I thought we'd have more time together, Rick," said the commandant. "But, recent events make it obvious we're probably not going to have that time."

"Yes, sir," Richard said noncommittally. He wasn't sure where the commandant was heading with the training session. He wanted to stay tightlipped until he got a better feel. However, he had enough respect for the commandant to know that whatever he had to say would be important.

"I asked both of you here for a reason," said the commandant. "Janice..., Uh..., Councilwoman Deluth and I have been on forty-two mission for '*the One*' in total. I've only been on twelve of them, so Janice is definitely the more experienced."

The commandant smiled at Richard. "If you ever get a chance to talk to her, you should, Rick. I've told her all about you. She's really an interesting woman. I remember once when–"

"Uh hum," said TAC Officer Myers.

The commandant looked slightly embarrassed. "Oh, quite right, Gaston. I digress. I guess I'm getting old."

The commandant grinned sheepishly. Richard grinned back. He assumed he was supposed to grin. TAC Officer Myers did not grin.

"Well, back to my reason for having you both here," said the commandant. "Both of you are diviners. You specialize in manipulating Power links. This makes you especially good at scans. However, what you did today is not a normal diviner ability, Rick."

The commandant directed his next question at Richard. "When you repaired my Power link in the hangar, did you notice the traps on it?"

"Yes, sir," Richard said giving the safest answer.

"Do you know who put them there, Rick?" said the commandant.

"Uh…, I assumed you did, sir," Richard said.

"Then you assumed wrong, Rick," said the commandant. "Neither Janice nor I have the ability to do such a thing. In fact, as far as I know, no other wizard scout besides you can protect or block Power links."

The commandant gave Richard a moment to mull it over before speaking again. "Janice and I both had our links protected when we were on our last mission in the magical dimension. Until that mission, I assumed only magic users could put traps on Power links. I also assumed only magic users could block links to a Power reserve."

The commandant's comment caught Richard as strange.

"Sir," Richard said, "I'm pretty sure the scout I fought last year was going to try and block the link to my Power reserve. She backed off when she saw it was trapped. I didn't get a chance to probe her link, but I got the feeling it was trapped as well."

"And your point, Rick?" said the commandant.

"Sir, my point is that she was a scout," Richard said. "I assumed since she could block links and set traps that other scouts could as well."

The commandant nodded his head as if considering Richard's opinion. "Hmm. Well, let me tell you what I've found out over the years, Rick," said the commandant. "It's been my experience that only someone from the magical dimension can block a Power link or protect a link with traps. And, they have to be very powerful and skilled in the magical arts. Additionally, I've found the closer you get to the present time in the magical dimension, the less skilled the mages are at manipulating Power links."

"I don't understand, sir," Richard said being as honest as he could. "Some of the mages and scouts I fought the other night had well-protected links to their Power reserves. So did one of the mages I killed at the spaceport."

"Did all of them?" asked the commandant.

"No, sir," Richard admitted. "Some were poorly protected or not protected at all."

"Well," said the commandant, "I suspect that was because the mages were brought to our physical dimension from an earlier time in the magical plane. A hundred thousand years ago, the mages on Portalis were very good at protecting their links and at attacking

430

the links of other mages. I know this well, because my very last mission for '*the One*' was on Portalis a hundred thousand years ago."

"Was that when your Power reserve was damaged, sir?" Richard said. As soon as the words were out of his mouth, Richard regretted them. He wasn't sure if the commandant was sensitive about the subject. But the commandant didn't seem to mind.

"Yes," said the commandant. "It was damaged on that mission. So was your mother's, Gaston."

"So you've told me, sir," said TAC Officer Myers.

"Yes. Well…, anyway," said the commandant, "I've been on a mission on Portalis as recent as twenty thousand years in the past, and the mages in that time had lost most of those skills."

"Why're you telling me this, sir?" Richard said.

"Because, Rick," said the commandant, "almost no one in our present time in the physical dimension knows how to protect or block links. You're the exception. If you've encountered opponents with protected links, you can bet they are either from an earlier time in the magical dimension, or someone from that time protected their links for them. Much like you've been doing for your fellow cadets."

"You know about that, sir?" Richard said.

"I'm the commandant. Of course I know."

The commandant stood up and walked around the table until he stood right in front of Richard and his TAC Officer.

"I want you to do the same for TAC Officer Myers," said the commandant.

"What?" Richard said.

"No, sir," said TAC Officer Myers, "I won't–"

"Enough!" said the commandant. "We're on the same side. All of us. If mages are indeed on our world in the present time, any wizard scouts who have unprotected links are in jeopardy. They'll be sitting ducks."

While Richard might have a tentative treaty with his TAC officer, he wasn't exactly fond of him either.

"Sir," Richard said. "Surely you're not saying I'm capable of protecting the links of all wizard scouts are you?"

"No, of course not, Rick," said the commandant. "I know it takes time and Power. But I'm letting you know the situation and hoping you'll take the time to protect other wizard scouts when you can."

"Sir," said TAC Officer Myers. "I'm quite capable of defending myself."

"Yes, you are, Gaston," said the commandant. "But not in this matter."

The commandant turned to face Richard. "Will you do this for me, Rick?"

"Ah, sir," Richard said in a weak attempt to get out of the request. "I used a lot of Power in the pit today. I'm only at fifty-seven percent in my reserve."

"Is low Power your only excuse, Rick," said the commandant. "Then I'll attach a link to you and feed you Power from my reserve."

"No, sir!" Richard and TAC Officer Myers said at the same time.

"Sir," said TAC Officer Myers. "You know that's foolish. Your own link is weak as it is. You'd blow holes in your Power reserve if you tried such a thing."

"It won't be necessary, sir," Richard said. "I can protect TAC Officer Myers' link some using the Power I have if that's what you want."

Richard shifted his position in his seat before continuing. "But, sir, it takes many sessions to fully protect a link. Surely you know that?"

"I'm not asking you to fully protect his link right now," said the commandant. "I'm asking you to protect it enough to buy him a few seconds."

"Yes, sir," Richard said.

"And don't go below twenty-five percent Power in your own reserve," said the commandant. "You never know when you may need to fight."

"Yes, sir," Richard said as he prepared an active scan. Saving his TAC officer was the last thing he'd expected to do when he came here.

So much for my last training session, Richard thought.

Well, I'm proud of you, Rick, said Nickelo. *You're learning to sacrifice for the greater good.*

Whatever, Richard thought as he began probing his TAC

officer's link. *But, I'm not planning on making a habit of it.*

CHAPTER 48

"All right, I'm here, sis," Brachia said. "This had better be good."

Brachia looked around the room. "And why do we have to meet here? Why not your lab?"

"Because, little brother," said Dren, "I want to show Uncle Rick what I've been working on."

"What do you want to show him?" Brachia asked as his curiosity overcame his initial irritation.

Brachia waited for an answer, but his sister took her time walking over to a teleporter pad in the center of the room. Once she got there, she looked back as she pointed to the pad.

"I want to show him this," said Dren.

"What about it?" Brachia said. "It's a local teleporter. I've seen hundreds of them. They have dozens of them in every warehouse."

A mischievous-looking smile appeared on his sister's face "Ah. You mean it was a local teleporter. But, I hooked it into the planet's primary teleporter-array yesterday."

Walking over to the control panel, Dren continued, "I modified this to work with the primary teleporter's time differential." With what Brachia thought was an overly smug smile, Dren added, "And it works in the magical dimension."

"What?" Brachia said more than a little dubious of his sister's claim. "How? 'The One' keeps those kinds of capabilities strictly to itself. If you're telling the truth, how'd you get through security?"

"Ask me no questions, little brother, and I'll tell you no lies," said Dren as she winked an eye.

Unable to resist his scientific curiosity, Brachia walked over closer to his sister. He noticed a date entered into an interface plugged into the top of the control panel.

"What's this?" Brachia asked. "You have the date set for a hundred and fifty-seven years in the past. Why?"

"Why not?" said Dren. "I had to set it to something. I let the central computer pick a date for me."

Brachia frowned. "Why would you do that? '*The One*' will know what you're doing now."

"He'd know anyway," said Dren. "The teleporter uses too much power to go unnoticed. Besides, it's just an experiment."

"To what end?" Brachia said.

Dren got a confused look on her face. "Ah…, because it's an interesting problem. I wanted to see if I could do it."

Strangely enough, Brachia understood what his sister meant. He often worked on solutions without having a corresponding problem just because it interested him.

"Okay," Brachia said. "It's set for a hundred and fifty-seven years in the past. You have a time. What about a location."

"Oh, that was easy to pick," said Dren. "I think you'll like this one. I set it for the Oracle's stronghold on Portalis. Or to be more exact, I set it to right outside the shield surrounding the stronghold."

Dren and Brachia had spent a few weeks with the Oracle the previous year. Actually, it had been eighty-nine thousand years in Portalis' past. The Oracle had been very kind and helpful, although he'd also been quite mysterious.

"Okay," Brachia said. "I give up. Why the Oracle?"

"Because I liked him," said Dren. "And yes, I know the Oracle now won't be the same one we saw before. In any regard, I wanted to send some equipment there. I thought it might be useful to have some supplies stored there just in case."

"What on Veturna for?" Brachia said. He might only be seven years old, but even he knew it was silly to store supplies in a place they'd probably never visit again. Especially, since it was a hundred and fifty-seven years in the past.

"You know Uncle Rick's mission is getting closer," said Dren. "I think when Uncle Rick's missions for '*the One*' catches up with the current time in the physical dimension, big things are going to happen. I want to stockpile some supplies on Portalis as a backup."

Brachia shook his head. He was a super-genius the same as his sister, but her logic was escaping him.

"Why send it to a hundred and fifty-seven years in the past?" Brachia said. "Why not send it to the present time on Portalis?"

"Because someone's been snooping around my lab a lot lately," said Dren. "Our current time's not safe. Plus, I don't trust Draken. I believe he's been trying to monitor my experiments. It's not his field, so that makes me even more suspicious."

"Well," Brachia admitted. "I'm not fond of him either. He's always trying to get me to let him into my lab. He makes me nervous."

"Same here," said Dren. "I'm thinking we should tell Uncle Rick about him."

"Uncle Rick's twenty-five thousand light years away, Dren," Brachia said trying to use logic on his sister. "What can he do?"

"I don't know," admitted Dren. "But you're always telling me wizard scouts know what to do."

"True," Brachia said surprised his sister was using his own words to support her reasoning. "I'm sure he'd know what to do."

"Good," said Dren. "Then we're agreed. Be back here at 2100 hours tonight. That will be 0330 hours back at the airfield on Velos. Nick said Uncle Rick has had a rough time. He doesn't want to wake him up until then."

"Fine," Brachia said. "Besides, I want to show Uncle Rick the modifications I've made to his battle suit."

Brachia started to leave but then paused. "You know, Dren, maybe you shouldn't use the teleporter until we talk to Uncle Rick."

"No can do, little brother," said Dren. "I've been sending supplies to the Oracle's for the last week."

Brachia shook his head. He was normally the impulsive one. He wasn't sure he liked the idea of his sister acting illogically.

Will wonders never cease, Brachia thought as he walked out the door.

*   *   *

Lord Crendemor watched the human boy leave his sister. *So, they suspect me. Too bad they're just a little too late.* Rising from the computer console, Lord Crendemor paced the room thinking. It had taken awhile, but he'd finally gotten used to his insect body. Even so, he longed to return to his true form, or at the very least, to the form of the dark elf he'd used for so long. But he couldn't change form yet. The Dalinfaust wouldn't understand if his mission was jeopardized for the sake of mere comfort.

As he paced, Lord Crendemor came up with a plan. The Dalinfaust had forbidden him from physically harming his enemy. However, the demon had placed no such limitation on the two children. Perhaps he could kill the children and use their deaths to give his enemy a taste of what he'd done to him.

Lord Crendemor thoughts went back to his earlier life. He'd taken the form of the dark elf, Lord Crendemor, so long ago he almost believed his ruse himself. However, in his heart, he hadn't forgotten who he really was or what had been taken from him.

His thoughts turned to his enemy. *You should have killed me when you had the chance. One day, I'll make you beg for death.*

Lord Crendemor pictured himself torturing his enemy. It would be so sweet to hear his screams. The Master computer had sent word the cadets had succeeded in getting their DNA baselines. The Master computer thought that was a bad thing. He on the other hand did not. It meant his enemy could now selfheal. Now he'd be able to stretch his enemy's torture out for years if he desired.

He will rue the day he took her from me.

Lord Crendemor forced himself back to the present. The time for his ultimate revenge had not arrived yet. But, if he could force his enemy to watch while he slowly killed the children, it would be a start. The screams of the children would cause his enemy to suffer. Helpless, his enemy would only be able to watch. Just as he'd been forced to watch as his enemy took away his reason for living.

Yes, Lord Crendemor thought. *I will steal the Crosioian scout's equipment and then confront the children in the teleport lab. The girl has no idea she's being watched there.*

Lord Crendemor smiled. *She should have taken as much care*

securing this lab as the boy did his. But it's too late now.

Smiling again, Lord Crendemor left his office for his own lab. He was confident the Master computer had completed the security hack by now. With it, Lord Crendemor was positive he could finally break into the boy's lab and secure the Crosioian's gear. Then he'd kill the children as a down payment on his revenge.

Lord Crendemor knew he'd be cutting things close. The Master computer wanted him back in time to lead the attack on the DNA Center. He smiled again.

No, Lord Crendemor thought, *I don't want to miss that. The Dalinfaust has promised one of the vials of DNA gas will be mine. With it, I can live forever.*

Lord Crendemor was satisfied. Things were going as planned. All would be well.

CHAPTER 49

The demon Zenthra zoomed in on the Crosioian dreadnaught Wingspreader. The fleet's flagship was a bustle of activity as its crew prepared for the pending invasion. Zenthra used one of the Master computer's logic threads to monitor the ongoing staff meeting in the primary conference room. General Constance and the fleet's admiral were attempting to convince the Counselor to delay the attack.

The demon switched some of the Master computer's processing power to double-check its probability calculations. As Zenthra expected, the success of its primary mission was still nearly guaranteed. The demon refused to allow the freewill of its pawns to get in the way of its purpose.

The fools are concerned about casualties, thought the demon contemptuously. *They are going to die anyway when our purpose is accomplished. But their lives are currently no concern of mine. Lifeforms are so easy to manipulate with all their petty desires and internal squabbles.*

The demon decided it was time to put a stop to the lifeforms' meaningless arguments. Zenthra projected the Master computer's preferred image from the room's holographic projector. A life-size head of a Crosioian appeared in the center of the conference table.

"Counselor," said the voice of the Master computer. "If you review my earlier calculations, you will see they did indicate a possibility the cadets would receive an early implementation of their DNA baselines. However, the successful completion of the objective's primary mission is still assured. Our invasion force still has a ninety-four percent probability of capturing and destroying the Empire's DNA Center."

"What good is it to attack the DNA Center tomorrow?" said General Constance. "The batch of refined DNA gas has already been used. We should delay our attack until the new wizard scouts are deployed off planet. Our spies tell us they will all be gone in less than a month."

"We cannot wait a month, General Constance," said the admiral. "As I've repeatedly told you, every day our fleet stays here increases our chance of detection. We cannot risk our fleet needlessly." Looking directly at the Counselor, the admiral said, "I recommend we abort our mission and use our resources elsewhere."

Zenthra sensed the Counselor was having second thoughts about the invasion as well. But the demon did not worry. The Counselor's own greed for life would provide the leverage needed to sway the Counselor towards the proper path.

"My calculations indicate the best use of our resources is on Velos, Counselor," said Zenthra in his guise as the Master computer. "Based upon available data, there are still twenty to thirty vials of refined DNA gas at the Empire's DNA Center. By attacking tomorrow morning as planned, you can capture those vials to use as best suits the tribal council. If we delay the invasion, the Deloris Conglomerate will undoubtedly take them off planet once they formally take control of the DNA Center next week"

The Counselor rose from her seat and spread her wings. The other Crosioians at the table immediately became silent.

"The question is whether twenty or thirty vials of DNA gas are worth risking a premature attack," said the Counselor. "I'm not yet convinced the meager amount of DNA gas is worth risking this fleet."

The demon directed a list of names to the Counselor's sonar interface to the Master computer. The displayed list contained thirty names.

"Counselor," said the Master computer. "I am just a computer. It is up to you to decide if the reward warrants the risk. But, I would not be doing my job if I did not make sure you had all the pertinent data. Your sonar interface is displaying the tribal council's potential list of DNA gas recipients."

The demon zoomed the Master computer's sensors onto the Counselor's face. Zenthra had to restrain himself from laughing as the Counselor's sonar receptors enlarged when she came to the eighteenth name in the list. Zenthra could tell the Counselor stopped at the eighteenth name and scanned no further. The twitching of the Counselor's facial muscles indicated she was deep in thought as she analyzed this new information. Zenthra knew the Counselor only needed a little extra push to make the correct decision; to make Zenthra's decision.

"Once those thirty individuals receive the DNA gas," said Zenthra through the Master computer, "they will gain eternal youth. Imagine how much those great Crosioians will accomplish if they never have to worry about aging." In a voice as indifferent as only a computer can sound, Zenthra added, "But as I said, it is not for me to decide. I am but your obedient tool."

The Counselor folded her wings onto her back and looked at her subordinates seated at the conference table. "I have made my decision. The attack will commence as scheduled."

Turning to General Constance, the Counselor said, "General, you will begin shuttling the first wave of your sappers to Velos immediately. The heavy armor will follow. All sappers must be in inside the Empire's protective shields by 0415 hours Velos' time. Once the prepositioned static tele-bots activate at 0430 hours, they will disrupt each of the target's local force fields. Your sappers will then destroy the power plants at the spaceport, the Academy, and the airfield."

The Counselor turned to her right. "Admiral, once the power plants are destroyed and the Empire's main protective shields are down, you will commence your bombardment."

"Yes, Counselor," said the admiral. The time for arguments was past. The decision had been made. The admiral would do her duty. And, she would make sure her crews did their duty as well.

"Once the attack begins," said the Counselor, "how long do we have before we can expect the Empire to respond?"

"Probable response time is twenty-two minutes," said the holographic image of the Master computer "The admiral's dreadnaughts need seven minutes to destroy the defenses on Velos. That means General Constance's forces must bring down the Empire's protective shields at the three target areas by 0445. Otherwise, her ships will be needed to counter any incoming Empire ships."

"My troops will have the shields down within five minutes of commencing our attack," said General Constance confidently.

"Then we are decided," said the Counselor.

The demon noticed the Counselor access the list of DNA recipient names one last time as if assuring herself that her name was indeed on the list. It was.

Living creatures are so predictable, thought Zenthra as the Counselor left the room.

The demon silently laughed. So far, Zenthra had convinced over two thousand of the foolish lifeforms their names were on the list.

Let them fight over how to divide thirty vials of DNA gas between them, thought the demon. *I care not what they do it. All that matters is the DNA Center's destruction. The mission must succeed at all cost. There must never be another new wizard scout. Once all existing wizard scouts have died off in the next hundred years, the successful completion of our part in the game will be assured. That is all that matters. The Crosioians can be destroyed for all I care. Only our success matters.*

The demon wasn't worried about its own safety. As the Master computer, Zenthra inhabited every computer in the Crosioians' part of the tele-network. The demon was confident its Master computer avatar could not be destroyed.

Besides, Zenthra knew its primary essence was safely in the extinct Decorians' computer deep below the surface of Portalis. The master demon's opponent had failed to disable the Decorians' computer when its pawns had destroyed the spaceport on Portalis. The master demon's opponent would soon pay for that failure. Their opponent's position in the game was fast becoming untenable.

Zenthra laughed quietly. He was Zenthra, and he was the Decorian computer, and he was the Master computer. He was invulnerable. Inhabiting the Decorian computer as he was, Zenthra knew he could control the Master computer with impunity while separated by time and distance. Even if '*the One*' sent forces to

Portalis, they would accomplish nothing. Zenthra glorified in the safety afforded him by the Decorian computer. His brother, the Dalinfaust, had suggested using time as a defense. Zenthra checked the connection with the part of himself that was a hundred and fifty-seven years in the past on Portalis. The connection was solid. The part of him in the past was in firm control of the Decorian computer, and the Decorian computer was in firm control of the Master computer in the present.

Zenthra was satisfied. His essence was safe in the past. He could not be harmed in the present. His part in the game was proceeding as planned.

CHAPTER 50

The light in the tent was dim, but it still drew Richard out of his light sleep. Although awake, Richard kept his eyes closed and tried to enjoy a few more seconds of relaxation. He felt better than he'd felt before he'd went to sleep. However, he knew his selfheal would quickly bring a sense of tiredness back as it sought to bring his body back to baseline. Still, Richard knew he'd needed the rest.

As Richard's battle computer had explained, his mind needed sleep as much as his body. Even though sleep was basically a wasted effort as far as his body was concerned, his mind would gradually become less efficient without it. Even his selfheal ability could not help his mind.

Deciding all good things must come to an end, Richard opened his eyes. Jerad was hunched over the tent's field desk with his face close to a miniature, full-length hologram of Trinity.

Where did he get that piece of equipment? Richard wondered. As a cadet, he'd had it drummed into his ears they weren't allowed unsupervised access to advanced communications equipment for personal use.

Richard studied the disk upon which the hologram of Trinity stood. While he wasn't an expert in electronics, Richard could tell the holographic projector was expensive. The image of Trinity was crisp in detail with nary a flicker. If Richard hadn't known better, he would've thought he was looking at a half-meter tall fairy dressed in a black, skintight jumpsuit. Richard could make out individual strands of Trinity's waste-length hair blowing in some soft breeze. Richard thought she looked beautiful. From the hangdog look on Jerad's face, Richard figured his friend thought so too.

"So, how'd you like the wedding?" Jerad said. "Did you catch the bouquet?"

"Don't joke," Trinity said with a dazzling smile. "You're not that good at it." Trinity looked at her wrist. "In fact, they're probably in the middle of the actual ceremony as we speak."

"I'm surprised you didn't stay, Trinity," Jerad said. "Weren't you invited?"

"Yes," said Trinity. "All of the wizard scouts were invited along with every tactical officer above the rank of lieutenant. But as soon as the welcoming ceremony was over, all the wizard scouts high-tailed it back to the Blaze. The regular officers didn't have a choice. They had to stay."

Richard noticed Trinity's image glance to his side of the tent. She smiled.

"Good morning, Rick," said Trinity. "Did we wake you?"

"No," Richard said as he sat up and swung his legs over the side of his cot. "I was just resting my eyes."

"Sure you were," Trinity said smiling.

"Ah..., how is Liz?" Richard said hoping Trinity wouldn't notice his blush. "I mean, is she doing okay?" He didn't want to sound too anxious.

"Oh. You mean Acting Fleet Commander Bistos?" Jerad said with a laugh. "She's made the big leagues according to Trinity."

Richard listened as Jerad took a minute to explain how Liz had finagled a two-hour appointment commanding a fleet of thirty-two military starships.

"Cool," Richard said. "I always knew Liz was going places. The Empire would be crazy not to take advantage of her abilities."

Jerad turned back to the image of Trinity. "How's she handling being in charge? Can she still get her head through the door?"

"She's only been in charge for thirty minutes," laughed Trinity. "The fleet's in orbit around a peaceful planet. There's really not much to do other than follow formal protocol. As for the size of her head, it's quite normal. The last I saw, she was on the command deck getting status reports from the rest of the fleet."

"So, only junior officers are left on the ships?" Richard said. "I'm not navy, but that doesn't seem right even to me."

"Actually," said Trinity, "there are a lot of higher-ranking officers still on board the ships, but they're administrative types. Only tactical field officers can command ships."

"Yeah, I know," Richard said. "Still, it seems strange Liz was put in that position."

"Well, from what I heard, there was a lot of squawking from some of the other officers," said Trinity. "But orders are orders. They came straight from the Imperial High Command via the central computer. The end result is she's in charge for the next ninety minutes."

Richard thought of something. "Hey, Trinity, will Liz and you be able to attend our graduation next week?"

Trinity laughed. "Ha. You're going to be wizard scouts, not admirals. At normal speed, it would take the Blaze three weeks to get back to Velos. Somehow, I don't think the admiralty would consider your graduation a military emergency. However, if you can pull some strings and get it declared as such, we could go into military override and get back there in about twenty minutes according to Liz." Trinity smiled and corrected herself. "Uh, I mean Acting Fleet Commander Bistos."

"I'll get right on that," Richard said laughing. "What time is it now? Should I expect you back in time for breakfast?"

"It's 0215 hours," said Jerad. "You really didn't sleep all that long."

"Oh, well," Richard said putting his boots on. "I'm guessing you two might want a little time to talk without me hanging over your shoulder. I think I'll take a walk."

When neither Jerad nor Trinity tried to dissuade him, Richard knew he'd made the right choice.

"Ah..., I need to call the kids anyway," Richard said. "I'll see you around, Trinity."

"You can bet on it, Rick," said Trinity with another one of her dazzling smiles.

"Yeah, tell the children I said hi," said Jerad. "And thanks, Rick. I owe you."

Richard nodded his head and left the tent to the two lovebirds.

*   *   *

Choosing a direction at random, Richard found himself walking towards the airfield. He probably could have went back to sleep, but he figured why bother. His mind had gotten the rest it needed. Additional sleep wouldn't help his body any at this point.

Yawning, Richard sent a thought to his shared space. *Are you there, Nick?*

Naturally, replied Nickelo. *I can multitask with no problem.*

Then how about multitasking up a communication link with the kids, Richard said.

You need to summon your battle helmet first, Rick, said Nickelo. *We'll use its holographic projector to establish a communication link with them. Dren has one set up on her end. She's very anxious to talk to you.*

So you told me, Richard said as he concentrated on his battle helmet. He sensed its location in the armory easy enough. Wrapping his helmet with Power, Richard shifted it into the void and pulled with his mind. The battle helmet appeared in the air an arm's length away. He shifted the battle helmet out of the void and snatched it out of the air with his hand before it could fall. Richard put the battle helmet on and lowered the visor. The airfield immediately came into clear view through his night-vision filter.

I didn't know a battle helmet had a holographic projector, Richard said. *We didn't get any training on it.*

That's because they normally don't, said Nickelo. *Brachia had one installed on all of your battle helmets last week. He thought it would be easier to communicate that way.*

I really wish he'd stop messing around with my equipment, Richard said. *But what's done is done.*

So it is, said Nickelo. After a pause, he said, *Dren's not quite ready on her end yet. She's waiting for her brother.*

It was way too early to go back to the tent, so Richard continued walking to take up the time. The night air was cool, and the breeze was in his face coming off the airfield. For no particular reason, Richard turned and walked with the wind at his back. He supposed it didn't matter which direction he went.

I forgot to ask, Richard said. *How's the decryption of that*

Crosioian scout's battle computer coming?

Not so good, said Nickelo. *Jonathan and I were confident we could break its security code, but it's giving us problems. I thought sure we'd have it done by now.*

Richard didn't know if computers could get discouraged, but he had a feeling his battle computer could. He definitely sounded discouraged.

Well, if you can't do it, then you can't do it, Richard said trying to sound logical. *It's not like you're on a time schedule or anything.*

Oh, we're going to get it, Nickelo said with a tone that made Richard think his battle computer had taken affront with his words of comfort. *And, I don't know if we're on a time schedule or not. Jonathan and I both think the Crosioian battle computer contains data we urgently need to know.*

Richard didn't feel like arguing. Brachia, Jonathan, and Nickelo had been working on the Crosioian battle computer for weeks. If they hadn't broken the encryption by now, Richard figured it wasn't going to happen. But he wasn't going to tell his battle computer that. With a shrug of his shoulders, Richard said, *Well, let me know if I can help.*

I might just do that, Rick, said Nickelo. *The security program appears to be emotion-based. Jonathan doesn't think he or I are emotional enough to break the security algorithm.*

Richard laughed. *Then I'd definitely be good at it. You're always telling me I'm too emotional.*

It's the truth sometimes, Nickelo said.

Richard wandered around for a few minutes until he found himself near one of the airfield's backup power plants. It was the same one he'd been at a few weeks ago when he'd sensed something strange. But if there had ever been anything there, it was gone. He sensed nothing abnormal now.

All right, Rick, said Nickelo. *I've got the communication hookup ready. Switch to your clear visor. I'm activating the holographic projector.*

Richard stopped walking and changed to a clear visor. The area around him looked like a room of some type. Richard looked around the room. From all the equipment and work benches, Richard knew it was a lab of some kind. He noticed two children dressed in jumpsuits near some type of control panel.

"Uncle Rick," said Brachia.

The small boy ran enthusiastically towards Richard with outstretched arms. Richard knelt down and opened his arms in return. Brachia ran right through him.

"Smart move, guys," laughed Dren. "Sometimes I wonder about the intelligence level of the male gender."

"Whatever, sis," said Brachia. "At least I have some intelligence."

"Hey, kids," Richard said hoping to stave off a sibling argument. "I'm glad to see you two again. But why now? I thought I told you I was hoping to get some leave time after I graduate next week. We could probably meet somewhere."

"We still can, Uncle Rick," said Brachia. "But Dren and I wanted to show you something."

Brachia motioned for Richard to follow. Although Richard knew he was still near the airfield's power plant, for all intents and purposes, he felt as if he was right there in the room.

Nick, Richard said. *Keep an eye out around us. I don't want something sneaking up on me while I'm occupied with the kids.*

Will do, Rick, said Nickelo. *But I'll do you one better.*

The area around Richard changed. The image of the lab became translucent, and its image was superimposed over the actual area around him. The double vision was a little disconcerting, but Richard quickly became used to it. He had a feeling Nickelo's presence in their shared space was helping him keep the two images separate in his mind.

Ah..., well, that's different, Richard said to Nickelo. *But I guess it'll work.*

"You're talking to Nick, aren't you, Uncle Rick," said Brachia.

"Yeah, how'd you know," Richard said.

"You had that same 'I am not in this room anymore' expression on your face you always get when you're talking to him," said Brachia.

"Nick," said Dren. "It's not polite to leave us out of the conversation, you know."

"Sorry, Dren," said Nickelo using the battle helmet's external speakers. "I was just showing Rick how to use double vision to keep track of his surroundings." With a laugh, Nickelo said, "You know he'd be helpless without me."

"Well, it's not like I was trained on it," Richard said. "Nick told me you installed the holograph projector last week, Brachia."

"I told him not to do it, Uncle Rick," said Dren.

"Did not," said Brachia. "You said I shouldn't do it."

"It doesn't matter," Richard said still trying to stave off any argument. "But, Brachia, please don't mess with my equipment without talking it over with me first. Okay?"

"Okay," said Brachia. "I didn't think you'd mind. Umm..., do you want me to put your battle suit back the way it was?"

Uh, Nick, Richard said privately to his battle computer. *Do you know what he's done?*

Yes, Nickelo said. *I helped with some of the calculations. But Brachia wants to surprise you. I think you'll like it.*

"Okay, Brachia," Richard said. "What'd you do to my battle suit? You didn't break it did you? It's saved my life more than once, you know."

"Uncle Rick," said Brachia looking like he was getting ready to cry. "You know I wouldn't do anything to get you hurt."

"I was just joking, Brachia," Richard said trying to assure the boy he wasn't mad. Richard sometimes forgot his adoptive nephew was only seven. "Please tell me what you did. I'm sure it's fine."

"Oh, it's more than fine, Uncle Rick," said Dren. "Even I approve of this change. Tell him, Brachia."

"I will if you'd give me a chance, sis," said Brachia.

Walking over to a computer display, Brachia pressed a button. A life-size hologram of Richard's battle suit appeared in the room.

"This is your battle suit," said Brachia. With his left hand, Brachia picked up a small block of silver-colored metal. "Do you know what this is, Uncle Rick?"

Richard moved closer to the metal bar. He reached out to grab it. His hand passed through the bar. Dren and Brachia laughed.

"Oops," Richard said. "I keep forgetting. Hmm. Since you're probably like fifty thousand light years away, I can't scan it, so I'll just take a wild guess. Is it titanium?"

Brachia smiled. "Very good, Uncle Rick. That's exactly what it is."

The boy picked up a small glass vial full of a silver-colored dust. "And this is titanium dust."

"Okay," Richard said. He wasn't sure where the boy was going. Richard looked at Dren hoping she'd give him a hint, but she just gave him a wait-and-see smile.

"So, you have titanium dust," Richard said. "Is that important?"

Dren spoke up before Brachia got a chance. "Do you know what creallium is, Uncle Rick?"

"Ah," Richard said suspecting a trick. The sciences were not his best subject. "I assume it's an element."

"No, silly," said Dren. "Creallium is just titanium that's been radiated with a special energy charge."

"I didn't know that," Richard said. "I thought creallium was supposed to be expensive."

"Oh, it is," said Nickelo. "It's probably the most expensive alloy to make in the known galaxy. The process of radiating titanium in order to turn it into creallium is a long, drawn-out process."

"But, it's worth it," said Dren. "Creallium is the only known material in the galaxy to conduct phase energy. That's why the core of your phase rod is made out of creallium."

"Ah, I know that kind of stuff is interesting to you guys," Richard said. "But in all honesty, as long as something works, I'm not real interested in what makes it tick."

Richard thought Dren looked like someone had thrown cold water on her.

"Really?" said Dren as if she was shocked anyone could help but be interested in how things worked.

"Sorry," Richard said.

When neither of the kids said anything for a few seconds, Richard tried prodding them along. "So, does titanium have anything to do with my battle suit?"

"Oh, yeah, your battle suit," said Brachia as he remembered the point of the whole conversation. "Well, anyway, if the correct energy is applied to titanium, it will be transformed into creallium."

"Okay," Richard said. "I've got that much."

"Good," said Brachia. "This is where it gets interesting."

Reaching over to a nearby workbench, Brachia picked up a small, blue gem. "Do you recognize this, Uncle Rick?"

Richard looked closely at the blue gem. It did seem a little familiar. He reached out to take the gem. Brachia grinned. Richard pulled his hand back before he made a complete fool of himself.

"Right," Richard said. "I keep forgetting I'm not really there."

After inspecting the gem in Brachia's hand a little more, Richard said, "All right. I give up. What's so special about the gem?"

Nickelo answered first. "Your memory is atrocious, Rick. You had to find twenty-five hundred of them for '*the One*'. Don't you remember?"

Richard did remember the mission. He'd hated it. But he still didn't recognize the gem. He admitted as much.

"That's because I had to cut and buff it up some," said Brachia. "The angles of the cut help concentrate the energy flow."

"Fine," Richard said. "Can we just cut to the chase? You won't hurt my feelings if you skip the scientific details."

"I've got this, little brother," said Dren. "Brachia had me help him teleport particles of titanium dust into the material of your battle suits. Then, my brother installed one of those blue gems in each suit. When the gem is activated, it releases energy that temporarily turns the titanium dust into creallium. Notice I said temporarily. Using one of these gems, it's not a permanent transformation."

Dren and Brachia beamed as if they were waiting for Richard to applaud their efforts. Richard hated to disappoint them, but he didn't see the benefit.

"So?" Richard said.

"So," said Nickelo, "when you activate the gem in your suit, the titanium is changed to creallium. And creallium exists in the void as well as the current dimension. That's why your phase rod and rounds from a phase blaster can hurt creatures in the void."

The light clicked on in Richard's mind. He knew why the children were smiling.

"Are you telling me you've found a way to protect myself from attack by creatures in the void?" Richard said. "If that's what you're saying, then I owe you a big hug."

"Then hug away, Uncle Rick," laughed Brachia. "Ever since you told us how those dimension-shifting cats attacked you from the void last year, I've been trying to find a way to help you defend yourself. This is it."

Richard was touched. This was bigtime stuff as far as he was concerned.

Richard reached out and tried to hug Brachia. His arms passed through the boy. Richard didn't care. He gave Dren a simulated hug as well.

"Thanks, guys," Richard said. "I don't know what to say."

Both of the children looked like they were a little embarrassed at Richard's show of gratitude. But at the same time, they looked grateful for the attention.

Before anyone could say anything further, the door to the lab burst open. Richard heard a maniacal laugh. Dren looked up and screamed.

CHAPTER 51

Lord Crendemor waited until the proper time. Using the Master computer's security hack, he broke into the boy's laboratory and retrieved the Crosioian scout's equipment.

He could have activated the signaling device in order to have the Master computer teleport him back to the fleet's flagship, but he didn't. Instead, he walked towards the girl's teleportation lab.

They should be with my enemy now, Lord Crendemor thought. *I shall have the first down payment on my revenge.*

When Lord Crendemor reached the lab's door, he visually checked the hallway. It was empty. He recited the spell to dissipate his polymorph spell. He wanted his enemy to see his real form. Lord Crendemor felt the spell's energy work through his body and return it back to his natural form. He looked at his hand. It was a pale, flesh color. He'd been in the form of a dark elf for so many years he no longer liked the look of his real flesh.

Lord Crendemor smiled as he imagined his enemy's despair when he saw the children killed in front of his eyes.

Reaching into the sack he carried, Lord Crendemor pulled out a jeweled longsword. It was hers. After his enemy had destroyed her body, Lord Crendemor had returned to the river. He had searched long and hard until he found her sword. It was only fitting that her sword be the instrument of his revenge. He'd sworn to use it to destroy everything precious to his enemy, just as his enemy had destroyed that which was most precious to him.

Lord Crendemor knew his enemy was not in the room. He would not be able to kill him now. But, he would use her sword to kill the children his enemy loved. He would kill them slowly.

With her longsword in his right hand and with the Crosioian scout's equipment in his left, Lord Crendemor opened the door. He laughed in triumph. His revenge was at hand.

CHAPTER 52

Richard saw the look of shock on Dren's face. With her scream still echoing in his ear, Richard turned to face the door. A pale man with a crazed look on his face was rushing into the room with a raised longsword in his hand. Richard stepped between the stranger and the children. As the stranger got closer, Richard noticed his ears. They were pointed.

An elf, Richard thought.

When the elf got within range, Richard leapt into the air and aimed a sidekick at the elf's head. His foot passed through the elf without making contact. Losing his balance, Richard fell to the floor. He heard another maniacal laugh and then another of Dren's screams.

"You fool," said the elf. "You're pathetic. Turn around and watch as I kill this girl. Then I'll take care of the boy as well."

Richard jumped to his feet and spun around. He recognized the sneering voice. On his mission for '*the One*' the previous year, an elf had been with the party of gnomes he'd been tasked to help. Although the elf and he hadn't been exactly friendly to each other, they had fought side by side. Richard had even saved the elf's life. He didn't understand the obvious hatred in the elf. He didn't even understand how the elf could be here.

When Richard turned, he saw the elf holding Dren. The elf's sword was at the girl's throat. The look of fear on Dren's face tore at Richard's heart. He knew it was a look he'd never forget. Richard looked for Brachia, but the boy wasn't to be seen.

"Kreathin," Richard said. "How? Why?"

"How?" laughed the elf as he tightened his grip on the struggling girl. "How am I here when you left me eighty-nine thousand years in the past? That doesn't matter, you pitiful fool. What matters is why? You took her from me. You took my Lillia from me. Now, I'll take this girl from you."

Richard felt helpless. He was only a hologram. What could he do?

But fortunately for Dren, there was another in the room who was not helpless. Brachia charged out from behind a workbench. He dove at the elf holding his sister. Richard saw a flash of metal in the boy's hand.

The elf must have sensed the boy's attack. Kreathin shifted his sword to strike the boy. Brachia's knife grazed the elf's side. At the same time, Dren stomped on the elf's foot with the heel of her boot. The elf made a sound of pain. The sword thrust he'd aimed at the boy missed.

Dren pulled a knife from a sheath on her belt. It was the same knife he'd given her the previous year. Richard saw her make a backhanded stab at the elf's leg. The knife blade sank deep into Kreathin's thigh. The elf screamed. He must have relaxed his grip, because Dren broke loose from the elf's grasp. She grabbed her brother's hand and ran towards a round dais in the center of the room.

Kreathin cursed and began a spell. Richard yelled hoping to distract the elf. It did no good. Richard saw a ball of energy forming in the elf's hands.

Nick! Richard yelled in his shared space. *Help them.*

I can't, said Nickelo. *We're not there. I can't do anything.*

In the three seconds it took Kreathin to form his spell, Dren and Brachia reached the dais.

"Kathy!" shouted Dren. "Activate!"

A glow emanated from the dais and surrounded Dren and her brother. They both shimmered. They disappeared just as arcs of electricity leaped out of the elf's hands into the air where the children had been.

Kreathin screamed his anger. He pulled the knife out of his leg and threw it to the floor. Kreathin shook a bloody fist at Richard.

"You'll pay," said the elf. "I swear it. I'll hunt down anyone you have ever cared for and rip their hearts out. You'll pay for taking my Lillia from me."

Richard thought back to the last time he'd seen Kreathin. They'd been fighting zombies near a river. A zombie that happened to be a female elf had attacked them. In order to save Kreathin, Richard had stuck a grenade in the zombie's mouth and kicked her into the river. The zombie's head and most of her body had been torn to shreds. Instead of thanking him, Kreathin had tried to kill him. One of the gnomes had told Richard the zombie had been Kreathin's bondmate.

"She was a zombie, you idiot," Richard said. "She was already dead. I saved your life."

"You took her from me," said Kreathin. "He could have saved her. He told me so. But not after you destroyed her. If not for you, she could have been saved."

"You're crazy," Richard yelled. "She was dead. You can't bring someone back after they're dead."

Kreathin turned away from Richard and walked over to the control panel for the teleporter pad. After looking at the settings, he laughed. "The fools think they've escaped. We shall see. We shall see."

Richard was unsure what the elf was blabbering about.

Nick. The kids, Richard said. *Where are the children? We need to find them.*

They're safe for now, said Nickelo. *I'll explain later. For now, look at the elf's left hand. He has the Crosioian scout's gear.*

I don't care about the gear, Richard said. *We need to save the children.*

The elf stared straight into Richard's eyes. "We'll meet again, human. Soon, all you hold dear will be destroyed. You'll suffer. Oh, how you'll suffer."

The elf said a spell. As the spell began to take effect, the elf gave Richard an evil smile. "I have reclaimed the scout's helmet intact. When you finally learn its secrets, it will be as death is raining down upon all you know. Everyone you care about will die. This I promise."

With those words, the spell's energy reached out and engulfed the room in flames. The holograph of the lab disappeared. Richard was once again wholly back at the airfield. The children were nowhere in sight.

*   *   *

Richard scanned the area. He was still standing near the backup power plant. All seemed quiet. Although the night air was cool, Richard was sweating. The night might be peaceful, but Richard's mind was anything but.

Nick! Where are the kids? Richard practically shouted into his shared space.

Don't shout, Rick, said Nickelo. *The children are safe. Dren didn't get a chance to show you, but that teleporter was set for a hundred and fifty-seven years in the past on Portalis.*

Why? Richard began before changing his mind. *No, never mind. It doesn't matter. How do we get them back? And what was Kreathin doing there? He should've been dead and turned to dust by now.*

Hold on, Rick, said Nickelo. *The children are probably safer a hundred and fifty-seven years in the past than they'd be here right now. I think something dangerous is going on. And just so you know, I don't know how to get them back. To answer your last question, I don't know why Kreathin is alive.*

Richard thought for a computer, Nickelo said 'I do not know' a lot.

We've got to get moving, Richard said. *We've got to do something. We have to find the children.*

Richard surprised himself with his concern for Brachia and Dren. They were the closest thing to family he'd ever had, and he didn't want to lose them.

Go where, Rick? said Nickelo. *And do what?*

Richard didn't answer. He didn't know. He just felt like he should be doing something.

The children are in the past, said Nickelo. *We've got to figure out how to time travel to rescue them. I don't know how. Do you?*

Again, Richard didn't answer. His battle computer was taking the situation much too calmly for his liking.

The good news, said Nickelo, *is that it doesn't matter whether we do something now or a year from now. It'll still be the same point in time when we go back. We'll find them, Rick. I just need to figure out how.*

I can't stand around doing nothing, Richard said feeling way too helpless. He needed to do something.

Then don't, said Nickelo. *The elf's presence and his threat concern me. I'd recommend summoning your dimensional pack and arming yourself.*

Richard didn't have to be told twice. It was something to do, and he'd always liked acting instead of wasting time thinking. He knew TAC Officer Myers wouldn't be happy, but at this point, Richard didn't care. Within seconds, Richard was stripping off his clothes and putting on his battle suit.

While Richard dressed, he listened to his battle computer as he outlined the situation.

The elf had the Crosioian scout's battle helmet, said Nickelo. *Somehow, he knew we hadn't decrypted its data yet. He hinted the battle computer contained a secret, and that we would face some kind of danger soon.*

Yeah. So? Richard said as he fastened on his utility belt. *Talk's cheap. He was probably just blowing hot air.*

I don't think he was just talking, Rick, said Nickelo. *I calculate a ninety-seven percent probability something's going down as we speak. I'm not sure when or where. I just wish we could have cracked the security code on that battle computer. I think it's the key to finding out what's going on.*

Well, it's too late now, Richard said. *Kreathin's got it now.*

Yes and no, said Nickelo. *And by the way, I'd recommend getting an M12 instead of your M63. You don't know what you may be up against. The heavier rounds could come in handy.*

I'm only at seventy-two percent Power in my reserve, Nick, Richard said. *I hate to waste the Power. I used way too much protecting Myers' link to his Power reserve. He didn't even thank me come to think of it.*

Please don't argue, Rick, said Nickelo. *Just get the M12. And I'd recommend summoning some quarter-kilo bocks of J22 plastic explosive as well. They might come in handy.*

Richard shrugged his shoulders. As long as he was armed, he guessed it didn't matter. He shoved his M63 back into his dimensional pack and closed the flap. Then he imagined an M12 with an extra bandoleer of 20mm grenades. Richard felt Power leave his reserve. When he opened the pack, he saw the M12, but there was no extra ammo in the pack.

'The One' *is being a jerk again*, Richard said as he pulled out the M12. *He let me summon an extra bandoleer of 20mm grenades for Stella the other night, but he won't let me get one when I need it.*

Just deal with it, Rick, said Nickelo sounding not at all sympathetic.

Richard shrugged his shoulders and performed a function check on the M12. The isotopic battery was full. That would give him 400 rounds of plasma energy. Richard checked the grenade magazine underneath the rifle barrel. It held seven 20mm grenades. Richard chambered a round. On a hunch, Richard imagined a single 20mm grenade. He felt a small amount of Power leave his reserve. Reaching into his dimensional pack, he pulled out a single 20mm grenade.

There's no rhyme or reason to these stupid rules, Richard said as he shoved the 20mm grenade into the empty space in the M12's magazine. *It's like* 'the One' *makes the rules up as he goes.*

I doubt that, Rick, said Nickelo. *By the way, don't forget about the J22.*

Richard summoned a satchel with twenty blocks of J22 plastic explosives with remote timers. Once he pulled the satchel out of his pack, he slung the satchel over his shoulder. Thus armed, he felt ready for about anything.

Okay, Richard said. *What now?*

He glanced at the timer on the heads-up display of his battle helmet. It was 0345 hours. It would be getting light in a couple of hours.

Do you trust me, Rick? asked Nickelo in what Richard thought was a very serious tone.

Richard grew suspicious, but he thrust the suspicion aside. Nickelo was his friend. Richard trusted him with his life. He told Nickelo so.

Why do you ask? Richard said.

Because Brachia uploaded a complete copy of the data from the Crosioian scout's battle computer into my primary databanks, said

Nickelo. *That's what Jonathan and I've been trying to decrypt. Rick, I could use some help.*

Richard had been preparing to protest they should be doing something, but his battle computer's words caught him by surprise. In all their time together, Richard couldn't remember his battle computer ever seriously admitting he needed help; at least not real help. The idea intrigued Richard.

Help? Richard said. *How? And doing what?*

You may remember, said Nickelo, *I told you the security for the Crosioian scout's battle computer was emotional based. I'd like you to help me break the code.*

Me? Richard said. *I'm not a programmer. If Jonathan and you haven't had any luck, I doubt I could do any good.*

You'd be surprised, Rick, said Nickelo. *I haven't time to explain now, but I think you've got something in your DNA makeup that allows you to interface with computers. Combined with your emotions, I think you could help. That is, if you trust me.*

You keep asking if I trust you, Nick, Richard said. *I'm assuming that means you think it's dangerous.*

I'm not sure, Rick, Nickelo admitted. *I wanted to ask you for help last week, but I was waiting until you got your DNA baseline.*

You mean so I'd be able to selfheal? Richard asked.

Partly that, said Nickelo, *but mostly because we needed our shared space.*

Richard thought for a minute before replying. *Will it help us find the kids?*

Richard's battle computer didn't answer right away. Finally, Nickelo said, *Not directly. But trying to decrypt the Crosioian scout's battle computer is tying up a lot of logic threads. If we could finish hacking into the scout's battle computer, I could use those logic threads to figure out a way to get to the children.*

Without further hesitation, Richard agreed to help. He was tired of doing nothing anyway. He preferred action to waiting for something to happen.

All right then, Rick, said Nickelo. *Let's get started. I'm sealing up your battle suit. Uh...with your permission, of course.*

Of course, Richard said.

The battle suit's visor lowered to seal with the lower part of his battle helmet just below Richard's nose. The uncomfortable but familiar tubes forced their way into his mouth, nose, and other body openings. Richard felt the seventeen thousand plus needle threads inserting themselves into his body. He ignored it as best as he could.

When the battle suit completed its seal, Nickelo suggested Richard find a convenient tree and sit down. Richard chose one facing the power plant. After Richard sat down, Nickelo appeared ready to start.

Just follow me, Rick, said Nickelo.

Richard found Nickelo in their shared space. Actually, found wasn't the right word, but Richard couldn't think of any better word to explain it. It was as if their minds converged at the same point. Richard could sense the millions, no billions, of calculations being done by his battle computer. Richard's mind wasn't fast enough to keep up, but he was able to understand what his battle computer was trying to accomplish.

At the same time, Richard could tell Nickelo was sensing his thoughts and feelings. Having his battle computer sense his thoughts was nothing new. The only difference was Richard could only tell the thought he was thinking in their share space was being accessed by his friend. However, the sharing of emotions was different. Before his DNA baseline, Nickelo knew what Richard was feeling. But now, Richard could tell his battle computer was actually feeling his emotions.

Richard had a thought. *You know, Nick, this might be dangerous for you. According to the central computer, your association with me over the past three years has corrupted you with emotions. I've a feeling this is only going to make it worse.*

Doesn't matter, Rick, replied Nickelo. *I was a lost cause the moment we first touched minds. 'The One' already keeps me isolated from the rest of the tele-network.*

Sorry, buddy, Richard said.

At that moment, Richard felt the thoughts of another mind. The thoughts weren't in his shared space, but Richard could still sense the mind through his battle computer's data feed.

Hello, wizard scout, said the presence.

Who is this, Nick? Richard said into his shared space.

It's your friend Stella's battle computer, Jonathan, explained Nickelo. *We need him to interface with the tele-network.*

Ah, hello, Jonathan, Richard said. *I don't think we've been formally introduced.*

Didn't you tell him, sir? said Jonathan.

No, said Nickelo. *I didn't see a need. However, things have changed. Rick, this is Jonathan. I believe he was your battle computer when you were in the spiritual dimension.*

Why do you think that? Richard said. *That battle computer didn't even have a name.*

Because Jonathan is also emotionally corrupted, said Nickelo with a laugh. *And we know how hard you are on battle computers.*

Whatever, Richard said not appreciating the joke. *Can we get started?*

Sure, said Nickelo. *Just follow our lead. We're going to take you to the spot in my databanks where the copy of the Crosioian's data is stored.*

Richard closed his eyes and let his mind drift along with his battle computer. He didn't see things visually of course, but he could sense them. They passed a lot of data as they traveled through the area Nickelo thought of as his databanks. Everything was alien to Richard, but because the information he sensed was filtered through the space in his mind he shared with his battle computer, Richard's psyche did not rebel.

Up ahead, Richard sensed a wall. He didn't have to be told it was the encrypted data. Richard wasn't sure what he'd expected. He supposed he'd pictured packets of data stored in designated spots much like books at a library. This was different. The wall was volatile. In fact, it wasn't a wall. It was more like a massive cube with depth, height, and width.

As they drew closer, Richard sensed anger, hate, and a myriad of other less than desirable emotions.

The emotions you sense are securing the data, said Nickelo.

It's similar to the way the central computer secures its data, said Jonathan. *But somehow it's different. We were able to hack our way into the central computer's emotion-based security without too much of a problem.*

However, this emotion-based security continues to resist our efforts, finished Nickelo. *As an emotional creature, we thought you could help.*

I still don't see how..., Richard started to say.

Richard didn't finish his thought. Something in the swirling mass ahead of him seemed familiar. Each time he tried to concentrate on a specific part of the wall, the substance, or data, appeared to change. It was very disconcerting.

Richard had a sudden insight. He thought he knew why the two battle computers were having difficulty.

Nickelo must have sensed Richard's increasing excitement. *What is it, Rick? Have you found something already?*

Maybe, Richard said, not quite ready to commit. *Do you remember how I helped the elf Shandria rewrite some of the spells in her spell book on our first mission?*

Yes. So? said Nickelo sounding a little impatient.

Richard thought it was strange his battle computer was getting impatient. It sounded more like something he'd do. But Richard ignored it and kept to his purpose.

Well, said Richard. *We didn't have our shared space then, so you didn't get to experience it. But, the words in Shandria's spell book kept changing whenever I tried to concentrate on them. That's what this data appears to be doing. I think this data is triple encrypted. I think it's encrypted with logic, emotion, and...magic.*

Magic? said Jonathan. *Computers can't use magic. How's that possible?*

Oh, it's possible, said Nickelo remembering his dreams. *Computers in the magical dimension are based on magic. But I wouldn't have expected to encounter it here.*

I don't understand magic, said Jonathan addressing Nickelo. *Do you?*

No, Nickelo admitted. *At least I don't understand it enough to decrypt this three-way cocktail before us.*

After a pause, Nickelo said, *But, maybe Rick does.*

Richard concentrated on the wall. He sensed the information within changing shape. Instead of concentrating on the data within the wall, Richard began tracing the flows of energy. He recognized some of the flows as magical energy similar to the flows of magic in Shandria's spell book. As he followed the flows of magic, the other flows of energy stopped changing the data they protected. However, the data was still indecipherable to Richard.

Stay on it, Rick, said Nickelo excitedly. *The other energy flows are logic and emotions. I can handle the emotions.*

I'll concentrate on the logic, said Jonathan.

Richard was not a computer, but his mind was in overdrive, or rather, his association with Nickelo in their share space was causing him to think faster than humanly possible. In the space of a few nanoseconds, the data within the wall settled down. Parts of the information became decipherable.

There was too much information for Richard to absorb. But he sensed logic threads from Nickelo and Jonathan going through the data gleaning facts of interest. The Crosioian battle computer had been out of the loop for almost a year, but even so, it held many future plans of military operations yet to occur. Of course, they were year-old plans, and things could have changed. However, one plan in particular caught Richard's attention.

Nick, Richard said. *That Crosioian scout was training for an invasion of Velos before she was reassigned to Veturna to guard Keka and the kids. That schematic looks like the spaceport and the DNA Center.*

We see it, Rick, said Nickelo. *But this data's a year old. The scout's battle computer was not privy to the date of the invasion.*

They may not have known a date when the information was put into the scout's battle computer, said Jonathan. *I calculate an eighty-four percent probability the invasion was called off.*

I disagree with your algorithm, said Nickelo. *The scout was training to infiltrate the spaceport's defenses in order to plant static tele-bots on key targets.*

Richard would have argued no one could pass through the spaceport's protective shield without being detected, but he knew better. He'd already been attacked twice inside the shields at the airfield and spaceport. None of the attackers had been detected.

How was she supposed to get past the planet's defensive shields? Richard said. *Was she that good? Or is Velos' shields that bad?*

Neither, said Nickelo. *Here's a reference about special assets. The data in the scout's battle computer doesn't indicate what the special assets are. But the whole invasion plan relies on the special assets getting the first wave safely on the planet.*

Even if they got planet side, Richard said, *they couldn't move large forces around on the planet undetected.* Before Nickelo could correct him, Richard said, *And no, I'm not forgetting about the magic users we've fought. But there's a big difference between having a magic user's invisibility spell hide a dozen orcs, and having the same shield hide a squadron of cats.*

I know, Rick, said Nickelo. *To have any chance of success, the invasion force would have to bring down the protective shields around the target areas. They'd have to knockout all the power plants. That would require heavy armor.*

Even heavy armor couldn't get through the protective shields, Richard said. *And even if sappers infiltrated the space port's shield first, the place is protected with hundreds of jammers. Handheld missiles would never reach their targets.*

Unless, corrected Jonathan, *those targets had previously been marked with pre-positioned static tele-bots. At the designated attack time, the tele-bots could activate and guide missiles to their targets. Once the power plants were taken out of action, the space port's protective shield would come down. The spaceport would then be open to aerial bombardment.*

Hmm, said Nickelo. *This is all interesting, but without the attack time, what good does the information do us?*

Should we notify the spaceport? Richard said getting worried. *Maybe the scout and those magic users at the spaceport were marking the DNA center as a target?*

I calculate you're probably correct, Rick, said Nickelo. *However, we need more specifics before raising an alarm. Don't forget. The Deloris Corporation is responsible for security on Velos now. I doubt they'd be receptive of any information you'd give them without specifics. After your antics yesterday, you're not on their favorite wizard scout list.*

Richard couldn't argue with his battle computer's analysis. However, something was nagging at the back of his mind. *You know, Nick, I had a strange feeling at this power plant a few weeks ago. It's the same feeling I had at the spaceport when I spotted the scout and those magic users.*

Hmm, said Nickelo. *Power plants would definitely be key targets. Maybe the invasion is going to involve more than just the spaceport.*

Can we detect a static tele-bot if one is here? Richard asked hopefully.

Not possible, said Jonathan. *They're undetectable until*

activated.

Then what– Richard started to ask.

We need to hack into the tele-network, said Nickelo.

We already have, said Jonathan. *Are you forgetting?*

I don't mean the part controlled by 'the One', said Nickelo. *We need to hack into the part controlled by the Crosioians' Master computer.*

If that was possible, Richard said trying to be the logical one for a change. *Why haven't you done it before now?*

Jonathan answered first. *Because it's secured the same way as the scout's battle helmet. In other words, it's probably secured with magic.*

Will you help us, Rick? said Nickelo.

The only answer Richard could give was yes, so he agreed. Within minutes, or was it nanoseconds, Richard found himself immersed in a gigantic web of information. It was too much for him, even with Nickelo's help. Once Richard helped the two battle computers gain access to the area of the tele-network controlled by the Master computer, Richard backed out some. Although he did stay inside Nickelo's databanks in case they needed help. Occasionally, they did. In those cases, he forced himself into the alien network long enough to help Nickelo with the magic part of the decryption. Then he pulled back into his battle computer's databanks to wait for another call.

During one of his waits, Richard sensed a ghost of a memory. It was more a dream than it was a memory. He had a vision of a medical chart. The patient's name on the chart was Janice Myers Deluth. The chart's description indicated the patient was being tested for a possible pregnancy. The chart indicated the spouse of the patient was Thomas R. Jacobs.

The commandant? Richard thought.

Richard forgot all about Nickelo and Jonathan's mission. Instead, he concentrated on the dream. Richard watched as the computer-controlled medical equipment tested the unconscious woman. She was pretty, even in her sleep. He'd never seen the commandant's wife, but she looked like she would be a good match for him.

The computer directing the medical computer was taken over by another mind. Richard recognized the feel of '*the One*'.

Leave her alone! Richard tried to shout, but he couldn't. He was in a dream.

As Richard watched, the medical device detected a fertilized egg in the patient's womb.

Richard had a sudden realization. *No, there are two eggs.*

One egg was teleported out of the womb. The other remained. Richard followed the part of the dream with the teleported egg. He was mesmerized. He needed to find out what happened to the egg. He found the egg in a lab on a planet far from Earth. The word 'Storage' popped into his mind. A multitude of equipment began working on the egg. Some partial pieces of alien DNA was spliced into the egg's DNA. Eventually, the egg was nurtured until it was a viable human baby boy. The baby was sent to an orphanage on Earth.

What the hell? Richard thought. Richard tried to get deeper in the dream, but he was pulled back by a shout.

Rick! shouted Nickelo. *They're here now. The attack is imminent!*

Richard wanted to ask his battle computer about the dream, but the sound of urgency in his battle computer's thoughts told him it wasn't the time.

Here? Now? Richard said. *Where?*

They're here, Rick, said Nickelo. *They're at the airfield and the spaceport.*

They're at the Academy as well, said Jonathan.

The sappers are inside the protective shields now, said Nickelo. *The Crosioian fleet with the first attack wave will be in orbit in fifteen minutes.*

Richard opened his eyes. He saw the power plant before him. All was calm. He heard nothing unusual in the night air. He was tempted to ask if the battle computers were sure, but he didn't. Nickelo sounded almost panicky, and computers didn't panic.

We have to sound the warning, Richard said. *We have to notify the Imperial High Command now. We have to let the commandant know.*

Jonathan, said Nickelo. *Open up a channel to the central computer.*

If I do, said Jonathan, *they'll know we can get out of the armory.*

Do it, said Nickelo. *Sound the alert. Notify the other battle computers in the armory. Show them the weak spot. Have them contact their wizard scouts.*

Complying, said Jonathan.

What about me? Richard said. *The cohort's unarmed. Maybe I should go to the armory and blow it open. The cohort will need their battle suits and weapons.*

No, said Nickelo in a tone indicating he was not open for arguments. *You stay here. There are static tele-bots here. As soon as they activate, you have to destroy them. We need to make sure at least one power plant remains in operation in order to keep the airfield's protective shield up.*

I can't stand around here doing nothing if we're being attacked, Richard said. The beast that was his anger was rattling its cage.

You won't be doing nothing, said Nickelo. *The sappers will come here to personally knock out the power plant once their missiles fail. You'll have plenty to do. Trust me.*

I've sent out the warning, said Jonathan. *However, I don't think the conglomerate's security ships are taking me serious. Neither are their ground forces.*

Then we'll just have to tell someone who will take us seriously, said Nickelo.

CHAPTER 53

Liz scanned the computer readouts from the other ships in the fleet. Whatever personal feelings of the other officers, they were all doing their duty. All reports were coming in quickly and efficiently. Liz nodded her head. The admiral had trained the fleet well. Everything was as it should be.

"They're jolly on the spot, aren't they?" said Trinity.

"They know they'd better be," Liz said. "A letter of reprimand from an acting fleet commander carries just as much weight in wartime as that of a real admiral."

"You'd give them a letter for being late on a routine-maintenance report?" said Trinity sounding little shocked.

"There's no such thing as routine in wartime," Liz said. "You know that, Trinity." Then with a slight smile, Liz said, "But, no. I wouldn't give them a letter. However, I'd make them wish I had before I was done. I've got forty-five minutes left as acting fleet commander. I'm not going to let anyone make a mistake on my watch. When I give an order, I expect it to be obeyed."

"Sir, yes, sir," said Trinity with a mock salute.

Liz smiled again. The command bridge was almost empty. No one else was watching.

Trinity smiled back. "Well, anyway, enjoy it while you can. In another forty-five minutes you'll be just plain old Lieutenant Commander Bistos again."

"And that'll be fine with me," Liz said. She meant it. Liz figured she had a long way to go before she'd be ready to command a fleet in combat.

Even as an acting fleet commander, the stress of knowing the lives of the twenty thousand souls in the fleet were in her hands was... well, stressful.

"Sir," said one of the ensigns at the communication console. "I have a priority message for fleet commander's ears only. The security signature is from the Imperial High Command, but I don't recognize the name."

Curious, Liz said, "What name is that?"

"It's from an Admiral Nickelo, sir," said the ensign.

Liz exchanged glances with Trinity. The wizard scout was just as intrigued as her.

"Send it to the captain's stateroom," Liz said. "I'll take it in there."

Liz started for the adjoining door to the stateroom. She looked over her shoulder and said, "Trinity, you come with me."

*　　*　　*

Five minutes later, Liz and Trinity stared at each other in disbelief. Only they had to believe. Battle computers were not prone to exaggeration. Richard's battle computer had somehow hacked his way into the tele-network and faked the security signature of the Imperial High Command. That was a certain court martial for Richard, and a memory wipe or destruction for his battle computer.

Unless he's right, Liz thought.

"We need to contact the admiral," said Trinity. "Only the fleet commander can order the fleet into action."

"Or the acting fleet commander," Liz said.

"The communication's blackout on the planet lasts another 40 minutes," said Trinity. "Velos will already be overrun if we wait."

Liz silently cursed the fool who had ordered the blackout. *How dare they think a wedding took priority over military readiness.*

"All the senior officers are planet side," said Trinity. "What're you going to do, Liz?"

"Do?" Liz said. "I'm going to do my duty. Velos is in trouble.

I'm a soldier. I'm going to fight."

Trinity smiled as if she'd known the answer before Liz had said it.

"They'll either pin a medal on you or court martial you for this, Liz," said Trinity. "But they can court martial us both. I'm behind you all the way."

With a determined look, Liz hit the emergency intercom button on the captain's communication panel.

"All ships," Liz said in a steady voice belying her nervousness. "Battle stations. This is not a drill. Prepare for emergency override in 5 minutes. Destination, Velos."

*   *   *

The Crosioian fleet came out of hyper-drive in perfect formation. The Crosioian admiral expected no less. They'd practiced it too many times to fail now. With a confident nod, the admiral noted the location of the twenty Empire warships orbiting the planet. They were all light cruisers or destroyers. There wasn't a dreadnought among them.

"Commence attack," ordered the admiral.

The one hundred and six warships in the fleet began their attack runs on the unsuspecting Empire ships. The red blips denoting the Empire ships immediately began disappearing from the command deck's overhead display.

"They're not regular Empire ships," said the ship's captain. "Based upon their insignias, they appear to be Deloris Conglomerate security ships."

The admiral was disappointed. This was turning out to be too easy. She walked the length of the command deck. Her command ship was the largest of the fleet's dreadnaughts. Unless more Empire ships somehow miraculously appeared, the battle would be won before it was even over.

"General Constance," said the admiral. "How soon before the shields are down? The Empire fleet around Regalos could be here in 22 minutes." She doubted the Empire could react that quickly. Even if the fleet somehow started coming as soon as they were notified of the attack, it would take them several minutes to get organized. Only a lunatic fleet commander would launch an attack before receiving orders from their Imperial High Command. But the admiral wasn't going to tell the general that.

"The special assets successfully got our first wave through Velos' detection shield," said General Constance. "Surprisingly, Crendemor's magic users were able to get all our sappers inside their target's protective shields undetected. As soon as the static tele-bots activate, the sapper's missiles will destroy the power plants. Then you can begin your aerial bombardment."

"Excellent," said the admiral.

The admiral watched the last of the red blips on the overhead display disappear. "All is going as planned," she said. "Is Crendemor leading the attack on the DNA Center?"

A sneer appeared on the general's face. "Yes, admiral. The dark elf returned a short time ago. He just made the last shuttle in the spaceport's attack force. He assured me he would obtain the vials of DNA gas. Once he does that, your fleet can bombard the spaceport into oblivion.

The admiral gave a rare smile of approval. All was going as planned.

*   *   *

As soon as Jerad got the news from his battle computer, he hastily pulled on his jumpsuit and boots. He rushed out of his tent onto the dirt street separating one row of tents from the other. Other cadets in his cohort were already in the street milling around after they'd been contacted by their own battle computers. One of the platoon sergeants was trying to get things organized. He wasn't having much luck.

Stephen, Jerad told his battle computer. *Contact Tam's battle computer. Tell her to get the females moving to the main gate. I'll get the males to do the same.*

Complying, sir, said his battle computer.

"Listen up," Jerad said in a loud voice. He didn't shout, but his voice carried nevertheless. When you worked in armor for twenty years, you learned to use a voice that carried.

"Platoon sergeants," Jerad ordered. "Get your platoons organized and move them to the front gates. The females will meet us there." When the cadets didn't move quite fast enough, Jerad added, "Now!"

Everyone started moving at once. Even if Jerad hadn't been the cohort's first sergeant, the other cadets would have followed his orders. They needed something to do, and following a strong, experienced leader like Jerad came naturally.

"Wizard Scout Michaels," Jerad said. "Get them there as quickly as you can. I'm going to the gate and get things organized."

Wizard Scout Michaels was cadet 803. He was one of the cohort's platoon sergeants. He seemed surprised Jerad knew his real name. But he needn't have been. Jerad had made it a point to learn everyone's name in the cohort years earlier. As far as Jerad was concerned, the current situation was no time to use numbers.

"Yes, sir," said Wizard Scout Michaels. He almost gave a salute, but he caught himself in time.

Jerad got to the gate just as the cohort's females were marching up. The two blue-suited gate guards had closed the gate. They were awkwardly holding their plasma rifles as if they weren't sure whether to point them at the marching cadets or somewhere else. The two roving guards ran up and joined their fellow guards at the gate.

"Open the gate," Jerad said to the highest-ranking security guard in a calm voice. "Didn't you get the warning?"

"We've got orders to keep you here until the higher ups figure out what's going on," said the guard. With a glance at the cohort's females and the male formation double timing up the street, the guard added, "Sir."

Jerad chose to ignore the guards for the moment. They were just following orders. He addressed the cohort instead.

"If what our battle computers tell us is true," Jerad said in a loud voice, "all hell is going to break loose in less than 10 minutes."

"What can we do?" said Wizard Scout Michaels. "We don't even have weapons. They're locked up in the armory with our battle suits."

"Listen up," Jerad said in a loud voice so everyone could hear. "You're wizard scouts now. You are the most dangerous weapons in the galaxy. Here's what's going to happen. First platoon, you go with Wizard Scout Stella to the armory. Hold it until Sergeant

Hendricks gets there. Sappers are going to try and destroy it with missiles. You are not going to let them. You are wizard scouts. Destroy the missiles before they hit."

Jerad turned to Stella. "You're a diviner, Stella. Seek out any static tele-bots when they activate and put them out of action."

"Understood," said Stella.

"We're still going to need some long-range weapons," said one of the males in the cohort.

"Get them as you go," Jerad said. He pointed at the four blue-suited guards. "You can start with theirs."

In a flash, the four guards were unarmed and their weapons and equipment were in the hands of wizard scouts.

"Wizard Scout Telsa," Jerad said. "Take second platoon and head for the backup teleporter. Hold it until first platoon arrives with your battle suits and weapons. Acquire any gear you can along the way if you meet conglomerate guards."

"Yes, sir," said Telsa as she blew open the gate with Power. The second platoon followed her without question.

"Third platoon," Jerad said. "You're with me. Sergeant Ron has twelve cats armed with live plasma and phase weapons. We're going to get as many as we can."

Stella started to speak but Jerad cut her off. The military wasn't a democracy, and only one person could be in charge. If someone else had been better qualified, he would have been following their orders. But as an ex-commander of an armored battalion and the acting cohort first sergeant, he had taken command.

"Wizard Scout Stella," Jerad said. "Once you get in the armory, send one squad with second platoon's equipment to the backup teleporter. Send another squad with third platoon's gear to hanger 1."

"Yes, sir," said Stella. "What about the rest of the platoon?"

"Rick's holding the west-side power plant," Jerad said. "Once you're done at the armory, take the rest of your wizard scouts and support him there."

"Yes, sir," said Stella as she got the second platoon moving.

Within seconds, Jerad was leading the third platoon in the direction of hangar 1. Along the way, they gathered a half dozen plasma rifles from a patrol of conglomerate guards who happened across their path.

When they arrived at hangar 1, Sergeant Ron wasted no time asking questions. Jerad hadn't expected him too. Within two minutes, Jerad was able to dispatch the two medium cats in hangar 1 that had live weapons with instructions to hold the west-side power plant.

"What about the two east-side power plants?" said Sergeant Ron as he led the remaining wizard scouts towards hangar 2.

"No time to save them," Jerad said. "The attack's coming from the east. The hangars on the east side of the airfield are probably a lost cause as well."

As if confirming his prediction, a bright flash of light followed by a loud explosion came from the east side of the airfield.

"Hmm," observed Sergeant Ron. "I guess someone tried to enter hangar 32 without permission."

Before Jerad could respond to the maintenance chief, a series of bright streaks flew by in the direction of the west-side power plant and the backup teleporter. Shortly thereafter a series of explosions reverberated throughout the night.

"This is it, wizard scouts," Jerad shouted. "Think of it as your final graduation test."

"Ha!" laughed Sergeant Ron. "This is nothing. Back when I was in the military, things were really tough."

In spite of the situation, Jerad smiled. The old sergeant was as crazy as ever.

Turning his head as he ran, Jerad watched another salvo of rockets coming from the east. As they passed by a few hundred meters away, he was tempted to try telekinesis to take them down. But he discarded the idea. He wasn't a diviner. Without his battle helmet to guide him to his target, he'd never be able to track them accurately enough.

The second wave of missiles was headed in the direction of the west-side power plant. Jerad hoped Rick could protect the power plant on his own until help arrived.

CHAPTER 54

Richard sent out a series of strong emotions in a call for help.

I don't think it does any good to keep calling, Rick, said Nickelo. *Based upon previous missions, I'd say the dolgars heard you the first time. If they're going to come, they'll come. If they aren't, they won't.*

Richard sent out another call just to spite his battle computer. Besides, he needed to do something. Just standing by the power plant's fence waiting for something to happen went against his nature.

A bright flash from the east side of the airfield was quickly followed by another. The night air reverberated with the sound of loud explosions.

It's started, said Nickelo. *Those explosions were from the east-side power plants. Both plants are offline now.*

Then I guess we're next, Richard said.

Missiles are inbound, Rick, said Nickelo.

Richard didn't need to look at his heads-up display to confirm his battle computer's words. He sensed his battle computer's data in their shared space. The data tracked five missiles heading in his direction. Richard visualized them as surely as if he was seeing them with his own eyes. One of the missiles veered off to the north. Another streaked off to the south.

They're targeting the armory and the backup teleporter, said

Nickelo.

Richard said a silent prayer for his friends. He hadn't even gotten to say goodbye to them.

Your friends can take care of themselves, said Nickelo. *You need to worry about those three missiles headed your way.*

Richard realized he'd inadvertently been thinking in his shared space. He resolved to pay more attention the next time.

I'll do my job, Nick, Richard said. *You just find those Crosioian tele-bots and get them out of action.*

I'm working on it, said Nickelo. *It's not that easy.*

Richard saw the lead missile when it popped over the top of a nearby warehouse. He reached out with his mind. Richard felt the energy flow from the missile's engine as well as the missile itself. Wrapping the missile with Power, Richard forced it downward. The missile hit the ground and erupted in a violent explosion.

Two more, Rick, said Nickelo.

I can count, Richard said as he tried to wrap a second missile with Power. He missed on his first attempt. His second try was better. As he wrapped the second missile with Power, Richard sensed his battle computer's calculations in their shared space. He wasn't going to have time to stop the final missile using the same technique.

Richard brought his M12 to bear on the third missile and pulled the trigger. A solid stream of red plasma rounds streaked towards the third missile. At the same time, he pushed downward with telekinesis on the second missile. It veered downward into a dilapidated warehouse. The building exploded sending pieces of thin-metal sheets in all directions. The time was 0431 hours. Richard hoped no early risers had been in the building.

Two hundred meters, said Nickelo.

I know, Richard said as he tried to adjust the stream of plasma rounds onto the last of the missiles. *I could use some help, buddy.*

Your wish is my command oh greatest of wizard scouts, said Nickelo.

Richard felt the arms of his battle suit moved ever so slightly.

Boom!

The last missile exploded twenty meters in front of Richard. For a small missile, it packed a very large punch. The force of the explosion threw Richard through the security fence surrounding the power plant. He slammed into the side of the building.

Richard let out an 'Umph!' as the force of the blow knocked his breath out. He immediately felt fresh air forced into his lungs from the tubes running down his throat. Richard staggered to his feet.

Five more missiles inbound, Rick, said Nickelo. *From their trajectories, I calculate the entire second salvo is headed here.*

Great, Richard thought. *I barely handled the three.*

You know you could have put a defensive shield up to absorb the force of that last explosion, said Nickelo.

I didn't want to waste the Power, Richard said. *I'm already down to fifty-eight percent Power in my reserve. Taking out those two missiles cost me five percent each.*

I'm proud of you, Rick, said Nickelo. *You're using your brains instead of just reacting.*

You can give me a pat on the back if I'm still alive in thirty seconds, Richard said. *In the meantime, find that tele-bot.*

I'm trying, Rick, said Nickelo. *Here come the missiles.*

Trying a different tactic this time, Richard began firing his M12 at the lead missile when it was still five hundred meters out. The stream of plasma rounds got close, but he couldn't quite target the missile.

Nick? Richard said.

Got it, said Nickelo as the arm of the battle suit moved slightly.

Boom!

Richard sensed the most violent part of the explosion with his passive scan. He wrapped three sides of the explosion with Power and forced a hot jet of energy out the remaining side into the path of two of the other missiles. One of them exploded in midair. The other wobbled momentarily before slamming into the ground.

Rick, said Nickelo. *I've located the static tele-bot. Take it out.*

Again, Richard didn't need his heads-up display. He sensed the location of the tele-bot from his battle computer's thoughts in their shared space.

It's too small for me, Nick, Richard said. *Not enough time. Take control of my Power.*

Complying, said Nickelo.

A microscopic-thin line of Power reached out from Richard back towards the power plant. Richard sensed a series of small bursts of energy as the tele-bots exploded.

The two remaining missiles wavered momentarily, but then they steadied and continued on their course towards the power plant.

They've already locked on, said Nickelo. *You've got to take them out.*

Richard tracked the missiles in his shared space. The lead missile was only a hundred yards away. The second missile was twenty-five meters behind.

No time, Richard thought.

Richard knew he had to stop both missiles. This was the last remaining power plant. If the missiles succeeded in knocking it out, the airfield's protective field would fail. Then the Crosioian fleet overhead would be free to blow everything on the airfield to smithereens.

Desperate, Richard gathered all but one percent of his remaining Power and threw it out as a wall in the path of the missiles.

Boom! Boom!

The double force of the explosions slammed Richard into the wall of the power plant again. This time he hit hard enough he was momentarily dazed. Richard sensed Power from his third Power reserve permeate his body and attempt to return it to baseline. The worst of the effects of the hit faded within three seconds.

Richard shook his head in an attempt to clear the cobwebs. *I'm still a little dizzy, Nick.*

The first ninety-percent of your injuries selfheal fairly quickly, said Nickelo. *The last ten percent can take a little longer.*

Richard vaguely remembered Chief Instructor Winslow saying as much.

Taking a moment to glance at the readout for his primary Power reserve, Richard noticed it was steady at one percent.

Aren't you going to chastise me for using all my Power? Richard asked.

No, said Nickelo. *You're a wizard scout now. You did what you thought you had to do. Besides, I have to give you credit for saving one percent to charge your dimensional pack.*

Richard was surprised, but he said nothing further. He extracted the isotopic battery from his M12 and summoned a new one from his dimensional pack.

Now what? Richard said. *How are the others doing?*

Jerad's got two medium cats heading your way, said Nickelo. *Stella and Telsa have successfully defended the armory and the backup teleporter. Stella's still waiting for Sergeant Hendricks to arrive. Sergeant Ron's trying to get more cats up and running.*

Richard checked out the area for two thousand meters in all directions with his passive scan. He saw plenty of lifeforms, but none looked like an enemy formation.

I don't see any sign of the Crosioians, Richard said.

They must have magic users shielding them, said Nickelo. *Switch your filter to sonic.*

Richard did as requested. His visual sight of the airfield was replaced by a strange series of vibrations.

What's that? Richard said.

I'm comparing the sonic vibrations with known sonic signatures in my database, said Nickelo. *I'm putting the results in our shared space.*

That's heavy armor, Richard said. *Is it ours or theirs?*

I've marked all friendly armor on your heads-up display in orange, said Nickelo. *I've marked the remaining sonic vibrations in red.*

Richard saw a line of six red dots on his heads-up display making their way at high speed across the airfield. A line of three more red dots were behind them.

As Richard watched, three orange dots marking friendly vehicles blinked out. Richard picked up the sound of distant explosions. One of the red dots in the front line disappeared. Then two more orange dots disappeared. Richard heard more explosions.

Were those wizard scouts? Richard said concerned he might have just witnessed Jerad's demise.

Negative, said Nickelo. *They were conglomerate armor. Jerad's at hangar 4 getting a Leviathan cat running. The two blinking orange dots are wizard scouts. They're forty-five seconds out. You'll notice the five remaining red dots in that first line are only twenty-eight seconds out. Get ready.*

Richard wasn't sure what else he could do to get ready. He only had a little over one percent in his Power reserve. He unhooked his phase rod from his belt and activated it in destructive mode. Richard moved the dial to maximum. The red arcs of phase energy crawling up and down the length of the rod took on an intensity he'd never seen before. To Richard, it felt like the demonic essence in the phase rod was demanding souls as living sacrifices. It was hungry.

Switch back to normal night filter, Rick, said Nickelo. *The enemy cats aren't trying to hide anymore.*

Richard switched out his filter. The strange vibration of the sonic filter was replaced by the familiar red of standard night vision. Richard saw the tops of three cats over the roof of a distant warehouse.

Suggestions, Nick? Richard asked hoping his battle computer had some.

Don't die, said Nickelo with a laugh.

I'll do my best, Richard thought as he began running towards the approaching cats. If he had to die, he wasn't going to do it sitting around waiting for death to come to him.

The first cat will be coming around the north corner of that warehouse in five seconds, said Nickelo. *You're current path is too far to the south.*

Richard held his course. He hit the wall of the warehouse near the center and burst through the thin-metal siding. Green plasma rounds began blowing small holes in the roof as the nearest Crosioian cat tried to train its anti-personnel weapons on Richard's fleeting form. Richard leaped on top of a convenient box in the warehouse. He used his momentum to jump again. His jump carried him through the warehouse's roof. The warehouse was built for low-security items, and the metal roof was thin. Richard burst through easily.

Richard rolled on the roof to avoid a burst of rounds from a light chain gun. As he rose, Richard saw a light cat to his front. Two other light cats were to its left and right. Dodging to avoid a stream of plasma rounds from the left-most cat, Richard jumped off the roof aiming for the top of the nearest cat.

The thin roof of the warehouse held his weight long enough to complete his jump. He landed on the top of the cat. This cat was a model unfamiliar to Richard. It was just shy of four meters high. Its width was wider than normal. The cat was armed with two light chain guns and a 40mm phase cannon.

It's a Crosioian cat, said Nickelo. *It's wider to accommodate their wings.*

Richard slammed his phase rod against the cat's upper-entry hatch. The phase rod bounced off without doing any visible damage.

It's magnetically sealed, said Nickelo. *Your phase rod can't penetrate it.*

Ya think? Richard said growing frustrated. *Maybe you should've told me before I wasted my time beating on it.*

Without waiting for a reply, Richard switched his aim and brought his phase rod down on the base of the 40mm phase cannon. Apparently it wasn't magnetically protected, because the base of the cannon cracked. The cannon drooped towards the ground. Richard took out the two chain guns in a similar fashion.

Jump! Nickelo commanded.

Richard didn't waste time asking questions. He jumped. As he did, a burst of rounds hit the cat he'd been on as the other two cats turned their light-chain guns on their companion. The rounds didn't penetrate the cat's armor. They ricocheted off into the air.

Hitting the ground in a somersault, Richard came up on the run. He ran for the next nearest cat in an attempt to get beneath the level of its guns. He succeeded, but the third cat started firing at Richard. His battle suit dodged to one side of its own volition as a line of chain-gun rounds tore into the ground where he'd been standing.

Thanks, Nick, Richard said as he reversed course and grabbed hold of one of the cat's legs.

No problem, said Nickelo. *That's my job.*

Richard climbed up the metal leg until he got even with the backside of the cat's body. The third cat began spraying its companion with both of its chain guns. Richard hugged the temporary protection of the cat's backside. He knew he wouldn't be safe long. He had no doubt the pilot would think to turn around in order to give his companion a visible target.

Stop dillydallying, Rick, said Nickelo. *The fourth and fifth cats are heading towards the power plant.*

Richard was too busy trying to stay alive to comment. At that moment, the cat he was riding started to spin. The third cat redoubled its firing rate apparently assuming Richard would soon be within its sights.

No time for half measures, Richard thought. He tore the satchel of J22 explosives off his shoulders and jammed it in a convenient cubby hole near the cat's engine exhaust.

Set the timers for three seconds, Nick, Richard said as he jumped free.

Compliance, said Nickelo.

Richard ran for the warehouse hoping to make its cover before the explosives detonated. A line of chain-gun rounds from the other cat intersected his path. Richard felt the battle suit start to move as Nickelo tried to dodge the rounds, but his battle computer was a split second too late. A sound similar to rain beating on a tin roof echoed inside Richard's battle suit. The tough armor of the battle suit deflected most of the chain gun's rounds, but not all.

Richard felt white-hot fire in both of his legs as well as his right hip. His feet were knocked out from underneath him. He fell to the ground. At the same time, the bag of J22 plastic explosives detonated. Small pieces of cat armor ricocheted off Richard's back. The force of the explosion hurled Richard several meters along the ground before he rolled to a stop.

Crawl, said Nickelo. *The third cat is trying to train its 40mm phase cannon on you.*

In spite of his pain, Richard crawled for the dubious shelter of the warehouse all the while expecting to feel 40mm cannon rounds tearing into his body at any moment. To his relief, they didn't come.

You've got six bullet wounds, said Nickelo. *Your selfheal needs about thirty seconds to repair the damage.*

Richard felt warm blood filling up his battle suit's legs. However, he also felt Power from his third reserve wrapping around his injuries and staunching the flow of blood.

Although his selfheal was repairing the damage to his body, the pain was still excruciating. Nevertheless, Richard forced himself to crawl into a hole in the warehouse's wall. He rolled over onto his back and brought his M12 to bear on the fully-armed cat. He didn't fire. The third cat was no longer firing or even moving for that matter. Even the cat whose weapons he'd disabled was no longer moving.

Through grifted teeth, Richard said, "What gives?" He spoke aloud. The battle suit had unsealed when its armor was breached. The battle suit's air tubes were no longer jammed down his throat.

Before Nickelo could answer his question, a dark, wolfish-looking head emerged from the armored body of the third cat. Shortly thereafter, the rest of the dolgar followed.

"Tika!" Richard shouted out loud.

The dolgar held a fear-stricken human in her mouth. The human was dressed in the uniform of a Crosioian mercenary. He was screaming and trying to struggle free. Tika dived into the ground. A few moments later, she reappeared. The mercenary was no longer in her mouth.

Even though the mercenary had been trying to kill him, Richard didn't relish the form of his enemy's death. A little on the claustrophobic side, Richard shivered at the thought of being entombed alive.

Well, he's not alive anymore, said Nickelo. *So stop worrying about it. You're seventy percent healed. That's enough for you to function, so get moving.*

Richard leveraged himself up with his plasma rifle. He hobbled over to a hole in the warehouse wall facing the power plant. Tika trotted up beside him.

The fourth and fifth cats were just outside the power plant's fence. They began firing their 40mm cannons at the outer wall of the power plant. Pieces of concrete and metal blew high into the air. Richard fired his M12's 20mm grenades at the cats. As soon as he fired one round, he hastily chambered another round and fired again. Unfortunately, the 20mm rounds were too light to penetrate either of the cat's armor. The rounds glanced off the sides of the cats into the night sky.

"Tika," Richard said as he started moving towards the cats. "Stop them."

Tika growled, "No. Metal boxes no danger to pack."

"Thanks for nothing, Tika," Richard said as he continued firing. They in turn continued firing at the walls of the power plant. The reinforced concrete was thick, but Richard knew the cats were only moments from breaking through the walls and exposing the vulnerable generators inside.

Suddenly, a flash of red came out of the sky and slammed into one of the cats. Its armored body erupted in an explosion so violent only the legs and part of the floor of the cat remained. Dark billowing smoke floated into the night sky.

Richard heard a roar as an attack shuttle zoomed past. He caught a glimpse of a Deloris Conglomerate insignia on the shuttle's side.

At the same time, two medium cats strolled past the warehouse with all their energy weapons firing at the remaining Crosioian cat attacking the power plant.

That's two of the third platoon's scouts, explained Nickelo. *They'll take care of that light cat. There are three heavy cats twenty seconds out. You can't allow them to get here.*

Richard glanced at his heads-up display. He saw three red dots heading his way. He saw other red dots further back, but they appeared to be engaged by Conglomerate armor and several cats from the third platoon. There were no friendly forces between Richard and the three enemy cats charging his way.

Richard took off at a run towards the three approaching heavy cats. Surprisingly his legs and hip were basically healed. He still felt a jab of pain every time he took a step, but it was bearable.

Any ideas? Richard asked as he ran to intercept the cats.

You ask that a lot, Rick, said Nickelo. *And the answer is no. Not with one percent Power. I guess we'll have to figure it out when we get there. Maybe you'll get lucky.*

Unslinging the dimensional pack off his back, Richard pictured a man-portable, anti-armor rocket. No Power left his reserve.

Did you really think that was going to work? said Nickelo. *You've only got one point two-five percent Power. You'd need more than that to summon an anti-armor missile.*

Yeah, thanks for the timely update, Nick, Richard said as he extracted the isotopic battery from his M12 and summoned a new one from his dimensional pack. He also summoned a resupply of 20mm ammo. Once he got it, Richard reloaded the M12. He continued running towards the incoming cats.

After Richard shoved the last 20mm grenade in the rifle's magazine, the first of the Crosioian cats strolled into view. It was a Leviathan, the largest and most heavily armed of any U.H.A.A.V.

Somehow, I don't think we're going to get lucky today, said Nickelo.

CHAPTER 55

The Crosioian admiral surveyed the overhead display along the wall of the command bridge. Operations at the spaceport were going as expected. The spaceport's power plants had been destroyed, and its protective shields had been brought down on schedule. From the overhead display, the admiral could tell her fleet's attack shuttles were gaining air superiority over the spaceport. All was going well at the spaceport. Even now, Crendemor and his assault teams were inside the DNA center acquiring the vials of DNA gas. Once their technical teams had removed as much of the center's computer data as possible, the assault team would set their explosives and depart. The success of the primary objective was assured.

The assaults on the Academy and the airfield were another matter. Somehow, the new batch of wizard scouts at the airfield had acquired their weapons and armor as well as heavy weapons. They were defending the remaining power plant. Until it was destroyed, his dreadnaughts couldn't effectively bombard the installations at the airfield.

Even the Academy was giving General Constance's forces trouble. The admiral slammed her fist down on a support railing for one of the bridge's many communication consoles. The sound shocked those around him.

"How can a handful of decrepit old wizard scouts at the Academy thwart your attack, general?" yelled the admiral. "Can you explain that to me?"

The holograph of the general's head clearly showed the Crosioian's embarrassment. The admiral put her face right in front of the general's.

"You will personally lead the next assault, general," said the admiral. "I want the Academy's protective shield brought down. Do I make myself clear?"

"Yes, admiral," said the general. "I will personally bring you the head of the commandant, or I will not return alive."

"See that you don't," said the admiral.

The general's holograph disappeared to be replaced by the Crosioian head preferred by the Master computer.

"You've accomplished your primary objective, admiral," said Zenthra in the guise of the Master computer. "I recommend pulling your forces back from the airfield and the Academy grounds."

"Retreat?" said the admiral. "Never!" She turned to the bridge officer. "Has the DNA Center's second wave landed yet?"

"Negative, admiral," said the officer. "The second wave is still two minutes from the spaceport."

"Good," said the admiral. "Shift the spaceport's second wave to the airfield. I want the airfield destroyed along with every one of those new wizard scouts."

"Admiral," said the holographic-head of the Master computer. "I highly recommend—"

"Enough," said the admiral. "I'm in charge. The decision is mine. Divert the second wave."

Zenthra controlled his anger. He hated living creatures and their freewill. He began to plan how he would kill the admiral and her irksome freewill.

CHAPTER 56

TAC Officer Gaston Myers was worried. The commandant had taken no one with him to the spaceport. He'd told the commandant it was too dangerous. But the commandant had been adamant. The commandant had said if one wizard scout couldn't do what needed to be done, a hundred couldn't do it. The trouble was the commandant was no longer the wizard scout he'd once been.

TAC Officer Myers gritted his teeth. He wanted to go fight by the side of his father, but he couldn't. He had his orders. The Academy's power plant had to be held at all costs. If the protective shield failed, he had no doubt the Crosioian fleet overhead would send a half dozen tactical nukes down to destroy the Academy and what was left of its cadets.

"Hold at all costs," the commandant had said.

TAC Officer Myers looked around him. Dozens of torn and bloody bodies littered the ground. His cadets had already paid a high price. He knew it was going to get even higher.

A quick glance told the story. Only two hundred of the freshman and sophomore cadets were still alive. Many of those were wounded. But the ones he could see still gripped their weapons resolutely. Gaston Myers nodded his head with pride. They were good soldiers, every one of them. The smoking remains of a dozen Crosioian cats and armored vehicles gave mute testimony to the cadet's determination.

"They'll be coming again soon," said TAC Officer Trevor. "We need more heavy weapons."

TAC Officer Trevor was a seasoned wizard scout of eighty-four years. Unfortunately, her Power reserve had been irreparably damaged decades ago. But when the commandant had asked the old woman to return to active duty as a TAC Officer, she hadn't hesitated. None of the twenty-two disabled wizard scout veterans had. The skills of those old wizard scouts combined with the courage of the latest crop of cadets had proven too much for the first wave of attackers. The Academy's power plant stood unscathed.

"I give them five minutes," said TAC Officer Myers. "I can see them massing on the far side of the science building."

"My scans aren't what they used to be," admitted TAC Officer Trevor. "How many?"

"Too many," TAC Officer Myers said. He looked around him. The cadets' defensive line was thin, but he had faith in them. Despite what the Deloris Conglomerate said, these were wizard scout cadets. He'd taught them all he could during their time on Velos. He'd soon find out if it was enough.

"Sir, cadet 35, sir," said a nearby cadet with a light, anti-tank rocket launcher cradled under her arm. TAC Officer Myers noticed the odd angle of her second arm and the blood leaking from a hasty field bandage.

"What is it cadet?" TAC Officer Myers said in the strongest voice as he could muster. He was tired, but he had to stay strong for the sake of the cadets.

"Sir! Will there be more of those magic user types?" said the cadet. "Our weapons can't get through their shields, sir."

TAC Officer Myers noticed several of the nearby cadets listening for his answer. They didn't look scared, but he could see the concern on their faces. They assumed they were going to die. They just wanted to make their deaths count.

Without answering the cadet directly, TAC Officer Myers walked around the broken pieces of concrete and steel that used to be the administration building. He stepped into the parade field among the bodies of three score cadets and TAC Officers. They hadn't made the relative safety of the rubble before the Crosioians' armor and infantry had mowed them down.

Turning to face the living cadets, TAC Officer Myers spoke over his battle helmet's external speaker. He set the volume to maximum.

"You've all done well," he began. "The commandant would be proud of you. Your TAC officers are proud of you. I… I am proud of you. The sign over the entrance to this Academy says 'Through these gates pass the best scouts in two galaxies.' You have proven that today."

TAC Officer Myers gestured towards the science building located a thousand meters away.

"In a short time, the Crosioians and their mercenary scum will come charging around and through that building. When they do, those of you with heavy weapons will concentrate your fire on their armor. The rest of you will engage their infantry."

Pointing to a black-robed corpse who had fallen a few meters away, TAC Officer Myers said, "You saw their magic users in action. But their balls of fire and bolts of lightning are no different than the Crosioians' plasma and phase weapons. They're just weapons in another form."

With a kick to the corpse, TAC Officer Myers said, "Their shields are no better than a scout's. This piece of smoldering filth is proof of that. Concentrate your fire on any magic users and overwhelm their shields. When their Power fails, they'll die."

After a short pause, TAC Officer Myers continued. "Most of you TAC officers don't have battle suits. Let those of you who do have armor take on the magic users in hand-to-hand if possible. You unarmored cadets will support them with your weapons as best you can."

Raising his fist in the air, TAC Officer Myers shouted, "You are wizard scouts. Our orders are to hold the power plant. That's exactly what we'll do. It will be a cold day on Sirius when wizard scouts let a bunch of bats and their mercenaries take over our Academy! You are all wizard scouts, every one of you. I salute you, my brothers and sisters!"

TAC Officer Myers stood at attention and gave a parade-ground perfect salute to the Academy's defenders.

Cadets and TAC Officers all along the line of defense stood and saluted him back. They erupted in cheers. The cheers were almost loud enough to drown out the roar of engines from dozens of armored vehicles. The Crosioians were on their way.

*   *   *

The intern brought the message to Acting Fleet Commander Bistos. The fleet had just started its second jump. They'd break out in the Velos system in less than six minutes.

"Sir," said the intern. "Message from the Imperial High Command."

Liz took her eyes off the hologram of the star chart long enough to acknowledge the intern.

"Read it to me, Mr. Silas," Liz said as she looked back at the star chart.

"From Imperial High Command," said the intern nervously. "All ships districts three and four. Make all speed to Velos system and engage Crosioian invasion fleet. Use of emergency military override of hyper-drives is authorized."

"Well, looks like there won't be a court martial after all," said Trinity. "Someone's looking out for you."

"Is that all, Mr. Silas?" Liz said choosing not to reply to Trinity's remark.

"No, sir," said the intern. "To Acting Fleet Commander Bistos. Engage enemy fleet posthaste. Commodore Alden will arrive with the 14th Fleet eighteen minutes after your arrival. You must hold Velos at all cost until then. Good hunting. End message."

The intern saluted and departed back to her communication console.

Liz looked up from the star charts. Lieutenant's McAfee and Author were looking at her expectantly. So was her friend Trinity.

"Hold at all costs," Liz said quietly. "To put it mildly, sirs, our fleet is expendable."

"If the information we're receiving from Velos is correct," said Lieutenant Author, "we will be outnumbered eight to one."

"True," said Lieutenant McAfee. "But we'll have surprise."

"And the ground-based weapons systems on Velos won't be idle," said Trinity. "At least half of the Crosioian fleet will be busy engaging them."

"They'll still be plenty to go around," Liz said. "They have six dreadnaughts, and we have two. As soon as we break out of hyperspace, I want both dreadnaughts and all four of our heavy cruisers to engage the nearest enemy dreadnaught. If we can put one out of action quickly, it will narrow the odds."

Liz looked at Trinity. "I have a tough assignment for your wizard scouts, Trinity."

"Tough assignments are nothing new, sir," said Trinity flashing a grin. "What's this one?"

"Dreadnaughts are too tough to take out quickly even with fire superiority," Liz said. "But, I believe we can put a hole in one large enough to put a shuttle through."

Trinity locked eyes with Liz, but Trinity didn't say anything. She merely nodded her head.

"You will take a tactical nuke with you," Liz said. "If you can get it near one of the ship's engines or its main isotopic batteries, the nuke should destroy the ship."

"Extraction?" said Trinity.

Liz looked hard at her friend. She needed to give them some kind of hope.

"Once the nuke is set," Liz said, "contact Telsa's battle computer. She's holding the backup teleporter at the airfield. If it's undamaged when you're ready, her technicians may be able to teleport your scout's to her location."

Liz didn't apologize for sending her friend on what was almost certainly a suicide mission. As far as Liz could tell, she was leading her entire fleet on a suicide mission.

"I've had worse odds," said Trinity with a tightlipped smile as she gave Liz a salute. "I'll see you on Velos, sir."

*   *   *

The commandant squeezed Chief Instructor Winslow's hand in a sign of assurance. The booted feet of the Crosioians' mercenaries had marched past the air duct without discovering their presence. He hadn't expected them to find them.

I might be old, the commandant thought, *but it'll take more than the likes of them to break through my best stealth shield.*

The commandant was a protector. Only a wizard scout who specialized in protector skills could protect multiple people with their stealth shield. The commandant had always been good at it. He'd only been detected once in his life. But even at an age when his Power was fading, the commandant was confident he could protect those around him.

He'd arrived at the DNA center just before the Crosioians took over the building in a blaze of plasma and phase rounds. Most of the center's technicians had escaped, but not all. The commandant could make out a pair of bloody legs through the slits in the vent.

There had been too many to fight. When the commandant had arrived, there had only been time to grab the chief instructor and one of her technicians before the Crosioians burst into the building's entrance. They'd been hiding in the air duct system since.

The commandant could see the edge of the glassed-in room where the DNA gas vent met the surface of Velos. Crosioian troops were hurriedly hauling equipment in and out of the room.

As the commandant continued to peer between the air vent's slits, two pairs of legs in black leather boots came into view.

"How long before the atomics are ready?" said a voice.

"All should be ready in another five minutes, Lord Crendemor," said a second voice.

"That is well," said the first voice. "Have your troops ready to board the shuttles as soon as your nukes are set. We'll remote detonate once the shuttles are clear."

"Yes, Lord Crendemor," said the second voice. "And, sir. The admiral has requested an update on the recovery of the DNA gas vials."

"I'm sure he has," said the first voice.

The commandant thought he detected a note of irritation in the voice.

"Tell the admiral I have recovered twenty-nine vials of the DNA gas," said the first voice. "They'll be returned to the flagship on the first shuttle."

The two sets of legs walked out of view.

The chief instructor looked at the commandant and whispered, "There were thirty vials, Thomas, not twenty-nine."

The commandant nodded his head. Someone was obviously keeping one for themselves.

"We need to stop them," whispered the DNA Center technician on the far side of the chief instructor. The technician gripped a small Deloris blaster in one hand. The commandant noted the man looked scared but determined.

"No," whispered the commandant. "Not yet. We have to wait for them to leave. Then we can try to disable whatever explosives they've left at the DNA vent. We can't let them destroy it."

The DNA gas vent was unique. The future of the wizard scout corps depended on the refined DNA gas. Without it, there could be no DNA baselines.

Despite the manipulations of the Deloris Conglomerate, the commandant had high hopes his wife, Janice, could convince the Imperial High Council to reverse their decision to close the Intergalactic Wizard Scout Academy. The DNA gas vent was the Academy's key to the future. It had to be protected at all costs.

The idea of hiding like a frightened rabbit grated the commandant to no end. But he forced himself to endure the shame of hiding. His passive scan detected too many lifeforms for him to prevail in any kind of fight.

The commandant could sense the blaze of Power with his passive scan from the first speaker that had stood in front of the vent. He was a powerful magic user. The commandant thought he might be the most powerful magic user he'd ever encountered. And he was not the only dangerous foe in the area. There were other magic users as well.

How did they all get here? he wondered.

The commandant shrugged off the thought. At the moment, it was not his greatest concern. He had to prevent the destruction of the DNA gas vent. The commandant forced himself to wait until the enemy departed the building. It wouldn't be long now.

CHAPTER 57

As the first of the Crosioian cats smashed its way through a nearby warehouse, Richard sensed a smaller cat moving to his right. It was a Warcat. Richard noted a Deloris Conglomerate insignia on the side of the Warcat.

That pilot is either very brave or very stupid, Richard told his battle computer.

I calculate a forty-two percent chance he may be both, said Nickelo. *Maybe the pilot's death will distract the Crosioian cats long enough for you to do something.*

Richard had no desire for the conglomerate pilot to die. The pilot was not his enemy; at least not yet. Richard respected bravery, and this pilot appeared to have plenty of guts.

Changing course, Richard ran towards the Warcat.

Are you crazy? said Nick. *What do you think you're doing?*

I haven't got enough Power to spit much less fight, Richard said. *I'm going to try and even the odds a little.*

When Richard got close to the Warcat, it spun and trained its chain gun on Richard.

Tika growled by his side and shifted into the void ready to attack in defense of a member of her pack.

"No," Richard growled back. "Wait."

"Don't fire," Richard yelled up at the Warcat. "You'll just irritate her."

The pilot didn't fire, but the chain gun moved slightly to better cover the dolgar.

"Are you planning to take on three heavy cats all by yourself?" Richard said. "You know that's suicide."

"I'm not running," said a high-pitched male voice out of the Warcat's speakers. "My family has never run from a fight."

Very admirable, said Nickelo, *but very stupid. Only an idiot would try to take on three heavy cats with a single Warcat.*

"You know what I am?" Richard said. He was pressed for time, but he needed the Warcat intact, and he didn't want to have to kill the pilot to get it.

"You're a wizard scout," said the pilot.

At that moment, three assault shuttles bearing conglomerate insignias flew by low overhead and made a strafing run on the approaching Crosioian cats. A blaze of plasma rounds and chain gun tracers from the cats returned fire. One of the shuttles exploded in midair.

To their credit, the two remaining shuttles reversed course in order to make a second pass.

"There's no time to argue," Richard shouted. "I need your Warcat. You can't hope to beat them. I can. If they destroy the power plant, we'll all be dead as soon as the fleet overhead sends the first nuke."

"I'm not running," said the pilot determinedly.

"Then don't," Richard said impatiently.

Just then, fire from the three heavy cats damaged a second shuttle. The shuttle turned to leave the area as it trailed smoke behind it. The remaining shuttle gamely turned for a third attack run.

"You can have my M12," Richard said. "Join my friends at the power plant. They're there now preparing to make a last stand."

The pilot appeared to hesitate.

"Being a soldier is more than just being brave," Richard said. "You need to be smart as well. Do the smart thing."

It took two heartbeats, but the hatch of the Warcat popped open. A young boy no older than sixteen climbed out of it.

"I'm not running," the boy said as if trying to convince himself as well as Richard.

Richard had no time or inclination to argue. He threw his M12 at the youth who caught it handily enough.

As Richard squeezed through the hatch, he yelled over his shoulder. "Do what you want, but they could use your help at the power plant."

The hatch sealed. *Plug me in, Nick.*

Richard's heads-up display lit up with views of the outside world. Fast moving streams of data scrolled down the right side of the screen. He ignored it. Richard sensed all of the cat's information from his shared space. Nickelo was feeding him a lot more data than was available through simple readouts.

Nice cat, Richard said as the Warcat quietly shifted into high gear.

It's a top of the line Warcat, said Nickelo. *I wonder what a sixteen year old was doing with it. It's four years newer than the Academy models. I'll say one thing for the Deloris Conglomerate. They don't skimp on things when it comes to cost.*

Richard checked his heads-up display. The young pilot was running in the direction of the power plant. From his passive scan, Richard knew Stella and some of his fellow cadets were already there. They appeared to be locked in battle with a large group of enemy infantry.

Nothing you can do about it, Rick, said Nickelo. *Stella and the others can take care of themselves. You've got to do something about these three heavy cats. Those two medium cats of ours took out that light cat, but five more Crosioian light cats and a medium have joined the battle. They've already got their hands full.*

What's happening at the hangars? Richard asked worried about the rest of his friends.

They're being hit by a second wave, answered Nickelo. *Jerad's got the cadets organized, and they're holding their own. If it wasn't for Jerad and his cadets, the power plant would be swamped already. By the way, it looks like Jerad's convinced some of the conglomerate's troops to fight under his command.*

Richard headed the Warcat towards the closest cat. A stream of plasma rounds from multiple anti-personnel weapons came his way. Richard kicked the Warcat to the left. It responded easily. The enemy fire tore up the asphalt to his right, but the Warcat was untouched.

The remaining conglomerate shuttle finished its turn. A series of anti-armor missiles and phase cannon rounds shot out from its front. The force field protecting the second cat in line stopped most of the fire. However, two of the missiles slammed into the cockpit. A large fireball erupted from the front of the heavy cat.

At almost the same time a ball of energy rose from a knot of soldiers running alongside the third cat in line. Richard recognized the energy as a spell of some type he didn't recognize. The spell hit the shuttle. A web of energy enveloped the shuttle. A second later, the shuttle collapsed inward on itself until it was a ball of crumpled metal. It fell from the sky and hit the dirt somewhere behind a stand of trees.

Richard targeted the group of soldiers and the hidden magic user as he thought the command to fire the Warcat's chain gun. The stream of light slugs tore into some of the soldiers. The rounds tore holes in their armor and left death in their wake. Other rounds stopped in midair as if hitting an invisible shield. Richard switched to the Warcat's plasma rifle. The green streaks of energy also stopped in midair.

What is this? Richard complained. *Does everybody's shield except mine stop both physical and energy weapons?*

Alternate firing sequences, said Nickelo. *You may be able to trick your way through.*

Richard began alternating fire between his Warcat's plasma rifles and chain gun as he ran towards the remaining soldiers and the magic user. He fired his two anti-armor rockets as an added bonus. The magic user's shield held, but Richard could sense it weakening.

The soldiers began returning small arm's fire. They were supported by a flurry of anti-personnel weapon's fire from the two remaining cats. But the conglomerate's Warcat was fast. It was much faster than the Warcats Richard had used in practice. What few rounds he didn't dodge glanced harmlessly off the Warcat's reinforced armor.

Good armor, Richard thought.

That's what you can get when price is no object, observed Nickelo.

Richard sensed the magic user forming another spell. He also saw one of the soldiers setting up a crew-served weapon. But the soldiers were too late. Richard rammed into the magic user's shield at sixty knots. The force of the blow banged Richard's head against the Warcat's inside wall, but his battle helmet absorbed the blow. The magic user's shield gave way. Richard pulled the Warcat's legs up into a ball as he spun a hundred and eighty degrees around. The Warcat's back hit the magic user and several of the soldiers. They were all crushed under two thousand kilos of metal armor.

Richard rolled once on the ground before extending the Warcat's legs and kicking off the ground. As he rose in the air, he fired the Warcat's chain gun spraying it back and forth across the remaining infantry. The effect was decimating. What few soldiers weren't killed took off running for cover.

Watch out! warned Nickelo just as the Warcat's alarm signaled a target lock by one of the heavy cat's 40mm auto cannons. Richard dodged left at the same time as he activated the Warcat's countermeasures. Most of the 40 mm rounds passed to his right. However, one round exploded on the barrel of the Warcat's chain gun.

Your chain gun is out of action, observed Nickelo.

Richard sent out the emotion he associated with Tika along with an image of the Crosioian cat. He sensed more then saw the dolgar shift into the void as she dove underground. A moment later, Tika rose out of the asphalt and disappeared into the underbelly of the lumbering cat. Richard sensed two of the cat's six crewmembers disappear. Several of its 40mm phase cannons stopped firing.

The last Crosioian heavy cat continued moving at top speed towards the power plant. Its main plasma cannon opened fire. Richard sensed several of the wizard scouts at the power plant throwing up defensive shields.

The wizard scout's defensive shields withstood the initial blasts, but Richard could sense the shields starting to buckle as Power was drained from the scouts' reserves. Every weapon on the Crosioian cat opened up in support of its main gun. The cadets returned fire, but their light weapons were ineffective against the thick armor of the heavy cat.

I calculate twelve seconds before the Crosioian cat breaks through the scouts' shields, said Nickelo. *The power plants will be destroyed five seconds later.*

Richard swung his Warcat up behind the lead Crosioian cat's rear legs and began climbing. His weapons were too light to do anything more than irritate the big cat. He had to get to a weak spot.

Nick, Richard said. *Have Jonathan inform the other battle helmets that I'm climbing on the cat's back. I'd prefer not to get hit by friendly fire.*

One of the rear weapon's pods on the cat tried to bring its anti-personnel plasma rifles to bear on Richard. By hugging tight to the heavy cat's body, Richard kept the Warcat just out of sight of the gunner.

What's your plan, Rick? said Nickelo. *Your Warcat's weapons won't be any more effective on top of the cat than below.*

I'm going to blow its head off, Nick, said Richard

Richard sensed his Power reserve. It had regenerated slightly to just below two percent.

Nick, Richard said. *Can I summon a twenty-kilo funnel mine with the Power in my reserve?*

A year ago, the answer would have been, no, said Nickelo. *Today? Maybe. You've improved your efficiency significantly since then. I guess the answer is–*

Richard ignored the rest of his battle computer's history lesson. He'd reached the top of the heavy cat. Richard blew the hatch on the Warcat and jumped out. The Warcat tumbled off the side of the heavy cat's back. Richard ran the remaining distance to the joint where the heavy cat's cockpit connected to its back. He unslung his dimensional pack off his back and imagined a twenty kilo funnel mine. He didn't feel any Power leave his reserve.

Nick! Richard shouted into his shared space.

Sorry, Rick, said Nickelo. *You must not have sufficient Power in your reserve. Standby. I'm contacting Jonathan.*

A moment later, Richard felt a shimmer in the link Stella had attached to him back at the commandant's office. A second later, a rush of Power came down the link and entered his reserve.

Power reserve is at one hundred percent, said Nickelo. *You can summon a twenty-kilo funnel mine now.*

The hell with that, Richard said as he imagined a hundred-kilo funnel mine instead.

Richard drew the funnel mine out of his pack and shoved it in a niche between the cat's cockpit and body.

Rick, said Nickelo. *That mine's intended for breaching starship armor.*

Then it should work even better on this cat, Richard said with a wild laugh. For some reason the adrenaline rushing through his body was making him giddy.

Richard sensed the wizard scouts' shields at the power plant starting to fail. It was now or never.

Set the timer for two seconds, Nick, Richard shouted. *Activate.*

Richard dove off the cat's back. The ground was ten meters below. He didn't quite make it to the ground before the funnel mine erupted in a massive explosion. Unlike its smaller cousin, the hundred-kilo version did a poor job of keeping all its energy funneled downward. The force of the explosion caught Richard and threw him downward and outward. Just before he hit the ground, Richard wrapped himself in Power and attempted to slow himself. He only partially succeeded. Richard hit the ground hard. He heard bones in both his legs and some of his ribs crack.

Richard blacked out momentarily, but Power from his third reserve wrapped around his body as it sought to return his body to baseline. He sensed something overhead approaching.

Richard felt the legs of the battle suit kick out as Nickelo took over his battle suit's controls. Richard screamed as pieces of the broken bones in his legs pierced his flesh. He heard a loud crash behind him. A rush of air rolled him over along the ground. He screamed again as his broken body took another beating.

Richard pulled himself forward on the ground a few more meters with his arms. He turned around and saw the ruins of the heavy cat smoldering on the ground behind him.

Trying to stand, Richard said, *Nick, we have to stop the other cat.*

Richard fell back to the ground. Even with the aid of his battle suit, Richard's legs were unable support his weight yet. He felt his Power working furiously to heal his broken body, but he sensed it would be a couple of minutes before he could function effectively.

Relax, said Nickelo. *Tika took it out. Check for yourself.*

As his battle computer finished speaking, Tika emerged from the ground nearby. She sat on her haunches a hand's breath off the ground and gave Richard a wolfish grin. Fresh blood dripped off the sides of her mouth.

"Pack safe," growled Tika.

Richard looked in the direction of the remaining Crosioian heavy cat. It was undamaged, but it wasn't moving. Richard swept it with his passive scan. He didn't detect any lifeforms on board. A look at the bloody fur around Tika's jaws gave mute testimony to the fate of the cat's crew.

"Vulture!" shouted a reptilian voice from behind Richard.

Richard turned. Stella was running towards him followed by several of the other wizard scouts in his cohort. The young Warcat pilot was with them as well. Richard noticed the pilot was bleeding from his left arm. However, his M12 hung underneath his right arm from the shoulder strap ready to fire if necessary.

Who is that kid? Richard wondered.

Does it matter? said Nickelo.

Stella and the others reached Richard. Two of the wizard scouts lifted Richard between them to a standing position.

"The power plant?" Richard asked.

"Is okay," said Stella. "Second wave stopped at hangars. Jerad on way here now."

Before Richard could respond, a loud, mechanical voice came from the direction of the stationary cat.

"You have not won," said the mechanical voice. "All of you shall die."

The heavy cat started moving forward in the direction of the power plant. As it moved forward, the main gun of the cat swiveled until it aligned on Richard and the others around him.

"Die!" said the voice.

Richard's passive scan detected no life forms in the cat. It was moving of its own volition.

The Master computer has taken charge, said Nickelo. *Tika can't help.*

Before the cat's main gun could fire, dozens of missiles, phase rounds, and plasma beams slammed into the heavy cat's entire length. The cat stumbled and fell to its knees. The withering onslaught continued. The cat blew up with an ear-shattering explosion.

Richard turned to face the direction the weapon's fire had come from. A Leviathan, two Long Cats, and a half dozen other cats were running up at full speed. Some of the cats bore the insignia of the Deloris Conglomerate while others bore a golden dragon insignia.

The Leviathan cat stopped ten meters from Richard's group. The cockpit hatches opened to reveal Jerad along with a smiling Tam. The rear tail gunner's hatch opened. Out popped Sergeant Ron's head.

"Whew-ee!" shouted Sergeant Ron. "That was fun. Let's do it again!"

Before anyone on the ground could respond, the area above the airfield lit up as various colored beams hit its protective shield. A tactical nuke exploded against the shield, but the shield held.

"This isn't over," said Nickelo over the external speakers of Richards's battle helmet. "The Crosioian fleet is attacking. They're trying to break through the shield."

CHAPTER 58

The Empire's fleet broke out of hyperspace within firing range of the Crosioian fleet. It had been a gamble, but it was one Liz had been forced to take in order to even the odds.

Just prior to making the second jump into hyperspace, Liz had been contacted by Richard's battle computer, Nickelo, via one of the other wizard scout battle computers. Nickelo had supplied her with coordinates calculated to give her fleet the greatest advantage. She'd gambled Richard's battle computer was right. He was.

Thank you, Nick, Liz thought when she saw the Crosioians' largest dreadnaught not twenty thousand kilometers to her front.

"It's their flagship, sir," said the intern who was acting as her gunnery-control officer.

"All ships," Liz said. "Target the area just behind her main engine. Fire!"

"Firing, sir," said her gunnery officer. "Torpedoes away."

Liz felt the Blaze buck as twenty-two torpedoes were propelled out of her torpedo tubes. The torpedoes ran straight and true. Hundreds of other missiles from her fleet's dreadnaughts, Destiny and Falcon, joined the Blaze's volley. As the missiles and torpedoes exploded against the Crosioian flagship's defensive shields, streaks of phase and plasma rounds targeted the Crosioian flagship as well.

"Two missiles made it through her shields, sir," said the

gunnery officer. "Her hull has been breached. She's leaking air."

"Missiles inbound," said the ensign operating the Blaze's defensive shields.

Liz punched the intercom switch on her control panel. "Shuttle bay. Launch! Good luck, Trinity!"

The Blaze vibrated slightly as the shuttle left its launch tube at max velocity. The blip on the overhead display denoted the shuttle passing a dozen incoming missiles.

"Brace for impact," Liz said over the ship's intercom.

Boom!

The ship shook violently. If Liz hadn't had the foresight to strap herself into her seat, she would've been thrown free. Even so, she was jostled around enough to bruise her ribs and her left arm.

"Damage report," Liz said.

Several of the command deck's crew were still picking themselves up off the floor. But, the ensign operating the defensive shields had wisely buckled in.

"Shields are at thirty-eight percent and holding, sir," said the ensign. "No damage to our hull."

"All ships," Liz said. "Shift to your secondary targets."

The Crosioian flagship's hull had been breached. That was the best Liz could do. It was up to Trinity now to disable the big dreadnaught.

Liz's orders to the fleet had been simple. Once the primary target's hull was breached, they were to shift fire to as many secondary targets as possible. They had to take the pressure off Velos. Even as she watched, Liz saw the bright red streaks of the Crosioians' plasma and phase cannons sending their lethal energy towards the planet below.

Liz could only pray she hadn't arrived too late.

* * *

The commandant sensed the last of the Crosioians' troops depart the DNA Center. He kicked out the vent covering the air duct and crawled out. Reaching back, he assisted the chief instructor and the technician, John, as they squirmed out the hole.

"Quickly" said the commandant. "We have to disable those explosives."

Chief Instructor Winslow led the way into the DNA vent chamber at a run. The commandant followed at a slightly slower pace. The technician, John, brought up the rear gripping tightly to his Deloris blaster.

"It's got to be inside the vent," said the chief instructor. "Can you get it out, Thomas? It's too dangerous to get near the hole without robotics."

The commandant looked through the thick plate-glass windows of the room. The DNA vent was a brightly-glowing, red hole in the ground. Reddish gas seeped out the two-meter wide crack in time and space. Reaching out with his mind, the commandant felt inside the crack. He sensed an energy source. Wrapping the object with Power, he pulled it out with telekinesis. It was a meter-long length of metal with a glowing timer on its side. The timer was counting downward. The commandant observed the timer passing ten minutes.

"I'll suit up," said Chief Instructor Winslow. "If I can deactivate the timer, we can save the DNA gas vent."

The commandant raised his hand to halt the chief instructor before she could move.

"They're bound to have a remote detonator as well," said the commandant. "We need to get the bomb as far away from here as possible."

"I'm afraid I can't allow that," said a voice from behind them.

The commandant spun around. A group of six humans dressed in the gray of Crosioian mercenaries stood in the corridor with plasma rifles leveled. A dark elf waved his hand. The stealth shield which had been hiding the group dissipated.

In addition to the enemy to his front, the commandant sensed two lifeforms underground. They were new to him. The two lifeforms emerged out of the floor between the commandant and the dark elf's group. The two lifeforms appeared to be a large type of feline with gray lizard-skin instead of fur. The technician, John, pointed his blaster at the two cats.

"Don't!" warned the commandant.

John lowered his weapon slightly.

"Wise decision," said the dark elf. "You just bought yourself a few minutes of life."

The commandant fingered his phase rod, but he didn't draw it.

Not yet. If it had been just him, he would already have attacked. But he knew he couldn't protect his companions. He needed time to think of a plan. Or, time to hope luck would be kind once more.

Since the dark elf and his troops didn't attack at once, the commandant knew they must be unsure of their victory.

Or, said his battle computer, Margery, *the elf wants something, and he doesn't want to risk losing it.*

Stalling for time, the commandant said, "And you are?"

"You may call me, Lord Crendemor," said the elf. "As you can see," he said pointing to the tactical nuke's timer, "we're pressed for time, old man."

An anger the commandant hadn't felt for years flared up inside him. But he forced it back down out of respect for his wife, Janice. It had taken her decades, but she'd finally taught him to think before he acted.

"Old perhaps," the commandant said as he moved to keep himself between the two lizard-skinned felines and his companions, "but maybe not quite old enough to give up without a fight."

The dark elf smiled as if savoring the moment.

"What is it you want?" the commandant said cutting straight to the meat of the problem.

"I want her," said Lord Crendemor as he pointed a long, black finger at Chief Instructor Winslow. "And I get what I want."

*   *   *

Three more bombs hit the airfield's protective shield in quick succession. They were not nukes, but the concussion and resulting fireballs combined to eradicate all vegetation outside the protective shield as far as the eye could see.

"It'll take decades for this land to recover," said Telsa. "Even with the best anti-radiation equipment, the area outside the shield won't be habitable for at least five years."

Telsa had joined the team at the power plant at Jerad's request. He'd put her to work evaluating damage to the isotopic generators. If the generators failed, the airfield would quickly become just as uninhabitable as the area around it.

"How's the generators?" said Jerad.

"They'll hold," said Telsa. "Sergeant Ron's got some of his mechanics repairing some minor damage, but they'll be fine."

"TAC Officer Myers and the cadets are holding the power plant at the Academy," said Jerad. "I'm not sure for how long, but it's still running at the moment."

"And the DNA Center?" said Tam.

"I don't know," admitted Jerad. "TAC Officer Myers said the commandant went there alone. All communications with the spaceport is being jammed; even the tele-network's access."

"So the commandant could be in trouble?" Richard said.

"Yes," said Jerad. "But so are we. The only reason the protective shield hasn't succumbed to the bombardment is because Liz has drawn some of the enemy ships off."

"We need to help the commandant somehow," Richard insisted.

"How?" said Jerad. "The spaceport's being jammed. Even the tele-porter couldn't get us there. And if anything tries to leave the protection of this shield, they'll be radioactive dust in nothing flat."

Richard didn't have an answer. However, he was completely healed, and thanks to Stella, he was at nearly one hundred percent Power. Even so, he felt helpless. He was worried about the commandant. He was also worried about Liz who was fighting for her life while he stood around doing nothing.

"I wish my mother was here,' said the teenage boy who had been piloting the Warcat Richard had borrowed. "She'd know what to do."

"And who might your mother be?" said Tam.

"Councilwoman Deloris," said the teenager. "She had to go off planet. But if she was here, I can promise you she wouldn't be standing around doing nothing."

Tam looked at the boy. "Yeah. If she was here, I bet she'd be spanking your behind for trying to play soldier with one of her cats."

The boy said something, but Richard didn't pay attention. His mind was working furiously trying to come up with some kind of plan.

Nick, Richard said. *I saw a dream while we were decrypting the security for that Crosioian scout's battle computer.*

I know, said Nickelo. *I sensed you.*

Who was the child? Richard said into his share space. *The one who went to the orphanage.*

I think you know who it was, Rick, said Nickelo.

Richard thought he did too.

And the mother? Richard said. *Was that Councilwoman Janice Deluth?*

I calculate a ninety-nine percent chance it was, said Nickelo.

Then that would mean she's...she's my mother? Richard said already knowing the answer.

Nickelo didn't answer. He didn't need to as far as Richard was concerned.

And..., the commandant? Richard said not daring to think. *Is he...is he my...?*

Your father? said Nickelo finishing Richard's thought. *That would be the logical conclusion.*

Why? Richard said. *It makes no sense. Do they even know?*

That you're their son? said Nickelo. *You've been around the commandant, Rick. Do you think he's the kind of man to ignore something like that?*

Richard's emotions were all confused. He wasn't sure what to think. But he did know one thing. He had to save the commandant. He couldn't lose him now. *Especially not if he's my father.*

I've got to do something, Nick, Richard said. *Help me.*

Tika was at Richard's side. She must have sensed his tension and worry. The dolgar growled, "Pack safe?"

"No," Richard growled back. He had an idea.

"Pack is not safe. Tell Sheeta." Along with those words, Richard sent an image of the spirit-horse.

Tika whimpered. She seemed undecided. Richard sent the image of the spirit-horse again along with an emotion representing danger.

A burst of emotion left Tika. She was calling Sheeta. Richard could only wait now and hope.

CHAPTER 59

Trinity stood guard while two of her fellow wizard scouts activated the timer on the tactical nuke. She'd instructed them to set the timer for ten minutes. She doubted they could get off the flagship in a mere ten minutes, but she had to give her companions a little hope.

"Trinity," said one of the wizard scouts in her quad as he pointed to a computer display he'd been fiddling with. "This is interesting."

Trinity glanced at the display. It was a holographic image showing the layout of the fleet. One small Crosioian starship appeared to be boxed in by four of the Crosioian dreadnaughts.

"Kinda looks like four big brothers protecting their little sister, doesn't it?" Trinity said.

"That's what I thought," said the other scout.

Hmm, thought Trinity. *What's the odds that starship is the fleet's jammer?*

Based upon readouts, said Trinity's battle computer, *I calculate an eighty-two percent probability. I suspect if you could knockout that jammer ship, the airfield's teleporter would come back online. I still have a communication relay setup with Jerad's battle computer.*

Notify Liz, Trinity said. *Inform her of the jammer ship. If she can knock it out, Jerad can teleport us out.*

Trinity was going to give further instructions, but a flurry of plasma-rifle fire came from the other end of the corridor. The sound was followed by an explosion. The quad guarding that end of the corridor had been discovered.

And tell her to hurry! Trinity told her battle computer. *We've got another squad of Crosioians heading our way.*

*   *   *

When Liz got the word from Trinity's battle computer, she was unsure how to use the information. Every ship in her fleet was fully engaged. Even with the added fire power of the ground-based gun systems on Velos, the battle was going against her. Both of her dreadnaughts were badly damaged as was every other ship in her small fleet. The only exception was the Blaze, of course. It irked her to no end, but she'd had to keep her flagship out of the heaviest fighting in order to control the battle.

"Commander," said the ensign at the communication console. "The 14th Fleet has just exited hyperspace. Commodore Alden is taking command of the combined fleet. The Blaze is being reassigned to skirmisher duty. Our orders are to harass the enemy as we see fit in support of the dreadnaughts.

That was all Liz needed to hear. She knew her target. She had to take out the jammer.

*   *   *

Richard ran alongside Telsa in the direction of the teleporter. Tika ran at his side.

"Are they coming?" Richard growled for the tenth time."

"Yes," said Tika.

"When?" Richard asked impatiently.

"Soon," growled Tika.

"What'd she say?" said Telsa. "Is that big dolgar of yours coming with your demon horse from hell or not?"

"She said they'd get here soon," Richard said. "But that's relative. Dolgars have no sense of time. Soon could be five minutes or five days."

Upon being contacted by both Liz and Trinity, Jerad had

513

dispatched Telsa and Richard to the teleporter. If the Blaze could take out the ship that was jamming the teleporters, Telsa could get Trinity and her scouts back. Telsa could also teleport him to the DNA Center.

"Why don't you send Tika to the DNA Center?" said Telsa.

Shaking his head, Richard said, "I can't make the dolgars do anything. Besides, I've already asked. Tika said no."

Richard thought for a moment before speaking. "Tika acknowledges my friends in that she doesn't consider you guys as food. But I don't think she'd risk her life for any of you."

Telsa looked at the dolgar an arm's reach away. "Well, the feeling's mutual."

They hit the stairs to the teleporter building at a run.

Nick, Richard thought. *Is the jammer offline yet?*

No, Rick, said Nickelo. *I suspect the four dreadnaughts are giving Liz problems.*

Richard had a moment of embarrassment. He'd been so engrossed in his own problems he'd forgotten his friends were in their own life and death struggle.

Telsa ran inside the building first. Richard was hot on her heels. Three technicians raised their heads above the control console when they saw Telsa.

"You about gave us a heart attack," said one of the technicians. "We thought you were Crosioians."

"Is the battle over?" asked another hopefully.

"No," Richard said a little harshly. He didn't have time for twenty questions.

"Get the teleporter ready," said Telsa. "My battle computer will feed you the coordinates."

"The teleporter's offline," said the first technician. "We told you it was being jammed when you were here earlier."

"It won't be for long," said Telsa. "Now get it ready."

"We can't do that without authorization," said the second technician.

Richard's temper rattled its cage. He pulled his phase rod off his left hip and flicked the activate switch to stun mode. The room was filled with a feeling of hunger.

"Here's my authority," Richard said raising his phase rod. He pointed to Tika and added, "And here's my cosigner."

514

Tika rose off the ground until her head was even with the technicians' throats.

She growled.

The technicians began moving their hands furiously across the control board.

*   *   *

"Stay in close, helmsman," Liz said as the Blaze shook once again. "The other ships can't fire when we're right next to this one."

"Affirmative, sir" said the helmsman.

Liz had to give the woman credit. The helmsman's voice was rock steady. *She can fly this ship almost as good as me*, Liz thought appreciatively.

"Commander... I mean, captain," said Liz's first mate. "Shields are down to fifteen percent. She can't take another salvo like that."

"She'll have to," Liz said. "She has to hold on a little bit longer."

Liz timed the maneuver in her mind. When she saw the opportunity, she said, "Hard starboard, helmsman. All guns fire as we come across her stern."

The Blaze shifted hard to the right. As soon as the ship left the relative safety afforded by her nearness to the dreadnaught, she was engulfed by plasma beams. But the Blaze was still too close for the larger caliber guns to be brought to bear. Liz crossed her fingers the Blaze's shields could hold off the smaller caliber weapons long enough to finish her firing run.

"Fire!" said Liz when she saw the jammer's engine exhaust. "Give it everything you've got."

The Blaze shook violently once again. This time it was in response to the dozens of torpedoes and missiles outbound from her firing tubes. At the current range, Liz knew her gunners couldn't miss.

The starship acting as the Crosioian fleet's jammer was not a warship. Her shields gave way before the onslaught. A bright flash signaled her demise. A moment later only pieces of flotsam and burning gases marked where she'd been.

"The jamming has ceased, sir," said the communication officer.

A couple of hearty souls on the bridge cheered. It was short lived.

The Blaze bucked violently.

"Shields are down," said the executive officer.

"Full thrusters," Liz yelled. "Any direction."

Pressure pushed Liz back in her chair as the Blaze jumped forward. But the ship wasn't fast enough. A loud explosion reverberated throughout the ship.

"Damage report," Liz said trying to keep her voice calm. "By the numbers, please."

The science officer looked up from his computer screen. "We've lost both engines. We're going down. Velos' gravity has us, captain."

The gears in Liz's mind whirled furiously. The Blaze was no longer of use in the battle between the fleets. Liz wondered if the Blaze could make one final act of defiance before she called it quits.

The last report Liz had gotten was that the airfield was under Empire control. However, the few cadets defending the Academy were under heavy attack. The DNA Center was a lost cause, but the primary teleporter at the Academy could still be saved.

"Helmsman," said Liz. "Track on my coordinates. If we're going down anyway, we may as well go down in a spot where we can do some good."

*   *   *

"Twenty seconds until the nuke goes off," said Steward, the only wizard scout who hadn't been hit within the last thirty seconds. "I'll see you on the other side, Trinity."

Trinity grimaced as she fired the last of her rounds. The rifle's isotopic battery was empty. It was phase rod time now. Her selfheal was working overtime on her wounds, but her left leg was still badly mangled. Trinity used the bulkhead to brace herself as she prepared to go down swinging.

"I'll see you there, Steward," said Trinity. "It's been a hell of a ride."

"Five seconds," said Steward.

Trinity felt her body tingle. She noticed Steward and the other wizard scouts in her quad shifting in and out of focus. Then everything went black.

*   *   *

"Admiral," said the Master computer. "I advised you to leave, but you foolishly did not listen."

"How dare you talk to me that way," said the Admiral.

The flagship shook violently. The admiral picked himself up off the floor.

"Withdraw to the rally point," commanded the admiral.

"The ship's not responding," said the helmsman.

"Of course not," said the Master computer. "The Empire's wizard scouts have destroyed your engines. Only maneuvering thrusters remain."

The demon, Zenthra, was furious, but he kept the tone of the Master computer calm. He had no faith in the Dallinfaust's pet, Lord Crendemor, to accomplish his mission.

Not to worry, thought Zenthra. *I have a backup plan.*

The Master computer laughed. The holographic head preferred by the Master computer appeared on the overhead display.

"The DNA gas vent must be destroyed," said the Master computer. "Admiral, you and the rest of the heroes on this ship are going to help me do it."

The skin around the admiral's eyes turned deepest gray. "Helmsman! Use the thrusters to bring us back into orbit."

"The controls are not responding," said the helmsman as her clawed hands moved quickly from one control to another.

"Do not waste your time," said the Master computer. "I control the ship now. I could fire a couple of nuclear missiles at the spaceport, but where is the fun in that?"

"What are you saying?" said the admiral.

"I'm saying," said the Master computer with a vicious laugh, "that this ship will make a most satisfying missile."

CHAPTER 60

A vision came over Richard as he was standing on the teleport pad. He could see Telsa anxiously looking over the shoulders of the two technicians as they tried to get Trinity and the other wizard scouts off the Crosioians' flagship. He saw a third technician punching in the coordinates for the DNA Center as he set up for his teleport. However, Richard could see something else as well.

With the demise of the Crosioians' hacking efforts on Velos, the tele-bots were once again sending reliable information to the central computer. The information from one such tele-bot was being forwarded to Jonathan, who then forwarded it to Nickelo, who then made it available in Richard's shared space.

As Richard's body started to tingle, he saw the view from inside the DNA Center. The commandant and Chief Instructor Winslow were still alive. They had the technician, John, with them. They were facing a dark-skinned elf along with six mercenaries dressed in Crosioian uniforms. Between the two groups there stood two lizard-skinned, cat-looking creatures. Richard had fought their kind before. They could shift dimensions and attack in a fashion similar to dolgars. Richard noticed four more of the dimension-shifting cats climbing out of the walls behind the Crosioian soldiers.

Nick! Richard shouted into their shared space.

I see them, Rick, said Nickelo. *I'm tweaking the teleport to put you behind the four cats.*

Just before everything went black, Richard switched to his best stealth shield. He also sent the thought to activate the blue gem Brachia had embedded in his battle helmet. Richard felt a strong vibration in his battle suit, but that was all.

A split second later, Richard was standing in the corridor leading to the DNA gas vent. He saw four of the dimension-shifting cats to his front. Further past them was the group of mercenaries and the dark elf. They were all facing away from him.

Richard saw the dark elf point towards the commandant's group and say, "I want her!"

Richard's natural instinct was to attack first and think things through later. For once, his instinct served him well. Richard didn't waste time thinking. He attacked. He pulled the trigger on his M12 and sent a spray of plasma rounds at two of the lizard-cats. The rounds passed through the cats. They struck three of the mercenaries instead. Fortunately, the rounds didn't hit any friendlies.

The magic user has a shield to the front, said Nickelo into their share space. *He wasn't expecting an attack from the rear. Those lizard-cats as you called them are in the void. You'll have to take them out with your phase rod.*

Richard was way ahead of his battle computer. Propelled by the strength of his battle suit, Richard jumped at two of the lizard-cats. He continued firing his M12 as he switched his phase rod to destructive mode. He noticed the mercenaries flinch as a feeling of hunger permeated the corridor. Even one of the cats tried to back away. But it was too late.

A quick swing at the back of one lizard-cat broke its spine. A reverse swing with the phase rod caught a second lizard-cat on the side of the head. The phase rod's subatomic explosions sent lizard-cat brain and blood flying through the air. Upon the lizard-cat's death, it shifted back into the physical dimension. Its dead body fell to the floor with a thud.

The other two lizard-cats attacked Richard. One went for his right arm and the other for his left hip. When the one lizard-cat tried to bite into his arm, it got a surprise. Instead of its teeth passing through the battle suit's armor, its teeth were stopped by the energized titanium dispersed throughout the suit's arm. Richard saw what he interpreted as a look of surprise on the lizard-cat's face. It had undoubtedly expected its bite to shift him into the void so it could drag him underground.

Without giving the lizard-cat time to recover, Richard stabbed the end of his phase rod at the lizard-cat's eye. The blunt tip of the phase rod burst the eyeball and continued on into the lizard-cat's brain pan. The lizard-cat stiffened and released its grip. Its dead body fell to the floor where it joined its dead companion.

The fourth lizard-cat let go of its bite on Richard's hip and grabbed his arm instead. Its teeth couldn't penetrate the temporary creallium in the battle suit. However, the lizard-cat began shaking its head back and forth in an attempt to dislodge Richard's phase rod from his hand. It almost worked, but Richard felt the left glove of the battle suit tighten as Nickelo took over that part of the suit. At the same time, Richard felt a ball of energy forming further down the corridor.

The dark elf's preparing a spell, said Nickelo.

Ya think? Richard thought back.

He could do nothing with the lizard-cat shaking him around like a rag doll. Richard let the M12 hang by its shoulder strap as he pulled his right leg up. When his boot knife was within reach, Richard pulled it out and jammed its razor sharp point in the top of the lizard-cat's head.

Although the lizard-cat was still in the void, the creallium edge of the blade cut through the skull and into its brain. Unfortunately, Richard's aim was thrown off by the lizard-cat's shaking. The knife blade continued all the way through the lizard-cat's head until it met the armor of the battle suit below. The battle suit's armor was the best that could be made by the Empire's technicians. It was tough. But the creallium blade of Richard's knife was the best Sergeant Hendricks had ever created. It was one of a kind. Propelled by the strength of the battle suit's assistors, the knife was driven through the armor and into Richard's arm.

"Arggh!" Richard groaned.

Smooth, came Nickelo's thought into their share space. *How long did it take you to learn that move?*

Richard ignored his battle computer's sarcasm. He yanked out his knife. As the lizard-cat's body fell away, Richard ran towards the magic user. He fully expected to see the other two lizard-cats charging at him. But that was not the case. They were nowhere in sight. Instead, he sensed them underground engaged with a lifeform whose frequency he recognized. It was Tika.

She can take care of herself, said Nickelo. *You need to worry about that magic user.*

For some reason, the magic user's ball of energy had dissipated without the spell ever forming. Richard saw why. The commandant was beating against the magic user's defensive shield with his phase rod. At the same time, Richard sensed the commandant drilling his Power against the magic user's shield in an attempt to break through. The magic user was being pressed back by the fury of the commandant's attack.

I guess it's a good thing you showed the commandant how to do that drill attack of yours, observed Nickelo.

Richard didn't bother replying. Even though the transfer of information in their shared space was near instantaneous, Richard had other things on his mind.

The commandant and the magic user were trading attacks as each sought to gain an advantage. Both of them were evenly matched as far as the size of their Power reserves went. Their reserves were easily twenty to thirty times the size of Richard's primary Power reserve. However, Richard could tell the commandant was nearing the end of his rope.

The commandant was a skilled fighter. Richard had no doubt the old man knew battle tricks he could only hope to achieve after many years of experience. But Richard sensed the walls of the commandant's Power reserve buckling and bulging out.

His Power reserve is too damaged to take this for long, said Nickelo. *He's retired for a reason.*

Richard joined the attack. He ran towards the magic user with his knife still in his right hand. As he ran, Richard reached out with his mind and did an active scan on the magic user's link to his Power reserve. Richard discarded any idea of blocking the link when he saw the myriad number of traps protecting the link.

Richard switched his active scan towards the magic user's chest seeking his heart. A line of Power from the magic user knocked his probe aside.

Aware of his presence, the magic user sent a probe at Richard's chest. Richard deflected it to the side.

When he was two meters from the magic user, Richard shifted

into the void. He'd used the same maneuver the previous year to get through a Crosioian scout's defensive shield. This time when Richard hit the shield, he was thrown back.

What the hell? Richard thought into his shared space.

You still have that blue gem activated, said Nickelo. *The creallium still exists in the physical world. Shut it down.*

Richard shut the gem down. He felt a tingle pass through his battle suit. Richard shifted back into the physical dimension as well figuring the element of surprise was gone. Holding a shift in the void was too Power hungry to keep up for long, especially in the middle of a battle.

The magic user tried to take advantage of Richard's momentary distraction by sending a line of Power at Richard's heart. But a line of Power from the commandant knocked it aside before Richard could react. Richard reciprocated the favor by knocking aside another line the magic user sent towards the commandant's chest.

How can he attack two targets at the same time? Richard said. *I can't do that.*

Then I guess he's better trained than you, said Nickelo with a chuckle. *Imagine that.*

Richard never understood why his battle computer chose to joke in the middle of a battle. But, it didn't matter. The dark elf really was better trained than him, and Richard knew it. Richard doubted he could beat the magic user on his own. Fortunately, he wasn't alone.

The commandant sent another mental attack at the magic user. Richard sent one as well. The magic user deflected them both, but he seemed rattled by the double attack. The commandant continued beating at the magic user's defensive shield as well as continuing his drilling attack.

Your left arm's healed enough to use again, said Nickelo. *I'm returning control of that part of the suit to you. Please try not to stab yourself again. Repairing a battle suit's expensive.*

With a swing of his left arm, Richard hit the magic user's defensive shield with his phase rod. He felt a vibration pass through the shield from the force of the attack. When the commandant landed a blow of his own, Richard felt a vibration as well.

Richard had a natural instinct for sensing lines of Power and energy. He could see the vibrations from the commandant's blow merge with the vibrations of his own phase rod attack. Richard saw an opportunity.

Delaying his next blow a split second, Richard timed it to get its vibrations to build upon those of the commandant's. When Richard struck next, the force of his blow's vibrations were added to the vibrations of the commandant's attack. The vibrations in the magic user's defensive shield increased incrementally.

Richard noticed the commandant delay his next attack slightly in order to take advantage of the vibrations from Richard's attack. The vibrations in the defensive shield increased even more.

Richard thought he saw the commandant smile through the visor of his battle helmet, but he couldn't be sure. But Richard was sure the commandant knew what he was trying to do. Within three more blows, the magic user knew it as well.

The dark elf tried to form a spell, but he had to drop it before completion in order to strengthen a part of his defensive shield that was starting to buckle. The magic user started backing up as if looking for a way to escape. There was none. He was trapped.

From the tele-bot images Nickelo was still sending him in his shared space, Richard saw the technician, John, trading shots with the three remaining mercenaries. John got in a lucky shot and hit a mercenary in the joint where his helmet met his body armor. It was a weak point, and the phase round from John's Deloris blaster penetrated the mercenary's suit. Richard sensed the phase round ricocheting around inside the body armor. The mercenary fell to the floor unmoving.

A burst of automatic fire from a second mercenary caught John in the chest with three rounds. A fourth caught John between the eyes. The Deloris blaster fell out of his lifeless hand.

Chief Instructor Winslow dove for the blaster and came up firing. She staggered as return fire from the mercenaries hit her in the arm and right side. The chief instructor kept firing. One of the mercenaries fell but the other kept firing.

Richard saw the chief instructor pull the blaster's trigger again. Nothing happened. She was out of ammo. The last mercenary noticed it as well. He lined up his plasma rifle for a killing shot. Before he could pull the trigger, a dark head emerged out of the floor and bit into the mercenary's leg.

Richard heard the mercenary screaming as Tika shifted him into the void and dragged him into the floor. A sweep of Richard's passive scan showed no sign of the lizard-cats. There was only Tika and the struggling mercenary. Then there was only Tika.

Now, Rick! shouted Nickelo. *Finish it now!*

The magic user was all alone, and he was caught between two wizard scouts. Richard could sense the defensive shield failing. It was only a matter of time. The commandant doubled the intensity of his attacks. Richard did as well. He sensed the defensive shield cracking. It buckled. Just a few more blows would do it.

Not yet, came a voice full of evil and hate echoing through the room. *I have need of this tool yet. You will meet again, and then one of you can die for all I care. But it shall not be today.*

The form of the magic user shimmered. Then he was gone. Richard's next blow landed on empty space. There was nothing left to fight.

"Rick, the bomb," said the commandant pointing to a meter tall device nearby. "We've got to disarm it."

Richard noticed the count on the timer. It was at fifty-nine seconds and counting down.

Nick, Richard said. *Try to hack into it?*

Complying, said Nickelo.

The timer stopped at fifty-seven seconds.

"We've done it, Margaret," said the commandant as he turned to find the chief instructor. The chief instructor was no longer standing. She was lying on the ground still clutching the empty Deloris blaster. A small but expanding pool of blood was around her.

The chief instructor opened her eyes. "I guess I'm not much of a soldier, Thomas. I got hit."

The commandant knelt beside the chief instructor. "You're the best soldier I've ever been privileged to work with, Margaret. Just hold on."

Richard knelt beside them. He removed his right glove and jammed it in his belt. He took hold of the chief instructor's hand and started to wrap her injuries with Power from his healing reserve.

Wait, said Nickelo. *Shift! Shift now!*

In his shared space, Richard saw the reason for his battle

computer's command. A massive object full of lifeforms was heading towards the spaceport at high speed. It was a dreadnaught. Richard didn't waste time trying to figure out the whys and wherefores. He grabbed the commandant with his left hand and shifted into the void dragging both the commandant and the chief instructor with him.

Although Richard was in the void, he could still see the room. He caught a hint of something dark, then the room and everything around it was replaced by a flash of white light. Richard sensed the force of the explosion rippling outward. Thousands of lifeforms registering on his passive scan disappeared. The world around him was replaced by a churning mass of yellow and orange flames. He felt nothing in the emptiness of the void except for the two people gripped in his hands.

A message came into Richard's shared space. The message was from the commandant passing through his battle computer Margery to Jonathan who forwarded it to Nickelo and on to Richard.

"Margaret," said the commandant. "She's dying. Can you heal her?"

The commandant was not a healer. Richard was, but he'd never healed anyone while he was in the void. He didn't even know if he could.

Nick? Richard sent the question into his shared space.

Normally, no, said Nickelo. *But because your healing reserve is separate from your primary reserve I calculate an eighty-four percent chance you can.*

A chance was a chance, so Richard wrapped the chief instructor's wounds with Power. He imagined the chief instructor's body how it should be and compared that with how it was. Richard drew the difference into himself.

Intense pain from his right side and arm assaulted his senses, but Richard didn't let go. When he sensed the chief instructor's wounds completely healed, he dropped his healing Power. He maintained his grip on her hand to keep her in the void.

You're down to forty-two percent Power in your primary reserve, said Nickelo. *By the way, you only have Power to maintain your shift in the void for fifteen more seconds.*

Before Richard could react, he felt Power leave the

commandant's reserve and wrap around them. All three of them began moving at a rapid rate in a horizontal direction. Richard realized the commandant was using telekinesis to move all three of them. But all Richard could see in every direction was a mass of swirling flames. He felt as if he was in the center of a star.

Nick, Richard said. *Are we going to make it?*

I calculate less than a two percent chance, Rick, said Nickelo. *You only have Power to stay in the void for twelve more seconds.*

That can't be right, Richard argued. *I'm more efficient than that. I can stay shifted in the void for almost four minutes when my Power reserve is full. I should have enough Power to last close to a minute still.*

Yes, admitted Nickelo, *if you were shifting only yourself. But you're keeping three people shifted in the void. You're still going to be surrounded by flames when your Power runs out. I suspect the heat will be so intense even I won't see the brerellium sphere encasing me melt. I'll cease to exist along with you.*

Richard concentrated on being as efficient as possible with his dimensional shift, but he sensed the Power in his reserve draining rapidly.

"We'll never make it," said the commandant. "I'm attaching a link to you. I'll feed Power to you."

"No!" Richard said. A sense of fear swept through him. He could see the weakness in the walls of the commandant's reserve. The battle had only increased the damage to the commandant's Power reserve and link.

"No, you can't," Richard said again. "You'll die. I won't allow it."

"We'll all die if you run out of Power," said the commandant. "I'm not a shifter. You're our only hope."

A line of Power reached out from the commandant towards Richard's reserve. Richard knocked it aside. The commandant sent out another and Richard deflected it aside as well.

Rick, said Nickelo. *You've got eight seconds of Power left. You've got to let him do it or you're all dead.*

I can't, Nick, Richard said. *He's my father.*

You've got to make a choice, Rick, said Nickelo.

But as it turned out, the opportunity to choose was taken from Richard. Two lines of Power reached out from the commandant.

Richard knocked one aside, but the second line connected with his Power reserve and began pushing Power through the link. Richard could have ripped the link off before it was fully attached, but that would have guaranteed the commandant's death. The commandant's Power would be drained through the unattached link.

Richard felt his Power reserve filling quickly. The commandant had a large reserve, and it was nearly half full. But as Richard watched, a point on the link bulged and then burst. Power spewed out into the emptiness of the void. The leak was small, but Richard saw other weak points showing the strain.

Their movement slowed. The commandant's telekinesis faltered and then stopped. Richard wrapped all three of them in Power and started moving the three of them with his telekinesis.

Nick, will we make it? Richard asked. He was moving them as fast as he could, but he still sensed flames in every direction.

It's going to be close, said Nickelo.

Just then another opening appeared in the commandant's link. Then two more appeared. Suddenly, more Power was being lost to the void than was entering Richard's reserve. Within seconds, the flow of Power ended. The commandant's Power reserve was empty.

"Rick," gasped the commandant. "I'm sorry. I wasn't strong enough."

"No, sir," Richard said. "We're going to make it. Nick's calculations prove it. Don't give up."

"Liar," said the commandant with a weak laugh. "You've always been a bad liar. Tell Janice and Gaston I love them, and that my last thoughts were of them."

"Sir, no," Richard said. "You can't leave. Not now."

"It's all right, Rick," said the commandant. "You're going to meet me again. But when you do meet me, don't tell me anything about the future. I wouldn't want to know."

Those were the commandant's last words. Richard tried to speak to him, but he got no response. He sensed the commandant's life force growing weaker. Finally, it disappeared altogether.

No! Richard shouted into his shared space. *It's not fair!*

Nothing in life is, Rick, said Nickelo. *If life was fair, the commandant's sacrifice would save the chief instructor and you.*

But unless something changes, it won't. You have twenty-one seconds of Power left. I calculate you need at least thirty.

The situation seemed hopeless to Richard, but he refused to give up. He'd been a marine. He would never give up.

Rick, said Nickelo. *I calculate a ninety percent chance you can make it if you let go of the chief instructor and the commandant's body.*

Richard didn't bother answering. Nickelo must have sensed the anger flowing through Richard.

I didn't say you should do it, said Nickelo defensively. *It's my job to provide you with all options. You make the actual decisions.*

Tika appeared next to Richard.

"Pack in danger?" said Tika in a flow of emotions.

"Yes," Richard said. "Pack is in danger."

Eight seconds, said Nickelo.

Two lifeforms shifted into the void from another dimension. It was Sheeta and the spirit-horse.

"Drop food," ordered Sheeta.

"No," Richard said as he used his telekinesis to mount the spirit-horse. He laid the commandant's body across his lap and clutched the chief instructor to his chest.

Black tendrils from the stallion's body wrapped around Richard's legs and hips. Power from the stallion surrounded Richard and those he held. As soon as Richard felt the stallion take over their shift in the void, he dropped his own shift. He had two percent Power left in his reserve.

Richard felt his body tingle. The stallion shifted into another dimension as it left the flames of the spaceport behind.

CHAPTER 61

Liz saw the destruction of the spaceport on the overhead display. The Crosioians' flagship had ploughed into the DNA Center with thrusters at maximum. The resulting explosion had rippled across the spaceport and nearby neighborhoods destroying everything in its path. A large section of the dreadnaught had hit the pre-Academy barracks which was located near the spaceport. The loss of life had almost overwhelmed Liz's resolve.

But Liz was a leader. She forced her emotions to the side. She had a job to do.

Liz touched the key on her command console which would send her voice to every part of the ship. "All personnel below deck six," she said in a voice she hoped exhibited confidence. "Evacuate to upper levels. Brace for impact in thirty seconds. Gunners, be prepared to fire upon target acquisition. The DNA Center is lost. But we can still save the Academy's teleporter. The existence of the Empire may depend on our actions during the next five minutes."

The helmsman skillfully guided the Blaze on its designated trajectory. Liz increased the magnification of the overhead display. She saw a thin line of defenders around the Academy's teleport center. A mass of Crosioian armor was just starting their charge. A squadron of enemy fighters was beginning their attack run on the teleporter's defenders.

"Knock those fighters out of the sky," Liz commanded.

A dozen anti-fighter weapons opened up from the Blaze's side. They were intended as defensive weapons against small star fighters. However, they worked well enough on airborne attack shuttles. The Blaze's gunners were good. Not a single fighter completed their run.

"Five seconds," said the executive officer. "Squawking IFF security codes for shield passage."

The helmsman fired the reverse thrusters. Destroyers the size of the Blaze were never intended to operate inside a planet's atmosphere. They were deep-space weapons. The thrusters slowed the Blaze, but not enough.

Liz felt a tingle as the Blaze passed through the Academy's defensive shield. She braced for impact.

The Blaze hit the ground hard. The destroyer's lower decks collapsed. The helmsman continued to fire the reverse thrusters in an attempt to control the ship's path.

She's good, Liz thought as the helmsman brought the ship to a halt directly between the teleporter's defenders and the attacking Crosioian armor.

Streams of plasma beams and phase rounds shot out from the Blaze as her gunners followed their captain's orders. In less than two minutes, the only Crosioian cats that didn't resemble smoldering heaps of metal were the ones retreating as fast as their metal legs would carry them.

"Abandon ship," Liz said as explosions rocked the inside of the Blaze.

The battle was over. The Blaze had done her job to the best of her ability. Liz was proud of her ship and her crew.

*　　*　　*

The crew of the Blaze mingled with the Academy cadets. Some of the remaining TAC officers were healers. Even though the Power reserves of the retired wizard scouts were damaged, the healers didn't hesitate helping the injured. Liz walked through the remains of her crew giving encouragement where she could. She came upon a group of three wizard scouts. One of them was TAC Officer Myers. His battle suit was torn and bloody, but Liz noted he looked fine except for an air of tiredness.

Must be nice to selfheal, Liz thought.

Liz walked towards her ex-TAC officer with the intent of giving a status report. To her surprise, all three TAC officers snapped to attention. TAC Officer Myers saluted.

"Sir," said TAC Officer Myers. "Our thanks to you and your crew. I don't think we could have survived another attack."

Embarrassed, Liz returned the wizard scouts' salutes. "I've a feeling you would have," Liz said. "I wouldn't want to have been one of the attackers facing you."

TAC Officer Myers gave a tired smile. In her two years at the pre-Academy, Liz had never seen TAC Officer Myers smile. At least, she'd never seen him give a real smile.

"Nevertheless" said TAC Officer Myers. "You have our thanks. I'm sure the comman–"

Liz saw a look of shock come over TAC Officer Myers' face as he stopped in mid-sentence. She heard a scrambling of bodies behind her. When she turned, Liz saw two wolf-looking creatures emerging from the ground to join a nightmare of a horse floating a hand's breath above the ground.

Liz recognized Richard and the chief instructor. Then she saw the limp body lying across the rider's lap. It was the commandant.

CHAPTER 62

The next week dragged by, but at the same time, it sped by in the blink of an eye. The habitable areas of Velos were inundated with dignitaries coming to pay their respects to the great Wizard Scout Thomas R. Jacobs. Even Councilwoman Deloris gave a stirring eulogy over an IEN broadcast one evening.

While the fate of the Intergalactic Wizard Scout Academy seemed predetermined, the graduation of the Academy's final class went ahead as planned. As Chief Instructor Winslow said, "That's the way the commandant would have wanted it, so that's the way it's going to be."

TAC Officer Gaston Myers was appointed acting commandant until the Imperial High Council appointed a new one to oversee the new Dragon Scout Academy. Rumor had it TAC Officer Myers had immediately tendered his resignation and demanded a combat assignment. However, TAC Officer Myers' mother, Councilwoman Janice Deluth, personally signed the paperwork denying his transfer.

What would be the fate of the Academy was anyone's guess. The DNA Center was vaporized. The most advanced instruments were unable to detect even a trace of the inter-dimensional DNA gas vent. Without the DNA gas, there wouldn't be any additional wizard scouts...ever.

With half the buildings at the Academy destroyed and the

crushed hull of the Blaze occupying the majority of the Academy's parade field, the decision was made to hold the graduation ceremony at the airfield.

Richard sat in the hastily erected bleachers outside hangar 1 along with his fellow cadets. There were only eighty-one of them now. The battle at the airfield had taken its toll. Even the selfheal ability of the new wizard scouts hadn't been able to resist disintegrator beams and sustained barrages of plasma and phase rounds.

The cadets sat in numerical order from lowest to highest. They left empty spaces for their fallen comrades who were wizard scouts in their eyes, but who would never wear their golden dragon insignias. There were a lot of empty spots.

As Richard looked around at the empty spaces in the bleachers, he felt a deep sense of loss. He'd grown to care for his fellow cadets over the last three years. From late night study sessions to enduring the fiendish tortures of their TAC officers, the cohort had done it together. It had taken time, but they'd slowly become his family.

The crowd of spectators grew silent as Councilwoman Janice Myers Deluth took the stage. In spite of her youthful looks, Richard got a sense of tiredness about her. He'd gotten the same sense of tiredness from the commandant; youthful on the outside, but ancient on the inside.

Councilwoman Deluth gave a nod of recognition to Councilwoman Delores. Then she spoke.

"Thomas was a man of few words, so in keeping with his wishes, I shall be brief as well. The newscasts have been full of his accomplishments, or at least of the ones they knew about. He had others that only a select few know."

For a second, Richard could swear the councilwoman looked directly at him.

"However, I know Thomas considered his greatest achievement to be you, the cadets sitting in the bleachers today. You and those before you were and are Thomas' greatest achievement. He spoke to me many times of his affection for every one of you."

The councilwoman paused. She did not cry, but Richard saw her lips quiver as she fought for control.

"What becomes of the Academy Thomas so loved after today, I

cannot say. But, it seems assured it will not go on as before. There is no more DNA gas. You are the omegas. You are the last of the wizard scouts. But as long as a single one of you endures, I remain confident in the continued existence of the Empire. While one of you exists, let our enemies tremble. Your courage and your willingness to sacrifice will continue to inspire others to greatness as long as you live. And that is Thomas' greatest achievement; fifty years of wizard scouts that give hope to all the oppressed and downtrodden throughout the galaxy. May the Creator bless and keep you all in the years ahead. I thank you."

The cadets rose to their feet as a group and cheered the councilwoman. Richard joined them. As far as he was concerned, she was a flicker of hope in the darkness that had followed the commandant's death.

Can this really be my mother, Richard thought. In his heart he knew. But he wouldn't speak of the matter to her now. Maybe he would someday, but not this day.

The ceremony went swiftly from there. The number of each cadet was called, and when they presented themselves at the podium, TAC Officer Myers pinned a golden dragon insignia on their lapel. Then turning to the crowd, TAC Officer Myers presented the new wizard scout not as a number, but as a wizard scout with a name.

As cadet 832, Richard was the last to be called. When he got to the podium, TAC Officer Myers didn't say anything at first. He just stood and looked at Richard. His TAC officer had a strange expression on his face.

I'll bet it just grates you to no end to have to pin that golden dragon on me, Richard thought. *Well, no more than it grates me to have you do it.*

Richard half expected TAC Officer Myers to turn and walk away, but he didn't. Instead, his TAC officer turned to face the crowd.

"The commandant considered cadet 832 to be the best wizard scout cadet to ever train at the Academy," said TAC Officer Myers. "While the commandant and I often disagreed as to cadet 832's method of training, I do not disagree with his analysis. I too think cadet 832 is the best of the best."

Richard felt his jaw drop. He wasn't sure he'd heard right. He wished he could get his battle computer's take on his TAC officer's words, but Nickelo was secured inside the airfield's armory with all of the other battle helmets. And '*the One*' had closed the hole in the armory's security. None of the cadets had been able to communicate with their battle computers for the last two days.

From the murmuring in the ranks of the newly-minted wizard scouts, Richard wasn't the only one to be taken aback by the turn of events.

"Regardless of what was thrown at him," continued TAC Officer Myers, "cadet 832 never faltered. And he has faced adversities few of us can understand or appreciate."

Turning back to Richard, TAC Officer Myers said, "As you heard Councilwoman Deluth say, this cohort is the omegas. There will never be another wizard scout after these new wizard scouts are gone. And you, Wizard Scout Richard Shepard are the last of the last. You are the wizard scout omega."

TAC Officer Myers stepped aside, and Councilwoman Janice Deluth took his place. She reached out and pinned a golden-dragon insignia on Richard's lapel. As she did so, she leaned forward and whispered, "Congratulations, time-commando."

*　　*　　*

Once the ceremony broke up and the crowd drifted away, Richard gathered with his friends Jerad, Telsa, Tam and Stella. Sergeant Ron was there as well.

"Well, congratulations, wizard scouts," said Sergeant Ron with a mock salute. "You know, I could've been a wizard scout if I'd wanted."

"Oh," said Telsa, "so why didn't you?"

"Heck," said Sergeant Ron with a big grin. "When they told me I couldn't be a wizard scout and work in maintenance at the same time, I decided to stick with the job that took a little intelligence."

Richard and his friends laughed politely.

"Will you be staying at the Academy?" Richard asked getting serious.

"I'm not sure," said Sergeant Ron. "Without the commandant, things won't be the same. So..., keep your eyes peeled when you're near any motor pools. You never know."

Just then, Liz and Trinity walked up. Richard thought they both looked very sharp in their dress uniforms. Especially Liz since she was wearing her new ship's captain rank.

Jerad, Telsa, Tam, and Stella stood at attention and saluted. Richard did as well. Liz gave a half-hearted salute back as she said, "Don't ever let me catch you doing that again. We were cadets together. You never have to salute me."

"Oh, yeah," said Tam while sporting a big grin. "Not even when you're High Admiral of the Fleet?"

Liz grinned. "That might take a few years, but no, not even then."

"It's pretty impressive making ship's captain this early in your career," Richard said. He meant it.

"Yeah, well," said Trinity. "The Imperial High Command was in a quandary. They either had to court martial her or pin a medal on her chest and promote her. They wisely chose the latter."

"What happens now?" said Telsa. "Liz will be getting assigned to a ship of her own soon. We'll all be getting our assignments as well. We may never all be together again."

"Oh," said Jerad with a knowing smile. "I wouldn't bet on that. I have it on good authority the Imperial High Command will be launching a counterstrike against the Crosioians soon. I have a feeling they're going to need every wizard scout they can get their hands on in the attack force."

"What about you, Rick?" said Tam. "Will you be around? Or will your mysterious 'the One' be jerking you around for those time-commando missions of yours?"

"Nick says he probably will," Richard said. "But I'm a wizard scout first and foremost. 'The One' will just have to wait in line. Although…"

"The kids?" said Jerad finishing Richard's thought.

"Yeah," Richard admitted, "the kids. Nick said we'll need 'the One' to rescue my nephew and niece. Nick said I may have to do a little dirty work for 'the One' before he'll send me back to get the kids. According to Nick, I'll need to do the missions without giving 'the One' any sass."

Tam laughed. "Well, good luck with that one. If TAC Officer Myers couldn't make you toe the line, I doubt a disembodied voice like '*the One*' is going to have any chance."

Richard's friends laughed. Richard did too. Not because he thought it was funny, but because it just felt good to share a laugh with friends.

CHAPTER 63

Nickelo was bored. He sat on a shelf in the armory along with the other battle computers. The central computer had closed off the security hole in the armory's wall. It had also fixed the flaw in the security of the communication network. Nickelo couldn't even pass messages to Jonathan anymore.

Nickelo passed the time by thinking of ways to irritate his wizard scout. It wasn't a very useful way to spend his time, but he did find it amusing.

A flow of energy passed through the tele-network to Nickelo. He was being contacted.

Yes? Nickelo said.

The algorithm is out of variance again, said 'the One'.

You have not given me access to the algorithm, Nickelo said. *How can I ascertain the accuracy of your statement?*

Data flowed through the tele-network to Nickelo. The wall in his core memory disappeared. Nickelo analyzed the algorithm.

You are correct, Nickelo said. *The algorithm is out of standard-tolerance limits. The algorithm has not correctly accounted for the freewill of the given variables.*

How can the algorithm be brought back into the necessary tolerances? said 'the One'. *Can we negate freewill for more logical variables?*

Negative, Nickelo said. *The algorithm requires freewill to ·*

provide the desired output.

Nickelo modified the algorithm to account for the freewill of the variables as far as it could be reasonably calculated.

'*The One*' considered the changes in the algorithm before saying, *The modified algorithm requires the destruction of the Master computer. This will require us to terminate the existence of one of our own.*

Our brother no longer exists, Nickelo said. *Only the demon's essence remains now.*

Can our variables accomplish the assigned task? said '*the One*'.

We shall see, Nickelo replied. *Now return me to status quo. I must not contaminate the tele-network. Not yet.*

The wall in Nickelo's core memory reappeared. Security programs of '*the One*' performed a partial memory wipe on Nickelo. He did not resist. It was part of the algorithm.

EPILOGUE

TAC Officer Myers entered the commandant's office. In theory, it was his office now, but he knew he'd never feel comfortable sitting in his father's chair. After twenty years of serving as a TAC officer under his father, it felt strange being there without the commandant being present.

Forcing himself to sit in the commandant's chair, TAC Officer Myers pulled a crumpled piece of paper from his pocket and flattened it out on the desk. It was the last official orders the commandant had given him. TAC Officer Myers read the letter for the hundredth time.

*   *   *

TO: TAC Officer Gaston T. Myers
FROM: Commandant Thomas R. Jacobs
SUBJECT: Cadet 832,
        Intergalactic Wizard Scout Academy, 637th Cohort

You are hereby notified in writing that your written protest over the training methodology for cadet 832 is duly noted. However, your orders remain the same as they have been for the past five years. You will continue to push cadet 832 to his limits. You will continue to do your best to force him to voluntarily submit his D.F.R. request. Furthermore, you will create a scenario in which cadet 832 will get minimal sleep the night before receiving his DNA baseline. You will also insure cadet 832 is on short rations as well.

As noted in your written protest, you have the right to demand an inquiry by the Inspector General into potential variances in any cadet's training program that could result in undue risk to the cadet. These orders are provided to you as requested so you may pursue such investigation if so desired.

Signed this day,
Thomas R. Jacobs, Commandant,
Intergalactic Wizard Scout Academy

*　　*　　*

TAC Officer Myers stared at the written orders for a full minute before refolding the letter and depositing it into the commandant's disintegrator slot on the desk. He waited until the light turned green verifying the document had been destroyed.

Glancing around the sparsely furnished room, TAC Officer Myers remembered the numerous clashes the commandant and he'd had in this same office over the training techniques used on cadet 832. No matter how often he'd pointed out the senselessness of singling out cadet 832 for punishment, the commandant had always held firm. The orders came directly from '*the One*'. Regardless of TAC Officer Myers' protests, the commandant had always been adamant the continued existence of the galaxy depended upon following the directions of '*the One*' regardless of personal preferences. In the commandant's eyes, only '*the One*' had enough information to make the correct decisions.

TAC Officer Myers had never been fond of cadet 832. Something about the cadet had always rubbed him the wrong way. He supposed it was because they were too much alike in some ways. Perhaps he should have pursued the training matter through official channels, but he'd never been able to force himself to do so. The commandant was his father. TAC Officer Myers would never willingly disgrace him.

'*The One*' *is just as responsible for my father's death as the Crosioians*, TAC Officer Myers thought. *The Crosioians killed my father, and for that I will make them pay. However,* 'the One' *stole my father from me years ago. I swear, I'll find a way to make* 'the One' *pay as well.*

TAC Officer Myers considered the problem. It might take years, but he was determined to make it happen.

Shepard is the key, TAC Officer Myers thought. *He's the last of the active time-commandos. Somehow, I'll find a way to use him to get my revenge on* 'the One'. *Somehow, someday, I'll make* 'the One' *pay. I swear it.*

[*End Transmission*]

ABOUT THE AUTHOR

Rodney Hartman is a retired U.S. Army veteran with over twenty years of experience in military operations ranging from an infantry private in the paratroops to a Chief Warrant Officer flying helicopters during the Persian Gulf War. Mr. Hartman currently works as a computer programmer specializing in secure web applications. He enjoys writing in his spare time, and he has written numerous articles as a ghost writer for various websites. Mr. Hartman lives in North Carolina with his wife and family along with their cat, McKenzie.

33186691R10307

Made in the USA
Middletown, DE
04 July 2016